SULHA

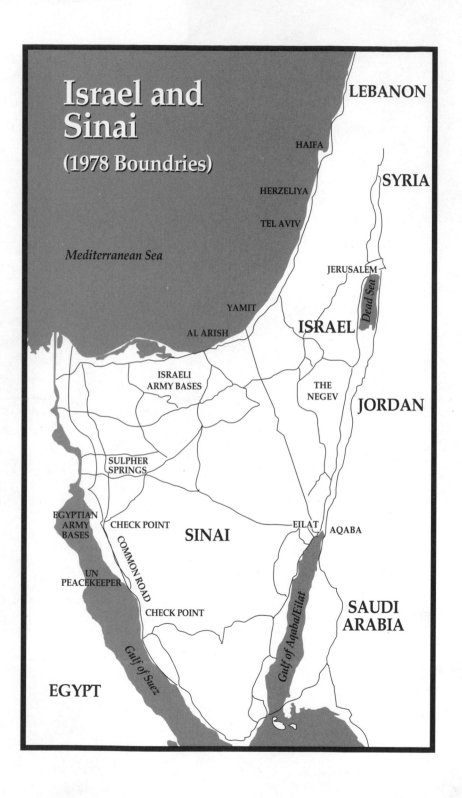

Israel and Sinai
(1978 Boundries)

LEBANON

SYRIA

HAIFA

HERZELIYA

TEL AVIV

Mediterranean Sea

JERUSALEM

Dead Sea

YAMIT

AL ARISH

ISRAEL

ISRAELI
ARMY BASES

THE
NEGEV

JORDAN

SULPHER
SPRINGS

EGYPTIAN
ARMY
BASES

CHECK POINT

SINAI

EILAT

AQABA

UN
PEACEKEEPER

COMMON ROAD

CHECK POINT

Gulf of Aqaba/Eilat

SAUDI
ARABIA

Gulf of Suez

EGYPT

Sulha

Malka Marom

Malke marom

אלכי מרום

KEY PORTER BOOKS

Canadian Cataloguing in Publication Data

Marom, Malka
    Sulha

ISBN: 1-55263-053-6

I. Title.

PS8576.A747S84 1999   C813'.54   C99-931103-4
PR9199.3.M368S84 1999

The author is grateful for permission to reprint from the following:

"After my death," by Chaim Nachman Bialik. Copyright © by Dvir Publishers, Israel.

"The Silver Plate" by Nathan Alterman. Copyright © by the author, Acum, Israel.

Two lines from poem 1249, reprinted by permission of the publishers and the Trustees of Amherst College from *The Poems of Emily Dickinson*, Ralph W. Franklin, ed., Cambridge, Mass.: The Belknap Press of Harvard University Press, Copyright © 1998 by the President and Fellows of Harvard College. Copyright © 1951, 1955, 1979 by the President and Fellows of Harvard College.

The Canada Council | Le Conseil des Arts
for the Arts | du Canada
SINCE 1957 | DEPUIS 1957

The publisher gratefully acknowledges the support of the Canada Council for the Arts and the Ontario Arts Council for its publishing program.

Canada

We acknowledge the financial support of the Government of Canada through the Book Publishing Industry Development Program (BPIDP) for our publishing activities.

Key Porter Books Limited
70 The Esplanade
Toronto, Ontario
Canada M5E 1R2

www.keyporter.com

Electronic formatting: Heidi Palfrey
Design: Peter Maher

Printed and bound in Canada

99 00 01 02 03 6 5 4 3 2 1

In memory of my sister Yehudit

For Alexandra Hillah, Marva and Ellai

Rarely, in the regions inhabited by Arabic- and
Hebrew-speaking people, will the two agree on any one thing.
The word *sulha* is the exception. In both
languages it has the same meaning: a forgiveness;
a reconciliation; a joining, repairing, making whole that
which has been torn asunder—peace.

Prologue

Today the great riverbeds of the Sinai are paved. Troops can move in the desert faster than ever—it was for them, the peacekeeping forces, that the great wadis were blacktopped. Yet, fast or slow, sooner or later, the flash floods will surely tear up the asphalt and sweep it downstream, just as they did the mines from the minefields.

Fast or slow, huge signs spin by every few kilometers on these highways, signs that say: "It is forbidden for stranger-foreigners to get off the main roads." Thus, paved or not, the great riverbeds, the great, ancient passageways of the Sinai desert, are now borders within borders.

But ever since time remembered, the Sinai has held restrictions within restrictions. The ones written on bejeweled veils have been as binding as the ones carved in granite.

To this day, no place in the Sinai is more restricted to stranger-foreigners than the home ground of the mountain Badu. Even stranger-nomads are reluctant to venture there, not only because the wadis and the tributaries are difficult to traverse for even the best of camels or four-wheel drive, but also out of fear of the mountain clansmen and the strict nomadic law that dictates: Honor and blood will be avenged, if it takes five generations to track down the offender's descendants. Even in words, very few people dare enter.

Only in whispers of whispers do people rumor that the most beautiful women in the peninsula have lived in solitude, for the past fifteen hundred years, in those mountains where no one except a person directly related to them by blood or marriage is ever allowed to see them, veiled though they may be. That is why their tents are called "the forbidden tents."

To this day, only one stranger-foreigner has entered the forbidden tents. Her name is Leora—Nura, the Badu named her.

❧

It was in spring 1978 that Leora first entered the forbidden tents.

For once, since she was war-widowed in the Sinai War, Leora elected to forgo the memorial ceremonies held on Mount Herzl. She chose instead to touch the ground that had claimed her husband, the scorched wilderness over which his fighter plane had last been sighted. She embarked on her journey in time—ample time, she thought—to reach that site on Memorial Day.

But the desert laughs at what we mortals predetermine. You head to one place but end up at another. That's the desert—the unexpected, the detours that change your life.

Leora didn't know it. She didn't know the desert. It was the first time she had ventured to the Sinai.

There was only one paved highway in the whole peninsula on that spring day in '78. Every few kilometers, this highway climbed a hill or a mountain, rising so close to the Gulf of Aqaba–Eilat, Leora didn't have to step out of the Land-Rover to see the desert mountains and the Red Sea forming an almost perfect circle of blue in the Valley of the Sun; and grains of sand glittered like gold dust on the beach, where stranger-girls wearing topless bikinis attracted Badu youths and nearly bewitched them—or so the Badu elders said—with their unveiled faces, uncovered bodies, and upbraided hair that swayed in tandem with the motion of their hips.

And when the sun disappeared behind the mountain range west of the highway, the sister range swelled east across the gulf, in Jordan, and farther south, in Saudi Arabia. The faint image of the gulf looked like the creation of an artist who had no desire or time to finish his picture, choosing instead to paint half the gulf on half of the canvas and to fold it precisely while the paint was still wet, in order to press an exact copy.

Now, soon after the Land-Rover turned from the gulf to the interior, Sinai became a chain of circles, no two links alike, and every highway—every road, every path, every track—was a wadi, a river caked dry. At forty or fifty kilometers an hour, and sometimes over sixty, the Land-Rover rolled on a river of dust banked by mountains—a towering massif locked tight, with no opening, no way out, in sight, and just when it seemed you were going to smack into it head-on, the mountains would part, the river would bend, a new circle would open up. You would exhale in relief—only to gasp when you notice that this circle, too, is locked tight. Solid stone ahead. Looking back, you see no sign of the spot where the mountains parted, as if by miracle, only a minute ago. An opening must be there—you know in your head, but not in your blood.

A drought had been ravaging the Sinai for the past seven years, like in Egypt during Joseph's days. And still the Sinai won't let you forget that, in this desert, more people die in water—flood-water—than in thirst.

Upon the stone-hard banks of the dry riverbed, floodwaters had painted a white line. Whenever you see it, you cock your ears for the clap of a thundering flood and you itch to climb above the white line, no matter how innocent the sky. Rainfall, even a drizzle kilometers away, could flood here in a flash, tearing boulders off the cliffs and sweeping them downriver.

Deep in the interior, Sinai dwarfs the living—and the dead.

Here Leora felt she was in the right place at the right time. And though she wished she knew the desert well enough to tra-verse it by herself, in her own vehicle, her respect grew all the more for Russell, a distant relative who had offered her a ride in his Land-Rover.

Professor Russell—El Bofessa, the Badu called him in recogni-tion of his knowledge of the desert and its inhabitants—was con-sulted by Badu elders on the event that had shaken the whole region as none other in the past thirty years. For, never before in thirty years—thirty years of war—had any Arab nation agreed to negotiate a peace treaty with Israel. Yet the previous autumn, the president of Egypt, Anwar Sadat, had flown to Jerusalem, and there, for the whole world to hear, he had declared: No more war!... No sooner did he say that than the prime minister of Israel, Menachem Begin, offered to return the Sinai to Egypt in exchange for peace.

At that very moment the Israeli occupation of Sinai changed from permanent to temporary—just as, in 1967, it had started to change from temporary to permanent when the Arab leader decided in Khartoum to reject the Israeli peace offering. But now, almost as soon as the peace talks started, they began to collapse. From day to day, no one knew if they would lead to no more war or to no more peace talks, let alone peace. And so, a period of waiting began—not unlike the one in 1967.

"The mirror image of time is staring you in the face at this very moment. For once you can see the full measure of the moment we are living in," Russell told Leora. "Nothing stays the same here for very long, yet everything stays the same here forever," he added, by force of habit, forgetting she was not his student. "Words change meaning from day to day now. 'Peace,' for instance, is invested with Messianic dimensions today, but if Egypt signs a peace treaty with Israel, the word 'peace' would shrink to mean 'no war.' This, in turn, is bound to shrink the soul..." Russell applied the brakes, skipped out of the Land-Rover, and picked up a couple of rocks, "work tools from the Stone Age..." He rested them on a ledge above the white flash-flood line.

It was not until they reached the Gates of the Wadi that the detour—the unexpected—materialized in the form of a nomad who hailed their Land-Rover to a stop. The nomad and Russell exchanged salutations. Still short of breath, the nomad said, "A child-boy possessed of demons must be rushed quick-fast to the *darwisha*—the healing woman—of the mountain Badu..."

Russell told Leora he'd take the detour; drive the Badu child-boy to the *maq'ad*—the men's guest-receiving-place—of the mountain Badu, and then drive her to her destination.

But when they arrived, the mountain *maq'ad* was deserted.

"Stay here and don't wander off," Russell said to Leora and to the Badu child-boy. And then he went to look for Abu Salim, the elder of the mountain Badu, or one of his clansmen.

As fate would have it, Abu Salim was far away from the mountains that day. He and all the men of his mountain clan had gone to track down his first-born son, Salim. In the folly of youth, Salim was covering his tracks for a far distance.

Abu Salim was married to two wives at that time. One, Salim's mother, Azzizah, was the *darwisha*—the healer—of the mountain Badu. The second, Tammam, was a new girl-wife who had given birth to her first child, a girl, five-six months before that day. Their forbidden tents were pitched on a plateau, invisible from their husband's *maq'ad* and from the road—the wadi—as well.

The plateau held a lookout point from which the two wives could see only a small stretch of the wadi that led to the *maq'ad*. The granite mountains, though, carried the sound even of the soft stride of a camel. A Land-Rover or a Jeep the wives could hear ten, fifteen, even twenty minutes before it reached the small stretch visible from the women's lookout. And because few vehicles dared risk the climb to Abu Salim's *maq'ad*, the wives could tell, by the sound alone, that it was none other than El Bofessa's Land-Rover approaching.

No child old enough to walk down to the *maq'ad* was in the tents that day. Therefore the women had no one to dispatch to Abu Salim's guest-receiving-place, no one to inform El Bofessa that he would be waiting for nothing. And no one to brew honor— *ya'ni*, coffee—for their favored stranger-guest. Or even to brew for him tea.

Adhering to the age-old Badu edict that forbids contact between outsiders and the women of their mountain clans, the two wives returned from the lookout point to their women's work. And when they heard the tooting of the horn, they knew a child was in the *maq'ad*, playing with El Bofessa's Land-Rover. But then, suddenly, the women heard screaming and yelling—a shrill chorus of the first wife's name.

It was the Badu child-boy possessed by demons, the first wife knew right away. For that child-boy had been sent to her for healing once before. She did not know what to do now, and neither did the second wife. The two wives waited and waited, and still the screaming and yelling continued. Only when it sounded as if the child-boy would expire from his screaming did the two wives decide to edge down toward the *maq'ad*—just close enough for the child-boy to hear them calling him to run over to their hiding-place.

There were many granite boulders to hide behind along the winding footpath. And so, from boulder to boulder, the two wives, carrying the infant-girl with them, were dodging and clinging when, abruptly, the yelling stopped. All they could hear were happy sounds coming from the child-boy; happy sounds growing closer and closer—too close. For they could see him now, tugging with both hands the arm of a demon taller than the tallest tent pole. But what scared them most were the eyes.

Not once in their lives had the two women seen a human being, or even a demon or a monster, with eyes so big, so dark, and almost like a mirror reflecting the sun. It was a monster-demon new even to the senior wife, who was a *darwisha*, daughter of a *darwish*, a healing man. The monster-demon had possessed the child, the first wife thought. Small wonder she had no power to exorcise it. She had no power to even move her legs, she was so afraid; she did not remember how she returned to the plateau, and neither did the second wife.

There would be no hiding-place from such a monster-demon, the two wives thought. And so they huddled next to the cooking fire, for they were cold. Though the fire was hot and the sun was high when the demon appeared on the plateau, the Badawias' hands and feet, and even their tongues, froze, refusing to obey them and move. Neither one knew how it happened that the monster-demon found them hiding inside the tent of Abu Salim's girl-wife.

Happy, the child-boy leaped over to them. But right behind him the monster-demon entered the tent, crouching low, and it took off the monster eyes. Underneath was another pair of eyes— *Aywa*—yes—another pair of eyes the color of which not once in their lives had the wives seen. Not brown like human-being eyes. And not blue like the stranger-eyes the men had described. But like the color of the mountains in springtime—in years of bounty, not drought, when the sun has not yet dried the dew. Eyes the color of bounty had to be a good omen; surely no harm would come to them now, the two wives thought. And just then the monster-demon greeted them.

"*Salamat...marhaba*," it said in greeting, its voice sounding like a woman's. But how could it be a woman when it wore no veil to cover its face, no *thowb*—long tribal dress—to cover its body? And so uncared-for it looked; so unloved, unloving, and uncaring—not even one bracelet adorned its wrists, not a necklace on its neck, not an anklet, an earring, and no kohl dust on its eyes. It did, however, wear gold on one of its fingers and gold around its neck, as a Badawia does when unclean and envious of every woman with a child planted in her womb. And its hair was braided like a Badawia maiden's. But its hair was not dark like human hair.

"Because it is the hair of a woman-stranger," said the Badu child-boy possessed by demons. "El Bofessa said that many woman-strangers have hair this color."

"Cannot be," said Abu Salim's wives, even though they did remember the men describing how strange the hair color of strangers was. And how immodest woman-strangers were, how unloved and uncared for. And how they dressed in clothes called "shirts" and "trousers," which is also what man-strangers wore. And how some were even taller than Badu men. But a Badu who does not pepper his story—does not stretch it taller and wider than life—is not a Badu, the two Badawia wives knew. And from the lookout point, all strangers looked no bigger than tiny ants. Not once in their lives had these mountain Badawias seen a stranger-man or -woman so close—and in their tents, yet. It cannot be a stranger-man or -woman, the two wives decided at once. And at once they told it to the child-boy. "For no stranger-man or stranger-woman has ever entered our tents," they said, "and no stranger-man or stranger-woman ever will."

"But it is a stranger-woman," insisted the child-boy. "*Wallah*, how happy my mother will be when I tell her that you are no longer better than her. Strangers corrupt your tents also…."

His mother pitched her tent only a short distance from the Gates of the Wadi, where a huge water tank was drawing every passing stranger. And sometimes a woman-stranger driven by curiosity, or thirst for knowledge, as well as for water, would enter his mother's tent. His mother was of Abu Salim's tribe but not of his clan, which she considered to be her good fortune. For she believed the horizon of the women in Abu Salim's clan was all too narrow. Or so the same child-boy had said the last time he had been healed here.

The child-boy lacked discretion. Nothing else was wrong with him. But a Badu, even a Badu child, who lacks discretion is not a Badu. That is why there was no doubt in the Badu's mind that he was possessed by demons. Still, he was a loving and a lovable child.

"He must have dragged the woman-stranger to the tents to make his mother happy," the girl-wife whispered. The first wife laughed. She could not be angry with the child.

But she was angry with El Bofessa. Even though she had never met him, the senior wife held El Bofessa responsible for the transgression of the woman-stranger. For the first wife had been told that El Bofessa knew what was allowed and what was forbidden, not only in the mountains, but in Badu compounds the world over. And she was sure he knew that the Badu child-boy, lacking in discretion, was bound to tell of this transgression to one and all he happened to meet, thus exposing the blood, not only of El Bofessa and of the intruding stranger-woman, but of the girl-wife, and hers as well.

It was clear to her then that she and the second wife had no choice but to convert the intruder from a woman-stranger to a woman-member-of-the-clan, a member close enough to be allowed to enter their tents. For this conversion, however, Abu Salim's wives had to hand the infant-girl to the intruder. And though the intruder's eyes were the color of bounty, the wives were apprehensive, even afraid.

Wallah, the two wives had to muster all their courage even just to urge the intruding woman-stranger, "Quick-fast, give your breast to the infant-girl. Let the infant suck your nipple once-twice. For that is all that is required of a woman to become the infant's mother third-removed," they explained. "The infant's mother is first-removed, the first wife is second-removed, and now, *Inshallah*, you will be third-removed. Quick-fast now, give your breast to the girl-infant, for no stranger is allowed to be here."

The woman-stranger understood not a word the two wives said. Or so it appeared.

"You have to feed words to a stranger *wahada-wahada*—one by one," the child-boy said. That was what El Bofessa had told him, said the boy.

But even when the two wives fed their words to the woman-stranger *wahada-wahada*, she did not seem to understand. She would not uncover her breasts.

"Perhaps she has no breasts. *Wallah*, woe to us if this stranger is a man," the first wife said. Then, just as she reached over to tear open her shirt, the woman-stranger withdrew, looking startled, even afraid, and as if the woman-stranger thought the Badawia wives to be monster-demons.

And so to assure the woman-stranger that they meant no harm—and to show her what was required, for her own good as well as for theirs—first, the girl-wife gave her breast to her infant-girl; then, the older wife; and then they passed the infant-girl to the woman-stranger. And *wahada-wahada*, they told the woman-stranger to do the very same thing.

Now finally the woman-stranger understood, or so she said. But in the strangest way of speaking . . . The woman-stranger laughed. Then she explained that she could not help but laugh because she was familiar with all sorts of greetings: shaking hands, kissing, and even rubbing noses she had heard of, and of greetings like passing a pipe. But never of a greeting like passing an infant from breast to breast.

Let her think it is the way we Badu greet, the two wives

decided. Later on, *Inshallah*, they would correct her thinking. It did not surprise the two wives that the infant-girl would not take to the breasts of the woman-stranger, for the woman-stranger's smell was fragrant yet repulsive. Still, the infant was coaxed to suck the nipple once, twice, if not three times—which was more than was required for her to be the infant's mother, third-removed. And so the two wives said, "*Bas*—enough," and they took the infant from the lap of the converted woman-stranger.

"*Mabrouka! Mabrouka!*—May you be blessed!" the two wives and the Badu child-boy kept repeating, for they thought Allah was not accustomed to blessing strangers. And also not accustomed yet to her—the woman-stranger—being a close member of the family, the clan.

To welcome her into the clan now, the wives brewed only tea, for the last of the coffee to brew honor was down in the *maq'ad*. And she, the stranger-no-stranger, said El Bofessa would think she had lost her way in the mountains if she did not return to the *maq'ad* soon. So there was not enough time to prepare for her a feast.

Quick-fast Abu Salim's wives began to brew the tea. And to their amazement, just as quick and fast, the stranger-no-stranger began to heap upon them questions, the likes of which the two wives had never heard, questions like: How do two wives and one husband make love? Three at once, or two and one watching, or withdrawing to the other tent? ...

"*Ayb*—shameful, not proper," said the older wife, Azzizah.

So now the stranger-no-stranger asked: How do two wives divide the household chores? Does each wife have equal standing, or does the first wife rule over the second, or is it the other way around? And does your husband favor one wife over the other? Does he have enough to satisfy both your needs? Are you not jealous of each other? Did you, yourselves, sew, bead, embroider your beautiful veils, dresses, jewelry? Where do you buy the cloth, the beads, your food? ...

"It is not proper to ask questions," the first wife replied to all her prying.

Such ignorance the Badawia woman had never seen. Even more than the child-boy, the woman stranger-no-stranger lacked manners and discretion. The poor woman, the first wife thought, the poor woman will soon be divorced, if she is not divorced already. For surely not even a stranger-man would remain married to a woman so ignorant, unmannered, indiscreet, immodest, unruly, and . . . lazy. The senior wife had never seen a woman with such lazy-looking hands. The skin of her hands was almost as soft as the infant's. This woman-stranger-no-stranger was obviously too lazy to even carry water and gather wood, the first wife thought; the burden of her workload fell, no doubt, on a kinswoman who took pity on her, for obviously she was ill-fated—until today.

It was all the work of fate, the older wife was convinced of that now. Just as the child-boy was fated to be possessed by demons, the woman-stranger-no-stranger was fated to be where she was, and who she was—deficient, lacking in everything but bounty in her inner eyes. And so the senior wife told her, "It was the dictate of almighty fate, *Wallah*, that compelled you to enter our tents, which is very fortunate for us, as well as for you and El Bofessa. For our men would have been bound to punish us all had there been anything any mortal could do but submit to fate."

"How would your men have punished you, me, and El Bofessa?" said the woman stranger-no-stranger.

"You will see, *yaa-Rabb*, if you disclose to anyone even the shape of my bracelet," the Badawia replied. "Swear on the life of the rain that for as long as you live you will not reveal to anyone what you see here and what you have seen, what you hear and what you have heard, and not even what you smell or sense—now, before, and until you leave—not unless or until you are permitted to do so by my husband, my brother, my son, or his son's son."

"Why?" The woman-stranger-no-stranger was still at her questions.

"Swear!" the first wife demanded in a voice so alarming that the stranger-no-stranger's voice trembled when she said, "I swear."

"On the life of the rain," said the first wife.

"On the life of the rain," repeated the woman-stranger-no-stranger, her voice trembling still.

"But surely the woman-stranger-no-stranger can reveal that she is invited to visit-stay in our tents whenever she so desires," said the girl-wife, for she was as curious about the woman-stranger-no-stranger as the woman-stranger-no-stranger was about her.

Abu Salim's first wife thought it was only proper to invite the woman-stranger-no-stranger now. And so she told the stranger-no-stranger, "You must come and visit-stay with us for a week, a month, even a year. And this you can reveal to anyone you wish, but only this invitation, not who invited you. And if El Bofessa asks you, Where is the Badu child? tell him: Safe and sound in Abu Salim's tents."

The mountains echoed the tooting of the horn just then. And the girl-wife said, "Children must be playing in the *maq'ad* with El Bofessa's Land-Rover." For the girl-wife wished the woman-stranger-no-stranger would not leave as yet, and the first wife also wished she would stay. But the two wives knew the woman-stranger-no-stranger was right when she said El Bofessa was sounding a direction for her to return to.

And so, while the first wife pinned onto the shirt of the woman-stranger-no-stranger an amulet to ward off the evil eye, the girl-wife picked from the fire a twig burning at one end only. Then with her fingers the girl-wife rubbed the glowing ashes at that end—rubbed and rubbed until that end came to a fine point. She then dipped the fine point into a vial of kohl dust and said to the woman-stranger-no-stranger, "Give me your eyes, your inner eyes."

The first wife, afraid the fine point would harm the woman's inner eyes, held steady the stranger-no-stranger's face with both hands. And now the woman-stranger-no-stranger, groaning in pain, tried to wrestle her face free. But the first wife, not realizing how strong her hands were, and how rough and hard from hard work, released her hold and said, "You do not trust me, I see."

"Oh, you mean this is a ritual of trust—or of parting? In greeting, you women pass an infant from breast to breast, and in parting you kohl eyes?" said the woman-stranger-no-stranger.

Abu Salim's wives laughed and laughed.

Professor Russell tooted the horn of his Land-Rover as soon as he returned to the *maq'ad* after searching high and low for Abu Salim—only to find there neither Nura nor the Badu child.

Their blood would be on his head if any harm were to befall them, Russell knew. Frantic now, he went to look for them. Again he searched and searched. And when he could not find them, he tooted and tooted, until Leora reappeared—without the Badu child-boy.

"What happened to the boy? Where is the Badu child-boy?" asked Russell.

"The child-boy is safe in Abu Salim's tents," Leora replied.

"What?! The forbidden tents?! The women's tents?!" Professor Russell was livid. For all the way to Abu Salim's *maq'ad*, he had told Leora how they, and even their descendants for five generations, would be punished if Leora were to enter these tents that the mountain Badu forbid all strangers to enter. "Where is your brain! Your ears! Why did you not listen to me?" Russell asked Leora, more angry and afraid than ever in his life.

"I cannot tell unless I am granted permission by Abu Salim, his sons, or his sons' sons," Nura replied. And not another word would she tell Professor Russell about the forbidden tents.

As soon as Abu Salim and the men returned to the tents, the child-boy told them everything—just as the wives had thought he would.

The Desert

August 14, 1978
Kfar Sabba, Israel

"Who is it? Who is it?" my mother answered when I rang the bell. Her voice was full of sleep; my parents start their nap earlier with each advancing year.

"It's me, Leora."

"Wake up ... The girl-child is here ... Quick-fast ... Come on ...," I hear her saying to my father in the bedroom. As if every second is precious when the "girl-child" makes a flying visit.

"The girl-child is here alone," I tell them. But still they keep me waiting outside their front door; they don't want me to see them without their teeth. I return my key to the holdall and wait—outside the same door, in the same corner where I had first kissed Arik in such heat of love, branded my passion just under his jaw. For days I walked around blushing while Arik, beaming, craned his neck for all to see how crazy about him was the girl he was courting ... Feels like a lifetime has passed since then; yet, at the same time, it feels like only a month has gone by since that evening.

My parents have yet to open the door, and already being back home warps time. Mind you, if I were to count the days I've actually been here since I left home, nearly a quarter of a century ago, they would probably add up to no more than one or two years, three maximum.

I manage to sneak a good hug before my parents pull away from my embrace. And right away, as if the world is on fire, my father brews tea in the old aluminum *feenjon* and my mother pulls from the pantry the old Frumin cookie tin. As soon as she opens the lid, the apartment is permeated with the primal feel of home; of life first lived.

"Go get the cups, my child," I can almost hear my mother saying, just like she used to in the dilapidated one-room farmhouse in Kfar Sabba—my childhood home. So, I go to get the cups, but as I approach the cupboard, my mother tells me, "Sit down, my child. You are a guest."

One by one, she sets on the table the mismatched remnants of the old special-occasion set of dishes. Then she gives me a quick appraisal. I must look terrific if she spits behind her back to ward off the evil eye of envy.

"What do you think of that, Arik?" my father says inside. I see the glint in his eye as he turns to look at the all-too-enlarged and grainy old photo that's been hanging on the wall for the past twenty years—of Arik, forever smiling, forever young, framed in mourning-black.

Below it—pressed under glass on top of the credenza—Arik, forever happy in the faded photos, is surrounded by snapshots of the whole family, a few friends, and one of our old neighbors, pointing to the havoc the Tommies wreaked on our shack the night they stormed in to search for the skeleton children and grownups who had escaped from There.

Illegal immigrants, the Tommies called them, but my parents called them uncles, aunts, cousins. "Even if they visit only for an hour, keep it secret," my parents told me, so I kept it secret, locked it deep inside, even though my parents hadn't hidden anyone from the Tommies that night—except their guns, secreted in the hollow legs of the kitchen table. That table is the only thing the Tommies didn't tear apart.

"A *Goyishe copp*," my mother said in Yiddish, after the Tommies left that night.

"Don't be smug," my father told her in Hebrew. "Woe to the smug of Zion."

"What means '*Goyishe copp*'?" I asked my parents.

"You see what you are teaching the child," my father said to my mother. Still angry, he advised me, "Don't ever underestimate the *Goyim*—the Gentiles—or you will end up like The Millions There."

So, the next time the Tommies stormed into our house, I didn't underestimate them. I am trembling only because the Tommies search and destroy late at night, and I awaken to their smashing, tearing, and shouting. And my father is not at home—now, during the curfew, of all times. The Tommies know my father is in the Underground. They'll hang him on the gallows, I think, and I tremble even more.

My glance goes to my mother. She is pretending that the illegal uncle hiding in our house is my father. So I also pretend. And when she plops me on his knee, I snuggle up to him as if he were my father. I can't tell if it's his fear or mine that trembles through his knees, his chest, his arms.

Yet my mother says to the Tommies, "Look at how you are frightening the child."

The Tommies don't understand Hebrew, but they do understand trembling and shaking. They look at me as if I am afraid of them. That's what they like to see—a Jew scared shitless. Every child in The Land knows that. How can my mother reduce me to that, I think, and now I pretend there is a valve in my throat. I close it and it blocks my tears—but not my trembling.

So now the Tommies suspect that the illegal uncle is not my father, and they bark, "Papers! Papers!" which, in English, means a card that says who you are.

I don't know why the Tommies grab him and my mother. The valve in my throat bursts open, so I hide my tears in my mother's dress, and with all my might I cling to her. But the Tommies tear me away from her with such force that my head hits the cupboard, stars pop into my eyes, and waves roar in my ears as if a couple of conch shells are clamped to them.

"You killed my girl-child! Murderers! Nazis!" my mother shouts over the waves.

"*Shurrup*! You bloody bitch! You bloody Jew!" shout the Tommies.

"Nazis! ... Nazis! ..." my mother yells from very far away.

Next thing I know, I'm in my neighbor's house, lying on a cot, a compress on my forehead. The neighbor's face looks troubled, sad, worried.

"The Tommies took my mother to There, the ghettos, the death trains, the death camps, didn't they? It's all my fault, my fault," I say.

"No. No. Hush. Hush," says the neighbor. She is even a better mother than my mother. Her puddings are better and she hides no illegal uncles, or guns...

The only thing my mother tries to hide this afternoon is how incapacitating she finds the pain caused by the arthritis in her knees. Try as she might, though, she can't get up from the chair as she does on her better days—by pressing her hands on the tabletop and hoisting herself, sort of like a pushup. My father has to help her today. But no matter what toll the years exact on her, in my eyes she is the fearless heroic giant she was even the night the Tommies dragged her to prison—the night the neighbor who took me in had served a pudding better than my mother's...

When this neighbor went out to work, she took me over to another neighbor, whose puddings were even better, and song after song she sang, much better than my mother. All the neighbors were so much better mothers than my mother. I want to stay with them. But when my father came home from work, he said we should give our neighbors a rest.

Before I sleep, I wish: Let the Tommies detain my mother for another day at least. Then I hide under the blanket so that God will not find me and strike me dead, not just for that wish but for meeting Ahmed in the meadow as well—the meadow that rolls between his Arab home town, Qalqiliya, and my Jewish home town, Kfar Sabba.

"I have no grandfather—and not a grandmother also," I once told Ahmed in that meadow. "We Yahodi children have no grandparents."

"Everyone has one grandfather and one grandmother, and many—even bastards—have two of each," said Ahmed.

"You mean picture grandparents, not real grandparents," said I.

"What means 'picture grandparents'?" asks Ahmed.

"'Picture grandparents,'" I explain, "means 'grandparents who hang on the wall, and even when framed in silver or gold, they make your mother very sad and your father very angry with God.' It will kill him, my mother says; 'Have faith,' she tells him; so, with faith, he goes to check the lists, but——"

"What means 'lists'?"

"Names, one under the other, all from There," I say, which is not even the half of what "lists" means, but Ahmed doesn't even know what "There" means.

"Where?" he asks me. And I try to explain, but every second word he asks me, "What means . . . ?" and I cannot explain even half of what each word means, so these words are only words to him. Meaningless.

A train is a train to Ahmed, but not to me. To me it is There, and Here, and deep inside myself in a locked compartment that shakes and shakes, especially when my father comes home after work and says to my mother, "Nothing . . ." Again he could find no one in the lists; I know, every night after work he goes to check the lists, every night he comes home and tells my mother, "Nothing." Then he gets angry with God, so angry it will kill him.

Quickly, before God strikes him dead, I run out of bed and I tell him, "But they are here, Abba—even inside me in the compartment, they are breathing, moving . . . Feel, you can feel them. Feel," I say, taking his hand and placing it on my chest where you can feel the compartment inside shaking.

"Oh, my child," says my father, his face sad. "You are not afraid, Leora, are you?"

"No, Abba. I am not afraid." And really I am not afraid.

The kettle whistles on the Primus like a train on tracks of fire—flames rise up from the sides. My father says, "Come, Leora. Have some cookies and tea." So I have some cookies and tea, then go back to bed. My mother stays up very late; she has to sew sleeves. She gets paid by the number of sleeves she sews by machine in the factory, and at home by hand at night. While she sews, my mother, in a voice that flutters on her breath like an angel, sings the lullaby that her mother sang to her.

Her mother hangs on the wall across from my bed. The glass that covers her starts to drip like candle wax—drip, shimmer, and blur—and in that blur my father appears and says, "Cookies and tea... Nothing... Cookies and tea... Nothing..." again and again like a train on flames, gathering speed, faster and faster, chugging "Cookies and tea... Nothing... Cookies and tea... Nothing..." I'll die if I don't jump off, I know. The teacher told us at school about the trains.

"Stop it. It's a nightmare..." I tell myself. "Stop it. It's a nightmare..." again and again. But my voice has no sound. And now the train, speeding like mad, is chugging "Stop it. It's a nightmare... Stop it. It's a nightmare..." faster and faster.

Quick-fast, before it's too late, I jump off the train. Run as fast as I can, struggling for breath and sweating because the Swastikas run after me, and they have trained dogs. I run and run. Cry and cry for help, but I have no voice. The train comes after me, even when I run downstairs. Four steps at a time I skip. Still, at each landing, at the door of each neighbor, the train whistles louder and louder, and even louder at the Marimskis' door. With all my might I try to escape from our apartment building. But just as I reach the front entrance, the neighbors whisper to keep my mouth shut or they'll lock me up. They think I know that the second-floor neighbors are an illegal uncle and aunt, and that the neighbor across the hall is fighting Underground in the Palmah, and that the other neighbor is fighting in the other Underground, in the Etzel. All our neighbors are hunted by the Tommies, and their lives are in my hands.

I swear I breathe not a word to anyone. Yet, one night, late, Mrs. Marimski knocks on our door and says, "I have a premonition my son is dead."

My parents know that her son is fighting Underground. They stay with her all night. At five o'clock the next morning the newspaper arrives, and there, in black and white, it says that Mrs. Marimski's son was killed by the Tommies.

"He was only seventeen," Mrs. Marimski whispers, looking at me as if it were my fault.

"No. I swear, I breathed not a word," I want to tell her, but, like in the nightmare, my voice has no sound. I can't even say that perhaps I talked in my sleep and the Tommies heard. Now he is dead. And I'm sure that even my parents think I betrayed him. They'll let the neighbors lock me up.

When all the grownups tear their clothes in mourning, I run away—to the sea. And when it gets dark, I run to the boulevard.

The power is not off tonight. Lovers are burning the benches, and up in the balconies people are playing cards, or cracking sunflower seeds, or even singing and dancing as if nothing happened—as if nothing happened Here or There, only in our apartment building. Now for sure I'm not going back.

Instead, I go and sit on a vacant boulevard bench. My eyelids are so heavy, I can open just a crack to see the street-lamp overhead starting to drip like candle wax—drip, shimmer, and blur—and in the blur I feel the mark of Cain on my forehead... Maybe because I talk in my sleep. Or because I sneak a look when the skeleton children gobble up the school lunch so fast, like the goats when we couldn't go out to feed them because of the Tommies' curfew.

The skeleton children don't understand Hebrew. Still, the teacher whispers when she says, "They are afraid you will steal their food. That's what happened to them There." Then she explains and explains, and after all her explaining she says, "You understand, don't you?"

"Yes," I say. And really I understand—I understand that I understand nothing. People are getting killed Here and There, and still people are playing cards on verandas, even singing and dancing, and lovers are burning boulevard benches. And a mark of Cain is stamped on my forehead.

After the War of Independence, in '49, a cease-fire is called. Just when the siren is howling for everyone, everywhere, to stop, stand, and remember, I think my father is going to die. All of a sudden he loses his booming voice, and in a scary whisper he tells my mother and me to stand at attention in our tiny kitchen. And his strong, huge construction hands are so shaky. When he finally succeeds in striking a match, it can barely meet the wick of the thick white memorial candle. Desperate for air, he's gasping deep before he tells us that his mother and father and his brothers and sisters, and everyone in his family and in his little Polish town died today. "Today"—his lips are quivering—"today, when we bury sons and daughters who had sacrificed life for the rebirth of the Nation . . ."

My father is not aware that the official day to remember them from There is not today. And I'm too stunned to tell him. He looks like he's going to die any minute, any minute. Blood drains from his face, and air from his lungs. But I can tell he's struggling with all his might not to cry. My father never cries.

When he whispers, "Now I will say Kaddish—the mourner's prayer—for my mother and my father and my . . ." his whisper cracks. But I see his teeth guarding his quivering lips. He pauses forever before he starts to recite.

Instead of a quivering whisper, out comes the thunderous wail, held in his throat year after year.

"*Yitgadal ve'yitkadash.*" Again and again the same words. "*Yitgadal ve'yitkadash.*" My father's face is blood red, glistening with saliva and tears. "*Yitgadal ve'yitkadash.*" My father wails and wails the same words his father had recited in prayer, praising God, raising God, sanctifying God . . . Seeing God in a grain of sand.

And after you went, Arik, my father recited the Kaddish at the first *minyan*, early at dawn, every day for a whole year, like a father for his fallen son. To him you are a son.

"Leave it, Leora . . ." my mother tells me, as I'm about to clear the dishes. Her fingers start tapping the tabletop—a war drum. Her eyes, clamped to my father's, demand he fire the first shot.

He shakes his head and ever so reluctantly, in that loud voice of the hard-of-hearing, he tells me, "Worries your mother, Leora, your going to Sinai tomorrow."

"You've just returned from Sinai," my mother interjects.

31

"Three months have passed since I returned from Sinai," I correct her, a girl on the defensive.

"Yes," my mother fires back, loud for my father to hear. "Three months of such coming and going. No sooner did you return from Sinai to The Land than you flew to Canada . . . only to fly back to The Land with *shmates*, knapsacks, sleeping bags, desert boots, like the foreign students. Here, you buy a *fakklapte*—beat-up—old Jeep . . . take shots and pills to ward off TB, cholera, typhoid, malaria, any plague the doctors think you might catch in the wilderness . . . Why? . . . Why are you going to all this trouble to look for trouble, stay in Arab tents—enemy tents . . ."

"Bedouin tents," I mutter to stop her before her fear for me infects my confidence and resolve.

"What? . . . What?" my father shouts, his hand cupping his ear.

"Leora thinks the Bedouins are not our enemies because they serve in our army"—that's how my mother amplifies for my father. "Leora lived so long a time in Canada, she no longer remembers that Bedouins of Jordan serve in the Jordanian army and even that the Sinai Bedouin had served in the Egyptian army, maybe in the platoon that shot Arik down."

"It's one thing to visit Bedouins for an hour or so, like you did three months ago when you entered their tents by accident, but to prepare and buy and pack like for a visit-stay of months . . . Worries not only us, but also Arik's brother and your sister," my father booms.

"Do you know what your sister's husband told us?" my mother says, in a voice barely audible for my father—and the neighbors. My father moves his chair closer to my mother's when she continues, "It is not only crazy, your sister's husband told us, but out-and-out stupid, asking for trouble, to stay, a woman alone yet, with Bedouins   primitive, if not savage enemy Arabs encamped in some God-forsaken part of the Sinai desert. Even if you were to fire SOS flares, no one would see them, let alone come to your rescue . . .

"You should go to a psychiatrist, not to the desert. That's what

Arik's brother told us." My mother's eyes, drooping with the weight of worry, seek a spark of reason from mine.

"Arik's brother, of all people," my father says, shaking his head. "Remember what he used to say? 'Go to the desert, not to a psychiatrist. There is something clean about the desert—clean, cleansing, liberating...' Who would have thought then that a dreamer like him... legends are made of dreamers like him who turned the Negev desert into fertile land, would... You know, he told us that the Negev Bedouins are stealing dry the irrigation water we've rationed to farmers, and chopping for firewood any branch or twig they can lay an ax on... 'The nomads are not the sons and daughters of the desert, but its father and mother,' he told us...'"

"Is it running to, or is it running from, that drives you to go to Sinai?" my mother interjects.

"No one really knows what compels one to venture to the desert, until one truly enters it," my father says before I can reply.

"I would have gone to Sinai, as you do, had I been your age," my mother mutters.

Like that my parents give me their blessing.

On my way to my Jeep, from the sidewalk I see they went out to their balcony. Side by side they lean on the railing to take an extra look. Who knows if it won't be the last one, they think. I see it in their sad waving to me. *Shalom ... Shalom ...*

2

I have parted from everyone but you, Arik. From this window, here, in the hotel room, you can see lovers' fire-circles, like the ones you and I used to light right here, on the beach of Herzliyya. Do you remember how we would wait for the coffee to bubble and simmer seven times before adding the cardamom, and the wind would blow a few grains of sand into the *feenjon*, our lips would add sea salt to the mugs, and only then would the coffee taste just right. Oh, I wish you were here ... Tonight, more than ever, I wish you could travel with me not only in spirit, but in body ...

Early tomorrow, barring the unforeseen, I'll be heading to the compound of the mountain Bedouins who have forbidden all strangers to enter their tents ever since time remembered—until three months ago, when they invited me. Why did they break their age-old restriction? Your guess is as good as mine. Professor Russell asked me, "Did they convert you to a Badawia—a daughter of their clan? ... By what rite? ..." I kept my promise—breathed not a word of what transpired in the tents—except that I had been invited to visit-stay. Russell spared no effort and time to prepare me for this visit—even though he finds it hard to believe the mountain Badu would invite me or any stranger to stay in their forbidden tents. He thinks I misunderstood their Badu Arabic.

Maybe I did. Maybe I just heard what I wanted to hear.

I don't know what compels me to venture to Sinai this second time—yesterday's justifications and rationalizations don't hold tonight. But, thank God, so much brain power is packed into this place (after all, The Land is inhabited by the descendants of King Solomon the Wise) that I can't bump into a person who doesn't volunteer a seamless explanation—your brother's, Arik. "It's sheer madness ..."

Even the hotel porter took a swipe. Into this room he walks, sees the desert gear piled up in one corner, and the suitcases stacked in another. "Which corner do you want me to cart off to the storage room?" he asks. "The corner of adventure, of *keif*?" He points to the desert gear. "Or the corner of *galut*—exile?" he says, pointing to the suitcase he carts whenever I fly to The Land. Year in, year out, I fly in and out of The Land—in and out, in and out, like the waves below. Wave after wave beats and retreats, beats and retreats, again and again, like a lover longing to possess the shore. Even when I'm here, I long to be here. I can't shake the feeling of exile, even here in Herzliyya, where I know every shifting current and tide. Even here in The Land that we—you, my Arik, and I—touched as one would a lover.

Oh, but what a jealous and demanding lover, The Land.

"There was a man, but look, he is no more. No. Not on a silver platter shall the State be delivered. No, each man shall pay with his blood. Each man shall pave with his bones..." Such eulogies are dumped year after year on the stone that bears your name, my Arik.

Just another training flight, I thought, so damn classified was the Sinai War. Night fell, and there was no blackout, except on the news—and the phone was silent. Well, I thought, Arik's playing in the hangar with the new jets, like a child with new toys. He doesn't know how late it is. And I waited by the window, watching for the arc of your headlights.

As the darkness gathered, our upstairs neighbors argued at the top of their voices about some textile strike: the burning issue of the day when the war was still "classified." Oh, I'll never forget the angry shouts, the clock, the dark, the waiting for headlights to beam in our window.

I clung to the window long after the voices stopped, leaving quiet and the clock ticking on into the night. The cold night seeping through the dark glass was too ominous to take. So I called the base. It was bad form, I knew. If every pilot's wife called whenever worry prompted, every hand at the base would be busy with telephones, not planes. A good pilot's wife wouldn't call. But I did. I couldn't get through. They were busy with the war that I didn't know about as yet. I dialed and redialed for hours. And when I finally got a line, they told me you were sleeping. Sleeping, yes. They wouldn't—couldn't—break it to me on the phone. I was kept in the dark about that. Nor did I suspect that war demanded all their time and attention. It was only the second all-out war we had engaged in, and we didn't have it down to a science yet. Disorganization meant they had no intention of sending anyone to tell me anything that night. But I kept phoning—every pilot and ground-crewman I knew, and the drowsy wives of the whole damn air force. An hour or two later, your base commander showed up.

The minute I saw him I knew.

"A terrible tragedy . . .," he said. And I remember thinking: What's wrong with me? I feel nothing. The emptiness was strange, and the puzzlement it caused absorbed me. I couldn't squeeze a tear, not even when I glanced over at our little Levi's crib.

"Should I bring you a glass of water?" the base commander asked. And I remember thinking: What an idiot. A glass of water? What in the hell for? Later he said, "You will remember Arik just as he was, always."

I couldn't hear it, couldn't see then how hard it had hit him. He'd served with you for the whole eight years of the air force's history. It wasn't much of a force then. So small it was, like a tight-knit family flying makeshift planes patched together from recycled junk by ingenious ground crews who crossed their fingers each time their creations took off. I can see now how hard hit your base commander was; and he felt so personally responsible that he had to come to tell me himself, no matter how heated the battle that night, or how much he feared for the safety of the others he had sent aloft. And, in the morning, he said, he would inform your parents.

"I'll inform them tonight," I said, thinking your mother would have had a premonition that her son had fallen in battle. She didn't. Deep inside, a part of her—the part that responds to the order in classic works of art, music, and literature—held on to the belief that you would be spared because your brother had been badly injured in the '48 War of Independence, and because of the loved ones she and your father had lost There, in the Shoah. To your parents you were like Joseph to Rachel and Jacob. And when I told them straight—"Arik fell in battle, killed in action"—they looked at me as if I, like Joseph's brother, was repeating a malicious lie.

And then life further echoed that story. Three days after your casket was buried at Mount Herzl, two representatives of the religious authorities tell us that no one is to mourn you because you are not among the killed-in-action, but among the missing-in-action.

"Great! Wonderful! Arik, like Joseph, is alive in Egypt. Imprisoned. A prisoner of war!" I cry out, fucking delighted in a roomful of mourners, all of whom react as if I have swallowed false hope dished out by messengers as false as the false Messiah, Shabtai Tzvi.

"Get off it before it drives you mad, breaks your parents and mine," your brother said. "Face reality, not only for their sake and yours, but for Levi, Arik's only living trace..." And then the strangest thing happened. To all those who believed you dead, you became larger than life. A terrible loss to the *whole nation*, you were now part of The Price. Compounded by thousands, The Price had gained a tyrant's power; it wouldn't let the living live, or the dead die.

"The wife of a man missing in action is not a widow," stated one of the two religious reps before they left. "For seven years, she is to be *agunah*—anchored to him, bound to await his return."

"Your father will come home much sooner than that," I told our Levi.

I went mad, people said. She would never have dropped out, abandoning The Land to marry some Canadian only a year after her husband, Arik, went missing, were she not clear out of her mind, they said. Even now, some say that, sane, I wouldn't be venturing to Sinai. Those infected with madness are never cured, some people think. Like malaria, madness can flare up any time.

So, all these years I tell no one of this feeling that visits me from time to time, that you are still in Sinai, living with Bedouins... Such a notion—call it wishful thinking or fantasy—is not out of line, according to the guidelines for the wives of the missing-in-action. In fact, such a notion must have visited most everyone in the family; otherwise, they wouldn't have suspected that I am going to the Sinai this time to track you down, my Arik. And they wouldn't be saying that I should go to a psychiatrist, not to the desert, would they?

Who knows, they might be right.

But, wouldn't it be something if I tracked you down after all these years, found you in some compound of some Badu clan that forbids all strangers to enter, not only their tents, but their *maq'ads*—their guest-receiving-places? No outsider would have heard even a rumor that this clan exists, in such complete solitude has this Badu clan lived—for centuries perhaps, or maybe just since you bailed out of your flaming plane.

Landing in some deserted dry riverbed, you cracked your thigh bone, like Jacob; dislocated your left shoulder; and smashed your right arm. You could barely crawl to a spot of shade, a drop of water, a twig to build a fire. And when the pain didn't knock you out, you cried for help. But no one heard you for days. The desert nights assailed you with frost. Then, each day, the desert sun first thawed your bones and then broiled you. You were unconscious, frost-bitten and dehydrated, by the time a couple of camel-riders found you.

A Yahodi pilot—a Jewish Israeli pilot—they knew as soon as they saw your tattered uniform. *Wallah*, Israel will pay a fortune to ransom him, the camel-riders thought, and Egypt might pay twice as much for this pilot of their arch-enemy and the military secrets he is sure to divulge under torture. So, as fast as they could, and careful to keep you alive and hidden from smugglers, raiders, spies, soldiers—Israeli or Egyptian—or from anyone who might snatch you from them, the camel-riders carried you to their forbidden mountains.

And there, in a Badu compound so remote and isolated, inaccessible even to camels, they nursed you month after month, until you walked with only a slight limp and used your left shoulder and right arm only slightly awkwardly. But, even after all these months and all the Badu remedies, amulets, and care, you remembered nothing from your life before the war; you couldn't remember your name, never mind military secrets that would interest Egypt. You knew only whatever the Badu had taught you during the months they cared for you.

Now, having invested so much of their heart in you, they couldn't part from you—not even for the fortune Israel was sure to pay...

"Oh, there was a man, but look, he is no more. His plane engulfed in flames plunged into sandstone mountains... But not on a silver platter shall the State be delivered... No, each man shall pay with his blood... Each man shall pave with his bones..." The pine by the gravestone that bears your name has grown tall. So has your son, my son, Levi. He is as tall as you were the last day you stepped out of the room-and-a-half that we called home.

It's our son's turn, my Arik. Our Levi starts his army duty three months from now. He wants to serve in our air force, like you, to be a pilot like you. He even took flying lessons in Canada, and now has such a head start, he's licensed to fly jets, not only in Canada, but here as well. Still, he cannot serve in our air force as a pilot like you. The law of The Land does not allow an only son to serve high-risk duty, in the sky or on the ground, without the parents' written consent—yours, my Arik, and mine. But only on me does he work for this parental consent. And he is not a child now. I don't like to see him nagging his mother for permission like a child, and God knows it is not his fault that he is our one and only child. But how in the hell can I consent to waive a law devised to protect his life—the only living trace of you? What right have I to strap him to the altar? I see no sign of the angel that had spared Isaac. I see no end to the war here. Is it not a life-and-death decision your son is badgering me to make—alone?

I will not decide alone, not this time. This time, my Arik, you damn well better assume your share of responsibility for this boy that you and I brought into this world. Ever since he was six months old, I have kept you alive for him—alive in the present, not merely in the past; not larger than life, but part of it; not as the carrot or stick, to encourage or to punish him, but as a man, with demands, expectations, disappointments, self-doubts, conflicting emotions, contradictions, ambivalence, and opinions. Oh, it was a terrific workout for my imagination. But, in this decision, I am not going to imagine. Do we give him our consent or not?

Come on, give me a hint, a sign ... It's midnight, the seven heavens are wide open. Open up to me for once when I need you ... Oh, tonight, more than ever, I wish you were here—or gone from my life, once and for all ... The more I miss you, the angrier I get, and tonight—I long for you more than ever.

"There was a man, but look, he is no more..." Only in dreams can I feel your breath on my face, my beloved Arik.

"Woe to you if you waive this law that exempts from high-risk duty our only living link with our son Arik and, God forbid, Levi gets killed. We will hold you responsible," your parents told me when I parted from them yesterday. I shouldn't have allowed Levi to take flying lessons, they added. I shouldn't have told the kid that he's as good a pilot, if not better, than you; I should have flatly said "no" when he first asked me for my consent ...

Your parents were not telling me anything I hadn't told myself—and Levi—in moments of weakness. In moments of strength, I would illuminate for him the dark crevices of fear that had compelled me to overprotect him. In moments of strength, I had reinforced his courage to fly, to overcome fear—his and mine, if not your parents.

Neither Levi nor I will ever know the state of fear your parents have lived in ever since they lost everyone and everything they knew and loved in the Shoah. "If such unimaginable expression of man's inhumanity to man could happen in a country as civilized as Germany, it could happen even in America and Canada," your parents believe to this day. "In a fool's paradise, millions of Jews live in America and Canada, like we did in Germany." No one is happier than your parents that Levi decided to return to The Land.

But you know, Arik, Levi didn't exist for them in his first five years of life. After you fell, for nearly five years they couldn't muster a drop of love for anyone alive.

And then, one winter day...

Levi was five years old. It was one of those February days when the sky was blue, the sunlight gold, the almond trees in their celebrated bloom, and the scent of the jasmine hedge drifting with the sea breeze up to your parents' front balcony, where Levi was building a model airplane. I managed to coax your parents to come out of their shuttered rooms and away from the fumes of their oil heaters. It was warm on their balcony, but your parents didn't feel it. I don't remember how long they sat wrapped in layers of sweaters, jackets, and shawls. Then, just as it seemed they were dead to the world, your father peels off his shawl, and your mother heaves a sigh and says, "What a beautiful day for someone."

"Yes, for us," pipes up little Levi, turning his head just as you had in the photo your parents snapped when you were his age. And all of a sudden your parents' eyes met and they looked like they used to, before you went. Then, just when they turned and looked at Levi, as if they saw him for the first time, your father covered his eyes with his hands and kept shaking his head, "No! No! No!" Yes, yes, yes—your mother nods her head and, weeping, leads your father back to their shuttered room. Halfway, she turns to me and says, "You better take the child away..."

"I'm not leaving until I finish building my model," the child announced. He had a mind of his own even then.

"You'll finish later," I told him.

"No!" he balked. "I have to build it now... because now I see how to fit all the pieces, and later the glue will be too dry to build with."

"I'll buy you another tube of glue," I snapped, torn between a compulsion to withdraw with your parents and the instinct to protect my child. And Levi was hitting and running now... and carrying it way too far, even before he grabbed the mugs of tea I had brewed for your parents and flung them in their direction. Too angry to think, I was slapping any part of him my hand could

41

flick-flack, when I heard your parents yelling, "Stop beating the child! Leora! You are killing him! Stop it! Stop it!"

I couldn't believe my ears, my eyes. Just as Moses beat the stone and water gushed out, I beat the child and your parents snapped to life, opened their arms to shelter their grandchild.

"Go … Go to your Abba's Abba and Imma," I whispered to him.

But he muttered, "I want to go back to Canada, Toronto, to be with Gingie …"

"Is Gingie your dog?" your mother asks him.

"No." The child cracks up.

"Gingie is a boy, your friend?" says your father.

"Yes," says Levi, stepping over to your parents. And now, hardly pausing to breathe, he goes on to fill their ears. "Gingie's name is not really 'Gingie,' but because Gingie's hair is red, everyone calls him 'Gingie' …"

I looked after Gingie then, while his parents studied in Toronto. We lived like an extended family for my first seven years in Canada. Had it not been for them, would I have stayed Outside in exile? God only knows.

Soon after Gingie's parents finished their studies in Canada, they bundled Gingie off with them back to The Land. Levi and I were the only Israelis in Toronto then. Or so it seemed.

It was the same Gingie who had talked me into buying a rusty old clunker for this desert journey—and for the desert trips he is planning to take with his best friend, our Levi. I never saw a kid as crazy about Jeeps as this redhead. That's the only secular *keif*—pleasure—Gingie couldn't give up when he became a born-again Jew. In search of the Great Find, as he calls my tired old Jeep, he combed the whole of The Land, then skipped his religious studies to overhaul it. It probably ate him up that he yielded to this secular "weakness" of his. He had kept postponing our departure date, as if I have nothing better to do with my time than wait—for him to escort me to the desert; for Dave, the Canadian I married, to decide to move to The Land. And for you, my Arik, to share the responsibility for the decision your son nags me to make …

Around midnight, seven hours before our departure time, the phone rings in my hotel room—the redhead is calling up to postpone again, I think. But I pick up the receiver and a voice I've never heard before says, "Hello. Leora?"

"Yes."

"My name is Tal. Tal Granot. I phoned to tell you that Gingie has transferred your Jeep to me. I'll escort you to the desert, if that's all right with you."

"What happened to Gingie? Is he all right?"

"Yes. Gingie tried to reach you before he set out for the Territories. He was offered a job there, starting this morning. He told me your departure time had been set for seven o'clock this morning. That's too early. The Jeep still requires a bit of work. I'll collect you at nine."

"What did you say your name was? I'm sorry, I didn't catch it."

"Tal. Tal Granot."

"You don't sound like Gingie's friends from the Block or the Faithful."

"No, I'm a kibbutznik, Gingie's former commander." He chuckled. "See you at nine."

"*Shalom. Le'hitraot*—see you."

"*Shalom. Shalom.*"

Only at home, in The Land, would a man and woman who had never met decide, after a brief phone call, to embark to deserted terrain that demands they trust each other with their lives. Only in Hebrew could I tell in but a few words this Tal—his mettle, his values, even his madness and the bond that bound us: that invisible indivisible bond forged by a shared dream, the prophetic spirit imbued in our ancient ruins, the unremitting heat of our long summers, the stinging salt of our seas...

He must be free of commitments to job or family, for the next seven days at least, this Tal, I thought, and he probably loves the desert, craves challenge and adventure—otherwise, unless he owes Gingie a hell of a favor, why would this Tal have agreed on

43

short notice to roll in the Sinai Peninsula with a woman Gingie had probably described as "the mother of my best friend, whose first husband, my friend's father, was a pilot shot down in the Sinai War..."

Ah, Arik, I can hear your brother, my sister, and her husband now:

"Mad to travel to the desert with a person you don't know from Adam... The Land today is not like The Land you remember, not like what Arik had dreamed of..."

3

First day in the forbidden tents
August (?) 1978
One week (?) after leaving Herzliyya

"Wake up, wake up," a voice whispered. Sounded like a man's voice, but it could have been the wind or just another dream. The eyelids opened, but it was just as dark as when they were closed. Dark and silent and still—as if God were holding his breath. Then, suddenly, it was shivering cold, and the blanket felt heavy and soggy, like after a rainfall. The next moment, or so it seemed, it was sauna hot; the blanket felt bristling dry, and blinding red circles started to grow and ripple inside my eyelids, as if I were watching a stone sink into a blazing lake. And when I opened my eyes, all I could see were black dots popping out of a painful white light. And all I could hear was the roar of the wind against my ears. And, with the wind, a smell arrived that slowed the pulse as though the blood sniffed danger, an enemy—an ambush; no, fresh-baked bread.

Yes; smells like bread and ambush both.

I'd smelled them before, long ago.

Get up, I told myself. Shouldn't have waited so long to take that sleeping pill last night. Where in the hell did I put my sunglasses? Sun, wind, blasting, like fire in the eyes. Tearful, I groped for the sunglasses.

There. After I put them on, I could see slumbering goats, saluki dogs, the infant-girl also sleeping, and the two Badawia wives sitting by the fire and refueling it with dry goat dung, just as Ahmed used to do in the meadow that rolled between Qalqiliya and Kfar Sabba.

There were meadows where houses, shops, and factories stand today, and a blazing carpet of bewitching wild poppies conjured by the first rain. The poppies were as potent in death as in life.

That is why, in the summer, no one would venture into the meadows. Even police dogs avoided the place in their search for Jews and Arabs fighting each other and the Tommies.

I kept it secret in my heart as a child, how I wished to cross that divide, and be inside the Arab houses—so close to my home town, Kfar Sabba, I could almost touch them from my window in the enclosed porch. At night they looked like a constellation of stars. In daylight they changed colors with the shifting angles of the sun. And in the heat of summer, the plain that stretched in the divide would shimmer like a lake, so wide I could barely see the hills. Only for a moment or two in the early morning, just before the summer sun would steam-dry the dew, could I see the Arab houses clustered uphill. At high noon the summer sun would bleach them out, and, in the late afternoon, a purple haze would veil them. But, when the winter rain washed away the dust that clogged the air, the horizon became wider than ever, and it seemed but a short walk from my home town to Qalqiliya.

From opposite directions, Ahmed and I led our goat to the meadow. Ahmed seemed as surprised to see me at first as I was to see him, and just as afraid. He was as little as I was. And, like in the scary movies, the meadow earth was steaming after the rain. And purple cyclamen bloomed among the poppies, white and yellow narcissus scented the air and beckoned the bees. But snakes crawled up on the rocks to warm their blood in the winter sun. Like albinos, they were sun-shy in summer and kept under the rocks and the tangled thistles and thorns that shaded the weeds that the goats loved to munch on.

"*Dir balak*—watch out. Step on a snake and you will die of snakebite," Ahmed would tell his mother's goats and mine. The first words of Arabic my mother's goats—and I—knew, we learned from Ahmed. "My kinfolk would kill me if they knew that I even looked at your shepherd-child-girl," Ahmed told my mother's goats.

"My kinfolk would punish me if they knew *I* looked at your shepherd-child-boy," I said to his mother's goats.

"Why, because I am an Arab?"

"No, because the men of your tribe are like the poppies: one glance, and you are bewitched for life. That is what I heard my kinfolk say."

"But that is what I heard my kinfolk say about the women of your tribe..."

Bread and ambush.

Thirty or forty goats are napping only a few feet from the blankets by the fire. The two Badawia co-wives are sitting on one blanket. Next to them, the infant-girl is sleeping on another. The blankets are spread on the ground—littered with animal dung; goats', saluki dogs', camels'... Two camels, out in the blinding sunshine, seem to be munching gravel, sand, and stones.

Not a blade of green around here. But farther up, or down—I wish I knew where north is here; I can't even tell if that speck of shimmering green is far or near, if it's a tree, a bush, or a dream-image like the dream-lake of dancing light across the fire smoke. But now the wind shifts direction. The lake disappears with the smoke, and the Badawias start coughing and spitting. They have to lean down, almost to the ground, to avoid spitting on their veils. Why do they veil their faces when there is no one to see them but each other?

Bejeweled and painted, the two co-wives are covered with exquisite shawls, glittering veils, and embroidered dresses, as if they are sitting in the harem of some oil-rich Arabian sultan and have to compete for his favor. Their face veils alone must weigh a few pounds and be worth a small fortune. Row after row of coins and beads—it is impossible to see what color the cloth that carries them is. The top row of coins digs into their cheekbones and nose; the bottom row dangles down almost to their breasts. How can they breathe under all that silver and gold? Clanking like a cash register whenever they bend down to spit.

And the flies keep buzzing from their spit to my face, to the animal dung, to the infant's lips, to the saliva dripping from the trembling tongues of the saluki dogs, to the Badawias' bloodshot eyes.

Only their eyes, and their leathery feet and hands, are not covered. Their eyes watch every move I make.

I try to ignore their eyes and their silence. I don't like the feeling here in the tents. The Badawias seem to be sorry they invited me; to say I'm not wanted here is an understatement.

"Don't form opinions," Russell had advised me. "Don't judge. Don't project. Don't assume. Don't anticipate. Don't romanticize. Don't take the initiative. Don't impose. Don't corrupt. Don't interfere... Keep a diary or journal, keep writing and before long you'll find the notebook will become a shelter, a companion, a private corner..."

But I didn't come here to be stuck in a paper shelter. I've been stuck way too long in the biggest private corner of them all—Exile...

Two p.m.? Can't be! My watch must be wrong. The angle of the sun reads... Can't tell east from west here, so it could be 2:00 p.m. or 10:00 a.m.—ten or two, it makes no difference here, I guess.

The two Badawias don't let me out of their sight. Even when I went to relieve myself in a ditch behind a cluster of huge boulders, halfway there I noticed the girl-wife following me, silent and dark like a shadow, and only a few steps behind me. She stood and watched me take a piss, then wash my hands and face, and brush my teeth with the last drops of water from my canteen (I didn't want to use their water without permission; a few jerricans stand here near the fire, but who knows how far their water source is from the tents). The girl-wife didn't utter a sound. Like a dancer, she glided soundlessly behind me back to the blankets. The senior wife must have moved the blankets over next to the fire; they look like carpets now, which is what they are—hand-woven, rough wool, faded, frayed, dusty, stained, and—infested with lice and fleas. The Badawias keep scratching, and me with them now.

I should have packed something for lice, flea bites. If the Badawias possess such a concoction, there is no evidence of it. This itchiness keeps spreading, as if God-knows-what is crawling all over the head and body. Nerves? Exhaustion? Allergy? The sun? The shade?

The sun–shade contrast is amazing here. That walk from the blazing ditch to the shade of the tent took me from a furnace to a freezer.

Tea bubbles in a cracked enamel pot. A horde of flies fights for space on the rim of the steaming tea glass. The senior wife fans them away, her bracelets, a dozen at least on each wrist, jingling like silver bells. How gracefully she moves. Her bloodshot eyes, torn wide with kohl and blue tattoos, spark fiercely, almost savagely. She rests a small steaming glass of tea on the sand in front of my carpet—fills her glass last, but drinks first. How can she, under her veil? She empties her glass in a deliberate manner, as if to show me the tea is not poisoned. Why? Do I look like I need such reassurance, or is it part of a ritual, a custom? Is she that mistrustful of me?

The tea glass is scorching hot. I can't hold it.

"Yaa-salaam," mutters the senior wife, breaking the silence. "Yaa-salaam—good heavens," she says, but seems to imply, "What a pain. This guest spills precious water on the carpet."

"Yaa-salaam," echoes the girl-wife, as if to say, "Amen." Then she utters what sounds like a torrent of curses. She talks so fast, I can't understand a word she says.

I ask her to repeat her words slowly, wahada, wahada—one by one.

And she, her eyes fearful, her voice high in her throat, almost like a muffled scream, says, one by one, "Take off your eyes, your dark mirror djinn-demon-monster eyes."

The senior wife, her voice husky and fearless, tells her junior co-wife that she thinks the women of my tribe veil their eyes with dark mirrors.

"The sun is burning my eyes, just as the glass burned my hand," I say. Then I wrap my kerchief around the refilled tea glass and explain that, as the scarf protects my hand, the dark mirrors protect my eyes. But when I offer them my sunglasses to try, to see for themselves, they both refuse, recoil, as if afraid some alien calamity will strike if they touch them.

"*Guwwa*—power to you," says the senior wife, urging me to drink another glass. "Drink up so your hands, your eyes will grow strong, will need no protection." She wishes me power, it seems, so that my hand will be busy with her strong and oversweet tea and not with this notebook, another *djinn*-demon-monster. As soon as my hand picks up the glass, she whispers to her junior co-wife something that sounds like "Now, go snatch the *djinn*-demon-monster from the hands of the woman-stranger and throw it into the fire."

"You throw it into the fire, I'm afraid—*wallahi*—afraid . . . afraid . . ." the girl-wife whimpers at her senior co-wife like a frightened daughter at a mother. But when she addresses me, her voice is strong. "What are you doing?" she demands, a wild, hostile look in her eyes. "What are you doing?"

"Writing," I reply.

"What are you doing?" the child-wife repeats, the third time now, her fury growing.

"I am writing," I say slowly, enunciating each word carefully. I continue to scribble deliberately, like the senior wife and her tea—my own reassuring ritual.

"Why are you doing writing?" she asks.

"To remember and to learn," I say.

"You mock us." The senior wife grunts, almost like a TV comedian imitating an Arab.

And I also hear myself sounding like Johnny Carson doing his Arab routine on late-night TV. So flowery, formal—swearing upon my life and by Allah that I do not mock them. "*Wallah*, I'm offended," I say; how can they think that I would mock my gracious hosts.

"*Yaa-salaam*, she talks like a *rajol*—like a man," whispers the girl-wife. Don't men and women talk alike here? Do Badu women here skip the ceremonial bullshit? Is their talk straight, informal, because they're isolated and communicate only with their blood-kin?

"I did not mean to mock you," I say, as a woman should, I guess. Next I'll close this notebook, take off my sunglasses, my desert boots, my jeans; I'll dress like a Badawia and lose my identity.

"*Yaa-Rabb, yaa-Rabb,*" the older wife says with a sigh, "you remember—learn not from doing writing, but from generation to generation—*min jil le-jil.*"

"How do you do that?" I ask.

"*Allah alem,*" she replies. "Allah knows how I remembered-learned everything my mother had remembered-learned from her mother and also everything my daughter remembered-learned from her daughter."

"And you?" I ask the girl-wife.

"*Wallahi,*" she says, "I remember everything my father did remember from his father's father."

"You've been blessed," I say. "Myself, I can't remember your names, for example, because I did not write them down. But you—do you remember my name?"

The two co-wives huddle, and all the hardware on their veils, wrists, ankles, necks (looks like real amber, turquoise, silver, and gold) *jingle-jangles.* I can't hear a word they whisper to each other.

"How can we remember your name when you did not tell us what is your name?" said the girl-wife. An out-and-out lie, straight to my face, without a blink.

"Did I not tell you my name right after I gave my breast to your infant-girl?" I say to the girl-wife.

"*La*—no," she replies.

"Well, you see how, without writing, I cannot even remember if I told you my name or not . . . What is your name?" I ask the senior wife.

"It is not proper to ask questions," she replies.

"But did you not ask me questions?" I say.

"Ask me, ask me," says the girl-wife like a girl-child. "I wish to see my name."

"No, *haraam, ayb*—shameful, forbidden," says the senior wife to her junior co-wife.

"But who will see tomorrow?" mutters the girl-wife.

"Are you ill?" I ask her.

Silence.

"Is she ill?" I ask her senior co-wife.

"*Allah yaa-aref*—Allah knows," replies the senior wife. "Everything takes the time it is inscribed to take."

"I wish to see my infant's name, and mine, and also hers," whispers the girl-wife, as if it was her dying wish. The older wife doesn't say this time, "*Haraam, ayb*—shameful, forbidden."

"*Yalla, yalla*—quick-fast—do writing," says the girl-wife, surly and impatient. "*Yalla*, write, show how names look."

The senior wife's name is *Azzizah*, meaning "joyful," "happy."

The girl-wife's name is *Tammam*, meaning "complete," "whole."

"For, when we were born," explains Tammam, "Azzizah's mother saw her daughter was born Azzizah. And when I was born, my mother saw I was born Tammam. And when my daughter was born, I saw she was *Salimeh*—meaning 'peaceful,' meaning 'whole,' 'complete,' like when I myself was born, and also 'joyful,' 'happy,' like Azzizah." Only the infant looks like her name, Salimeh— peaceful, sleeping wrapped in her scratchy carpet among the goats and the flies.

Tammam asks me to point to her infant's name. I hand her the notebook, but she won't touch it. She is so afraid of this *djinn*-demon- monster that she uses me as a shield, crouching behind my back, peeking at the names over my shoulder. "*Wallahi, wallahi*," she mutters when I point to her daughter's name. "Come look at the names," she calls out to her senior co-wife, but Azzizah... How can she light a cigarette, smoke under her veil? Her cigarette smells like hashish. Tammam also rolls a cigarette—bends down almost to the ground, sticks it under her veil... Smoke drifts as if her veil was on fire... "Show me my name. I lost it," she says. "Show again. I lost it, I lost it."

I point to her name and explain that I do not know to write in Arabic, and so I write her name in English.

"Does 'English' mean 'writing'?" Tammam asks. She doesn't seem to grasp that there are languages other than her own.

Tammam

52

I write it separately for her, frame it, so that she won't lose it again.

She asks me to turn this *djinn*-demon-monster notebook from side to side; from each and every side she wishes to see her name.

"What do you see?" I ask her.

"*Wallah, Wallah,* I see my name is small and little and hiding in a cave like a pouch," says Tammam. "Now I see a tree ... *il siyal* (acacia?) and a black goat-hair tent, and two mountain peaks and a gorge plunging—*yaa-Rabb*—how deep in between ... But now, from this side, I see a mother and father, and another mother and father and one standing here, you see? ... Here, one standing all alone to one side like an orphan—no, like a palm tree—no, like an eagle, yes ... and I see edges ... sharp edges, *yaa-Rabb*, sharp edges like daggers pointing ..."

"*Bas—bas*—enough, *yaa*-Tammam. Go away from the *djinn*-demon monster," says Azzizah, the senior wife.

Tammam obeys her, glides away to her infant, cradles her daughter in her arms, rocks back and forth, back and forth—tears glued to her eyes. Again and again, she repeats each verse, "O hear what my mother had told me before she departed ... Behold, my life leaves me at the time inscribed ... And going to Allah I take my leave of you, my love, my child, my daughter, so take what is left of my life and enjoy it ..."

The infant's laughter delights her girl-mother.

How beautiful Tammam's eyes are. Maybe, as the rumors have it, the men of this tribe hide their women because they are so very beautiful. I haven't seen their faces unveiled, but how they carry themselves—the senior wife also, her bloodshot eyes wrinkled and sometimes fierce, but how regal and sensuous she carries herself, moving like a graceful dancer, her jewels like delicate wind chimes when she turns to the infant. Salimeh leaps to her arms, squealing, delighted.

"What is your name?" Tammam asks me, all traces of tears in her eyes and voice having drifted away like smoke with the shifting wind.

"My name is Leora."

"Leora? What does 'Leora' mean?" she asks.

"'Leora' means 'Light unto me'," I reply.

"But that is not a good name," says Azzizah.

"My name is not good? Why?" I ask.

"Not good, immodest to call a woman so endearingly 'Light unto me'," Azzizah replies. "Only your husband can call you 'Light unto me' ... and only in your tent. *Aywa*—yes ... It is not a good name, for if your husband were to hear another man calling you, his wife, so endearingly, 'Light unto me', he would be bound to kill him ... Our husband cannot call you 'Light unto me'. No, *wallahi*— by God—no, he cannot. No stranger can call you that, but I remember now ... *Wallahi*, I remember you did tell us your name was 'Nura', meaning 'light'. Yes, that is your name ..."

And so she has invented a new name for me, just like that.

"How did you know I have a husband?" I ask her.

"Every woman has a husband," replies Azzizah, "unless ... *yaa-Rabb*, did your husband divorce you, *yaa*-Nura? Did he cast you off?"

"No."

"Pray he never will," mutters Azzizah.

✞

"Arik must be turning in his grave ...," people said when I married Dave.

You would be dizzier than hell, Arik, had you spun in your grave each time they said so.

"Arik must be turning in his grave ...," they said when your friend Yehoshua, in his telegram of condolences, proposed to marry me the day he heard you fell. (Yehoshua was in Washington then, when the Sinai War broke out.) Can you imagine how it shocked the mourners sitting *Shiv'ah* for you?

His telegram arrived before you were shifted from the killed-in-the-line-of-duty to the missing-in-action. Your brother was so livid you would have thought Yehoshua was encroaching on his territory; that a widow was still bound by law to marry her husband's brother, unless he released her and himself from this legal obligation.

Almost all the mourners were secular, but you wouldn't have guessed it from their reaction. It seems that age-old tribal laws and customs can't be shrugged off in three or four generations. So deeply were they entrenched in tribal mentality that virtually in unison the murmurs began: "Arik must be turning in his grave... How could Yehoshua... not wait a year, or at least thirty days, let alone seven days of mourning to pass, before he offers to marry Arik's Leora... As if no man but a friend as fiercely loyal to Arik as Yehoshua would be willing to be so helpful to Arik's family, to go even as far as to marry a woman ten or eleven years his junior, still vital and attractive... As if his offer was honorable and not simply an attempt to possess her..."

Everyone knew that my paycheck alone couldn't cover our mortgage payments, Levi's and my medical care, our water, electricity, and grocery bills, and the taxes, of course. Everyone offered to help. And my parents insisted that Levi and I move from that room-and-a-half that you and I called home to their apartment. Your brother thought Levi and I would fare better if we moved to the *Moshav* that he and his circle had founded in the Negev. My mother's aunt thought Levi and I could use a breather in Toronto, Canada, so she mailed me a plane ticket. And Yehoshua, knowing how proud I was, how I liked to think of myself as independent, even of you, proposed to marry me, not only as a favor to me, you, and our son, Levi, you'd say, but because Yehoshua loved me secretly—or so he liked to think...

It didn't occur to him, or to anyone, me included, to ask a government ministry or agency for financial assistance, so accustomed were we to give, not take. Even my paycheck, hard-earned though it was, caused me embarrassment. It's hard to believe today that we were so inexperienced and short-handed, it didn't seem unusual that a girl not yet nineteen, without any qualifications other than a high-school diploma and a few months of army service, would be hired to take charge of a community center. God only knows where I found the audacity to run that center of that tin-shack town that housed thousands of newcomers, some of whom had never seen running water or electricity. Some, like the Badu, didn't know how to read or write, and ate with their fingers. Others ate an apple with a fork and knife, and could read, write, and quote philosophers, poets, and scientists in nine languages. That diverse assortment had to be integrated, or The Land would quickly become like the Tower of Babel. And the women, thousands of women—unlike the men and the youths who picked up Hebrew at work, in city streets, and army service—were stuck in that town, caring for infants and children, elderly parents, and fellow survivors who made you wonder if insanity was not the sane response to the suffering inflicted in the ghettos, the mass expulsions, the extermination camps…

During the Sinai War, in a newspaper ad framed in black, the newcomers of that tin-shack town conveyed how they sorrowed with their war bereaved—and with me as well… It didn't dawn on them till years after that war that their government had managed to scrape the funds needed to launch the Sinai War, but not the funds required to provide them with decent living quarters, or to support those widowed and orphaned by the damned war. Twenty years or so later, these newcomers realized they had the power of majority to topple the leaders who had ruled The Nation for thirty years and install instead the leaders of the opposition— among them none other than our Yehoshua.

Yes, he's a cabinet minister. Our Yehoshua, can you imagine, Arik? He quit his tin business soon after the Sinai War, got into politics, joined the opposition, and became such a shit-disturber— almost as if he couldn't live with the thought that you had been wasted for nothing; as if he had vowed that mistakes like the war that claimed you, my Arik, won't happen again, not if he could help it. Such a noise he made about any leader, general, or minister he believed to be negligent, unscrupulous, self-serving, or corrupt—people, inside and out of The Land, were saying he was irresponsible, or tunnel-visioned, or just plain dumb if he didn't realize that his shit-disturbing was giving fodder to Jew-haters the world over. But Yehoshua kept at it in the opposition—and now in the coalition—without giving a damn what people said about him—even here, in this Land, where people give a hell of a damn what anyone, anywhere, says about them or any Jew.

You liked it, Arik, that he was like a wild card. But your brother hates him now more than ever. The Nation is in peril, your brother thinks, if one of our cabinet ministers is a man who offered to marry his best friend's wife, war-widowed only a day.

That telegram of Yehoshua's, or rather the story of it, was circulated over the years as a sort of a character reference, and it circled ever wider, the higher Yehoshua rose in prominence. Even in Canada you can see Yehoshua on TV and in magazines and newspapers. In person, I hadn't seen him in years.

So imagine, on the eve of my departure to this forbidden compound, I get back to the hotel. And as I pass the terrace, perched on the cliffs sheltering the beach, I hear a man calling out my name. The voice sounded familiar, but I couldn't place him. I shaded my eyes from the sun setting behind him, and I saw Yehoshua inviting me to join his table, just like he used to, with a wave of a wrist.

For a moment, I could almost touch you by looking at him, my Arik. I couldn't take my eyes off him. He looked better in person than on TV, and much better than in his younger years. He looks distinguished now, successful, happy—would you have aged like that? I wonder.

It took but a word, a gesture, a glance from Yehoshua to unleash the memories, tugging the past into the present, and spinning emotions up, down, sideways—as if it was only yesterday that his kid sister, Ya'el, and I were in Grade 5 at public school. And after completing our chores, we'd get together to do our homework and play at her parents' apartment, or mine, in Tel Aviv at that time—where the back balcony faced the back of Ben-Gurion's house. On evenings when it was too hot to close the shutters, Ya'el and I would watch Ben-Gurion doing his "homework," as we called it, dressed in pajamas, just like my father's and Ya'el's. And, like her mother and mine, Ben-Gurion's wife, Paula, would give us

hell whenever we got carried away by the energies of our innocence. "Be quiet . . . Ben-Gurion can't think, can't sleep!!" Paula
would yell from a back window, and we loved it that we had such
power to serve The Nation by keeping quiet . . .

I don't remember if it was Yehoshua, his wife, or Yehoshua's
host or guest—an American yachtsman—who insisted I sit down
with them, for a cup of coffee at least.

"Leora is related to me—by marriage, you might say," Yehoshua
told the American yachtsman. "Leora's first husband and I were
closer than most brothers . . . We were classmates since kindergarten, till we graduated from the Technion, with our degrees in
architecture, when there was no milk and honey in this land of
milk and honey, and when hundreds of thousands of newcomers
expelled from Arab lands, and the survivors of the death camps,
had to be housed. So, for free, my friend Arik went and designed a
dream town to house them. But the civil servants, being civil servants, couldn't believe that such a beautifully planned town could
be built at such a low cost. And there was no convincing them.
'Your town is a dream unattainable for years, if not decades,' I told
Arik. I urged him to quit architecture, as I had, and go into the tin
business with me. Or to sign up to serve in the standing air force."

"Arik was an ace pilot," said Shoshana, Yehoshua's wife—knows
you from his stories, no doubt, which she must have heard
umpteen times . . . The longer you don't fly, the better a pilot you
become—such is the nature of nostalgia.

"Yes, but as much as Arik loved to fly, he hated even the
thought of a permanent army or air force here in The Land,"
Yehoshua went on. "The war would end any day, any day, Arik
believed. So he continued to serve as a pilot in the reserves and
earned his salary by teaching architecture. He and his students
built a model of his dream town. Soon afterward, the Sinai War
broke out and Arik fell—"

Shoshana interrupted Yehoshua to remind him friends were
expecting them for dinner, and we dispersed; them to their lives,
and me, back to limbo.

I had no idea what Tal would look like when I went to meet him next morning. (A week or ten days ago. Yesterday? A decade ago? Feels just the same.) Who was Tal among the men in the hotel lobby? The place was crowded with Israelis, wound up as if they had overslept. Ever since the bus was attacked on the coastal highway, only a few kilometers away, very few tourists had checked into this seaside hotel, even now, in August, the height of the tourist season. It was Sunday, the first working day of the week in The Land, and half the crowd was waiting, it seemed, for the other half to check out. I recognized not one face in that crowd, other than the hotel staff. As I stood there, I felt like a tourist myself.

I *did* remember Tal saying on the phone the night before that he was a kibbutznik. But that didn't help; no man in that lobby looked like a kibbutznik, definitely not like any of the ones who used to assign me shit-duty in the border kibbutz where I was supposed to do army service. I also remembered Tal saying that he was Gingie's former commander. But in a lobby filled with men drafted to serve regular and reserve duty from the age of eighteen to fifty-five, how could you tell, when no army has more commanders per soldiers than our defense force, and most, like Arik, look like they didn't rank above private.

One man in the lobby seemed to wonder if I was looking for him. But he was standing in the corner, like a security man—a handsome security man. No, on second glance, he was not more handsome, or less so, than the next man. If he was a commander, his men would have followed him into the line of fire because he appeared to be so much like every man; they would think, if he can do it, so can I. Ah, but he exudes that certain something that you, my Arik, had; that unmistakable something of a man reclaimed by the reclamation of his land, by the gathering of his people, by the defense of his nation. He looked years older than Gingie, closer to my generation than to Gingie's. Even a kibbutznik couldn't take a week off to go to the desert on a minute's notice from Gingie, I thought; he must have a wife, children, a job. His eyes traveled from me to the glass wall, behind which sat the Jeep that Gingie had picked for me to purchase.

Parked there, next to the shiny, pristine luxury cars, my Jeep looked like a throwback to the days of austerity in The Land when you rarely saw a vehicle that didn't look like it would conk out had it not been for the ingenuity, the prayers, and the sweat poured into maintaining the engine.

I was about to go outside, to wait by the Jeep, when the man from the corner walked over to me.

"Leora?"

"Yes. Tal?"

"Yes. *Boker tov*—good morning."

"*Boker orr*—morning bright."

"*Boker tov . . . boker orr*, Leora," chimed a couple behind me— Yehoshua and his wife, Shoshana, and a few feet behind them, Yehoshua's bodyguard, wearing over his plainclothes the tell-tale safari jacket that bodyguards wear to hide their weapons. The guard was like a banner of office, announcing that Yehoshua was a cabinet minister.

"What are you doing up so early in the morning?" Yehoshua asked me. And I could almost taste the life I lost when I lost you, my Arik.

I was about to introduce Tal to Yehoshua and his wife, when a hotel guest, who looked like the only sweat he broke was on a tennis court, came to pay homage to Yehoshua.

"All honor to you," the tennis player said. "You were speaking for me, I must tell you, when you were saying, on TV, that we should pause to consider if it would not cost us the Promised Land to give Sinai to Egypt for a promise of peace. You took the words out of my mouth, upon my life, when you said that we should pause to remember how dearly we paid for giving Sinai to Egypt after the Sinai War, and what a buffer zone the Sinai desert was in the Yom-Kippur War—only five years ago and already all too many of us forget."

"A people who forget the past won't have a future," pronounced Yehoshua.

"Oh, we won't have a future. We'll be finished in the next war, if we give Sinai to Egypt," said the tennis player. "We can't trust Egypt or America, or any country in the world. War after war, we see we can't depend on anyone but ourselves. But, war after war, we forget..."

That xenophobic hawk was straining Tal's patience and tolerance, I sensed. Tal was clearly itching to get going, to get away—from me?

He was evaluating my character now, I sensed, in the harsh light of this resort hotel, its guests, their shiny new cars, the tennis player, my friend the cabinet minister and his wife, their bodyguard, the security men in army uniform and in plainclothes—and that lobby. A new addition, it looked like it had been designed by a committee that couldn't agree on the hotel's location, half seeing it in the Middle East and half in Europe. On the walls behind the reception desk, a huge mosaic mural has been inlaid as a sort of invocation of the ancient ruins at Bet-Alpha and Kfar Nahum. Persian carpets, faded with dignity like in the old European hotels, were carefully scattered over floors of local marble. A jungle of tropical plants, in imitation ancient Roman and Greek fired-clay vessels, flourished by the glass wall facing west, toward the Mediterranean. The glass wall facing east, toward Jerusalem, looked over the parking lot.

Tal kept watching the Jeep beyond the glass wall, as if he feared that someone would steal it, or perhaps hoping someone would. It must have registered that I am tall, but slender, with no muscle bulk—not a good bet to be much help if the Jeep was to roll over in some deserted wadi, pinning us beneath it. Besides, Gingie must have told him that I don't know the desert—where his life would depend on me, mine on him... As I watched his jaw clench, I was sure he was kicking himself for being all too quick to volunteer for this journey with a woman he had never met, in a dented old Jeep, with no safety bar, on roads-no-roads into which flash floods had swept mines from battlefields long buried under the sand . . . Then his eyes met mine, and we laughed, both of us only too aware that our lives would never be the same if we didn't cancel this journey right now.

"*Boker tov, boker orr*," the hotel manager chimed, having come over to us once the tennis player had left. "I hope you enjoyed your stay." Addressing Yehoshua and Shoshana, the manager was text-book gracious.

"Oh, we did." Yehoshua was as well. "The food, the service—everything was first rate. I feel like new after a weekend here. You run a first-class seaside resort, I must tell you."

"Kills me to hear it." The hotel manager was confessional now. "We are full only on weekends, you know, and only with Israelis. We spend a fortune on advertising all over the world, but after the latest terrorist attacks, the tourists stay away as if this hotel was in the middle of a war zone."

"Next time we meet with the Egyptian delegation, we will hold the peace-talks at this hotel. Your reservation lines will be jammed after that," Yehoshua said to the hotel manager. Then he looked at me as if I had made the mistake of my life in not responding to his wedding proposal.

I was bursting to ask: Will it be the mistake of my life if I give my consent to Arik's only son—my Levi—to serve as a pilot, like his father? Should I give my consent? Tell me, Yehoshua: What did you guys in the cabinet decide—to trade Sinai to Egypt for peace or to keep Sinai and brace for war?

"We better get going, Leora, or we won't make it to the Gulf of Suez before nightfall." Tal pulled me back to the present, just as the sands of the past and the future were dancing out from under me like in a desert storm.

"You can't get to the Gulf of Suez without a military pass," said Yehoshua, seeming to, once again, like in the days before Arik went, be like a big brother to me. "It wouldn't take more than a phone call to get you a pass," he added, his eyes searching for a phone.

"No need to phone," muttered Tal. "We have all the required papers, permits, passes."

"Are you sure?" said Yehoshua.

"Yes," Tal replied.

"Meet Tal." I finally introduced him.

Yehoshua and Shoshana introduced themselves by their first names, just like in the old days. But then, Tal, it seemed, skipped a beat in a refrain familiar to them when he didn't acknowledge in any way Yehoshua's powerful position. And now they disregarded him, as just another piece of luggage.

"You are not going to the Gulf of Suez hoping that Arik, like Jonah, will step from the belly of the great fish, are you?" Yehoshua asked, as if my life revolved around no one and nothing but Arik, even after all these years, decades, of widowhood; as if the more inconsolable, devastated, the war widow, the more of a man, not only her husband is, but every man defending The Nation . . .

I am going to Sinai to reclaim the woman buried in the rubble of widowhood, I wanted to say, but I knew it was way out of line.

"Yehoshua and Arik, my first husband, fell in the Sinai War, were friends, closer than most brothers," I said to Tal, to bring him in from the periphery to which Yehoshua and Shoshana had banished him.

"Tal had the rank of commander in the Unit," I told Yehoshua and Shoshana, hoping it wouldn't impress them. But of course it did. After the rescue mission at Entebbe, the whole nation regarded the men of the Unit as a national treasure, albeit a top-secret one. Their names and faces were censored in all media coverage until they no longer served even reserve duty in the Unit—or until they died. Tal hadn't mentioned the Unit on the phone the night before, only that he was Gingie's former commander. But it didn't seem to surprise him that I knew Gingie served in the Unit, or that I used the Unit to lend him credence. I saw in his eyes that one too many had done it, as if he had been defined by the Unit as I was by war-widowhood.

"What was your rank?" Yehoshua asked Tal, clearly accustomed to having classified information declassified for him.

"Major," replied Tal, his face burning.

"Our finest all blush modest." Yehoshua chuckled, beaming as if Tal were his favored son. Turning to his wife, he added, "A major in the Unit is leadership material, you know ... You will have plenty of time to stop in Yamit," Yehoshua said to me.

"Very much like the model of Arik's dream town, Yamit," Shoshana explained to Tal.

Now, ask Yehoshua, I thought; your son's life might depend on it. But it smacked of corruption, of self-serving favoritism, even to ask him if it was true that the government would rather Yamit be destroyed than hand it over with the rest of Sinai to Egypt in return for peace.

"The model that Arik and his students built of his dream town is gathering dust in the archives of the Technion, you know," I muttered instead. Yehoshua looked at me as if I had said that the Zionist dream was gathering dust—me, who dropped out of The Land, the Zionist dream ...

"I'll find a place to display the model of Arik's dream town," Yehoshua responded.

"Display? Why? His model is of an unattainable dream in those days of austerity, you told Arik. But now—do you think it slipped through the cracks of time, it's a thing of the past, an artifact of history, some quaint object to be displayed?" I said, a mad war widow barely able to suppress her demons.

"I'll find a place to display the model of Arik's dream town," Yehoshua repeated.

"In your office?" suggested his wife.

"Yes, somewhere in the Ministry building ..." Yehoshua lost me then; the next thing I knew he and his wife were saying their goodbyes.

"It was good to see you. Drive safely."

"Somewhere in the Ministry building ...," I heard myself muttering as Tal and I headed for the exit door. "Arik is finished. Gone. A relic of the past. He wouldn't recognize Yehoshua now, his best friend ... thinks he is doing me a favor by sticking a dream he shared with Arik in some glass box somewhere in the Ministry building..."

"He was okay in the opposition, but now he's carrying it too far ... if the latest is true," said Tal.

"Carrying what? ... What latest?" I said, my pulse pounding a requiem for you, my Arik.

The soldiers guarding the entrance to the parking lot turned their eyes from mine as if I, like every other hotel guest, was aware that such cushy assignments went to soldier-boys who were cherished only sons—like our Levi—and whose parents refused to waive their exemptions from high-risk duty, or to those who barely passed their physical, psychological, or IQ tests.

If that is why Levi feels so pressed to get my written consent for him to serve as a pilot like his father, I would rather he guard abandoned luggage carts. And if his army record marks him for life, let him live and overcome it. I have had it with requiems.

"What's this latest about Yehoshua?" My tone—obnoxious, demanding—I was grasping for anything to fill that perpetual hollow of my grief for Arik. Seven days and nights of this neediness would be hell, even in a populated area with plenty of distractions available; in a deserted wadi giving was called for, not demanding. Tal had his own powerful reason to go to the desert, or to get away, I knew then, when he let it slide.

"Yehoshua is deploying dirty tricks to drive the Bedouins from the Negev," said Tal, "to clear space for the military installation we'd have to move from the Sinai to the Negev if and when we sign a peace pact with Egypt..."

"I can't believe it ... even of this new Yehoshua ... would kill Arik, if it were true," I added, sad-glad to see a black chuckle in his eyes.

The Jeep was already broiling hot to the touch, even at the coast, where the morning August sun was tempered by a sea breeze.

"There was no time, I see, to clamp on a couple of racks for the jerricans," I said.

"No. They didn't rattle too much on the way here, and in the wadis it doesn't matter if a jerrican or a knapsack bounces on your head—each knocks you out just the same. All the gear will be secured to the floor," said Tal, climbing into the Jeep through the passenger's door. From there we stuffed my knapsacks, duffel bag, sleeping bag, and parka into the back of the Jeep. It was much faster and easier than unhooking and unlacing the canvas flaps at the back or sides. I climbed into the driver's seat, and I could see that he had packed a tool box as large as the one Russell had carried in his Land-Rover, and an even larger first-aid kit. But only four jerricans.

"Aren't we a bit short?" I said.

"No. Two for water, two for gasoline. More than sufficient," Tal replied.

Plenty, if jerricans multiplied like rabbits, I wanted to say. But instead I told myself, Tal knows the desert and you do not. The gut instinct that said we were traveling too light was informed by fear, I reasoned, by fear and by that craving for more, more, more— that insatiable craving to fill the emptiness of loss. I was setting out to close that circle once and for all, and it was opening up, growing wider with my efforts.

"We better get going," said Tal, and waited for me to move. It was as if a new law of The Land decreed that a man shall sit in the passenger seat only when another man is driving.

I stuck to The Land I knew. "I am itching to drive, to be in control of this Jeep, at least. You too?"

"No," Tal replied, handing me the ignition key, but leaving his door open. The sea breeze kept blowing out the matches he struck, so I waited until his cigarette was lit, his door closed, his window open.

The Jeep rolled out of the parking lot, away from the sea, and on to the coastal highway. Soon, we were passing the Monument Boat. More of a dinghy than a boat, it was painted black and white, bore a plaque and had been raised on a sandhill fashioned to resemble a pedestal. But still it looked abandoned, left on that sandhill because it was too old for the sea and too new for the museum.

Traffic zoomed past the boat, only a school bus slowing as it approached. The teacher was probably telling of the days when the Tommies ruled The Land and slammed the doors shut, even to the survivors of the death camps... The schoolchildren probably yawned. Oh shit, *Exodus* again! They'd have seen the movie umpteen times on TV.

Here and there, west of the coastal highway, were the dunes where the counselor in the youth movement had dragged us to remember the boat people.

Into three sections, the counselor divided the dunes. One he designated as The Land; the second, as The Sea; the third, as The Next World. Then, after nightfall, he divided us into three groups. Those designated as the Underground Fighters had to smuggle the second group—the Death Camp Survivors—past the third group—the Tommies—and into The Land. Whoever got caught by the Tommies had to go to The Next World, as did the Tommies who got caught by the Underground Fighters.

The counselor sat on the water jerricans all day. After nightfall, he would say, "The boat people had no water, and neither did you. The boat people carried on despite it all, and so will you. The boat people measured up to the task, and so will you." His words were not mere slogans to us youngsters. Our generation was not battered to a stupor by banalities. The times were epochal. The extraordinary was as ordinary as our own parents.

Oh, but how earnest we were. What a humorless generation was ours. It was a dream night for youngsters to slip out in pairs. From horizon to horizon the sky glittered with the promise of love. In starlight, the dunes curved like an erotic backdrop, not a battleground. And we were juiced up like goats and rams in heat. But no one broke free of the mold that had shaped us to serve The Nation first and foremost. And no one giggled, uttered a curse, or even, heaven forbid, whimpered or groaned.

4

"*Yaa*-Nura, did you write-remember to bring us the gifts you had promised when you first entered our tents?" whispers Tammam, the girl-wife.

She wants to see what I brought to the tents. But the older wife keeps telling her, then me, "*Haraam*—not proper. Do not untie…"

"Is it proper for a guest to tell her hostess, 'No, I will not show you my presents'?" I ask her.

"No, it is not proper," replies Tammam. "Let us see the gifts now…"

The senior wife hushes her and murmurs, "Allah shall bless you for asking what is proper." Then, cutting her words *wahada, wahada*—one by one—she tells me, "A proper guest presents her gifts upon her arrival, but modestly she must leave her presents inside the tent, where the goats will not eat them and where the mistress of the tent will observe them but not see them." To her junior co-wife, Azzizah adds, "*Aywa*—yes—it is not proper for the mistress of the tent to see her guest's gifts because she welcomes guests for the honor, not for the gifts."

Tammam tells her—God, how fast they talk when they don't want me to understand, or when they are irritable—Tammam sounds like a teenage girl telling her mother to get off her back. It doesn't seem to bother the senior wife. "Will you show us your gifts or not?" Tammam snaps.

"What is it proper to do now?" I mutter.

"Whatever will please a guest is proper for a guest to do," replies the senior wife. She is curious also to see her presents. Yet when I empty the duffel bag onto the carpet, she gets up and glides away—to the ditch? Is she angry? At Tammam? At me?

"*Yaa*-Azzizah, come back, look at all the many gifts," Tammam shouts to her.

Azzizah doesn't turn around, does not even glance back. A gust of wind flaps her dresses and veils in our direction; she's walking against the wind, so maybe she can't hear.

Only ashes and stones remain in the scorched fire-circle. The saluki dogs run herding patterns around the goats, trying to keep them close to the tent, and dust chokes the lungs. The infant starts to cough; as soon as she cries, her girl-mother nurses her, the presents scattered now over her carpet. "What is for me and what for Azzizah?" says the girl-wife Tammam.

"Whatever you and Azzizah decide," I reply. "What did you mean when you said earlier 'Who will see tomorrow?'" I add.

Suddenly, all glint of recognition leaves her eyes. It is as if I were some ghost. She sits among the barking salukis, the goats, and the flies, bejeweled and kohled, and wearing an exquisite embroidered dress. Around her are stones, sand, and goat dung, and facing her is the carpet covered with presents. She nurses her infant, crying, delighted, "*Yaa-Allah, yaa-Allah*" and sorting out gifts—one by one, she heaps them all to one side—all for herself? Why does she pretend that I'm invisible?

I scratch like a monkey infested with lice, and she looks straight at me but doesn't seem to see me. "Did I say something wrong, improper?" I ask. "I didn't mean to intrude, to bother you in any way," I add.

The girl doesn't respond—not a word—not a grunt of recognition. I have never seen anything like it. She doesn't seem to take in the stranger-woman scratching like a monkey. But where could she have seen a monkey, even a photo of a monkey? It is hard to grasp that Tammam and Azzizah have never seen a book, newspaper, magazine, movie, TV; have never been to the zoo, or walked on a sidewalk, seen a street, a house, a chair, a bed, a kitchen, a bicycle, a garden, a rose, a green lawn, a forest, a restaurant, a bank, a store, a policeman, a doctor … It is hard to grasp that people can live so isolated only a journey of two days by Jeep from Eilat, yet we know next to nothing about them.

Azzizah seems to appear from nowhere, doubled over under a sackful of grain. Her back is sore; she rubs it to soothe the pain when she straightens up. The goats stamp over to the sack, driving the saluki dogs mad. The mountains echo Azzizah's call—"*Eerrrrjjjjuuuuu-yaa-rrruuckooo…*"— as she shoos away the goats, like Ahmed used to. Her back might be killing her, yet she glides light on her bare feet over sun-hot stones, and lifts and empties the sack. The goats finish the grain off too fast for me to see what kind she fed them. Where do they buy grain? Where do they store grain here? "Do you transport the grain from far away or from nearby?" I ask Azzizah.

"From far away Abu Salim transports the grain on camelback," she replies. "But nearby, we store the grain in one of the many caves."

Shadows shrinking—it must be close to noon. The Badawias serve for lunch what they served for breakfast—tea. They take their tea like my father—three pregnant spoonfuls of sugar to a glass, maybe even four. Not exactly a balanced diet, especially for Tammam, who is breastfeeding her infant.

"Look, Azzizah, look how many presents, all good, beautiful, look," Tammam bubbles as if Santa Claus, not I, had invested the time and thought, care and sweat, not to mention money, to purchase and lug from Canada everything she and Azzizah had asked me to purchase for them, and more.

But it was Azzizah's response that surprised me more than Tammam's.

"Look, Azzizah, look how beautiful the sweaters for little Salimeh," says Tammam.

"Beautiful, yes. But not good, worthless. Salimeh will soon outgrow them," says Azzizah to my face. "Not good, worthless," she says when she sees the black yarn. "It is not wool," she complains. "Worthless… not good," she mutters.

Only now I notice how worn Azzizah's clothes are: faded, frayed at the hem, dusty and stained like the carpets, and full of tiny burn holes from her cigarettes and fire sparks. But the embroidery work looks like a precious antique. It blinded me to the rest. By comparison, Tammam's clothes look new, well kept.

"*Aywa*—yes—worthless, not good, the yarn, the sweaters. But did you ever see such rainbow beads?" Tammam says to Azzizah.

At Dressmakers' Supply they thought I owned an embroidery shop. Here Azzizah mutters that I didn't buy enough rainbow—iridescent—beads, and not enough of each color, and not enough embroidery thread . . . Next, Azzizah sees the gold chains I brought—three, eighteen-carat gold, one for each wife and a tiny one for Salimeh. "The ring is missing." Azzizah frowns now.

"Where is the ring on the chain like yours?" Tammam asks me; finally she acknowledges my existence. And what am I going to tell her? That only war widows wear wedding bands on chains?

I told them that I didn't write-remember when I met them three or four months ago, but I'm writing it now so that next time I visit I'll not forget to bring the missing gold rings.

"By the will of Allah, it shall come into being—not by will of man, woman, stranger, or Badu," said Azzizah, in one word: "*Inshallah.*"

"Which one is for me and which for Azzizah?" Tammam asks me, pointing to the wristwatches.

"You and Azzizah decide," I reply.

"You can have them both . . . Not good, both worthless," mutters Azzizah to Tammam.

"I want only one," says Tammam, turning the watches from side to side, not able to choose. "What do you think of this one? . . . And that one?" she asks me, like the widows accustomed to having their late husbands make all the decisions.

"It makes no difference which one. The two watches are identical," I reply, "identical also to mine."

"Identical inside perhaps, but not identical outside," says Tammam. "Look, this watch looks like a bird flying, the other like a deep wadi, and yours like a mountain peak. Even the red shepherd running fast to gather straying sheep is a faster runner in this watch . . . But a faster runner will lose his breath, so maybe that watch is better?"

"The watches are not synchronized," I explain, then show her how they are all identical now.

"*Yaa-Allah, yaa-Allah!*" exclaims Tammam. "Show me how to move the wadis and mountains."

"The watch will break," Azzizah tells Tammam when the girl-wife tries.

"*Yaa-Allah, yaa-Allah*, look, Azzizah, look how you make a bird fly, how you erect a tent . . . bend a wadi!" Tammam's excited high-pitched shouting startles her infant. And Azzizah pulls out her withered breast to pacify Tammam's child.

The girl-mother seems to be completely engrossed with the watch. "How do you call the hour of the flying bird?" she asks.

"Fifteen after three," I reply. Corrupting her? Too late to worry now.

"*Wallah*, Azzizah, look, the hour of the flying bird is called 'fifteen after three'," says Tammam. The minute she learns a new thing, the junior wife shares it with her senior co-wife. "Look, Azzizah, the hour of the deep wadi is called 'five minutes before one', the hour of the mountain peak is called 'thirty-five minutes after five' . . ." The girl is fast—too fast?

"Who taught you to read a clock?" I ask her.

"You did, *wallahi*. What a good teacher you are," she replies.

"I think someone else was a good teacher before me," I say, and Tammam tells me not to worry, she and Azzizah will not tell their husband that I taught them the name of the hours.

"Why hide it from your husband? Does he forbid you to learn how to read time?" I say.

"What is the name of the hour now?" Tammam says in response. But ever since she and I moved the wadis and mountains to make the watches look the same, every watch shows a different hour.

"I don't know. Do you?" I reply.

"You see, worthless. The watches like all the other presents," says the senior wife Azzizah. And now she takes off her beaded necklace—incredible beadwork; it looks like a miniature Agam painting—and she presents it to me. "We Badu call this necklace *galb*, meaning 'heart'," she says, as if only the name is of value.

I refuse to accept it. "This gift is not good . . . worthless," I say, and Azzizah cracks up. But then she spits and tells me she'll dump all my gifts into the fire if I will not accept her gift. So I put on her necklace.

"*Mabrouka, yaa*-Nura—May you always be blessed," Azzizah tells me.

"Allah shall reward you," I say in response.

The girl-wife stares at her rings—three, four bands on each finger—then examines all the silver on her ankles and wrists, hides the tangle of necklaces under her shawl, takes off the turquoise ring, winces as she puts it back on her finger, then takes off one of her silver bracelets and puts it back on again. Again and again, she takes off a piece and puts it on again, wincing all the time.

"*Aywa*—yes," mutters Azzizah. "A gift—a favor—is as heavy as a mountain, brought over on a donkey but returned on a camel..."

And now Tammam hands me one of her silver rings, thinks for a moment, then hands me her turquoise ring also—as if the silver band was not sufficient.

"*Wallah*, more than sufficient," I assure her.

Her eyes light up. She takes her turquoise ring back, sticks her silver band on my finger, and mutters, "*Mabrouka*—May you always be blessed."

The goats nearly trampled little Salimeh. That child speed-crawls one moment, then *boom!* she crashes... Like Levi at that age when Arik went.

For days, weeks, that child was crawling, and looking for Arik behind this door, that door, like he used to whenever Arik played hide-and-seek. His tiny face would light up whenever it sounded like Arik was skipping up the stairs that led to our apartment. But the steps would pass by our front door, or a relative or friend would enter, and Levi would cry and cling to me as if he feared that I, like Arik, would disappear if he let go for a second...

❧

Levi was clinging to me when we boarded the El-Al plane, as though he knew it was nothing like the air force plane his father used to take him and me joy-riding in. The air force was very informal in those days, sort of like a family concern.

It was a sad winter day, that day I first flew out of The Land.

Raindrops, like tears, streaked the window of the El-Al plane—a prop plane, mostly empty. Very few among us Israelis had the means, in those austerity days, or the inclination, to fly abroad. Touching another land was almost like betraying your lover. And so small a village was The Land then, the pilot of our El-Al flight knew Arik, Levi, and me. We received the royal treatment, till we landed in London, where I had to switch airlines. (El-Al didn't have landing rights in Canada then.) So, in London, the El-Al crew escorted Levi and me to the transit lounge. Soon after we parted I discovered that my flight to Toronto was delayed—mechanical failure or weather conditions. I don't know how Trans-Canada had arranged for Levi and me to stay in London without a visa. The ground hostess spoke English too fast for me to understand and, when I asked her to speak slower, she addressed me as if I was an imbecile who was hard of hearing.

"We get you a taxi to take you, and baby, to very good hotel in London city," she told me. "You no have to pay for taxi, hotel stay, or food. You, and baby, eat in hotel." She was almost shouting. But she meant well. She scribbled the name and address of the hotel on a note she gave me just in case I got lost—which of course I did, even before I left the airport.

How Arik would enjoy this airport, I thought, as I wandered with Levi cradled in my arms through the maze of corridors, lounges, restaurants, bars, and shops, thinking Arik had never seen so many planes landing, taking off, refueling, parked in one place. And so many people under one roof—bigger than any in The Land—dressed in fancy clothes, like in the movies, rushing so fast, in so many different directions. And not one familiar face in a crowd. No one said "Shalom" in greeting or parting, or "How cute your infant, how old is he, what's his name?"... No one stopped to tell me what a terrible blow to the nation is Arik's loss, or that he probably hadn't fallen into Egyptian hands and probably wasn't being tortured in some Egyptian prison...

I was never more certain of that than when I passed by the check-in counter of Egypt Air and saw the Egyptian Arabs, not very far from the check-in counter of El-Al. (Terror attacks then were carried out only in The Land.) Like in a dream I passed by check-in counters of airlines of Arab nations at war with us. For eight years, not a day goes by that they don't embargo us, besiege us, threaten to drive us to the sea … yet here their sons and daughters—dressed in opulent *abia, kaffiyyes*, veils, and even fur coats over *thowbs* and *jalabeeyas*—were under the same roof with Levi and me and no one fired at us even a hostile glance. Perhaps they couldn't tell that I was Israeli. Your own people you recognize immediately. I saw no Israelis in the crowd; the El-Al counter was closed by the time I reached it.

For the first time in my life, I found myself in a place where no one knew who I was, where my parents came from, what I feared, dreamed, hoped. I had no idea how liberating the anonymity of exile could be until that moment. For the first time in my life I didn't feel compelled by the times, the place, the values instilled in me, to assume responsibility for anyone but my infant son and myself. For the first time, I wasn't compelled to meet anyone's expectations but my own, or conform to the mold that shaped my generation … Only for a few brief moments did that freedom last—moments as sweet as stolen water.

Levi, an independent soul even then, kicked and squirmed himself free of my arms. And before I could pick him up, the child crawled away, like he did at home whenever he wanted to play hide-and-seek. The faster I ran after him, the faster he crawled. Soon, he had scooted out of my sight. I called out his name, but the child, thinking he was in a crowded park or beach in The Land, waited for someone to pick him up and return him to me. Here, at the airport, though, the rushing crowds ignored me, as if, like in the nightmares, I had no voice.

'Watch out for the child!… Watch out … for my child!… Stop!… Be careful!' I was afraid the rushing crowd would trample him underfoot.

'*Leeevvviii!* …' I cried as soon as I spotted him, only a few seconds after I thought I had lost him in that wilderness of indifference.

I couldn't wait to get out of the airport. But almost everyone I approached to ask directions to the bus or taxi stand kept on rushing by; the few who stopped shrugged or muttered, even before I finished my question: 'Sorry, I don't know … don't understand …' And Levi, sick of being captive in my arms, wanted to crawl in the airport like at home, to eat in the airport like at home, to nap in a crib like at home … He was overtired and hungry. And I had no English pounds and only a few dollars. I wasn't allowed, by law, to take much foreign currency out of The Land. And I didn't know how much anything cost—how much to get to the hotel by cab. Or if I might need the dollars allotted to me—or more—for God knows what emergency. Never before had I been forced to wonder: Who do I know here? Who can I ask to back me up in an emergency?

So, this is exile, I thought, homesick already.

But London—What a surprise to find London festive and bright, not gray and drab as I had imagined. Display windows on Regent Street towered to the sky like mountains of emeralds, rubies, and diamonds. "Christmas lights," the taxi driver explained. It boggled my mind that anything Christian could be so beautiful, joyful, peaceful … I didn't expect to find Christians with Swastikas stamped on their foreheads, or Tommy guns slung on their shoulders, but the Tommies I knew when they ruled The Land were not of this place.

Incredible how their occupation tactics didn't corrupt the Tommies at home. Amazing how nice and polite the Tommies were in their London, saying, "Beg your pardon," even when you stepped on their toes, and "Excuse me" … "Please" … "Thank you." They weren't patronizing when they said it, like they used to be in The Land. No, it seemed natural, almost inbred.

I tried it once. "Thank you … Please … Excuse me," I said, but I associated the words with the hypocrisy of the powerful, the groveling of the weak, the brown-nosing of the collaborators, the misguided trust of the assimilated, the resignation of the ghetto. So heavy these words, even eight years after the Tommies had left The Land.

What a thorn in the butt we must have been for the Tommies. It must have been hell for them to put their lives on the line in a land arid, parched, hostile to them, decade after decade, night and day, to fear that every step they took might be their last. Many got killed, wounded—for what? Why did they have to fan the embers of war, not only between Arab and Jew, but between Arab and Arab, and Jew and Jew?

How could they have stayed away from such a London? Where in The Land could they see a river as mighty as the Thames, a lawn as green and wide as Hyde Park, or a hotel like the one in which Trans-Canada reserved a room for Levi and me?

The King David Hotel in Jerusalem had seemed like a palace until I saw this hotel. If there was ever in The Land a palace like this hotel, it had been destroyed in one war or another, one crusade or another; and so were the trees, if there was ever a stretch of peace long enough for them to grow as tall as the Christmas tree that stood inside the lobby of this hotel. Nowhere had I seen a tree so tall outdoors, let alone indoors; or such fancy molding on such a high ceiling; such a plush carpet spread on such a wide wood floor; such a huge stonework fireplace; or such logs stoking the fire— huge they were, like the ones my parents had described when they told me of the logging camps in Poland where my father had met my mother; where they worked for *Hakhsharah* (developing muscle and stamina for the pioneering work of rebuilding The Land).

Up in the room was a beautiful booklet for room service. I ordered, and they served. It was incredible: Whatever I ordered, the Tommies served; my wish was their command. I ordered and ordered, thinking the next order would give me a taste of justice.

I'd never felt so ugly, cruel—and sick. I had never seen butter before; it was too rich. Even the smell nauseated me.

5

The slanting sun rays tease color out of stone. The mountains, boulders, and rocks are streaked with ancient hues of bronze and rust, copper green, iron red, yellow, purple and pink, gray and brown. The sky bands the horizon with cloudless blue. Afternoon shadows stretch long to the east—

North! South! West!

The tents are facing east. Because the mountain peaks to the east shield the tents from the morning sun? The camels are still grazing on gravel and stones. But that shimmering green spot, I see now, is a tree—looks like an acacia—not very far from the tents.

The Badawias seem to be racing against the sun now, so busy preparing food they don't notice Salimeh starting to crawl toward the fire. Her tiny elbows keep collapsing, dropping her head to the stones, dust, and dung. She stops to play with filthy balls of unspun wool and hair, chews on a rusty rim of a pail, licks off the sand stuck to a tea glass—too close to the fire.

The infant-girl cried and screamed as soon as I picked her up. Her girl-mother sprang to her feet and grabbed her child from my arms, spewing a torrent of curses. Her senior co-wife, Azzizah, also cursed and cursed. You wouldn't suspect that, only three or four months ago, the same Badawias demanded I give my breast to this infant—as part of a ritual that converted me from stranger to stranger-no-stranger? that made me little Salimeh's godmother, her adopted mother, and therefore a member of her clan, her tribe?

Maybe they only sound like they're spewing curses because their language is harsh to my ears and you never see a smile on their veiled faces. And maybe I hear my own anger in their voices. Day before yesterday, I knew what compelled me to come here; now, I don't. Day before yesterday, I thought my night-school Arabic would serve me well here; now I find it's good enough only for classroom tests. Day before yesterday, I believed I was welcome to visit-stay here a week, a month, a year; now I catch a snippet like "People hear my blood is exposed and they come to visit-stay like vultures" and I start to spin-curve like a question mark.

But the minute I tune out their speed-talking, the minute I concentrate on their body language, I see these two Badawia co-wives working together like a team, with no sign of rank—no seniority, no privilege of youth. They consult each other—Enough salt? More oil?—both crouching by the cooking fires in front of Tammam's tent, next to the jerricans and a large pail that serves as their kitchen sink. Whenever one leaves to fetch a bowl or spice, the other takes her place. There is no sign of discord between them, only harmony.

Their cooking utensil is a *shibriyya*—dagger. Their kitchen counter is a torn sack spread flat on the ground. They store their ingredients in dented tin boxes, cloth bags, and bundled rags. Rice is boiled in a chipped enamel pot. They bake their pita over a flat iron disk that looks like the top of a rusty gasoline barrel.

It is impossible to keep dust and sand away from the food because of the goats, the saluki dogs, and the wind—and because they cook first, clean house later.

They use bunched twigs to sweep the ground, raising dust, sand, and coughs. Now they shake out the blanket-carpets, spread them back flat on the ground around the fire. Tammam glides over to Azzizah's tent and comes back dragging two more carpets; rolls them up like bolsters. Then, stuffing all the presents back into my duffle bag, she asks me if I remembered to bring a gift for their husband.

"Yes," I reply.

"Good," she says. She doesn't ask what I brought.

It is not proper for a guest to work, Azzizah told me when I offered to give them a hand. "Recline, recline on your welcome-carpet," the senior wife says, as she gives a sponge bath to Tammam's infant. She dips the dusty hem of her dress into a few drops of murky water. The baby cries and kicks, and after her bath her face seems to be covered with gray powder. Azzizah brushes the dust away with one of her shawls. They save every drop of water, it seems, and serve the rinse-water to the goats.

Now, all of a sudden, Tammam and Azzizah tense up. Each sits down on her own blanket-carpet, pulls a mirror from her red wool sash-belt, straightens her veil, and sticks some kohl in her eyes.

"Should have changed Salimeh's dress," Azzizah mutters. Then she and Tammam fall silent.

I turn to see if anyone is approaching, but I see no one. I hear only the wind, and the saluki dogs running away. A moment later they run circles around the master of the tents, Imsallam Suleman Abu Salim.

"*Ye-massikum bil-khayr,*" he mutters, his voice dark and raspy.

His wives murmur something under their veils—a reply to his greeting, I guess.

The dogs sit behind his carpet even before he folds his legs.

Silence. This is the second time today that a greeting is followed by silence. The fire hissing and a coyote, hyena, or fox howling far in the distance, the sound bouncing from mountain to mountain. A purple shadow falls on the plateau—the mountain peaks in the east glow like the sun.

Imsallam Suleman Abu Salim breathes like a heavy smoker. Commanding, regal, dignified, intimidating . . . such a presence. Though last night, when Tal and I arrived at his *maq'ad*—men's guest-receiving-place—I saw this Badu being gracious to a fault. I sense a sort of quietness in him, the inner stillness of a man who is not afraid to die.

A slash above his jaw looks like someone was aiming for his neck and missed—not by very much. His scar glistens dark through his white stubble like a wild streak. His white *kaffiyye* headdress doesn't fall down in majestic folds but is wrapped around his head like some rag, as though he couldn't care less about his appearance; he hasn't shaved in a week, hasn't bought a new *jalabeeya*—shirt-dress—or a new *abaiah*—cloak—in years.

And his shoes—he wears them without socks; dusty, scruffy black shoes with the laces missing. He takes them off before folding his legs on his carpet and puts them on before getting up. His feet must be swollen or his shoes too tight—how else could he keep them on, walking without a shuffle, without a sound?

His two wives own no footwear, by the look of their feet.

His hands look like those of a top executive, not toughened by manual labor like his wives. He wears a ring—only one, but what a ring, a scarab set in gold. Plundered from an Egyptian tomb? In his smuggling days? Why doesn't he upgrade the living conditions here in his tents? Surely he can afford it if he can afford his ring, and the silver and gold and gemstones on his wives.

Cooing like a dove now to her father, little Salimeh breaks the silence. Her girl-mother lays her down on the carpet and ... oh, how that infant smiles and laughs, crawling straight to her father. I don't know where I got the impression that Bedouin men value sons more than they do daughters. Maybe they do, and only here does Imsallam Suleiman Abu Salim hold his infant daughter like a testament to his virility.

Unlike his wives, Abu Salim doesn't live isolated and remote in forbidden tents. He has met strangers, and not only in his *maq'ad*. His wives must know this, but they don't seem to comprehend it.

"She is doing writing, you know. Her name is Nura," says Tammam. "Nura remembers-learns by doing writing, for strangers cannot remember from generation to generation—*min jil le-jil*—like us Badu. We Badu are blessed."

Silence... God, what a silence.

The Badawias stare at the fire as if praying or escaping. The wind shifts and blows smoke in Abu Salim's direction. He coughs and spits, buries his spit with a handful of sand.

"*Aywa*—yes," he says finally, handing his infant daughter back to Tammam as if to say, "Mind your infant and your tongue. Remember your place ..." "Hormmah," he calls her. Doesn't "Hormmah" mean "shameful," "disgraceful"? "Say, tell me, *yaa-Hormmah*, what was your guest writing to remember?" he asks her. His tone, his manner, would intimidate the hell out of me, but if his girl-wife feels intimidated, she gives no sign of it.

"Your guest is doing writing," Tammam says, "to remember-learn everything we Badu remember-learn without doing writing… because we Badu are blessed."

"Is that what your guest told you?" Abu Salim asks his girl-wife. Silence.

"Supper will get cold," mutters Azzizah. To protect Tammam? Me? Should I interfere now, tell him "Yes, that's what I told Tammam"? But that's what his wives could say—

"What were you writing?" he asks me.

And now I understand why you need a bit of time here before you open your mouth.

"I was writing not to forget," I reply. "My memory is not as good as it was when I was young."

"*Aywa*—yes," says Abu Salim. "We Badu have a saying, 'All is carved in stone when one is young, and carved in sand when one is old.' But you are not old. You told me a story, I know. You strangers call stories 'lies.' Telling story-lies is not good, I heard you strangers say. We Badu like to hear a story and also to tell stories, to spice up life. We Badu have a saying, 'A man who tells no lies—no story—is a man with no pepper'," he says, flashing his brown teeth.

His girl-wife Tammam brings him a dented jug, and a frayed towel that was once white. Her husband washes his hands first, then tells me to do as he did. After the senior co-wife washes her hands, she holds the jug for Tammam to wash up.

Their dinner table is the gravel ground in front of their husband's welcome-carpet. Dinner is rice heaped on a round bronze tray.

"But where is the *samn*?" Abu Salim mutters. "Where is the honor of guest?"

And a lot of honor Azzizah pours over the rice. It looks like pukish green oil, thick like grease and smelling of mildew.

"Eat, eat," says Abu Salim, and when he sees me hesitating, he explains that *samn* is clarified butter Azzizah prepared, not from goats' milk, but from camels' milk. "Azzizah watched over it for a month—*yemkin*—maybe a year."

"Eat … *guwwa*—strength, power to you," Abu Salim and his wives say, as we say "Bon appetit."

So I told them, "*Guwwa*—eat, eat—*bon appetit*," but they wouldn't touch their food.

"For it is improper," says Abu Salim. "A proper host never eats with his guests, only after … only what is left on the tray after his guests have their fill." They would rather starve than be "not proper," it seems.

I was famished. But, like the tourists I used to laugh at when I was a child, I couldn't even look at that tray, and the rice kept sliding from my fingers.

"*Wallah*, how ignorant Nura is," the Badawias mutter. "Even her fingers are ignorant … not even knowing how to roll rice properly from a tray."

"Yes. Would you show me, teach me … eat first?" I say.

Abu Salim has obviously seen a stranger or two who didn't appreciate Badu delicacies. "Welcome a guest even if he arrives in the late night, even if he had wronged you, even if he offends you," he says, spitting behind his back. He covers his spit with a hand-ful of sand and, with his other hand, starts to roll the rice into spoon-size balls.

His wives follow, digging their fingers into that same tray. Each person seems to have a territory in the tray, as if the rice, like a pizza, was divided into four portions. Each hand rolled off rice from his or her territory only; they didn't touch the rice in my ter-ritory, the invisible triangle in front of me. Each showed me how to roll rice with my fingers. And when they saw my fingers pick-ing only white grains of rice, they shoved the rice, dripping with thick green grease, over to my territory.

The Badawias' faces are covered with veils at dinnertime also, and yet they polish off their rice while my territory is still full. I turn the tray around—turn my territory over to them.

"*Wallah*, I had my fill," I say, three times, and only then do they stop urging me to eat, eat.

Only the Badawias eat the leftovers. Their husband doesn't

touch even a grain of rice in my territory. And when Abu Salim sees how I devour the pita bread, he tells Azzizah to prepare a bowl of dip for pita. Fried onions and tomato paste never tasted better and I polish off the bowl.

"*Wallah*, I had my fill," I say.

"*La*—no, a guest who has had his fill would leave a bowl more than half full," says Abu Salim. "Your guest did not have her fill. You should have prepared more," he tells Azzizah. Then he orders Tammam to fetch coffee beans.

"But the coffee beans to honor guests are in your guest-receiving-place—your *maq'ad*," says Tammam, her girl-eyes betraying that Abu Salim rarely, if ever, has made such a fuss over a woman-guest. She looks to Azzizah for an explanation. "Women-strangers are not women ... but not men also," she mutters to Azzizah, adds a torrent too fast for me to understand.

"*Oskoti*—hold your tongue," snaps Abu Salim at his girl-wife. Then, turning to me, he says, "Your Arabic teacher taught you well, but he is not an Arab; I can tell by your manners. And by your accent, I can tell he taught you in Syria."

"No, he taught me in Toronto, Canada, but he is an Arab from Syria," I say.

"Cannot be," says Abu Salim. "A Syrian is but a Syrian ... A Jordanian but a Jordanian, a Palestinian but a Palestinian ... Like Egyptians, Lebanese, Iraqis, and all the rest, all are *fellahin*—peasants. Only we Badu are Arabs, true Arabs.

"Are you ready?" he says all of a sudden, "Are you ready?" His face casts longer shadows than the sinking sun.

"Ready? Ready for what?" I whisper.

"Ready to record on the cassette, like El Bofessa." Abu Salim turns to his wives, tells-orders them not to utter a sound for as long as the Record button is pressed. And now in the sing-song voice of Badu legend-telling, he says, "It was from the wind that circles the earth that Allah had created the Badu. And so, like the wind, the Badu roams and wanders, and like the wind, the Badu is free ... And from the arrow Allah created the horse. And so, like the arrow, the horse is fast, and, like the arrow, the horse gallops straight... Then from the heavy cloud that bears blessings unto the earth, Allah had created the camel and so, like the cloud, the camel is heavy and, like the cloud, the camel bears blessings... And then Allah had picked a bit of dust from the earth and created the donkey-mule—demeaned and oppressed till dust... And when the donkey stood and defecated, Allah had created from the donkey's defecation, the *fellah*—the peasant.

"Now, play it back," Abu Salim orders me.

Again and again his wives wish to hear the playback. Again and again Abu Salim tells me, "Forbidden to record and photograph the women. Only the men you can record and photograph..."

"Why?" I say.

"Stay here and you will learn, *Inshallah*," says Azzizah.

Tammam opens her eyes wide, as if a *djinn*-demon had suddenly possessed her senior co-wife, Azzizah. The last thing we need is a stranger-guest, Tammam thinks, it seems.

"She, the stranger-no-stranger guest, Nura, presented us, your wives, with wristwatches," says Tammam, openly breaking her promise to me. Again Tammam empties my duffel bag. But now she looks at the heap on her carpet as if it is a heap of bribes and corruption.

Abu Salim stares at the heap and says, "You favored us too much, Nura. A favor is as heavy as a mountain; brought over on a donkey but returned back on a camel." Abu Salim and Azzizah were raised on the same parables, it seems. Tammam looks young enough to be their daughter, or granddaughter.

It is Imsallam Suleman Abu Salim who decides which wife gets what. His mother had named him after King Solomon the Wise. And, like King Solomon, Imsallam Suleman Abu Salim divides the presents, share and share alike, to each wife. It is for Tammam, and not for Azzizah, that Abu Salim picks the more colorful and glittering of ribbons, beads, and clothes.

"Not good... worthless," says Abu Salim as Azzizah had, but only when he sees the one and only toy I brought for his infant daughter, a stuffed animal, a Canadian beaver. "Worthless . . . not good. The infant girl will grow up thinking animals are harmless," says Abu Salim. His face beamed with delight when he saw the binoculars Professor Russell had suggested I buy for him. "My eyes are too old now to see far," says Abu Salim.

"No, a Badu who suckled on the heart of a crow can see through mountains till the day he dies," says Azzizah.

And Tammam sits there, cradling her infant in her arms, as if she can't understand what the hell has gotten into her senior co-wife, and their husband also, now that he has ordered Azzizah to fetch the firewood.

And if Azzizah had hit a rock with a shepherd staff like Moses, it wouldn't have surprised me more than the stack of fragrant firewood she fetched. It's beyond me where a person can find a stick of firewood here. Only a lone tree on this rock, and all around only tall granite cliffs, boulders, stones, and sand and sky . . . maybe a bush or two down in the wadi leading to the *maq'ad*. Firewood is probably as precious as water here. It looks like Azzizah saved it for a special occasion. She and Abu Salim seem to know something about which Tammam and I don't have the foggiest notion.

What is it? . . . Not proper to ask questions.

A complete stranger they'd invited to visit-stay with them, no questions asked—not even "What is your name?" . . .

"Lee—what? . . . Orrrra? . . . How do you spell it?" I'm asked in Toronto.

Laura, or Lorna, or Lee, my Canadian relatives called me at first.

I was dressed in the latest fashion when I first landed in Toronto. I didn't want my relatives in Canada to think of us in The Land as poor cousins. I landed wearing nylons and high heels— purchased in Tel Aviv, a pair of delicate suede pumps the salesman had showed me were featured in some high-fashion magazine. In these delicate shoes I stepped off the plane right into the slushy Canadian snow. Real snow was not at all like the snow in the movies, I discovered that day; real snow was soupy and brown, and the air was so cold—I had never imagined such cold. Levi and I were shivering, even indoors, when the heat was raised way too high for the Canadians. They said it was the blood—too thin, or too thick. I think it was the trauma of drastic change, sudden loss, grief, homesickness...

But I loved my great-aunt Sheina and her husband, Eizer. He was fluent in many languages, Hebrew among them, which he spoke with such a Diaspora accent, I could hardly understand a word. He had retired from the successful tailor shop and store he had founded; his son was running it now. But still he wore a three-piece suit, even at home, complete with a tie and a gold watch and chain; his white goatee was immaculately groomed, and his head always covered by a kippa or hat. He was observant and he'd get up at four o'clock in the morning to study the Talmud, or the Mishnah, Gmara, the Bible and one of its many interpretations, most of which he knew by heart.

His wife, Sheina, my mother's aunt, the sister of my "picture grandmother," embodied, in my eyes, the grandparents I wished I knew—even from stories; the grandparents that my mother couldn't tell me about, it so pained her how they had perished There, in the Shoah. Maybe because Sheina looked sort of disembodied by the vicissitudes of her long life, which seemed to have shriveled her, all but her remembering and her spirit. A spirit that shined through her skin, which was almost like onion skin, so translucent; and lit up her eyes, which were hazel like mine; and illuminated a way of life buried under the ashes There, and under the mountains of skeletons, and the continent of shame...

Nine years older than her sister, my mother's mother, Sheina remembered the day when her mother birthed my grandmother, as well as the day when my mother was born, and the days when they bolted the shutters, and the trap door to the cellar in which they took shelter during the pogroms. Sheina also told me that her father, my mother's grandfather, had seven daughters, like Shalom Aleichem's Tuvya. But, unlike Tuvya, her father was a *gevir*; endowed with a gift of seeing far, not only in business dealings. And so, years before his seven daughters were of age, he looked for seven husbands. From town to town he traveled, since he was exporting and importing grain and coal, not only from cities and towns, but from Austria, Hungary, and Poland. And wherever he happened to be on *Shabbat*, he went to the synagogue, prayed and listened. By and by he discovered who is the most brilliant of boy students—the *talmid hakham*—in this or that province. Seven such outstanding boys he found, and through all their years of schooling, he paid for their tuition, for all their needs—theirs and their families'—as part of his daughters' dowries. Like that he found my great-uncle Eizer, and my mother's father, my grandfather Yossef. Yet, until they got married, he kept his daughters in the seclusion of his home and his synagogue. Sheina, like Azzizah and Tammam, didn't know how to read and write. She learned to pray by remembering—from generation to generation. Her mother's tongue was Yiddish, and so was her love language. *A tayere neshome… mine tayere kind*—Precious soul… my precious child—she called Levi and me. She saw nothing wrong in my marrying Dave a year after Arik went, while still grieving, still unable to comprehend inside my inner self that Arik was gone…

There were only a handful of *Sabras*—native-born Israelis—in Toronto then, or so I've heard. I didn't meet even one, until Levi caught tonsillitis. I took him to the doctor, and in the waiting room I found a mother and son, both red-haired, both speaking good Israeli Hebrew. That's how I met Gingie and his mother, Riva. It turned out that she and Mottke, Gingie's father, had known Arik's brother in their Underground days.

Mottke was specializing then at the Western Hospital in Toronto, and Riva, Gingie's mother, was doing her doctorate in psychology at the University of Toronto. I looked after Gingie while they were studying and working.

And after Dave and I were married, come summer, Levi and Gingie would move with me to the log cabin that Dave had leased by a lake in Algonquin—a provincial park as big as The Land, if not bigger… with lake after lake, river after river, amid vast forests.

Oh, how we could have used such a wealth of water in The Land, not to mention such a treasure of treasures—peaceful borders. That's what I thought first time I drove to that cabin. Never before had I traveled hundreds of kilometers by car in one direction and seen no ruin, no town rebuilt in a defensive cluster surrounded by walls or security fences. No bullet-pocked walls, no border minefield, no loops of barbed wire, no military installations, no army base, not one soldier. And no one afraid to live tens of kilometers from the nearest neighbor.

But, the first summer that Dave leased the cabin, the nearest neighbor moved to Muskoka, where there was a gentlemen's agreement not to sell a parcel of land or a cottage to a Jew...Good riddance. The new neighbor had a couple of boys the same age as Levi and Gingie and they taught Levi and Gingie how to canoe, portage, navigate, and survive in that wilderness.

Dave was crazy about Israel then. Riva, Mottke, and I loved to see The Land through his eyes. It flattered us, did us proud, the picture Dave would reflect to us. We never tired of the stories he told of the summer he first flew to The Land and met Arik, Levi, and me. It was in the summer of '56, only a few months before the Sinai War.

Dave flew to The Land for a study mission, with a group of Torontonians. Their group leader had advised them to pack, for their stay in Israel, Nescafé, if they liked coffee with their breakfast, and salami if they liked meat for lunch or dinner. "And if you think that lugging a salami to a Jewish country is as ridiculous as lugging ice to Iceland, you've got another think coming to you in Israel," their group leader told them. "You are flying to a Jewish country where a bowl of chicken soup, never mind coffee, is a luxury rarely available." "Oh, cut the fundraising crap," Dave thought when he heard it. He couldn't imagine that Jews in a Jewish state, of all places, lived in conditions found in third-world countries.

It was news to Riva, Mottke, and me, the reality seen through his eyes—how The Land, smaller than some of the lakes in Canada, inhabited by a fraction of the number of people who live in Manhattan, was besieged by neighboring enemy-nations inhab-

ited by more people than live in the whole of Canada—four times
more... "Just to fly there for a week made us Canadians feel like
heroes... But you had to be there to believe how fired up the
Israelis were, by their destiny... You could get a sunburn just from
talking to them," Dave would tell us. We lapped it up.

No one in his study mission expected to find in the Holy Land
a beach like in Rio de Janeiro, and sidewalk cafés, like in Paris,
crowded with great-looking girls—Jewish girls—and Israeli men,
direct, warm, friendly, uninhibited. Dave had never met so many
extraordinary people per square foot. Nearly all—even the taxi
drivers, the hotel waiters, and the construction workers at the lecture hall—would tell them, "Why waste your life in Canada.
Come join us. All you have to do to be what you were born to be is
to be here in The Land." Dave saw us like that.

It was during that study mission that Dave walked by a barber
shop, and on the sign above he saw his family name printed in
Hebrew and English. It's not a common name. His father and
uncle have been checking phone books for years in search of relatives lost in the Shoah.

"Do you have an unlisted phone number?" Dave asked the barber.

"Me no speak English," said the barber. "You speak no Hebrew?"

"No."

"Yiddish?"

"A *bissle*—a bit," said Dave. But his Yiddish was sprinkled with
so many English words, and the barber's with so many Hebrew
words, they got nowhere until Arik happened to drop in for a
haircut.

"You are not listed in the phone book, are you?" Dave asked the
barber, and Arik translated.

"No. Soon I'll apply for a phone. Meanwhile you can use the one
in the pharmacy only a few steps from here," replied the barber.

"Is that your name on the sign?" Dave asked the barber next.

"Yes, I haven't changed it," replied the barber. And after Arik
translated, the barber explained to Dave that many in The Land followed Ben-Gurion's example and changed their names to Hebrew.

"Ben-Gurion changed his name?" said Dave.

"Yes, from 'Green'," replied Arik.

"My son also changed his name to Hebrew," said the barber, "but I kept mine, thinking I might have family somewhere in exile, how will they find me if I changed my name..."

"Same as my father's name and mine," Arik translated for Dave.

It soon developed that Dave and that barber were related. Right there and then, the barber closed his shop and dragged Dave and Arik to his home to celebrate with him, his wife, his children, his neighbors, his friends, the family's reunion.

Later that day, Arik brought Dave home. Levi loves to hear Dave tell how a small electric fan barely ruffled the mosquito net draped over the crib where he, Levi, lay fast asleep. Only a baby could sleep through this noise, Dave thought to himself as Arik led him to the balcony; you couldn't hear your own voice for the radios blaring through wide-open windows and the conversations carried out like shouting matches over the din of the radio broadcasts. Then, all at once, everyone fell silent and only the radios squealed now—the news, in Hebrew. Dave understood not a word... Dave understood not a word even of the *Haftara* he had chanted at his bar mitzvah.

Dave is twelve years older than me, and only a year older than Arik. Yet he seemed much older, exile old, and sweating in a tie, and a jacket bearing a crest with the maple leaf and the Star of David intertwined.

"Take off your jacket, your tie. Feel at home," I told him.

He had studied Hebrew not in school but in a *heder*, Dave told us soon after the news broadcast. *Heder*, to Arik and me, was a Hebrew word loaded with ghetto; and with a striving to transcend the ghetto, the pogroms, the poverty; and with a love of Torah, with enlightenment, with Bialik's poetry, with *Shabbat*. But, to Dave, *heder* was a room in the back of a synagogue, reeking of stale snuff, spittoons, dour old men with long white beards who got angry at him and his classmates whenever they would laugh. Bar-mitzvah Hebrew that they didn't understand their teacher whipped into their memory with a strap and a ruler. There was no love, laughter, or understanding in the *heder* Dave knew; it was forced labor after school hours—a punishment for being Jewish.

To get to the *heder*, Dave had told us, he had to pass by a place called Christie Pits, where Gentile thugs would gang up on him and his Hebrew-school classmates and beat them up, humiliate them. And it was just as humiliating to take the long way round and avoid Christie Pits, he said. Doing that made him and his classmates feel like cowards.

"Why did you remain in Canada then? Why didn't you and your Hebrew-school classmates move to The Land?" Arik asked him.

"I nearly did," Dave replied. "In '48 I was all set to move to Israel, join the battle for Independence. But when my parents heard I signed up, they told me they'd donate a plane to the Israeli air force if I'd stay in Canada. A plane will serve Israel better than you, they told me. I agreed. And they kept their end of the bargain."

"No plane could ever serve Israel better than you," said Arik to Dave.

Now Dave is pushing Arik's son—my son, Levi—to be the pilot he never was. Dave doesn't want Levi to make the same mistake he made...

6

The special-occasion fire is crackling, fragrant, warm, and so bright you could read and write by it. I pick up the notebook. No one objects. Tammam stacks the cooking utensils and the bowls and tray, but doesn't bother to wash them up. The flies disappear with the sun.

You can see nothing outside the rim of the fire-circle light, the night is so dark—and so cold: the wind is blowing cold shivers at my backside, while my frontside is fire-hot when Imsallam Suleman Abu Salim asks me, "From where did you get this beaded necklace around your neck? From where did you get this silver band on your finger?"

Silence.

A show-nothing mask is pasted across the Badawias' eyes.

Demons lurking in the darkness like the mountains in daylight, echo after him, "Who gave you the necklace and the ring?"

"Surely you know who gave me these gifts," I say, shaking inside.

"Say-tell who presented you with the necklace and with the ring," he says, the fire dancing on his face. And the demon-mountains echo, "Say-tell . . . say-tell."

"But . . . you know. You know. . . . Azzizah—Azzizah and Tammam, your wives . . ."

"No! No wife of mine gave you her necklace. No wife of mine gave you her ring. No wife of mine gave you her name. Necklace . . . ring . . . No . . . Whenever a person asks you, 'Say-tell who gave you this necklace,' you must reply, 'A friend from Sinaa.' Say-reply—repeat after me," insists Abu Salim.

"A friend from Sinaa," I repeat.

"*Aywa*—yes," he says. "Whenever a person asks you, 'Say-tell who gave you the ring,' you must reply, 'A friend from Sinaa.' Say-reply repeat after me. Repeat . . . Repeat."

"A friend from Sinaa . . ."

"'Where in Sinaa?' the person will ask, and what will you reply? Repeat. Repeat. Repeat after me: 'In the vast expanse of Sinaa.' 'Which friend? What is her name? The name of her tribe?' the person will ask, but you must reply with silence. Repeat again, one more time."

Again and again, Abu Salim rehearses my replies. He won't let me write to remember. "Writing could evaporate in smoke. This you must never forget," he says. "Repeat again, one more time." He drilled me as if his wives were secret agents, the ring and necklace smuggled like top military secrets. If they would ever be traced to him, he would be charged with spying... or drug-trafficking, or... What in the hell *do* the Badu smuggle across borders?

Scares the hell out of me, his badgering: "Repeat... Repeat," as if his life and mine were at stake. So I take off the necklace and the ring and I ask him to safekeep them for me.

"Gems of trust you take off... How ignorant you are," says Abu Salim. He tells-orders me to put them back on. And then again he starts...

"Who gave you this ring? Who gave you this necklace?..."

Together with the ring that sealed our marriage, Dave gave me his promise: Next next year we'll move to Israel. I took it as a gem of trust, more valuable than any jewel Dave could give me. He even stapled to the *ketuba*—the marriage contract—three return tickets to The Land. But the next year his father had a heart attack and Dave had to take over the business. The year after, one of his partners pulled out and Dave had to restructure the business. Then his mother suffered a stroke and needed looking after. "Next year, we'll move to The Land," he said after that, year after year, like the observants have said, day after day, for the past two thousand years. "Next year in Jerusalem..." Now Dave says Israel has become just like America and we might as well move to Phoenix, Arizona.

Why did he marry me? I don't know. He says he had never met a girl as beautiful as me, but the girls around Dave were much more beautiful, and definitely less trouble. I was a wreck, war-widowed and with an infant son who clung to me. He had no idea whom he was marrying, and neither did I. I didn't know him then; I doubt I ever will.

I had no idea he expected me to weep when he showed me Christie Pits. I was bound to disappoint him, having been raised to do, not weep. I had no tears for Arik, not even when his bones were buried, and none under the wedding canopy with Dave—where I felt I was betraying Arik . . .

"One tough cookie . . . tough as nails," Dave called me that day he had driven me to Christie Pits.

The world changed for me that day, narrowing from a conglomeration of countless tribes to two: those who had lived through war, and those who hadn't. Dave was not of my tribe, but one of the things I loved most in him was that he didn't know war, except from movies and books.

His den is lined with war books, even Clausewitz, and shelves full of histories of the First and Second World Wars, in the Pacific and in the European "theater," as they call it. But it is the Middle East wars that take up a whole wall full of shelves. Dave has read it all, and talks of war like an academic does of poetry. His war experience smells of books, of leather-upholstered armchairs, and of a cozy fire crackling in the fireplace. I wouldn't mind it a bit if he were not a superhawk, eager for Israel to "bomb the shit out of the Arabs." And who should do the bombing? My son?

What gave him the impression that I'm a wild *Sabra*? I don't know. I've had no wild moments with him. What I do know is: Dave loved it that I am a proud Jew, as he called it, but he wished I could keep my pride under wraps. So did his closest friends, the survivors of Christie Pits, his fellow veterans.

Dave was no hawk in that war, allowing a few Gentiles into his camp. He introduced them to me at a cocktail party, a week or two after we got married. I had a few laughs with his friends, and then one of the Gentiles congratulated Dave for having got himself a great gal—nothing Jewish about her, or something like that, he said. He obviously expected Dave and me to take it as a compliment. And Dave came through, "Thank you," he said without a sliver of cynicism, by rote, force of habit, without thinking. That's a good strategy for surviving cocktail parties, but what did I know then of such tactics. I was new to pretence, to the meaningless scripts of peaceful coexistence. "How are you?" "Fine, thank you. Couldn't be better, and you?... Good, glad to hear it." There was a rhythm to the ritual, but it was alien to me.

Dave didn't like to make waves, I knew even then. Appearances were important to him. Usually his appearance was elegant, understated, and unruffled. But how could he be unruffled by that Gentile compliment?

"Would you risk your butt to hide me," I asked that Gentile, "if Jews were hounded here in Canada, like in Nazi Germany? Or do you think I could pass, if I worked at it, and save you the trouble?" Something like that I told him. I felt sick. I was dying to go home to The Land. No plane was fast enough.

"Let's get out of here," I whispered to Dave. "Let's go home..." The Land, I meant, but he thought I meant to Briar Hill. As he was helping me with my coat, I heard one of his Jewish friends, a Christie Pits survivor, whisper to him, "Tell your wife to smarten up and remember where she is..."

That night Dave started to teach me how to kill the very thing that he loved in me. I was making more than waves, to his way of thinking. By addressing that one Gentile as I did, Dave seemed to think I had stirred up anti-semitism in all the Gentiles at that party; now each Gentile would tell two friends, and so on. Singlehandedly, I had loosed upon this Canadian earth a fucking anti-semitic plague. Such power, one Jew in exile had, it seemed.

I wonder now if what happened there, at Christie Pits, left Dave believing that the only real power a Jew has is the power to stir up hatred for Jews.

Tone it down, he told me; button it up and keep a lid on it. It? The *Sabra* wildness he claimed to love in me? I'm a bit of a WASP, he says—or, more correctly, a bit of a *Goyishe copp*—because I don't have the seventh sense, that extraordinary gift that Yahod like him, born and raised in exile, possess. "It's like radar," he told me. "A way to detect danger, to sense what's bad for the Jews."

Where was that extraordinary radar during the Shoah, I asked him, outraged. How could he believe—*boast!*—that exiled Yahod possess any such sense, after what happened There?

"It's no use even trying to explain it to you," Dave said.

Did he know even one Gentile who would risk his or her life to shelter him? I asked him.

He'd never thought about it, he said. "It serves no purpose to question it," he said. "Everyone can be a hero in a hypothetical situation, but, when it's for real, no one knows what risk he'd be prepared to take."

Exile is this uncertainty. Exile to a Yahodi is more than just exile.

Strange, how even though The Land is torn by war, and Canada is blessed with peace, Dave, not I, grew up in an atmosphere of uncertainty. And what a difference that makes. Even today it stands between us, a barrier wider than different languages or tribes.

A different time zone—seven hours behind The Land, this desert, is Toronto—evening here, morning there...

Every morning, Dave read *The Globe and Mail* carefully, hoping to find that Canada had finally opened a door for a Jew, if not to become a prime minister, then at least a faculty dean, or maybe even a provincial cabinet minister or a judge. But when the newspaper *did* finally report that a Jew had risen to a judgeship, Dave told me it was not good for the Jews: if this Jewish judge made one unpopular decision, the Gentiles would take it out on all Jews. And if he made only just and popular decisions, such brilliance was bound to engender envy and resentment of all Jews. That is why it is bad for the Jews when a Jew is awarded the Nobel Prize.

A good edition of the morning newspaper didn't use the word "Jew" at all, according to Dave, unless a Gentile used it to say something like "the long-suffering Jews." Even that was iffy: Some Gentiles can't stand the thought that Jews are outstanding in anything, even suffering.

But no edition of the *Globe* presented as many problems to Dave as one that mentioned The Land. On the one hand, he believes that if the Jews in The Land were not outstanding soldiers, The Land would fall. And that is one thing that Dave would not like to see, his feelings about today's Israelis aside. On the other hand, Jews being outstanding in battle is much worse than Jews being outstanding in suffering...

The rescue at Entebbe, though, was good for the Jews. Why that particular outstanding operation was good for the Jews is probably beyond the understanding of lesser mortals lacking the "seventh sense."

The worst possible item the *Globe* could report, or allude to, or imply, is that a Canadian Jew is torn between his loyalty to Canada and to The Land. Dave said it was an expression of anti-semitism, and anti-semitism is not supposed to exist in Canada. Anything that suggests it only rocks the boat...

Dave talks about making waves and rocking the boat as if he thinks that all the Yahod in Toronto are huddled in a boat riding just at the waterline; the slightest wave could capsize us. But when I'd urge him to abandon that boat and fly home to The Land, he'd tell me, "It was always like this," as if anti-semitism were a rule of nature, or a divine act that couldn't be changed by man. The sooner you accept it and learn to live with it the better.

The man was dead, desensitized, or he wouldn't—couldn't—tell me "It was always like this," without any feeling, any fight, *muruah*—balls. That's what exile does to you.

Aywa, it was clear to see why one of the names for God is the place. Maybe Dave and I thought, felt, or hoped that we would complete each other, and that wholeness would make up for the place.

I don't know why I married him. Sometimes, when he's at the log cabin, busy repairing last winter's damage and preparing for the fast-approaching autumn—splitting wood, fixing the roof, replacing the chimney, rechinking the logs—his unruffled appearance is defeated by the sweat, the heat, and the beauty of the place. And I glimpse the Dave I married—Dave in the right place.

Levi follows Dave like a shadow up north. And Dave sees the boy as a legendary child of a legendary father and mother. In turn, that elevates Dave, or so he feels. How Dave did it, I don't know. The man was buried under umpteen lids, yet he instilled in Levi the conviction that he, Arik's son, is of the aristocratic Yahod, in and out of The Land. And me, Dave elevated even higher—out of this world, out of his reach; Arik's widow, the eternal flame burning for Arik and for him. Even in the realm of myth and legend Dave sees himself in second place.

"You don't know how lucky you are to have your mother for a mother," Dave would tell Levi. But the child wanted a mother like Allan had, and Ron and Jeff, and all his Toronto friends.

"I want a fat mommy," he'd whimper whenever I'd say, "Oh, come on. It's just a sore throat. In a day or two you'll be all right..." "You are not a good mommy. I want you to be a fat mommy!" he'd whine when I wouldn't chauffeur him around. "You're old enough to take the bus, travel by yourself, on your own power like a man. You can do it, I'm sure." And then I'd tremble until I'd see him back, safe, in Briar Hill.

That's what Dave loved in me. But now that I hesitate to give Lev my consent to serve high-risk duty, both Levi and Dave call me a fat mommy—a Jewish mother—as if a Jewish mother was not good for the Jews.

Dave doesn't know war. Who would have thought when I married him that what I had loved most in him, might end up killing my son.

7

"Does your husband sleep one week at Azzizah's tent and one week at yours?" I ask Tammam. She stokes the fire, as it is about to be engulfed by the darkness that dwarfs us even more now that only the girl-Badawia, her infant-daughter, and I are here at the *maharama*—the place of the women—by the fire-circle in front of Tammam's tent.

"No," she replies. "One night he sleeps at Azzizah's and one night here."

"But I am here two nights, and both nights he went to sleep at Azzizah's tent. Why? Is he displeased with you?" I ask.

Silence. The girl-wife unfastens the gold chains I gave her. One she draped round her neck, the other round the infant's—limp with sleep. "*Mabrouka ... mabrouka*—may you be blessed," she whispers twice, once to her infant, once to herself. Then she hands me the tiny safety pin that was hanging from her infant's bracelet like a charm, and she says, "This is Salimeh's gift to you." Next, Tammam takes off her most beautiful bracelet—turquoise embedded in silver—and presents it to me, insists I keep it. "You must. You must ..."

"Why? Will Abu Salim favor you more because you gave me this bracelet?"

"No," replies Tammam. "No bride was more favored than Abu Salim has favored me."

The bride-price that Abu Salim paid for her exceeded the sum that any man before him had paid to purchase a bride, Tammam said. Her father had purchased all her jewels, veils, dresses—"all my possessions, with the bride-price he had received from Abu Salim," she says.

"Is that the custom?"

"*La*—no," the girl-wife replies. "Only a good, loving father like my father would not keep his daughter's bride-price for himself, or for to purchase brides for his sons … *Wallah*, I miss my father. I wish I was a maiden back in my father's tents."

"Does your father know you miss him? His tents?"

"Yes," replies Tammam. "Every father knows how his daughter misses him, and every mother too. But my mother died soon after she birthed me. My father's wives mothered me. It was my father's wives who arranged my marriage to Abu Salim. But my father did not buy even one bead for his wives with my bride-price." Stepmothers fare no better here than in "Cinderella," it seems.

"Why did your father agree to this marriage arranged by his wives?" I say.

"What questions you ask, *Wallah*. Not proper to ask questions. *Dir balak*—watch out—Abu Salim will kill you if you betray his trust. He will track you down no matter how wide and far you escape. No one remember a better tracker than Abu Salim."

"Do you wish I did not come to visit-stay with you?"

"No," replies Tammam. "You were fated to visit-stay with us, or you would have died on your way up the mountains, and your escort-guardian would have died on his way down."

"Who told you that my escort-guardian did not die on his way back?" I ask her.

"No one. That is how I know that he did not die," replies Tammam.

&

Soon after, my escort-guardian, Tal left the *maq'ad*, Abu Salim loaded my desert gear onto his she-camel. He chose to walk up the steep winding path to his tents. He kept up the walking pace, ahead of me. But as soon as he heard me huffing and puffing, he waited until my breathing steadied, and only then did he continue ahead. He didn't ask me the purpose of my visit, or how long I intended to stay. He said not a word till a turn or two before we reached the tents, then he told me to lock up my valuable things. "One can never tell who may wander into the tents while you women are out tending goats," he said. "And when the goats return home to the tents—the encampment—you women will be talking and talking and the goats will eat everything that is not locked safe."

"I carried no lock to the desert," I said. "But I did carry money and passports. Could you lock them up for me, or would it burden you?"

"Are you certain you wish me to safekeep your passports and your money—valuable things?" he said.

"Since I trust you to keep safe my honor and my life, I think I will also trust you to keep safe my passports and my cash," I replied.

Abu Salim chuckled. Still, he told me to count the money three times so that I would not say later that money is missing. I remembered, then, Russell telling me that a thoroughbred she-camel costs as much as a brand-new Rolls-Royce... I don't know if Abu Salim's she-camel was a Rolls or a Chevy. But he reacted to my sleeping bag as if I had carried a lousy mattress to a palace of a thousand and one bedrooms, each equipped with a lavish four-poster bed...

"Put it away. There is no need for a sleeping sack here," he told me, then assigned me to sleep in Tammam's tent.

The goats sleep in Tammam's tent. She, her infant, and I "bed" down by the scorched fire-circle outside her tent. Last night she wouldn't let me write by flashlight. "Blow the torch out! Blow the torch out!!" she said, stress and fear sparking in her voice, her eyes. Tonight she played with the flashlight beam, catching a wildcat flashing yellow eyes on top of the boulders that grow on the mountainside.

The night is long and lonely when everyone else sleeps and you can't. And ever since I synchronized my watch to Azzizah's and Tammam's, I have had no idea what time it is. As soon as I switch off the flashlight, the cold of desert night creeps into my bones, and the lice itch like hell, and I pray a scorpion or snake doesn't crawl into the carpet-blanket... I took a sleeping pill last night; felt like a dope-head all morning. I should have brought some escape reading—printed with fluorescent ink. Has anyone invented such a thing?

Tammam sleeps with her infant cradled in her arms. Both sleep wrapped in one carpet-blanket, the same carpet-blanket Tammam sat on all day. Both sleep in the clothes they wore all day. If Tammam took off her veils and her jewels, I didn't see it. The carpet-blanket covers her head—and the infant's.

The temperature drops thirty degrees, if not more, at night. It takes only one day and one night here to see that Jacob didn't exaggerate when he told Labban, "Heat ravaged me by day and frost by night." Did our forefathers live like Abu Salim and his wives?

"*Wallah*, I miss my father ... Wish I was a maiden back in my father's tents. *Ma tovu ohalekha Ya'akov*—How good are your tents, O, Jacob." Rachel, Leah—Tammam, Azzizah—Sarah, Hagar—Ishmael, Isaac—Arab, Jew. Both direct descendants of Abraham ... like Moses: *Mousa*, in Arabic, *Moshe* in Hebrew—married Jethro's daughter—a Badawia.

Here I can feel the hardships—or, more correctly, only a taste of the hardships—my parents experienced in their pioneering days, when they lived in a small, threadbare leaky tent from the day they landed in The Land until my mother was eight months pregnant with me.

✤

"What do you think? Should I waive Levi's exemption from high-risk duty?" I asked my mother a few days before I set out on this journey. It was Thursday evening. My father was still at work, at a building-supply store now, no longer in construction.

"I can't think now. The supermarket is about to close and I have to buy produce for *Shabbat*," my mother says.

"But you've had months to think on it, you love him as much as I do...," I say.

"And as much as the nation his father gave up his life to defend," my mother says, cutting me off. I think she loved you, Arik, like a woman, not like a mother-in-law.

"You mean you are torn...?"

"If you want to discuss it now, come with me to the supermarket.

We'll talk on the way." My mother feels her arthritis when she walks downstairs. The supermarket is kitty-corner to where my youth movement's shack used to stand. Gingie was working on my Jeep, outfitting it for the desert, so I suggested we grab a cab.

"You grab cabs here, stay in hotels. You have no idea how life has changed here in The Land," my mother says. There is such a spark in her eyes, I have no doubt she is dragging me to the bus and to the supermarket so that I'll see how life has changed here and understand why she thinks I should or shouldn't give Levi my consent.

The meek don't get on the bus here, let alone inherit the earth. The lineup was long at the bus stop. It was evening rush hour. And when the bus arrived, they charged, nearly trampling my mother. The bus pulled away before she and I, and a few elderly people, managed to elbow our way in. The next bus pulled in before the lineup had a chance to regroup, but this one stopped meters from the curb, and the first step is too high for my mother. The bus driver doesn't move to lend her a hand, hoist her up into the bus, so I give a push from behind. Then a fresh batch charges in, and the driver takes off with such a heavy foot on the gas that all of us in the aisle are flung to the back. My mother's fall is cushioned by the crowd squashing her. No one gets up to offer her a seat, and when someone gets off at the next stop, five race for the vacated seat, shoving my mother out of their way. The force of the next acceleration flings us farther back; the driver shifts to second gear and we are propelled in the opposite direction. I am bracing myself for the shift into third when my mother, charging to the exit door, snaps like a paratrooper commander: "Follow me. Quick-fast, Leora! Jump out as soon as the doors open ... Jump before you get caught between the doors and break a hand, like Arik's mother did ..."

My mother's intention behind this expedition is starting to form in my mind. Territorial skirmishes are a part of daily life now, and daily life and its assumptions have become a strategic weapon.

The bus driver, it seems, was out to punish the passengers who drove him crazy, day in, day out, when he had better things to do with his life, which he nearly lost in the last war and might lose before the next stop. Terrorists rig buses with explosives every day of the week. No one can figure out how those who recently machine-gunned a busload of passengers slipped through security, but my mother has a theory: "Those terrorists eluded capture by pretending they were old enough to be grandparents." My mother has no doubt about that.

"You see?" she tells me after my handbag, but not hers, was searched at the entrance to the supermarket.

"Stupid! . . . I could have been a terrorist, for all you know," she tells the civil-defense guy on handbag duty. She could have been talking to the wall. "Like that, our elderly are dismissed here these days," she mutters. "In the health clinics also, whatever the elderly tell a doctor or a nurse falls on deaf ears; even the receptionists treat us as if we've outlived our use. And in the hospital, Arik's mother was treated as if healing her was a waste of effort, time, medicine, money, because she will soon die anyway. That's a very bad sign, Arik's father thinks, and you know what a student of history Arik's father is. From history he learned that a people who illtreat their elderly have no future."

"Don't tell me you believe the lessons Arik's father learns from history," I tell my mother. "Don't you remember, he learned from history that it was ruthless, irresponsible to declare a Jewish state in '48? Remember Arik telling us his father was sure the Arabs would finish us off the day the Tommies pull out of The Land?"

"It would break Arik's heart if he saw how our elderly are treated," she says.

"No, Arik would say we are new at having elderly here. Give us a couple of days and we'll learn to treat them better than most," I told my mother. Here I am again, I thought, keeping Arik alive by expressing his opinion, feelings, doubts . . .

"You know, I forgot how young we all were in those days. I wasn't much older than you are today the day Arik fell . . ." My mother was transformed that instant by some recollection from her youth, or by sheer necessity.

Her eyes, fearless as ever, fired menacing shots at everyone and everything they met, and she was psyched up for battle: her elbows sharp for the push, her hand at the ready for the grab; her cart poised for action. The supermarket was yet another war turf. Whenever I allowed someone to pass me or to cut in, she would look at me like she thought that I had lost my survival instinct in Canada, and that this was a training mission to reignite my self-preservation.

The air in the supermarket, like that in the streets, bristled with angry frustration and frantic animosity, as if the people had been cooped up in shelters, and now, during a tentative cease-fire, had to make up for lost time. The people behind the counter were on the defensive, seeing each customer as out to abuse them. The shoppers were desperate but wary, as if they thought the supermarket might run out of food, like in the days of austerity and rations, and meanwhile was out to cheat them.

No one bought a loaf of bread without squeezing the crust and smelling it first, and the staff at the meat and fish counters were inspected carefully, in case the blood, bile, and guts on their aprons weren't all that fresh. The fruit and vegetables, stacked in pyramids that were reconstructed hourly, did look good and fresh. Still, all hands seemed to grope for the prize in the middle of the bottom row. My mother, though, trusted the bottom row even less than the top. The supermarket didn't stay in business by being dumb, she told me. Exactly where it is most difficult to reach is where the supermarket sticks the rotten produce . . .

On to the last testing ground. My mother pushed me and the cart to grab a place in the shortest lineup at the checkout counter. We were squeezed to the back by all, except one. Dressed in a dusty paratrooper's uniform, he looked like a field commander transported in a time capsule to a battlefield bereft of gallantry and honor; there were no brothers' keepers here—no covenant, no compass, no sides for or against; no hope of peace or victory; no threat of defeat; no sorrow, no joy, no purpose; there was no need for him to be here.

No one in the line moved aside to let him check out first. As I moved our cart to make room for his, my mother stopped me, snapping in my ear, "What's with you! Everyone here is a front-line soldier. Serving active duty, he is entitled to shop in the *Shekem*—the army's supermarkets and department stores—where prices are cheaper than in civilian stores. Obviously money is no object for him."

"He probably thinks he won't live to spend it," I mutter.

"Naa," says my mother. "Youngsters his age just say that, like we used to, in cynical jokes and songs, like, 'If I die, bury me in the winery of Zikhron L'Zion...'. But, deep down, youngsters think they are immortal. Our Levi, too, or he wouldn't nag you for your consent..."

"I wonder whether he nags me, hoping I won't give him my consent—counting on me to know that deep down he fears his life will be cut as short as his father's."

"No, you made sure he conquered that fear," says my mother. "You think I don't know... don't know what a gift you gave your son, don't know what it cost you... But it's Levi who has no idea what you go through. Not till he lives to parent a child his age will Levi realize the price of letting him climb into a cockpit, even of a civilian plane. It's beyond me where you drew the courage..."

"From you," I told my mother.

"Really?"

"Really."

"You did a terrific job raising that kid."

"Yes. Best thing I did in my life. But it has used up my courage. I have nothing left to give to deciding on that damn consent."

"Give me your hand," my mother says. She puts her fist into my hand, then says, "There. I gave you a fistful of courage. Now you can decide."

8

What a surprise the morning dew was. It has fallen in such bounty, the carpet-blankets are soaked through. Shivering with cold, I was about to unroll my waterproof, warm, dry sleeping bag, and crawl into it. If that offends the Badu, well, it's either that or catching pneumonia, I was thinking when I saw Abu Salim's white *kaffiyye* glowing in the dark, the salukis trailing him, panting, shivering.

"Wake up. Wake up," Abu Salim whispered, bending over his girl-wife, Tammam.

Was it his voice I heard yesterday morning—or was it the day before yesterday?—whispering "Wake up, wake up"? I didn't drift back to sleep this morning. If Abu Salim was aware of it, he took no notice. And there are no walls here, no doors. Tammam and her infant were sleeping under a heap of dew-drenched carpet-blankets only a meter or two from mine. I couldn't help but hear Abu Salim trying to wake his girl-wife with whispers of endearment, *Ayuni, galbi*—my eyes, my heart.

Tammam didn't stir until Abu Salim murmured something that sounded like "If your brother comes while I am gone..."

"*Yaa-Rabb*," Tammam moaned, as one would moan "Oh my God." She turned to her sleeping infant-daughter and, like yesterday—oh, it would make your hair stand on end if you heard how she whispered, "Take what is left of my life and enjoy it..."

"Surround yourself with dignity while I am away...," Abu Salim whispered.

Her jewels *jingle-jangled* as the girl-wife heaped dew-damp dung, firewood, and twigs into the scorched fire-circle. One match after another Tammam struck, but only they caught fire.

"*Sabar*—patience—*ayuni, galbi*—light of my eyes, my heart— patience is better than thinking," Abu Salim counseled her, and lacking no patience—and with bountiful matches and a few dry twigs—he started the cooking fire. Blowing life into it, he also started to cough—terrible coughing spasms that wouldn't quit. It must drain him. He should quit smoking, see a doctor. Or at least use a bellows for the fire. His wheezing, spitting, and coughing awakened his infant daughter, Salimeh.

As soon as she started to cry, Tammam, cradling her in one arm, breast-fed little Salimeh. With the other hand, Tammam brewed tea and rinsed glasses, as if Abu Salim was not suffocating—choking red, his face glistening with beads of sweat, his bloodshot eyes bulging out of their sockets. His girl-wife didn't seem to see it. With the self-absorption of the young, she babbled about her brother to herself or Abu Salim, to their infant daughter or me, I don't know which. For an instant it looked as if the girl's indifference to him so pained Abu Salim and aggravated his cough that it would kill him.

Just then his senior wife, Azzizah, rushed over from her tent with some cough remedy she had concocted, making him cough even more, until she rubbed his back to stop it. Her layers and layers of veils, shawls, and long flowing *thowb* covered up her body and face, but not her love for Abu Salim—unrivalled by that of her junior co-wife, Tammam.

In no way did the girl-wife indicate she vied for Abu Salim's favor or love. Neither wife treated the other as a rival; rather, they seemed to be allies—friends, sisters. And, in a way, Abu Salim also treated his wives as if they were sisters, or mother and daughter.

"You see Azzizah and yet you do not learn from her," Abu Salim told his girl-wife. "Had you done as Azzizah does, stored your firewood in your tent, your firewood would not be drenched through with dew, and you would be able to light a fire in the morning without your husband having to expand not only the last of his matches to kindle it, but the last of his breath, causing him to cough."

"It is his cigarette smoking more than anything, that is causing him to cough," Tammam said, her beautiful eyes catching mine. "That is what I have been told, not only by Azzizah, who is a *darwisha*—a healer, daughter of a *darwish*, son of a *darwisha*—but also by my brother, who once saw a *Yahodi darwish*—a Jewish-Israeli doctor—driving a huge white Jeep with a huge machine inside that can see your lungs coughing, and your ribs, even your heart."

"But not your soul. No machine can see the soul of a man," says Abu Salim. "Yet with such nothing-machines you Yahod—Jews—win the hearts of our Badu young, and even some of our Badu elders.

"One Badu elder, or so I had heard people tell, went to consult a *Yahodi darwish* who had such a machine. And after the *Yahodi darwish* looked through the machine, he told the Badu elder that the desert's dust and sand and fire-circle smoke, and even morning dew, were not good for his lungs. 'But the desert, the dew, and the fire-circles are good for my soul,' said the Badu elder to the *Yahodi darwish*. 'Is cigarette smoking also good for your soul?' the *Yahodi darwish* said to the Badu elder. 'No,' replied the Badu elder. 'Cigarette smoking is my weakness. A man without weakness has no soul, no capacity to understand, to forgive, to love.'"

Last thing I expected to hear from this fierce-looking mountain Badu.

Nothing here is as I had expected it to be. Even time … drags and speeds here, at once. It feels as if I entered this forbidden compound only a minute ago and that I've been here forever, sipping over-sweetened tea brewed over a fire fueled by goat and camel dung.

And overhead, now that dawn has lifted the sky, the white tail of a jet plane, flying too high to be heard, looks like a wisp of hair in the vast blue. Flying high or low, the aircraft that took to the sky this morning links this isolated Badu compound, and the remote mountain chains that surround it, to grounds familiar to me, and lends a sense of security—to me, not to Abu Salim.

"*Shufi, aywa, shufi*—look, yes, take a good look," he tells me, pointing to the wisp of white hair in the sky, dispersing now. "It evaporates almost like the morning dew. *Aywa*—yes, the dewdrops that come and go, yet never fail to give life to the plants and herds that sustain our Badu way of life, rust your Yahodi airplanes and Jeeps, your tanks and cars, if you fail to waterproof them. But a camel, *Wallah*, a camel needs no gasoline, no waterproofing … A camel can traverse vast deserts without water for days and with great speed, *aywa*, a camel can gallop at thirty or forty kilometers an hour in wadis that no Jeep can traverse. And what do you get from tending Jeeps? Nothing but dirty hands. But, *Wallah*, what knowledge you gain from tending camels—there are no caves in the desert, no rocks, no plants, no animals that a Badu, even a child-boy or -girl, does not know from tending camel and goat herds. *Aywa*, a Badu is not a Badu if he does not possess this knowledge, valued most highly ever since anyone can remember until your tribe, Israel, took rule of this desert in a stunning victory you won fighting from airplanes, tanks, and Jeeps.

"*Aywa*, ever since anyone can remember, and to this day, Arab kings send their sons to learn from us Badu *adabb*—nobility, character, manners. But now our Badu young prefer your airplanes and Jeeps to our camels and goats, *aywa*. Now they think power is derived from such vehicles—and from cassettes of songs sung by singers who know nothing about the desert, nothing about our Badu way of life. Yet such cassettes our young now prefer to the words we Badu press from our hearts into poems, legends, stories …

"In one generation, *Wallah*, our way of life is bound to die if your tribe, Israel, continues to rule in this desert and to ride in our wadis and skies with your *tayyarat* and *sayyarat*—airplanes and Jeeps—and your unveiled maidens that entice our Badu young to stray more than any witch or demon"—Abu Salim spits, covers his spit with a fistful of sand. He glances at his girl-wife, Tammam, as if she embodied the Badu young who stray, as if she were his weakness, without whom he would not have the capacity to understand, forgive, love.

She hugged her infant daughter tight to her chest and cried out, "Like vultures they will descend upon me all too soon. Oh, my child, my daughter, take what is left of my life and enjoy it." Her umpteen bracelets *jingle-jangle* as Tammam points her finger at me and declares, "She is the first of the vultures—"

"*Oskoti*—hold your tongue!" Abu Salim snaps at her, startling his infant-daughter, Salimeh. She cries. He spits, then spews a torrent of words too fast for me to understand. And all too abruptly, with a tough hand, his senior-wife grabs my arm, shows Tammam how my hair stands on edge of goosebumps, and says, "Look at how your words frighten our guest."

"*Aywa*. I see you are truly my sister," says Tammam, her tearful eyes almost pleading.

And so I am transformed—just like that, faster than I can jot it down—from vulture to sister.

Why did I ever think that life in Badu tents was tranquil?

Nothing prepares you for this place. The drastic contrasts—dew and drought, sun and shade, open desert and the claustrophobic compound, the serenity of the surroundings and the Badu: tense, strained, volatile. It is almost as if they are swimming, fighting the current, in a river beneath a river. The river they show us—the river of customs and manners, poems and legends, a thousand and one Arabian nights—is calm and flows inexorably out of some ancient headland. And the river they wish to hide—the one they forbid all strangers to glimpse, even stranger-friends and scholars; the one in which they keep their secret of secrets, shame of shames, fear of fears … and the mysterious magnet that draws you to them—is treacherous and changeable. Tammam can barely keep her head above water.

Azzizah throws her a line time and again. Her secret-river talking is not as fast as it was, or else I'm starting to catch more words, and parables. I can imagine a hundred and one tales when I hear her telling Tammam:

"We, who are accustomed to the tents of the high are not about to descend to the low—a falcon, not a sparrow, you lift your hood and bring your prey—tongues twisted by evil eye of envy—blood exposed, *dir balak*—watch out, be careful—honor, reputation, patience …"

"*Aywa*, yes," responds Tammam. "Patience is better than thinking, if only you can manage it, oh self——"

"You frightened your stranger-guest," Abu Salim muttered to his wives.

"No, no, I'm not afraid," I protested, too much…

Silence. Abu Salim rolls himself a cigarette, slowly, deliberately, prolonging and compounding the feeling of uncertainty, suspense, and fear that creeps into my gut with nearly every Badu silence. Like an idiot I brace myself now, as if I have said or done something wrong and Imsallam Suleman Abu Salim is going to lash out at me, punish or reward me, as he does his wives. He coughs and coughs. His tobacco smells like hashish.

"The desert is a place safer for a woman than for a man… Are you ready? Write it to remember," he demands.

"We Badu so value a woman," he dictates, "that one of our names for woman is *amarat a'beit*, meaning the main pole of the tent, the pillar of the house. If a woman is violated, it is as if the house or tent has collapsed. Thus, the curse of curses, *Yekhrab beitak*—May your house be destroyed—means: May your woman be violated. And even in blood-price, a woman is valued more than a man. *Aywa*, if a man is killed in battle or in a fight, someone from the other side, the side that spilled the blood, must be killed to avenge the death, or a blood-price must be paid in his stead.

"Blood price: forty camels for killing a man; one hundred and sixty camels for killing woman; three hundred and twenty camels for killing a pregnant woman.

"Even a wealthy tribe can become impoverished if one of its sons harms a woman, even if in error. That is why women wear black, to prevent error. Even in the old days, when Badu tribes raided one another and plundered, the men would flee if too weak to drive back the attackers. But the women and children stayed. They knew that, no matter how their menfolk fared, no other Badu tribe would stoop so low as even to frighten a Badawia, let alone harm her.

"*Aywa*, we Badu are Arabs, true Arabs, not *fellahin*, like the *Felastiniyiin*—Palestinians—who have slaughtered your Yahodi children in Ma'alot." Abu Salim spits behind his back. "You are surprised, I see. You think we Badu know nothing.

"Did your men kill the killers of your children?" he asks me.

I can't remember what reprisal if any followed the slaughter in Ma'alot.

"Sometimes the killers escape," I mutter.

"Not from us Badu, *Wallah*—by God," Abu Salim says. "With us the Tribe, the *Hamula*—the Clan—and the Family are held responsible for any wrongdoing by any man, *Wallah*. If I were to kill a man, then run and hide in the vast expanse of Sinaa, his kinsfolk would be sure to avenge his blood with mine or my brothers', my sons', my nephews', my uncles', or my cousins', their children's children's or mine, even if it took five generations," says Abu Salim, raising five fingers. "Even a Badawia married to a son of the family who spilled the blood is bound to kill even her husband to avenge her blood kin.

"It is maybe the biggest mistake you can make, to let pass even the slightest transgression, for it can but lead to very great trouble—as with the old Negev Badu who had heard that the virility of his youth would return if he ate the meat of a bird from the distant land of Habbash, a bird called *Habbashat*——"

"I never heard of such a bird remedy," mutters Azzizah under her veil. "*Ghul...Ghul*—Tell on ... Tell on."

"*Aywa*. The old Negev Badu bought the bird and kept it and fed it twice a day so that it would have more meat to restore his strength." Abu Salim goes on, in the lilting voice of Badu legend-telling: "And then, one day, his *Habbashat* bird was stolen. Right away he gathered his sons and told them, 'There is great danger, unless you find my *Habbashat* bird.' But his sons answered that he was well rid of the bird, for it was making an old fool of him. It matters not what his *Habbashat* bird was making of him, the old Negev-Badu told his sons, 'the only thing that matters now, important for us all now, is to find my *Habbashat* bird and bring it back to our compound...' But his sons thought his desire to restore his virility got the better of him, and before long his *Habbashat* bird escaped from their remembering. And then, a few weeks later, three goats were stolen from the family's herd. High and low they searched the whole Negev desert for these goats, but found not even a hoofprint.

When they came to their father for advice, 'Find my *Habbashat* bird' was his advice, which they ignored, as before. But then, a few weeks later, their camel herd was stolen and the robbers violated their women. 'Because you did not avenge the theft of the *Habbashat* bird, the whole desert thinks us easy prey,' the old Negev Badu told his sons. *Aywa*, in this world of wolves, never be the sheep.

"We Badu can wait forty years to seek revenge, and even then think we are hasty. We Badu can wait, *Wallah*, we true Arabs do not lack patience like you strangers, always looking at the minutes strapped to your wrists. We Badu have as many minutes as there are grains of sand in Sinaa. Forever—*daimann*—Arabs will condemn you Yahod to live with the fear that the Arabs will push you into the sea—for, if the fathers fail, the sons will try, and their sons." Like Arik, his son will fall, and his son's sons, forever and ever—*daimann*...

"How can a war, or a bloody tribal dispute end in a *sulha*—in peace—if you must always avenge blood for blood, or for a blood-price that depletes all the resources of your tribe?" I ask him.

"*Oshrobi, oshrobi*—drink, drink." Abu Salim hands me another glass of tea. "For, even as you sit in the shade, the dry desert air and the ever-blowing wind dehydrates you." Imsallam Suleman Abu Salim, wrapped in layers and layers of clothes, advises me to do the same, "For layers of clothes keep you warm in the shade. And in the sun, they protect you from sunburn and dehydration." One pot of tea after another is brewed. We sip glass after glass of steaming tea. And still it's cold, damp, dismal...

Why are they fussing over their stranger-guest? Their enemy-guest? Why did they invite me to tents they forbid all strangers to enter?

Why did I fly halfway around the world and back to come to this God-forsaken place?...

❧

To escape—from myself. That's what my sister thinks. That's why I ventured to the desert, to this wilderness. That's how my sister sees me.

Yes, the little one who used to insist we call her "Lallik" because it sounded like "Arik" and "Leora." She was not yet nine when you went, my Arik. All the grownups she loved were stricken by grief. And some of the children around her told her that I would have to be chained-anchored to your grave stone for seven years, if the air force doesn't find you or your body. Other children told her that you were dead and buried and I'd have to marry your best friend, Yehoshua, in seven days or seven weeks. But next she heard from her little friends that her sister, Leora, flew to Canada with little Levi—just as she was about to be chained to your grave. From other children she heard that I flew to visit-stay with my mother's aunt in Canada for seven days, or seven weeks. Seven months later, she got it from nearly everyone around her that her sister, Leora, was a low-down dropout, a deserter, barely in mourning for her husband, Arik, before marrying that wealthy Canadian, Dave … A good war widow would never have done such a thing. No, I should have become a living, breathing monument to you, my Arik. My kid-sister didn't shun me, as others did. She simply refused to let me get close to her.

On one of my annual trips home I saw that, suddenly, she'd grown up, in her high heels, fashionable clothes, trendy hairstyle, skillful makeup, and wearing a diamond engagement ring … Her house is only a ten- or fifteen-minute walk from my hotel at Herzliyya on the beach, but the distance is too great for her. And, on more than one occasion, she invited me over and I was greeted by a locked door and an empty house. No explanations, no apologies.

I ask for neither, of course—not from her, not from anyone in The Land. And yet, no matter what I do or don't do, someone, inside or outside our circle, will confront me directly or whisper behind my back that a dropout has no rights here in The Land no right to demand, criticize, question, or state an opinion, and certainly not to complain, especially not about anything remotely connected to The Land, the Nation, the State. I have effectively been gagged for more than two decades, silenced not only in person, but long distance, by mail, by phone, and . . . I allowed it to happen.

By now, it doesn't seem strange to anyone but me that no matter what anyone says to me, I don't voice disagreement, disapproval, criticism, or anything that might be interpreted as negative. I revert to the positive, supportive, encouraging, uplifting, for something to say—and to the very people who have tried to silence me. But so draining is the effort to censor myself that even those I love have become a burden. I've got to take a break, be by myself for a while. But they, uplifted by me, urge me to stay—until they are all talked out. Then, almost like an opera singer after an aria, sounding the last note of the finale, they expect me to applaud. After a week or two of that, whether they have reserves of fresh material or not, they get tired of performing. And then the questions begin to build like a chorus: "Don't you have to get back to Canada . . . to your work . . . to your husband?"

Had it not been for Levi, your brother would shun me. I've betrayed everything you lived and died for, he believes, and he clearly can't stand the sight of me. So, I've erased signs of my presence when he was around, uttered not a sound, hardly breathed. But a day before I set out for this desert compound, I drive over to your parents' to part from them and I see him there.

"Would Arik give or deny his consent for Levi to serve high-risk duty? What do you think?" I ask him.

He frowned, as though thinking that only a low-down dropout would ask such a question of a man whose sons were serving high-risk duty this very minute. Seemed he was itching to tell me what he thought of a person who would consider using any law to get her son out of front-line service. But Arik's parents were sitting with us, so he said instead, "Whenever Levi's number will come up, he'll be a goner, be he in Canada or in The Land, serving high- or low-risk duty."

His parents, heaving a sigh, gave him that look. It's even sadder now that he's their only son. Your brother shrugged, as if reconciled to the notion that your parents would never give him his due; to the day they die, they'll regret that you got killed, not him. And then, to add insult to injury, your parents went on to remind him how in the last war—the Yom-Kippur War, fought only five years ago—he was sick with worry for his sons—not for his daughter, even though she was also serving compulsory army duty then, because she had been exempted from high-risk duty, as are all women-soldiers in The Land these days. "How quickly we forget," your father said.

Next your mother turned to me and said, "How can you even think of waiving the boy's exemption after your sister tells the whole country that your son wants to serve front-line duty, to risk his life to atone for your sin..."

My sin—dropping out of The Land.

That sister of mine, thinking I'll let it slide, no doubt, like the umpteen times she stood me up, greets me with her practiced smile when I finally track her down at my parents'. She and my parents haven't heard me raise a voice here in many years, the shock when I explode at her is all too obvious, scary, painful.

"Where in the hell did you dig up this crap about Levi feeling he has to atone for my fucking sin, even if it kills him?... To *you* I'm a dropout, but not to Levi... To *you*, not to Levi, it's such a sin that you shut me out for more than twenty years, not only here but Outside... Six thousand miles you fly to New York, only an hour by plane from Toronto, but not once have you been moved by curiosity, never mind love, to fly the distance, see where Levi grew up, how he lives, how I live... And you think you know enough to make such a pronouncement!... For more than twenty years, I've been sitting on a suitcase with one foot in The Land, the other in Canada. And you think I dropped out!

"You have no idea how I wish I could... no idea what a peaceful country Canada is. No idea what Levi is giving up to return to The Land. No idea what a burning idealist the kid is. No idea how he loves to fly, how good a pilot he is. As best as he knows how, Levi wants to defend The Land, the Nation, in the front lines—like his father, Arik's brother, his sons and the best of his friends, Gingie...

Why is that so inconceivable to you, you have to invest him with such a puny motive—atoning for his mother's 'sin' reduces him, and you, the Nation, The Land ... For so little was Arik wasted?

"Or are you afraid Levi will fall like Arik? Is that why you invested him with such a motive? No way would I waive my son's exemption for that. Is that what you thought?"

All the while, my sister stroked my mother's arm and my father's, like when she was little, to take the pain away, make it better.

I phoned her later. She was sleeping, her husband said. A while later I called again, and she says she's about to sit down and eat.

"I just phoned to say goodbye. I'm going to Sinai first thing tomorrow, you know," I told her, and before I could add, "Let's make a *sulha*—a forgiveness———"

"Shalom," she says, and hangs up on me.

Would you be as unforgiving as her, my Arik, or would you remember and count in my favor the devotion of my youth? Remember how beautiful I was in your eyes? Remember how you loved to hear me laugh, how you whispered, "Your thighs are like a palm; let me climb, drink. Your lips are ..." How I long to caress you, to kiss you, to love you now. Oh, how I remember the muscle of your youth ...

In my requiem years I couldn't make love without feeling unfaithful to you, my Arik. Dave knew it before he married me. He said he understood it, respected it. I believed him, took his waiting as an expression of his love for me. But now ...

Dave thinks, or rather pronounced, unequivocally, that I'm going through a midlife crisis, as he calls it. That's what compelled me to make an eighteen-thousand-kilometer U-turn—from Sinai, to Toronto, to Sinai—he maintains.

"Dad" is what Levi calls Dave.

"Abba" he calls you, Arik. He looks like you, your son, Levi, speaks Hebrew like you—and English like a Canadian, like my husband, Dave.

His dad won't move to The Land, not even for one year, let alone the three years of Levi's compulsory service.

Levi thinks I'm running off to the desert because he and Dave have put me in a situation whereby I must choose between my husband and my son.

I have no life of my own, our Levi thinks; no dreams of my own; no fantasies, yearnings, cravings that have nothing to do with husbands or sons.

9

In a grand swoop, the sun rises above the cliffs and, in minutes, the carpet-blankets, even the firewood, has dried up. Only the dewdrops trapped in the desert plants remain: "The pasture that sustains our camels and goats," says Abu Salim, "which in turn sustains our Badu way of life." We are dwarfed by a desert splashed in sunrise gold, while sand carried on the wind prickles like shards of glass.

Azzizah makes shade, propping open the side flap of Tammam's tent like a sort of a veranda awning, with a couple of rusty poles that were once water pipes.

Next she moves the welcome carpets to the shade. where it's so cold I put on my parka. Instantly, it seems, Azzizah has lit a fire in the scorched fire-circle here in the shade at the side of Tammam's tent.

Some of the goats and saluki dogs move back and forth between sun and shade, as if they can't decide which curse is worse. Others, parched, hungry, edge toward the water jerricans and feed bags, but *ffflllliiinnnggg!* Tammam throws stones at their feet. They move away, only to circle back when Salimeh cries, distracting her girl-mother, her father, and his senior wife.

No matter what they do, little Salimeh cries on and off, as she has done since her father's coughing spasms startled her from sleep—like an infant in pain from teething or hunger. Little Salimeh needs not only mother's milk but solid food three times a day. I should have loaded my Jeep, not with trinkets, but with cases of baby food, and powdered eggs and milk, and tins of sardines, salmon, tuna ...

I'm famished. The Badu eat only one meal a day, in the evening, rice or pita. Their camels and dogs eat twice a day. Morning and evening, Abu Salim feeds them. And now Azzizah, taking pity on the goats, puts out some feed on tattered sackcloths.

The two tents—Tammam's and Azzizah's—are pitched thirty meters apart, give or take. Both fronting east. Pointing to the northwest is the only spot of green—the lone acacia tree, braving the winds near the edge of the plateau. On the opposite edge, in the southwest, is the top of the path that leads to Abu Salim's *maq'ad*. And almost directly opposite, in the southeast, you can see the top of the path that leads to the waterhole. It wouldn't surprise me if the Badu consider this plateau to be choice real estate because of its symmetry. They love and crave the order and harmony inherent in symmetry, you can see it in the patterns and colors of their hand-woven welcome-carpets, and camel saddles, and their hand-embroidered *thowbs*—dresses—and *abia*—cloaks.

The latrine—the ditch, or, more correctly, a bit of a crack in the hard granite ground that traps layers and layers of wind-blown sand and gravel—is by the outcrop of boulders at the foot of the cliffs that tower in the east and shade the first fire-circle of the day. The Badu move the fire-circle with the ever-shifting sun and shade.

You don't see their water source in this sketch of this forbidden encampment. I have yet to walk the path leading to it. "Is your water source as far a distance from the compound as the *maq'ad*?" I asked them.

"Not very far going down to it empty, but all too far coming back up full," Azzizah replied.

"Why do you pitch your tents so far from water then?" I ask her.

"Not proper to ask questions," she snaps. And, really, their water source is their most precious and envied inheritance, especially now, in this sixth or seventh year of drought. Hell, I wouldn't ask my closest friend where she kept her most valuable inheritance. Why did I ask them?

Little Salimeh, as if feeling the pain of the whole world, bursts out crying again. Tammam, crying with her, offers her a breast, but the child screams, her red face covered in tears and saliva; she is kicking, wriggling out of Tammam's arms and almost into the fire.

"My milk ran dry! My milk ran dry!" Tammam screams. "*Yaa-Rabb, Yaa-Rabb*—my God, my God—my milk ran dry!"

"Your milk turned sour from worrying," Azzizah tells her junior co-wife. "Patience is better than worrying."

"My milk ran dry, and you talk of patience!" snaps Tammam. "You . . . *you* feed the infant with patience, not milk." The girl-mother plunks her infant on Azzizah's lap and walks toward the lone acacia tree. Her sun-bleached desert appears to be as infinite as her sun-bleached sky; her compound, confining.

Spewing a slew of curses, Abu Salim disappears, perhaps to the ditch. His camels, their front legs hobbled, munch gravel not far from the fire-circle. Azzizah pulls out a withered breast from the nursing slit at the side of her *thowb*. Her purple nipple is wrinkled like a dried prune, yet little Salimeh accepts it.

"What would so worry Tammam that her milk turns sour?" I whisper to Azzizah. Her bloodshot eyes drill holes through me, her eyebrows knot.

"You came here knowing nothing . . . nothing," she mutters, and leaves it at that.

"Is Tammam ill? Is that what worries her so?"

Silence.

"Is Tammam pregnant, afraid she will die, like her mother, soon after birthing her second child? Is that what worries her? Is that why she keeps telling her infant daughter, 'Take what is left of the rest of my life and enjoy it'?" I ask Azzizah, breaking the silence.

"Not proper to ask questions," Azzizah replies, then says, "It is the drought. The drought first dried up the milk of the she-goats, then the milk of the she-camels; now the milk of Badawias the desert over."

Raving mad, Tammam returns to the fire-circle—or so it seems. With her *shibriyya*, the dagger she used last evening to pry open the tin of tomato paste and to chop the onion, she chops at the ground by the cooking fire; her jewels *jingle-jangle* furiously. She chops and scoops out the gravel—chops and scoops, chops and scoops, *jjjjinggggle-jjjangggle*; chops a hole about a third of a meter wide and deep, into which she puts the red-hot ashes from the cooking fire. On a tattered old rag she pounds flour, salt, and water into a wad of dough. Anger powers her fists. Azzizah doesn't say a word to calm her. The dough is now flat as a pizza, and oval-shaped, yet Tammam pounds still. Out of the tattered old rag she scoops it, plunks it on top of the red-hot ashes, then layers on more ashes and adds a final topping of gravel. Now she picks up a fire poker and tamps down the gravel over the grave in which she has buried the dead treat. *Tap. Tap. Tap. Jingle-jangle, jingle.*

"What are you doing, *yaa*-Tammam?" I whisper to the girl-wife, her girl-infant cradled in Azzizah's arms, fast asleep.

Silence. *Tap, tap. Tap. Jingle-jangle, jingle.*

"What is she doing?" I whisper to Azzizah.

"*Wallah*, I never never, never, saw a woman so ignorant as you," whispers the senior wife in response. "You do not even know how to be a lazy woman."

"A lazy woman?" I ask her, thinking I didn't hear right.

"*Aywa*," replies Azzizah. "Tammam is preparing lazy pita. One pita from one piece of dough, not five or six pitas—five-six times more work, but five-six times better pitas———"

"Hush!" snaps Tammam. *Tap, tap, tap.*

"She hears, by the sound of her tapping, if the lazy pita is done," explains Azzizah.

The tea is brewed, and still Tammam taps.

"Sounds like it is done," the senior wife whispers to her junior co-wife.

"Not yet," mutters Tammam.

"My hearing is getting old." Azzizah sighs.

It sounds to me like cardboard buried under the gravel by the time Tammam decides the lazy pita is done. She scoops off the top layers of gravel and ashes and, using her *shibriyya* dagger like a fork, digs out of the smoldering cavity a flat chunk of steaming charcoal, which she plunks on the dented bronze tray. Now, she bends over, like when she is lighting a cigarette and doesn't want her veils to catch fire. Gravel and ashes cloud out from the sides of her veils as she blows to dislodge sand, gravel, and ashes from the loaf of lazy pita.

Soon after devouring most of the loaf herself, Tammam pulls her breast out of the nursing slit of her *thowb* to see if the lazy pita restored her milk.

The fire and the sizzling heat work such optical illusions that, for a moment, I'd swear I was seeing an apparition—a shimmering ghost dancing and thrashing directly across the fire. Then, just when I feel the onset of an adrenalin rush, I realize it's Abu Salim rejoining the fire-circle.

Now, through the veil of fire-smoke, he looks like Jacob, the day he first caught sight of Rachel.

Azzizah's glance drops to the ground, the hurt heavy in her eyes, like Leah's.

Tammam, like Rachel, rounded up her goats and Azzizah's, as shepherd-boys from the neighboring compound came to lead her goat herds and Azzizah's to water and pasture.

A cloud of dust trails after them, and you can't shake the feeling that our ancestors walked here only yesterday.

I get a real taste of those long-ago days as I bite into my lazy pita bread, embedded with grains of sand. Every nerve explains why the Badu-young prefer the loaves of bread they see in the restaurants that dot the coastal highway, and at the airport, not far from the mountain that people believe is Mount Sinai. At its feet, at the Santa Katerina Monastery, a lousy imitation of the Burning Bush that never consumes itself draws hundreds, thousands, who cannot help but see the red light-bulb that "burns yet doesn't consume itself . . ." Still, it doesn't stop the longing for what never was—except perhaps in myths, you say to yourself in Santa Katerina. But here, this morning, when the dew washed clean the desert, I could almost touch those long-ago days—be they myth or not—days when the world was a purer place, when underneath everything there was a sacredness, when a pillar of fire-smoke-dust pointed the direction to The Promised Land.

This morning I can also feel the strain in Jacob's tents—Rachel's and Leah's—and the passion.

And the flies-bugs-lice. God, what I wouldn't give now for a good long shower, a clean change of clothes, a big breakfast, a long walk—a straight answer to the question: Why would Tammam think me the first of the vultures to come here? Why would vultures come here? To prey on what? Why would Tammam look mystified when Azzizah tells me, "You would be wise to stay here," and when Abu Salim presents me with a *kaffiyye*—headdress—exquisite, heavy with red embroidery.

"Invite a guest and honor him, but whether he'll partake of your hospitality or not, only fate will decide," Azzizah mutters, almost as if she could sense how I wished I could take off in my Jeep now.

Abu Salim spits behind his back, then addresses me, "You go in circles like a Badu forced by drought to wander from waterhole to waterhole, grazing-ground to grazing-ground."

"You would be wise to stay here," Azzizah tells me again, and Tammam's eyes pop wider in amazement.

"What makes you think I go in circles?" I ask Abu Salim.

"You strangers look at the dust of our *abia*—cloaks—and you think we Badu know nothing," Abu Salim replies, rolling another cigarette.

"From the Gulf of Suez to the Gulf of Aqaba–Eilat" Abu Salim glues the fine cigarette paper with a lick of spit, his bloodshot eyes addressing me, "round and round you went, in circles and zig-zagging ever since you and your escort-guardian entered this Sinaa Peninsula—not from the east, by way of Aqaba–Eilat, but from the west, by way of Al-Arish–Yamit you entered."

"*Wallah*, it's true, how did you know?" I ask him.

"Are you ready?" he responds, like a monarch ready to dictate to his scribe.

"Yes."

"Good. Write what you hear me tell you to write, so that whoever reads it will know that, without you or anyone else telling it to me, I know that from the desert town Al Arish or Yamit, you and your escort-guardian went on to the sulfur springs, then to the Common Road, the wadi of the bitter waters, the ever-shifting sand mountains, the ancient temple at Sarabit al-Khadim, the ancient turquoise mines, the greatest of all the great dry river beds, Wadi Feiran, the man-made oasis at the monastery Santa Katerina, the tip of the peninsula, Ras Muhammad, the spectacular wadi... Too narrow and steep to traverse is the last wadi, even by camel; you have to dismount and walk very carefully for one wrong step could start a rock slide. Yet I am sure you crossed it by Jeep."

"We did, *Wallah*. How did you know, *yaa*–Abu Salim?" I heard it in my voice—"amazement" is not the word. Abu Salim wasn't telling me half of what he knew, by the look his wives gave me.

"Like the *fellah* you ask, 'How did I know?'" says Abu Salim, one eye amused, the other annoyed, disdainful.

"*Aywa*, it is a true story, or so I have heard. Six or seven years ago it was, before the onset of this drought, it happened that a *fellah* lost his camel," Abu Salim elaborates in the sing-song voice of Badu storytelling. "His precious she-camel galloped away, far into the desert. The *fellah* went to search. High and low he searched, and farther than far, the desert over he searched. And then one day he met a Badu. And the Badu asked the *fellah*, 'Are you looking for your camel?'

"'*Wallah*, yes,' said the *fellah*.

"'And is your camel a low camel, with a short neck, red hair, and blind in the left eye?' asked the Badu.

"'*Wallah*, yes,' said the *fellah*, thinking in his heart: 'This Badu is all too familiar with my she-camel. He must have stolen her away for himself.' But the *fellah* was not completely sure of it. So he asked the Badu, 'Where did you see my camel?'

"'I did not see your camel, only her footsteps,' said the Badu.

"Now the *fellah* grew even more suspicious. And he told the Badu, 'Only her footsteps you saw and you know she is a low camel, her neck short, her hair red, her left eye blind?'

"'*Aywa*—yes,' replied the Badu. 'By her footprints I knew your camel was lost. For any rider astride a camel would move with purpose, in a straight line. But your camel, *yaa-Fellah*, zigzagged from this bush to that. And by the leaves that your camel chewed, only on one side off that bush, I know your camel is blind in the left eye. For a camel chews on the right side of the bush only when blind in the left eye. And by the footprints that were so very close to the bush, I know your she-camel's neck is short. And by the hair your she-camel left on a branch, I know her hair is red. And by the urine marks in the sand I know your she-camel is short, *yaa-Fellah*. For a she-camel urinates against her tail. And whipping her tail until she was done, your she-camel left clear marks on the sand. Not large and wide as a tall camel, but narrow and small I saw, and I knew the lost she-camel is short.'

"Yes," Abu Salim waited for my pen to stop.

"And by the layers of dust I saw on your Jeep the moonless night that you and your escort drove into my *maq'ad*, I knew the circles and the zigzags you had made from gulf to gulf. And from the way you were leaning to the left, as you were approaching the fire-circle, I knew that your escort drove most of the way. And from his desert shoes, I knew that he was of the Yahodi border-crossing soldier-of-soldiers. And by the way he dismounted the Jeep, I knew that his knees had been injured. And from the late hour he decided to drive into my *maq'ad*, and from the Badu words he had asked you to teach him, I knew that he saw only the dust on a Badu's *abaiah*, and therefore he thought he could outwit us Badu."

"You see?" Tammam's eyes said, meeting mine. "I told you Abu Salim is a tracker better than the best of trackers."

"Is it possible even for the best of Badu trackers to track a man who disappeared in the desert twenty-one years ago?" I ask Abu Salim.

"It is possible, until it is impossible," he replies.

"*Oskotu*—utter not a sound," Abu Salim tells-orders his wives. Next breath he tells-orders me to record his words for El Bofessa—Professor Russell. "*Oskotu*—not a sound from you, women, while I record," he orders, as I'm about to press the red Record button. His infant daughter won't obey him. She whimpers even in her sleep. Azzizah collects the child and glides over to her tent.

On and on, for nearly a full side of the cassette, Abu Salim issues a torrent too fast for me to understand. He sounds like a person directing his anguish, frustration, and anger at the whole world.

Before he redirects it at her, Tammam decides to leave. She can't have taken more than a couple of steps when he stops his harangue to snap at her, "Where are you going?!!"

"To the child and Azzizah," she replies, in that arrogant voice the young use when the old get on their nerves.

"Stay here!" Abu Salim orders her. "You have a guest…" He waits until she obeys him, rejoining the fire-circle, then he tells her to shut up while, on and on, he resumes his recording.

She picks up her embroidery work and jabs at it and squirms, as if it's hell for her to sit so imprisoned and gagged for five minutes, let alone for however long he intends to record.

"Something doesn't feel right in this forbidden encampment. I wouldn't stay with these Bedouins if I were you," Tal had cautioned me soon after we parked at Abu Salim's *maq'ad*. I'm glad I stayed, but now something definitely doesn't feel right here.

Fear.

My fear…

10

"Leora!" Tal cried out just as a motorcycle swerved in front of the Jeep and over to the next lane.

"You startled the hell out of me," I snapped. The wind and the clanking engine garbles my words; his also. "Bolt your window. I can't hear you," I motioned to him.

"Keep your hand on the wheel. Your eyes on the road," he motioned back.

The wind tousled his hair over his furrowed brow. He looked like a kibbutznik now—a kibbutznik who can't chew gum and walk at the same time; a kibbutznik unaccustomed to city life, to the fast-paced jockeying for position—pushing, shoving, swerving in and out.

North of the country club, a heap of fresh flowers swelled on the roadside. This memorial bears no plaque. It is not long ago that a busload of families who had chartered the bus for their annual picnic were killed in this terror attack. Now even the Israeli Doves travel armed here on the coastal highway, a major artery here, not unlike Highway 401 in Toronto.

Tal was armed as well. I hadn't noticed it until the wind flattened his t-shirt to his gut, outlining the handgun tucked into his belt. It was sad, but small wonder he was trying to hide the need to carry a gun when we were just fifteen minutes from downtown Tel Aviv.

I turned east onto the highway that leads to Jerusalem and Mount Herzl, and only then realized I didn't know which road leads to the Gulf of Suez, or even to Yamit. "Turn back?" I gestured to him when I saw him shaking his head.

"Keep going," he motioned back. "I'll direct you."

This highway was not congested. A diesel tanker, "Flammable" blazoned on its side, crawled from a roadside diner onto the highway with complete disregard for the Yield sign and stuck to our tail, zigzagging behind, blowing diesel fumes and blasting my ears off. I waved him into the passing lane, but he kept sounding his horn. I couldn't tell if he was trying to warn me that something was wrong. Just as I was about to pull off the highway, Tal hoisted himself over the gap between our seats and shouted over the tanker's horn: "Don't touch the brakes! The man is a lunatic. Step on it until you catch a good distance from him, then get off the highway."

The road felt slippery, even at eighty klicks. The Jeep was tuned for crossing desert wadis. The loosened bolts, cables, and screws were cranked so tight that the pedals, clutch, and gearshift required muscle. The steering was quick to the touch—too quick for paved roads. I felt as if I were pressing full speed on an icy road in Canada. I don't remember when the tanker passed us. I just remember how relieved I was when the Jeep pulled to a stop on the soft shoulder.

The tension showed in Tal's face. But his hands, lighting a cigarette, were steady, unlike mine.

"And I wanted to drive, to be in control."

"I wouldn't take it personally. It's a national disease," Tal responded. "Now you see why more people get killed here in road accidents than in all the wars and terrorists' attacks put together," he said. After a hesitation, he added, "My father was killed in a crash. Many years ago. Whenever I see such a lunatic I remember that my chances are better in the battlefield than here on the roads."

"That's obscene. I mean, I saw the statistics but——"

"Yes, obscene. But true," he said. "Your services would be in demand here, way more than Gingie's mother's. You're wasted in Canada."

"So, Gingie told you that I'm a social worker who——"

"A social worker? No, I thought you were like Gingie's mother, a psychologist. Gingie told me you work with bereaved parents, widows, orphans—not the war-bereaved, like his mother, but accident-bereaved..."

"Was your father driving alone the day he was killed?"

"Yes. He died alone ... but he lived long enough to realize his dream."

"What was his dream?"

"To come up to The Land. Settle in a kibbutz."

"Where did he come from?"

"Belgium ... If my parents had moved to The Land a year before the War of Independence, I would have been born in The Land, in the kibbutz."

Tal was thirty-one years old, I knew now. Years younger than he looked. Thirty-one years old means he had battled in the '67 war, the War of Attrition, the Yom-Kippur War, and, in between, took part in reconnaissance missions and commando raids behind enemy lines.

"Did Gingie also tell you that I am forty-two years old?"

"No. I figured you were in your forties when Gingie told me your first husband, Arik, fell in the Sinai War," he replied. "But when I saw you in the hotel lobby, I thought you looked closer to thirty. That's why I hesitated to approach you, to ask you if you are Leora."

He was like the kibbutzniks I remembered now, I thought, laughing to myself. Those kibbutzniks would tell a woman over forty that she looked closer to thirty, not as a compliment or a come-on, but as a matter of fact. And, like those kibbutzniks, I had to pull his story from him. Tal was obviously not accustomed to telling it. Everyone knew everyone's story in his kibbutz, most likely; he was probably unaccustomed to talking about himself, didn't know how to tell his story.

"How old were you when your parents—you—came up to The Land?"

"Six," Tal said; "seven when my father got killed."

"Did your mother remarry?"

"Yes. A redhead like Gingie. My brothers, half-brothers, are also redheads. Both are serving regular duty now. One just made it to the Unit."

"No——"

"That's what my mother said when she heard it. 'No. One in the Unit for nine years is more than enough.'"

"You served in the Unit for nine years?"

"Yes, with a few interruptions, for training courses, a field command, and the Yom-Kippur War." Tal butted his cigarette underfoot. The dry thistles and thorns in the roadside ditch could easily ignite into a brushfire.

"What is your job in civilian life, Tal, in the kibbutz?"

"I'm on leave of absence from the kibbutz."

"Why?"

"We have a day or two in this Jeep, right?"

"Yes."

He filled the gap between our seats with our sleeping bags so that we could continue to talk without having to shout over the noise of the engine, the traffic, the wind.

We switched seats and, now, in his driving, I saw what a commander Gingie had.

Tal drove like a person magnanimous by nature, discipline, or habit. For the first time that morning, he didn't look awkward, embarrassed, or uncomfortable. Confidence suited him. He looked handsome now—a hundred untold stories were plowed into his face.

❧

"Where did Abu Salim ride off to? . . . To work?" I ask his wives after he left abruptly, without a word.

"Only women do work, women and *fellahin*," replies Azzizah. "Men have more important things to do."

"Like what?"

"Not proper to ask questions," Azzizah responds, as she refills the teapot with the last drops in the jerrican. "*YaahhAhh* . . . the older I grow, the farther the waterhole and the faster the water skins empty." She heaves a sigh.

"I will fetch water," says Tammam. She is picking at something—lice?—in her infant's hair.

"I will go with you." I can't wait to stretch my legs, wash my face, maybe even take a sponge-bath. "Is it the custom to pitch your tent some distance from your water source?"

"*Aywa*—yes," replies Azzizah, spinning camel hair into weaving threads.

"It is a good custom," says Tammam. "For had we pitched our tents right by our *bir*—waterhole—all the women who fetch water from our well would forever be in our face."

"*Aywa*, fetching water is woman's work, made difficult by the distance from the *bir* to the tent," says Azzizah. "Yet it is good to distance our tents, because it is forbidden for strangers to enter our women's tents, but not to quench their thirst at our waterhole."

"And also because we Badu would be bound to extend not only water, but shelter and food, to friend and foe alike. For we Badu are measured by our hospitality. Yet, few of us can afford to be as hospitable as we wish to be," says Tammam.

Azzizah chuckles under her veil. "Years ago, my tongue was as blunt as Tammam's. Now it is almost as smooth as the tongue of a man."

No water in the compound, except a few drops in the teapot. Doesn't seem to bother the Badawias. Me—just the thought of it dries up the spit in my mouth. The constant desert wind, an emissary from the sun, dehydrates you before your throat feels it. I'm all too aware of it now.

"Were you ever so parched you thought you would die?" I asked them.

"A proper Badawia will never roam thirsty, for she will never leave her goats, never allow them to wander far from the *bir*—water source," Azzizah replies. "But once ... only once, I strayed. Once, when I was a maiden tending my mother's flock a distance of three days and nights from my mother's tent, I heard Abu Salim calling my name in the night. Abu Salim was but a boy himself then, tending his mother's flock, but even as a boy Abu Salim knew how to cover tracks. No one ever suspected we strayed."

"Were you too young then to become pregnant?" I said.

"*Wallah*, what questions you ask," says Azzizah, chuckling. "I did not become pregnant until I married Abu Salim. For many years I bore him only daughters. Four lived and five died. And Abu Salim wanted a son, so he divorced me."

"Only to marry her again," says Tammam.

"*Aywa*—yes," says Azzizah. "Time and again Abu Salim divorced me, only to marry me time and again. For whomever he married bore him only daughters."

"So why is he called 'Abu Salim'—'father of Salim'?" I asked.

"Because my last-born was a son, and I named him 'Salim,' meaning 'peace,' 'perfect peace.' For then I knew that Abu Salim would not divorce me ever again, and I would not lose my daughters to the service of his new wife. My son I would never lose, for his wife is bound to live here, in his parents' compound, just as my daughters went to live in their husbands' compounds." Azzizah heaves a deep sigh, then mutters, "Two of my daughters come to visit me often, for their husbands' compounds are pitched only a day or two by camel from here. But the other one, and my son, Salim, I have not seen for nearly a year."

"Is your son staying with his sister, far away from here?" I ask her.

"Not proper to ask questions," replies Azzizah, dropping the curtain. This much and no more would she reveal.

And Tammam's eyes mirror the distance, revealing nothing.

Silence. In a tiny hammock-like sling extending from her head and swinging down her back, Tammam carries little Salimeh toward the lone acacia tree rooted by the spot the Badawias call "the lookout point."

Azzizah grunts and sighs, her bloodshot eyes sorrowful.

"Why are you sad, Azzizah?"

Silence.

"What got into Tammam?"

"Her longing," Azzizah replies.

The sky was a cloudless backdrop for the August sun. The thorns and thistles, and the wildflowers were scorched brown, but the orange groves and fields of carnations and gladioli, avocados, tomatoes, and eggplants cultivated in between the new sprawling suburbs of the Shfelah—the plain—were green. You wouldn't know there was a drought. Sprinklers by the thousands rained on the cultivated fields as Tal and I drove by. Then, all of a sudden, they were switched off. The water rations had been used up, Tal explained.

"The water for these fields, for the whole country, and the Negev, Sinai, and Judean deserts, is draining our reservoir, the Kinneret—the Sea of Galilee—at an alarming speed," said Tal, as we drove by that green stretch. "Another year of drought and it won't take a miracle to walk on the waters of the Sea of Galilee—not at the deepest point, anyway. In the shallows, you can already walk on the rocky bottom, and it's not a long swim from any bank to the deeps this summer. You can skip across the Jordan River, this summer."

The Jordan Valley, rimmed by the Golan Heights and the Galilee mountains, is home to Tal. The Sea of Galilee is a stroll away, and the Jordan River runs—trickles, these days—through the lands of his kibbutz. No one is taking long showers this summer, he said. To conserve water, the kibbutzniks had installed a new irrigation system regulated by a computer to release just the right amount of water and fertilizer directly to the roots. Not a drop of water is squandered to the wind—not on the lawns, the flowerbeds, the banana plantations, the cotton fields... The textile mill is also equipped with computerized machines, as is the dairy farm and the plant that processes and packages the dates grown on the kibbutz.

Like this, Tal let me know that the kibbutz, not only Yehoshua, had changed with the times. And yet, a few kilometers later, it appeared that, like the kibbutz members I remember, Tal had very little cash on him. We had to take a slight detour to pick up his paycheck and a bit of an advance. He also wanted to check the Jeep; it had sprung an oil leak—half a drop a minute, if that. "Probably just a loose bolt," Tal said, "but, with an old Jeep, even overhauled like this one, you can never tell."

"Maybe it's a sign," I said, thinking about the desert ahead.

"We'll know soon enough," he said. A few kilometers later, he pulled in to a Delek service station that looked like any new Texaco, Shell, or Esso station at a busy intersection in Canada. "That's my workplace these days," he said, as he pulled up in front of the service pits.

I don't know why that surprised me. It was not uncommon in the kibbutz to see "leadership material" like Tal, or cabinet ministers like Yehoshua, working in the garage or in the communal dining room. It was uncommon, though, to see a kibbutznik working in a city service station. Even if the per diem the kibbutz offered him to study in the city was peanuts, he would moonlight only to buy a book or a tool he couldn't borrow.

"Are you a student, Tal? Is that why you are on leave of absence from your kibbutz?" I asked him.

"No. I'm a recovering soldier," he replied, as if soldiering were an affliction or an addiction. And then he added, "Recovering from surgery to reconstruct a pair of knees."

"Wounded?"

"No, just wear and tear." He got out of the Jeep with a slight hesitation, almost like my mother, who never steps down without bracing herself for the inevitable shot of pain from her knees, worn out by age and arthritis.

"No one in his right mind would go with you, or me, to the desert," I muttered, and we both laughed.

He wasn't treated like an employee by anyone at that service station, and he certainly didn't behave like one; rather, he exhibited the same authority with which he drove—that of a commander, outstanding among the extraordinary, elite among the privileged elite. One thing about the kibbutz hadn't changed, apparently: Some members are more equal than others. After all, God is not a communist. He doesn't dispense equally to all, and Tal got more than enough to spare, it seemed.

He didn't object when a young man, built like the hefty roughnecks you see in the movies, but with a face like a cherub when he smiled, suggested playfully to Tal, "Let a real mechanic repair the Jeep." More seriously, he said, "There's something I want to discuss with you. You won't believe what happened here this morning. You won't believe the news I heard."

"Leora, meet Shabbo, my employer," Tal interrupted. "Shabbo is the 'real mechanic' who gave Gingie the okay to buy your Jeep."

"Only a temporary, part-time, employer," Shabbo corrected Tal, as we walked over to his office.

"Shabbo? Is that a Brazilian Portuguese name, or is it a nickname?" I asked him.

Shabbo looked at Tal, as if waiting for permission to reply. Tal nodded, and I half-expected Shabbo to tell me he served in the Unit. Instead, Shabbo said he was a mechanic in the Unit, where he picked up his nickname. Like a *shablool*—a snail—he'd always be curled under a chassis, or the hood of a command car or a Jeep; and also because he'd always keep his tail in the home base of the Unit. He couldn't go out on missions and raids because his medical profile was stamped "Not Fit for Combat Service"—a faulty heart valve, Shabbo explained. As if he had to excuse his service at home base.

Would Levi feel the need to explain, if I deny him my consent? Let Levi live to feel inferior, like Shabbo. It's The Nation's heart that's damaged if Shabbo feels he must explain. The Nation itself is a casualty of war if a person is valued according to how high the risk in his military service.

Shabbo dispatched one of his "real employees" to bring a tray of coffee to his office. "You wouldn't object if Tal were to put your Jeep to good use for two-three weeks, right?" Shabbo asked me, once we had seated ourselves around his desk.

Tal laughed. "All right, Shabbo, what have you got up your

sleeve this time?" he said, his eyes still laughing. Turning to me he added, "Shabbo is one of our up-and-coming entrepreneurs. His dream is to be a multi-millionaire."

"In three years, you and I can each be a multi-millionaire, easy," Shabbo said to Tal. "All you have to do is to get in with me on this deal—fifty-fifty. Don't laugh, Tal. Remember the Mercedes? The guy who owns that big, blue Mercedes, one of my best regulars? Do you know how he made his millions? Our Defense ministry contracts him for jobs, big jobs ...

"Well, this morning, his Mercedes pulls in and he tells me, 'Come, Shabbo, I'll buy you a cup of coffee.' So we walk over to the diner, and he starts to grill me, like: How did I get started in the service station? How much do I still owe to relatives, friends, the bank? How much do I gross a year? He says he might have a business proposition for me. He has to know first how I operate. So I tell him how I operate, and he tells me I'm a natural ... Here I bust my butt eighteen hours a day and he tells me I'm a natural. All right, I think, let him think I am a natural, the main thing is: We're in business.

"But then he asks me what I did in the army, what corps I served in. All this he wants to know when I can't even tell him the Unit exists. So I say, 'Why are you asking?' And he tells me that, for the job he has in mind, he needs someone who knows how to take charge; command operations; move men and equipment. So I think: What do you know, Tal lucked out; my turn will come another time. So I tell him, 'I know the man for you.'

"'Is your man like you, a natural in business?' he asks me. So I tell him, my man is a kibbutznik—served in the standing army six years on top of the three regular; just got discharged with honors, decorations; ranked major; has a good head. He'll do better than any natural. But the Mercedes says, 'Naa, kibbutzniks know how to spend money, not to make it. But why don't you two hook up, become partners?' So I tell him, 'No problem, if the job is right.'

"'The job is a subcontract for the pullout from Sinai. Is that right enough?' he tells me. Can you imagine, Tal. 'Peace with Egypt is in our pocket,' the Mercedes says. 'This is classified, but the army is pulling out of Sinai right now.'"

"No way!" said Tal.

"That was my first reaction, too," said Shabbo. "'No way!' I told the Mercedes. 'Nothing is signed. The newspapers are full of ultimatums Egypt gives us every Monday and Thursday, that she'll pull out of the peace talks if we don't give Gaza and the West Bank to the Palestinians, and every foot of Sinai to Egypt, and sovereignty over Jerusalem … Why, you can't crack sunflower seeds in a group today without people yelling and screaming and knocking heads over whether or not it's suicide to give Sinai to Egypt, let alone the rest,' I told him. But the Mercedes tells me, 'The government decided already, it's fixed; the people are the last to know.' So I think to myself: The guy has friends in high places; he's one of the biggest contractors for Defense; he must know what he is saying; why, in the Unit, we knew classified stuff that the people don't know to this day.

"Do you know what a subcontract for the pullout from Sinai means? We're talking millions of dollars, according to Mercedes, American dollars, Tal, not shitty local currency, and millions of dollars in three years.

"If he wasn't bullshitting me, all Egypt wants from us is every fucking foot of Sinai, not later than three years from now. According to him, the government is planning to give back to Egypt the Sinai that Egypt 'gave' to us—a bare wasteland.

"Yamit is going to be like it never was three years from now. Everything we've built in Sinai is going to be leveled to the ground or pulled out—must be pulled out in three years. That's why Defense is contracting out part of the work," Shabbo said.

And I was thinking: It would break my father's heart to hear even a rumor that Yamit would be leveled to dust. Only photos would remain of the dream he had shared with Arik, and memories, and Arik's model displayed *somewhere* in Yehoshua's ministry building. Did Yehoshua know this latest about Yamit? Or does the Mercedes know something that the cabinet minister doesn't?

Peace in our pockets, he said, my Arik. Now Levi will stop nagging me to consent to his combat duty. What a messenger, Shabbo.

"'This pullout job was made for my partner and me, I told the Mercedes,'" Shabbo said. "I told him, 'My partner's military-service record is classified, but I can give you his name. You have friends in high places, you can check him out. The pullout pressure will be nothing for him. You can count on him to deliver. No one fucks around when he's in charge. And me, you know for five years, you know my work. A natural, you said, with machines, with money, business.'

"And the Mercedes said: 'Oh, I know your word is as good as your work. But this pullout subcontract is different, a big job; it involves a partner, and it might save us a hassle later if I see how you'll deliver now.' Then, right on the spot, he offered us a tryout job up in the Golan Heights. Can you imagine, Tal? To try us out, he'll subcontract to us a little job he got from Defense. Made me laugh how he set a limit of ten days to see if we can deliver under pressure. Ten days to stretch up a few security fences in the Golan Heights. This is pressure to him. So, I didn't laugh, and he said he'll supply the materials, the rest is up to us. So I told him: No problem, we'll deliver in seven days—not ten. And the minute he pulls out of the station I hired a few guys and borrowed four Jeeps. Leora's will make five, and that should do it. What do you think, Tal? In three years you and I are going to be set for life.'"

Shabbo turned to me and asked, "You won't need the Jeep for that week, will you?"

"Forget the Jeep," Tal told Shabbo before I could open my mouth. "Dragging bales of barbed wire on the basalt boulders and over rocks would wreck the Jeep."

"But I'll return the Jeep in better shape than it is," Shabbo said.

"You can't return kilometers, Shabbo," countered Tal.

"All right, no problem, we'll borrow another Jeep," Shabbo said, his face still flushed with excitement.

But then Tal told him, "I'm sorry, Shabbo, you'll have to count me out."

"Why?" Shabbo asked him. "The kibbutz holds no challenge for you. Every young kibbutznik with a brain is leaving and you————"

"I won't have anything to do with war-profiteering, Shabbo. Count me out."

"Where do you see war-profiteering? This pullout job is for peace. I thought you were a peacenik." Shabbo's voice was raised now.

"Oh, come on, Shabbo. You're dealing with a war profiteer—a contractor, like the ones who milk Defense and cut corners to buy a Mercedes. You know who pays in the end for the cut corners. Are you that hungry, Shabbo? Did you think *I'm* that hungry? I could never understand the paper-shufflers in Defense, and it looks like I never will. Whenever we sent in a requisition, they'd cry that they're broke; and here, a fat civilian contractor bribes them, or whatever, to squeeze from them millions of dollars for jobs the army can do. The borders are relatively quiet these days; men and equipment are sitting idle; why can't they do both jobs? You would think we'd have learned something from the Yom-Kippur War, but it looks like we haven't. Same mistakes—same corrupt paper-shufflers, same war profiteers, same contractors, same vultures. *Dir balak*—watch out—Shabbo. You know what smell attracts vultures."

"If you think I smell, you don't know where you live, Tal. Don't be a dreamer. The Land is not the Unit." Shabbo's face was flushed; his tone was cynical. "It's a land of milk and honey, all right. A land of fucking milkmen, each one for himself, Tal, like in California. But here, each one milks as if, next war, he'll go to the next world; so what the hell, milk whatever you can from Defense, from Commerce, from any ministry. And isn't the government milking whatever it can from any tit it can find? And isn't the war the richest tit of them all? That's what everyone is milking.

"More than half the country is shuffling papers for the government, or sweating their butts off in government munitions plants or the aircraft industries, or selling jeans, coffee, and rock-'n'-roll to the government workers, and you think they are not war profiteers? And isn't your kibbutz milking the government for all the subsidies and interest-free loans it can get? It has no fucking compunction, that's for sure, about collecting your army officer's paycheck month after month, year after year . . .

"In the army you see only Defense contractors, so you think only contractors are war profiteers. But after a couple of years of civilian life you'll see the whole country is living off the fucking war. You want to change it? Here's your chance.

"Remember in the Yom-Kippur War, Tal? Remember you said: 'First thing we do when the war is over is bust our butts to replace the old guard, kick them out of their fucking cabinet chairs. We owe it to the ones who went.'"

"That's what every soldier says in every war," Tal said.

"Oh, don't give me that. 'A military record is the ladder in The Land. Just look at who's running the country,' you said. Well, let me tell you, it took me a good two civilian years to see that money is what determines rank in civilian life. The generals you see in power are only puppets of the money men. That's how it is. Some generals are voted into power, other generals are voted out; but the same money men are pulling the strings. You want to replace them, then enter their arena, play their fucking game—only better. Grab the opportunity or someone else will; and he'll not do half the job that you or I will, and you know it . . . Look, sleep on it. But let me know soon as you get back from the desert."

"No need to sleep on it, Shabbo."

"How do you know, you might see the light in Sinai."

"You mean, light reflecting off the golden calf?"

"No, Tal. The Hebrew slaves who built the golden calf wanted to go back. I want to go forward, to be partners with you. If the Mercedes wasn't bullshitting me, if we really pull our forces out of Sinai, it's going to be like Switzerland here. A whole different world, a whole different life. Look ahead, Tal, not in the rear-view mirror."

"I've heard it said of war widows that they look backward not forward, and of dropouts and of the exiled, but not of kibbutzniks, elite commanders like you," I say to Tal when we are alone in the Jeep, heading southwest to Yamit.

"Would you reconsider Shabbo's offer of partnership, if and when we trade Sinai to Egypt for peace?"

"No."

"Why?"

"I want to reap the crops I plant," Tal replies. "I am a farmer . . . a farmer who likes the smell of a field freshly plowed, the sight of a field of tall sunflowers brimming with seeds, the sound of the breeze rustling the eucalyptus trees . . . For me, the kibbutz is the place."

"So, why are you on leave from the kibbutz?"

"Leave it for now," he replied, almost like Azzizah says, "Not proper to ask questions," when she drops the curtain, indicating that, beyond this, no more would be revealed.

⚜

"Forbidden," Azzizah decreed when I asked her if she could tell me what Abu Salim cassette-recorded earlier in the day, much too fast for me to understand. "Forbidden," she said.

"But Abu Salim recorded the cassette in front of me and Nura, therefore he clearly thought it is not forbidden for her to know what he cassette-recorded," said Tammam. Curious to learn all about the cassette recorder, she convinced Azzizah to relent.

Their veils-upon-veils can't conceal their delight in the power they have over Abu Salim's voice. Play, Off, Pause, Forward, Rewind . . . Tammam keeps pressing, while Azzizah mutters in between bursts of laughter—hers and Tammam's, "Not proper . . . Not proper . . ."

"Abu Salim starts with many many . . . *Wallah*, how many greeting-blessings to El Bofessa," says Tammam.

"The longer the greeting, the more troubling what follows," says Azzizah. *Wahada-wahada*—one by one—she and Tammam cut Abu Salim's talking-too-fast-for-me-to-understand, like my mother amplifies for my father.

Neither wife comprehends her husband's men-talk at first listen or at second or third. Time and again they played and replayed the same sentences. (Each time I caught a few more words.) Time and again, Tammam presses Rewind, Play, then Stop, while she and Azzizah discuss what their husband could possibly mean by this or that expression.

"Whatever he means, it is not proper to put Abu Salim's men-talk into women-talk," Azzizah decides, "for no woman is as well informed as a man."

"*Aywa*, we can but say what we think Abu Salim was cassette-recording," says Tammam.

"What we think Abu Salim was maybe saying," Azzizah corrects Tammam.

"*Aywa*," says Tammam, "Maybe what troubles Abu Salim is that we Badu were not invited to the *maq'ad* where the elders of the mighty tribes of Egypt and of Israel are peace-talking, as if our Badu elders are but women who have no voice, no say, no power…"

"*Wallah*, it is truly troubling…," mutters Azzizah.

"And maybe it also troubles Abu Salim that not one tribe in the world alliance of all the stranger-tribes the world over (meaning: not one nation in the United Nations) demands that we Badu rule in our Sinaa, even though Sinaa is ours."

"True, *Wallah*," says Azzizah, "the waterholes, be they full or empty, are ours, as are our home grounds—be they green or parched by drought, as are the passageways—smuggling routes?, all ours…"

"We Sinaa Badu are treated like *Harrah* (shit), for we Sinaa Badu are but thirty or fifty or sixty ten-hundreds (thousand) strong, Abu Salim is saying here," says Tammam. "He says that all the stranger-tribes the world over, even the stranger-Arab tribes, care only for the stranger-Arab tribe called the *Felastiniyiin*—Palestinians. For they are stronger than us Sinaa Badu by many many ten-hundreds … stronger only in numbers they are."

"Yet they were as powerless as us Badu," Azzizah corrects her.

"*Aywa*—yes," Tammam agrees, "This stranger-Arab tribe Abu Salim calls the *Felastiniyiin* was as powerless as us Badu, in the days before the world alliance of all the stranger-tribes had empowered the *Felastiniyiin* in a land called Lubnan—Lebanon…"

"*Wallah*, how wide the horizon of our border-crossing men...none wider than your father's, Abu Salim's," Azzizah says to little Salimeh. The child squeals in happiness to see what wonders the cassette translation of her father's words are working on her girl-mother and Azzizah. Like a magic carpet, it transports them far beyond the narrow confines of their compound to a realm they are forbidden to enter—except in rare stories told by their men.

"And in this part of the cassette recording," continues Tammam, "what troubles Abu Salim is that the alliance of all the stranger-tribes gave us Badu not even one grain of rice. Not even the stranger-Arab tribe called the *Felastiniyiin*, who had supplies to spare now. For the world alliance of the stranger-tribes supplied them with money and food to spare, and also with clothes and carpet-blankets to spare, and schools, and clinics, even dwelling places... And with so much fire-power they were supplied, night and day they fired in the air, just for the *keif* of displaying their newly supplied power..."

"*Yaa*-Allah!!" exclaims Azzizah. "I will remember forever how the noise of fire-power convulsed our mountains in the last war, as in the war before the last, and the one before..."

"Here, too, I think Abu Salim is saying that the *Felastiniyiin's* pleasure-firing gave the people of the land called Lubnan a headache. Therefore, the Lubnan elders told the *Felastiniyiin*, 'Stop your firing.' But the *Felastiniyiin* replied, 'We will do with our fire-power as we desire,'" says Tammam, cutting her words, *wahada, wahada*—one by one.

"Clearly, the *Felastiniyiin* were abusing the hospitality extended to them by the people of Lubnan," says Azzizah.

"*Aywa*," says Tammam. "Strange are the ways of the stranger-tribes of the world over, for they did not stop their flow of supplies to the *Felastiniyiin*, not even when the *Felastiniyiin* sparked a war of brothers (a civil war) in this land called Lubnan, and not even when, under the very heart of the place called Beirut, which had offered them refuge, the *Felastiniyiin* had sheltered the blood of their fighting men in many many caves... And their fire-power they stored at the very heart of their dwelling places, right next to the clinics, the schools, and the dwelling places... *Yaa-Rabb*..." Thus the *Felastiniyiin* exposed the blood of their women and children.

"Sip your tea, *yaa*–Abu Salim," Azzizah tells the cassette recorder now when Abu Salim coughs.

"*Aywa*," says Abu Salim on the cassette, slurps his tea with much noise, almost as if he could hear her. Cracks us all up.

Tammam doesn't have to hear a section more than once or twice now, before she goes on to cut his words *wahada, wahada*— one by one. "'*Wallah*, if we do not disarm the *Felastiniyiin*, they would overpower us all, as they do in this land called Lubnan,' one stranger-Arab tribe said to another. That is what I think Abu Salim is saying... 'We know how to disarm the *Felastiniyiin*,' said mighty Egypt. And without further words, the mighty sheikh of mighty Egypt flew in a *tayarra*—aeroplane—to the place called Al-Quds— Jerusalem. And there, for the whole world to see and hear, he declared that mighty Egypt would battle Israel no more. But only on condition that Israel would evacuate Sinaa—only Sinaa, not the land called *Filastin*—Palestine... And just like that, right there and then, the *Felastiniyiin* were disarmed of their most powerful loyal and constant ally, *Wallah*."

"*Yaa*-Allah, Tammam, you talk like a man," says Azzizah, a glint of amazement in one eye and apprehension in the other. "Tell on... Tell on," she urges her junior co-wife.

"*Aywa*," says Tammam. "And in this part, I think Abu Salim was saying that for thirty years, no tribe—not even the *Felastiniyiin*— had sacrificed as many sons as Egypt for the liberation from Israel of this place called *Filastin*... *Aywa*—yes—for thirty years Egypt had favored the *Felastiniyiin* even more than her own sons, let alone our Badu sons. In prison, *Wallah*..."

"A fate worse than death is prison," Azzizah mutters, almost touching the ground as she bends and lifts up her veil to spit.

"And yet, in prison, *Wallah*, mighty Egypt would lock our Badu sons whenever our Badu sons would refuse to serve mighty Egypt in her army, and her battle for the liberation of *Filastin*. That is

147

what I think Abu Salim was saying here. And next he said that when our Badu sons died battling for the *Felastiniyiin*, not even the *Felastiniyiin* acknowledged it ... and not even Israel. *Aywa*—yes, not even as an enemy are we Badu of Sinaa recognized. The world does not see how we Badu of Sinaa are disregarded. But why us Badu and not the *Felastiniyiin?*" (Abu Salim spoke now like a person bereaved: "Why me?")

"*Inshallah*, fate will right this wrong," says Azzizah.

"*Inshallah*," says Tammam. "That is what Abu Salim was saying, '*Inshallah*,' he said. This wrong will be made right by one of the men high up, who is destined to do so before or after he hears these words that he, Abu Salim, was recording now ..."

"It is too hot now to continue ... too hot to fetch water ... too hot to move from the shade," says Azzizah, as if in the past two-three days we have moved more than a few steps from Tammam's *maharama*—the place of the women—by the fire-circle in front of Tammam's tent.

12

Tal has probably crossed three deserts by now—the Sinai, the Negev, and the Judean—if he's returning to Tel Aviv by way of Jerusalem; two—the Sinai and the Negev—if he decided to get back by way of Beer Sheba; and only the immense expanse of Sinai if he's driving back through the western gateway: Al-Arish–Yamit. Tal had driven through that gateway countless times, always duty-bound—until the morning he and I took that route to the peninsula. For the first time, Tal was entering the western gateway to the peninsula *by choice*. He could barely conceal his excitement, elation, and joy—and I, my sadness.

Kilometer after kilometer, we kept passing war helmets, rust chewing rings around the bullet holes in them, lying on the roadside next to rusting chunks of tank chains. And past the bend, a wilderness unlike any I had seen or imagined. From horizon to horizon, battleground and battle training grounds... From horizon to horizon, the wilderness that had claimed you, my Arik, orphaned our son, widowed me, and trained Tal to know war: a wasteland flattened by God or man and covered with army bases.

I didn't know we had such a huge army... a desert full of army tents at the ready for peace or for war; prefab barracks on wheels; weapons camouflaged by nets that undulate for kilometers like wind-swept wheat fields; and kilometers of practice rigs, target ranges, and simulated battle conditions—man-made mountains, canyons, and canals; and flags flags flags—blue and white and every color of every unit, as if life were a movie, war were a game.

The higher the sun climbed, the more flooded with illusions that flat wilderness became. You could swear a sea—so calm, it shimmered like a mirror—stretched as far as the eye could see. And, just like the Red Sea in the Story of Stories, it parted for the Jeep to pass on a dry paved road, reverberating with the thunder of the mighty hooves and wheels of the Pharaoh's chariots.

"Couldn't be an earthquake, could it?" I asked Tal.

"It's a convoy heading our way," he replied.

I couldn't see a sign of a convoy then. You couldn't tell up from down at that hour, almost like in a whiteout in the snow-covered Canadian wilderness. So brittle was the air that it almost cracked, fragmenting all distant images, until a dark dot zoomed in out of nowhere.

"It's the first of the convoy," Tal explained. He knew that the huge army truck, carrying a load wider than the two-lane road we were traveling on, was heading toward us, even though it looked like a cracked-mirror reflection of a camel galloping in place. Blink, and it seems as if the Jeep is going to crash into a skyscraper reflecting the sun's blinding rays. Tal pulled over at a safe distance; still, the slipstream rattled the Jeep like a bomb blast. No sooner had we recovered than we were hit by another, and another...

The convoy rolled north with no end in sight. The parade of monster double-load trailer-trucks shrouded with swirling camouflage nets stretched back into infinity, raising dust, diesel fumes, scorching heat; and rumbling with such thunder that Tal had to yell for me to hear him. "Look at what we are giving up for a piece of paper from Egypt that might be good for nothing but wiping butt...." He considers himself a peacenik, but he sounded like a hawk—a hawk who looked sorry for the soldier-boys assigned to that convoy. "The older you get, the younger the new recruits look," he shouted, as if he was as old as Methuselah.

"Do you think peace with Egypt is in our pockets, as Shabbo said? Is that why this convoy is pulling out of Sinai?" I asked him at the top of my voice.

"They could be heading north to shore up our defense at our border with Syria and Lebanon," he shouted. Then, as if he suddenly remembered that he was out of the army, that his time was his own, he switched on the ignition, released the brake, turned the Jeep's tail to the convoy, the paved road, and floored the gas pedal, like a person intoxicated with newfound freedom.

There was no clock in the Jeep, no radio, no safety bar, no locks on the doors and windows. Winds from all directions blew in through the cracks between the canvas top and the steel frame. The fenders had a few dents; the bumpers, rust spots. But the tires were brand new and the engine had been completely overhauled. Spare parts were stored in the toolbox; wine and brandy in the provisions cartons; combat rations and field dressings in the first-aid kit. The Jeep was no place to be careless.

I couldn't find a sliver of shade by which to navigate. The sun was directly overhead, and that part of the desert was so flat and barren; not a trace of a Badu's fire-circle, tent, goat, camel; not even a chewed-up skeleton, a thistle, a thorn, let alone a bush or a tree. And not a single landmark; not a wadi, or a knoll. There was nothing to bar the wind from sweeping away all tracks. The ground was packed hard, almost like a superhighway paved from horizon to horizon.

"Perfect grounds for tank warfare and exercises." Tal raced ahead, turned left, then right, as if signposts were staked at every turn.

"Where are we going, Tal?"

"Don't lean on the door It's only canvas," he tells me in response. Asking him how he could tell north from south was like asking a musician with perfect pitch how could he tell A from C.

"Are we heading south, parallel to the paved road?" I ask him, hoping he'll reply: "Yes. We'll get back to that road in ten-twenty minutes. The last of the convoy should be gone by then."

But he replies, "We are heading west."

"We can't be heading west," I said. "The Egyptian border lies only a few kilometers west of the road we just left, according to the map. And according to any report except Shabbo's, Egypt is still at war with us. We are heading south, right?"

"No. We are heading west," he insists, grinning. And in the pit of my stomach, fear is growing, seeded by a suspicion that he's really heading to Egypt, like a madman looking for trouble—and that I must have been out of my fucking mind to go to the desert with a man I don't know.

"Tal, we better head back to the road."

"Soon," he says, racing to a damn battle zone, judging by the smell of gunpowder that is growing stronger.

"Tal, it smells like we're heading into gunfire. We better turn back." I get no response from him. So I raise my voice above the rushing wind and clanking engine and I yell, "Tal, smells like gunpowder!..."

"Yes, it does," he yells back, pressing ahead into the wind.

"No, you are heading straight toward the gunfire."

"I don't hear gunshots, do you?" he says, shifting a hand from the steering wheel to give my cheek a quick stroke, as if I were a girl-child who was doing exceptionally well for her age, as if to say with avuncular arrogance, "Don't lose heart, kid. You couldn't be in better hands."

The patronizing bastard. "Turn the Jeep around, Tal. Why take unnecessary risks?"

"All right, brace yourself," he says, pumping the brakes. Then, he shifts to overdrive, and—wonder of wonders! Just as the ground disappears from under the Jeep and we seem to be heading nose first into hell, I see a burst of gushing water shooting skyward and splashing down to the center of a steaming pond, surrounded by a tall, thick hedge of cane shoots. Real cane shoots! Real water! Real sulfur springs! That's what smelled like gunfire. A green secluded spa, smack in the middle of a drought-plagued desert perfect for tank warfare.

This wondrous dreamscape he thought he had to sweeten with the element of surprise, lest I dismiss it as a mere piss puddle. To me, Niagara Falls and the Great Lakes were just water, but this desert pond was a wonder to touch, celebrate, experience—even if it killed me.

The lush cane shoots (God only knows how they could live here) screened off the wind, making that green spa a sauna. And the gravel felt like smoldering coals. The sulfur water stung like fire sparks, and the deeper I entered it, the more cuts, scars, and knotted muscles I discovered, as if I had been desensitized until now.

"Great for the knees," said Tal. "Don't!... Don't!... Don't you dare splash... Don't swim near me, Leora! This is no place for water games!"

No, only for fire games. For thousands of years, hundreds of thousands of men from all the corners of the earth have battled in this desert, and for what? Even the water here is fit only for patching up gashes and tears. Generations of warriors have bathed in that pond to heal their wounds, and still the water was clean—a white gusher untainted by the wellspring of blood. That was *the* wonder in that wilderness.

There was one little detail that Tal had overlooked.

So accustomed was he to traveling in that part of the desert in a military vehicle, he didn't know there were no civilian gas stations there. And it was forbidden by law to borrow gasoline from the army; just to make sure no one was tempted, military fuel was dyed to stain a civilian carburetor red. Tal didn't know what punishment awaited a civilian with a red carburetor, only that it was inescapable. Anyone who noticed that tell-tale red was bound by law to report it. That's what he told me as we approached the checkpoint at the entrance to the Common Road—the Caravan Route, as Abu Salim calls it. Both gasoline jerricans were jiggling empty in the back by then. And in the gas tanks about ten liters, he said. The needle on the gas gauge pointed to empty.

"How far to a civilian gas pump?" he asked the sergeant at the checkpoint.

"Two hundred and fifty kilometers, give or take," the sergeant replied. "But you are going nowhere for the next eight hours."

"Why not?"

"Because you arrived here five minutes late," said the sergeant, as if the road were a plane that had taken off five minutes ago, with everyone in that part of the desert on board; everyone except for the sergeant and a few soldier-boys, looking homesick, sun-scorched, and, like their roadside tents, so covered with dust that you couldn't see the khaki or the colors of the flag hoisted atop the rickety command barracks, ruffling in the wind, almost like an apology. "My instructions were to block entry five minutes ago," the sergeant explained. "Your Jeep couldn't clear the Common Road before the U.N. guys shift the road from us to Egypt. You'll have to wait here till the U.N. shifts the road back to us."

"Eight, nine, ten hours from now ... Oh, come on, let them go," one of the soldier-boys said to the sergeant.

"What a dream—a Jeep, a woman, a vacation in Sinai," said another.

"Come on, clear them, before the officer gets here," the other soldier-boys urged the sergeant.

"Let's see your passes." The sergeant relented, opening a ledger and entering our names, Tal's ID numbers, my passport number, the Jeep's plate number, the number on Tal's license to carry a handgun, and the numbers showing on his digital wristwatch. "Minus ten minutes, so press full speed, non-stop, and no detours. The U.N. slaps you with a hell of a fine if you don't drive straight through, even when the road is ours," he cautioned, as he handed back our military passes.

"Go! Before the officer shows up," the soldier-boys said. "Go already, go!" They slapped the Jeep's back fender as if it were the rump of a cowboy's horse, sure to clear the Common Road, like in the old Western movies, just as the enemy came within range. An obstacle like an empty gas tank was all too predictable in such a script, because the United Nations (read: the Cavalry) would, at the very last moment, come to the rescue.

It turned out almost like that. The angel that protects idiots must have been watching over Tal and me.

"Go already, go!" said the soldier-boys. But Tal, obviously itching to go, hesitated.

"Go, already. What's with you?" the sergeant said.

"We might not have enough fuel to ..." I start to say, and before I can add another word, Tal fires a look at me, as if I'd told the soldier-boys that he can't get it up. Next thing I know, he bolts out of the checkpoint and onto the Common Road, red-faced and angry. It pissed him off, I assumed, that he of all people, a major with nine years' service in a unit independent of logistical support from the rest of the army, miscalculated something as basic as fuel supply.

"It's only human to err," I tell him. But that only adds fuel to his fury.

"Your very humanity can kill you here," he snaps. As can human error, which nearly finished us off in the Yom-Kippur War, I think. And only last week, a terrorist-guerrilla fighter masquerading as a frail old woman asked a boy scout to help carry a bag of groceries rigged with explosives. That scout's humanity killed him, all right.

"But when your very humanity is a threat to your survival, isn't it next to a miracle that your humanity survived," I said, then urged him to turn back to the checkpoint.

"Don't look at the gas gauge," he responds, racing ahead.

"Why? Is the gas gauge inaccurate?" I ask him.

"With my luck, it is. I can always count on luck to come through in the crunch," he says, like every warrior spared by the grace of God, luck, fate...

"Must have been my luck, not yours, that brought on this—"

"No, it was my mistake." He cut me off.

"My mistake too." I had counted on the Badu, as Tal had counted on the army. "The Badu are storing gasoline in the desert's sands," Russell had told me three-four months ago, when I first ventured to the peninsula. "The Sinai tribes are hording truckloads of food supplies in caves all over this desert. And deep in the sands, the Badu are storing heaps of gasoline drums and spare parts for every Jeep, Land-Rover, and Peugeot pickup truck they can buy or steal ... just in case the peace talks lead to war. Yes, whoever tells you that Bedouins never prepare for the future, or that Bedouins are basically happy because they have zero expectations, zero disappointments, doesn't know the Sinai Badu..."

But it was inconceivable to me, even as I was experiencing it, that we could roll in Sinai for hundreds of kilometers without seeing a sign of Badu; inconceivable that this Common Road, of all places, would be off-limits to the Badu, of all people, or to anyone who couldn't secure a pass from the Israeli army, *or* from the Egyptian army *or* from the U.N. Peacekeeping Force.

There was nothing here, but promise—of peaceful coexistence, cooperation, sharing...

"Is it because of the peace talks that we have been sharing this road with Egypt?" I asked Tal.

"I don't know," he replied.

"Is this road always empty, or has it been cleared of traffic for the transfer with Egypt?"

"I don't know."

"Is this part of the desert off-limits to the Badu?"

"I don't know."

Again and again, he said "I don't know," as if Egyptian troops were lying in wait for us in the stretching shadows, ready to apprehend us, and the less I knew the better. It would have been better still if I didn't know that he had served in the Unit, and if I practiced to be an imbecile like him.

"Are you afraid, Tal?"

"No, but at least one of us is still normal, still afraid," he replied.

The Jeep conked out just then. Tal skipped out, lifted the hood, and checked; slid under the chassis and checked; squatted by each tire and checked, as if the Jeep had died because of some mechanical malfunction that he could repair. Last, he checked the gas tank, then climbed back into the driver's seat and told me, "The gas tank is empty. But the Jeep is okay." Then he turned the ignition key and pumped the gas pedal—again and again, again and again, as if it were February in Canada and one more try would convince the engine to start.

"One more try and you'll flood the—whatever it is you flood in a Jeep," I said, without thinking.

His luck held. Next try, the engine started, running on the last few drops.

My eyes were riveted now to each spot where the road curved or dropped. And soon my watchfulness was rewarded:

Egyptian troops! Only about a hundred meters west of my window.

So close. Egyptian barracks rush by, one after another, almost like train carriages, moving on the other side of the barbed wire— the other side of the border, according to Tal. Another flock of flags—were it not for the fact that none was blue and white, the Egyptian bases would look no different from the Israeli bases. Same barbed wire. Same sun-faded barracks and tents. Same dust shrouding the soldiers. Some looked young enough to be my sons; others, dressed in shorts, with a towel slung over a naked shoulder, looked like Israeli soldiers itching to take a shower after a grinding day of war maneuvers.

For the first time, I feel how deeply rooted in us is the longing to transcend the loneliness imposed by man, nature, or God knows what ... For the first time in my life, I see Egyptian troops, up close, and, like a child who turns her head to the window and sees beings from outer space, I wave to the Egyptian soldiers across the barbed wire—wave across the decades of grief, across the decades of fear, killing fields, rivers of blood.

One Egyptian soldier waved back, then another and another— across the decades of war, the decades of siege.

"That happens sometimes during cease-fire," Tal said. "Sometimes the lines are close enough to exchange jokes, curses, cigarettes, even names. Then the cease-fire breaks, and it's back to 'us or them.'"

The waving soldiers looked like prisoners behind the barbed wire. Did one of them fire the shot that downed Arik's plane? Perhaps, the father of one? Did he see Arik's plane plunging to the sands of this desert?

God only knows what hold this place has on me. I hate the hold the dead have on any place of last resort, any last stand—the Wailing Wall, Masada, the Stations of the Cross—places that trigger not only strong emotions, revelations, hallucinations, but wars that turn men like Arik into mere statistics.

The next bend reveals nothing but a lone acacia, its branches twisted by the lashing winds. And east of the road, the last slanting rays tease the color out of the stones, and the peaks of the mountain chain glow like the Pharaoh's staff with stripes of gold and purple, bronze, turquoise, yellow, red, and copper-green, spinning by at top speed. The Jeep will roll on for eight days on one drop of fuel, like the miracle of Hanukkah, I imagined, as the road twisted and turned, sloping like a river drawn to the sea.

It was past Abu Zenima that I saw the Gulf of Suez for the first time. As wide as the sea, the gulf stretched to the north and the south, and to the west it spilled beyond the horizon. But not one fishing boat was in sight, not one ship, tanker, sailboat, or gunboat. The gulf was deserted like the Common Road and the wilderness around it. We were the only people on earth, it seemed.

And then an ambulance, or one of our Clinics-on-Wheels that served the Badu, switched on its top light to let us know it's heading toward us.

"Lucky the Jeep is rolling now," Tal muttered, as he switched on the Jeep's headlights.

"Flash the lights to signal distress," I suggested.

"What's with you? That's a United Nations Jeep," he replied. To Tal, the U.N. soldiers sheltered and aided Arabs who make no secret of their intention to destroy Israel, even here, on the borders and roads that we have entrusted to the U.N. for peacekeeping.

But, to me, at that particular moment, the United Nations was a Canadian soldier—glad to assist us any way he could, including an offering to us of a Canadian cigarette and a cold Canadian beer. Never before had I so wished to see a Canadian. Never before was I so glad that a part of my Canadian tax money was allocated to the United Nations.

"Pull to a stop, Tal."

"We'll make it on our own power. No need..."

"Stop!" I snapped. "Don't make me beg."

Only then did he pump the brakes. But he wouldn't signal distress, wouldn't budge from his seat. "I won't be a party to it," he said, keeping his door shut.

I got out of the Jeep, ran to the middle of that damn Common Road, and waved my arms to signal distress. But the U.N. driver flicks his headlights on and off, then sounds his horn to blast me out of his lane.

"The bastard is not slowing down, Leora. Move aside!" Tal cried out, as if the U.N. driver was a Tommy and we were back in the British Mandate days.

I would rather die than live as if it was for nothing, the price we paid. I didn't budge, even when it now looked like the U.N. driver was amusing himself by playing chicken with me.

"It's not legal for you to stop on this road!" the U.N. peacekeeper snaps, before I could explain why I was blocking his lane. "Go back to your Jeep! Drive away, or I'll give you a money penalty," he tells me in English, sounding and looking like a Scandinavian who wished he was ice-skating now in his native Finland, Sweden, Denmark, or anywhere but here; driving alone at this bewitching time of day on a road thousands of kilometers away from his home, his family, his wife. A gold wedding ring glittered on his finger, and his open collar revealed a gold cross on a gold chain. Heat rash covered his face, and sweat oozed over it, like salt on a raw wound. His eyes were protected by Ray-Bans, like mine; his hair was fair, like mine; his uniform was blotched with sweat and dust, like my clothes; his lips were chapped, like mine.

"I am sorry to detain you, but we are down to our last liter or two. I was hoping you had gasoline to spare," I said in English, doing the polite and proper, WASP routine. Small wonder he was suspicious.

"I saw you driving full speed before you stopped. No one drives at full speed with only a liter left. The checkpoint soldiers permit no one to drive on this road without adequate fuel. Your checkpoint soldiers told you, I am sure, that it is not legal for you to stop on this road." He sounded like someone who is sick and tired of being taken for a sucker by the locals.

"You can check our Jeep and see for yourself. We have no more than one or two liters of fuel," I said. Tal looked at me as if he thought that I was the last of the naïfs in the Middle East. But the U.N. peacekeeper seemed to think that Tal's look was directed at him.

"I can see from here that your gas tank is full," the U.N. peace-keeper said. And before I could ask him how in the hell he could see how full or empty the tank was, he adds: "I see your license plate is yellow, Israeli, and I know that Israeli Arabs *never, never* send a woman to ask a man for gasoline—only *you people* would do that. And *you people* know how much gasoline to carry to the desert. *You people* just want more gasoline—more land, more everything. I have no extra gasoline."

"The poor bastard is afraid we are laying an ambush for him," Tal said in Hebrew. "Look at how he holds his radio transmitter at the ready. From where you're standing you can't see it, but his automatic is ready to fire. So don't scare him."

"Would you tow my Jeep, or radio to *my people* that we cannot clear this Common Road without assistance?" I asked him, as nice as could be.

Yet the poor bastard snaps, "Assistance?!! Assistance you've already received from your checkpoint soldiers, I am sure. *You people* help your own people, and only your own people. Drive away now, or I will give you a money penalty for stopping." He lets go of his radio transmitter and his automatic weapon, and pulls out a ball-point pen and a clipboard stacked with forms—the fine, the "money penalty," I assume. He fills in a box or two, then looks at me as if waiting to see me skip back up to the Jeep. When I don't, he seems to wonder if the tank is really empty, or if I am bluffing to get more gas, or if I am laying an ambush for him.

Bluffing, he decided, it seemed, as he filled in another box or two on his "money penalty" form. Then he stopped, as if it had finally dawned on him that the checkpoint soldiers kept a log-book of names, license numbers, and entry and exit times. Our meeting spot could be calculated almost to the kilometer. He'll be in deep shit if we don't clear off this road before the U.N. transfers it to Egypt. His radio transmitter will be very busy with inquiries from his checkpoints, Egypt's, and *my people's* . . . God only knows what commotion would ensue if Tal and I were apprehended by Egypt in these peace-talking days. You couldn't help but feel sorry for the poor bastard once you saw how the Common Road linked his destiny to Tal's and mine.

"If you have a siphon, you can transfer gasoline from my tank to your jerrican," he said finally, looking like he didn't want my thanks, appreciation, or any acknowledgment of his generosity. Getting me out of his life was thanks enough. I don't know why he decided to offer us fuel. I like to think it was an expression of generosity.

The desert is a place where good and bad are wedded like sun and shade, where a stranger is always received and always shut out, a place where the common language is often silence or guns, where the horizon is wide and the boundaries narrow. A place where I had lost Arik and found Tal.

13

Hauling bucket after bucket of water from God-knows-how-deep in the waterhole wasn't as easy as Tammam made it look. It didn't take long for me to feel the cumulative effect, not only of the weight, but of the rope. It was like pulling a line of thorns.

"Abu Salim owns the water rights to this *bir*—well—and three others... Only this one has not run dry as yet," Tammam told me, her leather-tough hands scuffed from again and again pulling and dropping the dented bucket. It's really a waterhole encircled by rocks—like the ones in Abu Salim's *maq'ad*—round and smooth, but still rough enough to fray the rope that rides them like a pulley. The fraying marks the history of this waterhole, showing how full it was when the rope was new and how far down the drought has forced the rope to travel. But at least the waterhole is shaded by the mountains, the breeze there is cool, resting there is a pleasure—luxuries you forgo once you embark on the path that leads from the well to the tents; a blazing hell, uphill all the way, steeper by the step, and not a spot of shade except the ones thrown by Tammam and me, shrinking by the minute, or so it seemed. Don't believe anyone who tells you that a desert broiled by the August sun wouldn't bother a desert nomad. At each uphill step Tammam cursed the desert, the summer, the pitiless sun turning the gravel to coals that seared her bare feet and squeezed from her streams of salt-sweat that greased her grip on the water jerricans and stung her eyes.

And she had to watch where she were going; the path narrowed or angled away every few feet; she and I could kiss this world goodbye if we didn't watch every step.

I had no idea how segregated, cut off from the rest of the world these mountain Badawias were, until I walked this path. Its direction is almost opposite to the path leading down from the tents to the *maq'ad*. Men receive guests in the *maq'ad*; women and children draw water from the well. The slopes that separate their paths—jagged granite ridges—would be a challenge for mountain goats to scale.

Tammam wouldn't let me help her carry even one jerrican, except for a few steps. "Not proper for a guest," she insisted, carrying all three. One in each hand, almost dragging on the ground, her back doubled under the weight of the third that was strapped to her head sort of like a papoose. Every few steps she took a break, not just to relieve the burden from her hands and back, catch her breath, wipe the rivulets of sweat that stung and blinded her eyes, and curse the desert heat, but also to wait till I stopped huffing and puffing.

She and I were giddy with relief when we finally made it back to the welcome-carpets spread in the shade Azzizah had created by propping up the side flap of her tent.

Azzizah, knowing how drained Tammam was, tried to pacify Salimeh with the nipple of her withered breast, but the parched and famished child wouldn't take it. "Oh, let her take what is left of the rest of my life and enjoy it..." said Tammam. The senior wife relaxed her hold on the child, and little Salimeh crawled straight to her mother's milk. And only now did Azzizah pour a bit of water into her cupped hand, and bit by bit quench her thirst.

"Not even one neighboring woman was to be seen at the well," Tammam reports to Azzizah. "At daybreak the neighbors must have heard that my brother is cutting his distance short, and already they are keeping their distance long."

It is a mystery to me what she means. Is it a parable? riddle? poem? Or are the neighbors staying away out of fear of her brother? Should I, too, be afraid?

Azzizah spits. "Patience is better that worrying," the senior Badawia says under her veil. "Maybe the neighbors' waterskins are still full today, because yesterday their tents were empty of guests, their evening was short, their night was without spice, their fires did not burn long—or maybe they went to fetch water when the paths to and from the well were still cool and moist with dew. And maybe"—Azzizah chuckles under her veil—"maybe the neighbor-ing Badawias stayed and gossiped at the *bir*, for there is no cooler place in the desert than the well when the mountains still shade it. But then, maybe, like us the first time we saw our stranger-guest approaching, wearing her *djinn*-demon eyes as she does today, our neighboring Badawias fled in fright when they heard or saw her coming with you closer and closer. It could also be that our neighbors made themselves scarce because their men-folk had told them what they had said to Abu Salim—*ya'ni*—that is—that our stranger-guest, being of the tribe that rules this desert, had been dispatched here by the authorities."

Me. A spy. Can you imagine? What could possibly lead their neighbors to think that the authorities would dispatch a spy to this God-forsaken place? What could these Badu be hiding in their forbidden mountains? Treasure or information smuggled from Arabian deserts and kingdoms? Is that what Abu Salim and his clansmen do that's more important than work?

Their neighbors' suspicion doesn't amaze me as much as Abu Salim and his wives' disregarding it. Ever since I entered their tents I have wondered how they could invite me—or anyone connected to their foreign rulers—to their forbidden tents. If I live to be a hundred, I'll probably never see foreign rule as benign. So deeply entrenched are these childhood impressions, preserved like the scar from a terrible blow, I am shaken by the thought that anyone here or anywhere would distrust, despise, resent me, my tribe, even half as much as I had the Tommies.

I wanted to assure the two Badawias that I was neither connected to the authorities nor dispatched by them. But I thought the more I tried to assure Azzizah and Tammam of that, the less assured they'd be. I underestimated them. Azzizah and Tammam transcended the divide—of the tribal bad blood... That is what I was to discover—soon after this little misunderstanding.

"If it would please you, let one of the waterskins be for you to be bathed with," said Azzizah, her eyes addressing mine but her words echoing through time, almost straight out of Genesis. Ah, I thought, she is storytelling the Badu version of the day her ancestor and mine, Abraham, received his stranger-guests.

"Let your bathing be in my tent," Tammam went on to tell me—the Badu version of Abraham's guest-receiving story, I thought.

"In her tent or mine, as you wish," said Azzizah, her eyes inquiring how I liked this story-legend, and did I wish to hear the rest of it?

"*Aywa*—yes—tell on," I urge both Azzizah and Tammam. But, in response, the two Badawia co-wives stare at me, astonishment and disappointment in their eyes.

"She did not understand," Azzizah mutters to Tammam. Now Azzizah turns to me and, as she keeps repeating "Bathing...washing...*fahemti*—understand?" Her hands mime a woman soaping her breasts. And, pointing a finger at me, she adds, talking like Tarzan or Jane in Badu Arabic, "You—bathing—washing—"

"Yes, that is how I bathe-wash," I reply, barely able to keep a straight face.

"Good. That is how you can bathe now, here in Azzizah's tent, if you wish, or in my tent," says Tammam.

"That is what I have been trying to tell you, to offer to you," says Azzizah.

I was too moved for words, and I had no idea then what a surprise this promised bath would turn out to be. More than anything just then I wanted to convey to the two Badawia co-wives what their offering meant to me, what memories and longings it stirred. But I didn't know how.

It was an invitation to enter the cherished landscape of the forbidden other. Gaining entry to the forbidden tents was, to me, like visiting Ahmed's forbidden home in Qalqiliya. The houses and purple hills of his home town were a mere ten or fifteen minutes' journey on my father's bicycle, as I knew from the single time my father had taken me to buy cracked olives and *za'atar*, virgin olive oil and fresh-baked pita in the Qalqiliya markets. That trip had another purpose, I realized then. It was not only to buy food, but to face and defeat the fear that threatened to steal our freedom, the fear that we would be killed by our Arab neighbors, in their home town or our own. The bloodier the hatred of our Arab neighbors toward us, the friendlier and more loving I imagined life inside the forbidden homes. Ah, I would be so loved in those places, I thought, by Ahmed and his parents, and by the Arab prince who employed Ahmed's father and mine. The more threatened I felt by the radio reports of violence in the streets, the more powerful I imagined my position in those forbidden palaces. The more burdensome my chores, the more palace servants I appointed myself. It was at once a hopeful and a shameful dream, and I carried it as a secret in my heart.

And now I was being welcomed into and offered the precious gift of water in another forbidden palace.

I had yet to see a drop of drinking water wasted here, or a Badu washing but hands before digging fingers into the communal food tray. Since I arrived, only little Salimeh has had a change of clothes—but not a bath. Like Tammam, Azzizah, and Abu Salim, I have slept in the clothes I have worn all day since I entered this compound. I felt dusty, clammy, and lousy, and I probably smelled like I could use a bath. Maybe that's what prompted the Badawias' offering. I was dying to take a bath, but not here, not after seeing what it takes to fill a water jerrican, let alone to lug it up here to the tents.

"With your permission I'll bathe at the waterhole," I told Azzizah and Tammam, a breath after blessing them for their water offering.

That shocked them.

"Shameless, she does not veil her face ... shameless, she wants to undress and bathe at the *bir*," Azzizah muttered. "Never in my life did I meet a woman so shameless, so ignorant. Does not even know it is not proper to bathe at the well."

"For you can never tell who might wander to the well just as you are undressing, bathing," Tammam, her eyes addressing me, went on to explain, doling out her words, *wahada, wahada*—one by one. "Not only did I tell you, but with your own eyes you saw that, at a distance all too far to carry water, we Badu pitch our tents, so that no one would stare us in the face ..."

166

"Knowing nothing—nothing—she came here, knowing nothing...," Azzizah was muttering under her veil.

One of the all too few things I did know when I came here was that, in Badu Arabic, like in ancient Hebrew, there is no word for "privacy." Yet look at how these mountain Badawias guard theirs—from each other, as well as from their neighbors and strangers. Both their tents open up to the east, in such an angle that you cannot see the opening—the interior—from one tent to another, nor the fire-circles of one tent from those of the other.

"It is not good to bathe at the well, even if you were to know for certain that no one would happen to stare you in the face there when you are bathing. For there are bad winds at the well," says Azzizah.

"Bad winds? At your water-source?" I answer.

"*Aywa*—yes. Azzizah knows, for she is a *darwisha*—a healing woman, daughter of a *darwish*," says Tammam, exhausted still from dragging the water she and Azzizah were offering for my bath.

A part of me was glad not to go back to the waterhole in this heat. Yes. I accepted their offering. I rationalized it, of course. Not just with piddly little justifications: They can't wait for me to take a bath, they can't breathe near me I'm so stinking filthy. But with big rationalizations: Rejection of his offering moved Cain to kill his brother, Abel...

"I like both your tents equally well; therefore, I ask you to advise me, in which one would it be proper for me to bathe?"

"In mine," Tammam was first to reply, "for Azzizah always has women guests, not only her daughters, but many Badawias in need of a *darwisha*, whereas I never had a woman guest before you came and, by my fire-circles, you sat, feasted, even slept."

"*Aywa*—yes," said Azzizah. "A camel-saddle weighing heavy to one side needs to be balanced lest it would slide off, and all the goods contained inside would be lost to the sand. It was for this reason—to correct the imbalance somewhat—that Abu Salim decided to receive you at Tammam's fire-circles. And it is for this very same reason that I also advise you to be bathed in Tammam's tent."

The Badawias escorted me to Tammam's tent. As they watched me pulling a fresh, clean towel out of my duffel bag—not a face towel, for once, but a bath towel—Tammam muttered to Azzizah, "A towel like that she takes with her to the ditch, only much smaller, small enough to fit in her pocket ... Then, in another pocket, she stuffs a long strip of paper she tears from a white roll, paper not like the paper she writes on to remember, but paper like my brother had told me of, paper softer than the softest Egyptian cotton. And then, after she defecates at the ditch, she wipes her tizzie with this softest of paper, does not wash it with water like a human being ..."

(Whenever Tammam follows me to the ditch to relieve herself, discreetly, under one of her many veils, she carries a tin can filled with water—a sort of portable bidet.)

As soon as Tammam dropped the tent flaps ("For you can catch bad winds, even if you are bathed inside a tent," explained Azzizah), I realized how good the constant desert breeze was, not only at cooling but at deodorizing. During the first few minutes it took to adjust, even the Badawias had to fight the impulse to get the hell out. "The sky caved in, just for a moment, just for a moment," they whispered, reassuring themselves, and me, as though claustrophobia hit them harder than the stifling heat and the smell of goat and infant and fire-circles and woman. And now that the wind was not stealing away all other sounds, a frenzied hum filled the ears and, once my eyes adjusted to the darkness, I could see the swarming flies.

The inside of Tammam's tent is not the same as Azzizah's. The senior wife has a sort of a lean-to in which she keeps her goats penned up behind a gate improvised out of branches and rope. A few goats escape whenever she opens and closes this gate. Still, Azzizah doesn't have to sweep out heaps of goat dung, or choke on dust raised by her broom of twigs, like Tammam, whose goats stay in and around her tent when they are not herded out to pasture. Unlike Tammam, Azzizah stores firewood inside her tent, sparing her the coughing and frustration of lighting up and blowing life-fire into dew-drenched dung, firewood, and twigs.

Each wife stores in her tent sacks of provisions. Azzizah's swell full;

Tammam's are nearly empty. Next to the sacks of staples, Azzizah stores a trunk, the likes of which Tammam does not possess; it looks like a treasure chest pirated off some ancient schooner. Neither wife would reveal to me what Azzizah keeps locked in that trunk. Azzizah's remedies, potions, and amulets, or smuggled goods, perhaps, and maybe the passports and cash I had entrusted to Abu Salim for safe-keeping as well. In both of the Badawias' tents, bundles of God-knows-what, wrapped in rags, hang high up the tent pole, out of the goats' reach. High up there, Azzizah also hangs a real waterskin full of that Badu delicacy *samn*. Only at that main center pole could I stand at full height; everywhere else I had to walk in a crouch.

"Did Abu Salim purchase your tent in Al-Arish? Or in Baghdad, Damascus, or Amman?" I asked the Badawias as I waited for them to step out so that I could undress and bathe, "Badu-proper," without anyone staring me in the face, as the Badawias would say.

"We Badawias each weave our own tent," explained Azzizah.

"From the black hair of the goats," elaborated Tammam.

"Three years, *yaa-Rabb*, three years it takes a woman to weave her *bit sha'r*—tent woven from goat hair." Azzizah sighed. "Then, every year, a woman has to weave patches to repair the damage done to her tent by the sun, the wind, the sandstorms. For thirty years, *yaa-Rabb*, I patched and repatched my tent. Then, one day, I see my tent is but patchwork. So, for the next three years I weave a new one. And in the old one I keep my goats now..."

"My *bit sha'r*—tent woven from goat hair—was bequeathed to me by my mother the day she died birthing me," said Tammam. "Whenever I touch my tent I feel my mother's hands. That is why I weave to patch and repatch it, but never, ever will I weave a new one, *Inshallah*—God willing."

"Was the tent your mother's to bequeath, or was it your father's and he fulfilled your mother's wish?" I asked Tammam.

"My father fulfilled my mother's wish, *ya'ni*—that is—he kept the tent for me year after year, all my child years, but it was my mother's to bequeath, for a woman's tent is hers, not her husband's," replied Tammam.

"Not only a woman's tent, but everything in it, including the goats, for her to keep and to bequeath," added Azzizah. "That is why, whenever Abu Salim divorced me, I kept not only my old and new tents, but everything in them, including the goats."

"And what did Abu Salim keep whenever he divorced you?" I asked Azzizah. "What is Abu Salim's to bequeath?"

"The waterholes," replied Azzizah. "And the passageways"—her term for the smuggling routes?—"also the camels."

"All have empowered Abu Salim, and greatly enhanced his reputation," stated Tammam, as she unhooked from high up her tent pole a bundle of crumpled sackcloth bags.

"Many, many, many Badu the desert over are beholden to Abu Salim, for the use he gave them, their herds, and all in their household, of his passageways and waterholes in years of drought as in years of green, of plenty," said Azzizah. "It is such giving that has enhanced Abu Salim's reputation, and such beholding to him of many, many that has empowered Abu Salim."

Sackcloth bags that once contained flour, rice, and sugar were stored in the bundle Tammam unhooked from the center pole. Two or three, she spread flat on the ground. Then, as if they comprised a spanking-clean tile floor in a shower stall, Tammam instructed me to "step onto them after you take off your stranger's shoes and all your stranger's clothes, even your stranger's head scarf." She and Azzizah made no move to leave the tent.

"Is it not improper for me to undress in front of you?" I asked the Badawia co-wives.

"No, for we are all sisters here, *yaa-okhti*—my sister," Azzizah told me in reply.

What would you say to that, Ahmed, *yaa-akwhi*—my brother— what would you say to that?

"*Yaa okhti* my sister," Tammam said, reaffirming Azzizah.

The Badawias are just tossing out these words like a couple of empty shells, yet I grab them like a starved goat. Is that what you would say, *yaa*–Ahmed?

As soon as I had shed my layers of stranger's clothes, Azzizah demanded, "Now get ready to be bathed." As I step off the sack-cloth to fetch one of the jerricans from the closed-off entrance to the tent, intending to carry it over to the designated sponge-bath area, Azzizah and Tammam simultaneously cry out, "*Laa!*—No! No! No!" Thinking that they noticed a snake or scorpion hiding between the water jerricans, I break out in that unmistakable sweat that reeks of fear; then Tammam mutters to Azzizah, "Look at how afraid she is of being bathed—like little Salimeh."

I breathe in relief.

"Yes, breathe deeply, deeply, and step back onto the sackcloth." Azzizah instructs me in how to prepare for being bathed. "Now, holding your breath, you are to crouch and close your eyes——"

"And hold your head down. Stay like that, even when we instruct you to let out the breath you hold, breathe deeply again, then again hold your breath." Tammam voices this set of instructions while her hands, as strong as my father's construction worker's hands, force my shoulders down and me to crouch.

Then, all of sudden, splash! and ice-cold water breaks over my head and shoulders. God, I think, so quickly do you adjust to the heat in the tent that jerrican water as warm as piss feels frigid. I grope for the wash-towel and soap, then lock my knees to stand up and—*splash!*—straight into my face—and a hand grabs the towel and soap while another forces my shoulders back down to crouch position and a foot unlocks my knees. *Splash!*

"*Yaa*-Allah, give me a minute—*dagigah, dagigah*—a minute to shampoo, soap..." I try to say through a mouthful of water. *Splash!*

"Now you can stand up and breathe," Azzizah says, showing me that the water jerrican in her hand is empty. Chilled and shivering, my teeth clacking, I reach for my bath towel. It's soaking wet.

"*Dagigah, dagigah*—one minute, one minute," Tammam mutters as she and Azzizah towel me dry with their hands, massaging and rubbing, massaging and rubbing—warmth and vigor—but then they forget how powerful their leathery hands are. "*Bas!*—Enough!!" I cry out in pain. They curse, draw back, and proceed to read my body as if it were a map of my life.

"Oh, *yaa-Rabb, yaa-Rabb*—oh, my Lord, my Lord," Azzizah cried out, her eyes troubled, angry, sorrowful, addressing mine. "Now I see why your nights are sleepless," she tells me. The Badu tradition of receiving guests, no questions asked, keeps her and Tammam from expressing what has obviously been on their minds, even now as I stand naked in front of them.

"Oh, my *yaa-Rabb*—my Lord—be careful, careful, *yaa*-Azzizah," Tammam cautions, wincing as Azzizah's fingers gently examine blue and black bruises that have faded completely from my memory if not altogether from my skin. The eye could barely detect them in the dim light-no-light that filtered through the thick black weave of Tammam's tent. These bruises are just travel souvenirs I picked up on the road, when the Jeep gathered speed to fly over a sand trap but sank instead and catapulted the jerricans and desert gear into the front seat. But what are these travel tribulations compared with the desert hardships Tammam and Azzizah endure—not just for a week or a month or two, but every day of their lives. It is their endurance more than any past glory that invests the Badawias and their clan-tribe with legendary dimensions.

It doesn't always follow that the hardships of life harden a person's heart; the opposite is often true.

"O, *yaa-Rabb, yaa-Rabb*," Tammam mutters, pointing to my bruises. "If that is how your husband beats you, rid yourself of him. There is no shame in divorce. Keep it secret, but sometimes it is better to be a woman divorced than a maiden, for a woman divorced can marry whomever her heart desires, whereas a maiden can marry only him whom her kinsfolk decide she must."

"But a woman divorced must leave her children with her husband; otherwise, few would be afraid to be divorced from a wife-beating husband. *Aywa—yes—*if you were to divorce your wife-beating husband, you would be bound to leave with him the one and only child you bore him—only one I see," Azzizah says, checking the stretch marks on my hips. "Faint, seven or nine years old, meaning the child is old enough to stay with his father.

Strange that your husband did not divorce you, even though your womb has been closed up for the past seven to nine years," Azzizah muttered, then she examined my stomach and thighs.

"Now, I see why he did not divorce her. Look at the scars of her struggle with fate." Azzizah's fingers direct Tammam to the old burn scars on my thigh, souvenirs from the War of Independence. (I was twelve, with the fearlessness of the young, when an Egyptian Spitfire dropped a bomb next door, and I ran in, without thinking, to pull the screaming kids from the wreckage. I didn't feel a thing until afterwards. It seemed natural at the time; now people remember it as heroic—or plain dumb.)

"Here you can see," Azzizah said to Tammam, her fingers tracing my old souvenirs, "how, ever since her son was born, she went from one *darwisha* to another, trying to reopen her womb. See how the *darwishin* tried and tried to cure her?"

Badu fertility remedies for women burn-scar the thighs, it seems. The Badawias didn't connect the scars to appearance or beauty. When they consoled me they said, "Next month, next year, *Inshallah*, you will conceive … next month, next year, Allah shall increase …," they said, just as we Yahod say "Next year in Jerusalem …"

"For the past seven or nine years, clearly no *darwisha* pressed burning rods to Nura's thighs to fertilize her womb, for no *darwisha* doubted that her husband's loin sacks had dried up, that he cannot implant a child in her womb," Azzizah said.

"Surely you beseeched your father and brother to demand your husband divorce you," Tammam said to me.

"Of course she did," says Azzizah. "Of course she did. Only to discover to her bitter disappointment that her kinsmen refuse to demand her husband divorce her. For her kinsmen do not wish to return to her husband the bride-price he had paid them."

"Her kinsmen spent her bride-price, no doubt," mutters Tammam, then spits in disgust.

"Still, I would not lose heart, if I were you," Azzizah tells me, her fingers assisting mine to unbraid my tangled hair.

"Were it so easy to undo the ensnaring tangles of fate."

173

Tammam sighs, joining in the task of untangling my blind fingers' braiding. The Badawias' fingers are patient and gentle.

"If I were in your place," the senior Badawia went on to say to me, "I would wait for a moonless night, then I would escape with my child, escape from my husband's compound; run and cover my tracks and my child's, even after we crossed the boundaries of my husband's home ground and mine; run and cover our tracks until we were well into the boundaries of another clan, another tribe. Then, quick-fast, I would touch the tent flaps of a Badu elder there. For, as soon as you do that, the Badu elder is bound to shield and shelter you and your child for as long as you live."

"I know where you and your child can escape, even from capture of the authorities," Tammam whispers, barely able to restrain her excitement.

"Our tents," Azzizah and Tammam say in unison.

"For no stranger, no matter how high among the authorities, would dare enter our tents," explains Tammam.

"And here, in Abu Salim, you have an elder of power to persuade the whole clan to shield you and your child. He might even persuade your kinsmen to uphold your honor and theirs. Here you also have me and Tammam to help you mother your child."

"May you be blessed with good fortune, and good health, and long life and rainfall and peace . . .," I muttered, overloaded with emotion, then I added, "These fading bruises were caused, not by my husband, but by——"

"By another man, *yaa-Rabb*!" Tammam cuts me off. "Your blood-kin better avenge this abuse with blood or with blood-money paid to your blood-kin, else one and all of your blood-kin will be chipped at by the whole desert until nothing is left of your honor, reputation, power, possessions, just like in the story of the *Habbashat* birds that Abu Salim told you."

"Still, your kinsmen would be wise not to demand too high a blood price, and to refrain from mouthing words pointed like a sword during the negotiations of the blood-price, else a blood-feud would ensue," said Azzizah.

"A blood-feud would ensue from bruises you can barely see?" I asked.

"Words you can barely hear have been known to spark a blood-feud lasting for generations," Azzizah tells me in reply. "But more often a price is paid for blood or for whatever transgression to bring about a *sulha*—a reconciliation, peace, forgiveness. But such a payment can strip your clan of all the best of your goats, camels, waterholes, passageways, and sometimes even the best of your daughters, whom you must give in marriage to the person you, your blood-kin, or clansman had injured, so that a *sulha* can be brought about and sealed. Oh, it is such a punishment that the burden of one's guilt falls on all you love and hold dear, just the thought of it has been known to drive a human being—even one only rumored to be guilty—to flee from home and wander from waterhole to waterhole, for weeks, months, even years. That is why everyone the desert over is careful to restrain anger, passion, desire, envy, greed, and to hold back a heated tongue, fist, dagger, sword, *zubi*—prick—or *cous*—pussy."

"Not everyone is so restrained, else no blameless person would be rumored to be guilty," mutters Tammam. "Oh, take what is left of the rest of my life and enjoy it." The girl-wife heaves a sigh, her jewels *jingle-jangle* as her hand gently swishes the swarm of flies from her infant's face. The flies scatter, then land once more on little Salimeh...

14

From a distance, they looked like fireflies flash-dancing by a checkpoint roadblock, the crossbar and barrels glow-painted blue and white. Then, like moths, ten or twelve more swarmed out of the darkness into the high beams. And then suddenly the windows were full of men. Nearly all of them looked like they had been serving reserve duty at the tail end of the Common Road for thirty years, not thirty days, and had not seen a woman in all that time—a woman like the one sitting in this Jeep, a woman like their own back home, and as if I reminded them of why they were stuck in a wilderness, being ravaged by heat all day and by frost all night, they looked at me with a glint of swagger in one eye and sorrow in the other.

The checkpoint at the dark periphery of their base was lit by the soldiers' flashlights. I saw now why they had resembled fireflies from far away.

"Good evening," they muttered, almost in unison.

"Good evening," Tal and I replied, almost in one voice. "Is this the last checkpoint out of the Common Road?" said Tal.

"Yes." Not one made a move to enter us in the ledgerbook or to lift the blue and white crossbar that blocked our passage to the open space beyond.

"Smells like you bathed in the sulfur springs. What a place!" said one.

"Nothing compared to this place," said another.

"This place! This place is the tail end of the world," muttered a surly voice from the group that crowded Tal's window. Like a chorus in a play, the group parted to make room for a dark Adonis to approach Tal's window. He was so attractive, my face was burning—and my insides.

"It's a shame...," says a soft-spoken voice from behind me—Tal looks like he has seen a ghost over my shoulder—"... a shame to travel so far and reach the tail end of the world when there's no light to see what a beautiful tail the world has. If I were you, I'd bunk overnight at our base, and tomorrow, when the Common Road is ours again, I'd return to the gulf and drive to the beach just north of the turn."

"Look at this reservnik and you'll have an idea of what my father was like," Tal whispered, leaning close to my ear. I saw a fellow who gave off the feel of a teddy bear, worn out and frayed, sort of like an old security blanket.

"Nothing to see there," the dark Adonis cuts in. "There's nothing for hundreds of kilometers around. But it's warm in the barracks. And there's hot water to shower off the sulfur, smells like rotten eggs. I'd camp overnight in the base if I were you."

"Too cold tonight to camp outdoors," said a reservnik with a birthmark on his face, wrapped up in an army *doobon*—parka— like most everyone else, including Tal. "Too dark now to find firewood," he added, "and the cook on duty at the base tonight is, in civilian life, the head chef at the Hilton Hotel in Tel Aviv."

Tal presented our pass to the Adonis by his window.

"Keep it. We'll check you out tomorrow," said the one with the birthmark. "Marble Cake," the Adonis called him, as did the others—rank and file all, it seemed. There was no sign of a stripe on any shoulder or sleeve.

"Doesn't your base have a commander who has any say about inviting two—terrorists, for all you know," Tal said.

"I am the commander," said the one who gave off the feeling of Tal's father. "Let him consult with her," the commander told his men. And they allowed us a meter or two of privacy.

"You'll be the only woman at the base if we stay the night. They might billet you to a barracks full of men. Did you ever sleep in a barracks full of men?" Tal asked, looking as exhausted as I felt, and he was clearly drawn to this reservnik who reminded him of his father . . .

"No, but what the hell. Let's camp here overnight," I whispered.

"You got yourselves a couple of guests," Tal said to the reservniks.

Nothing but a black void beyond the belt of light surrounding their base—or so it seemed from the inside. The powerful security beams, fed by a powerful droning generator, picked up only dust particles and a tiny desert mouse that scuttled into the base through a hole in the mesh security fence and disappeared under the Jeeps that were parked next to crates, barrels, and rolls of cables piled in heaps only a few steps from the barracks.

It was just a three-barracks base—mobile barracks, squatting on blocks as if ready to be hauled off at a moment's notice. You wouldn't have suspected it from the outside. From the checkpoint, the base looked huge—and permanent.

The barracks closest to the gate was "off limits" to us, the commander told us. He and his men bunked in the second barracks, he said, directing us to the third, the "kitchen mess hall," he called it. He stomped the sand off his desert boots on the straw mat by the entrance. Tal and I followed suit.

It was clean and tidy inside—and strictly kosher, like in every army base. Two sets of dishes on the shelves, two sets of cutlery, two sets of pots and pans—one for meat, one for milk. And over the two sinks, it had two taps for running water—hot and cold. The stove was restaurant size. In the mess-hall section, there was one table, with room for only one chair at the narrow top and bottom; at the long sides, benches without back support could fit five, or seven squeezed in tight. The commander sat at the head of the table; Tal on one bench, I on the other. Directly across me sat the dark Adonis. Leaning forward so that I could hear him over the commotion, he said, "I checked the showers. Give it an hour and the water will be good and hot. The shower stalls are in the open because only men are based here. But no one will look, I'll make sure of that. I'll close off the stalls with blankets if you want."

"Thank you," I said, flushed by the male sparks all around me. "How many men are based here?"

"Bad luck to count troops," replied a reservnik wearing bubble-lensed glasses. His Hebrew sounded like Russian.

"Russki," the Adonis called him, "it's all right." He turned back to me, "Twenty, twenty-four men are based here."

They all had to file in sideways behind us, the space in the mess hall was so cramped, and only when there was no standing room, even in the kitchen part of the barracks, did they realize that no one was out on patrol duty, guard duty, checkpoint duty, and God-knows-what duty they served in that barracks that was off limits to Tal and me.

Shifts changed at various times, in various numbers, without as much as a signal or a nod from the commander or anyone else. "How do you know when, and whose turn it is?" I asked the commander. He scratched his head like the man who was asked if he slept with his beard under the blanket or on top.

"After serving together for twenty-seven years, you just know when and how," piped Marble Cake, and the barracks shook with the laughter of men who had known each other—and served one month each year side by side—since Tal was four years old. All except the Russki, the dark Adonis, and two or three more who seemed to be in their mid-thirties. Replacements, the commander called them.

"Not all of us made it to this table," the commander said when the laughter died. His eyes went to Arik's wedding ring, strung on the gold chain around my neck. I didn't want him to ask me, When? How? Children? Remarried? Dropped-out? I didn't have the strength to get into that now, so I covered my neck with the white *kaffiyye* draped on my shoulders. And the Russki thought I was cold.

"A shot of vodka would warm you up in a minute. But there is no vodka in this Jewish army base of ours." The Russki was amused by the thought of an army base without a drop of booze.

"We do have liquor on the base," said a deep bass voice that belonged to a tall, rangy reservnik who looked like he had gone on a crash diet just before being called up. His crumpled fatigues were hanging on him like a scarecrow's costume—"The Turk" his fellow reservniks called him. He handed me a glass of sweet sacramental wine. "Liquor on an empty stomach makes a person dizzy," he cautioned, handing me a slice of bread. "Eat it first," he said, "Eat ... Eat ... Don't be shy ... eat, then gulp the liquor and you won't feel the cold."

Tal was laughing inside, it seemed, one moment; the next, he had tensed as if I were public property confiscated from him for the war effort. The men were claiming me here, with their eyes at least, as their own woman. Innocent, *Shabbat*-bride, home, family, love—I was all of these to them, but not a person. The air sang with the festive goodwill these attributes stirred. And, after years of being needled, gagged, shunned by my own for dropping out, deserting, betraying, a part of me so enjoyed being claimed by my own, I didn't want to lose it.

One by one the commander introduced his men, as if they too were emblems of something larger, as his names for them showed: the Turk, the Pollack, the Hungarian, the Electrician from Tiberius, the Accountant from Beer Sheba, the Photographer from the artist colony Ein Hod, the Carpenter from Nes-Ziona—himself, the Taxi Driver from Jerusalem. Marble Cake owns a bookstore in Tel Aviv; the Moshavnik grows and exports oranges and gladioli; the Kibbutznik is an expert on breeding and raising carp in man-made ponds; and the Russki is a newcomer to The Land and to the community of scientists at the Weitzmann Institute of Science in Rehovot, and also to reserve duty.

"What a shaft, reserve duty here. Thirty days and thirty nights stuck far away from everyone and everything. Stuck! Stuck! Stuck!" The dark Adonis kept banging the table with a clenched hot fist, rattling everything and everyone—except the Russki. Even the commander seemed to be wary of this dark Adonis, shutting him out of the introductions. Why? Was the Adonis a gangster or a pimp from the Kerrem? Or was it his dark skin, his Arab-ghetto origins? Was street prejudice spilling into the army? A *Chukh-chukh*, my brother-in-law would call the dark Adonis. "*Chukh-chukhs* hate the Arabs who had expelled them and confiscated all they had possessed in their Arab lands of origin. But check the military cemeteries and you'll see they don't volunteer to serve in elite, high-risk units; they know that idiots like us are all too glad to be heroes. Tell it to a *Chukh-chukh*, though, and he'll accuse you of being prejudiced, spreading out-and-out lies—that is, if he doesn't just pull out a knife and slice your tongue off... *Chukh-chukhs* talk with knives and with fists..." Is that why no one at the table told the dark Adonis what they thought of his rattling steam—no one except the Russki.

"You are stuck, stuck, stuck in the Soviet Union, believe me," said the Russki to the Adonis. "Nowhere in Russia was I as free as I am here, even on army duty."

"Yeah," agreed the Electrician, irritation in his voice. "My father also came from Russia, also suffered there, struggled there, and when he came up to The Land, he received *kadahat*—fuck-all— except malaria. Fifty years later, you come up to The Land and you receive a dream of a job, and an apartment complete with a telephone, and a car and all the modern conveniences, duty free. Yeah, you're free here all right."

"This is the first time you serve reserve, so you don't know the half of how free you are here... Ah, what a vacation reserve duty is, the best vacation a man can have," the Carpenter told the Russki. "Thirty days away from the pressure of work, whining kids, nagging wife. Thirty days of a quiet head. Thirty days for the wife to appreciate what a load you carry at home, not to mention at work. Thirty days for her to worry about unpaid bills, and spanking the kids, and fixing the stove now that the Electrician is here serving reserve duty."

"And how she greets you after thirty nights," said the Turk. "And thirty days a year of army exercises keep you in shape—trim, young. And it's like family, the closeness of the men in your unit."

"Closer than family," Marble Cake said to the Russki. "No one could ever replace the ones you lost in the death camps, or the ones you left behind in Russia, but here you will not go through life alone. The men of your unit will join in your celebrations and will be the first ones beside you in your times of need."

"It's too bad your first time serving reserve has to be in a base too far for our wives and children to drive over and visit us for a few hours, as they usually do, even when we're on high alert, like in '67," said the commander, and the reservniks chuckled.

"You know, we were combat soldiers in '67, front-line soldiers," the Accountant told the Russki. "We had to dig in, but it was so quiet that if we hadn't switched on the radio we wouldn't have suspected that such unbelievable turns of events were taking place; not only did Egypt demand that the U.N. peacekeepers vacate the whole of this buffer zone—the whole of Sinai, but the U.N. complied, exposing us to Arab armies aiming to push us to the sea."

"That's what our wives and children were hearing on the radio, on top of the hour every hour for one week, then another," said the Hungarian. "I will never forget how tension was mounting by the minute, and our leaders were still afraid to make a move because we were so outnumbered. Not one of us could leave our position even for an hour, let alone for *Shabbat*."

"So, after two weeks," said the Carpenter, "we decided that if we cannot go home next *Shabbat*, our families will come to us. What a picnic we had, all of us together with our families. You wouldn't have suspected that an all-out war was imminent."

"But a week later . . .," muttered the Moshavnik.

"Speak up. Speak up," the Turk urged the Moshavnik, almost like the Badu do; turning to Tal and me, he added, "Wait till you hear this."

"A week after that picnic," continued the Moshavnik, "my wife had had it with that 'imminent' state of war which had dragged on for three weeks. She had to work the orange groves and flower fields now all by herself, like ten men. It tired the hell out of her. So she decided to take the day off. Early dawn she packs the children into the car, and off she goes to visit me. The roads are empty, but she thinks nothing of it, because, by now, nearly all the nation's men were away, like me, in defensive positions along the borders . . ."

"She was sick and tired of the same radio bulletins, the same news of war to finish us all off once and for all, every hour of every day," Marble Cake cut in. The reservists knew one another's stories by heart, it seemed, like couples married for twenty-seven years. "For her, the radio was like the fellow who cried wolf."

"Yes," said the Moshavnik, "my wife was looking forward to a beautiful day; she was heading to the place we had held a picnic the week before. I would be there, she thought. But when she arrived, my wife saw that my unit had moved. Where to? She had only one clue. My unit, my division, belonged to southern command. She figured my unit had moved to another position farther south. And so, farther south she drove to look for me. It was like a game of hide-and-seek for the children, and my wife also enjoyed the drive."

"It was a very beautiful morning," said the Turk, "blue and quiet."

"For an hour or two, my wife felt like she had the country all to herself. And then she started to pass one tank after another. But that was only to be expected in the situation, my wife thought, especially so close to the border, where she was driving. So she thought nothing of it and continued to press south. Then one tankist stopped her and asked, "Where are you heading, *maydeleh?*"

"*Maydeleh*—my girl—the tankist called her. And really my wife was but a girl then, and more shy than today. Too shy to tell the tankist that she was looking for her husband, my wife tells the tankist that she is just taking the children for a drive.

"'A drive?! We're in the middle of an all-out war, and you are taking your children for a drive?!!' The tankist shakes his head. But my wife tells him, 'That's what my mother has been saying for the past three weeks.'

"So the tankist hands her his transistor radio and my wife hears: '. . . in a pre-emptive strike this morning, the Israeli air force struck a heavy blow . . . and heavy battle in the south . . . and according to the latest reports from the east . . . our forces in the south are advancing . . .'. All the tanks that my wife had just passed were with our forces in the south, which were advancing—my wife was fully aware of it now."

"She trembled for the children now, and for her husband, and for herself, and also for the tankist who stopped her from advancing ahead of our advancing forces," said the Turk. "The tankist didn't laugh when he saw the jalopy she was driving. 'You must have courage to spare if you drove this all the way here,' the tankist told her."

"We called the car Charlie Chaplin, 'cause every time we saw it we laughed," interjected the Electrician.

"Soon as my wife heard the tankist say she had courage to spare, she knew he couldn't spare even one man to escort her and the children back home. So she said to the tankist, 'I'll be all right. Don't worry . . . You take care . . .'

"'Ah, *maydeleh*, there are no girls like our girls,' the tankist said, and he told her, 'Drive back home as fast as you can. And the minute you see a plane not ours, jump out of the car with the kids and dive into the ditch by the roadside.'

"My wife followed his instructions. But Charlie Chaplin heated up. The car stalled. And the ditch was no place to wait for the engine to cool down, my wife thought, because the sky was busy now with planes flying too high to see if they were ours or theirs.

"The only risk worth taking now was to get the children to a proper shelter, the sooner the better, my wife thought. So all the time that the engine was cooling down, my wife pushed the car on a road fried by the sun, the asphalt sizzling under her bare feet. As always, she had left the house barefoot. She liked to feel the land skin to skin, if you know what I mean."

"It was no 'Six-Day War' for this unit," said the Turk. "We didn't return home after six days, and not even after thirty . . ."

"Yes, for weeks my wife had to look after the children, and the house, and the fields, and the groves, all by herself," said the Moshavnik. "I don't know how she did it. And six years later, in the Yom-Kippur War, it was much more difficult. On top of everything else, she couldn't export the gladioli and the oranges because the Arab states threatened to cut off their business ties with any nation that dealt with us.

"My wife figured she could save the oranges by storing them in refrigerated depots. But it's now or never with flowers, like with people. And all the gladioli died in the fields," said the Moshavnik. "And now my wife didn't know if she should plant a new crop."

"All the nations, bar none, deserted us, abandoned us really, in that war in '73, the Yom Kippur," said the Accountant. "Almost like in the days of the death camps."

"'They don't deserve our flowers,' my wife said to herself. Then, when she heard that the Egyptian air force was pounding my division, she thought, 'Let the world have a winter without flowers...'.

"But after the cease-fire," the Moshavnik went on, "I returned home and saw her in the fields, sweating over a fresh crop swelling already with buds. 'Let *us* have a winter filled with flowers,' she said."

Tal shook his head when our eyes met. I couldn't read them as yet, couldn't tell if he didn't want me to ask him, even with my eyes, any questions about that, or any war.

"We didn't return home till winter from a war that started on Yom Kippur," said the cook on duty as he sat down next to me.

"I know you are hungry. Supper will be ready sixteen minutes after I finish this cigarette," he said to Tal and me. The others didn't laugh, even though the only preparation he had made for supper so far was to tie an apron over his faded fatigues. If he really worked as chef at the Hilton in civilian life, it was probably as the short-order cook, not the head chef, as they had claimed. He took a long drag, savored it like a man who cannot smoke on the job. "I used to love Yom Kippur. This day that God checks out the columns of your good deeds and your bad in his ledgerbook is the only day of the year I could make it into his good book; the only day I do nothing but catch up on my reading and my sleep. It's my favorite holy day also because it is the only day in the year on which the radio and TV are off the air from sundown to sundown. And the silence in Tel Aviv is such a contrast from the daily noise—and such a wonder to the tourists at the Hilton, once I overheard a tourist saying, 'You've got to be here to believe that three hundred thousand city Jews could be so quiet for twenty-four hours.' Can you imagine what a shock it was when the radio announced a general call-up?"

"My son was called up, hours before the radio announcement," said the Electrician. "We were in the synagogue, to please my father mainly. My father is so happy to see us in the synagogue, on Yom Kippur at least. Three generations side by side—his old cronies made a big fuss about that. My son was only nineteen and a half, but they worked him so hard in the paratroopers that he kept nodding off, like the old men. It was just before noon; I remember checking my watch and thinking how slow time moves in the synagogue. It was just a few minutes before noon that one of the boys from my son's unit shows up in our pew, whispers something to my son, then my son leans over to me and whispers that war has broken out, he must rejoin his unit in the front. 'But you are still a child,' I told him. I'll never forget what a child he looked to me that moment.

"'You have no combat experience,' I told him, 'I'm an old war horse, I'll go, you stay.' I had no say, of course. Neither did he. Just like that, without a minute to adjust, his place and mine changed. He was the man in the family now. I understood how my father felt in the '56 war, when I was called up. Now my father was draping his prayer shawl even over his head, and the gold band covered his forehead and his eyes, as always. It used to scare my son when he was little, to be shut out from his grandfather, so he would tug at my father's shawl and say, 'Let me in,' until my father would envelop him also in his prayer shawl. Now, my son was taller than both my father and me; he had to bend down to whisper to his grandfather, 'Let me in, let me in ...'.

"I could feel my father's tears on my face when I also parted from him to rejoin my unit. But, like everyone in this unit, I rushed only to wait—finding the main roads plugged with tanks, supply trucks, reservniks, and regulars ...".

"But no civilians," said the Commander. "You have to be a taxi driver to appreciate what a mistake the Arabs made when they chose to attack us on Yom Kippur, the only day in the year that our roads are not clogged by civilian traffic. And they compounded their mistake when they didn't bombard the traffic jam;

they could have destroyed our whole defense force before we even had a chance to regroup."

"First time in my life I saw religious reservniks and regulars driving on Yom Kippur," said Marble Cake. "It was that, more than anything else, that made me realize we were in deep shit."

"The last thing I expected," said the Electrician, "was to find our unit trucking troops from one front to another, like a child using his fingers to block a pipe bursting from more holes than he has fingers for..."

"The last thing I expected," said the Commander, "was that we would lose seven hundred men in seven days. The tourists in my taxi don't know what it means, until I tell them that seven hundred men killed in one week here is comparable to the number of Americans killed in a decade in Vietnam, even more. Here, I tell them, there wasn't a person who didn't lose a loved one."

"I don't remember a week when the morale was so low," said Marble Cake. "Of all weeks, our minister of defense chooses that week to disappear. No explanation. As if all those years Dayan was just a figment of the nation's imagination."

"A general like Dayan we didn't have since Joshua, I believed," said the Accountant. "That black eyepatch of his was almost like a symbol to me, a symbol of courage, resolve, triumph against all odds. I couldn't believe Dayan disappeared for any reason but to hold secret talks with leaders the world over, to secure a cease-fire, or supplies at least. But then I heard that Dayan had given up—no use putting up a fight, he believed, no hope of a chance for us to survive this war."

"Really, that's what it looked like," said the Turk.

"Ah, all you had to do to feel like a hero was *not quit* like Dayan did," said Marble Cake. "The troops we trucked from one front to another buzzed with the latest: Dayan quit the war effort, but not his cabinet post..."

"That's not the way I heard it," said the photographer from Ein Hod. "Dayan's daughter is my next-door neighbor and according to her, Dayan, her father, offered to resign."

"Me," said the Commander, "I felt I was living through a biblical event—a biblical turning point, if not a biblical punishment, calamity. In seven days, in front of my very eyes, we turned from a nation of idealists to a nation of cynics. The youngest soldier in my truck told me sarcastically, 'We are going to survive this war for sure, else our ministers and retired generals wouldn't bother to promote themselves by putting down even the chief of staff.' Daddo—the chief of staff—was not up to the task, we heard."

The Chef exhaled a long stream of smoke. "We heard that General Sharon would deploy the atom bomb if he were chief of staff—let the Philistines die with us... And Dayan—by the time our leaders finished with him, even the king who wore no clothes fared better. For years the gossip columnists wrote about Dayan's womanizing and archeological digging and hoarding. For years the people knew all about it. But only now the people called Dayan, 'Zayan'—Fucker... Even the people from his own party said that Dayan stole not only the nation's antiquities and another man's wife, but another man's thunder. The credit we gave Dayan in the '67 war belonged to Levi Eshkol; the credit Dayan gave himself in the Sinai War belonged to Ben-Gurion, who was the prime minister then and the defense minister as well..."

"To me personally," said the Commander, "there was something biblical about Dayan. Even in his downfall, he was a unifying force. Like the nation, Dayan was an idealist in his youth. I hope his downfall is just a warning and not a foreshadowing of things to come in this modern state of ours."

"What downfall? Dayan is our foreign minister today," said the Turk. "It was a grief-stricken nation that dumped on Dayan. A grief-stricken nation, battle-fatigued, fighting on the losing side, with no supplies, no ammunition, no leader to rally behind, no hero..."

"No hero?!... Trucks full of heroes we saw day in, day out," said the Electrician. "One more exhausted than the other, and my son... never have I seen my son looking so exhausted as on the day we trucked his unit from the front in the north to the front in the south. It was ten days after Yom Kippur, I remember, the first time I saw him since Yom Kippur. He was in the first line of fire, I could tell. He didn't have even one quiet minute in that whole time to shave, wash up, change a shirt ... And now he couldn't unwind. It wouldn't sink in that we were rolling safe now, out of range. 'We shouldn't be sitting in the same truck,' he told me. 'Mother will kill us if we catch a direct hit,' he said, had a good laugh, then added, 'Did you hear the latest? The only man in the government is Golda. Steel balls this woman has, if she can launch a counter-offensive now ...'"

"He was at the spearhead," said the Commander to Tal and me. "The Electrician's son, I mean. He was with the paratroopers who spearheaded the counter-offensive that crossed the Suez Canal, and stopped advancing only ninety-seven kilometers from Cairo, and only on the condition that Egypt sit with us at the cease-fire table. And Egypt agreed. I didn't think I'd live to see the day that an Arab nation sat at the table with us. These first direct cease-fire talks led to the peace talks in Camp David today. So that counter-offensive that Golda launched was a turning point, not just in the Yom-Kippur War, but in our destiny ..."

"I wake up in a sweat some nights, so well I recall that turning point ..." The Photographer was lost in memory. "I'll never forget how the Egyptians pounded everyone and everything that tried to reach the bridgehead at the Suez Canal ... So many bodies were floating in the Canal, you couldn't see the water ..."

Tal's men were among those, I could sense-see it in his eyes.

"Naa ... the only person who suffered an injury in the Yom-Kippur War was General Sharon," said the dark Adonis, and every-one laughed—except the Russki. "Come election time, and you'll understand, *yaa*-Russki. Come election time, and you will see The Land plastered with the picture of Sharon walking around during the Yom-Kippur War, wearing a bandage around his head like a crown, 'Sharon *Melekh Israel*—Sharon, the King of Israel!' His party people on the right will shout come election time, you'll see. And the people on the left will shout back."

"Aaah … you will never know how I dreamed to vote in democratic elections with shouting for and against," said the Russki. "Best thing I like in this country is that I can criticize everything and everyone from first moment I come to this country … even before I know Hebrew. Very loud I like to criticize now, for all the years I had to be a silent Jew in Russia."

"But if everyone will do here what he couldn't do outside, will this country survive?" asked the Turk.

"Okay … clear the table. Supper will be ready, sixteen minutes from now," said the Hilton chef. True to his word this time, he rustled up a delicious *kalabash*—Moroccan omelet—and a sumptuous vegetable salad, with a fruit salad to finish.

And, just like at home, someone got up to bring over a jar of olives, and the others muttered, "Bring over the pickles, while you are at it … and the cheese … the jam … and more bread."

Bedtime. Tal and I find we are billeted in the barracks that serves as sleeping quarters for all the reservniks at the base.

"You can't say I didn't warn you," Tal's eyes, sparking amusement, say to mine.

"You should be so lucky," my eyes reply. His eyes dance with laughter, imagining himself sleeping in a barracks full of women.

15

The Badawias watched me putting on my clean change of clothes with disappointment and disapproval.

"Surely these are not your tribal clothes," says Azzizah.

"They are not," I reply.

"Now that you are bathed clean, I thought you would be wearing, not your stranger's clothes, but your tribal clothes," says Tammam. "Surely you brought your tribal clothes in one of the travel sacks."

"Tammam wants to see your tribal attire," says Azzizah.

So do I, I think to myself. For all I know, Tammam and Azzizah are wearing my tribal attire—that is, if my tribe had tribal clothes. Were they destroyed with the Temple? Did my tribe lose them in exile? Was it Isaiah or Amos who had described the daughters of Zion wearing anklets, bracelets, rings, shawls, and veils like the ones that Tammam and Azzizah are wearing today? Which tribe originated them? The Badawias? Mine? The Babylonians? The Aramaics? Or some other tribe erased from history in the devastating tribal wars fought throughout this region ever since the ancient days?... Such questions didn't seem to have entered the Badawias' minds.

"Are you wearing your tribal attire?" I ask them.

"*Taba'an*—naturally," Azzizah replies.

"What would you say if someone were to tell you that your tribal attire resembles mine?" I ask her.

"Cannot be," she responds. "The only tribal clothes resembling ours are worn by Badawias of our tribe."

"It is from our tribeswomen who dwell at the Gates of the Wadi, and from my brother as well, that I heard how strangers the world over admire our tribal attire," says Tammam.

"Your tribal attire is truly admirable," I tell the Badawias.

"You can wear my clean change of tribal clothes and veils, if it is not forbidden for you to do so by your people," Tammam tells me in response.

"Only if it is not forbidden by your people," Azzizah emphasizes to me.

"*Wallah*, I would like to try on your tribal veils and clothes. It is not forbidden for me."

"*Wallah, wallah*," the Badawias exclaimed, sounding as happy as me.

First, the Badawias helped me get into a *tanorah*—underdress—which Tammam had given a shake to expel the creases and the dust and sand. Ankle-length and shaped sort of like a granny nightgown with ruffles at the ankles and wrists, the garment is made from fabric printed with iridescent blooms resembling nothing that grows or glows in the desert. Tammam's underdress feels light and soft to the touch, except for some rough spots on the bodice where her milk must have flowed over, and also below the waist—her discharge, I guess. (The Badawias wear no under-pants, I assume, since they were so amused to see me putting on mine.) Two nursing slits are hidden inside two wide folds tucked to a side seam that can be easily moved to the front, so wide is the cut of her underdress. The overdress—the traditional black *thowb*—weighted by yards and yards of heavy wool and exquisite embroidery, is even wider and sways sensuously around the hips. It keeps you warm in the chilling shade, and, out in the scorching sun, it keeps that film of sweat that acts like a sort of air-conditioner. These yards and yards get caught between my legs when I start to walk, cracking the Badawias up.

"*Wallah*, you walk like a camel with its front legs hobbled," says Tammam, still laughing.

"Both dresses fit you in width but not in length, for you are too long for a woman," says Azzizah as she and Tammam pull and tug the dresses to stretch them to my "length."

At each stage of this dressing up, the Badawias, almost as if they could sense I wished they had a full length mirror, inform me how it fits and how it befits me, as they probably inform each other whenever they try on a dress, or a veil, as they cut and sew it.

Next, the Badawias fold a royal blue shawl into a sort of a sash, which they knot around my waist snug enough to reveal the curves. "Now you look supple-curvy-beautiful, like a Badawia—caring and cared for, loved and loving," Tammam reflects. (And Russell thought it would offend the Badu if I wore anything that showed my curves. He couldn't emphasize strongly enough that I should wear an extra-extra large top over my jeans.)

In preparation for my tribal hairdo, the Badawias rubbed soap into my hair—wouldn't rinse it off. (Later, I discover that no hair spray or gel starches your hair like this soap job.) They braided my hair, into three—two thin side braids, and a thicker center braid shaped like a cone right above the forehead, sort of like a unicorn horn. Over that cone, they drape the long black veil that covers their heads and falls back to their ankles. My neck nearly gave way from the weight; but in front, over that unicorn-like braided cone, this veil, sticking out like the brim of a baseball cap, shades my eyes. It doesn't filter out the ultraviolet rays like "*djinn*-demon outer eyes," but you don't have to squint or clamp your hands to your forehead to see if you are heading for a sharp canyon drop.

And now that they have covered my forehead with beaded tassels and coins that dangle over my eyebrows, I understand why Azzizah and Tammam sit with their eyes downcast. Cast your eyes upwards or sideways and you see nothing but coins and beads, unless you crane or swivel your neck. "Improper, brazen," Azzizah admonished me, as she and Tammam secured this headpiece with bobby-pins fastened to the side braids that are twisted above the ears, sort of like a pincushion, with a knot so constricting the blood vessels above the temples that I see stars as I wobble around, until my blood—my mind—adjusts. Adjusting is far too easy for the liking of that inner driver in charge of self-preservation; keep adjusting at this rate, it warns, and before you know it you'll end up like the frog that kept adjusting to water that got warm, warmer, and warmer still, until it boiled the frog.

For last, the Badawias reserved the face-veil. They both examine Tammam's spare and decide that it is not as beautiful as the one

Tammam or Azzizah wears, but more beautiful than the one Azzizah keeps in spare. Then they debate whether or not it will do. Azzizah decides it is beautiful enough.

"Yes," Tammam agrees half-heartedly; a second or two later, mischief sparks in her eyes. Even before Tammam's hands go to unfasten her face-veil, Azzizah gasps—*yaa*-Allah, *yaa*-Allah—in amazement, delight, admiration of Tammam's gumption, gall, daring, or whatever it took Tammam to unveil her face to a person—man or woman, not her blood-kin—for the first time since she reached puberty.

How beautiful she is, this girl-Badawia sister of mine that Abu Salim married when she was sweet sixteen, if that (she can't be more than eighteen now). Look at her unveiled, and you understand how a man like King David could have lost his head at his first glance at Bat-sheba. Like Bat-sheba, Tammam is attractive. And like Bat-sheba, Tammam knows it. There is no mirror here, no lake, no still body of water to reflect her looks back to her, and no camera is allowed to photograph her, yet she knows it, has sensed it or seen it in others' eyes, loving, jealous, envious. She has that aloofness, that protective shield that the gifted build after receiving one too many knocks for their God-given gifts, and also the self-assurance of those with talents, genius, good looks, and good luck. She smiled when she caught me staring, entranced by her looks.

"*Wallah*, Tammam, your mother was right to name you 'Tammam,' for your beauty, like your name, *is* Tammam—perfect, complete," I say to her.

"So is your beauty," Tammam tells me in response. Then again her eyes spark with mischief and she adds, "If you want to see a woman endowed with beauty unequalled, look at Azzizah."

"No! Tammam! You are not taking off my veil ... You are not ... No! ..." Azzizah, protesting and laughing, retreats from Tammam.

"Yes, I am." Tammam, laughing, keeps advancing toward Azzizah, who keeps laughing-protesting-retreating in circles. You cannot help but sense now how these two Badawia co-wives trust and respect each other, how intimate their bond, how attuned one is to the other.

Tammam wouldn't grab Azzizah until Azzizah allowed her to do so, and Tammam sensed that permission was indeed granted. Laughing, they both fell to the shaded ground, then Tammam started to tug at Azzizah's face-veil—playful, as one would at a friend's braid. Swift like a tiger-cat, Azzizah grabs Tammam's tugging hand. Tammam just as swiftly tugs with the other hand, and on they go—to little Salimeh's delight; the child squeals as though having the time of her life—until Azzizah's face-veil drops. Azzizah covers her face with both hands, laughing at her own inhibitions. Then Azzizah's hands slip into Tammam's, and the woman who is Azzizah appears.

Under her veil, Azzizah wears a silver nose-ring so heavy it elongates the slit in her nostril; blue tattoos surround her lips, and her smile reveals brown teeth like Abu Salim's, quite a few missing. Her skin is creased by time and hardship, like the sandstone mountains assailed by the ever-blowing desert winds, yet tower in a precarious, misshapen, unique beauty, like Azzizah's.

"Now you see how beautiful I am," Azzizah says, her bloodshot eyes revealing she is not without vanity, vulnerability, and cunning.

"*Aywa*—yes," I tell her. "I see you are endowed with beauty like your mountains, enduring. And, like your hospitality, noble, and ennobling those fortunate to see, enjoy it."

"*Wallah*, how well put," Tammam says.

"Put smooth like a man, not straight like a woman," Azzizah mutters, half-frowning and half-loving every smooth, flattering word.

Now the Badawia co-wives secure Tammam's face-veil by tying the tail ends of its band behind my head with a knot so tight that the veil dents the bridge of my nose and digs into my cheekbones. All the rows of coins and beads worked into the cloth block the air—the blessed desert breeze; with every breath, the cloth is sucked closer to your mouth, giving you the taste of Tammam's salt, sweat, and saliva, the bitter nicotine she smokes, the over-sweet tea she drinks. I had no idea how this exquisite-looking veil shrinks the field of vision. This is how the Badawias eat, drink, smoke a cigarette. For every morsel, sip, or puff, they have to tilt their heads down—as though bowing in deference. I turn my eyes upwards and see only the brim of the head veil. Looking downwards, of course, I can see the exquisite beadwork and coins. From the corners of my eyes, I can see not much farther than my elbows. So I swivel my head sideways, and the massive veils whirl centrifugally to my ear, revealing my face. That, for Tammam and Azzizah, is the equivalent of walking nude on Bloor Street, 5th Avenue, or any thoroughfare in Jerusalem. "Not proper, forbidden," the Badawias tell me after they have a good laugh. "No part of your face is to be seen when you wear this veil."

Do they know that I couldn't begin to understand what they, my sisters, sense—feel—even superficially, until I got into their clothes; glimpsed into their lives from inside the veil—sister to sister—bridging the divide that has separated us since the days of Sarah and Haggar.

Now you tell me, why here in Sinai—in this remote compound—and not in The Land, Ahmed and I—his people and mine, Arabs and Jews, like Azzizah, Tammam and me—

Three naïfs, Tal would say, no doubt. He can't see an Arab, even an Arab child, without seeing an enemy. An Arab child led one of his friends straight to a minefield. Naïvety can kill you in this part of the world, Tal thinks, and he might be right.

We three naïfs nearly died laughing when I tried to lift my butt off the welcome-carpet. Folding your legs is relatively easy in the dresses and veils, but getting up—now, for that you need serious muscles. Abu Salim cannot get up from a welcome-carpet without hoisting his *jalabeeya* up to his knees. But that is forbidden for Azzizah and Tammam. They can't reveal more than two or three inches above the ankle, and the women, unlike Abu Salim, are also encumbered by veils. I try rocking to gain momentum to take me up off the ground, and raise my hand like a Buddha over my head, imagining a rope is pulling me up. The Badawias, collapsing in laughter, offer me a hand, and I gladly accept.

They pull me up. Now, walking in these contraptions should be a cinch, I think, having seen how graceful the Badawias glide. But the back veil trailing behind me winds itself underfoot, yanking out the bobby-pins that secured it to the cone-shaped braid; that, in turn, yanks out the bobby-pins that held the unicorn horn-like braid, and the side braids which held the headband. The mass of tassels, beads, and coins came crashing to the ground, and the unicorn-horn braid flopped down over my nose. Azzizah and Tammam found each part of the chain reaction more hilarious than the last, and I, caught up in it all, clowned it up a bit.

"Not proper, forbidden," I said, imitating Azzizah and lifting the *thowb*—overdress—to cover my face, thereby revealing not only my ankles, but my knees and thighs and my underpants.

The Badawias fell over, begging, "Stop … before we die laughing …"

Our laughter subsided, only to burst out again. The Badawias, wiping away laughter-tears, told me my ineptitude reminded them of the first day they had worn veils. Even after decades, Azzizah remembered that day, how constricting her veils, how cumbersome, yet how proud she felt, how eagerly she had awaited that day.

"And now, are you not encumbered by your veils?" I ask the Badawias.

"No, only some days, when I am overtired and there is no respite from the desert heat," Azzizah replied, heaving a sigh to catch her breath in the wake of our laughter.

"We wear no veils when no men are around, and from now on we will wear no veil when you are with us," said Tammam.

"No, forbidden …," muttered Azzizah.

"Do you cover your face with your blanket-carpet when you sleep because you do not want me to see your face unveiled?" I ask Tammam.

"No," she replies. "I cover my face with my blanket-carpet because the torch-light by which you write to remember all night disturbs my sleep."

"You should have told me."

"I did."

"True, but it was strange to you, I thought, then you said nothing, so I thought you did not mind it. Why didn't you tell me it disturbed your sleep?"

"Because," Tammam responds, "I could sense-see that you were writing to remember your loved ones—to be with them in the depth of night when sleeplessness is a torment."

"Take the night as it comes, bit by bit," Azzizah counsels me as she readjusts her cone-shaped braid. "Rest assured, *yaa*-Nura, my sister, rest assured one of your clanswomen is mothering your child-boy or child-girl."

"The son I left at home is full grown," I tell the Badawias.

"Cannot be," says Azzizah.

"You cannot be more than five-seven years older than me," says Tammam.

"How old are you?" I ask her.

"Seventeen or maybe nineteen years old," Tammam says. "You look twenty-three or twenty-five years old."

"Shows you how deceiving looks are, for I am forty-two years old," I respond.

"If you are forty-two years old then I am as old as Friday," says Azzizah, cracking us all up.

"How old are you?" I ask Azzizah.

"*Allah aref*—God only knows. I lost count of the years," Azzizah replies. "To tell you the truth, I did not menstruate for so many years because I was pregnant, or because I was breast-feeding, or because I was grieving over the loss of yet another child, or because of the drought or because of the overwork, that I do not know when I stopped menstruating because I was past my child-bearing years. Nor do I know when my teeth started to fall out because I was growing old; *ya'ni*—that is—past my child-bearing years. For my teeth started to fall out when I was in my child-bearing years, after I birthed my fourth or fifth child, I think it was. Or maybe after my second or third, as most women."

"I heard people say that strangers have all sorts of potions to keep your teeth from falling," says Tammam. Would her beautiful smile also be toothless after three or four pregnancies? There is hardly any calcium in her diet.

"Would you like to keep your teeth from falling out?" I ask Tammam.

"No, *Wallah*," Tammam replies. "The more teeth you lose, the more teeth you gain."

"True," says Azzizah, tying her face-veil back on. Then, in explanation she says, "It is only when a woman is past her child-bearing years that she has a voice—a voice almost like a man elder. A voice with teeth, *ya'ni*, a voice taken into consideration in matters small and big, like for example: where to tie and untie—move your household—when and if your waterhole runs dry."

"And if she is seasoned wise, like Azzizah, elder men would come to her fire-circles, to take her voice into consideration," says Tammam. "For it is forbidden for a woman, even past her child-bearing years, to sit in the *maq'ad*."

"*Aywa*, that has been the order of things ever since anyone can remember," says Azzizah.

"I mean no offense to your stranger-tribesmen, but I doubt it was a Badu man or woman, youth or maiden, who beat you up," says Tammam, addressing me.

"It was neither a Badu nor a stranger but my own inexperience of desert travel by Jeep," I tell the Badawias. "It was mostly by foot that I had traversed deserts until I first entered your tents three or four months ago."

"*Wallah*, by foot, like us Badawias," Tammam says, amazed.

"Does not amaze me to hear it," Azzizah comments. "Even when you first entered our encampment and stayed for but a brief moment or two, I knew you were a Badawia at heart."

"At heart, perhaps, but not at *cous*—pussy," mutters Tammam. Our laughter embraces little Salimeh, who laughs, glad to see us laughing. Laughter tears still springing from her eyes, Tammam goes on to explain: "Not at *cous*—pussy, because stranger-women are not circumcised. Therefore, stranger-women are ruled by their *cous*, not by their minds, or even their hearts … really. That is what my brother told me he had heard from the coastal Badu, who make love to stranger-women day and night."

"But surely you were circumcised, *yaa*-Nura, like me and Tammam and my daughters and women the world over, when you were four-five years old, for I have seen you have been modest-proper, not brazen with Abu Salim," says Azzizah.

"How were you circumcised?" I ask Azzizah.

The senior Badawia picks up little Salimeh, lifts her dress up, spreads her tiny legs apart, and, pointing to the infant's clitoris, Azzizah replies, "This is the part that Tammam or I will circumcise when, *Inshallah*, little Salimeh will grow up to be four-five years old."

"You mean, one of you will remove this part, cut it off, to circumcise little Salimeh?!!?" Damn the social scientists who observe female mutilation "objectively." And if I am no better than the worst of the imperialists for imposing my sense of right and wrong on the local natives, fuck it.

"Surely that is not how you were circumcised," Tammam says in reply, wincing from the thought of it.

"Surely, that part of your *cous* was but scratched with a *shibriyya*—a dagger—sharp and clean," says Azzizah, "scratched to bleed off the drops of lust."

"You mean, whoever circumcises little Salimeh will not bleed out of her the drops of love, and of her enjoyment of love-making?" I ask the Badawias.

"*Ayb*—shame. *Wallah*, what questions you ask," Azzizah mutters. "Whoever be she who is to circumcise little Salimeh is bound to do it proper, so that little Salimeh's horizon will not be as narrow as the narrow circumference of a she-goat *cous* in heat."

"Still, even a scratch in this part must have been very painful. You were old enough to remember when you were circumcised, were you not?" I ask them.

"A boy's circumcision is much more painful. That is why it is done when the boy is grown enough to withstand pain like a man," says Azzizah.

"When is that?" I probe.

"When a boy is nine or ten years old, or eleven or twelve, or thirteen or fourteen, depending on the boy, and on when his clan can afford to invite everyone the desert over to the circumcision celebration," replies the senior Badawia.

"Is a girl's circumcision also celebrated like a boy's?" I ask.

"You mean, your girls' circumcisions are celebrated the same as your boys'?" Tammam asks in response.

"Cannot be," decrees Azzizah. "Surely your circumcision was veiled."

"Veiled?" I ask.

"Celebrated, but by only the women in your compound," Azzizah explains, bending over the infant daughter of her junior co-wife, and the child, giggling, wiggles away from Azzizah's kisses and kicks her ankles free of her grip. Off she crawled, sensing that the water Tammam and Azzizah were warming was not for tea, but for her bath. More playful than fearful, the child began to screech.

Then, in one well-practiced, well-coordinated move, Tammam grabbed the child and Azzizah dumped the water on her, and on Tammam as well. Both Badawias began to rub-rub-rub and tickle the child. Little Salimeh laughed and laughed, as they toweled her dry with their powerful hands.

Now, Tammam decides to take a bath. Quickly, before the bad winds get her, she takes off her *jingle-jangle* jewels and layers of shawls and dresses, steps on the sackcloth, and—

Splash! Azzizah empties a jerrican over Tammam, crouching on the wet sackcloth—naked now, no veils, and no pubic hair...

So, that's why they had stared at my naked body, and whispered under their veils, "*Yaa-salaam*—good heavens..."

Good heavens, indeed. As if it is not enough that they circumcise—bleed the lusty woman out of themselves—and cover their womanhood in constricting veils and shawls, and don't take a step out of their forbidden mountain-chains, but they also remove their pubic hair, as if, like Samson's, their hair is the source of an extraordinary prowess.

Azzizah towels Tammam with her hands, rubbing-massaging this beautiful girl whom Abu Salim obviously loves. How could Azzizah not feel jealous, not show a trace of jealousy, in her eyes, in her hands. Tradition hasn't prepared me for this: Azzizah's foremother and mine, good old Sarah, was portrayed as a jealous bitch who bugged the life out of her husband, Abraham, until he relented to her demand that he cast Haggar into the desert, without any water and food; not only Haggar, the mother of his son Ishmael, but his son as well, when he was not much older than little Salimeh, and his mother as young as Tammam.

Azzizah rolls away the wet sackcloth, squeezing it dry right on the tent floor. *Jingle-jangle*—Tammam puts on the dresses and veils she loaned me. Does she have only two sets of clothes? She wouldn't try on my clothes.

"It is forbidden," Azzizah explained. "Your stranger-clothes are unbefitting a woman."

"*Wallah*, I feel empowered by the qualities you invested in my clothes when you wore them," Tammam exclaims, addressing me. She pins up the tent flaps with twigs like needles, and the cross-breeze is heaven.

"I feel the qualities you invested in everything you gave me," I said to her and Azzizah.

"That is why it is prudent to accept gifts only from a person of good qualities," says Azzizah, helping Tammam comb, untangle, and braid her hair.

"Is it a custom of your clanswomen to remove their pubic hair?" I ask them. They burst out laughing, little Salimeh with them, like a monkey. I can't open my mouth now without cracking them up. "Why are you laughing?" They howl anew. "Is it not a custom? Is it for beauty or health reasons that you remove your pubic hair? Is it only Tammam who removes it? How? With a razor? Wax? Burnt sugar? With what?"

Laughter.

"Do you bath once every two or three days or weeks now because of the drought?" I get off the subject of pubic hair, and now only Tammam giggles.

"Only once every two-three weeks you bathe-purify, or once every two-three days?" she asks me.

"Every day, when water is plentiful," I reply.

"Every day you love your husband?" she asks, but good and surprised.

"Why? Do you bathe only before, and/or after you make love with your husband?" I ask, like an idiot, forgetting she shares her husband with Azzizah.

"*Yaa-salaam*—good heavens," Azzizah mutters, then spits. But Tammam laughs under her veils.

"Even goats don't love every day," Tammam says, then bends forward, spits, and grabs a handful of sand to bury her spit like her husband does. "We Badu love proper-modest."

"How is that?" I ask Tammam.

"*Yaa-salaam*—good heavens," Azzizah mutters, then spits. But Tammam laughs.

"Did your husband tell you to bathe-purify for him tonight? Or did you wives decide that tonight will be Tammam's turn to sleep with him?"

"*Haraam, ayb*—disgraceful, shameful talk. *Bas*—enough," Azzizah snaps.

Silence.

My sister, a stranger ...

"No sooner do you take off your veils, *yaa*-Badawias, *yaa*-my sisters, than you put them on again."

"It is our veils, not our women's talk or men's talk, that reveal the Badawia behind the veil," Azzizah says. "It is in our veils that you see the representation of the jewels and gems, the silver and the gold—of character, blood, bones, lineage, nobility, and other such blessed attributes, virtues, good fortune, and pepper a Badawia was blessed with—or wished she was blessed with—to spice up life, *Wallah*, to lift her up above the *kharah*—the shit, and the pubic hair."

"Is it because of that, that you deem it not proper to ask questions?" I couldn't resist.

"*La*—no. It is because it is not good to know too much," Tammam says. "That is what I had heard from my mother's mother, who heard it from her mother's mother, that knowing too much makes you too old too soon."

"It is not only that," says Azzizah. "Knowing is like rain—too little leaves you impoverished and parched like the worst of the drought. But too much, like the worst of the flash floods, destroys, uproots..."

16

Salimeh, hungry, trying to extract a nipple, a breast, out of her mother's layers and layers, cried and cried. But Tammam—God knows how she could sleep so deeply—was on her stomach, her breasts hidden. Gently, I woke her up.

"*Wallah*, I am glad you are here," she whispered, half-asleep, breast-feeding her infant.

Across the fire from me, she sleeps now, enveloped with her infant-daughter in the same carpet-blanket. Her husband, Abu Salim, went to sleep by Azzizah's fire-circle tonight also...

A sliver of a moon and a dusting of stars only sharpen the contrast of the darkness circling the light thrown by my flashlight tucked in the folds of my sleeping bag, rolled up into an improvised night table.

❧

I stayed behind in the mess hall so that the reservniks could get undressed without a woman disturbing their privacy.

"You still here?" the Turk says, as he walks in at the first coffee break of his night shift, wearing more layers than a Canadian in midwinter, yet shivering all the same. He warms his hands on a mug of coffee, curses the cold desert nights. "They're keeping the light on for you at the barracks."

"Wouldn't it be more convenient for everyone," I say, "if I stretch out here, on a bench, or in a sleeping bag?"

"No," says the Turk. "The nightshift takes our coffee breaks here. It would inconvenience you, and us as well."

I waited in the mess hall until the only sound was the generator, clanking electric power.

White mosquito nets were hanging over all the field beds in the barracks, except two. In one, at the far corner, Tal, half-asleep, laughs as he motions to me that mine is the field bed at the farthest corner from his. I tiptoe over to that bed and see it is less than arm's length away from the mosquito net that veils the dark Adonis.

Just then one of the reservniks turns the light off. But the security lights spill into the barracks through the windowpanes. So I take off my desert boots, and slide under the blanket with my clothes on. The barracks smells of feet, sweat, toothpaste, and cigarettes. One man coughs, another clears his throat, then a choir of snoring starts. A couple of lizards cling to the ceiling; a third shoots across and hides in the corner above the dark Adonis. He turns toward me and, through his mosquito net, he whispers, "You sleeping?"

"No," I whisper back.

"I can't sleep," he says. "My wife is taking driving lessons. It's not safe."

"Why, I heard it's safer than ever to learn to drive in The Land these days," I whisper. "I mean, you can't get a driver's license if you don't take driving lessons from a certified instructor."

"Exactly," whispers the dark Adonis. "The driving instructors are not safe. Men, all of them, sitting almost on top of my wife when they teach her to drive, bound to touch her here and there, and my wife... My wife is very beautiful and... very hot blooded. She needs a man. And I am stuck here..."

"Your wife probably talks about you when she takes her driving lessons, like you talk about her now," I tell him.

"Do you think so?" He lights himself a cigarette, then says, "Me, I am stuck here. But you... it wasn't your idea to roll up in a Jeep in this part of the desert, of all places, was it?"

"Yes, it was," I reply.

"But there is nothing to do here," he whispers, "No night clubs, like in Eilat, and no restaurants, no movies, no swimming pools. My wife, she also likes the desert. But I take her to the best hotel in Eilat, not in a Jeep—a Jeep has no shock absorbers; the ride is too bumpy for a woman, especially here, the wadis are full of potholes and dust. Me? I wouldn't roll in dust if I could help it. But to each his own madness, to each his own dream..."

"What's yours?"

"Madness or dream?" whispers the dark Adonis.

"Oh, *shaa*, already!!! Let a person catch some sleep," one of the reservniks snaps, then mutters a string of curses.

"Ah, *shaa*, yourself!!!" the dark Adonis snaps back. "What's your rush?! From sunrise to sunset you rush, rush, rush. Nighttime, you can't wait to catch some sleep—catch a dream, big, small. But day breaks, and the sun melts all the dreams . . ."

"A puddle of dreams you rush to dream," he whispered to me. "That's what I discovered when I caught such a hit in the Yom-Kippur War, laid me up for months. All the dreams melt in the sun, I could see then . . ."

The generator kept clanking, and the lizards darted hungrily or slept upside down on the ceiling. Trying to sleep in that barracks full of men, snoring, mumbling, grinding teeth, dreaming . . . took me back to the hiking days in the youth movement; we traveled light, carrying only one light blanket—none of us owned a sleeping bag—but no one ever suffered from the cold, for we all pooled our blankets and slept in a cluster, often boys and girls side by side, all adhering to the honor code—no fucking, no teasing, no necking, no matter how tempted we were. And if you had to take a piss, you couldn't without unraveling the whole cluster. I was so busy trying to lie still like dead wood in that cluster, I couldn't sleep . . . Here, too, I couldn't toss and turn without waking someone in that barracks. So I tiptoed out.

It's like the plague of darkness outside the periphery of the security beams. And bone-chilling the air, already heavy with dew. There is no one round the johns; no one in the mess hall. A pot of coffee simmers on the stove. I help myself to a mug, light a cigarette, leaf through a stale newspaper I find on the table. Then Tal shows up. "Anything new?" he whispers.

"What are you doing up so early? I didn't wake you up, did I?"

"No, I was up. I wondered where you disappeared to." He also helped himself to a mug full of coffee and joined me at the table.

"Did you catch any sleep?"

"Yes. You?"

"Couldn't, too much excitement in one day ... Must have pressed a few buttons, their commander ..."

"Yes. Amazing how he even sounds like my father. He's lucky so many under his command made it to this table. All too many of mine didn't make it across the Canal ..." Tal lit himself a cigarette. "And three got killed a year later, in a reconnaissance mission led by me. Two got killed a few months after that, in a mission led by the commander who got killed at Entebbe. You lose a commander like him, and so many who covered the distance with you, it makes you wonder why you were spared. Can't be for what I am doing now, especially these days ..."

"That's what my father used to say when I was little. He is the only one in his family, and his little Polish town, to come to The Land way back in the pioneering days; the only one who didn't perish in the death camps. 'Why? What for was I spared? Can't be for what I'm doing, especially these days.' My father was tormented by that question. High and low my father searched for an answer. Nearly drove him mad ..."

"Did he find it—the answer?"

"I don't know. I never asked him. And he never asked me how I could live in Canada, drop out of The Land and live outside— especially after what the outsiders did to us There, and the price that Arik paid here, to make sure it would never happen again. He loved Arik, my father. And Arik ... it was Arik's idea to name our son Levi, so that my father's family name would live on."

"You don't have brothers?"

"No, only one sister. She lives a good, normal life here in The Land with her husband and children, only fifteen minutes from my parents' place."

"Is that the answer, you think?"

"You're asking me, Tal? I don't even know why I'm going to the desert. Do you?"

"One of the guys who survived the Canal crossing withdrew to the desert soon after his regular service," he replied. "Another sleeps whenever anyone drops in. A third became a workaholic. The religious fanatic, Gingie, became more fanatical. And I... a drifter. I never thought I'd see myself do that. The old excuse that it's only a reaction to the regimented life I led in the kibbutz and the army doesn't hold, not after six months. You should have seen the list of books I was planning to read when I got out of the army, became a civilian... I didn't read one, not one book in six months. Facing death I didn't see myself painted in this non-color. Facing death... Do you know what motivates a man to run into fire?"

"What?"

"The strongest motivating force, according to studies, is not courage or conviction, but peer pressure. We live in a small country; if you run away from battle—even a winning battle—the whole country knows it the next day. And if someone in your unit was injured or killed in that battle, you will not feel comfortable showing your face in the street—even though chances are no one will take you to task. Nearly every man in the street has faced in himself the urge to run away from fire. Still, and don't take this personally," he hesitated, then said, "the only men I know who dropped out of The Land were deserters before they dropped out.

"'The Land is not worth dying for,' they said. If they weren't bull-shitting themselves, they had *beitzim*—balls—*muruah*. Not many men can resist peer pressure, no matter what their personal conviction. That's what I like to think my drifting is. I mean, on good days I wonder if this drifting is not a rebellion against peer pressure, and values, taboos, imposed on me... On bad days drifting is like exile—alien, strange. You're not in the right place wherever you are; home is nowhere, not even in the kibbutz..."

"Is that why you took leave of absence from your kibbutz?"

"No."

"Do you have children, Tal?"

"No, not yet."

"Are you married?"

"No."

"Was Gingie with you on the rescue mission in Entebbe?"

"No, Gingie was deep in Syria then, driving through a terrain much more difficult than the airstrip at Entebbe. How did you know I was in Entebbe?"

"I didn't. Gingie didn't cross the Canal with you in the Yom-Kippur War, did he? He was not yet nineteen years old then."

"Yes, he did. It was the first time that Gingie went through fire with me. After the war he drove my command Jeep. You know, he can barely reach the pedals, he's so short, but he's a wizard with a Jeep—one of the best drivers in the Unit. That's why he is called to serve reserve more often than most men. Keep it to yourself, Leora. Everything connected to the Unit is classified, top secret. But only a fanatic like Gingie can clam up totally about the Unit. He wouldn't open up a crack—except to your son, perhaps. 'My kid brother,' Gingie calls your son, you know. You raised them like brothers, Gingie told me."

"Only for five or six years, while Gingie's parents studied in Canada."

"How old was your son when Arik fell?"

"Six months old."

"And you?"

"Twenty years old."

"Young. You must have gone straight from high school to the wedding canopy..."

"No, from high school I went to boot camp. My unit received more punishments than training in boot camp. Our commander would bark, 'Right turn, left turn—march,' and I or another would pipe up 'What for?' Boot camp was child's play for us—even the punishments. It was nothing compared to the paramilitary training we went through in the youth movement. The commanders in boot camp were glad to be rid of us. But the border kibbutz that we were assigned to, loved us. They gave us all the shit work that you kibbutzniks hate."

"Your unit belonged to the Nahal Corps?"

"Yes. Many from our corps live in that border kibbutz we served in."

"But you ... you didn't like kibbutz life?"

"No. I loved it. But Arik was a city boy—a city man; he was eleven years older than me. And he didn't want to wait till I finished my army duty to get married. It's almost as if he had a premonition that he didn't have much longer. He fell eighteen months after we were married. He was only thirty-one years old."

"Not so bad."

"Yes. Arik is the oldest in his block there in the military cemetery, up on Mount Herzl. His grave stone is there ..."

"Many of my friends are there."

"Now Arik's son, my son, Levi, wants me to waive his exemption from high-risk front-line duty. What do you think, Tal? Should I give him a yes or a no?"

"That's for you to decide."

"I don't even know if I have the right to decide, let alone what to decide."

"Yes, life is not a prick, life is hard all the time."

I burst out laughing. "You mean, practice doesn't make it easier."

"No, as a matter of fact, the longer you 'practice', the more men you lose, the harder it becomes to make a snap decision that might cost yet another life. But someone has to do it, as they say, until peace reigns in this region, if ever ... That is, if you think The Land, the Nation, is worth defending at any cost ..."

"That The Land might fall is unthinkable to me—as unthinkable as losing my son, Arik's son, in defense of The Land. It sounds selfish, but ..."

"It's to your son's credit, his striving to follow where his father left off, don't you think?" Tal replied.

"Sure. I wouldn't lose any sleep over it if it were not for one little detail—that his father got killed when he was your age," I said.

"My father got killed in a senseless accident when he was my age," said Tal, as if that was a wasted death, not redeemed by some heroic cause, like Arik's.

"Do you think the Nation would have fallen had we not launched the Sinai War?"

"I think … I know for a fact," he replied, "that we are living in a state of war that's been draining us for more than thirty years. Someone has to serve high-risk duty in the front line; if your son is exempted, the burden falls heavier on the shoulders of his best friend, Gingie, and on me …"

The night shift pulled into the base, and the morning shift pulled out. Tal probably knew why I asked the Commander if I could speak with him in private, but made no effort to stop me this time.

"We're short of gasoline," I told the Commander.

"How short?"

"The gas tank is nearly empty and not a drop in the jerricans," I replied.

And without further questions, the Commander went and filled up the Jeep's gas tank and the two spare jerricans. "Army fuel won't stain your carburetor red first or second time," he said, "but make a habit of this and you're stuck with a red-stained carburetor for life."

Tal and I thanked him and all the reservniks at the checkpoint while the Moshavnik was doing the paperwork. A few men were leaning on the crossbar that blocked entrance to the gravel road, a few sat on the barrels, a few leaned on the gateposts. Their base, nestled among sandstone mountains, seemed much smaller in daylight, and much closer to the checkpoint. It was only a quarter past seven in the morning, but already the sun shrank the distance, diminished the depth, and radiated such heat that Marble Cake's face looked more like strawberry and chocolate swirl.

Fifteen or twenty minutes east of the checkpoint, a command car overtook our Jeep, and the Turk at the wheel told us, "You left without your passes, your identity card, your passport …" Then he handed us the papers—and a bag of oranges: "From the Moshavnik, from his orange groves."

"But he also has flower fields. Where are the flowers?" said Tal, grinning.

"Try drinking flowers when you run out of water," said the Turk. "Have a safe journey. Enjoy your vacation."

⚹

We had guests today! Not long after we bathed, neighboring Badawias came to visit. I thought at first I was seeing double-triple when all around me Badawias appeared, veiled and bejeweled, just like Azzizah and Tammam. They're sort of like soldiers in uniform, these mountain Badawias, if you can imagine soldiers breast-feeding infants, or lugging kids on this hip or that, with toddlers holding on to their *thowbs*—tribal dresses. And flies-flies-flies attacking a child's running nose, the milk drops at the corner of this and that infant's mouth, this child's urine drip, that infant's diarrhea, and then the rim of all the steaming tea glass...

"Where are your gifts for our neighboring clanswomen?" Tammam nudged me.

"*Yaa*... I didn't know I had to bring gifts for your clanswomen," I replied.

"You came here knowing nothing," Tammam whispered, as if it was the height of ignorance to separate the individual from the clan, the tribe.

Tammam and Azzizah cover up for my ignorance by presenting to their neighboring clanswomen all the beads and embroidery thread I had purchased at Dressmaker's Supply in Toronto and lugged six thousand miles from Canada to present to Azzizah and Tammam and little Salimeh.

As a creature from beyond this world, an alien from Mars, the neighboring Badawias regarded me. The more they appeared to be afraid of me, the more it delighted Tammam, even Azzizah. Those two treated me as if I were a trained monkey: "Take off your *djinn*-demon eyes. Put them on... Write-to-remember. Show them. Show them how you speak... Write..." The least I could do was to return hospitality, right? I showed each neighboring Badawia what her name, and her children's names, look like in writing-to-remember on pages torn from this sketchbook and handed as an extraordinary gift to each neighboring Badawia. Azzizah and Tammam were delighted.

This place will never be the same.

In return, the neighboring Badawias presented me with jewels—rings, bracelets, anklets, necklaces. I *jingle-jangle* like a Badawia now.

17

The darkness was not as dense and confining now that the fire-circle in front of Tammam's tent was just a heap of scorched ashes and a skyful of stars dropped low and bright enough to reveal that the commotion that woke me and raised the dust was stirred up by the saluki dogs, running circles around the compound as if a predator was lurking below this plateau. My fight-or-flight response kicked in. A moment later, Abu Salim hushed the salukis, as if they were just imagining things. Without protest they ran to him in Azzizah's tent—pitched thirty meters, give or take, from my carpet-blanket. A few feet from me, Tammam sat still like a rock. Then she heaved a sigh, and whispered to herself, "Patience is better than thinking, if only you could manage it, oh self."

"*Esh hassal*—what's going on, Tammam?" I whispered. The tension emanating from her, and the loneliness, knotted my thighs, my gut. Her jewels *jingle-jangled* as she turned toward me and the worry in her eyes lifted. She was glad, it seemed, to have a person other than herself to talk with, think with—wait with—for the camel-rider.

Tammam had heard the camel-rider well before Abu Salim hushed the salukis. She knew then that the approaching camel-rider was the first son born to Abu Salim's sister, and that he had been riding a distance of seven-eight hours if his point of departure was anywhere near his compound; and that the salukis were stupid dogs not to have remembered the camel-rider; and that all too soon we were bound to find out what had brought him here at this hour of the night.

All that information the girl-wife imparted to me as might a woman who feared the arrival of news that her husband, brother, or son had fallen on the battlefield.

I had not picked up a sign that a camel-rider was out there, except for the commotion of the salukis. But so silent are the strides of a Badu riding a camel, most strangers can't hear them until the camel and its rider materialize in front of them—out of nowhere, it seems—startling the hell out of you. Only a Badu can hear the silent strides of a border-crosser's camel ten-fifteen minutes away. I found it an admirable ability in the Badu—until I waited tonight with Tammam.

The minutes stretched long; all I could hear was her heart beating—an echo of mine on the night I had waited for Arik, only to be told he'd never return.

Abu Salim's white *kaffiyye*, glowing in the dark by Azzizah's tent, signaled to the camel-rider to dismount there. Tammam, careful not to *jingle-jangle* her jewels, froze to a rock again as she strained to hear the exchange of whispers coming from Azzizah's tent.

"Why don't you walk over to Azzizah's tent if you want to hear what they are saying?" I asked her.

"I can hear from here what they are saying," she whispered back.

My ears caught only the secretive, conspiring sound of whispering and the long silences between that came from Azzizah's tent. After each silent pause ended, Tammam would invariably mutter, "*Yaa*-Allah . . . *yaa*-Allah," as if she couldn't believe her ears.

The exchange of whispering ended almost as soon as it began. And as the camel-rider left the compound Tammam sighed in relief. On second thought, it seemed, her eyes searched mine, as though seeking explanation, clarification.

"Did you not hear what brought the camel-rider to this compound at this hour?" I whispered to her.

"I did, but surely it cannot be that a bride is what had brought him here at this hour."

"A bride?" I asked her.

Silence. Tammam uttered not another word until it sounded like Abu Salim and Azzizah had fallen back to sleep. Then: "A bride that Abu Salim is wanting to purchase."

"You mean Abu Salim wants a third wife?"

"No," replied Tammam. "The whole desert laughs at a man who marries many wives. Abu Salim would divorce me or Azzizah before he married another wife. All he would have to do is to say 'I divorce thee' three times. My brother would come to fetch me, and I would return with him to my father's tents. But I am sure that Abu Salim would not divorce me. And I am even more certain that Azzizah does not want to be divorced from Abu Salim . . .

"Yet tonight, in her tent, I heard Azzizah whispering-urging Abu Salim to purchase the bride that Azzizah called 'She-camel,' which is also what Abu Salim and his nephew called her. For that is how we Badu talk of a bride when we talk of her purchase price."

"And what do you Badu call a she-camel when you mean a she-camel?"

"*Wallah*—we Badu have a hundred words for a she-camel, or maybe only fifty or sixty words."

"But do you Badu never call a she-camel a 'she-camel'?"

"Yes. Sometimes."

"So how do you know that Azzizah, Abu Salim, and his nephew were not talking-whispering about the purchase of a camel and not a bride?"

"Maybe they were . . . I will tell you what I heard them whisper and what I think of what they whispered, then you tell me if they were talking-whispering about the purchase of a bride or a she-camel," replied Tammam.

The girl-wife commenced filling me in, adopting the ancient sing-song lilt of the storyteller. "The owner of the she-camel does not wish to part from the she-camel, else he would not demand for her a purchase-price so high that the whole desert would laugh at the Badu who pays it. That was the first thing Abu Salim's nephew said-whispered. But surely it was not the purchase of a she-camel or bride that brought him here at this hour, I thought to myself. Yet the next thing I heard was the whisper of Abu Salim inquiring of his nephew, 'What is the purchase-price her owner demands I pay for his she-camel'?

"'Her owner demands you pay for his she-camel water rights to all your water sources, or passage rights to all your border-crossing routes,' replied Abu Salim's nephew.

"'And now I heard Abu Salim thinking it over, thinking and thinking to himself, and then to his nephew Abu Salim said-whispered, 'If that is the purchase-price her owner demands for his she-camel, he does not wish to part from her.'

"Surely they are talking of a she-camel, meaning 'bride', for no father wants to part from his daughter, I thought to myself. Yet, I clearly heard Azzizah urging Abu Salim to purchase the she-camel. So now I thought to myself, surely they are talking-whispering about a she-camel—meaning 'she-camel', not bride. For Azzizah would never urge Abu Salim to purchase another wife, I am certain of that.

"But next I heard Abu Salim say, 'The she-camel is blemished.' And now I was certain they were talking of a she-camel, meaning 'bride'. For I am certain Abu Salim would not purchase a blemished she-camel, no matter how cheap or dear her purchase-price. But in his eyes all women are blemished."

"Blemished—how? What is their blemish?" I whispered-asked Tammam.

"*Allah aref*—God knows: being women, not men, perhaps," replied Tammam. "Blemished she is, I clearly heard that. And then I heard Abu Salim say-whisper to his nephew, 'Tell the owner of the she-camel that I agree to purchase her at his asking price, and that after I consult with the elders of my clan I shall inform him, *Inshallah*, if her purchase-price be water rights or border-crossing routes.'

"Thereupon his nephew departed. But surely it cannot be that what has brought him here at this hour and has sent him off at this hour, is but a purchase of a bride, let alone a she-camel, blemished."

"Can you not ask Abu Salim or Azzizah, or both, to clarify it for you?"

"Of course, I can. But they are seasoned wiser than me. And whenever they deem it the time to clarify it for me, they will do so. Besides, it is not prudent to show you lack information, for information is power."

"Why is it not prudent to show you lack power?"

"Because you are treated like *kharah*—shit—if you lack power," replied Tammam. "Patience is better than thinking. Tomorrow, *Inshallah*, or day after tomorrow, I will know what is this blemished camel that Abu Salim wants to purchase."

"Would your kinsfolk be angry with Abu Salim if he were to divorce you so that he could marry this blemished bride?"

"No, there is no shame in divorce. And besides, Abu Salim is not divorcing me, I am sure of that. For Abu Salim thinks I am pregnant and Abu Salim is not a man who would divorce a pregnant wife."

"*Wallah, yaa*-Tammam, no one would know you are pregnant from looking at you."

"*Aywa*—yes. I neither look nor feel pregnant. But Azzizah told me and Abu Salim that she has no doubt I am pregnant. And Azzizah is a *darwisha* who can see in the alum crystal if a woman is pregnant or not. So maybe in this, my second pregnancy, it was fated that I be of the Badawias who neither look nor feel they are pregnant for the first three-four months. Or maybe my womb is not swelling, nor stirring with a child, because I am of the Badawias who neither menstruate nor conceive for as long as they breast-feed their infants. Or maybe the drought dried up my menstruation and my womb is barren this year. That happened this year, not only to the goats, but to many Badawias. The whole desert knows it. Still, you must swear—*swear*—you will not reveal to a soul that I doubt I am pregnant."

"I swear."

"Once you swear, you die if you do not do as you have sworn you will do," Tammam warned, her eyes torn wide by fear. Is Tammam afraid she might die, like her mother, the day she gives birth to her second child? Is that why Tammam urges her infant daughter to enjoy her mother's love, as if the child won't have too many days to enjoy it? Each moment of such love is more precious than anyone but an orphan like Tammam could appreciate. You would think her husband would be heartbroken to hear Tammam tell her infant daughter, "Take what is left of the rest of my life and enjoy it..." Why doesn't he empower his girl-wife with the information that more Sinai Badawias then ever these days are checking into the maternity wards of the Israeli hospital in Eilat, only a couple of days' travel from here by Jeep?

"Was Azzizah with you when you birthed little Salimeh?"

"Yes. If I am pregnant now, Azzizah will also be with me, *Inshallah*, when I birth my second child. But if I am not pregnant now..." Tammam heaved a sigh.

"Tomorrow, *Inshallah*, or day after tomorrow, surely it will be made clear to me why Abu Salim offered to pay such a high price—water rights or rights of passageways, *yaa-Rabb*—for a blemished camel or a blemished bride."

"You sigh like a woman tired out by her fears," I told her.

"*Laaa*—no—I am not afraid of my not knowing," said Tammam. "I am afraid only for—and of—my brother. Every Badawia is afraid of her brother."

"Of her own brother?"

"Yes."

"Why?"

"Because a brother is duty-bound to kill a sister if she strays or even if it is only rumored that she has made love with a man not her husband," replied Tammam.

"Her brother and not her husband is duty-bound to kill her for that?"

"*Aywa*—yes," said Tammam. "Your husband can divorce you for that. But if your husband kills you, your brother is duty-bound to avenge your blood, no matter how far you strayed. That is why it is said that the worst fate to befall a man is to have a sister who is rumored to have strayed, for no one loves you more than your brother—except your mother and your father. Your father also is duty-bound to kill you if people say you made love to a man not your husband. But my brother would never let my father kill me, for my brother loves my father and knows it would kill my father to kill me.

"O, take what is left of the rest of my life and enjoy it," Tammam whispers to little Salimeh, as she hugs and rocks the girl-child, sleeping cradled in her arms. "Day by day your uncle, my brother, is cutting his distance short on his way to visit us. Any day, any day, my brother will be here, *Inshallah*. Maybe then I will know why Azzizah urged Abu Salim to purchase a blemished she-camel or bride, no matter how high the purchase-price."

"Does it not kill your love for your brother, this Badu law?" I asked.

"No," Tammam replied, her eyes tearful. "I love this brother of mine. For many months I have longed to see him. My mother is his mother, too. She had only birthed him and me. And when she died birthing me, he was old enough to remember her, so, he told me everything about her. And when I was little and my father's wives mistreated me, he was the one who protected me. But he cannot protect a sister who is rumored to have strayed, no matter how much he loves her, not even if he is as powerful-respected as Abu Salim. For only blood can clear your blood-kin of the dishonor you bring upon them when you stray."

"And what if a Badu man strays, makes love to a woman other than his wife?"

"He, like a woman who strays, is bound to be killed by his brother, his father, or his blood-kin," replied Tammam, "for he dishonors his clan just the same, even if he is only rumored to have strayed."

"You mean to tell me that all a person has to do to dishonor your blood-kin is to start a rumor that you strayed?"

"*Aywa*—yes," said Tammam. "But the punishment for starting such a rumor, or for spreading it, is death. So *dir balak*—watch out—Nura. Spread malicious rumors about me, my blood-kin, or Abu Salim's, and your blood will surely be exposed for five generations. *Dir balak, Wallah*, I have told you before and I tell you again, for five generations your blood will be exposed if you reveal to anyone anything you see, sense, or hear in our tents, without permission from Abu Salim, his son, or his son's son."

"Why is it forbidden to reveal anything I hear, see, or sense here?" I asked Tammam. Blunter than Azzizah, she would give me a straight answer, I thought.

Silence.

"Why did you, Azzizah, and Abu Salim invite me to visit-stay with you?"

"Because you came here knowing nothing," Tammam replied. I cannot tell if she is joking.

"Now I allow you to write to remember by the light of your torch. It will not disturb me." Tammam advised me, as she was about to butt out her cigarette, almost as if she was afraid now of the dark, of the uncertainty and confusion that trailed the camel-rider, of the baffling whispers. "Patience is better than thinking…," she mutters.

If *she* can't understand what's going on here, how could I?… But, *Wallah*, she is right, I came here knowing nothing, neither the old wilderness, nor the new…

⚘

It was after nightfall when Tal and I reached Yamit. The headlights flooded the deserted beach, highlighting the lifeguard station, boathouse, showers, washrooms, and restaurant—all locked and shuttered. To the east, a band of powerful security lights blazed atop poles supporting the security fence around Yamit, turning the horizon into a tableau of war, of siege. To the south lay Gaza, and the dense and squalid misery of the worst of the Palestinian refugee camps in The Land. North, at the very edge of the high beams, was a tall meshed fence, squared off, as if to detain prisoners, and clamped to it at eye level, a sign in Hebrew and English said: No camping allowed on the beach outside this fenced area. That explained why the beach was deserted.

"Strange restriction. I've never seen one like that in The Land. Is it for security?" I asked Tal, as we checked the fenced-in area.

"I doubt it," he replied. "More likely, the maintenance crew didn't want anyone to camp on their beach. It would feel like being in a concentration camp to set up in this fenced-in area."

We decided to camp elsewhere and climbed back into the Jeep, and then… I can't remember how it happened. I only remember how I wept when Tal embraced me, drawing me close to him, and sliding his arm under my braid like you, my Arik, used to. And I, dry-eyed for years, sobbed on his chest … I tried to pull away, embarrassed by my outburst and need, but he held me closer, whispering, "It's all right … All right …" The more he accepted me, the more I convulsed with tears, a wellspring of pain buried for decades—of loss, exile, shame …

"It's all right … All right," he kept whispering, caressing, embracing. Then, suddenly, a blinding light, like a locomotive, sped through the darkness straight for us. Was someone up there determined to punish us for transgressing the sixth commandment with an embrace?

"It's all right … all right … It's only the searchlight on a border-patrol command-car," said Tal, brushing a tear from my face.

The search-beam flooded the Jeep. Two shadows flung open Tal's door, snapping, "What are you doing here? Didn't you see the sign? Can't you read? You don't have eyes? Let's see your ID, civilian and military."

"What's going on?" Tal asked the two men—one hefty, one slight, the Laurel and Hardy of the border-patrol.

"You can't park here after sundown, can't camp here overnight—only in the fenced-in areas," said the hefty one.

"Why only in that fenced-in area, like prisoners?" I asked.

"For security reasons."

"Don't explain anything, you don't know who they are …," the slight one, corporal stripes on his sleeve, ordered the other. Turning to us, he demanded, "ID, civilian, military." And when I handed him my Israeli passport, he raised his voice. "Give me your ID, not your passport."

"I have no ID," I told him, and Tal chuckled as if I was spouting metaphors. But the corporal looked like he thought I was mocking him. There was no comedy here. I explained to him that my ID card was taken from me when I dropped out of The Land, or when I got my Canadian passport. "Check my Israeli passport and you'll find my ID number."

"Don't tell me what to do!" He walked off to the blinding darkness, flicked on his flashlight, and checked our papers. "Come, look at who we have here," he called out to the rookie; just loud enough for us to hear, he continued: "You won't see many *military IDs* like this one. See here, in this box under rank, it says, 'Major.' And under name of the unit it says, 'Combat,' but no name. And look, in this box under 'Corps,' it says nothing. See? It's blank, blank, blank. That means we're not good enough to know we got us a hot-shot major in the Unit. You know, those sons of whores who walk around as if no one has a prick as big as theirs..."

"Let's have our papers back," Tal said, and I'm sure they heard the patronizing voice of those sons of whores.

"But look at how low this major stoops," the corporal said to the rookie, derision, hatred in his voice. "Look at his birthdate. Now look at hers..."

"*Yuuuh*, she's as old as my mother," said the rookie.

"He's eleven years younger than her. No one but a working cock would be caught with a woman eleven years older than him. He must be working for her. You know what the likes of him are called?" the corporal asked.

"No, what?"

"Gigolo." The corporal flicks off his flashlight. "Gigolo, a male whore ... Sells his cock for her Canadian dollars, and a visa to Canada, and the Jeep. Bet you her money paid for this Jeep..."

"The hatred at the borders has poisoned our patrolmen," Tal said after they finally returned our papers and we drove away. There was bitterness in his voice.

"Well, at least they didn't say, 'I wouldn't touch her even if you paid me.'" I tried to make light of it. "You know, Arik was eleven years older than me, and Dave is twelve years older. People here pressed Arik not to marry me. I was too young for him, they said, and too young is trouble. But that's nothing compared with the shit people dump on my colleague in Canada, married to a man ten years younger than her."

"Here … it's taboo," Tal said, hesitating, as if he only now realized what a line he crossed to embrace me.

"I had a thing about our war widows," he said quietly, as we headed to the town Yamit—the town inspired by the model of Arik's dream town.

"I don't know a man in The Land who doesn't have a thing about 'our war widows,'" I said.

"Neither do I …" He told me how he used to see the war widows in his home kibbutz, "like memorial candles, flickering constant, silent." The only war widows he had known before he was drafted were not widows like his mother; there was something untouchable about them, he felt, something that made him tremble. He didn't know what it was. Until one day, when he was not yet nineteen and still in training, he received a few hours' furlough and decided to explore the city. He got off the bus to stretch his legs for a bit when a boy, five or six years old, ran over to him, grabbed his hand, and said, "I knew I'd find you. Come. What are you waiting for? Mother is waiting." Thinking the kid had done something he shouldn't and had grabbed a soldier to protect him from his mother's punishment, Tal went along. The kid dragged him to the mother's flat, shoved him in front of her, and said, "Look. I found a father. So enough already, stop crying already." His mother apologized, then explained that her husband had fallen in the war of attrition; her son, only four years old then, feels the loss now, when he sees his friends doing those things that sons do with fathers. He wants to see his father just once, he says, just for a moment. She showed him every photo she had of his father, but the boy said that the man in the photos was not his father. He pictured someone big, much bigger than him, not smaller, like in the photos. And besides, the kid didn't want a paper father; he wanted a father who plays soccer with his son, who carries his son on his back and swims with him far out into the sea, where the lifeguard allows only boys with fathers to swim … The boy knows that fathers doing army duty wear a soldier's uniform. So, every week, he brings home a soldier or two.

He'll grow out of this phase soon, she said, looking like no memorial candle.

"I felt like moving in with them, like adopting that kid and his mother," said Tal. "Then, it dawned on me that all she needed was another one. All of a sudden it hit me that tomorrow, next week, next month, I could go, just like her husband. War widows began looking like the shadow of the Angel," Tal said. He stayed away from them; he understood now why they made him tremble—at least, he thought he did, until he came back from his fifth or sixth mission, one in which he had lost a friend.

"A friend who had joined the Unit after his regular service. He was a few years older than the others—had a wife already, and a couple of children. And I was ... I was twenty years old. I saw his widow, and I remembered every word her husband had told me about her. All the dreams her husband had dreamed for her, himself, and their children. I knew her loss better than most people, I thought. I had gone through a year and a half of training with her husband, had gone through fire with him, fought side by side with him. In some ways, I knew her husband better than she did, and missed him just as much, if not more. But I also remembered the bullet that hit her husband whistling past me. And how happy I felt that it didn't have my name on it ..."

When we embraced each other, Tal and I embraced the man within the war-hero, the woman within the war widow.

In Yamit he insisted on picking up the tab for coffee, as if my paying for a cup would make him a gigolo. He and I were the café's only customers. The owner was about to close it when we walked in.

"You couldn't find a seat in this place before this town of ours, like a sacrificial lamb, was put on the table of the peace-talks with Egypt," the owner of the café said, seating himself at our table. He began to pour his heart out—just like that, before he knew our names. "You know, sometimes, when this place is empty, like now, I tell myself, it's just a bad dream, a nightmare. As soon as I wake up, I'll find that, just like before we of Yamit were offered up like a sacrificial lamb, all us Israelis are one big family. You know, in the last war I battled with the Golani, and not once did it occur to me, I swear to you, that I was risking my butt for the people of Galilee or the people of the Jordan valley, their towns, *kibbutzim, moshavim.* To me they were family. The last thing I expected from this family is that they would even think of sacrificing everything I laid my life on the line for, everything my buddies lived and died for, every-thing my wife and I dreamed of, worked for, mortgaged for. It can break you when it happens. What gets you is the crumbling of that trust in the family—that gets you, much more than the dream of a home and garden in a dream of a place. Such friction in the family might ignite a civil war—a brothers' war. And here, in Yamit, in almost every home, husbands and wives are fighting day and night."

You wouldn't have suspected any of it, sitting in that café, sip-ping another cappuccino, this one on the house. Radiant light and soft music spilled out of open windows; whiffs of honeysuckle, rose, jasmine, and sea salt drifted on the breeze; a couple of lovers, walking by hand in hand, wished us "good evening."

"That couple are among the few who are of the same mind. Both believe we'll never give up Yamit," said the owner. "Most oth-ers can't agree: One is willing to trade Yamit for a promise of peace; the other is not. In one house, one says, 'I put everything I have into this place. They'll have to kill me before they move me out of here.' But the other says, 'No one will ever pay us more money for our house and garden than the Nation will . . . it's guilt and shame compensation, but what the hell, we'd be able to retire on it . . .' 'Stop fighting,' the children cry. They don't want to move away from their friends, school, teacher.

"And at the same time, outside your window, Arab men from Gaza, Al-Arish, or Rafah are already bickering over your house. 'I was first to claim this house . . .'; 'No, it was I, by *Allah*, it was I . .'; 'No, it was I . . .', says a third, pulling a weed out of your lawn as if your garden was already his.

"My wife wanted to shoot him. 'I'd rather destroy this house, this whole town, than give it to these Arabs,' she says. It drives her crazy the situation. She went to stay with her parents, took the children with her. I never thought it would happen to me, to my children.

"And already the camping grounds at the *dikliya*—the palm grove are closed. The only place you can camp overnight here these days is on the beach, in those fenced-in areas." With that, the owner of the café invited us to stay overnight in his house. And only now did he introduce himself: "I'm Amos."

Amos thought that Tal was my husband, not my gigolo.

I could almost touch Arik's presence in Yamit. Just like in Arik's model, the public space was on the first floor of Amos's house. No wall separated the living room from the kitchen and dining area; and the private space was upstairs. But Arik had tremendous respect for the desert sun and winds; his windows were narrow slits, almost like those slits in Badu tents which afford a gentle cross-breeze.

"Be they narrow or wide, the fine desert dust blows even through the concrete blocks, you'd swear," said Amos. "During a sandstorm, no matter how tight you seal windows, doors, shutters, and concrete walls, the floors and every surface in the house are covered with sand." He was watering the tropical jungle that grew on the window ledge in his son's bedroom. (That's where Tal slept; I had his daughter's bedroom.) His separation from his wife and children was temporary, Amos believed, or so it seemed. The tricycles were still parked at the entrance, and in the master bedroom, his wife and children looked very happy in the photos on the dresser. The scarred plaster behind the headboard of their double bed was a testament to the passion of their love-making—or to how shoddy the plaster work was.

The morning revealed Yamit . . . Oh, how Arik would have loved to see it, flaws and all. Amos's house butted up against the next house. And some houses were semi-detached—compromised, like in Arik's model, to cut building costs. Arik had railed against such compromises. He would have probably called the gray stucco an eyesore, and been grateful that it was nearly hidden by the network of climbers. The bougainvillea was old enough to reach to the second floor; the climbing roses framed the kitchen windows; the honeysuckle shaded the terraces in the backyard; and the jasmine hedge screened off the front courtyards. Only the fig trees and the grapevines gave evidence of Yamit's newness and how determined her inhabitants were to be rooted to her shifting sands. A tangle of roots was probably fighting for room under the flowerbeds and the sprawling lawns, which absorbed the harsh sun and reflected a gentle green light onto the houses. Arik would have liked the way the houses curved on both sides of the paths, which led to the public square. The wide square he would have envied—multileveled, and with palm trees, benches, a playground equipped with all the toys, and a bubbling fountain that worked—and a huge memorial for all who fell in battle here. East of the square, across a wooded area, stood the school and the library. And, bordering the square to the southwest, was a huge L-shaped structure that housed a supermarket, department store, movie house, offices, bicycle repair shop, beauty salon and barbershop, kiosk, bakery, and Amos's café, with a bus stop at the back. The communal parking lots, and the only road that allowed traffic, were situated on the periphery of the town, only a few meters inside the security fence that bound Yamit. Outside the fence, to the west, sand dunes spilled down to the sea, and palms shaded the sun-bleached beach, stretching wide and long as far as the eye could see. Had it not been for the skeleton of an apartment building, "abandoned by the builders ever since the peace talks had begun," Amos said, you could easily forget, especially when the paths came to life with schoolchildren, that you were strolling through a town that might be evacuated if and when she is traded to Egypt for a promise of peace—"or most probably destroyed," Amos said.

"But nothing will ever be the same again in The Land, even if we keep Yamit. It changed everything, the willingness of so many to sacrifice Yamit. Like in America, it's each man for himself, not one big family any more. Even real peace with Egypt would be no consolation to me for losing that, never mind all the rest I stand to lose …" Amos couldn't see the emptiness in his life, the emptiness in his soul, ever being filled. "To me, loss is loss. The soul is no perennial rose bush, where you prune a branch and another grows to bear more blossoms," he said. The thought of such renewal is almost an insult to everything he holds dear, he said. "I can see no phoenix rising from the ruins of Yamit, can you?" he asked Tal.

"Peace with a neighbor like Egypt is no phoenix to sneeze at," Tal replied. "I wouldn't hesitate to trade Yamit for that, had the mainstay for our defense, for our survival here—our secret weapon, you could say—not been to hold on to a settlement at all costs."

Tal sounded like my father then. It'd been years since I'd seen my father so torn; he argued with himself, like he used to argue with God: "How can we even think of giving Yamit to Egypt, even if Egypt were to keep her word, wage no more war against us?" he boomed one day. The more hard-of-hearing he gets, the louder his voice is. "I say this, not because Yamit is like Arik's dream town and mine, but because Yamit is a Jewish settlement. How can we give away a Jewish settlement when for more than thirty years we have ordered our boys to hold a settlement of ours at all cost … How many boys who followed this order are buried right next to my son-in-law Arik?

"Is it time for a change of values, even basic values? Am I being just an old man fearing that such change will kill a good thing and give birth to a monster? Or is the opposite true? Will this change give birth to a good thing and kill the monster? Is it against what we Jews hold to be most sacred—life—to order our boys to hold a settlement at all cost, to the last man? Is a settlement just real estate? Overnight you raise, overnight you trade off? Is even Jerusalem just real estate?

"Is life not more sacred than Jerusalem? Does life not come before and above Jerusalem? Would my grandson, Levi, end up like his father, Arik, if we give Yamit to Egypt, or will he be spared?"

18

Where do all the flies disappear to after nightfall? Wherever, good riddance.

I dozed on and off all day. My neck is covered by welts, like black-fly bites up in Algonquin, Canada, at the stinging hot and itchy stage, and my eyes—swollen, almost glued shut and sore as hell, especially when the wind shifts fire smoke to my direction. Doesn't help to wear my *djinn*-demon eyes, but I keep them on. The Badawias are all too worried as it is.

"It is a good sign that she writes-to-remember now," the senior wife mutters to Tammam, talking as if I were not here, by the fire-circle at Azzizah's *maharama*—the place of women. "It means she is not as ill now as when she felt too ill to write-to-remember." Not exactly, but what a switch from my first day here when Azzizah cautioned Tammam to stay away from the writing, as if she thought it might be some instrument of the devil.

What worries them much more is that their husband, Abu Salim, hasn't returned from wherever he went this morning "to do more important things than work." And he hasn't dispatched anyone to explain his tardiness. Explanation, information, is power, *Wallah*.

The two wives had expected Abu Salim to show up, as he had done since I've been here, soon after the neighboring kids returned with the goat herds at sundown. But night fell and the desert vastness contracted to a circle of firelight that expands and shrinks, expands and shrinks, at the whim of the fire tongues, and still no sign of Abu Salim. Tammam's stomach and Azzizah's rumbled hungry, before mine for once, and they decided we would eat supper without him. Just rice, plain and dry; they skipped the *samn*, thank God, and there was no dip of fried onions and tomato paste, and no pita, lazy or regular.

Aside from this variance, Abu Salim's wives continue to obey his dictates and wishes and to anticipate his likes and dislikes. But until my strange ailment started to worry them, the atmosphere was not as tense; there was even a sense of liberation in the compound. I was wearing a clean layer of clothes. It felt good not to itch and scratch, and I hated the thought of sleeping in lice-infested carpet-blankets, as Abu Salim had told-ordered me to do. So I unrolled and unzipped my sleeping bag and said to the Badawias, "With your permission, I'll be sleeping in my own sleeping sack tonight."

They giggled under their veils and their eyes popped wide with amazement and fright, as if it was wonderful that I would ask the permission of women, and that I would want to sleep in such a strange contraption, but alarming that a woman, even a stranger-woman, would even think of doing what she wants and not what she is told to do.

"Abu Salim will be very angry with you, and with us, if you disobey his wishes," said Azzizah. And Tammam added, "He will punish us if we permit you to disobey him."

"How would he punish you?" I asked them, like an idiot. It's so hard to grasp, even here, where it's staring you in the face, that a tribe, a way of life that has endured for centuries, would put their women-mothers-daughters-sisters-wives at the mercy of any and all male relatives, even for such basic staples as flour and rice. Abu Salim comes and goes, but his wives stay put. Imsallam Suleman Abu Salim has a say, a voice; his wives, a whisper, barely audible. He carries money, not on veils, for decoration, like his wives, but in his pocket, for purchasing power.

"I think he went to visit his brother or sister," said Azzizah. "He will get back in but two-three days, *Inshallah*."

"Maybe he went to meet my brother, *yaa-Rabb*, take what is left of the rest of my life and enjoy it, *yaa*-my little Salimeh." Tammam yawned and yawned like when anxiety-fear depletes your oxygen reserves.

"Are you afraid of Abu Salim?" I ask her.

"No," Tammam replies.

"You?" I ask her senior co-wife.

"*Wallah*, I am, for I love him," replied Azzizah.

In no apparent way did Tammam betray to her senior co-wife that she had overheard the exchange of whispers that came from Azzizah's tent.

"Did Abu Salim go to fetch this blemished camel or blemished bride?" I asked Tammam when we were alone at the ditch. She looked at me as if she didn't know what I was talking about, as if she had wiped it from her mind, and it was dormant now in the realm of denial.

I can't continue to stay here much longer. I'm not feeling well.

BBBBBBOOOOOOOOOMMMM!!!!!! A jet breaks the sound barrier. And under that fractured sky, Tammam and Azzizah, weaving on a loom pegged to the ground like in Methuselah's days, wait for their husband, like Penelope did. Time and time again they decide that they'll wait so long and no longer. Now they decide that if Abu Salim is not back in the compound by the time the sun clears the shade from their loom, and if my stranger's remedies fail to cure the ailment that plagues me by then, Azzizah will consult the alum crystal to foretell a remedy to heal my ailment.

Azzizah has been weaving a camel-saddle for her son Salim nearly every day for months and months. Or so the Badawia told me. Long wool threads in the colors of her desert mountains, stretched tight in long neat rows, are secured at each end to spikes she hammered into the ground, weeks, perhaps months, ago. Not one spike has budged, so hard is the ground of this plateau. Tammam, helping her today, returns the runner, bulging with threads of many colors, back to Azzizah's side of the loom. Every move they make is accompanied by the *jingle-jangle* of their jewels and veils. Crouching close to the ground, they weave a colorful geometric pattern, like an enlarged version of the beaded necklace gift of trust that Azzizah presented to me the first day I stayed here. Both the miniature and enlarged versions look like the design of Agam. His tapestries, paintings, and prints were probably inspired by a camel-saddle he saw belonging to one of Azzizah's clansmen. "From generation to generation we Badawias remember how to weave this pattern for our clansmen's camel saddles," Azzizah told me. Back-breaking work, this weaving like their great-great-grandmothers; even Tammam can't crouch for very long without taking a break to stretch her legs and rub her back ... and keep her infant-daughter a safe distance from me.

"Blood is blood—*a-daam daam*," Azzizah mutters, her bloodshot eyes addressing me, worried I'll die on her. "We can be better sisters than blood-sisters, but if it was fated that you breathe your last here in our compound, your clan, sure to lay the blame for that on my clan, is bound to attack my clan to avenge your blood, for *a-daam daam*—blood is blood—*yaa-Rabb*, and such a strange ailment as yours never, never did I ever see in all the many years that I have been a *darwisha*—a medicine woman. Nor did I ever hear of such a strange ailment as yours, even from my mother, who was a *darwisha*, daughter of a *darwish*, son of a *darwisha*."

And really, picture a face with eyes almost swollen shut like Mr. Magoo's, and lips protruding almost as far and wide as Donald Duck's. With the sunlight and fire smoke that is everywhere, the only relief came in sleep. But as soon as I would doze off, Tammam would wake me up to see if I was dead or alive. A few hours ago— was it a few days ago?—the swelling spread from my neck, eyes and lips to my jaw. Thought I'd caught the mumps; then the swelling shifted to my cheek, my forehead. Now my face looks distorted, as if the mirror had grown bunions, and my bones ache like in the early stage of flu. My forehead is burning, yet I'm chilled. Malaria from murky jerrican water?

I took some anti-malaria medication—not, as prescribed, two weeks before I ventured to the desert but, like an idiot, when I got here. I've taken antibiotics just in case this swelling is God-knows-what infection; and antihistamines, just in case it's some damn allergy; and painkillers on top of that. Now I probably look and sound like I'm zonked out of my skull.

The Badawias stare as if they wish I'd go somewhere else to die.

"Woe to us if the alum crystal reveals that fate holds in store for her to die of her ailment in our compound." Azzizah sighs. "Her tribe is sure to blame us, attack us Badu, to avenge her blood."

"*Wallah*, how it dries your spit, the fear of your blood exposed," mutters Tammam, hugging little Salimeh. "Take what is left of my life and enjoy it, my child, my daughter…"

"*Ana assifa*—I am sorry—to have encumbered you with such worries," I apologized, then I told them I would pack up and leave, go down to Abu Salim's *maq'ad*—guest-receiving-place—and wait there until I could catch a ride.

"*Stana*—wait!" snaps Azzizah, spewing a string of curses on fate for inflicting me with such a strange ailment, and for inflicting me on her. And another slew of curses on my husband for allowing me to travel to her compound. And yet another volley of curses on her husband for inviting me to visit-stay then riding off.

"You cannot leave, go out of our sight, until Abu Salim gets back," she informs me, the sun obliterating depth, stealing the third dimension from the surrounding mountain chain, a cardboard backdrop in the glare. "For until Abu Salim gets back, your blood is on our heads." Azzizah strings a few more curses on my tribe for its might and power and rule over Sinai, and on her tribe and clan for its lack of might and power and for being reduced to live under the *frangi*—foreign rule—of my tribe.

She and Tammam can probably weave here only when the cliffs shade this flat ledge chiseled into the slope by desert winds that reshape all in view here, except the Badawias' way of life.

I couldn't bring myself to ask the Badawias if it was possible to dispatch a neighboring camel-rider to fetch a friend of a friend of my son's stationed at the post that houses the health clinic by junction of Wadi E. and Wadi M.—all too many mountain chains away from this one, and a journey through treacherous canyons. And besides, I look worse than I feel. And that friend of a friend of my son's might not be there.

Tal had referred to him as the Haifa'ee—the one from Haifa.

The Haifa'ee had served with him and Gingie in the Unit, Tal said as we approached that junction. Tal wasn't sure if the Haifa'ee was employed by the military administration, or by the Society for the Protection of Nature, or by the Red-Shield of David, only that he was stationed at that post.

A half-dozen ambulance-helicopters could land at once in front of that post, so wide was that junction. The architect who had designed the post must be one of your colleagues or students, Arik. Like you, so mindful of the environment, from a distance you couldn't tell the stone-walled post from the mountainside behind it. A few camels and one Jeep were parked by the stone wall that fronted the post, and Tal wondered if the Haifa'ee had parked there for a change. "Whenever you phone him, you are told he is out," Tal said. He decided not to stop, not to intrude on the Haifa'ee or to allow the Haifa'ee to intrude upon us.

But on his way back from Abu Salim's *maq'ad*, the hour was late, the night moonless, and the terrain tricky. The minutes stretched long until he reached that post by the junction and found his friend the Haifa'ee at the post. After a good supper, a cold beer or two, and half a pack of cigarettes, he told the Haifa'ee, as he had told me, that he didn't feel right about leaving me at Abu Salim's *maq'ad*. Tal's intuition was off, warped by the war, the Haifa'ee thought, as I did. But three days later, or is it five days later, the Haifa'ee hears from a camel-rider that he must dispatch my escort-guardian to Abu Salim's compound, quick-fast, before I get carried away by longing... and wishful thinking...

✣

He fell on me like rain on a land plagued by drought. Out of the blue came this man, Tal, "dew" in Hebrew, who restored me like rain a desert land and, like dew, evaporated only from the surface.

Life had never afforded him the opportunity to travel with anyone from outside his circle, the kibbutz and the army, until the day we met. A new sphere opened up for both him and me that day—a sphere we referred to only as "The Jeep." And maybe because we were traveling in the interior of a wilderness where manna dropped from heaven and mountains parted for you at the moment of impact, we believed the Jeep was invested with metaphysical powers.

From the start, not one moment in the Jeep was like another. Gears were shifted by him, by me. We took turns at the wheel, but rode out the bumps together. Classified maps and information were declassified. The gap between our seats was filled with sleeping bags so that we could sit closer together; could talk without yelling over the rushing winds and the rumbling motor—at least, that's the rationale we gave it the first day.

It was on just such a beautiful day that Tal had first set foot in The Land; "I thought we landed in paradise...," he told me soon after we passed the Haifa'ee's post. Tal was a city-child in Belgium, six years old the day he and his parents flew in to the kibbutz. "In that same day my family grew from three to three hundred and sixty," he said, and everything that his extended family—the kibbutz—had, was his for keeps.

"Mine, for keeps?" He was incredulous at first. "For me it was a dream come true to ride, not a wooden carousel horse but a real horse, to gallop in open space—my fields, my horse... And you didn't have to ask your parents for money to buy a toy or a sweet. And your parents didn't have to pay money for anything. My mother didn't have to drag parcels from the market. There was no marketplace in the kibbutz. Fish, you could net from your lake. Eggs, you could gather from your chicken coop. Tomatoes came from your garden, melons from your fields, bananas from your plantation, milk from your cows, honey from your beehives. My parents and I had found the fabled land of milk and honey, just as my father had said we would. A child born in the kibbutz takes it all for granted, but for me, the kibbutz was paradise."

Tal, obviously unaccustomed to telling his story on our first day, needed no prodding to tell it now, on our last wadi crossing. "Back in Belgium, in wintertime, it was gray and cold, and windows had to be kept shut. But here, in the Jordan Valley, wintertime was—is—bright and warm, and windows are wide open. And summertime is like the Garden of Eden. You swim nude in the Sea of Galilee and the Jordan River, with your kibbutz classmates, no grownups. We lifeguarded one another. And no grown-up forced a child to do anything—not even homework, in this Garden of Eden. No teacher patrolled the classroom during exams in this paradise. If you cheated you were stripped of honor, not by a grownup, but by your peers—your classmates, your roommates. "We kibbutz children roomed with our classmates in the children's house, a mini-paradise, where the child had full autonomy. Boys and girls roomed together; classmates shared everything, even our parents...

"Four or five o'clock in the afternoon, we'd visit our parents in their living quarters. And if your own parents didn't indulge you with their undivided attention, you walked over to visit a classmate's parents. Six or seven o'clock in the evening, the whole kibbutz, children and grownups, would gather in the dining room, which was bigger than any restaurant in Belgium. The pots in the kitchen were so big that a child could play hide-and-seek in them.

"*Shabbat,* the kibbutz would swell with so many guests that dinner was served in two or three shifts. And even though all kibbutz members were secular, on the eve of *Shabbat,* everyone in the dining room would wear a festive white shirt or blouse. After supper, everyone would gather on the great lawn for a play by the national theater—the Habima—or a concert by the Israeli Symphony Orchestra, or some dance recitals, concerts, plays, and puppet shows performed by members of the kibbutz. But everyone had seen and heard so many rehearsals that the performances would put most of the audience to sleep."

His performance would be a surprise, Tal decided at age nine or ten. In secret, bit by bit, he borrowed the gunpowder from a box of ammunition to make fireworks.

"Fireworks? How did you know how to make them?" I asked.

"Same way I knew how to swim and how to speak Hebrew—by osmosis," Tal replied. "The difficulty was keeping everything secret. On a rare quiet evening, as soon as it got dark, I set off the fireworks, but the minute they exploded, the siren howled and the whole kibbutz shifted to red alert. At that time, years before the '67 war, there wasn't a day that Syria didn't pound the valley with heavy artillery from the Golan Heights; and Jordan always unleashed artillery barrages, and terrorists to boot. Their activity often singed the night sky, but never fireworks. My classmates had never seen fireworks, except in the movies. I wanted them to see the real thing—the real, colorful paradise."

It hadn't occurred to him that anyone in his kibbutz would mistake his fireworks for enemy fire, Tal went on to say, driving slower and slower, almost as if he didn't want to reach Abu Salim's *maq'ad*, where he and I would part.

"*Saper*—tell on," I urged him, like the Badu do a storyteller. "*Ghul*—tell on ..."

"There wasn't a child in the kibbutz who couldn't tell, just by the whistle of a bullet or a shell, its calibre and target," Tal went on. "Far or near, whenever the siren howled, everyone was supposed to take cover in the nearest shelter. Everyone, that is, except the grownups, who were assigned to treat the injured, or release the livestock if the barns caught fire, or secure the kibbutz against infiltrating terrorists. The kibbutz will never forgive me for triggering a false alarm I thought, or worse: the kibbutz will forgive me because I was an outsider, a newcomer from Belgium—I was a boy who wanted to be like all my classmates, a native-born kibbutznik."

He ran away that night and went into hiding before anyone in the kibbutz even as much as suspected that the siren was a false alarm. "I stayed in hiding for two nights and two days," he said.

"No way," I said. "No way you could hide in that valley for more than half a day, if that. Not in the valley I know, the border kibbutzim I remember. Even if you had the courage and the cunning to scrape together enough water and food to sustain you for two nights and two days, heads would be counted in the shelters of your kibbutz. Life would be on hold in the whole valley until you were found. Such consequences must have flashed through your mind before you went into hiding…"

"No. All of that would flash through the mind of an Israeli child, born and raised in The Land," said Tal. "You *Sabras*—native-born Israelis—can't begin to imagine what it's like to be a newcomer to The Land, to the kibbutz.

"My fantasy in hiding," Tal continued, "was that my classmates would find my hiding-place and beg me to come home. 'Only if you promise,' I'd say in response, 'that all would be forgotten, especially that I'm a newcomer,' and that never again would they laugh at my mother's broken Hebrew or at her Belgian accent and foreign ways…"

His mother was a city woman in Belgium, Tal explained. To her, the kibbutz was a group of farmers who had come through for her and her children when her husband was killed. A reliable bunch of farmers, and heroic, but also crude, provincial, narrow. "And worst to her were the farmers' children—a wild, undisciplined bunch whom she regarded as a very bad influence on me.

"It surprised me, to put it mildly, how much I missed that wild bunch after two nights and two days in hiding. I was also tormented by the thought that my mother would be sick from worry for me.

"I headed to her room after nightfall. Everyone in the kibbutz was fast asleep, it seemed. Her door, like all the doors in the kibbutz, was unlocked; she didn't go to sleep as early as the farmers. But she had predicted to the minute when I'd show up. A cup of steaming chocolate was waiting for me on her table. And supper, piping hot.

"'How did you know?' I asked her.

"She told me that the whole kibbutz had known for two days and two nights where I was hiding. It had taken only minutes for the farmers to locate my hiding-place. After that, they took turns keeping a watchful eye on me. Not for a second in two days and two nights was I out of their sight, she told me. As soon as I came out of hiding, a farmer came over and told her that I would, no doubt, come to hide now under her apron. 'These farmers know you as well as your own mother,' she told me. However, she said, I would find no protection under her apron this time. She had never dreamed that I could be a bad influence on the wild bunch. Now, for once, she agreed with the farmers. One child learns from another in the kibbutz, they told her, and she agreed. My escapade had to be turned into a lesson to all the children in the kibbutz. I was to be made an example of.

"I was too stunned, too humiliated for words, or for hot chocolate and supper. My mother could see it. Still, she wouldn't let me sleep that night in her quarters. My father wouldn't want me to hide under her apron, she said. Before I left, I asked her if the whole kibbutz knew also that I was preparing fireworks.

"'No, that was a surprise!' she replied. 'A surprise that fell hard on the whole kibbutz, the whole valley.'

"'Because it triggered a false alarm?' I asked her.

"She didn't know, she said, she couldn't understand the farmers. They take so much in stride: No matter how heavy the enemy fire, they don't evacuate the children; they don't give up. They sleep in underground shelters. They drive armored tractors. They plant a forest of barbed wire around their living quarters to keep out terrorists. All this is natural, but a child sets off fireworks, and it shocks them. She said she will never figure them out; she would always be a newcomer. So will I, I thought as I left her room.

"But just then, when I'd finally accepted it, I entered the children's house and discovered that I was no longer a newcomer, but a kibbutz child, same as my classmates." Tal asked me to light him a cigarette and then he went on to say that to be a kibbutz child was not exactly what he had imagined.

"The night-light was just bright enough to show all my classmates sleeping. I tiptoed to my bed and crawled under the blanket. The bedsprings creaked, and one of my roommates woke up. He opened an eye and whispered, 'Shalom, Tal.' Then I heard a whisper rolling from room to room: 'Tal is home ... Tal is home ...' Next thing I know, all my classmates are gathered around my bed and from all directions I hear, 'You put us all to shame, Tal ... You are one of us ... We kibbutz children ...'

"Now, I was no longer just I, but Us, We. Mine was Ours. And Ours was mostly leased or entrusted to Us by the Nation, which was also Us, We, Ours ... I had confused one Ours with another. And so had my mother. The boundaries of public and private were clearly defined in the city, in Belgium. Here, they were clear to my classmates—bred in their bones. They gave no thought, no words to the idea, until one bone cracked. My classmates didn't know at first how to infuse this marrow into my bones.

"They told me that the Nation is so strapped for cash, it's counting bullets—bullets for defense, security—and I blew a whole box of ammunition on fireworks. And worse, my classmates said, I blew a moral value held high by us, the Nation. Then they gave me a list of never-evers: 'Never ever forget that ammunition is to be deployed only for the defense of our nation. Never ever play with any weapon like a child corrupted by war. Never ever forget that nothing frightens our nation more than the idea that children can be corrupted by war, except the fear that we children would get killed; that is why children serve the Nation best by staying in shelters and by staying away from firearms. Never ever forget that we kibbutz children are the best the future has to offer to our Nation ...'

"In those days you couldn't turn on a radio or open a newspaper without knowing how impressed the whole world was by the way the grownups were teaching us kibbutz children to adhere to the moral values that have elevated the kibbutz to a model of democracy and equality ... there were no juvenile delinquents in the kibbutz, no destitutes, no underprivileged—and no lenders, no conniving dealers, no underhanded pushers. That was the attraction the kibbutz had held for my father, but had he lived in the kibbutz for more than a year, he would have missed the spice and energy of the city, or so my mother thought. It would have disturbed him to see me behave like the farmers, lacking Jewish flavor, Jewish smarts, Jewish humor.

"My classmates didn't have to tell me to never ever forget that the best thing in the world was to be a kibbutz child. Or to never ever forget that, of all the children in The Land, we kibbutz children were the most privileged. That is why our Nation expected us to be better than all the children in The Land, my classmates explained.

"That list of never-evers generated tremendous peer pressure and rivalry. We were unaware of it, until we left for army duty, volunteered to serve in elite units, and the war claimed many . . .

"The more classmates you lose in battle, the more you expect of yourself, your nation, your leaders, the more disappointed you get . . . the more classmates leave the kibbutz and move to pursue the I-me-mine of city life."

On the battlefield he had observed more than once or twice, Tal went on to say, how the truly courageous can be seized by such fear that they had to be hospitalized. "Makes you wonder if a person doesn't have a limited amount of resources; instead of 'use it or lose it,' you lose it when you use it. Maybe that's what happened to my kibbutz classmates, if not to the nation. After all these decades of war, we can't resist the urge to live it up today for it might be your last. But the longer you squeeze today for all it's worth and fuck tomorrow, the more you reduce the odds that you, the Nation, will make it to tomorrow. So our gut is torn between two basic survival instincts. It's schizophrenic: When you live it up, your thinking shrinks to the singular—I-me-mine. But when you serve in the army, your thinking had better expand to the plural—We-us-ours—or you won't live to see tomorrow."

Tal didn't say it in those words. His Hebrew is rooted in the Jordan Valley, the kibbutz, the Unit; mine is a drop-out Hebrew, along with drop-out English and night-school Arabic.

"Your Hebrew isn't bad—a few outdated idioms, one or two grammar mistakes, a misused word here and there, but from your accent it's impossible to tell you dropped out," he said at one point.

"English also, I speak with a good Hebrew accent. Now if I could get my butt to park where my accent is."

He laughed. "I can't imagine you living outside," he said. "A native like you. How did you happen to end up in Canada of all places?

"Tell on," Tal urged me. After being gagged here in The Land for more than twenty years, he had no idea how it moved me. I was unaccustomed to talking about myself to anyone but you, Arik. A cool evening wind fanned away the heat, but my face was burning when I opened up to him.

"I was dressed like a high-fashion model when I landed in Toronto. You wouldn't have recognized me," I said, forgetting I was talking to Tal, not to you, Arik. Tal laughed, so incongruous to him, to imagine me dressed like a mannequin in a glossy magazine...

                           ✼

I've got to get to a doctor. As soon as the Badawias get up, I'll insist they ask one of their neighboring clansman to escort me to the nearest clinic—the one at the Haifa'ee's Nature Conservation post is the closest, I think. I don't have the energy to even imagine breaking through these mountains. What in the hell am I doing here? And how in the hell do I get out of here?

Just tell Abu Salim that you want to leave and he'll arrange a ride for you, Russell told me. Well, tell me what I do when Abu Salim is God-knows-where.

19

My throat was so constricted last night, and I was plagued with such a case of shivers, that I thought I was breathing my last. It took forever for the antihistamines to kick in, and when they did they knocked me out. I slept through a whole day and night, according to the Badawias.

Now it's tea time, again. Tea, the Badu's chicken soup. I've had so many glasses, my stomach sloshes with every move like a full jerrican.

This morning only Azzizah is here, working her loom. Tammam went with little Salimeh to "catch the wind, ventilate…" It can get to you, I guess, the narrow confines of this forbidden compound—especially when your stranger guest has been afflicted by a devil not known to you.

I groaned all night in pain, "and in longing for your loved ones," Tammam told me first thing this morning. I could barely hold the tea glass then, or lift it to my swollen lips. No wonder she fled to "catch the wind…"

"You surely feel better now if you write-to-remember," Azzizah told me while weaving, weaving. "But, *Wallah,* how it can ail you, remembering." She heaved a sigh.

"How did it ail you, remembering?" I asked her.

Silence.

"How did you heal the ailment brought on by remembering?" I pressed.

"Not proper to ask questions," she replied, weaving, weaving.

"The best of my friends, Riva, is also a *darwisha*—a medicine woman, not unlike you, *yaa*-Azzizah. So is her husband, Mottke— *Wallah,* he is a *kebir darwish*—a big medicine man," I told her.

"So was my father, *Wallah.* What a big *darwish* my father was," Azzizah said, weaving, weaving…

❧

Ah, *yaa*-Mottke, I wish you were here. I could use a doctor now, *Wallah*... All the shots you had advised me to take, and the pills you had insisted I pack in my desert gear, have helped fuck-all so far.

Ah, *yaa*-Mottke and Riva, why don't you get into my Jeep and ask that redheaded son of yours to drive you to these remote mountain chains and see, like I have, why the Book mentions the desert on every second page but attempts no description. It is impossible to capture this place—in words or in a photo. The desert shows you a different face every minute, a kaleidoscope of vistas powered by the ever-changing angle of the sun. No camera aperture opens wide enough to hold the sky, mountains, canyons, and the lone acacia tree you see in most photos of this desert. As the sages say, you need background to see, to appreciate foreground...

If it weren't for Mottke, Levi would have reported for compulsory duty when he was eighteen, like everyone else in The Land.

"But in Canada you graduate from high school after Grade 13, not 12, like the kids in The Land," Mottke told the boy. "You are not like the kids in The Land. Recognizing it, the law of The Land entitles you to a three- or four-year deferment. But in your case I think the law doesn't go far enough. In the case of the likes of you, who are all too eager to be soldiers or combat pilots, I think the law should deem you unfit, and advise you to get your kicks elsewhere. We run a clean service here, or at least as clean a service as possible."

The boy likes to think that Mottke is like you, Arik, even though I had told him that, unlike Mottke, you had held beauty, joy, and adventure in high regard; you had bent the law, broken speed limits, and tempted the Angel whenever you straddled a motorcycle and climbed into a cockpit; you wasted rationed fuel to tip your wings over the tin-shack town during my working hours, and at all other times over the room-and-a-half we called home; and how that declaration of love touched the newcomers and our neighbors. I also told Levi that the bane of your life were civil servants—some of whom were Mottke and Riva's best friends, old underground friends—who had nixed every plan you submitted for your dream town because they considered beauty a luxury we could ill afford, even though your design cost

246

little more than the ugly tin-shack towns those civil servants favored. But no matter what I told our Levi, he idolized Mottke. He keeps picking father figures. It bugs Dave—it reflects badly on him, Dave thinks, and you know what store Dave puts on appearances. Still, Dave was more of a buddy to him than a dad. "No man can take your father's place," Dave told the kid, time and again. It was out of loyalty to you, Arik, that Dave said it—felt it. But the boy needed a father to idolize and emulate, and he could do worse than Mottke.

Mottke is probably one of the few people in the world—never mind The Land—who considers the rescue mission at Entebbe to be a flagrant abuse of power, trust, and sovereignty. "What right have we to land in Uganda and shoot left and right, even on a mission to rescue a jumbo jet full of hostages, be they all our people?" Mottke would tell you. "If our people want to fly Outside, to see France and have a good time in Paris, let them do it in good health—and at their own risk, not my son's."

To Dave, The Land is like a movie—a vicarious adventure that is dust-free, risk-free, blood-free. The West Bank is vital to *us*, Dave believes, just like Gingie—Mottke and Riva's son—does. But let Gingie pay the price for the West Bank.

Gingie is Dave's boy, and Levi, Mottke's. But Dave doesn't tremble for Gingie, or for Levi. Mottke trembles for both boys. The irony! The one who trembles grew up to believe he was so *powerful* he could change the course of destiny. And the one who does not tremble grew up to believe he was that *powerless*, whatever he does, good or bad, makes no difference.

Exile, paradox is thy name, *Wallah*. Dave, the man who takes as a compliment a cocktail-party comment that his wife is not at all like a Jew, secretly wishes he could wear his Jewishness like a badge for all to envy, and fear—just like Gingie … Dave sees the redhead as a sort of vindication for Christie Pits. Here is a pint-sized redhead, wearing a *tzitzit* and *kippa* like a ghetto Yid, yet serving in *the* crack commando unit in The Land—in the world, after Entebbe.

Soon as they finished their studies in Canada, Riva and Mottke returned to The Land. Dropping out to exile is a form of suicide,

Riva thinks. That's what I tried to do when Arik got killed—tried to stop living, growing, aging, according to her. "Why do you think you keep braiding your hair just as you did twenty years ago?" she said, "And wearing the same Nimrod sandals, the same hand-embroidered *shmates*, as if you ran out of clothes coupons, just as you did twenty years ago in the days of austerity?" Riva thinks only a self-hating people would choose to live in exile. We are a self-destructive people, she maintains. Both our temples were destroyed, not by outsiders, but by our own, and no one could destroy the third except us. That's why Riva doesn't give a damn about what a Gentile thinks or writes or broadcasts about us. But when one of our own drops out or talks like a dropout, she reacts as if Samson had gone mad, shaking the pillars of his Temple, and screaming, Let my own people die with me.

Feeling torn is alien to Riva. Opposite pulls, she believes, are a Diaspora exile's disease. She hates Shalom Aleichem because he extols exile thinking: on one hand this, on the other that. An exile copout, Riva likes to say; that kind of thinking leads to death camps.

For years, Riva has been telling her friends that I didn't drop out, I just married a Canadian, next year I'll bundle him off to The Land for good. "You see?" she told them when Dave purchased a suite at the condominium hotel in Herzliyya on the beach.

Dave stayed in that condominium once, said he liked The Land but couldn't stand the people. They're no different from any Duddy Kravitz in Montreal, Toronto, or New York, he said. They'd sell their mother for a buck.

Every year I fly over; and the taller Levi grows, the longer I stay at that damn hotel suite—alone.

Riva, torn now between marriage and The Land, doesn't know what to advise me. She can't stand the thought that I'd have to choose one or the other, so she stuffed The Land in my veins, sparing me exile, self-destruction, suicide.

"Deep inside herself, Leora carries The Land," Riva started to tell her friends. She took my recollection of her as the embodiment of The Land in Toronto, and switched it around.

"Let go of your power over your son," Riva, of all people, tells me. How can she see me as manipulative when she knows I am the reluctant holder of power dumped on me by the law of The Land? Why, I want to know, would the law so protect the only child of a family and so persecute his only parent, his mother? The decision is his mother's, mine alone. Now tell me, how could Levi be an exception in the eyes of the law, but not in his mother's eyes?

The law is primitive, Mottke thinks, primitive as blood. Mottke speaks from both corners of his mouth at once: Rise above blood, but die to defend your nation, your land.

Primitive—*Wallah*, what a two-faced beast. Blood is detestably primitive, but primitive art is great. Take the art, dump the blood. Pick and choose your heritage: blue and white; red is out ...

The primitive ignites war, Mottke believes. So how come the most peaceful tribes in The Land are the very Badu tribes that he considers to be primitive?

Ah, *yaa*-Riva, Mottke, wish you were here. I feel drained, listless, isolated ... Even the fear of isolation saps a person's strength. It's tempting to surrender to the desert, to break the chain of connections and responsibilities ...

Dave's contribution to The Land dwarfed even my parents', you would think if you saw how the prime minister of Israel, Menachem Begin, recognized it, and honored Dave—and other big U.J.A. contributors like him—at a ritzy dinner at the Hilton in Jerusalem four or five months ago. It didn't occur to Dave to invite my parents to the reception. Levi and I had to suggest it to him. Yes, good idea, Dave said. My parents declined with thanks. I didn't go either. Levi accompanied Dave. Their photo with Begin, framed in silver, is displayed proudly in Dave's den.

Such honor is like junk food: the more it swells you, the more you crave it. And now, at every United Jewish Appeal, Dave's cronies will slap him on the back, no doubt, and say, "What a great contribution, Dave." Your contribution—Levi, Arik's son, my son.

If Dave had served army duty, he'd know what it's like to get a furlough for *Shabbat*. And Levi, like a orphan, will stay at the base, or crash one *Shabbat* at Riva and Mottke's, the next at my parents', the next at Arik's parents', the next at my sister's, or Arik's brother's. Like a homeless, motherless, fatherless bastard, he of all sons, after the price his father paid to make Levi feel at home in The Land. The thought of it is unbearable to me.

The Badu would say Dave and I were fated to be married these twenty years, then fated to be divorced ... so be it. My days of sitting on my suitcase with one leg in Canada and one in The Land are over.

You were favored by fate, *Wallah*, Dave. Don't blow this opportunity to correct the mistake you made in '48. Move to The Land with me this year, or we both must accept the consequence.

With the setting sun, my list of fears grows, as does the crowd in my head—Arik, Riva, Mottke, Gingie, Levi, Dave, my parents ... I tuck them all in my bundle—like Rachel did with the idols she stole from her father when she was afraid to travel with Jacob to the Promised Land, to independence ...

20

Magic. Azzizah, a *darwisha* now, grunting and groaning, searches inside her remedy sack-bag, glides over to the other side of the fire-circle at the side of her tent, squats and stares at "the alum crystal to divine," Tammam informed me; her hand vise-like around my forearm to make sure I stay-sit right here at the entrance to Azzizah's tent. "Not good to distract the *darwisha's* divining," Tammam explains.

Azzizah decided to practice her medicine on me only now that the swelling is almost gone and I feel much better. Tucking her alum-crystal into her bundle of Badu remedies, Azzizah now demands I rejoin her by the fire-circle at the side of her tent. She grunts, groans, and stares into my face again and again as darkness closes round the fire, and the wind delivers the evening cold.

"Have you divined, *yaa*-Azzizah," whispers Tammam. Is she reciting a line in a ceremony? Is Azzizah's grunting and groaning also part of a healing ritual? "Have you divined?" whispers the girl-Badawia again.

"*Aywa*—yes," Azzizah says, her voice now a drone. "The alum revealed a man discontent with his fate, with Allah; *yaa-Rabb*, lacking faith, his heart empty, his soul a void . . . a hollow dark cave . . . the dwelling place of *al-shaytan*—Satan—the devil . . ."

"*Yaa*-Allah!" exclaims Tammam. Little Salimeh must have seen Azzizah practice her medicine many times before; she snuggles against her girl-mother as though settling in for a good, scary show.

"*Aywa*—yes. The alum revealed *al-shaytan*—the devil—looking like a snake, but flying like a bat, his head like a camel, but with two horns like a he-goat . . ." Azzizah drones on. "The alum showed *al-shaytan*, looking like a flying snake, had found a void in a man's soul to raid-rob the thinking from this man . . . and so, not thinking of the plentiful bounty Allah had lavished on him, this man roams the desert feeling discontent with his own fate and envy of your fate, my fate.

Aywa—yes, this man cast the harmful glance of the eye ... Did you notice-see the glance of the evil envious eye?" she asks me.

"*La*—no," I told her.

"*Aktar al-qubur min as-suudur*—Most graves are dug by envy in men's hearts." Azzizah repeats these words again and again. Her remedy for the evil glance of envy is a stone amulet, blue "like the blue eyes of someone who stands at the side, *ya'ni*—meaning, a stranger ... Strangers' blue eyes are most harmful," Azzizah says, fastening the blue stone amulet to the beaded necklace she gave me.

"Harmful how?" I ask her.

Silence. Badawias' eyes stare through slits in their veils.

"Most graves are dug by envy in men's hearts," Azzizah intones, pulling a tiny leather pouch from her remedy sack-bag. She says I'll have to wear it just like she, Tammam, and little Salimeh do. She pins it to my blouse with the safety pin that Tammam said was little Salimeh's present to me. "The name of Allah is tucked inside," says Azzizah, "for *al-shaytan* fears nothing but the name of Allah," she adds, then forbids me to open the pouch, to look at the name of Allah. Strange how the Badawias sprinkle "Allah" liberally in every second sentence they utter, but I have yet to see either one facing Mecca to pray.

"Where did you get these leather pouches containing the name of Allah?" I ask.

Silence. Like in a trance, Azzizah stares at my face, grunts and groans as if she feels the discomfort of my ailment. I can't make out a word she drones except "*Fahemti*—understand?"

"No, your moon is up before your sun is down. I don't know if you mean night or day," I reply.

"*Wahada, wahada*—one by one—cut your words, *yaa*-Azzizah," says Tammam, *jingle-jangling* the flies away from little Salimeh. "What do you see?"

"I see," says Azzizah, her bloodshot eyes drilling holes in my face, "the swelling lumps, shifting like the sands, and like a nomad roaming, wearing shoes."

"Meaning?" Tammam asks Azzizah.

"Meaning the ailment was caused by roaming in shoes, meaning not seeing where going, for wearing shoes is like wearing blindfolds on the soles of your feet," replies Azzizah.

"Abu Salim also wears shoes," I remind Azzizah. "Yet you told me that he can see-sense through mountains, remember?"

"Abu Salim would see much better if he were not wearing blindfolds on the soles of his feet," responds Azzizah. "You have to be very careful when you walk without shoes, for you can step on *kharah*—shit—and that can make you very sick," Azzizah adds. I laugh.

"It is no laughing matter," snaps Tammam, "stepping on ejaculated semen can also make you sick."

"And stepping on a snake or scorpion can kill you," adds Azzizah. "So can stepping on broken glass..." She grunts, groans, stares, and drones: "I see your shifting swelling was caused also by bad winds blowing, *min el ard*—from the earth..."

"Don't be afraid. Azzizah will provide a remedy for that," whispers Tammam.

"*Aywa*—yes," Azzizah says, then she tells me to lie flat on my stomach, and next thing I know she is dancing on my back to squeeze out the bad winds from my lungs. Her bare feet, surprisingly light, dance and massage my back. I feel a hell of a lot better now.

Three welcome-carpets Tammam spreads round the fire-circle in front of Azzizah's tent now. A fourth one she rolls into a bolster for Azzizah's aching back. "Rest, rest," she tells her senior co-wife. And it really looks like the divining, healing, and massaging has drained Azzizah. As soon as Azzizah reclines in the place of honor, close to the fire but away from the smoke, little Salimeh tugs at the nursing slits of her *thowb*, and the senior Badawia, heaping blessings on the girl-infant, pulls a withered breast and offers it to the child.

Meanwhile, Tammam cleans up glasses and brews tea—again, not a morsel of food, only tea, with loads and loads of sugar. She rolls a cigarette as she waits for the tea-water to boil. Bending almost to the ground so that her veils won't catch fire, she lights it. Smells a bit like Gauloises, the strong French cigarettes, Badu tobacco.

"Next year, *Inshallah*, may your womb, not your face, swell up," says

Azzizah, addressing me. She and Tammam both wish me to be blessed with many sons.

"Why only sons, not daughters?" I ask them.

"Because a daughter you raise only to lose her when she marries and moves to her husband's compound, but a son you have for the rest of your life," replies Azzizah (switch genders and you've got the Hebrew and Canadian saying: A son you have till he marries his wife, but a daughter you have for the rest of your life.)

"And also because—write-to-remember—as I told it to you before, *yaa-Rabb*, how can a woman forget that her sons are her voice in the *maq'ad*; the more powerful your voice in the *maq'ad*, the more camel-riders you have crossing borders to gather information-power, and the more muscle you have to uphold your honor, your reputation, the story that remains when all else dies," Azzizah explains.

A gold coin—it looks ancient and priceless—Azzizah presses into my hand to keep as "an amulet to ward off your husband divorcing you. For, in a divorce, it is the husband who *daimann*—always—gets to keep the children. And the worst fate to befall a woman is to lose her children. Sometimes even this amulet cannot help, but sometimes it does help. Therefore, wear it always..."

"Did the alum crystal reveal to you that I will lose my son?!"

"I did not consult the alum for that," snaps Azzizah.

"Swear!" I snap back, like a Badawia.

Their bloodshot eyes, intense behind the slits in their veils, demand an explanation.

I put my writing-to-remember aside, and told the Badawias about my husband, Arik, and about my son, Levi, and about the written consent to waive his exemption from high-risk duty. "My fear of fears is that my son will end up like his father; therefore, I am afraid to grant him my consent, even though he is full grown and already a pilot as good as his father. And, who knows, maybe the times will change from war to peace. What would you do if you were in my place?" I asked the Badawias.

Silence. Water bubbles on the fire, yet neither moves to pick up the teapot. In this moment of silence, it seems they suspend life to lend solemnity and full weight to the burden of my dilemma.

"If you lose your men—if you have no sons, no husband—what for do you need your Land, oh, *yaa-okhti, yaa-okhti*—my sister, my sister," Azzizah responds, addressing me. Tammam picks up the bubbling teapot from the fire.

"Your fear is my fear, *yaa-okhti*—my sister," Azzizah goes on to say to me. "I also am afraid that fate might hold in store that my son, Salim, will end up like his father and my father and Tammam's."

"But that is good, *yaa*-Azzizah!!!" the girl-Badawia cries out, then spits three times, almost like my mother, to ward off evil eyes and ears.

"*Aywa*—yes. Abu Salim's reputation is unassailable. So is my father's reputation, as is Tammam's father's. But when Egypt ruled this our desert Sinaa," says Azzizah, heaving a sigh, her hands caressing Tammam's infant-daughter, fast asleep now on her lap. "ah, *yaa-Rabb*, in those days, when Egypt ruled this, our desert Sinaa, the authorities who were of Egypt decreed that our young Badu men must battle in the army of Egypt, else they would be imprisoned or shot dead. But we Sinaa Badu serve no foreign ruler. Therefore, our young Badu men, my father among them, also Tammam's father and Abu Salim, escaped from the reach of the Egyptian authorities.

"And, under cover of night, far away from us, their loved ones, they wandered from waterhole to waterhole, month after month, year after year. And no matter how homesick they were, Abu Salim, my father and Tammam's, and most of our young Badu men stayed away from our home ground. For that is where the Egyptian authorities kept coming to apprehend them. Then, all of a sudden, in the battle lasting six long days, your Yahodi tribe wrestled Sinaa from Egypt, and everything changed. For, unlike Egypt, your Yahodi tribe did not know how brave at heart our Badu men are; therefore, your Yahodi tribe did not decree that our young Badu men battle in your Yahodi army. And so all our clansmen came home from hiding, came home from their wandering under cover of night.

"O, *Allah*, decree my son be spared such a fate as taking leave of his loved ones, and far away from his home ground going into hiding, seeking shelter under cover of night, wandering from waterhole to waterhole, covering his tracks for months and months, years and years. The only fate worse than this, *Wallah*, is to be caught crossing borders or breaking any other *frangi*—foreign—laws. For then a camel-rider is imprisoned, and that is a fate even worse than death."

"*Aywa*—yes—that is what my brother thinks," mutters Tammam, her beautiful eyes tearful.

"May he be spared such a fate," says Azzizah. Little Salimeh, half-awake now, cracks a smile, and turns to her girl-mother, her arms flailing as if she can't contain her delight and love. Heaping blessings on the child, Azzizah hugs her tight, but little Salimeh wriggles out of Azzizah's clasp and crawls over to Tammam, who unties her veil to kiss her child, tears streaming down her beautiful face.

"*Yaa*, how glad my brother will be to see you. *Ayuni, galbi*—my eyes, my heart," Tammam says to her infant-daughter, "So much you have grown since he last saw you…

"*Aywa*—yes." Tammam turns to me. "Your Yahodi tribe did not compel our Badu men to battle in your army, but, *Wallah*, in the last war, I thought I saw the last of my brother."

"*Ghule*—tell on," Azzizah urges Tammam.

"*Aywa*—yes. It was in the big war that broke out four or five or six years ago," Tammam goes on to tell. "The drought was only in its first or second year when the last big war broke out, and I first menstruated, turning from girl to maiden. Therefore, I veiled my face. But, under my veil, I was still a girl-child, *yaa-Rabb*. Like a girl-child, I found it very exciting at first, that more tribesmen, women, and children than I had ever seen before pitched their tents near my father's compound and water source. Day and night they were tending goats or sitting around the fire-circle, *Wallah*. I had never heard so many men, women, and children tell so many stories, legends, and poems.

"But all too soon we all ran out of food. Our tribespeople who had fled from the Gates of the Wadi to seek shelter in our mountain brought with them food supplies only for six days, for they thought that this latest big war, like the one before it, would be battled only for six days. No one thought this last war would be battled for more than sixty days, *yaa-Rabb*."

"They could have stayed in their home ground, for in the all-too-many days of this last big war, all the battles had been fought a distance too far to endanger the lives of those who lived around the Gates of the Wadi," says Azzizah.

"*Aywa*—yes," says Tammam. "Everyone knew it to be so at the end of that war. At the beginning, no one knew if the war would be battled near or far from the Gates of the Wadi. All we knew after six days was that this latest big war was not like the war before it. And also that, in the past six days, our numbers had so swelled in our sheltering mountain compounds that in but three-four days we mountain Badu would not have food supplies to sustain us and our tribesmen. That was not bad news to us children. For we children thought that, when we would run out of flour and rice, the grownups would slaughter the goats, and we children loved goat meat. But, as soon as the grownups found out why we children were glad our food was running out, they told us that our Badu way of life would die if we were to slaughter our goats.

"And it was that evening, or the evening after, that our elders dispatched my father and my brother to fetch food supplies from Al-Arish, for they were among the best, the fastest of our camel-riders. Others were dispatched to purchase supplies in a place called Eilat, and across the border in a place called Aqaba, which is in a land called Jordan. And even to Saudia, and to Syria and Lubnan—Lebanon—our elders dispatched border-crossing men, to fetch not only food but information. For our elders did not trust the war stories they heard told on the machine called radio, that one of our tribesmen brought with him from the Gates of the Wadi. And the machine called radio did not tell in which market the stores did not run out of food.

"The desert's passes were fraught with new dangers in wartime. No one but Allah knew who would be fated to return with food supplies or with information-power to purchase food with, or maybe even the release of our clansmen who had been imprisoned for crossing borders or breaking laws. My brother was glad to be dispatched on a journey befitting a courageous full-grown man. And I was glad for him."

"Were you not afraid that a calamity might befall your father or brother, or both, on their way to or from Al-Arish?" I ask Tammam.

"No," she replies. "Their blood was far more exposed before the war. For we were pursued then, by a Badu clan bent on avenging the blood and honor of their blood kin. We were forced to stay in hiding for months and months, years and years, *Wallah*. And only a few weeks before the last big war broke out, our dispute with that Badu clan was settled. To firm up the *sulha*, the most pure of our maidens was given in marriage to the most cunning of their trackers. So that, even if that marriage would last but one night, the child conceived in that one night would be of our blood and theirs."

"Is that how your marriage to Abu Salim came about?"

"Let me answer one question before you ask another," snaps Tammam. "*Wallah*, I never met a woman who interrupts a storyteller like a child lacking discretion and craving nothing as much as quick satisfaction of curiosity. Such a child is made glad by none other than the stingy. For the stingy are the ones who tell their story narrow—to the point. *Aywa*—yes. Such a child is made but restless by the generous storytellers who tell their story wide, so they illuminate a world kept dark to me, to you. *Sahih*—right?"

"*Sahih, Wallah*," I agree, amazed by the change in Tammam. You wouldn't know it was the same girl who gave you the shivers whenever she lamented, "Oh, my daughter, take what is left of the rest of my life..." It was as if, while I was ill, Azzizah's medicine did wonders for Tammam, curing her of her volatile mood swings, of her fear that she will die...

"Tell on, *yaa*-Tammam," says Azzizah, rolling herself a cigarette.

"*Aywa*," Tammam continues. "The *sulha* of our blood feud and disputes meant that no cunning tracker out to avenge honor and blood with dagger and sword would lay an ambush for my father and my brother on their way to or from Al-Arish.

"*Wallah*, how disappointed my brother was that he and my father would cross no borders, break no *frangi*—foreign—law on their way to and from Al-Arish. But I was glad, because I knew that he and my father would be spared the worst fate to befall a camel-rider..."

"Which is to be imprisoned," Azzizah interjects, cigarette smoke drifting through the cracks in her shell of veils, shawls, and dresses.

"*Aywa*—yes," says Tammam. "It was a long long week, that week of my waiting. And then, one day, they both returned to our compound, but with only one camel."

"*Yaa*-Allah," exclaims Azzizah, almost like a child enjoying her favorite story. "Tell on."

"*Aywa*, with only one camel they returned," Tammam continues. "The other one they were forced to sell, my brother told me, to purchase the grain, flour, rice, sugar, tea, and coffee that he and my father fetched on the back of one camel only, so light was the weight of the provisions with a price so heavy—a thoroughbred she-camel, *yaa-Rabb.* 'Up and up and up, the price went, higher and higher, the more uncertain the uncertainty of the war,' my brother said. No one he and my father met on their way would venture even to guess how long this latest big war would last, or who would conquer to rule in this, our Badu desert. Badu from the desert over were riding to purchase food supplies in Al-Arish, only to find the stores in Al-Arish nearly empty, my brother said. And fresh supplies were not arriving to the Al-Arish stores because the suppliers, be they of the Yahodi or of the Egyptian tribe, were too busy with supplying food and weapons to their army men and machines. Therefore, there were hundreds upon hundreds of buyers for every sack of flour that remained. Like that, the price was raised higher and higher and higher, *Wallah.* Before they knew it, the money that my father and brother had carried with them did not suffice for even one sack of flour.

"And so, from store to store my father and brother went, from store to store," my brother told me, "until they entered a store in which the owner wished to purchase a camel. The owner of that store feared that this latest war might yet force him and his wives and children to seek shelter in the interior of the peninsula, where a camel would serve him and his household better than his truck, which was useless to the store owner now because the fuel for his truck, like the food-stuffs in his store, was commandeered for army use. Had it not been for this store owner, my brother told me, he and my father would have returned to our compound with the saddle-bags of both their camels empty."

"Did your clan—your tribe—compensate your father and brother for the thoroughbred she-camel they had to exchange for food?" I ask Tammam.

"No, *Wallah*. Our reputation was enhanced a hundredfold by the hospitality we extended to our tribesmen from the Gates of the Wadi during that latest war," she replied.

"Did you ever visit-stay with your tribesmen at the Gates of the Wadi, before or after that war?" I ask the Badawias.

"No, I never left these, our mountains—our home ground," the girl-Badawia replies.

"Neither did I," says Azzizah, "nor did my mother, Tammam's mother, her mother's mother and mine."

"The best home ground in the world is our home ground, my brother told me, and he knows, for he has traveled far and wide beyond our home ground," Tammam says.

Azzizah, refueling her fire-circle, not with goat and camel dung, but with the fragrant firewood she reserves for special occasions, starts to grunt and groan again. "The alum also revealed——"

"*Yaa-Rabb*—my God—what else did the alum crystal reveal to you. Tell, *yaa*-Azzizah," cries out Tammam.

"The alum revealed that maybe—*yumkim*—the cause of your ailment is your fear that your husband was fated to marry another wife." Azzizah's eyes are tearful from fragrant fire smoke as she addresses me. "Therefore, I shall cast a spell to spare you from the most terrible fate of sharing your husband with another wife ..."

"*Aywa*, it is not good," agrees Tammam.

"*Wallah*, I would not have suspected it from looking at you two," I say.

"We two are more fortunate than most," Azzizah replies. "I would rather my daughter be blind in both her eyes than be married to a man married to three wives, or even two ..."

"Cast your spell, *yaa*-Azzizah," says Tammam.

Silence.

Azzizah glides into her tent, muttering something that casts a spell on Tammam, it seems. The junior wife picks up a blackened poker and taps and beats the trio of rocks set in center of the fire-circle to hold cooking pots. Beats and taps, drums a slow gentle rhythm that changes tone with the striking of the various rocks. The echo, bouncing from mountain chain to mountain chain surrounding the compound, sounds like the heart-beat of the desert. And the dancer emerging from Azzizah's tent, draped in a huge black cape bordered with red embroidery that covers her veils, shawls, *thowbs*, and jewels, seems to have been conjured by the rhythm, like water from the sand. Out of the aridity of age and isolation has sprung a dancer vital-free as the *Hamsin*—the fifty desert winds.

Silence.

Tammam picks up the poker and holds it at a right angle: one end disappears under her veil, and it becomes a shepherd's flute. Her eyes close. Her fingers grope for invisible holes in the blackened poker and out comes the piping of a shepherd's song, the likes of which I have never heard. As Tammam plays her flute, Azzizah is stilled. And as she undrapes herself, shrugging off the voluminous red-bordered cape, she looks angry, pained, sapped of power. She is dying to run away, escape, it seems, but cannot. Tammam plays such a compelling flute, she pipes you to the limit, and then a breath beyond it, and another still, until the granite mountain chains tremble in response. You feel that if you don't hang on, brace yourself, you'll be drawn into the vast unknown.

ﬡ

ﬡ פ אול׳ ד

I dream I want to write my name in Hebrew, from right to left, but can't for the life of me. Can't breathe, sweating and drenched with dew, I wake up and pick up my pen ... What a relief to find I can write my own name.

ﬡ פ אול׳ ד

21

So bright is the sky tonight, you could read and write by it, and the moon is not yet completely full... The night was moonless when Tal and I drove up the wadi leading to these mountains—ten or twelve days ago, judging by the moon.

The Badawias hardly mentioned Tal, or our journey—our going in circles and in zigzag, as Abu Salim had called it. Their imagination wouldn't scale the confines of the familiar. It is forbidden for anyone but their blood-kin to escort them; therefore, Tal must be my brother, cousin, nephew, uncle... Did Azzizah divine that he isn't? Was it to purify me of straying with him that the Badawias had offered to bathe me?

Tal was quite sure that the drought had not yet forced Abu Salim to move his *maq'ad* from the spot Russell had circled in red on the tourist map. I don't remember the scale, but it was thousands of times vaguer than the maps Tal had borrowed from the Unit.

Never before had I seen a map so detailed, so up-to-date. One glance, and Tal knew if the nearest waterhole was dry or not. He could travel on those maps for hours, virtually see the terrain in three dimensions; see the color of this mountain or that wadi at this or that hour; and the length of the shadow this cliff or that tree would throw at this or that hour—even a lone acacia, like the one standing at the edge of this forbidden plateau, which Tal had never seen before "on the ground," as he called it. He was curious to see "on the ground" the "dead space" his maps concealed. It was an enigma to me that he could see on the map what was concealed, measuring how many kilometers from this point to that, triangulating coordinates, reading mysteries like headlines. It took years of reconnaissance missions and counter-terrorist raids behind enemy lines to acquire and hone such map-reading skills—skills he tested and retested as we roamed the interior of the peninsula, almost as if he feared he had lost them, and with them the best of himself, in the months it took his reconstructed knees to heal.

It was partly to test his new knees that he had offered to escort me to the desert instead of Gingie, he said. The doctors had refused to declare him fit, insisting he had not yet fully recovered from the reconstructive surgery. He thought they were being overly cautious, overly protective of their reconstructive work, and he couldn't wait to prove them wrong.

Soon after we entered the interior of the peninsula, he asked me if I'd mind taking a bit of a detour. He wanted to give his knees a test at one of his old training grounds. There's a bit of a climb, he said, as we neared a remote hilltop. It looked like a hell of a climb from the dry riverbed at the bottom, but even the few steep spots would have been manageable had he not been bounding in the lead, bugging me to keep pace, as if the Nation would fall if we didn't make it to the summit in record time. His knees were as good as new, he said, laughing at me for hauling along a camera like a tourist. He waved me off mockingly whenever I aimed the Pentax at him, but he stayed in the frame and even offered a bashful smile by the sheer wall that towered to the flat, table-top summit that looked like Masada from the distance, but without the welcoming path.

"It's a bit of a sweat to scale this mountain wall, but what do you say we give it a try?" Tal said. Twice before, he had scaled this mountain wall to that summit, he told me, both times with men who served with him.

"I'm not a draftee in the Unit," I said. "Let's get back to the Jeep."

"No man is drafted to serve in the Unit," he said. "The army sticks to the book on this one. *Devarim*—Deuteronomy—if I'm not mistaken: 'Who is the man that is fearful and faint-hearted, let him go return to his house ... lest his brother's heart be faint as well ...' Only volunteers serve in the Unit.

"This climb is not as difficult as it looks," he insisted. And really it wasn't—at least not until a toehold started to crumble underfoot, and then another, and another.

"Step light and fast. This mountain wall is made of a chalk-like substance. It crumbles easily," Tal cautioned me. More like powdered sugar, I thought, as it crumbled under his gut when he was lying flat at the edge of the tabletop, trying to reach my hand and hoist me to the summit.

"Move back, quick, before gravity and this fucking tabletop carry us into the next world," I snapped, cursing myself for my blind trust in him.

"Grab hold of my hand. Come on, Leora, before your foothold goes. Imagine yourself as light as a feather—too light to crumble the ledge ..." With that, he hoisted me to the summit—a sweaty, dust-covered feather, trembling with disbelief.

"Are you crazy!? How the hell are we going to get off this fucking mountain alive?"

You could see nothing from this vantage-point—nothing but deserted wilderness.

"Nothing but promise ... You are looking at the Promised Land," he said. "Aaron, the brother of Moses, is buried on this hilltop," he informed me.

"I'll be buried here too. I'm not going down that crummy slope," I said.

When he led me to the opposite side of that tabletop and I saw a gentle slope, a simple downhill jog, I could have killed him. Then I saw the toll his concession to me was taking on his knees.

"From now on we only go up, and stay up," I said. He shook his head, smothering his laughter, as if, like water, laughter would douse the fire of his anger. He needed the energy anger supplies, the tremendous power. But he laughed when I offered to carry him piggyback. For a moment or two he put his full weight on my shoulders, and I felt he was solid muscle. It was hard to imagine him light as a feather. When I managed to hold him up, he looked surprised, glad, relieved.

"You have the stuff it takes to make it into the Unit," he said. What was this stuff I had? To back him up in a crunch? To entrust my life to him? Was this test of his knees really a test of trust? A need to see promise in emptiness?

264

Tal intended us to stay a lifetime, you'd have thought if you saw how he went about setting up camp. He took charge by force of habit, it seemed. I didn't mind. It was something to behold how he checked a cove or an inlet we decided to set up in until he found an area of level ground, clear of anthills, scorpions, and snakes. Then, one by one, he'd clear sharp rocks and stones that might trip you and bruise your bones when you stretch out. Racing against the sinking sun, we'd comb the wadi for driftwood. In the last purple rays, we'd built a fire and spread our sleeping bags on the ground by the fire-circle, like welcome-carpets. He'd park the Jeep so that it would shield the fire-circle from the cold night wind. Next he'd unload the cartons of provisions and cooking utensils and place them by the back wheels. The water jerrican he put by the Jeep's front tire, so that we could wash our faces next to the side mirror, and far from the sleeping bags. "From now on, wherever we camp overnight, we must place the same things in the same spots so that we won't waste time and energy looking for this or that, or break a hip, nose, or wrist tripping over a jerrican, pot, or pan," he said. And he did all that, night after night, no matter where we camped. Every camp-ground looked the same, such a craving he has for order, for a constant, for home...

❧

Tal's craving for the extraordinary got us into the "spectacular" wadi.

"I saw an interesting shortcut on the map, through a spectacular wadi. What do you say we take it?" he had asked.

"Let's go for it," I said, excited, elated. Traveling with him was like traveling with Arik back in the days when nothing was impossible...

At first, the wadi had looked like many we had crossed. Circles open, circles close, mountain chains spin forty-sixty klicks an hour, and just when it seems the Jeep is going to crash into the mountains, they part, and another circle opens up. But this time the mountains opened onto a black gorge, plunging down to a tiny blue dot, barely visible, at the bottom.

It caught Tal by surprise. He pumped the brakes, standing up. Too stunned to fear or feel anything, I waited for the Jeep to overturn, to roll on its canvas top and crush us. He pumps and pumps, and the tires don't grip. The Jeep keeps sliding, tail up, and the gear in the back spills to the front. I keep shoving it back, but the noise tells me how futile it is. Jerricans and boxes of utensils and provisions, cans, cartons, bottles, pots, pans—all tearing loose, crashing, banging . . . The gear will tear our heads off if the Jeep doesn't stop skidding.

"Watch out, Leora! Brace yourself!" Tal is working the steering wheel now, like crazy. And the Jeep slides sideways, front and tail bumpers scraping the mountain walls. Then, the Jeep tilts to the side, nearly rolling over, rolling tail down, bumping, scraping, skidding— slows down, stops.

The wadi smells of burning rock, burning metal, burning rubber.

"Are you all right?"

"Yes, you?"

"*Haffffffffiiiiiiffffff*," he replies, and the echo trembles in that wadi, a mountain fissure opening to a different geological era. Way up, the sky is a sliver of blue squeezed between two towering walls. The sun has never been here, the cold and dark as old as time. In the shade, we can see history in the mountain walls—layers and layers of years, decades, centuries, in countless colors and shades. We can touch time here, polished smooth.

There is no sign of a white flood line. The floodwaters must have filled this canyon to the top, polished it smooth, as they gushed with a force that ripped away mountains along the way—boulders too large to clear this narrow. An avalanche of huge boulders blocked the exit at the bottom end. The way back to the entrance at the top was blocked by the same slippery bedrock that mocked the tires. On both sides, mountain walls scraped the sky. The Jeep was trapped.

"I didn't expect this wadi to be that 'interesting,'" he said, clearly kicking himself. I had no doubt he had seen this wadi in three dimensions after reading his classified maps. But, more than once or twice before, his maps had underestimated the danger.

"That was great driving," I said, my teeth chattering, in shock as it sunk in how close we had been to being killed.

"Where did you learn Morse code," he said, rubbing my body to draw the blood back to my face.

Just then the Jeep started to creak and to roll, and the two of us jumped out and grabbed a couple of rocks to wedge under the wheels. As if it mattered now . . . I averted my eyes from his; I didn't want him to see how sorry I was to lose this desert beast—this heap of rusted bumpers, dented green fenders, faded canvas flopping over a homemade wooden frame, plastic windows too scratched by wind-driven sand to see through, a hole in the dashboard where once was a radio, and two patched-up front seats joined together by the sleeping bags stuffed in the gap between them . . .

Tal picked his way down the avalanche of boulders and rocks, spry as a mountain goat. If his reconstructed knees were hurting him now, he gave no sign of it. Ordinary surgery had extraordinary effects in this spectacular wadi, it seemed. He went all the way to the exit at the bottom. Halfway back up, at the impossible obstacle—a crater between boulders, almost twice his height, he stopped and became so absorbed in surveying that obstacle that he seemed to be in a trance. Then, like a man possessed by demons, he began to choose rocks and stones to build a couple of ramps for the Jeep wheels to cross.

"Beware of scorpions and snakes sheltering in the crevices," he cautioned me when I arrived to lend a hand.

Those improvised ramps would support the Jeep if they'd support his weight, he thought, or so it seemed as he jumped and stomped on each ramp. Any wobble or slide he corrected with a rock or a stone.

No one will believe these ramps, I thought, as I reloaded the Pentax and snapped a long view of them from way below, close to the blue exit, my back glued to the mountain face as I scanned for a better perspective.

"*Staaaay wherrrre yooooou arrrrre . . .*" The wadi echoes Tal.

He must be far from certain that the Jeep will clear the wadi on those ramps we improvised or he wouldn't leave me out. I'm to go for help in case he gets pinned under the Jeep, it seems.

"*Waaait, Taaal!!!*" I call out to him.

But even before the echo stops bouncing, he's behind the steering wheel, aligning the wheels to the ramp, and releasing the hand-brake... The Jeep starts to roll, nose down, dead silent—no engine, not a breath... He must be standing on the brakes. Stone by stone, rock by rock, the Jeep keeps crawling, tilting from side to side, creaking, complaining... I hold my breath until the wadi roars with a sparked-up engine...

⚘

"Abu Salim has just returned from his journey. *Ashkor Allah*—thank God," Azzizah muttered, half-asleep when the saluki dogs ran to the top of the path that leads to the *maq'ad*.

"*Yaa-Rabb...yaa-Rabb...*" Tammam moans under her carpet-blanket.

"Go back to sleep," Azzizah mutters to herself or to Tammam. "Abu Salim has decided to sleep at his *maq'ad* tonight.

"*Rohu! Rohu*. Go. Go to the *maq'ad*," Azzizah ordered the salukis, and they took off like a shot.

"Is it the behavior of the salukis that tells you that Abu Salim has returned and has decided to sleep at his *maq'ad* tonight?" I ask Azzizah.

"Ah, *Wallah*, I have been married to Abu Salim for so many years, I can sense-see through mountain to his heart," Azzizah whispered in reply. "Patience is better than thinking," she counseled to herself, Tammam, or me.

The Badawias and little Salimeh are sleeping by the fire-circle in front of Azzizah's tent. Tammam was too tired this evening to move to her tent and start a fire to stave off the cold night air for little Salimeh. It's really a punishment to leave a crackling fire-circle by which you have been lying around, sipping tea, casting spells, and fighting off sleep. Soon after sundown the Badawia can't help but give in to sleep. Dusk doesn't stretch here for hours, like summertime up north in Canada. The birds would probably be chirping still at this hour in Algonquin—here you hear no chirp; the birds probably think it's way past midnight, but to me it feels like nine or ten o'clock—hours before my bedtime.

The classic desert vista—a vast expanse of sand—was nowhere to be seen in the interior of the peninsula. The wadis—the dry riverbeds, the desert's roads/no-roads—wound around the jagged mountain chains, closing in, then opening to release you. Closing, opening—closing, opening—circle after circle, hour after hour. It's a tremendous surprise when the circle of mountains parts to reveal a sea of sand ...

Sand dunes sprawl gentle, clean, untouched—except by the wind twirling the crest here and there. The dunes are speckled with fool's gold, glittering enticingly in the sun. The heat sears the nostrils like frost, and not a shrub or a tree is evident, even at the banks of the dry riverbed that forked a wide opening onto this ocean of dunes.

The fork to my left led to waterholes, dried up in the drought, judging from the looks of a Badu who ambled toward us from that direction, dragging his camel and sweating in the August heat under a heavy winter *kaffiyye* and a winter parka, over a tattered sweater, over an ankle-long *jalabeeya*—layers to keep the sun from drying him up like a raisin. The *shibriyya*—dagger—buckled at his hip underlined the fierceness conveyed by his bloodshot eyes and craggy face. His lips were parched white, yet he wouldn't touch our water canteen until he had greeted us with an endless stream of salutations.

"*Yaa*-Badu, I'm getting thirsty just looking at you," I told him. He laughed, exposing a mouthful of brown teeth. Then he dropped his head back, lifted the canteen like a waterskin, high above his lips. After a couple of gulps, he said, "*Bas*—enough" and screwed on the cap. "Keep the canteen," I said.

"Allah shall reward you," he said in response, tucking the canteen into his faded camel saddle. Then, he pulled out a pita, and, as if the whole desert was his *maq'ad*—guest-receiving-place—and Tal and I his guests, he peeled off his parka and sweater, spread them on the ground like welcome-carpets, and said, "*Ogodu*—sit down." Folding his legs, he offered us his pita: "Eat ... Eat ..."

Tal and I had packed enough provisions for a platoon. We spread my white *kaffiyye* on the ground, like a tablecloth, and served the

Badu a banquet lunch—sardines and tuna, pickles and olives, crackers, and, for dessert, oranges and grapefruit, courtesy of the reservniks. And water, of course, from our jerrican; the Badu drank now as if he thought he'd better save every drop in the canteen we gave him for his journey. To where? What brings him to this deserted sand furnace? Smuggling? Even after we have shared with him our water and food, the Badu is cagey, not volunteering any information about himself or about the water scarcity.

"Ask him no questions, and he'll tell you no lies. Respect him but suspect him," Tal muttered to me in Hebrew.

"The Tommies also used to talk like we weren't there," I say to him in Hebrew, then, switching to Arabic, I ask the Badu if he happens to know where could we find the nearest waterhole.

"*Aywa*—yes," replied the Badu, pointing to the horizon in the southeast—or the southwest, for all I knew. Then in a patch of sand he draws a map of the dunes, and of the wadi bordering the dunes—which, he assures us, should take us to the waterhole.

"His map is pretty accurate," said Tal. In one stroke he drew on the Badu's map a line straight across the dunes. "That's the route I'd take. The roundabout way is a waste of gasoline." We had purchased two extra jerricans of gasoline from a Badu driving a blue pickup, who charged us nearly ten times the going rate in The Land. Tal suspected the gas was diluted. And he didn't trust this Badu either. "He draws a good map, but he's probably giving us the runaround. No Arab would divulge straight stuff to a couple of strangers, no matter how much water and food they shared with him."

"Makes me sick such cynical stereotyping, coming from a peacenik yet. Your knees aren't the worst of your war souvenirs. Can your trust be reconstructed? Even if we don't find the waterhole, he could be mistaken or his information could be outdated."

Tal looked at me as if he thought me a child living in a dream world. He loved my innocence. I loved his knowledge.

"Not good to drive like he pictured, straight through the sand dunes," the Badu told me, "*Ahhsan*—better—to drive around the dunes, like I pictured in the sand. *Wallah*, these sand dunes are full of many

Jeeps and trucks, and even tanks, that sank in the sand, or ran out of gasoline, or melted in the heat. *Aywa*, it is the worst time of day now to cross the sand dunes, for the sun is too high to tell direction. Many many people lose their way in these dunes, even in the best of times…"

"We'll let some air out of the tires, and the Jeep will cross this sand ocean like a dune buggy," Tal said after I translated the Badu's words. A dune buggy on recon: we had loaded up with provisions for almost every calamity that could befall us, even with flares he had taught me how to fire back at the sulfur springs, just in case he got pinned under the Jeep.

Before we parted from the Badu, Tal showed him a small pocket compass. The Badu looked at it in puzzlement, turning it from this side to that. "Can I tell him what it is and how it works, or would that also would make you sick?" Tal asked me, sarcastically. Then he explained to the Badu in Hebrew how to read north by this instrument called a compass and I translated into Arabic.

"*Allahu akbar*—Allah is great," the Badu exclaimed. He then cautioned us to wait or, better still, take the roundabout route he had recommended, adding that this manmade north-finder can't be as reliable as the North Star or as your own shadow. Tal had no argument for that.

There was no stopping to check the compass once we ventured into the dunes. The briefest of pauses in shifting gears, and the Jeep swallowed a bellyful of sand. As we cut through that granular ocean, the magnetic fix went all to hell; the compass read north as well as I did—every direction was north. And in every direction sand dunes led to dunes like giant ice-cream cones sprinkled, like the Badu said, with rusty frames of command cars and Jeeps, and black shreds of tires, and charred wing or tail housings. Off your plane, Arik? Did you ditch in this ocean of sand?

The searing wind razored our faces with its invisible load of sand. But nothing bothered Tal. He seemed to thrive on the challenge, the risk, the adventure. Vitality lit his face and engorged every muscle. He seemed built for the motion: accelerate, clutch, pedal, shift, four wheels, high gear—and a roaring sprint up to the breaking edge of a dune, with the front wheels shooting for the sky, for the blinding sun.

Then, just as the gear in the back threatened to crash into our heads, he'd press full speed down a sandhill, giving us the momentum to clear the next peak ahead. One burst of momentum flung open my door, and when I reached out to close it a bottomless abyss waited below. The wind had chewed away the slope.

Sun above, sand below—the Jeep leaps over crest after crest and dives into trough after trough. A fairy mist of fool's gold swirls around us, and beyond the next breaking dune the wind whipped it into a giant dervish, gold-bedecked and -speckled. Another dune, and another, and the sand rippled down to the gentle slope that takes us—full circle back to the spot where we had entered the dunes.

I collapsed into laughter at the sight of the same Badu—sitting on the same parka, spread like a welcome-carpet in the same wadi, next to the same camel, and looking like nothing a stranger did would ever surprise him.

Tal, furious and cursing in seven languages, pulled a U-turn. Sweat blotches blossomed on his t-shirt, veins bulged in his glistening neck, his jaws quivering with anger. I decided to say nothing.

The shadows were starting to stretch now. Tal opened his door and threw it wide, using the angle of its shadow like the needle of a compass—one he could check only by leaning far out the door opening, while driving full speed. By the time we cleared the dunes, he had swallowed a lot of sand—and accolades from me.

Exhilarated, and tired of driving, we pulled to a stop in a deserted oasis tucked in a bend of Wadi R. As soon as he switched off the engine, a blessed silence engulfed us and the small cluster of date palms, a green miracle standing tall and proud at the bank of a riverbed that hadn't seen rain in seven successive years.

"What do you say we camp here tonight?" He was savoring a long-awaited cigarette, a warm bottle of beer, and the array of colors that the slanting rays were teasing out of the sandstone slopes surrounding the oasis. At sundown I gathered some driftwood. We built a fire. From his paratrooper's bag he dug out a *feenjon* and a small round canister. The oasis was perfumed with coffee and coriander...

"How come you didn't get married?" I asked him.

"I don't know," he replied. "Didn't find her yet... Maybe because I was preoccupied with other things... Maybe because no girl could match the allure of the Unit."

"That's what Samson said before he met Delilah," I muttered, and he laughed, tugging my braid like a boy in Grade 9 taunting the girl he loves, hates, fears, fucks in his most secret thoughts.

He said he's a very good cook and volunteered to prepare dinner. Well, he was certainly inventive. What I would give now just for the black and green olives, or the diced pickles and salami that he mixed into the pasta he cooked that night, adding a bit of olive oil, salt, pepper, oregano, rosemary. He opened a bottle of local dry red cabernet, then local 777 brandy to accompany a dessert of oranges and grapefruit flambé—so help me.

So highly classified were the nine years he served in the Unit, he hardly said a word during his furloughs at home, he told me. Such silence might be golden for the security of the Nation, "but not for your personal home life." He had seen it wreck the best of relationships, and even now, he said, it keeps him apart from everyone but the men who had served with him. "And in the kibbutz, the price of an error wasn't a life—yours, your men's, or your enemies'... It wasn't easy to adjust to a normal sense of responsibility. And it was very difficult to accept the authority of a person who hadn't earned your respect. You know how it is in the kibbutz—members vote for this person to head the banana planation, or that person to take charge of the laundry, not because this or that person is the best qualified, but because of popularity or animosity. If we ran the army like that, the Arabs would have finished us off in less than a week."

"Are you planning to sign up for another stint when your knees are healed?"

"No. I love the kibbutz, flaws and all. It's the place for me."

"So why are you taking a leave of absence from this dream, now that you can finally realize it?" I asked him, for the third or fourth time since the day we met. Still he hesitated. He lit a cigarette, puffed and puffed. The darker the night closed in on us, the brighter our fire-circle became...

"I was living with a girl in the kibbutz," he finally replied. "Her name is Ephrat. We lived together for three years, but we were together only on the occasional *Shabbat* and holiday that I was home on furlough. It was very different to have a normal life together. I loved her, very much. But I couldn't ... I mean, *we* couldn't live together and we couldn't live apart. The kibbutz is a small community. We bumped into each other ten times a day. She said she didn't feel free to see another man while I was there, and so she asked me to take leave of absence from the kibbutz till everyone stopped staring and whispering each time she was seen with another man ..."

"Aren't you carrying gallantry a bit too far?" I said—I could almost hear Riva saying, "I wonder if what really compelled him to take his leave of absence and maybe even to break his relationship with Ephrat, and to drift, was his craving for the extraordinary and the ordinary of life, both at once ... It's a textbook case, straight out of Returning Heroes 101 ..."

Ever since Riva's son Gingie had become observant, he had turned the most ordinary into the extraordinary, and to the divine, with his rituals and prayers. After a couple of months of that, the divine, too, became ordinary, and his craving for the extraordinary got him a criminal record for erecting an illegal settlement in the West Bank ...

⚘

In his whole life Tal didn't have as many photos snapped of himself—even of him refusing to be photographed—as he did on our journey.

On this our last night, before we built the fire, before we set up camp, before I forgot to give him all the rolls of film I shot so he could take them back to the city with him, I went to fetch them from the brown knapsack at the back of the Jeep. The knapsack was open; the cameras and lenses were all there, and the unused film in their yellow, blue, and green casings. But not one of the black canisters of film I'd shot, ten-fifteen rolls.

"Did you transfer them to your paratrooper's bag?" I asked him.
"No."

We searched every bag, box, corner in the Jeep. There was no trace of them.

"Where did you last handle that brown knapsack?" he asked. We backtracked through memory to every circle we had covered, every pissing stop we remembered, even to the place where he didn't want to stop—where, in a wadi, half-hidden by a boulder, I spotted a rare treasure: a dry tree stump to cook over and keep us warm all night. "Leave it," he said. "We have a sackful of driftwood, more than enough for one night."

"So, we'll give it as a gift to the mountain Badu," I cajoled. We had to move the brown knapsack to make room for that stump, and while I had it in my hands, I pulled out the Pentax, to finish the roll and tuck it in with others we had shot in the side pocket. "*Dai*—enough. Let's go ...*"*; he'd had enough of my detour. I fastened that side pocket too fast perhaps. And that wadi was bumpy. The canisters must have bounced out of the Jeep.

"That spot is a mere stroll from here, only a few kilometers," he said. He handed me the Beretta, flipped my braid across my face, and strode off to track down those canisters. Before I could open my mouth he was swallowed by the night.

"Those damn film rolls can wait till daylight. What's with you, Tal! Come back ...*"*

"I'll be back in no time," he responded from the darkness—almost the exact words you said, Arik, the day you went.

I'll be damned if I let that old war souvenir fuck me over now, I told myself. I lit up that stump, cleared the sharp rocks and stones away from the fire-circle, spread out the sleeping bags like welcome-carpets, parked the Jeep sideways against the cold night wind, unloaded the water jerrican, food provisions, cooking utensils. And when that inlet at the bend of the wadi looked like our camping-ground, when everything was in the same place, with everything in order, I started to prepare a feast: tuna in cream of mushroom soup on a bed of rice never smelled better; and, for dessert, I roasted the last of the sweet potatoes and carrots, spiked with a bit of honey and brandy ...

Then I waited.

I tucked my wristwatch in the knapsack. Time disappeared for a while. But then, the bottle of wine was empty, the stump half gone, the feast cold and soggy, and still no sign of him. He has x-ray vision, I told myself; he can see in the dark of night, there in Entebbe, Lebanon, Syria, Jordan ... He has tracked terrorists and guerrillas for nine years; film canisters are child's play to him. He is one of the best recon men in the Land. It's a moonless night, but a skyful of stars is as good a map as any ... It's a mere stroll, a mere few kilometers, from here, so what is keeping him so fucking long? Where in the hell is the North Star? Did we find that wood stump north or south of this inlet? Why are those damn photos so fucking important to him all of a sudden? That stubborn son-of-Moses will track them down, even if it takes till the Messiah comes. Nothing is impossible to him. Is this another test, or does he really want the damn photos? To validate this dream-journey of ours? Where is his damn romantic gallantry now?

How could he leave me alone in this wilderness, in this vast dense darkness?

It was closing in, edging tighter, shrinking the fire-circle light. The stump crumbled to ashes, and still, no sign of him. Only the sackful of driftwood left. A twig, a branch at a time, I fed the fire, and watched it shrink and expand, shrink and expand ... A silent wind was blowing smoke in every direction, cloaking the brilliant sky, stinging the eyes, stealing the breath, searing the face, but the darkness beyond it was cold and threatening. And creeping into that darkness beyond the winking fire-circle faces ballooned and burst, ballooned and burst ... Arik appeared, his pilot's cap jaunty—the prick. I'm done waiting for him—for any prick. One more cigarette, then I'm going to sleep. Or to fire the damn Beretta—

Now, Imma! Abba! What's that noise in the darkness, a rustling coming closer ... too close ...

"Hi, Leora. Shalom ..."

Over the fire-circle he leapt, like a madman, and took me into his arms. His lips tasted of salt, his hair drips sweat mixed with sand and dust. His pockets were full of film canisters—new souvenirs ... dream souvenirs ... ordinary souvenirs. Extraordinary.

Tammam rolled over in her sleep, almost to the rocks that ring the fire—a heap of coals still glowing red hot. She rolled right back, but it smelled like her carpet-blanket, *thowb*, shawls, or braided hair had got singed. It alarmed her, and me, until she smothered the glowing ember on her hand-woven carpet-blanket.

"You should not be sleeping so near the fire," she muttered to herself, and/or to me. "But the night is so very cold and long if you are not so near the fire." She wrapped herself and her infant daughter in that same carpet-blanket, and lay down, again very near the fire, but she kept tossing and turning, waking up, hearing things from all directions—camel-riders dismounting at the well, then camel-riders dismounting at Abu Salim's *maq'ad*. All I could hear was the wind, the hissing and crackling of the fire, and the distant echo of a wildcat in heat.

❧

... Later, with a sweep of his hand, Tal leveled the sand, then unzipped our sleeping bags and spread them out like a double bed, the army bag on the bottom, like a mattress, the down bag on top, a blanket, all tucked and without a single crease, stretched smooth ...

"Good morning," Tal greeted me, though the sky showed not even a promise yet of dawn. And then he opened our cover and read me as if I were the morning paper—with his eyes, his lips, his hands. "Extra good edition this morning," he whispers. "Just look at this article ... and that." The next one he finds engrossing and reads it through to the end ... Then he starts from the beginning again, pushing his morning edition out of my reach. "Wait till the next edition ..."

"Why? This edition looks outstanding."

"But it's hot off the press."

So I let the ink cool off a bit. Then I read him—slow, slow ... savoring each article, and he waits until I've finished. Then, just as we are about to light a cigarette, his wristwatch alarm beeps. *Beep ... beep ... beep*, echo the sandstone mountains.

The night Tal and I reached Abu Salim's *maq'ad* was moonless, the hour was late. Six or eight Badu men, one more fierce-looking than the others, were sitting around the fire. We parked the Jeep where the Badu parked their camels: outside the fire-circle light. Huge rocks were arranged in a semicircle for the comfort of Abu Salim's guests. They shielded us from the cold night wind, and when I leaned my back against them, I could still feel the warm rays of the midday sun. We all sat on hand-woven carpets—not stained and frayed like up here in the tents—and fragrant wood was feeding the fire, not dung. And coffee was brewing in an old, almost black, brass *bakraj*. I don't think I'll ever forget the sight of those fierce-looking men sipping coffee from tiny white-porcelain cups.

The Badu called Tal *yaa*-Jabbar—a man of great valor, "for only a man of great valor would dare traverse mountains so treacherous by Jeep on a moonless night," said one. Another, a toothless Badu with seashell earrings, said only one or two men dared drive a Jeep through the last few bends at dark of night; even a camel will often hesitate to cross that stretch. And the Badu with two fingers missing from his right hand, three from his left, asked Tal how could he see this and that crevasse, this and that bend ...

So impressed they all seemed—all except one. He looked like the whole desert was his domain. He also looked like no benevolent ruler.

"I am Imsallam Suleman Abu Salim," he said and then he asked me if I was the woman who had helped the sick Badu child-boy reach the *darwisha*.

"Yes," I said. Is that why Abu Salim invited me to visit-stay in his forbidden tents?

Abu Salim invited Tal to stay-sleep over in the *maq'ad*, until day light at least. But that place smelled of enemy to the Jabbar ...

Tal whispered in Hebrew that he didn't think it was wise for me to stay alone with that bunch—not in the *maq'ad* and not in the tents.

The mountains thundered when Tal took off, and the Badu sat as if they were watching a thriller: The Jabbar was the good guy, and the night, the desert, the mountains, were the villain. And as if Tal—the Jabbar—could hear them, they called out to him to watch out—a sharp bend was coming, a steep slope, a pothole, a crater, *yaa*-Allah, a narrow ridge, an abyss to the east... They continued to guide him until the mountain echoed a lonely hyena, then the barking of saluki dogs. And then the legend-telling lilt of the Badu with one missing eye. "*Wallah*, did you see?"

"*Wallah*, we did see," the mountains echoed.

"*Wallah*, did you see the Jabbar flying, though the night is moonless... flying through the wadi... through the sharp bend... the narrow ridge... the abyss to the east...," the Badu repeated, again and again, until the legend was carved on the mountain.

The Tents

22

"A Jeep is climbing up the wadi," Tammam announced while we were at the loom. Like the wind, she took off with little Salimeh; Azzizah and I trailed in her wake. We stopped at the spot the Badawias call "the lookout point"—from which Azzizah and I neither saw nor heard any sign of a Jeep.

"I can hear only the wind rushing. My hearing is getting old—slow, like the hearing of strangers," Azzizah said. "You cannot hear the Jeep, can you?" she asks me.

"No," I reply.

"*Aywa*, Abu Salim has told me how slow is the hearing of strangers," says Azzizah. "So slow, you can smoke up a whole cigarette and, maybe when you finish smoking it, you will hear the Jeep Tammam hears now, *Inshalla*." She rolls a cigarette for herself—seemingly to test how fast-slow my hearing is, and hers. She takes a puff—listens; another puff—listens...

You can see nothing but shimmering haze here, at this island in the molten mist. The sun is too high now for me to make out the mountain chain across the canyon that plunges so far below the lookout point you cannot see bottom, even if you stand upright and lean over—

"*Dir balak*—watch out." Azzizah cautions my every move; she and Tammam take turns holding little Salimeh. Curiosity could be fatal.

The only spot of shade is right under the acacia, the solitary green on this plateau. And the shade it gives is flimsy, tattered. It looks like Abu Salim's camels have browsed all the leaves they can reach, leaving only the thorns on the branches, and on the ground. "These thorns can spike right through your shoes, so *dir balak*," Tammam cautions.

Only in the early hours of the morning, and in the late hours of afternoon, can you see from this lookout point, and the view it gives is a single bend in the dry riverbed that leads to Abu Salim's *maq'ad*.

"Long before you see who rides in that bend, you can hear who is approaching the bend, especially Tammam. For Tammam's hearing is young, therefore sharp, sharper than mine, and even Abu Salim's," Azzizah explains, then takes a puff, but the wind has put out her cigarette. She doesn't bother to fight it, just tucks the dead cigarette into the pocket of her *qunah*—long black veil—that covers her forehead and falls back almost to the ground.

"Nighttime I can hear a distance much farther than daytime, and farther still on moonless nights," says Tammam, spreading one of her shawls as a welcome-carpet for her, Azzizah, and me.

Now she'll tell Azzizah of the night she heard Azzizah urging Abu Salim to purchase a blemished bride/blemished she-camel for the price of rights to waterholes, or smuggling routes... That's what I thought. But she makes no mention of it.

"Now I can also hear the Jeep," Azzizah exclaims. By this time Tammam can hear whose Jeep it is. I have yet to hear anything that sounds like a Jeep.

"It is Hilal's Jeep," says Tammam. "Maybe my brother is riding with him... Oh, my child, my daughter, take what is left of the rest of my life, and enjoy it..."

"Maybe Hilal is driving-coming to the *maq'ad* to take our stranger-no-stranger guest, Nura, back to her home tent," says Azzizah. Then, to me, she adds, "People will say our hospitality fell short if you cut your visit so short."

"*Aywa*—yes. I bid you stay, I bid you stay," Tammam inches off the turquoise ring her father had purchased with her bride-price and hands it to me. "I bid you stay..." All her most precious jewels, the girl-Badawia would give for a crack in the wall that confines her, Azzizah, and their clanswomen to this tiny world encircled by granite. They are exiles in their own home ground, these Badawias, as I am.

I do not, this time, ask the Badawias why they want me to stay, or why they had invited me. "No need to bid me stay with your ring, *yaa*-Tammam..."

"You mean you are going to stay?" the girl-Badawia entreats me.

"Yes," I assure her. "What makes you think this person you call Hilal is driving to the *maq'ad* to take me home?"

"He is your tribesman," Azzizah replies. "Abu Salim had told us Hilal is a Yahodi stranger-man of the authorities . . . a stranger-man thin and long, and walks bent like a quarter-moon. That is why he is called Hilal—meaning, 'quarter-moon.'"

"Today, as always, Hilal is driving to the *maq'ad* to see if Abu Salim has broken the law forbidding the cutting down of trees for firewood," says Tammam. "Then he stays to hear a story, poem, legend—and to tell how unruly are the women, even the maidens, of his Yahodi tribe. 'So disobedient and obstinate,' Hilal had told Abu Salim. 'No man could rule them; they rule man. *Aywa*, one Yahodiya named Golda Meir even became the sheikh of the Yahodi tribe, and the ruler of our Sinaa desert.'"

"Hilal is ill-fated to have been born a stranger," says Azzizah.

"I hear a horn tooting!" Tammam cries out as if she has heard the angel Gabriel blowing his horn.

"It is the horn tooting of my grandsons! My grandsons are riding with Hilal," says Azzizah. "Can you hear it now?" she asks me. I do, in the far distance, and the rumbling of a Jeep, finally.

Standing only a few meters from the edge of the lookout point, Azzizah and Tammam point to the spot where the Jeep was turning into the bend of the dry riverbed, conjured out of the haze that drifted above the dream-ocean in which we were enisled.

Azzizah and Tammam never entertained the sliver of possibility that it was a figment of their imagination, just wishful thinking, just auditory hallucination that Azzizah's grandchildren had caught a ride to Abu Salim's *maq'ad* with Hilal.

Elated, the Badawias lit Azzizah's special-occasion fragrant firewood in Azzizah's special-occasion fire-circle, round which they spread Azzizah's special-occasion welcome-carpets; they adjusted their veils and shawls and gave little Salimeh a bit of spit and polish. Then, they waited. Waited. Tried to keep the toddler from getting dusty-dirty again. Cursed and spat and waited, grunting, sighing, lamenting.

"It is not proper to keep Azzizah waiting too long to be paid respect by her grandsons," Tammam explained. "Abu Salim should have told-ordered them to come here long ago . . . It is not proper . . . not proper . . ."

"Not waiting for two grandchildren, but surrounded by many, many more I would have been all the time if fate had held it in store for me," Azzizah says, lamenting her fate. "I lost not only all my daughters—each one blood of my heart, fruit of my love, milk of my breast, each one from seed to flower I raised, only to lose her the day she died or the day she got married and moved to live in her husband's compound—but her children . . . O, *Wallah*, had fate held it in store for me to have eight sons and one daughter, not eight daughters and one son, eight more tents would be pitched in this compound, teeming with life, my many grandchildren would fill this compound. And I would not be pained now from knowing in blood, *yaa-Rabb*, how homesick my daughters are, how they wish they were here, together with their mother and father and sisters and brother. How it pains them that I miss them, that I am all alone now like a childless woman after birthing and raising so many . . ."

Tammam's eyes welled up with tears, as did mine.

"The salt of your tears and mine is one and the same, O my sisters . . ." Azzizah heaves a sigh, her eyes wet.

Silence. Waiting as the shadows stretch longer and longer. The special-occasion fire-circle demands more and more special-occasion fragrant wood. The longer she is kept waiting, the less she curses, spits, grunts, laments; the more lifeless Azzizah becomes, as if the only way she can accept her fate is to resign from life.

"I hear your grandsons approaching, *yaa*-Azzizah," whispers Tammam.

Silence. Flies buzzing. Fire hissing. No sounds of footsteps. Azzizah frowns, as if she thinks, this time, Tammam hears dreams approaching. Her jewels *jingle-jangle* as she rejects a cigarette with

285

the flick of a wrist. Tammam accepts it. I also light up one. Take a puff—listen. Take a puff—listen, like Azzizah did at the look-out point. Tammam fills the teapot and places it on the red-hot firestones.

"Now ... now I hear my grandsons approaching," mutters Azzizah. Her eyes reflect that she is pleased her hearing was slower than Tammam's by only half a cigarette, and mine by a full one.

The child-boys run to Azzizah. She bends to heap a long string of greeting-blessings on their heads. The oldest one, not older than ten or eleven, returns a breathful, then, in the next breath, adds regards from a clanful. The younger one, seven or eight, joins him, and saves for last regards from his mother. Both go over to Tammam. The girl-Badawia whispers greetings-blessings in their ears. They then heap greetings-blessings on little Salimeh. They fold their legs and sink to the special-occasion welcome-carpets. Both babble too fast to understand, one interrupting the other—like Mutt and Jeff. There is energy and mischief in their eyes as they sneak looks at me.

"Say each word *wahada, wahada*—one by one," Mutt tells Jeff. "Abu Salim said we ... have ... to ... talk ... *wahada, wahada*—one ... by ... one—in ... front ... of ... the ... woman ... stranger-no-stranger," he adds, enunciating each word so deliberately that all of us laugh.

"*Guwwa*—power to you," says Azzizah, serving a steaming glass of tea to Mutt—she calls him Faraj—and Jeff, Imbarak. They both wear striped *jalabeeya*—shirt-dresses—frayed, stained, covered with dust. Their curly hair is almost gray with dust. Amulets draped around their necks, their feet bare. Neither one flicks away the flies that pester the corners of their eyes, their lips, the rim of their tea glasses, and Faraj's—Mutt's—dripping nose.

"Did you see my brother on your way, or at the *maq'ad*?" Tammam asks Mutt and Jeff, her voice hard, her eyes soft.

"No," they reply, almost in unison.

She heaves a sigh of relief—or sorrow, I can't tell. Her eyebrows knot in a frown, like a person worried, disappointed, apprehensive ...

"Did you hear anyone tell how far a distance my brother has yet to ride before he dismounts at our tents?"

"*La*—no. No one mentioned your brother," says Jeff.

"*Ghul*—tell what you saw, what you heard in the *maq'ad*," says Azzizah.

"I want to tell... I want to tell..." demands Mutt.

"*Ghul*—tell on," says his grandmother, Azzizah, chuckling under her veil.

"*Aywa*, I wish to tell that Hilal came to bring word to the woman-stranger-no-stranger from her son in a paper called letter."

Oh, my God——

"*Ba'ad idhnikum*—with your permission—I'll go to the *maq'ad*, get my son's letter," I told the Badawias.

A letter, a phone call, a knock on the door—and that's it, the end of the world as you know it. Nothing is ever the same...

"We brought the letter," says Mutt, and Jeff pulls out of his pocket a white airmail envelope, bordered by red and blue teeth, and bearing Canadian, American, French, or English stamps, I couldn't tell. Tammam snatched the envelope from Jeff just as he was about to hand it to me.

"I want to see your son—his name, his words to you," the girl-Badawia explained.

Azzizah spits, then tells her grandsons, "You cannot trust Hilal, nor anyone who works for the authorities."

"But Hilal handed the letter to Abu Salim and Abu Salim told-ordered me to dispatch it to her," says Jeff, pointing to me. It takes every drop of self-discipline I have to restrain the urge to grab the letter from Tammam's hands.

"Hilal told me," cried out Mutt, "Hilal told me that strangers don't press their words to their loved ones in poems recited like us Badu..."

"*Aywa*," Jeff interjects, "strangers press their words on paper. Then they insert the words-pressed-on-paper into a paper pouch. And then they glue on a picture called 'stamp.' You see, this letter has many stamps, meaning many permissions to cross many borders.

And then the strangers, they take the paper pouch with all the many stamps to an airplane, and the pilot brings the letter to the authorities, to Hilal…"

"You cannot trust the authorities," mutters Azzizah.

"*Laaaaaa!* Tammam! Don't open it! Don't open the pouch! It is bad luck, bad luck! Hilal said it's bad luck to open the pouch, unless it is addressed to you!" Mutt and Jeff shout over each other.

Startled, frightened, Tammam threw the letter. The wind blew it to the rim of the fire-circle. I lunged to retrieve it.

"You ruined it!… Ruined it!! Now Abu Salim will say I'm not a man. I cannot be trusted even with paper———" Jeff lashed out at Tammam when he saw the letter was singed in spots. "Women can't be trusted even with paper. Hand it to me. Read it from my hand!" the little tyrant demanded, grabbing the letter from my hand. In the bit I held fast I saw that the handwriting was not my son's and that it was signed "Hillel—the Haifa'ee, as our mutual friend, Tal, refers to me."

"Let me have the part you tore, and I'll knead the two pieces into one in my writing-to-remember," I tell the little prick.

He spits like Abu Salim, curses all women.

"*Aywa*, as life must end, so women are lesser than men," his little brother declares.

"*Oskotu*—shut up you all!!" demands Tammam.

Silence.

"Like vultures they are descending upon us today," Tammam mutters, as if possessed by her old demons. Transfixed, she laments, "Oh, take what is left of my life and enjoy it … *yaa-Rabb* .. . *yaa-Rabb* …Oh, life who has sat me down square on hot ashes, why have you lashed me this way…"

"*Esh hassal*—what happened?" Azzizah asks the girl-wife.

"*Hushshsh*," Tammam hisses. "A camel-rider is approaching. Not on the path from the *maq'ad*, but on the path from the well," Tammam explains. "I think he is my brother…"

"Whenever you hear someone approaching you think it is your

brother," says Azzizah. Tammam by now is halfway to her tent, rushing into the wind with little Salimeh in her arms.

Tammam ululates—in honor of her brother? in celebration of his arrival? Her cry bounces from mountain to mountain. The whole desert can hear her trembling joy...

Hillel's letter

...You are staying in tents rumored to be embroiled in father-and-son violations that might end up in father killing son and brother killing sister—the girl Abu Salim married. His son Salim, rumored to have fathered her infant-daughter, might be subjected to Badu test for proof of paternity. If result positive, I'll return to the maq'ad *and take you home well before the crowd gathers to witness the double execution.*

...Bear in mind that after a year-long search Abu Salim finally tracks down his son, Salim, then only a couple of days later he breaks a law his clan has adhered to for as long as anyone can remember and invites you to visit-stay in his forbidden tents—to be your brother's-sister's keeper? To deter double-murder, arrest, imprisonment, by your mere presence? ...

If you would rather leave now, advise me of it via Abu Salim's grandsons. If you decide to stay, I'll back you up all the way.

Whatever you do, remember: the mountain Badu have been known to kill a person who spreads rumors of adultery, incest, illicit love...

> *Hillel—the Haifa'ee, as our*
> *mutual friend, Tal, refers to me*

23

"Are you ready? Write-to-remember!" Abu Salim orders me, as if this evening is no different from yesterday's, as if I am a scribe in his royal court.

"No," I'm itching to tell him. "Give me a minute to breathe, to recover."

"Are you ready?" little Mutt, emulating his grandfather, snaps at me.

His grandparents—Abu Salim and Azzizah—crack up. Oh, how their laughter irks Tammam and her brother.

The *shibriyya*—the dagger—peeking through the frock Tammam's brother wears unbuttoned looks like a sort of belt buckle, until he hands it to his sister and you see how the cutting edge slices the top off a can of tuna.

Tammam cuts open all the cans her brother brought. No one tells her to leave some for tomorrow. "Take what is left of my life and enjoy it," Tammam's eyes say to her brother.

Yes, I know the Badu well enough to read their eyes. It's Russell I can't read, and Hillel, and, perhaps most of all, Tal. Why have they waited to dispatch the police to this Badu encampment, even if they think the rumor is baseless?

Patronizing, arrogant, presumptuous—Hillel, Tal, Russell. Or was it only Hilal—Hillel—who presumed that a clan of Badu nomads who have endured for centuries without interference might suddenly find themselves to be such helpless, backward children, they couldn't survive a family crisis—a rumored family crisis—without the "mere presence" of a stranger? Then, to top it off, Hilal—Hillel—smuggles this letter past Badu who have lived by smuggling goods and information for centuries. There isn't a smuggler's ploy these Badu aren't wise to . . .

Tal must have stopped at Hillel's post after he dropped me off here. "Something didn't smell right there," he might have told Hillel. And when Hillel told him of the rumor, Tal probably wanted to drive back to Abu Salim's *maq'ad* to pull me out. But Hillel would have said, "She knows what she's doing. She must have heard the rumor and didn't tell you about it for fear it would endanger your life and hers, expose your blood for five generations... Is that how it transpired?

The Haifa'ee, Tal called Hillel, meaning "a native of Haifa." You can't walk upright in that city for very long; all the streets slope down or up the crests and ravines of the Carmel mountain range. Therefore, natives of Haifa walk bent like Hilal, meaning quarter-moon in Badu Arabic. In Hebrew, "Hillel" means "praise." The Haifa'ee—Hillel—Hilal—had served with Tal in the Unit.

Had he showed up in the *maq'ad* when I was sick and out of it?...

Daqq, daqq, daqq. Abu Salim pounds the roasted coffee beans to fine powder in a brass mortar. *Daqq, daqq, daqq.* The mountain echoed for all the desert to hear what honor, what welcome, Abu Salim is brewing for Tammam's brother.

Whatever Tammam's eyes say to her brother, he can't take it, or so it seems. His eyes shift to the cliffs in the east, reflecting the golden tail of the sun, sinking in gulfs, oceans, seas hundreds of kilometers west of this compound. In the slanted rays, the compound looks besieged by the mountains, circles within circles, their purple deepening by the minute. Dusk here is a tease, like a lover ejaculating prematurely.

Oh, what I wouldn't give now to be in the screened-in porch of the summer cottage in Algonquin with a glass of scotch on ice, not a pen, sweating in my hand.

Saluki dogs, chasing a herd of black goats to the tents, raise a cloud of dust and a fit of coughing and cursing. As soon as the dust settles, Tammam's brother looks at Azzizah as if she had brewed the rumors like poison to kill her junior co-wife, even if Salim, Azzizah's only son, must die as well.

Azzizah's eyes well up with tears—from the onion she is slicing? The senior wife drops the onion slices into a frying pan sizzling over the cooking fire eight to ten meters away from the welcome-carpets she and Tammam had spread round this fire-circle.

"Are you ready?" Abu Salim breaks silence as soon as my pen stops. Now, Abu Salim says nothing while my pen's moving. He frowns as if I take him for fool who doesn't know how long it takes to write three words. "Write what I tell you," says Abu Salim, pouring honor-coffee into dainty porcelain cups. "Largesse won't lessen your wealth/whereas avarice acts like a pail never full," he dictates, serves honor-coffee—"From the right, to avoid the guest's spite . . . *Uwakhad li'l theif/theni li'l seif/tallat li'l keif.* Now write what it means. Are you ready? . . .

"First coffee cup is for to honor the guests; the second is for the sword; the third is for the *keif*—the sheer pleasure. After that you must rest your cup face down on the ground. For only a *fellah* lacking *adabb, asl-agl*—nobility, lineage, character, manners—will extend his hand for a refill after the third cup of coffee-honor."

Tammam's brother sips, leaning forward for fear, it seems, that a drop might stain his light blue frock and pants—like his beige shoes and beige socks, spanking-white shirt and spanking-white *kaffiyye*, brand new. Nowhere in Sinai could he purchase such tailored clothes, except in Al-Arish—a week by camel from here, give or take a day or two. He rode straight from the tailor shop and shoe store to this compound, or else he saved this outfit for a special occasion.

"He dressed for a wedding," Azzizah said when he dismounted his camel by Tammam's tent. But it was in the season of the weddings that I first entered the interior of the peninsula, and not then, nor after, have I seen a Badu or stranger dressed like Tammam's brother. No man who has something to hide or to be ashamed of would dress up like that. Is that why he was riding like a prince, parading for God knows how many days, or how many travelers, shepherds, tents, or *maq'ad*s he passed? To dispel the rumor that might doom him to kill his sister? To show he has no doubt that Abu Salim's son, Salim, will pass the Badu test of innocence?

"How does your Badu clan test a suspect for innocence or guilt?" Ask them, Leora. Come on, what are you afraid of? I don't know. A hell of a lie detector you'd need to test a suspect in this place, where stories-lies are considered spice to enhance life and a person who tells no lies is considered to be a person with no pepper. Would a Badu of pepper conduct this test? When? When is Salim expected to reach this, his home compound? Would he be returning home if he were not absolutely certain that he would pass the Badu test of innocence?

"No," Tammam and her brother would reply.

"Yes." Azzizah and Abu Salim would disagree.

Or so it seems.

Abu Salim, looking like a pauper next to Tammam's brother, treats him like an old aristocrat indulging an upstart who has paraded his lack of cunning; his secret ambition; his craving for power, fortune, fame; and his vanity.

Tammam's brother places his cup upside down on the ground. He's had his fill of Abu Salim's honor; Abu Salim can keep his patronizing indulgence for his son Salim, his eyes seem to say. He's probably not more than two or three years past his teens; same age as my son. Maybe he also wants to be a hero. Maybe he dressed up in his best clothes because he thought all the eyes in the desert are on him; in tents and *maq'ad*s the desert over his name is mentioned; never before was he the center of attention anywhere, except perhaps in his father's compound, years ago when his mother died birthing his sister, Tammam. He was probably six or eight years old then. And ever since, he has taken care of his sister, Tammam; protected her, widened her world by telling her what he has seen and heard in the desert that stretches beyond her narrow boundaries. But now he's out of his league, Abu Salim seems to imply, otherwise he would have known that he would serve his sister best by acknowledging to no one that he had heard a rumor about anyone even remotely connected to him.

"Who gave you the Badu ring—the silver ring on your writing hand?" Tammam's brother breaks the silence like a tyrant—a tyrant who knows damn well that his sister gave me that ring, trusting I would not unveil her even to him, her brother.

Tammam utters not a sound. No one does. No one looks in her

direction, his, or mine—not even Abu Salim. Looks like Tammam was right: when it comes to her, her reputation, her ring, her brother ranks higher than her husband, Abu Salim, and higher than a woman-stranger of the tribe that rules his desert. Is that why he thinks he can test me like a tyrant? Like a tyrant schooled in the way of strangers; a tyrant who knows I can't pass this character test—that, if I'm straightforward, honest, I betray his sister's trust, her reputation, his clan's, his tribe's? Is he testing me to see if I will put his Badu moral code above mine and keep the silence even if and when he kills his sister?

For all I know, he's counting on me to call the police, but how? Does he think a Yahodiya stranger wouldn't dare sit alone in a Badu compound without a gun? One like Tal's that fires SOS flares? ... as if a Badu compound was an enemy camp.

"Who gave you the Badu ring—the silver ring?" He won't let up.

"A Badawia," I reply.

"What is her name?" he demands.

Silence. Abu Salim will snap his head off if he fires another question at me. Three questions too many for Abu Salim have been fired at me already, it seems. As soon as he saw his sister's ring he should have realized, taken for granted, that Abu Salim had prepared me for this test—a test that probably dates back to the days their clansmen were warriors or outlaws, and it took not more than a silver ring to lead enemy troops to their hiding-place or home base. The first question implied that Abu Salim was negligent, incompetent, incapable of keeping the Badu moral code in his compound; of keeping his son, Salim, from Tammam; of squashing rumors that might cost two lives and imprison Tammam's brother and Abu Salim for life. Does he hold Abu Salim responsible for all that?

Yes.

"To what tribe does she belong?" Tammam's brother drives the point home, sticking it to Abu Salim, by snapping at me. He knows, doesn't he, that he can snap at me like a tyrant; badmouth me, my tribesmen, my sheikh; even say to me: your sister fucked her own stepson—and nothing will happen to him, except perhaps a promotion to the status of a freedom fighter asserting himself against his foreign ruler. But for a critical whisper against an Arab ruler—not a king, a head of state, a sheikh, a mufti, but an elder like Abu Salim—hundreds if not thousands of young Arab men, true Arab young men like Tammam's brother, have paid the ultimate price. Beads of sweat cover his face now, as if it has finally dawned on him what it might cost him just to imply that a Badu elder is anything less than above reproach.

The boy is not himself; his brand-new clothes have gone to his head—that's what Abu Salim thinks, it seems. Abu Salim is acknowledging nothing this evening, not what the boy implies, not the rumor about Tammam and his son, Salim—not even that he prepared me for this test of trust.

"El Bofessa taught you well." Abu Salim breaks the silence, his eyes on mine and betraying in no way that it was he himself who had taught me.

I hide my eyes in this notebook and keep my mouth shut. I don't trust my gut. For all I know, I'm only seeing things, imagining . . .

"*Wallah*, El Bofessa taught her well," says Jeff, dragging a water jerrican from the cooking-fire-circle over to this one. "Had she been wearing a veil, she would be a Badawia."

"No, she can never be a Badawia, for she is not of Arab blood," says Abu Salim.

"That is why Hilal can never ever be a true real man," says Mutt, bringing the rusty tea container from the cooking fire. "But only because he is not of Arab blood; except for that, Hilal is a true real man."

"No, he is not," says Jeff, "because a true real man is complete, *ya'ni*, he is forty years old at least. For only then can his eyes be open; only then can he see who is true, who is false; only then can he have the wisdom to settle disputes; only then can he have a face in front of him—meaning honor, high esteem, reputation, respect, and boldness."

"But Hilal is bold," says Mutt, holding the teapot to catch water pouring from a jerrican that is too heavy for Jeff's hands. "Hilal is more bold than any true Arab, or he would not dare tell to a Badu elder like my grandfather, Abu Salim, that he cannot cut down this tree or that."

"*Aywa*, Hilal is bold, only to talk," says Jeff, tilting the jerrican back to solid ground. "Like a woman, Hilal is a pot that only boils and boils; like a woman, Hilal is not bold to punish not even one Badu who cut down trees, *sahih*—right?" Jeff asks his grandfather almost as if the kids on the block will laugh at him, gang up, beat the shit out of him, if Abu Salim will not reassert himself and, like a true real man, punish Tammam's brother for challenging his honor, power, manhood.

"*La*—no," replies Abu Salim, "Hilal does not punish a Badu for cutting down trees, *ya'ni*, firewood, because he knows that we Badu live on fire."

"Hilal knows also that we Badu could live on electricity fueled by a generator like the one that fuels the electricity in Hilal's post," says Tammam's brother.

"Fire," snaps Abu Salim, "fire fuels our Badu way of life, and Hilal knows it."

"You see? I told you. Like a true real man, Hilal is loyal to his friends," says Mutt to his brother, Jeff.

"No, Hilal, like a woman, has a womb, meaning: pity, mercy, compassion, *ya'ni*; like a woman Hilal is nice; and like a woman he is owed deference from no one. A true real man is not nice; a true real man is generous."

"But you told me yourself that Hilal is a true real man," says Mutt, resting the teapot on the blackened trio of stones set level in the center of the fire-circle.

"No, I told you that Hilal regards women like a true real man," says Jeff. "Only in that is Hilal a true real man; for, like a true real man, Hilal belongs to no woman, pays no heed to women——"

"For he likes trees more than women," mutters Mutt, trying to pry open the rusty top of the tea container with a twig that keeps breaking.

Jeff brings over from the cooking fire the sugar container—a small cloth bag, stiff like a kitchen towel that hasn't been laundered in days-weeks-months.

"*Aywa*, a true real man is not controlled by desire, hunger, or fear," says Tammam's brother, handing his *shibriyya* to little Mutt.

When Mutt has pried the top off the tea container, he goes on to say, "A true real man does not complain no matter how painful his pain. A true real man does not cry, not even when his mother or his child dies."

"But, first and foremost, a true real man is a free man," says Abu Salim, like a reigning old monarch, seasoned wise, accustomed to having the last, definitive word. "A true real man stands alone and fears nothing; a true real man is like a falcon—*shahin*: like a falcon, a true real man flies alone and fears nothing, and if there are two in the same territory, one must kill the other."

Must kill even his own son for invading his territory—his Tammam?

Was it here, by a fire-circle like this one, a family gathering with a guest or two, that Abu Salim's son, Salim, first saw this girl that his father married—to end a blood feud, seal a *sulha*—a forgiveness—with Tammam's clan? A girl in her teens, the purest maiden in her clan. Younger than Salim perhaps. A girl as graceful as a dancer, balancing her layers of veils on a head held high. Her black, full-length *thowb*, embroidered in dazzling colors and designs, is belted at the waist with a royal blue sash that reveals the subtle curves of a budding beauty. Her silver anklets glitter, and her wrists *jingle-jangle* with bracelets. Jewels cascade down her firm breasts, none more sparkling, more riveting, than her eyes.

Day after day, Salim hears his father—a true real man, like a falcon—waking Tammam with whispered endearments—*ayuni, galbi*—my eyes, my heart; yet, day after day, he sees his mother, Azzizah, treating this girl like a daughter, like one who could arouse Methuselah, perhaps, but not his father, Abu Salim. Now Salim thinks he understands why this budding beauty is as volatile as a goat penned up with an impotent ram. Now Salim thinks her riveting eyes are yearning for a potent ram like him.

And, evening after evening, Tammam brings Salim a bowl of water and a towel, and folds her legs on a carpet spread next to their common supper tray. His fingers and hers dig into rice oozing with *samn*. But he sticks to his territory, and she sticks to hers. Their fingers don't touch; their eyes don't meet. She, raised to be proper-modest, averts her eyes from his. He, raised to be a true real man, conceals his feelings evening after evening, week after week, month after month.

And then, one day, Tammam walks head on into the wind and Salim sees her stomach is not flat; she is pregnant. His father is not impotent. And suddenly it takes more strength than he has to control the rage and the pain that strikes a lover betrayed. By now he felt she was his territory, not his father's. Lest he kill them both, he takes off. A month or two after he leaves home, whispers circulate in the desert that Abu Salim had not fathered a child since he fathered his son, Salim, and as soon as his new girl-wife swells up with child, his son, Salim, runs away from home and covers his tracks...

Is that the way it happened? Or did it happen this way:

Tammam, younger than Salim perhaps, but not by much, is of his generation. Both grew up in these mountains, bumped into each other when they were children tending goats. Tammam was probably a scrawny kid then, too young to wear veils, too young to shepherd goats. One goat escaped, giving Tammam chase to a deserted wadi; just as Tammam is about to catch her, the goat scrambles up a mountain crag. Salim, wearing a tattered old *jalabeeya* he outgrew months ago, or a brand-new one that drags on the ground, waits with Tammam until her escaped goat, thirsty at last, reappears. Nearly every day after that, or once a week, once a month, Salim and Tammam meet in the same deserted wadi. Child-boy and child-girl games they play, and secrets of secrets they whisper for hours, year in, year out.

Then, one day, they fall silent and avert their eyes from each other—and from a ram that is humping a goat. The she-goat shakes him off. They lock horns, back off, then lock horns again, turning round and round, round and round, kicking dust. Dizzy and winded, she climbs on top of him. He, steaming, sweating, climbs on top of her. Blindly, in heat, his erection searches for her opening. She, maddened by heat herself, trembles, resists, groans, moans; then her knees wobble and he enters her. They shiver and tremble...

Next time Tammam and Salim meet, Tammam is wearing a veil. Salim vows to marry her. Both are of Arab blood. So Salim asks his mother, Azzizah, to arrange his marriage to Tammam. Azzizah approves of his choice. She asks Abu Salim to discuss the bride-price with Tammam's father. Abu Salim rides over to the compound of Tammam's father, and naturally is invited to stay over for supper cooked-served by Tammam—and, like King David when he saw Bat-Sheba, Abu Salim falls in love with Tammam, the girl his Salim has vowed to marry, the girl his Salim has loved since they were children.

Did Abu Salim invade his son's territory? Did he fear that his son, raised to be a true real man, like a falcon, would kill any who invades his territory—even his own father? Did Abu Salim dispatch Salim on some smuggling mission, like King David did Batsheva's husband, before or after he married Tammam and brought her to this compound? ...

Tammam is coaxing an empty tuna tin out of her infant's hands. Azzizah stops sifting flour—holds her breath, it seems, as if all too often she has seen the slightest cut develop into an infection that couldn't be cured by her remedies and spells. Veils *jingle-jangle* as Tammam assures Azzizah that little Salimeh isn't bleeding, hasn't cut herself. Only now does Azzizah go back to sifting flour. Tammam collects all the empty tins off the ground, places them on the sloping roof of her tent, near the tent pole where a section dips. I have yet to see a garbage can here. The ditch looks like a garbage dump.

Was it to uphold Abu Salim's reputation and to save her son's life that Azzizah has spread the word that Tammam is pregnant? No way could the father of this child be her son Salim, right?... No way could she be pregnant, Tammam had told me, "but swear you will not breathe a word of it to anyone..."

Tammam has brought herbs and spices from her tent and as soon as she sprinkles them into the pot of rice boiling on the cooking fire, delectable fragrances drift over to this fire. The tea is now brewed here by Mutt and Jeff. These two feel at home here. They helped themselves to water, tea, sugar—a couple of fistfuls Jeff dumps into the teapot for four or five glasses, if that. Mutt stirs the sugar in with a twig he has picked from a small heap of branches—chopped off a tree listed as an endangered species, no doubt. Hillel's job is protecting such trees. Or maybe it's just a coincidence that Hillel pops into Jeff's head now, again.

"Hilal told us that there are strangers who wonder if we Badu are true Muslemins," says Jeff, "for they see no mosque in Sinaa, except the one in the monastery, Santa Katerina, and they see but few Badu pray like true Muslemins five times a day, or even five times a week———"

"*Aywa*, we Badu are Muslemin, humbled by poverty and ignorance, for that is our fate," says Abu Salim. "We Badu cannot but submit to the will of Allah... Allah the compassionate, the merciful... Prayers and peace be upon the Last of the Messengers, Mohammad, the righteous Arab prophet."

"It was in Badu tents that the prophet Mohammad found shelter and hospitality," says Jeff, sipping his sugary tea with much noise, like his grandfather, Abu Salim.

"*Aywa*, that is what I heard my father's father tell," says Abu Salim.

The fire is now a circle of ashes, smoldering, hissing, cracking, crumbling. The wind shifts and flames up a twig. So precious is firewood here that Abu Salim feeds this circle of ashes a twig at a time. It gives heat but hardly enough light to read, write...

(I switched on my flashlight, tucked it into the top fold of my rolled-up sleeping bag. This improvised writing lamp tickled

Mutt, but Jeff frowns as if it was a travesty and he couldn't understand why Abu Salim and Tammam's brother allowed it.)

"Hilal told at the *maq'ad* today that Israel is pulling her troops out of Sinaa to show Egypt that she means to sign the Camp David Peace Accord," Abu Salim says to Tammam's brother.

"There will never be peace here," says Tammam's brother—no peace for him certainly, not since the rumor started.

Was it at his father's *maq'ad* that he first heard it? Or was it in Al-Arish, or in Dahab, at the Grill by the Red Sea, that Tammam's brother was sipping Coca-Cola, watching a tourist-girl in a string bikini smoking pot or hash, and dancing to rock-'n'-roll. But then Tammam's brother sees that all the Badu youths there at the Grill are watching him, not her. Round each table they huddle, whisper, pity or laughter in their eyes. He checks to see if his fly is open or if he has spilled Coca-Cola over his frock. Finds he is spotless, not exposed. Yet, everywhere he goes, the same thing happens. And whenever he demands an explanation, no one dares give him one word—the last one they would utter in this world, if Tammam didn't exaggerate: deadly to badmouth a woman; deadly to spread such rumors. So, after a month or two, he takes his best friend aside and tells him that he thinks he is possessed by *djinn*-demons, wherever he goes he imagines he sees Badu huddling, whispering, their eyes laughing at him or sorry for him. And only now he hears from his best friend that the whole desert is buzzing with a rumor that his sister, Tammam, fucked her stepson, Salim, leaving her brother with no choice but to kill the rumor-spreader if the rumor is false, or his sister, Tammam, if the rumor proves true...

"Never ever look at a man like you looked at Tammam's brother," Abu Salim snaps at me. "A woman modest-proper keeps her eyes downcast like you do when writing."

"Write-to-remember my brother's name is Akram, meaning 'generous and noble,'" mutters Tammam. She kneels by the cooking-fire at the *maharama*—the place of the women—"the kitchen"—cleaning trays for supper with a towel heavy with water, dust, and grains of sand. Abu Salim, in the "living room," by this fire, holds her infant daughter—his daughter or granddaughter?—on his lap. She wriggles out of his arms, and Tammam picks her up, telling her brother that my name is Nura.

"Nura told us women that Tammam's brother, Akram, looks like a prince from Saudia," Azzizah, putting her words in my mouth, says to Abu Salim.

"No prince in Saudia is of blood as noble as Akram's and mine," says Abu Salim, addressing me. "You strangers cannot see it, for you see only the dust on my *abaiah*—cloak." He spits and covers it with a handful of sand. "The royal house of Saudia sends their sons to us Badu for to learn nobility-character-manners, but you strangers look down on us Badu, for you only see the dust on our *abia*. Now, write what I tell you. Are you ready?"

"Many years ago," Abu Salim starts dictating, "there lived a man who had five sons. The first one, called Za'im, meaning 'leader,' went to dwell in Saudia. Many sons were born to him. All so arrogant like sheikhs who enter their guest-receiving-place only after it is full of men who have waited a week, a month, for a word of wisdom from their leader—their sheikh. Go to them, and they will give you not a word of wisdom-counsel-guidance, but only money, as if you were a beggar."

"*Wallah, wallah—Allah-lah*." The mountains echo Mutt and Jeff.

"*Aywa*," says Abu Salim, then in the sing-song voice of Badu legend-telling, he goes on to dictate, "now the second son, named Zak'am, meaning 'light-headed,' went to dwell in Egypt. Many sons were born to him. All love merriment and dancing. All will invite you to enjoy their merriment and their dancing. But you will die of hunger there.

"And now the third son, named Jamil, meaning 'handsome,' went to dwell in Syria. Many sons were born to him. All so handsome and so graceful, honor-upon-honor they think they heap on you if they let you see them from afar. Go to them and you will die of hunger there also. You will also find no shelter there.

"And now the fourth son was named Phaakar, meaning 'poor.' He and the fifth son—named Karam, which, like Akram—the name of Tammam's brother—means 'generous and noble'—went to dwell in no other place but this very desert, Sinaa. Many sons were born to them. All men of honor. Go to them and you will see poverty and dust on *abia*—cloaks. But no matter how poor, they are the ones who will offer you shelter and hospitality.

"*Aywa*, the King of Saudia and his royal sons are enriched by oil. But rich or poor, with great delight the worms will eat us all."

"Rich or poor, fate visits us all," says Tammam's brother, Akram, in the voice in which Badu declaim poems, verse—pouring their hearts out, as Russell had put it. According to him, a Badu rarely, if ever, complains, tells what he really feels, fears, hopes, or thinks of you, except in poems or verse, old or new. And if you want to respond, you say it in verse, or in a comment about the poem or verse just declaimed.

"*Ghul*—tell—*yaa*-Akram—*Akram-ram-ram*," the circles within circles echo Abu Salim, Mutt, and Jeff.

"*Aywa*," says Tammam's brother. "Be you a bird, an eagle soaring high between sky and star, fate will snare you wherever you are. The will of Allah shall be carried out."

"O, Allah!" the mountains thunder after Imsallam Suleman Abu Salim. "O, Allah! According to Your order, life is either wide or narrow. And if You decree life be wide, there shall be no wrong."

"*Inshallah—Allah-lah*."

Wide, infinite, the desert is now. All around the fire-circles, a dark void stretches as wide as the imagination; a dark void where time is poised and rushing past like a whirlwind, where far is near and near is far, where silence is not peace but a wild beast lying in wait for the kill. The salukis hear the howling, screeching, rustling silence, and are driven to patrol again and again the perimeter of the fire-circles. Abu Salim tells-orders the salukis to sit behind him. As soon as they obey, his camel—his Rolls-Royce—and Akram's, their front legs hobbled, make ungainly progress over the rim and park themselves closer to the fire-circle, where my face is burning hot and my back is shivering cold.

"The camel saddles are only a few steps beyond the rim. Go get the sweaters we left in Abu Salim's saddlebag," Jeff whispers to his brother, Mutt.

"You walk over to get them. I'm afraid," Mutt whispers back.

Jeff mutters a string of curses, and stays put.

Akram gets up, steps over the rim, and disappears into the darkness. Time stretches like an elastic band about to snap until he reappears with a bundle of sweaters. Mutt and Jeff layer them on, one on top of the other.

Abu Salim wears many layers under his *abaiah* mornings and evenings, the only times I see him, when the cold slices through to the bone.

I am wearing a parka over a sweater, over a blouse, over a t-shirt, but still the void at my back steals the warmth, chilling through to the marrow, and the wind trades smoke for the air, stinging the eyes and choking the lungs. And yet it feels like sitting, legs folded on a magic carpet that floats above it all—a magic carpet that has conquered time again and again on a thousand and one Arabian nights.

"*Ana bagul*—I wish to tell now," says Jeff.

"*Ghul, yaa-walad*—tell, my boy," says Abu Salim.

"Are you ready?" Jeff snaps at me. "You see the dust on my *abaiah* and you think I do not know that Hilal . . . Give me the package of cigarettes you keep in your pocket." Jeff clearly suspects I have concealed in it a forbidden something or other that Hilal has smuggled to me.

The magic carpet hits ground—

"No. Do not give him the cigarettes," Abu Salim says to me. "Do not reduce him more than he has reduced himself, his clan, his tribe—

"*Aywa*—yes," says Abu Salim to his grandson Jeff. "You did me proud, you thought, when you were shaming me, yourself, your clan, your tribe. For the measure of a Badu is his hospitality to friend and foe alike. *Aywa*, you are but a child, for you see the dust on her *abaiah*, and you fail to hear she speaks Arabic, not like El Bofessa, but like Hilal—meaning: She is of the Israeli Yahod, a warrior tribe so small in number that women, like men, had to battle the English, *Wallah*. Next, they battled all the armies of all the Arab nations. Then they trained their sons to be such warriors that in but a six-day war they wrestled from the Arab armies not only our holy city, Al-Quds—Jerusalem—but this our desert Sinaa. And only after this Yahodi victory did El Bofessa come to dwell in Israel from a land called Canada, where the Yahod, like the Saudis, give only lip-service and money even to avenge blood and honor. But, unlike the Saudis, the Yahod are duty-bound to avenge the blood and the honor of six million sons and daughters, meaning a thousand times six thousand, *yaa-Rabb*."

"Is that what El Bofessa told you?" I ask Abu Salim.

"No, El Bofessa never talks of Canada," replies Abu Salim, as he rolls a Badu cigarette for himself.

I pull the pack of cigarettes out of my pocket, take one, then put the pack on the ground.

"Now you can take one cigarette," Abu Salim says to Jeff.

"Me too?" says Mutt.

"Yes," replies Abu Salim.

Tammam's brother, Akram, also lights a cigarette, from his own pack of Marlboros.

"You see? Tammam's brother, like the rest of our Badu youths, smokes American cigarettes," says Abu Salim. "That makes them real true men of the world, men of tomorrow, our young men think. We of the older generation are men of days gone by, they think. Sinaa is a land of yesterday, they think. America is the land of tomorrow, they think. Canada also, for she borders on America, or so I heard. Not from El Bofessa. No, El Bofessa never talks of Canada. El Bofessa, I think, is ashamed of his parents. That is why I never pried. And only once I told him, 'a bastard is he who denies his parents, be they even slaves, as you Yahod were in Egypt.' But El Bofessa in response only asked me, 'Were you Badu ever expelled from your lands? Is that why you Badu tie and untie—*ya'ni*—move from one place to another?'"

"That is a good question," I said.

"No, it is not a good question," says Abu Salim. "For only a Badu who spills the blood of a brother innocent is expelled from his tribal grounds. We Badu are driven to tie and untie only when this mountain or that wadi can no longer sustain our herds. Or when this waterhole or that runs dry. Or when our foreign rulers tell us we cannot pitch our tents here and there—*ya'ni*—near their army camps, air bases, oil rigs."

"No move is more sorrowful than when a Badawia marries," mutters Azzizah, "for she is torn then from her father's tent and she moves-follows her husband to his father's dwelling-place. And if her husband divorces her, her children remain with him, his clan—his tribe. That is why the blood-kin of the bride never attend her wedding celebration."

"But," says Abu Salim, motioning to his grandsons to sit by his side—in the place of honor, close to the fire but away from the smoke. "No matter who your daughter marries, or how far from her clan she moves, she remains the daughter of her clan, her tribe. And if her husband kills her brother, she is duty-bound to kill her husband to avenge her brother's blood."

"See? I told you no story," Tammam's eyes say to mine.

"Hilal wants to marry a Badawia," says Jeff, unrolling the carpet that has been used as a bolster. He and Mutt drape it over their layers and layers of sweaters. They'll still feel the cold if they don't eat supper soon; those two must be starving.

"Hilal only says he wants to marry a Badawia for he thinks it flatters us Badu," says Tammam's brother. "Just as the Badu of the coast think it flatters a stranger-woman to hear that a Badu is willing to pay a thousand camels for her bride-price. But, of course, the Badu of the coast offer this bride-price only to a stranger-woman who wears a gold ring on her finger, like Nura does. For only by this gold ring can they tell that a stranger-woman is already married and has no intention of divorcing her husband."

"Nura wears gold to ward off the evil eye of envy," says Azzizah.

"*Laa*—no," says Akram. "Maybe the gold ring chained to her neck is for that. But the gold ring on her finger is for all to see she is a woman-married, of no intention to divorce her husband."

"For she is married to a Yahodi soldier-of-soldiers, are you not?" says Mutt, addressing me.

"Not proper to ask questions," Azzizah admonishes her grandson.

"I am married to a Yahodi who dwells in the land that El Bofessa came from—*ya'ni*, the land called Canada," I reply.

"Better Canada than Australia," says Abu Salim. "For although the world is round—as round as the moon when full—we are sitting on top of the world, and Australia is at the bottom of our bottoms," he explains. And even Tammam and her brother crack up.

"*Wallah*, what a story," says Mutt between laughs.

"It is not a story," says Abu Salim. "Dig a hole here a hundred thousand times deeper than a waterhole, and you will see the people of Australia. Canada is also on top of the world, like we are. Or so I heard Hilal tell. Had he traveled to Canada, Hilal would tell of Canada without shame."

It wouldn't surprise me if Abu Salim knows what Hilal smuggled to me, but I doubt he will ever ask me. He has asked no questions about my personal life, directly or indirectly, before or after he invited me to visit-stay in his forbidden tents. Such is the breadth of his hospitality—to friend and foe alike. If he is curious by nature, then, like a true real man, he restrains this natural trait also … Or maybe he thinks, know one Yahodi, know them all…

"My husband also would not be ashamed to tell you of his dwelling-place, Canada. In fact, the opposite holds true," I said.

"For your husband is a Yahodi born and raised in Israel," says Abu Salim.

"No, my husband is a Yahodi born and raised in Canada," I said.

"But surely your husband lives in Israel many, many years," says Abu Salim.

"No, like a Badawia, I moved-followed him to his dwelling-place," I replied.

"Your husband must be a man of honor and good reputation or you would have divorced him to return to your tribal grounds," says Abu Salim.

"A stranger-woman, be she divorced or a maiden, is free to

marry whomever her heart desires," says Tammam's brother, Akram.

"Information is power," says Abu Salim. "And like a gun falling into the hands of an infant, information can kill."

Kill? Is he talking to me? To Akram? Has Akram corrupted his sister, Tammam, by telling her everything he saw and heard in *maq'ad*s the desert over, filling her head with "wrong ideas"?

"Are you ready?" snaps Abu Salim. God, am I ready.

"A woman-stranger," dictates Abu Salim, "like a Badu man unseasoned, can but sit and listen in the *maq'ad*. For it is in the *maq'ad* that you gather-exchange-gain information—*ya'ni*—power. That is why a Badu unseasoned—young in age—can never be as informed-powerful as a Badu seasoned old. And even though the young in age have more strength to travel-gather information, even in deserts far, it is the Badu seasoned old who have the infor-mation—the power—to decide who to empower—*ya'ni*—when and where and if to dispatch this young man or that to gather information."

But at least a young man has the power to decide for himself when and if to relieve his bladder—or maybe Akram steps over the rim now and into the void just to stretch his legs or to fetch from his saddlebag a sweater for himself.

"Akram has never been dispatched to cross borders, gather information anywhere but here in Sinaa," says Mutt.

"*Oskot, yaa-walad*—shut up, *yaa*-child—for information is power," Jeff says to his brother, then turns to me. "It is men's work to gather information-power. That is why women can never be as powerful—informed—as we men are."

Akram reappears with a regal *abaiah* draped over his shoulders, lending him stature, and power perhaps—but not much protec-tion against the cold.

Abu Salim nods in approval, then turning to me he says, "Are you certain your husband would not be ashamed to tell of his dwelling-place, Canada?"

"*Wallah*, I am," I reply. "For Canada is a land——"

"*Stana*—wait—for permission to tell," Abu Salim cuts me off.

"Now, if you are certain that your husband and your father would not object, I, Imsallam Suleman Abu Salim, give you permission to tell of your husband's dwelling-place, Canada."

"*Ghule*—tell—*yaa*-Nura," Mutt and Jeff urge me, like grownups.

"Canada is a land blessed with peace and with great wadis that do not run dry in the summer months——"

"Cannot be," Tammam's brother, Akram, cuts me off. "Only the Gulf of Suez and the Gulf of Aqaba do not run dry in the summer months."

"Oh, *yaa*-Akram, the Gulf of Suez and the Gulf of Aqaba–Eilat are but a water jerrican compared to the sweet-water lakes in Canada," I say, and they all laugh in disbelief, as though I have added pepper to spice up life—all except Abu Salim.

"I had encountered many a lake of sweet water in my young border-crossing days," says Abu Salim, "and many a great wadi like the Nile, and the mighty Jordan that irrigates your land, Israel."

"*Aywa*," said I. "I knew no wadi more mighty than the Wadi Jordan until I went to my husband's dwelling-place, Canada. So, imagine how surprised I was to discover that the mighty Jordan is but a narrow stream compared with the great wadis of my husband's dwelling-place, Canada. I was wearing gold, but still I envied the people of Canada—envied their peace and their great wadis and lakes, but not their winters. For when the winter winds blow in Canada, the cold sears like fire. You cannot go out in bare feet, and some days not even in bare fingers."

"You mean you wear shoes-boots on your fingers?" says Mutt. The air seems warmed by laughter.

"*Bas*—enough—or her husband would be offended," says Abu Salim. "Tell on."

"The child is not far wrong," I said. "So cold are some winter days in Canada that you cannot feel your fingers unless you cover-protect them with what are called mittens or gloves; some are made of wool, others of sheepskin, and some are made of leather like shoes-boots, only softer. And some winter coats also are made of leather, others of animal fur."

"But why do they not build a fire to keep warm?" says Mutt.

"Because the authorities there in Canada, like Hilal here in Sinaa, like trees more than people," replies Jeff.

"*Laa*—no—look at her hands," says Azzizah. "Nura's hands have never gathered wood for fire, not because she is lazy, as I had thought, but because there is no wood to gather in her husband's dwelling-place, Canada."

"Oh, *yaa*-Azzizah," I said, "if all of Sinaa were to be covered with trees, one standing close to another, there would not be as many trees here in Sinaa as there are in Canada. For Canada is a land many times the size of Sinaa, a land of a peaceful, yet valiant people who battled in the two World Wars and, undaunted, brave their cold winter lands—and our all-too-hot Middle East as well."

"*Aywa*, they serve in the United Nations of all the nations of the world peace-keeping force," says Abu Salim. "Tell on, *yaa*-Nura."

"*Aywa*," I went on to tell, not about Christie Pits, as my son would, but as Dave would, and as the Israelis who drop out: "Canada is a land blessed not only with trees, water, and a people who are peaceful yet valiant, but also with soil that is fertile on the surface and below. Dig below the surface of the land Canada and you will find treasures more precious than silver and gold———"

"Oil," Tammam's brother interjected, cutting me off. "Now that Israel discovered oil here in Sinaa, she will never return Sinaa to Egypt for peace."

"Israel values her sons more than she values oil," says Abu Salim. "That is Israel's weakness and her strength. For oil, like glory, comes and goes, but sons from generation to generation tell the story of the oil and the glory that came and went. *Aywa*, nothing but the story remains of the great Lawrence of Arabia and the glorious days of his English—nothing but the story remains of the Turkish; nothing but the story remains of our own Badu warrior-of-warriors as well. For nothing remains when all else dies but the story."

Like a grain of sand, their family crisis—and mine. No matter how it gets resolved, sooner or later nothing remains of it but a story that will be carried in the wind or lie buried in this vast desert that witnessed the journey of the twelve tribes from slavery to freedom. Manna dropped from heaven when they complained of hunger. And when they complained that they were tired of eating manna day in, day out, breakfast-lunch-dinner, a flock of birds dropped from the sky. And when they complained that they were dying of thirst, water bubbled from a rock at the touch of a staff. Such miracles and wonders were performed for these twelve tribes who wandered forty years complaining every step of the way. The Badu have wandered for centuries, rarely, if ever, complaining—Badu like Abu Salim, who has overcome the hardship of this desert, day in, day out, for sixty years or more.

In the words he dictates Abu Salim refers to his story, and, by extension, himself, as a grain of sand. But would he be dictating these words if he saw himself, his story, so diminished; would he share his words with his stranger-guest, a daughter of these twelve tribes, if he thought she would see him so dwarfed by his desert? By his family crisis?

The smell of baking pita wafts over from the charred top of a gasoline barrel and silences these thoughts.

"I am hungry-famished." Mutt breaks the silence.

"*Oskot, yaa-walad*—shut up. You are whining like a child," says Jeff to Mutt. "You and I eat proper—after the guests have their fill."

"No, he is but a child, and one pita is ready," says Azzizah.

Mutt scrambles over to the cooking fire at the *maharama*—the place of the women—and Azzizah splits the steaming pita in two.

"Give half to your brother, for he also is but a child," she says to Mutt.

The fire-circle is cloaked in the smells of family now, of home—fresh-baked bread, fried onions, and tomato paste, tuna, and rice casserole.

"Are the dwelling-places in Canada made of leather also, and of animal fur?" says Mutt, his mouth stuffed with pita.

"Not as far as I know," I reply, my stomach rumbling.

"The dwelling-places in Canada are woven of goat hair like our Badu tents," says Jeff, eating before the guests.

"Cannot be," says Azzizah, picking up a second pita from the hot barrel top with her bare fingers. "Cannot be," she says, "for it takes a woman three years to weave a tent. And Nura's hands look like they have never even spun wool or camel hair for a carpet-blanket, let alone goat hair for a tent."

"The dwelling-places of the Yahod in Eilat are made of stone and cement," says Tammam's brother, Akram.

"So is Hilal's dwelling-place, here in Sinaa," says Jeff. "In Canada also?"

"*Aywa*," I reply. "Some dwelling-places in Canada are made of stone, others of cement; some are made of wood, others are faced with glass——"

"Cannot be," says Azzizah. "Only tea glasses are made of glass."

"*Laa*—no," says Abu Salim. "In Lubnan—Lebanon—there is a city called Beirut. And there I saw dwelling-places faced with glass like our tea glasses. Do they rise as tall in Canada as they do in Beirut?"

"I do not know how tall the dwelling-places faced with glass rise in Beirut," I reply, "but in Canada they rise almost as tall as the mountain chains here in Sinaa, maybe even taller."

"So, in Canada also, people live up high in mountain caves, just like us Badu in the cold winter months," says Azzizah. "Only our mountain caves are made of stone, and in Canada they are made of glass.

"*Sahih*—right?" Azzizah asks Abu Salim.

"You reply-tell," says Abu Salim, addressing me.

"I do not know how to reply," I say, "for I have yet to see your mountain caves. All I know to tell is that, in Canada, the dwelling-places that rise as tall as mountains are stacked one on top of another."

"Cannot be," says Azzizah. "For if Tammam were to pitch her tent on top of mine, her goats would topple my tent."

"The Badu tribes of Canada, like the Yahod of Eilat, have no goats," says Akram.

"There are no Badu tribes in Canada," says Abu Salim, "for, had there been Badu tribes in Canada, El Bofessa would have told of Canada and played cassettes recorded in the Badu *maq'ad*s of Canada."

"I wish to record cassette of legend-poem-story," says Jeff.

"Me too," says Mutt.

"Let Nura work her cassette recorder, for you might break it," says Abu Salim to his grandsons. "Are you ready?" he says to me, then to his wives, "Utter not a sound. The voice of a woman is not to be recorded—forbidden."

I couldn't fall asleep. Tonight, the carpet-blanket is more torture than comfort—a bed of steel wool—steel wool infested with armored lice and bed bugs; steel wool enwrapping me in the cold night wind; the cold gravel, hard-packed like rock. If there ever was a patch of sand on this plateau, the wind has carried it off, scouring even the cracks and the hollows. The flinty ground is uneven, and, wherever I turn, my bones spark with pain. And the night light—a luminous smile floating among the stars—changes the properties of color, like black and white film. The two fire-circles are obsidian now—the red of the embers, the white and gray of the ashes, the black, white, and gray of the smoke have vanished.

The fire was allowed to die when Abu Salim, his grandsons, and Tammam's brother left this forbidden compound to sleep in the *maq'ad*. Other than that, the sleeping arrangements are the same. Azzizah sleeps in her tent—or, rather, outside her tent. Tammam's goat sleeps in Tammam's tent, and Tammam and her infant, wrapped together in one blanket-carpet only a few feet from mine, sleep outside—on the front porch of her tent, which is also the back porch of her kitchen, and her living room—where the fire-circle was loaded with glowing ashes.

Soon after the ashes cooled and blackened, shadows meandered out of Tammam's tent. My heart pounds, until they materialize into a couple of goats. A foot or two from my face they stop to take a piss, then they plunk themselves down, almost on top of my carpet-blanket. I push, shove; they don't budge. I give up, and, just when I discover that goats are terrific heating pads, they meander back into Tammam's tent, and Tammam's infant-girl crawls after them. Halfway she hesitates, almost as if she has remembered that goats are the currency that sustains her way of life but is still puzzled by how highly they are valued. They are sheltered at night in a tent that took her mother's mother three years to weave, while she is outside, freezing. Little Salimeh wears no diaper, no underpants, no leggings—only a flower-print dress and the sweater I brought her from Canada. The sleeves, too long for her, roll up one hand and slide over the other; it drags behind her like a tail as she crawls back to her mother. Her progress halted by a rock in her path, she rolls over onto her side, then sits up, rubbing her gums with her bare knuckles. Her voice shivers when she whimpers—stops as soon as she hears her mother's *jingle-jangle*. Tammam stretches out an arm that opens a tiny crack in her blanket-carpet, and her infant scuttles into it like a puppy happy to be back at her mother's tit. It won't be long before she is weaned, even if the drought does not dry up her mother's milk. Girls are weaned sooner than boys here. Abu Salim believes that a boy should be indulged, so that he will gain a sense of power, superiority, dominance.

"A boy should be breast-fed longer than a girl," he said soon after supper. "A boy should not be disciplined as much as a girl, lest he be fearful. A girl should not be indulged as much as a boy, lest she be willful—overly strong, refusing to do what she is told, talking back, doing things without permission..."

"The more willful a boy, the better," said Mutt, repeating, obviously, words he had overheard ever since he was old enough to remember.

"A girl also, the more willful the better," said Tammam's brother, Akram.

"So long as she has a soft voice and not too long a tongue," said Jeff, frowning like his grandfather, Abu Salim.

"*Aywa*," said Akram, "a girl must be soft-spoken but willful also, or no one will respect her. Yes, a true real woman is a woman modest, obedient, deferential, soft-spoken. And at the same time, like a

true real man, she must be strong, courageous, assert herself...
even against her husband, if he or his blood-kin dishonor her
blood-kin or herself. Or she will not be respected..."

Not a sound did Azzizah and Tammam utter before and after
supper, when the cassettes were recorded, and when the recorded
cassettes were played back. Tammam's brother explained to his sister that, unlike a human being, a cassette recorder cannot talk and
listen—remember—record at the same time. Then he added that
the cassette recorder was recording only when the button with
the red dot on it was pressed.

Modest-proper, Tammam didn't tell him that she had translated
Abu Salim's cassette recording and knew how to use the machine.
The girl-Badawia waited until no button was pressed, and then she
said, "I wish to sing flute."

"*Ghanni*—sing on," said Mutt and Jeff, echoing Abu Salim.

"Are you ready?" Tammam says to me. "Cassette-record my flute
singing."

"No!" snaps Abu Salim. "Forbidden to cassette-record a woman's
voice in story, legend, poem, song, drum, flute——"

"But I wish to cassette-record my flute singing only for my
daughter to remember my flute singing," says Tammam as if it was
her dying wish.

"Forbidden," said Abu Salim.

"But you, or my brother, can safe-keep the cassette of my flute
singing, play it for my daughter, only for my daughter," Tammam
pressed on. Her mother died birthing her, leaving no record...

"No need to cassette-record your flute singing, for *Inshallah*—
God willing—your daughter will enjoy your flute singing for
many years to come," said Azzizah.

"*Inshallah*," said Tammam's brother, looking at Azzizah as if she
had the power-knowledge to cast a spell to dispel the rumor, then,
still staring at Azzizah, he added, "From gulf to gulf I have traveled,
and many cassettes of flute singing I have heard, but not in any
cassette, *maq'ad*, or tent have I heard a flute sung as well as my sister, Tammam, sings flute."

"Neither have I," muttered Abu Salim. But neither he nor Akram granted Tammam's wish. "Forbidden," they said, then they all urged Tammam, "*Ghanni*—sing on."

Tammam, disappointment in her eyes, and sorrow, pain, anger, just sat there tapping her fire poker on one of the stones that rings the fire-circle. Then she picked it up, and one end disappeared under her veil. Her eyes closed, she tried to coax her flute to sing. The only sound is trembling breath.

24

"Go tend goats today," Azzizah told-ordered me soon after "breakfast." She appointed her grandsons to be my guardians today. "Her blood is on your heads..."

"Tending goats is women's work. I want to stay with Abu Salim and Tammam's brother, Akram," declared Jeff. And little Mutt said he has no strength to entertain a stranger-guest... "And to carry her food and her water jerrican," added Jeff.

"*Adabb*—manners," Abu Salim growled, then he said that they had been dispatched here to tend the goats because their grandmother and Tammam were busy entertaining their woman-guest.

Abu Salim, Tammam, Akram, and Azzizah obviously didn't want me to stay in the compound today. Why today, of all days? Are they expecting Salim today and don't want a stranger to be there when he arrives—when they test him for proof?

It is inconceivable to me that Akram would kill his sister, Tammam, or that Abu Salim would kill his son. Is that why my gut tells me there is no need to worry, that everything will be all right? Or does the contrary hold true... "What a contrary breed we *Sabras*—native Israelis," Arik used to say. "In real trouble, emergency, wartime, we *Sabras* tell ourselves and one another: Don't worry. Everything will be all right... The rest of the time we worry like maniacs..." Like now, it worries me that I'm not worried; that I have become pragmatic, in pragmatic-land Canada: There's fuck-all I can do, so what's the use of worrying? It also worries me that maybe I'm not worried because I've become gutless, and too proud to admit it.

"I would rather go tend goats *bukra, Inshallah*—tomorrow, God willing," I told Azzizah.

"Would do you good to catch the wind, stretch your legs and your horizon... it is the best remedy for you," Azzizah insisted, as she packed a lunch box—wrapped leftover pita in a dusty rag—

and as she handed it to her grandsons, she told them again, "Nura's blood is on your heads..."

Mutt and Jeff walked, like "true-real-men," a pace or two ahead of their stranger woman-guest. The goat path twisted and turned down the plateau. The goat herd had reached the waterhole way ahead of us, as had scores of shepherd-children. Some of these kids are smaller than little Mutt; at kindergarten age, they have already been sent to learn on the job—how to survive in this awesome desert, how to traverse the treacherous and magnificent mountains and dry riverbeds of their home ground, and how to tend the goat herds that sustain their Badu way of life.

"Looks like you were mistaken when you said that tending goats was women's work," I say to Mutt and Jeff.

"*Laaa*—no—tending goats is women's work," they tell me, one interrupting the other. "But the women are always busy tending infants; or spinning wool; or weaving tents, welcome-carpets, camel-saddles; or entertaining guests; or ... like today, our grandmother Azzizah had no time to tend her goat herd because she has to help Abu Salim with———"

"*Oskot*—shut up," Jeff snapped, trying to crease his face into a copy of Abu Salim's fierce frown. "You don't know what to tell, and what not to tell..."

"Yes I do," says Mutt. "I was not going to tell what I am not supposed to. I know what to tell and what not to..."

Already the child knows how to swim with one foot in the river beneath the river, and the other foot in the masking river they show us.

Remember: these children are like a broadcasting station. Every word I utter, they repeat to Abu Salim, his wives, and God knows who else...

They stand next to me, like toy bodyguards. The other shepherd children huddle and whisper, giggle, and sneak looks at the woman stranger-no-stranger. But they ask no questions, and Mutt and Jeff volunteer no information—only cigarettes, my cigarettes. Jeff asks me to hand him my pack, then he presents to each child a cigarette and hands me back the pack, containing only one now for the rest of the day. The shepherd-girls, like the -boys, light up, and the mountains cough in sympathy, towering even taller above the children.

The children's clothes dusty, stained, tattered; their feet bare; their gray faces smeared by smirks. Pus drips from the corners of their eyes, and amulets like mine hang from their wrists and necks—leather pouches containing the name of Allah to ward off *al-shaytan*—Satan—and blue stones, like strangers' blue eyes, to shield against the evil eye. The shepherd-girls *jingle-jangle* with every move.

". . . The ones dressed in black veils and long robes are maidens; the others are still girls," Jeff whispers—so that no one will hear how ignorant is his woman-stranger-guest, I guess.

". . . A girl is like a boy," little Mutt explains. The Badu child-boy stands high on his toes even when I bend down, and whispers in my ear, "A maiden is a woman that looks like a girl . . ."

"A maiden looks like a girl, but she can bear sons and daughters, for she menstruates," Jeff elaborates. "That is why these girls wear veils. "Do you know what means 'menstruates'?" he asks me, as if he has just remembered that a stranger-woman is not a woman. No one has taught him the facts of life, I guess. Just like it was for me, when I was his age, such instruction is left to the goats.

The shepherd-children couldn't help but be aware that the waterhole, the only one around here that has survived the drought, is more empty than full. The bucket clatters on the rock bottom regularly. The girls and maidens, just like the boys, drag the brimming bucket up by a rope; after their goats are satisfied, the shepherd-children drink from the same bucket, and then they draw another bucket to fill jerricans. The splashing and spilling are reckless, as if they lived in water-rich Canada and not in a desert plagued by drought for the past six or seven years.

"The whole *hamula*—clan—owns the water rights to this well," Jeff whispers to me.

"But Abu Salim owns the well," says Mutt. "And, after Abu Salim will die, his son, Salim, will own the well . . ."

"Salim? Azzizah told me Salim has been away a long, long time,"

I say, playing on their innocence. "What will happen if Salim never comes back? Who will own the well then?"

"Salim is on his way to the tents," they tell me. "Tomorrow or the day after tomorrow, you will see-meet him, *Inshallah* ..."

"Maybe today?" I pry.

"Maybe today," replies Jeff.

"Perhaps we should go back to the tents," I suggest.

"What for?" snaps Jeff.

I wish I could answer him. God, I wish I could be straight and not devious. How I hate to manipulate. But I would hate even more to discover this evening that the double execution had been carried out, while I concentrated on remaining blameless.

"What if Salim returns today, shouldn't we wait for him in the tents, greet him proper when he arrives?"

"*Wallah*, we should," says Mutt.

"*Laaa*—no—even a giggling maiden would not leave her goats to wait and wait in a tent until her beloved arrives," says Jeff.

Both adamantly refused to let me help them water the goat herd. "The others will laugh, say we are not proper hosts ...," Jeff elaborates. Then, he and his little brother filled my canteen with water from the same bucket that served as a water trough for the goats ...

The water up in the tents comes from this well, this bucket. Is that what made me sick? There was a time I could drink water from any source. I was immune then. I've become a *kvetch* in antiseptic Canada; so damn refined I have to boil every drop of water and drink only tea.

Leading their goats, the neighboring shepherd-children leave like the grownup Badu—without a parting word. Each one runs to catch up with his or her herd, shouting, "*Urjah, yaa-urjah!!!* ..." During the mountains' mocking reply, they all disappear behind the shaded bend. Mutt and Jeff draw another bucket for their jerrican. We must hurry to catch up. There is no brake pedal on a herd of hungry goats.

I have never been happier to find a spot of shade. It is cool, paradise here, at this shepherd's cave, as the Badu call this shaded ledge. There is not a tree or a bush in sight—and not another shepherd; they all disappeared behind a bend in a wadi. The sky, the mountains, the riverbeds are bleached blinding white by the sun. My clothes are drenched through, and my water canteen is half-empty already. So much for not drinking a drop of murky water without boiling it first.

The last few hours felt like years of hard labor. Mutt and Jeff ran circles around the herd while I was dragging my butt—in a good, sturdy pair of desert boots which I had neglected to break in. My feet are blistered, pinched, swollen; if I take off my boots now, I won't be able to put them on again. More "refinement," I guess. Mutt and Jeff walk barefoot on burning gravel, stones, and thorns. They laughed when I asked them in what direction the tents lie. They pointed to a mountain that looks like every other one around here—bare, desolate, granite-hard. I see a barren desert where Mutt and Jeff see lush, green pastureland. They have shown me seven different shrubs and plants so far—"one more poisonous than a viper snake," they said, counseling me to look and to remember to never, ever, touch it.

"This one also," says Jeff, a cluster of leaves in his hand. "Look. Remember this plant."

Mutt laughs and laughs, then says, "If I drop this leaf into your tea, you will be bewitched."

"Meaning you will fall in love with him right here on the spot," Jeff explains, joining in his brother's laughter. "Bewitched love is not a good love," he adds, wiping away tears.

"What love is good?" I ask him.

"Married love is good," Jeff replies, "and loving your father and mother—parent-children love is also good, and love between brother and sister and all your blood-kin is also good. Love of friends is also good . . ."

"My brother is already promised to marry his cousin," says Jeff. "And I am also engaged,"

"*Laa*—no. You are telling a story," I say.

"I swear on the life of the rain that falls from the sky that I told you no lie," says Jeff. God knows where that child found a few dry twigs. Mutt lights a small fire and unties Azzizah's lunch box; with the pita she also packed tea and sugar and a rusty tin can. Jeff collects three rocks and plunks them into the fire; when he burns his fingers, he curses Mutt for lighting a fire before arranging stones to hold the teapot—the rusty tin can. As befitting a true real man, the child-boy ignores the pain, spits behind his back like Abu Salim, and curses Azzizah for packing tea, not coffee, to honor a guest, as is proper.

"My brother knows how to talk love," says Mutt. "Tell her, tell her ... But not all in one breath," he says to Jeff. "And if the words will run away, stop to catch them ..."

Jeff turns shy. His brother keeps nagging him. "*Ghul*—tell ..."

"Oh you fair one whose love is a hero—a hero among warriors ... The sight of your beauty releases prisoners. Your chiseled mouth is a gift to Allah ... from Allah ... and in it grains of sesame are scattered ..."

The mountains chuckle and mutter after Mutt, "*Yaa-salaam!* ... *Salaam ... laam.*"

"Where did you learn to love-talk like that?" I ask.

"Can I tell her? Can I? How you learned to love-talk from tending goats?" says Mutt.

"Not proper to tell," snaps Jeff. He can't resist, though, it seems, showing his power—his wealth of information. With much noise, he sips his tea, then he tells of Badu shepherds who talk love: "And some even do love where they think no one can see," adds the Badu child-boy.

"But before lovers marry, it is very forbidden—very, very, very dangerous—to do love," pipes up Mutt.

"That is why lovers wait until the wadis and hills around their tents are deserted," Jeff explains. "And then, when the herd is grazing a distance of three or four days away from their tents, Badu shepherd-boys and -girls do love. But first a Badu boy must learn to cover his tracks, for if he is caught doing love to a maiden, her father and brothers would be bound to kill her, and him also ..."

"*Wallah*, I love my uncle Salim," says Mutt. And the present is gone, swallowed up by the past and the future.

Jeff stares at Mutt but says nothing. Mutt chews and chews his dry, leftover lazy pita, and sips his tea with much noise, like his brother.

"My father told me that my uncle Salim knows to cover tracks better than all the Badu in all the deserts," says Mutt. "That is why no one could find his tracks for more than a year—not even my father, not even Abu Salim ..."

"*Laa*—no. Abu Salim is the best of all trackers, even better than his son, my uncle Salim," says Jeff. "That is why he was able to track down my uncle Salim."

"Why would Salim have to cover his tracks for a whole year? Did he do love to a maiden?" I am pushing it now, I know.

"You strangers know nothing," Jeff responds. "Shepherd-boys and -maidens do love one night, and maybe even three or four nights. Therefore, they have to cover tracks for one or three or four nights, but not for more than a year ..."

"Salim wanted to see the world," Mutt interjected.

"*Aywa*—yes," says Jeff. "My uncle Salim wanted to see the world, but his father, Abu Salim, said that it was not good to see the world. That is why Salim had to flee and to cover his tracks for more than a year. *Wallah*, he had to be even wiser, more cunning than his father and mine and the whole clan, the whole tribe, to do that."

"My uncle Salim will bring many gifts when he returns," says Mutt. "He will also teach me to cover tracks just like him."

"I know to cover tracks already," says Jeff. "Do you want to see?"

The mountains laugh with us when he walks backwards and then wraps our three *kaffiyyes* around his feet and ties two ropes to his ankles that twist and turn behind him, leaving the tracks of two snakes. Then he ties twigs to his ankles and leaves behind him the tracks of lizards and scorpions. With Mutt up on his back, Jeff demonstrates how to evade a tracker who is searching for two ...

Dropping Mutt, he shows how walking a looped path leads your tracker himself to cover up your trail. "Riding a goat leaves no tracks at all, see?" he says, climbing onto a scrawny black-haired goat, ravaged by drought, too tired to escape capture. "That is the best way to cover your tracks..."

"No, it is not," says little Mutt. He goes on to show me that the tracks of the unfortunate goat are deeper than normal.

"I wish to be a good tracker so that, if someone will steal my camel or goats, or rob my tent, or cause harm to my women, I will find him. *Wallahi*—I will," says Jeff.

"And a man has to be a good tracker for things that I cannot tell. I cannot tell, can I?" Mutt asks Jeff.

"No," says Jeff, and the little one beams, delighted.

"You see. I know what to tell and what not..."

They will have to know how to cover their tracks for smuggling at border-crossings, which I guess I'm not supposed to know. I should have brought the cassette recorder and camera. After being cooped up with Badawias who announce every other second that something or other is not proper, not allowed, I forgot that it's okay to record and photograph children.

"My father can even recognize camels grazing too far to see," says Mutt.

"So can I," says Jeff. "I will trap a crow and then you also will sense-see even through mountains, just like us Badu."

"Just like me," says Mutt. "My heart is like the heart of a crow because, when I was born," says Mutt, "my father gave me a tiny morsel of the heart of a crow to suckle so, like a crow, I will fly off before any approaching enemy comes into view—even an enemy like a snake or a scorpion, or even a *ghulah*."

"A *ghulah*?" I say, shocking the little one.

"Strangers know nothing..." Jeff mutters. "*Ghulah* means a witch that dwells-inhabits caves and mountain crags, like this one. She waits and waits until she sees a man or a boy traveling or camping alone. If she sees a man, she will entice him; a boy, she will snatch."

"But she only devours boys and men, not girls and not women. So you don't have to be afraid," Mutt assures me.

"My father had thought that a *ghulah* witch had devoured Salim," says Jeff, sipping his tea with his grandfather's sound effects. "But then, last week, he heard that Salim was well on his way home, so he went away to greet Salim——"

"I wish to go back to the tents to greet my father and my uncle Salim, proper, like she said," Mutt mutters to his brother, but Jeff tells him that the sun is still high, the goats still hungry, and my feet still sore; that we all need to rest.

"Perhaps we should borrow the camels I saw grazing down in the wadi, just for the ride back to the tents," I suggest. "Those camels looked lost... like they had wandered off from the herd..."

Mutt cracks up, runs behind a boulder and then back. It looks like he peed into the wind and sprayed his feet. He continues to munch lazy pita without washing his hands; their jerrican is nearly empty, and the waterhole is a hell of a hike from here. "*Wallah*, today I laughed and laughed more than any other day in my whole entire life," says Mutt.

"You want to borrow a camel, *yaa*-Allah, you strangers know nothing," says Jeff, shaking his head. "Look. You see the tent folded up here in the branches." He points to what looks like a nest of an eagle, or a hawk, or a family of ravens. "It's a winter tent. In the spring or summer, a woman folds it up like that, or when she goes to visit her father or mother, or goes to attend a circumcision or a wedding. Why does she need to carry her belongings or her tent when she can leave them on a tall tree, too tall for goats to reach, for only goats might touch it—no one else. *Wallahi*, the law is very, very strict on this. Remember, write, repeat," the child orders me. "Remember, never touch anything; never even borrow anything unless you receive permission—especially not a camel, *yaa*-Allah. Even after many, many years, everyone will recognize who owns it, and even if you deny and bring many, many witnesses to attest your innocence, once they suspect, they are entitled to demand that you swear..."

"And that you also test for proof," says Mutt. The rumor has risen again.

Jeff spits behind his back and gives Mutt such a look, the little one starts to cry and curse. "You talk empty," his brother tells him. "The test for proof is only in case of murder or in other criminal things like murder…"

"But stealing is a criminal thing like murder," says Mutt, wiping his eyes and nose. His face is a mess of tears and flies. "You think I know nothing," he mutters to Jeff, "but I know, I do."

"Write-remember," Mutt tells me, emulating his brother. "Write-remember to never ever swear you did no crime when you did, for you will die right on the spot—on the spot, *Wallah*… My father told that it was better to pay even many camels and many goats and many everything than to swear at the grave of a saint called 'a just man,' for even if innocent you can die on the spot just from the fright. My father told me it is better to test for proof…"

"How do you test for proof?" I ask the child, already guilt-ridden for using his innocence and losing mine.

"*Ana ma ba'ref*—I don't know," Mutt replies.

"I do," Says Jeff. "*Aywa*, once I even saw a *bish'ah*—meaning 'a licking of fire,' meaning 'a test for proof.' Only one family or two in the whole desert of the whole tribe knows how to conduct a *bish'ah*, my father had told me. From generation to generation they pass the knowing. The same one or two families conduct the *bish'ah*, my father said."

"Do you know how it is conducted, this licking of the fire?" I ask him, hiding my shame behind the veil of smoke from the last cigarette in my pack.

"*Aywa*—yes," replies Jeff. "The elder of the family builds a fire, then he rests a skillet on the fire—a skillet for roasting coffee but empty of beans. After the skillet turns white-hot, the elder takes it from the fire, then rubs his hand on the white-hot skillet three times to show how the innocent will not be harmed. And then he hands the white-hot skillet to the one suspected of crime. Now the suspected one must stick his tongue out to show all who gathered that his tongue is clean of blisters and sores before the licking, and only now he licks the white-hot skillet three times. *Aywa*, three times. Then the elder gives the one suspected a glass of water to rinse his mouth, to clean the ashes from his tongue, so that all who gathered will see the result. All fall silent and hold their breath when the one suspected sticks out his tongue. Now, if his tongue is clean, he is deemed innocent by one and all. But if his tongue shows a blister or a sore he is deemed guilty by one and all."

"My father said that you can bribe the elder to heat the skillet not so much as to blister the tongue," pipes up little Mutt. "That is why he said it was better to test for proof than to swear at the grave of a saint, a just one."

"You are talking ignorant, like a stranger," Jeff says to his little brother, then he tells me, "Write, remember. A bribe is a crime to give or to take. But it is better to test for proof than to swear, for if fear does not dry your spit, your tongue will not blister when you lick the white-hot skillet…"

"When are we going back to the tents? I wish to see if my uncle Salim and my father have arrived," says Mutt.

"Soon, soon," Jeff tells him, then sends the little one to fetch *la'anah*. Mutt picks up a few crusty leaves from some dried-out shrubs and brings them to Jeff, who chews a couple as if to show they are not poisoned, bewitching leaves.

"Eat, eat," he tells me, screws on his gruff, grownup face. "Eat, eat," he urges, like Abu Salim. They taste like salted juice. "*La'anah* leaves are as good as water. Write-remember. If you are ever lost, they will quench your thirst."

Mutt gets up and runs down to the wadi, disappearing around the bend.

The mountains shout after Jeff, instructing Mutt: "You better gather goat and camel dung on your way, else we will have no fuel for a cooking fire tonight."

"Is he going back to the compound by himself?" I ask Jeff.

"Yes," he replies. "My brother will not get lost. The little one only talks ignorant like a stranger, but he is a Badu—a true son of the Sinaa *sahrah*—the Sinaa desert—like me . . ."

The shadows were stretching long when I returned to the compound and found Azzizah rejuvenated, as spritely as a girl, and Tammam haggard, shoulders slumped, hands limp, eyes vacant and dazed like a woman stunned by sudden loss. Abu Salim looked like he could barely restrain his anger at her, at Akram, at Azzizah.

What went on here while I was away with the children? I wanted to ask. But as soon as we joined the fire-circle in front of Azzizah's tent, her sharp *darwisha*—medicine-woman—eyes caught sight of the nasty blisters on Jeff's fingers. "How could you be so careless to burn your fingers? Even an infant, a baby, knows that before you build a cooking fire you lay down three rocks and only then do you light the fire . . ."

Jeff dropped his head, flicking the flies away from his blisters.

"Do you feel pain-sore under your arm?" Abu Salim asks Jeff. The Badu clearly fears the blisters will burst, then fester.

"*Laa*—no," Jeff mutters, shaking his head.

Azzizah checks and rechecks his hands and arms and says he must dunk his blisters in the camel's urine, else his veins will turn black.

"You are not going to amputate my fingers," Jeff whispers.

"I may have to," mutters Azzizah, and Jeff starts to cry.

I took off my boots and showed the Badu the purple and yellow medicine I had applied on my blisters to prevent them from festering. Azzizah said she had never seen such remedies. But Tammam's brother, Akram, said that he had seen such a purple-and-yellow medicine stain on many a nasty cut and blister. "Some on my own flesh. It healed very clean and fast." Azzizah was convinced, but not Abu Salim.

"Did Hilal give you this medicine?" Abu Salim asked me, as if any medicine that came from his foreign rulers was poison.

"No," I replied. "I would give this medicine to my own son." Still, he kept saying no, and ordered Jeff to take Badu medicine—to dunk his blisters in camel's urine, as Azzizah had told him.

"But my father's veins turned black even after he had soaked-dunked his fingers in camel's urine," says Jeff.

"That was the will of Allah," mutters Abu Salim. "That was decreed by fate."

Azzizah is not as religious, nor as fatalistic. "Are you sure this purple-yellow remedy is so good you would give it even to your son?" she asked me.

"Yes," I replied.

"Go fetch it and give it to my grandson," Azzizah ordered me, overruling her husband. I was astonished, and relieved: She would not let him kill her son, Salim, it seemed clear now.

Abu Salim didn't say a word. Fierce as always, he looked, and angry as hell at Tammam, who sat there like a zombie while breast-feeding little Salimeh. That wild streak on his left jaw glistened red as Abu Salim watched me dressing his grandson's blisters, then he left, without saying a word in parting. That didn't seem to bother anyone but me.

Jeff wears his Band-Aids and purple and yellow medicine like a proud pioneer. I remind him again to keep his fingers dry and clean. God help me if his blisters fester.

"What happened here today while I was away?" I whispered to Tammam. I had followed her to the ditch. "You look like a terrible calamity has befallen someone near and dear to you."

Silence.

"I can't . . . I can't . . . You are truly my sister," she broke the silence, her eyes tearful, her voice raw with the sorrow of the ages.

25

"Visitors-guests approaching!" Azzizah is first to hear today.

"The vultures descending upon us," Tammam mutters, like a girl condemned. Azzizah is clearly shaken by this comment. It knocks me out—like a huge wave—engulfs me with terror, confusion, pain...

"*Dir balak*," Azzizah says to Tammam, the warning in her tone, her eyes, as well as her words. Watch out. One wrong word from you, one wrong move, in front of the vultures, and you are dead, she conveys silently. "*Ashow*—wake up!" Azzizah adds, implying: Snap out of it. Smarten up. Use your brain before it's too late...

But the girl-Badawia, almost like a girl-widow drained by grief, can't find it within herself to give a damn about anything, anyone, least of all her life.

And now Azzizah, frenzied, as if her life depended on it, takes action, sweeping the gravel ground of Tammam's tent and round the fire-circles; shaking the dust, gravel, and sand out of the welcome-carpets and spreading them out in a wide circle round the honor-coffee fire-circle; propping up tent flaps for shade; rinsing glasses, teapot, coffee *bakraj*, and skillet. For once she didn't tell me it is not proper for a guest to do work: Tammam sat by the side of her tent absently until I sponge-bathed little Salimeh and dressed the infant-girl in a clean change of clothes—a flower-print dress, sweater and bonnet to match.

"Hush, the visitors are but steps away." She whispers, by force of habit, it seems. *Jingle-jangle*; she and Azzizah adjust their veils and brace themselves for the vultures...

Running up the path leading to and from Abu Salim's *maq'ad* comes the retarded child-boy who had dragged me up to these forbidden tents months ago—a lifetime ago. A scrawny girl-child, trying to restrain him and catch her breath, mutters, "My brother, he ran ahead of my mother and my father and my sisters and my brothers…"

"First of the vultures," Tammam mutters under her veil.

"*Aywa*—yes." Azzizah grunts, frowns, heaves a sigh, rubs her aching back—they're a pain, these visitors. Both Azzizah and Tammam rise to their feet as soon as the saluki dogs run out to greet Abu Salim and the visitors. (Tammam's brother, Akram, is not with them. He rode away to greet Salim, according to Mutt and Jeff, who are tending the goat herd today also.)

Touching forehead to forehead, the Badawias exchange salutations, greeting-blessings. The Badu man-visitor kisses Azzizah's head, but doesn't go near Tammam, just throws the girl-wife a half-assed *marhaba*. Then he sits himself down on the welcome-carpet in the place of honor, close to the fire but away from the smoke. His children hang onto him like to a life preserver in rough sea. Five children—the oldest is the child-boy I met when I first drove into Abu Salim's *maq'ad* with Professor Russell. What a temper tantrum he had thrown then, frothing and jerking in spasms almost like an epileptic seizure until I relented and escorted him to this forbidden compound.

Silence. Even this child-boy—slightly retarded, according to Russell—observes the silence of greeting-ritual, or ceremony, or just a quiet moment to adjust to new group dynamics, to sense-see through to the river beneath the river… The child-boy looks at me as if trying to remember where he had seen me before, why he feels he knows me. He and his brothers and sisters have traveled barefoot and are wearing the same layers of tribal clothes as Mutt and Jeff and the neighboring shepherd-children; they have the same amulets and the same eye infection and runny nose, and their faces are busy landing fields for formations of flies.

Abu Salim starts to roast coffee beans in a blackened skillet—the one that his son, Salim, will have to lick when tested for proof?

The visiting infant breaks the silence. As soon as he begins to cry, his mother, sitting before Abu Salim, pulls out a breast. Her face is covered by a veil almost identical to Azzizah's, Tammam's, and the neighboring Badawias', indicating that she is of their tribe. Her shawls and *thowb* are embroidered and cut in the same tribal colors and style, and are laden with almost the same *jingle-jangle* jewels, coins, and beadwork, only much more of it. She checks me over with a pair of suspicious, disapproving eyes, heavily kohled, and bloodshot. Shocking-pink plastic sandals "blindfold" her feet, and running shoes her husband's. He has traveled with a *doobon*— a khaki Israeli Army parka or some imitation of it—over the same sand-colored ankle-length tribal *jalabeeya* as Abu Salim wears. The handle of his *shibriyya*—dagger—tucked in a leather holster, is inlaid with mother of pearl. A *kaffiyye* headdress that once was white is wrapped, rag-like, round his head, the same as Abu Salim's. He and his wife are probably of the same tribe, and also Azzizah's blood-kin and Tammam's; otherwise, it would have been forbidden for them to even enter this compound, let alone sit round the fire-circle with Azzizah and Tammam. Unless an exception has been made in their case, as in mine. Is it because these visiting Badu disapprove of such exceptions that my presence seems to annoy them? Or is it because Badu rarely show a friendly face on first meeting, showing instead, by their expression, that they are fierce, aggressive, intimidating, threatening, as befitting true real men and women. Maybe they are just tired of the sizzling sun that has dogged them all journey long, and they are parched and hungry, and their children must have been a handful...

Did their father come here to test Salim for proof? Is he of the one or two families who have tested their clansmen-blood-kin throughout time? Would he accept a bribe? Declare that Abu Salim's household was simply victimized by a malicious rumor?

"What have you got in your bag? Is it a *shibriyya*—dagger—or a gun?" the visiting Badu barks at me.

I check my bag and see that it contains nothing that resembles a weapon, only a pack of cigarettes, a lighter, an extra pen, a cassette, and my toilet kit, which I had pulled out when I sponge-bathed little Salimeh. The handle of my hairbrush sticks out, enough to arouse his suspicion. With such mistrust, paranoia, xenophobia, how can there be peace in this place? I say nothing, Badu-proper, like Abu Salim and his two wives. But I couldn't resist showing the visiting Badu how useful for brushing hair this weapon is. The tension dissolves with laughter; even Tammam and the visiting Badu joining in. The mountain chains send back the laughter and the delightful squealing of their eldest child-boy, who now remembers me and asks if I have any candies like the ones I gave him when he escorted me to the tents. His sister runs to pull him away from my side. "Leave him be. We are old friends," I tell her, and she hides, shy, behind her father's back.

"Is she the stranger-woman who stayed by your side when you were afraid to walk by yourself from Abu Salim's *maq'ad* to his tents?" the visiting Badu asks his son.

"*Aywa*—yes," replies the child. His parents heap their blessings on me, just as Abu Salim hands me a glass bubbling with honor-coffee.

I am about to hand it to the visiting Badawia when Abu Salim snaps at me, "What is your grievance against me, my household?! Did we offend you in any way?"

"The opposite is true," I respond.

"Why then did you reject the coffee—the honor—I served you, starting from the right, as I had told you to write-to-remember?" he demands.

"I thought you meant to serve your guests first," I reply.

"But you are also my guest," says Abu Salim, flashing his brown grin.

"Are you ready? Write-to-remember it better this time." He dictates: "Never, ever, reject honor-coffee served to you, unless you mean to say for all to see and hear that you have a grievance against your host, or that his companions are not worthy, or that you think his brew was poisoned..."

A person could start a war in this part of the world over a fucking cup of coffee.

"Who gave you this necklace?" Here we go again. The visiting Badu decides to test trust—not only mine, but Abu Salim's.

"A friend from Sinaa," I reply, just as Abu Salim had drilled me.

"And which friend gave you these rings?" the visiting Badu continues.

"My friend from Sinaa."

"Where is your friend's dwelling-place?"

"In the vast expanse of Sinaa."

"What is her name?" The visiting Badu laughs when I reply with silence. "You taught her well," he says to Abu Salim. But, next breath, he snaps, "What is she writing? I would not allow her to write . . . Did she bring a camera?"

"She did, but I trust she will not take pictures of the women. She knows full well it is forbidden," replies Abu Salim.

"What is the name of her camera?"

Silence. Abu Salim has had it with his tribesman's interrogation.

"Is your camera called Polaroid or Kodak?" the visiting Badu asks me. And Abu Salim, with a regal nod of the head, gives me his consent to reply.

"One is called Polaroid; the other Pentax," I say.

"I shall pay you one hundred dollars for your camera called Polaroid," says the visiting Badu.

Is my Polaroid the bribe? Abu Salim gives me no clue; neither does Azzizah or Tammam. So I light a cigarette, and then say nothing. And now he offers me two hundred dollars for the Polaroid. Before he raises his offer again, I tell him a lie: "The Polaroid is a gift I received from my husband . . ."

"She has no husband," he declares to Abu Salim. "No husband would allow his wife to visit-sit with people not her kin."

"I trust she has a husband and a son, as she has told she has," says Abu Salim, with obvious restraint.

"She has told you but a story," the visiting Badu tells Abu Salim. Then he turns to me and demands I show him pictures of my husband and my son.

"I have no pictures to show," I tell him.

"If she had a husband, and a son, and a camera, she would have pictures to show. All strangers show pictures," says the visiting Badu, casting doubt on Abu Salim's trust.

"Why do you have no pictures to show?" Abu Salim asks me, as if I'd betrayed him.

"I carry no pictures of my husband, or of my son, or of my mother and my father, for they are all carved in my heart," I reply, and I was about to tell the visiting Badu to keep the fucking Polaroid, when the children burst into excited cries as Mutt and Jeff return with the goat herd. The mountain-chains shout, laugh, screech as the children play a sort of hide-and-seek among the goats and saluki dogs, raising circles of dust. The infants cough and cry. Breasts are pulled out to pacify them. Not one grownup tells a child to shut up.

Imsallam Suleman Abu Salim himself, probably twice the age of his visiting blood-kin, now starts to unpack their camel, as dictated by Badu hospitality—extended to all, or just to visiting testers-of proof? It looks like they have come to stay for good, having packed everything they own: black goat-hair tent, blankets, carpets, pots and pans, and sackfuls of God knows what—flour for pitas, perhaps, and probably rice, onions, sugar, tea, cans of tomato paste, sardines, and tuna. The visiting man doesn't move to help Abu Salim; it's not proper for a guest to sweat, do work ... Is that why Tammam is pitching the visitors' tent—not in between Azzizah's and Tammam's tents, even though there is space, but about fifty meters southwest of Tammam's tent, where boulders and cliffs will protect the visitors' tent from the winds? Tammam is using stones to hammer in the tent pegs and poles. This tent, like hers and Azzizah's, is also facing east, at such an angle that no one can see into it, nor what is cooking at the fire-circles at the *maharama*—the place of the women.

※

Two cooking-fires this evening in front of Tammam's tent. On one, a huge pot of rice, on the other pitas, handed to the children as soon as they are done.

Azzizah grabs Jeff's arm when he comes for another helping of pita. She checks and checks his hand, and I was probably the most relieved of all to see that his blisters haven't festered. Abu Salim said nothing this evening, just frowned when I cleaned the blisters with alcohol and dabbed on a fresh coat of iodine.

The visiting Badu stuck his nose into my first-aid kit and asked if I had any ointment or pills to cure his son's ailment. Then he went on to tell me that he had dragged his son to every *darwish* and *darwisha* in Sinaa, even to Hilal and the Yahodi *darwish* at the clinic, but Hilal and the Yahodi *darwish*, like all the Badu *darwishin* he had gone to, could not exorcise the *djinn*-demon who had slipped into his son's head when the child was but two or three years old (that's when they noticed he was retarded, I guess). "My son is good, his heart is good... I will give you my camel, all my camels—everything I possess—if you will cure him," he said to me. "My son only lacks discretion, but a Badu who lacks discretion is not a Badu."

"There are special schools, special teachers, who could teach your son to be more discreet," I told him.

"Yes, that is what Hilal and the Yahodi *darwish* told me. But you know how fearful-irritable my son is when away from his mother. And she cannot go with him to these schools, for it is not proper for a woman... *Aywa*—yes, he told us how good you were to him. Allah shall repay you for that. What is your name?"

"Leora; the Badu call me Nura."

"I am Abu Hasan," he says, meaning the father of the child he was speaking of, Hasan. A father concerned about his child resides behind this wild, angry-looking, savage face—all teeth, bulging eyes, sunken cheeks, black stubble.

Dinner: the usual, pita, rice, dip of fried onion and tomato paste, and loads of sugar in the tea, which is served in shifts since there are not enough glasses to go around.

"I heard your son, Salim, is on his way home," the visiting Badu, Abu Hasan, says, rolling an after-dinner cigarette.

"*Aywa*," says Abu Salim. "My son is coming home to get married..."

"To get married?!... Married?!... Cannot be!..." The mountains cry out after Abu Hasan and his wife. There is outrage here, as if Abu Salim has robbed them of their bribe, or the bloody thrill of a double execution … They obviously didn't come here expecting a wedding.

"Not a word did anyone hear of it at the Gates of the Wadi, not even we, your blood-kin," says Abu Hasan.

"Tomorrow, *Inshallah*, the whole desert shall hear," responds Abu Salim, barely able to conceal his pleasure at surprising the whole desert, quashing rumors and pre-empting testers extorting bribes. "Tonight, *Inshallah*, the men shall gather at the *maq'ad* to decide what price for the she-camel, water rights, or rights of passage."

"Who sold you his she-camel for such a high price?" says the visiting Badu, as if he thought no one would be willing to marry his daughter off to a man of such a stained reputation as Salim, not for all the water rights and smuggling routes in the world.

"Iben Jahama, the honorable elder of the powerful clan," replies Abu Salim.

"Surely you did not purchase his eldest she-camel."

"His eldest and most favored she-camel."

"But she is blemished …"

"So is my son, Salim."

"Your son is blemished?" says the visiting Badu, as if he couldn't believe his ears. "How is he blemished?" asks Abu Hasan.

"Any son who leaves his father's tents to see the world is bound to be blemished," says Abu Salim, killing the rumor once and for all.

Tammam, cradling her infant daughter, sits folded into herself, a show-nothing mask silencing her eyes …

A blemished she-camel, meaning a blemished bride, Tamman, not for your husband Abu Salim, but for his son. Why did it not occur to you that Azzizah was talking of a bride for her son, Salim? Did her son promise, swear, he'd marry no one but you, *yaa*-my sister Tammam? No one but you, even if his father refused to grant you a divorce. Did he vow that, under the cover of darkness, together you would flee from this compound, with little Salimeh wrapped in your arms; covering your tracks, until you reached the shelter-tents of a Badu elder powerful enough to negotiate your divorce and license you to marry your heart's desire? Is that how you and Salim dreamed it would happen, *yaa*-my sister Tammam?

Is it for the death of this dream that you are grieving now—love-sick, as in the Song of Songs: O do not judge me for I am love-sick. No river of water could put out the fire of love, no fire could ever burn love out...

Was it to meet his son that Abu Salim disappeared when I was ill? Did he ride away to give his son the news that he had found a way for him to come home and live with his blemished bride in a tent next to yours? Is that what's killing you, *yaa*-Tammam? Would you rather your daughter be motherless, your brother be imprisoned for life? Would you rather Azzizah be a mother bereaved? Would you rather the whole *hamula*—clan—be destroyed, their reputation sullied in a story that remains when all else dies? Oh, Tammam, *yaa*-my sister, was it to avert all of that, that Azzizah urged Abu Salim to pay whatever price was necessary? Did Azzizah whisper that night, did she keep you in the dark for she feared you'd betray both her son and yourself, tell the whole world the rumor is true? Was your brother by your side when you were told of this wedding—the day I was dispatched to catch the wind and tend goats with Mutt and Jeff? Did he tell you, "*Ashow*—wake up—*yaa*-my sister Tammam. Smarten up. Grow up. *Dir balak*—watch out. All the eyes and ears of the desert are upon us, watching and listening for the story that we leave behind..."

26

"Go be my ears and eyes in Abu Salim's *maq'ad*," Azzizah instructs me soon after the evening sun sinks and the wind swallows the men's footsteps. They have gone to decide what price to pay for the blemished bride.

"But I am your eyes and ears outside the tents," Jeff protests, as if Azzizah has just demoted him for no good reason. "Your eyes and ears, and my mother's," he adds. Azzizah smiles. "You stay *fil bayt*—at home—with the women," Jeff tells-orders me. "It is forbidden for a woman to sit-stay in the *maq'ad*."

"Forbidden for a woman Badawia, but not for a woman Yahodiya, as is our guest Nura," Azzizah tells her grandson Jeff. And Tammam tilts her head as if Azzizah is now at a new angle, no longer rigidly upright.

Night rode out to meet us when we reached the *maq'ad*—Mutt and Jeff, the visiting children, and I. As soon as we got there, Hasan, the retarded child-boy, ran over to his father seated in the inner circle closest to the fire's crackling heat. His sister and little Mutt also crawled forward. Only Jeff remained at my side, his teeth chattering. I took off my parka and wrapped it round his shoulders. He organizes it into a sort of a tent, sheltering us from the wind, and my flashlight from the frowning faces of the elders, "who think you write-to-remember for to inform to the other side."

"Which other side?"

"The side of the bride," Jeff whispers back. "You better switch off the torch, for the moonlight is as bright, and not offensive to the elders." In a muted whisper close to my ear, this Badu boy who chuckles whenever I call him Jeff, guides me through his clan's customs and rules of debate in the *maq'ad*. Some men in the inner circle turn to him and frown. ". . . For it is not proper for anyone but the elders to speak here tonight. And it is also not proper for a woman stranger-no-stranger to sit here tonight, even outside the circle, in the dark," Jeff, defying the frowns, whispers in my ear.

Circles within circles round the fire-circle. In the inner circle, the elders and honored guests, including the visiting Abu Hasan; in the outer, their camels. Jeff and I are huddled in between, just outside the rim of the firelight, on the cold gravel, behind the backs of the Badu men, and they must have heard us way before we arrived. Yet no one offered a welcome-carpet to us, or a greeting or even a nod of recognition. The men continue to talk as if the children and I were shadows of saluki dogs or camels, or boulders arranged in a semicircle to protect the men against the cold night wind. From here, Jeff and I can hear only the crackling and the hissing of the fireheat. The wind taunts us with whiffs of the fire's warm fragrance.

A beautiful night, *yaa-Rabb*. A full moon lights the desert, as if it is midday and someone has decided to drape a pearl gray lampshade over the sun. The granite mountains seem buffed by the moonlight, their edges softened, feminine, inviting, enticing you to their bosoms. Woe to anyone enchanted by this mirage. The *kaffiyyes*, *abia*, and *jalabeeya*s are transformed into regal robes by the moonlight. The Badu look like desert monarchs and noblemen, even those who had looked like fierce outlaws on the moonless night when Tal and I first encountered them. Aside from Abu Salim and Abu Hasan, I recognize only three or four of the others. The Badu wearing a black eyepatch like Moshe Dayan—Abu Salim's brother and Azzizah's cousin, according to Jeff. And the Badu with seashell earrings—Azzizah's remedy for hearing loss, Jeff explains, "He is Azzizah's uncle." The toothless Badu whose face looks like a potato—"He is Abu Salim's uncle . . ." And the Badu with two fingers missing from his left hand and one from his right—". . . had tried to render powerless-harmless a land mine planted in Wadi M. by Yahodi soldiers, or Egyptians, or English, or Turkish . . . He is Abu Salim's cousin, and Tammam's . . ." Jeff doesn't know anyone in his clan who is not blood-related to him. His parents are first cousins, as are his parents' parents, "and most everyone's parents ever since time remembered . . ."

Not all the elders are old. Some are probably not yet forty, maybe not yet thirty, like the visiting Badu Abu Hasan. "Why does he have an elder's voice, here in the *maq'ad*?" I whisper-ask Jeff.

"*Allah aref*—Allah knows," he replies. "Maybe Abu Salim invited him to be a tongue speaking for our many clansmen who dwell at the Gates of the Wadi so that later they will not say they want no part of the decision, because they had no voice, in the decision making tonight... *Aywa*, I remember my father told me that no one disputes a decision if he has a say in it. That is why the host of the *maq'ad* lets all the elders have a say, and only then, after he hears all their opinions and their debating, their agreeing and disagreeing, he tells what he has decided to decide, and why he has decided to decide it..."

"You mean Abu Salim alone will decide if the bride-price is to be water rights or rights of passage?" I ask him.

"*Taba'an*—naturally. For Abu Salim owns the waterhole and the rights of passageways... and, after he dies, his son, Salim, will own it. And if Salim also is fated to die, it will not go to my mother, but to Abu Salim's brother, the brother who is the father of Abu Hasan; he is my uncle Salim's cousin..." Jeff points at the visiting Badu, Abu Hasan, the father of the retarded child-boy.

He stands to gain quite an inheritance if Salim is executed. Family rivalries, if not feuds, are bound to inform this debate.

"... One or the other, water rights or access to passageways—smuggling routes—is too high a price for this she-camel," says Abu Salim's nephew, Abu Hasan, his *abaia* wrapped round his retarded son. Here in the *maq'ad* he doesn't say that the she-camel, meaning the bride, is blemished, as he did in the tents. Here he has to take a long silence to gather the courage, it seems, to disagree with everyone who has had a say so far. None said straight out that the bride-price was too high, yet all implied it. "*Aywa*, cunning, rich, and powerful as a sheikh is the owner of the she-camel; his many sons and their large herd will drink our waterhole dry if we give him water rights for his she-camel, and they will take over our passageways if we give him a foothold in them. That is why I think one or the other is much too high a price for his she-camel."

"*Aywa*—yes," Azzizah's uncle, the Badu with the seashell earrings, agrees. It takes him ten minutes to say he agrees, and ten more minutes to say that one or the other is not too high a price—"For it is the price, not only for the she-camel but for our alliance with her noble owner and his powerful clan."

Silence... Silence is also a speaker here, taking a turn after each man. Each one talks in wider circles around the point, yet no one interrupts.

"*El haqq ma'ak*—the truth lies with you." All the men in the inner circle agree, in keeping with their tradition of *maq'ad* debating. Then a minute or so later comes the "But..."

"But I would pay for her, not water rights, but passageways, for they are worthless—only routes to prison," says a neighboring Badu.

"I agree; passageways are worthless these days, but tomorrow, if Israel is to trade this Sinaa desert to Egypt for peace, Egypt will rule in our Sinaa and, *wallah*, how valuable were the passageways when Egypt had ruled here in Sinaa...," says Azzizah's uncle and Abu Salim's.

"I remember... *Wallah*, I remember... It is very difficult to decide what price to pay when you don't know what Israel and Egypt will decide," says Abu Salim's cousin, the Badu whose fingers were taken by a land mine. "If they decide to sign the peace pact, then Israel will evacuate Sinaa, and soon after Egypt will rule Sinaa, and then our passageways will not be worthless. If that is what fate holds in store, I say let us keep the passage routes for ourselves and pay water rights for the she-camel. But if fate holds in store that Israel and Egypt will decide not to sign a peace pact, then Israel will continue to rule here in Sinaa, and our passageways would but be passage routes to prisons. *Wallah*, if I knew that that is what fate holds in store, I would say let us keep the water rights... *Wallah*, it is hard to decide, for only Allah knows if Egypt and Israel will sign a peace pact or not."

The last thing I would have expected is that a Badawia brideprice would depend on the peace talks at Camp David. No matter how well I know that Mid-East politics is just Mid-East politics in Canada, here it's a major consideration in any personal decision—something at the core of the inner-self, the spirit, the soul, mine like the Badu's, yearns to be free from the dictate of politics, fate, nature...

"*Aywa*," agrees Azzizah's uncle and Abu Salim's. "The only way to figure what to pay for the bride-price is to figure what Egypt and Israel will do... *Wallah*, if I were Israel, I would not make a peace pact with Egypt. First of all because, once before—twenty years ago it was, I think—soon after the war the Yahod call the Sinaa war, Israel returned the whole of this our Sinaa desert to Egypt for peace. Yet, ten or eleven years later, Egypt had attacked Israel again. Therefore, I think that now, as then, Egypt means to make a peace with Israel, but not a *sulha*. Surely Israel knows that; *Wallah*, the tribe of Israel is not a tribe of stupid bats. And the other reason is that Israel has built too many towns in Sinaa to give them away, and too many clinics and schools and army bases and air bases to give them away, and also too many roads and too many *biyaar*—wells, *Wallah*... wells and wells, of water and of black gold. *Aywa*, I think Israel is peace-talking with Egypt only to not offend her ally, America."

"I also say, let us pay rights to passageways, not water rights for the she-camel. For I think that Egypt cannot ever make peace with Israel," says Abu Salim's brother, the one with the black eyepatch like Dayan's. "The Arab *fellahin* of Filastin, Syria, Lubnan, Jordan, Iraq, Saudia, and many more the desert over, will never forgive Egypt if she makes peace with Israel. For their war with Israel is a holy war—*jihad*. A holy war should end with victory, never with peace. *Aywa*, yes, if Egypt makes peace with Israel, she stands to lose her honor. *Wallah*, the Egyptians will become a pack of hateful hyenas, crouching to drink from strangers' holes, lapping up water when no wind blows to convey their stink to all others..."

"I think Egypt values land more than honor, and Israel values life more than land, therefore Israel will give this desert to Egypt for peace, and Egypt will take it with both hands. Therefore, I say let us pay water rights for the she-camel, and keep the passageways for ourselves." The neighboring elder looks at Abu Salim, trying to see if his opinion has had an effect. Abu Salim simply nods his head, as he does after every speaker.

"*Aywa*, well put ... well put," says Azzizah's uncle, in the booming voice of the hard-of-hearing. His seashell earrings, Azzizah's remedy, are not much of a hearing aid, it seems. "But I am not sure that Israel values life more than land, for I have seen how the Yahod of Israel are willing to risk their lives for the land. *Aywa*, I have seen how small in numbers they withstood the onslaught of enemies, outnumbering them ten thousand to one, coming from all sides—Egypt, Syria, Jordan, Lebanon, Saudia, Iraq. And I remember how the Yahod of Israel had battled the mighty English, *Wallah*, with no weapons, only with courage and cunning. *Aywa*, look for yourself who rules in the holy land the holy city, Al Quds—Jerusalem—today. I see no English ruling there; I see no Arab ruling there ..."

"The Arab *fellahin* are bound to destroy Israel, even if it will take generation after generation to chip away at Israel, *Wallah*. The holy city, Al-Quds—Jerusalem—cannot be ruled by the tribe of Israel, for the Israelites are heathens, descendants of slaves ...," says Abu Salim's uncle, "and Egyptians slaves they always will be. For a person can never change his ancestors, nor what they did. *Aywa*, Egypt can never make peace with Israel because the Israelites' ancestors had plundered Egypt, robbed her of silver and gold, then stole away to the desert and buried the treasure in Wadi El__ not far from Mousa's Chair. *Aywa*, yes, the Israelites are ashamed to dig it out. But one day, after the Arab *fellahin* will defeat-destroy Israel, Egypt will come here with giant drilling rigs and they will unearth a thousand years or two, or maybe three thousand years of sand. *Wallah*, it may take a hundred years or two, or maybe three hundred years, but they are bound to discover the treasure that their Israeli slaves had plundered from them. Or else everyone will think that they can also rob Egypt, and Egypt will not mind, not remember—will even extend a hand for peace to her own slaves who robbed her." The Badu elder shakes his head, as if three thousand years ago was only yesterday—just like our fanatics argue whether Bar-Kokhba was a hero or a *schmuck*, as if their lives depended on what that hero-*schmuck* did two thousand years ago. Yesterday's sands burn under everyone's feet here—theirs and ours.

No one laughs when the Badu predicts Egypt aims to collect the golden calf and give her slaves three thousand lashes for escaping three thousand years ago and not staying on the job to finish the Sphinx or the pyramids.

Little Jeff crawled over to the inner circle by the fire to sip a hot glass of sweet tea. Abu Salim sends a steaming glass over to me with the visiting child-girl. She doesn't walk in front of the men but behind their backs, in the darkness beyond the rim of the firelight. She hands me the tea, and runs as if I were *djinn*-demon, *al-shaytan*—Satan. What can you expect from a child-girl who hears my tribe described as treasure-stealing, heathen slaves—and the evening is not yet over.

"Beware … beware, *yaa*-my fellow Badu, before you decide what price to pay for the she-camel. Let me tell you," shouts Azzizah's uncle, wearing Azzizah's seashell remedy, "not all that glitters is gold, but the opposite holds true as well … You would not think that such a tribe of slaves like the Yahod would have such a noble Badu king as King Daud—King David. *Aywa*, King Daud was a Badu—a Badu like us, slight of build, but his blood was pure, and his heart noble and courageous, and, like our ancestors, he led the caravans across borders when the ancient tribes used to visit raids on one another. Wise as the wisest of Badu, King Daud would raid the camels where the mountain trails widened. *Aywa*, every sheikh had put a price on his head, but no one could track him down, for he was a better tracker than all who were tracking him. Shelter he took in his father's tents, and day in, day out he tended his father's herd, when Allah touched his shoulder and said, 'Go to be the king of the Yahodi tribe.' Daud told Him, '*Wallah*, I am content to be a simple Badu, what have I to do with the Yahodi tribe?' Daud did not want to be the king of the tribe of Israel. But Allah told him that the Yahodi tribe had no son fit to be a king, for they were all slaves, not of noble blood …

"Why then would you want a kingdom and a king for them?" Daud asked Allah. And Allah replied that he chose the Yahodi tribe to be his whip to punish all the nations who strayed. They spared no one. Daud's Yahodi army conquered what we call Lubnan today, and also Syria, Iraq, Persia, Jordan, and Sinaa. But his son, Suleman, was not of pure blood. His mother was not of Badu blood; she was a Yahodiya, daughter of slaves. And her son Suleman liked the hole, not the sword. A thousand wives he married, and so a thousand palaces, one for each wife, he had to build. Only because Allah had loved his father did Suleman retain his kingdom. But his sons did lose that great inheritance, and I think the sons of the Arab oil kings will lose their wealth and their kingdoms just the same, for they have strayed…"

"You are right," says Abu Salim's brother, in the black eyepatch. "The Arab *fellahin* have strayed. Once upon a time their bellies were slim like a wolf on the prowl, but today, like the wolf of the hills, they cower beneath the pop of a hunter's shot. Only the sons of the poor they send to do battle for them. Every battle, you see the desert littered with their shoes, which they took off for to run away quick-fast from the battle, *aywa*. That is why Israel is bound to grow bigger—and heaven help us, for one day, not the Arabs but the Israelis will say: To us belongs the earth and all who dwell therein."

"Israel has no king," the mountains shout after the elder with the seashell hearing-aid. "She never had a king like her Badu king, Daud. But *Wallah*, I remember the first Israelites I saw, a long, long time ago it was—long before she was called Israel, up in the north border of Lubnan and Israel it was when we were sitting by the fire that a group of men approached us, riding horses like us Badu in those days, and one was even riding a camel. They all were wearing Badu clothes, even *shibriyya*—daggers. And, like true Badu, they greeted us; like us, they tended flocks, matched us poem for poem, story for story, hospitality for hospitality. *Wallah*, we could not believe they were Yahodi men. And they were good neighbors. *Wallah*, a good neighbor is better than a brother who lives far … *Aywa*, waterholes we shared, grazing land, and firewood. But they

346

are small in numbers. *Aywa*, the Arab *fellahin* are bound to win, for their sons are far too many to count. And many sons bearing weapons in their hands are like locusts, and you know what they say of locusts: One is a miracle, but many are a plague . . .

"*Aywa*, that is why I think the Yahodi tribe of Israel is fighting a losing battle . . . *Wallah*, if I were a tongue speaking instead of their tongue, I would go to the Arab *fellahin*, and to their rulers and kings I would say: 'We Yahodi are strangers and we loved you; we came to live among you. But our sons are few. We fear we will perish and so we ask you to fold us under your protection' . . ."

"The Israelis possess a new weapon more powerful than many sons. This new weapon is called 'the atom bomb.' That is why America, and even Russia, is afraid of Israel," says one of the neighboring elders.

"*Aywa*," says Azzizah's uncle and Abu Salim's, "You die just the same if a rifle is aimed at you or 'the atom bomb' or the sword. A battle you win, not by weapons, but by holding ground. *Aywa*, men hold ground, not rifles or atom bombs or even swords . . ."

"That is true," says Abu Salim.

Silence.

Everyone is waiting to hear his decision, it seems—whether to gamble on peace or on war, pay water rights or smuggling routes for his son's bride. But Imsallam Suleman Abu Salim takes his time. He stokes the fire, rolls a cigarette, spits behind his back, covers his spit with a fistful of sand. Finally, he clears his throat and says, "I think the Yahod of Israel had won every battle but lost every war. They cannot win because they are too few in numbers, and because they have no understanding of their enemies. *Aywa*, I agree that they had battled valiantly in the first battle they call War of Independence—thirty years ago, I think it was. They were men then. But after that battle they became women . . . *Aywa*, I have seen the Yahod of Israel in the second battle they call the Sinaa War, more fearful than women. And when the American sheikh—Eisenhower was his name—told them to give Sinaa back to Egypt, like women they did what they were told . . .

"And in the next battle, the one they call the Six-Day War, they won Sinaa from Egypt—but from the air, *aywa*, hiding in airplanes. And the Golan they won from Syria, hiding in armored tanks. Only the holy city, Al-Quds, they won from Jordan fighting like men—hand to hand, face to face, on their feet. But then they spared their enemy..."

"*Wallah*, they do not know their enemy," says Azzizah's uncle. That is their biggest failing. *Aywa*, had the Arab *fellahin* conquered Israel in but six days, they would have slaughtered every Yahodi, drunk his blood, and stuffed his belly with sand..."

"Spare your enemy and he will wait, gather strength to attack you again—even a woman knows that," continues Abu Salim. "Yet it caught Israel by surprise when that happened five years ago, in the battle they call the Yom-Kippur War. *Wallah*, how the Arab *fellahin* nearly destroyed Israel once and for all. *Aywa*, Israel won the battle but lost the war. And why? because they were afraid to risk their lives. *Aywa*, for the lives of thirty-fifty sons who had shamed her—sons who had surrendered in battle instead of fighting to the death—Israel gave Egypt the city of Suez and the fertile pasture lands around her. And now they surely will give Sinaa back to Egypt for peace/no-peace. For they have no understanding of their enemies..."

"*Aywa*," says Azzizah's uncle and Abu Salim's. "The Arab *fellahin* will never allow Israel slaves to rule the holy city Al-Quds—Jerusalem. I heard people say that Saudia is hording weapons for the next battle."

"Yes," says Abu Salim, "one day, *Wallah*, one day Egypt, Syria, and Jordan are bound to band together, and after they destroy Israel, they will destroy the *felastiniyiin fellahin*. And the oil king-doms too. And then they will battle each other until they also are destroyed..."

"And then we Badu will rule in Sinaa," mutters Jeff.

"*Inshallah*—God willing," the men responded, then chuckled, as if that was a dream—unattainable.

"*Wallah*, I will be sorry to see the day Egypt rules here in Sinaa," says the visiting Badu Abu Hasan. "For when Egypt ruled here in

Sinaa, she did not drive water trucks to our tents, as Israel does in years of drought. And she did not dispatch a helicopter to rescue a Badu injured or ill, as Israel does. And what will happen to all the clinics and all the schools that Israel had built for us here in Sinaa? The Egyptians will keep them for their own pleasure. And us they will imprison if we refuse to be her slaves—serve in her army instead of her sons, battle for her instead of her sons, die for her instead of her sons..."

"*Aywa*, Egypt was a merciless ruler, but I prefer Egypt's rule to Israel. For Egypt will not tempt our sons to sell their legacy for clinics and schools, water and roads," says Abu Salim. "*Wallah*, I long for the day when our sons will ride their camels like men in nights with no moon, on roads/no-roads, borders/no-borders..."

"*Aywa*—yes. But reading and writing means wealth today, not heavy saddlebags crossing borders," says Abu Hasan.

"True," says Azzizah's uncle. "Wealth is not measured by heavy saddlebags and not by reading or by writing. Wealth is *adabb*—character, manners, reputation. *Aywa*, reputation. If you tell me of a man who fans the fire, lets its flame bring people far from home, then I will say: that man possesses wealth. *Aywa*, if you tell me that a man is like a well never dry though the ropes are worn, I will say: that man possesses wealth. *Aywa*, everyone and everything dies, but the noble deed—the story of the noble deed. *Aywa*, only the story remains..."

"That is true," says Abu Salim. "A man grows to be noble not from heavy saddlebags, and not from reading and writing, but from the example of his father, his mother, his clan, his tribe. *Aywa*, I have seen *fellahin* reading and writing—Israelis also, and many, many strangers—but none were as noble as my son, Salim, before he was tempted to see the world."

"Salim is the very most best tracker in Sinaa, the very most best in the whole world—*Wallah!*" little Mutt shouts, and the mountains grumble in their ancient sleep.

Abu Salim asks the men if they have formed a decision, and in reply the men ask him what did he decide. He says, "I think Israel will surrender, give Sinaa to Egypt for peace/no-peace. But Israel's mistake is bound to be Egypt's gain. For Egypt will gain not only Sinaa but *zaman*—time—to rebuild her army and train a new generation of sons who will fight like men when Egypt will attack Israel again. But this time Egypt will hold her ground, *ya'ni*—hold the vast expanse of Sinaa. And even if she will not—*ya'ni*, even if Israel will capture Sinaa again—she will return Sinaa back to Egypt again. For her sons are too few to hold on to a vast expanse like Sinaa for more than five-ten years. That is why I think that the rights to the passageways will not be worthless soon. Therefore, I think we should keep them for ourselves, and for the purchase of the she-camel we should offer water rights."

Silence.

He doesn't ask if there are any objections—because he owns the well and her water rights, I guess. No dissenting voice is heard. No one seems to be happy or unhappy with this decision. For all their macho posturing, they are reined in even tighter than their women. They rely passively on Allah, say they are bound by the ropes of fate but otherwise would be free. But here they calculate possibilities, projecting long-term, short-term, almost like the CEOs of some multinational conglomerate. Everyone around them could be clobbering each other to death, even their Arab cousins, and the Badu are looking after their own interests—like pragmatic ultra-orthodox in Brooklyn and Mea Sh'arim? Is such pragmatism inherent in all of us? Is nationalism an acquired trait? Are we light years ahead of these Badu who see only delusion in the dreams of a universal bond?

A distant hyena howl is carried on the biting wind. In counterpoint, Abu Salim *daqq-daqq-daqqs* the beans for honor-coffee. They are going to toast their discussion, it seems.

They have decided to gamble on the destruction of Israel....

What does that say about my presence here? Is it a matter of indifference to them? Have I been insulted? Complimented? Assimilated into Badu culture? Or am I a pawn, invited to write-to-remember and cassette-record that no rumor was ever discussed or mentioned here in the *maq'ad*, or up in the compound?

Why would the Badu talk and talk about everything but this rumor? Is there even one Badu in this *maq'ad* who is not aware that Abu Salim is trying to convert a double execution into a wedding? Is this Badu diplomacy at work? Does deciding to purchase a blemished bride with their most precious possession enhance her value, her reputation, and, by extension, the reputation of her father, her husband, both their clans, and their tribe—the very men who sit here in this *maq'ad*?

Who sullied her reputation in the first place? Why would a people who roll in dust value reputation more than life? The story remains when all else dies: Is that why they didn't challenge Abu Salim? The Badu remember *daimann*—forever. All will remember now that Salim's father chose for him a highly valued, expensive bride.

27

The Polaroid camera transformed everyone in the compound—only for an hour or two, and not so much as to allow a snapshot of a Badawia woman or her forbidden tent. Azzizah, Tammam, and their Badawia visitor stayed behind me while I photographed every man and child in the compound, and also the camels, the goats, and the saluki dogs.

"*Bas*—enough! You will wear out the camera Polaroid!" the visiting Badawia kept saying after every shot.

I wish I could snap a photo of her now, staring at the image of all her children emerging from the moist paper in her hand, as if witnessing a miracle.

"*Shufi . . . Shufi*—Look . . . Look . . ." Her children and Mutt and Jeff are giddy with excitement at how handsome they are.

"*Yaa-Alllaaahhhh!*" Azzizah exclaims in wonder and awe, and *keif*—sheer pleasure—transported by the light-hearted, care-free merriment in her compound.

"Now you see why I wish to possess a camera Polaroid," her Badu visitor, Abu Salim's nephew, says to his wife and then to his uncle.

Abu Salim's frown barely conceals his amazement and delight over the stunning portrait of him and little Salimeh, the child looking regal, like she was next in line for his throne.

One glance at this portrait restored Tammam. Herself once more, it took her no time to learn how to use the camera, and she captured me with little Salimeh, and with Abu Salim, his grandsons, his nephew, his nephew's children—with everyone except the Badawia women.

Forbidden.

"Forbidden!" The visiting Badu snapped at Tammam, grabbing the camera from her hands.

"But I am not in the picture," Tammam protested.

"Yes you are. Your seeing is in the picture," decreed the Badu visitor. Then he demanded I throw into the fire all the photos Tammam had snapped.

"How can it be forbidden to show the camera-work—the seeing—of a Badawia woman, but not her beadwork—like in the necklace Azzizah presented to me?" I ask Abu Salim. "It would be a shame to destroy the only photos I have of me with you, with little Salimeh, with your grandsons, and with your guests. I'd like to show them to my husband, my son..."

Silence. Abu Salim has no idea what to tell me, it seems. There is too much newness here: never before he invited me to enter his forbidden tents had a mountain Badawia woman seen a stranger, or a camera, let alone having her seeing displayed in a photo. He coughed, he spat and covered it with sand. Then he spewed a few curses under his breath, sighed, and told me, "You need not destroy the pictures. But if anyone asks you who did the camera-work, your reply must be the same as when someone asks you who presented you with the Badu jewels, silver, and beadwork you are wearing."

"Your camera Polaroid is all used up now, spent, worth not more that fifty dollars now, but I will give you one hundred for her...," said the visiting Badu Abu Hassan, addressing me.

"Return the camera Polaroid back to her owner," Abu Salim ordered his nephew, his wild streak glistening red in anger, his bloodshot eyes narrowed in disdain. Then, like a king, he pulled off the ancient seal ring, a scarab set in gold, from his finger and presented it to me, as if to impress on his nephew and me that gifts are bestowed in his compound, not bartered for.

"But this ancient gem is too precious a gift to accept," I protest.

"*Aywa*, the gem is ancient and rare, but covered in dust, and does not sparkle like a new gem, or even like fool's gold," said Abu Salim. "You say it is too precious to accept because you are too polite to say you do not like it..."

"On the contrary, I am too polite to tell you how much I like it..."

"In that case, I wish you to accept it, for I presented it to you because it pleased me to do so. *Mabrouka*—may you always be blessed." He congratulated me, sort of like someone would say "Use it well."

"*Mabrouka ... Mabrouka ...*" everyone congratulates me, even the mountains.

"I like my picture more than all the precious gifts in the world," exclaims Hasan, the retarded child-boy, jumping in joy and kissing his photo.

"Nothing wrong with this child-boy," mutters Azzizah. "Nothing wrong ... except that he cannot grow from child to boy ..."

The visiting Badu brought no presents that I saw, but they did bring their own "kitchen" and their own food provisions. They ate separately, around their cooking fire-circle, and didn't invite Abu Salim, his wives, his grandsons, or his stranger-guest to partake.

"Listen to how they beat their coffee beans, as if afraid we will hear and come to drink," Tammam mutters, and for once Abu Salim doesn't berate her. Like one and all around this fire-circle, he muffles his laughter, so that the wind won't carry it to the fire-circle of his Badu visitors.

❧

Like a shadow, the visiting Badawia, Abu Hasan's wife, first followed me to the ditch and then to the shade of this huge outcropping of granite boulders where I sometimes write-to-remember. Here she folds her legs on the cool granite polished by the wind, bends almost to the ground to spare her veil when she lights her cigarette, takes a puff, and says, "I heard your name is Nura. Mine is A'ida."

"A'ida?" I couldn't believe my ears. She pronounced it almost like the opera title.

"Yes. *Aywa*—my mother named me A'ida, for she birthed me on the holy day Id el Adha," she replied, heaped on me a bounty of blessings for opening my heart to her retarded son, then went on to say that many Badu children are afflicted in the same way. "I heard you strangers think it is because we Badu have married our first cousins generation after generation, ever since time remembered. But I think so very many Badu children are afflicted by this very same ailment, which is but lack of discretion, because the times now are indiscreet. My son is but a child of the times…"

Aïda takes a long puff, butts her cigarette out, and says, "Azzizah told me you came to visit-stay here for to gain Badu knowledge. I will give you all the Badu knowledge you wish to gain if you give me your camera Polaroid, which you do not need anyway. For you have another camera, and with this one you already took pictures and pictures of everybody, alone and together with this one and that one, sitting and standing, from head to toe and only the face, *yaa-Rabb*. I do not mean to offend you but, if it were not for your Yahodi tribesmen, my husband would have been able to feed and clothe his children like a man noble and daring. *Aywa*, like a man noble and daring, my husband would have been a border-crossing camel-rider—smuggler—had your tribesmen not imprisoned every border-crossing Badu they catch. And prison… *Wallah*, no fate is worse than prison…

"Therefore it is even better to work taking pictures of tourists riding camels, *yaa-Rabb*. My husband needs your camera Polaroid for to feed and clothe his children, *yaa-okhti*—my sister. If you give me your camera Polaroid I will give you all the Badu knowledge you wish to gain. I have more Badu knowledge to give than both Azzizah and Tammam. For I know, not only the knowledge of the mountain Badu, but also the knowledge of us Badu who dwell near the Gates of the Wadi leading to these mountains…

"You tell me what Badu knowledge you wish to gain, and I shall impart it to you," she adds, reverting to temptation, the Snake in the Garden…

Impart to me the knowledge of the rumor, I want to tell her, but instead I say: "Can you impart to me the knowledge of Badu dreams and nightmares?"

"*Aywa*—yes," Aïda replies.

"And the knowledge of the heart of a Badawia woman who shares her husband with another wife."

"*Aywa*—yes."

"And the knowledge of the blemished bride—how she is blemished and why Abu Salim would purchase a blemished bride for his son?"

"Hush ... *yaa-Rabb* ... *yaa*-Allah. ..." In a whisper she hushes me up, saying that the soiling of a reputation is cause for spilling blood.

"But you and I have heard your husband telling Abu Salim that the bride is blemished," I remind her. And again she whispers, upset, saying that her husband couldn't have said that.

"The father of the bride would have cause to kill my husband if he were to say that his daughter is blemished. *Yaa-Rabb*, do you want my husband killed? His children orphaned? Me widowed? Breathe not a disparaging word about any Badawia woman or man, else you be killed, your son be orphaned. *Wallah*, this is the best, most valuable Badu knowledge I can give you—worth more than ten, more than one hundred, camera Polaroid ...

"For one camera Polaroid I give you this Badu knowledge:

"A Badu's nightmare of nightmares is to be imprisoned; a Badawia's is to be divorced for she must leave her children with her husband. Her dream of dreams, and his as well, is rainfall, green pastures, and a tent held by ten ropes spread wide, and power that's given by sons who are brave; and cover for daughters to shield them from shame, lest talk at a gathering stain; and black goats and camel herds that will need many shepherds; and paradise when you die, not hell, *yaa-Rabb* ...

"For your camera Polaroid I give you also this Badu knowledge:

"Sharing a husband with another wife is not good, for two wives receive only half of what a man can give—*ya'ni*, half his love, half his food for their children, half the clothes. And if he marries three wives, each wife receives only one-third of what he can give. Four wives receive only one-fourth. A man cannot marry more than four wives at one time. And if he does not satisfy his wife's need for love, for shelter and protection, food and clothing, he will give her cause to divorce him. Therein lies the secret of how to keep your husband from taking another wife..." She chuckles under her veil, an impish glint in her eyes. "I wrap my thighs around my husband and I draw him into me for more and more love. And when he tells me, '*Bas*—enough, *yaa*-woman, I am tired, my loin sacks are empty, how many times a night can you do love?' I tell him, '*Wallah*, how can you take a second wife when you cannot even satisfy one?'"

"You mean, you tire him out with love-making to keep him from marrying another wife?"

"*Laaa*—no. But, truth be told, I am more afraid of sharing my husband with another wife than of my husband divorcing me, *yaa-Rabb*. Sleepless would be my nights if my husband were to marry another wife. Sleepless I would lie the nights he lies with her, thinking the nights are not long enough for their play... Fearful I would tremble day and night, *yaa-Rabb*, if for a second wife my husband were to take a *darwisha*—medicine woman. Day and night I would wonder what spells and potions she concocts for me."

"Do you think Tammam lives in fear of the spells and potions Azzizah might be concocting for her?"

"*Allah aref*—God knows," replies A'ida. "But for your camera Polaroid I will give you this knowledge:

"I think Tammam likes to believe that Azzizah protects her like a mother. For her mother died of the evil eye soon after birthing Tammam. The poor woman died from one of the Badawias who came to visit-bless her newborn girl-child, Tammam. Or so I had heard. No one knows who this Badawia was, for many Badawias came to bless her that day. But Tammam's father, he had four wives the day Tammam was born, and maybe one of these other wives caused her to die by coming to visit her when she was menstruating."

"You mean to say you believe that a menstruating woman can kill a woman giving birth? How?" I ask her.

"By not wearing gold when she is menstruating and sees that again her womb did not conceive. Envious, such a woman can cause a mother who just gave birth to die, or to become barren, or even to cause the newborn child to die. That is why we Badawias are careful to always wear gold for to blind the evil-eye of envy ... *Wallah*, I would be afraid to invite you to my tent if I did not see you wearing gold around your neck."

"You don't think Azzizah protects Tammam like a mother, do you?"

"*Allah aref*—God knows," replies A'ida. "No matter how a guest offends you, treat her like a friend—even if her prattle brings your patience to an end," she mutters to herself, then, addressing me, she adds: "Now I shall give you Badu knowledge worth five cameras Polaroid.

"First: Let me caution you, *Wallah*, if to strange lands you go, get the lay of the land though the learning be slow. Two: If one balks at your questions, query him not; be as if on a peak far from winds that are hot. Three: If nothing of note should oblige you to leave, stay home your own guests to greet and receive. Four: The passer of gossip from your camp keep away, and don't ever, ever take to heart what he says; he conveys to you gossip, then brings it to me, not caring if truth or a lie it may be. Five: Throw no stone on a path where you are taking a trip; it will make either you or a friend of yours slip."

"*Wallah*, well put, *yaa*-A'ida."

"*Aywa*, it is from my father that I had learned these words, which he had pressed into verse," A'ida says. *Jingle-jangle*, as she flicks away flies. "My father was highly regarded for his gift with words, but a woman—a woman's value is measured by her reputation, *yaa*-Nura. A woman's reputation is held in much higher value than her gift for words, beauty, or gift of wisdom, or her working strength, or even her strength to deliver sons ... That is why it is prudent never, ever, to say or do anything that might tarnish a woman's reputation. This is the best, most valuable Badu knowledge I can give you, worth more than ten, more than one hundred camera Polaroid." A'ida knows that I know that she knows ...

She rolls a cigarette and hands it to me. "This is *baksheesh*—meaning for free. I learned this word, not from my father, but from the *Arayshiyyah*—meaning the marketplace that comes to our gates on a big, big truck, all the way from Al-Arish; therefore, we call it 'the A'rashiyya'... You know, our men cannot purchase provisions for us, for they are away from home all too many days, weeks, months, doing camera-work or construction work. But they leave us women money so that we will be able to purchase from the A'rashiyya food supplies, and clothing, and the latest things in everything, and even love curtains..."

"Love curtains?"

"Yes, *aywa*. Come, I will show you *baksheesh*," she responds, inviting me to her tent.

From the outside, her tent doesn't look much different from Azzizah's and Tammam's. Three years she spent as well weaving her tent, using the black hair of the goats she and her mother had raised and sheared, spinning it, rolling it onto their runners, and stringing it onto their looms. Inside, it was as dark and stifling as Azzizah's tent and Tammam's until A'ida pinned up the flaps like Azzizah and Tammam do, with twigs. And then she untied the strings that hold the white cotton "love curtain" to the "ceiling" of her tent and it drops down like a heavy mosquito net. Next she crawled inside, tucking the hem under a thin foam mattress, made in Taiwan to be used on patio loungers.

"Nighttime, the children cannot see us making love here. Even now you can barely see through, can you?"

"*Wallah*, I barely can," I reply.

"*Aywa*," she says. "We Badu from the Gates of the Wadi sleep, not like in the old days, as the mountain Badu sleep here. You are welcome to sleep here in my tent, I will even sew you a curtain all for yourself if you wish..." She invites me to crawl into the love-nest. Amazing how cozy and beautiful it is—a tent within a tent, and under the cone-shaped top, A'ida has worked colorful beads and ribbons, and done embroidery.

"For to please my husband when he rests on his back, and I mount him." She laughs. "My husband will never have the strength to take another wife, but I am also getting tired." She heaves a sigh, then asks me if I have pills "to prevent babies... My husband heard people say that stranger-women have such pills," she explains. "Is it true or but a story, as Azzizah says?"

"There are such pills, but I have none to give," I reply.

"What a shame," she says. "I do not know a day, ever since I married, that I was not pregnant or breast-feeding. I am blessed with good fortune, Azzizah tells me—your womb is fertile, your children alive, Azzizah says ... *Aywa*, I am, but I wish I could rest for a day, a month, a year ... If only I could get these pills to prevent babies, *yaa-Rabb*. I have tried Azzizah's remedies, but they do not help, for my husband plants his seed deep, deep, and my womb draws him in even deeper still.

"*Wallah*, I gave you much Badu knowledge, thrown wide and narrow, in verse and plain words, now give me your camera Polaroid," she says, closing the deal.

"I will, *yaa*-A'ida, if you will explain why you did not hesitate to reveal how you and your husband make love yet hold so firm your resolve to cover up the reason that compelled Abu Salim to overrule your husband's counsel and pay such a high price for the blemished bride for his son."

"*Hushh* ... You do not know her father," A'ida whispers. "He is more fearless than Abu Salim, more wealthy and more powerful, perhaps even wiser."

"Why, then, would he give his daughter in marriage to his inferior?"

"Abu Salim's son is not his inferior," A'ida replies, then walks away from the bargaining "table," leaving me alone in her love-room.

Holding the Polaroid as if it were a glass of water she was afraid to spill, A'ida glides toward me here, at the lookout point. "Better sit down here, for when you stand and look at lookout points, people think you are looking for your lover," she tells me. Is that why Tammam stands here for hours every day?

"The children were playing with your camera Polaroid, with all your belongings. You should lock them safe, away from children and goats," she advises me, her hunger for the Polaroid so hot in her eyes that I was about to tell her to keep the camera, but just then she says, "Do you promise to give me the camera Polaroid if I promise to tell you of the blemished bride?"

I couldn't resist. "I promise," I said.

"Swear you will not betray to anyone that you heard it from me."

"I swear."

She asks me for one of my cigarettes and bends down to light it. "*Ana bigul*—Now I shall tell," A'ida states in the manner of Badu story/legend tellers.

"*Ghule*—tell on," I urge her, in keeping with Badu custom.

"*Aywa*... The bride Abu Salim had purchased for his son is even more beautiful than Tammam, or so I had heard people whisper. Tall and graceful as a palm is this bride, I had heard it told; her voice like a flute, her heart like a man's—daring, wise, and noble, but her manner like a maiden's—modest. Her presence had filled every tent she entered with light...

"But then, one day, she was tending the flock, as maidens often do, a far distance—more than two or three days away from her mother's tent—and there she happened to see a Badu youth resting his feet in the shade of a tree like this one—a thorn tree. You know it is forbidden to cut down trees like this one, for they provide shade to shepherdesses and firewood for cooking fires. And the fruit provides fodder for the flock. And if you cut down a tree like this one, you will cut down the possibility of ever living here or anywhere trees like this are growing...

"And so, under such a tree, the Badu youth was brewing tea. And, like a proper Badu, he offered her—the bride that Abu Salim had purchased for his son Salim—a glass of sweet tea.

"And she was thirsty, *Wallah*. It was midday and the sun was high and hot. Her waterskin was empty, and the nearest waterhole was a far distance away. But she, being a modest maiden, waited for him to drink, to show her first that his tea was clean. She even waited for him to swear by the life of the tree and our worshipped Lord Allah and his prophet Mohammad that his tea was clean. And only then did she drink to quench her thirst...

"But that Badu youth was dirty, *yaa-Rabb*, filthier than tarfa bark, which gives off only black smoke when put into the fire. This dirty youth must have dropped a bewitching leaf into her tea for she lost her reason and, right there and then, without telling even her mother or her father, she left her flock and went off with the dirty Badu youth...

"Far, she followed him, *yaa-Rabb*, far across the desert and the border to another land—Jordan, I think is her name... And there, in Jordan land, the Badu youth, knowing that their blood was exposed, her kin bound to search for her far and wide—for forty years, or even four hundred, if need be—and that she, of such great beauty and tall as a palm, would not escape notice... Sooner or later someone was bound to tell her kin of their whereabouts, and her kin were bound to kill him and her. That terrible Badu youth knew all of that. And so, fearing for his life, the Badu youth vanished in Jordan land. *Yaa-Rabb*, he lacked the courage and the nobility to offer her even a marriage of destruction, meaning a marriage in a distant land, a marriage with no approval... *Aywa*, lacking character and *muruah*, he left her in that faraway land called Jordan...

"And she, her reason returning by and by, thought more and more of the hills and the plains of her home. She missed her mother and her father, her brothers and her sisters, longed to see them, even for the brief moment before they were bound to kill her. And so she decided to journey back.

"On and on she walked—*yaa-Rabb*, walked a vast strange desert all alone. Always at nighttime. Hiding behind the darkness so that no one will see-tell, shaming her and also her blood-kin. But one night she was border-crossing when Yahodi soldier-men caught her. And the Yahodi authorities, *yaa-Rabb*, as if she was a man smuggling information, imprisoned her—a fate worse than death...

"Day and night the Authorities asked her question upon question... But she, being a woman, how could she tell them even her name? She could not. How could she tell them why she had crossed borders without shaming herself and her blood-kin? She could not. And the Authorities, thinking she was ill, drove her to a clinic called 'asylum', and there they also locked her behind bars, for they feared she would escape.

"And there, in the asylum, she sat for many weeks, maybe months. Until, one day, a Yahodi *darwish*—Doctor, was his name—saw that she was proper-modest, not ill. But, not knowing her name, he did not know the name of her tribe, and not the name of her dwelling-place. And so he did not know how to reach her kin. He did not know what to do. He thought and thought, and then, one day, someone told him that Hilal knows all the Badu in Sinaa, and so he was bound to know the Badu maiden and her blood-kin. Right away, the Yahodi *darwish* fetched Hilal. And when Hilal saw how beautiful the maiden, how graceful and tall, he recognized her right away. For her father had favored her, even more than a son. And like a son, he raised her, even invited her to sit round the fire-circle in his *maq'ad*. It was there that Hilal had seen her. *Wallah*, so noble and courageous was this maiden, even here in this place called 'asylum', she greeted Hilal and blessed him, as she did every guest in her father's *maq'ad*. Hilal returned her greetings and blessings, and then he told her, 'How can I escort you to your father when I know he is bound to kill you?'

"'I am not afraid to die,' she said, 'but let me see my parents, my home, even if only for a brief moment.'

"Hilal, however, did not have the heart to escort her to her death. And so, he alone, without her, went to her father's *maq'ad*. And there Hilal waited and waited until her father's guests had all departed. When he was certain that no one will hear, Hilal told her father, 'Listen, *yaa*-my brother, the Authorities have searched and searched, and finally they have located your missing daughter. She is safe and well, I swear by the life of the rain that falls from the sky. But the Authorities will reveal her whereabouts to you only if you swear that you will never, ever harm her, or her sons, or her sons' sons...'

"Her father swore by the life of the trees and the plants, and by the life of the shield of Suleman, son of Daud... Her father swore by the life of everything sacred and dear to a Badu, and then he told Hilal, 'I pray, *yaa*-my brother Hilal, that one day you will believe a

Badu, even without all this swearing. *Yaa*-Hilal, why would I harm my daughter when I was the one who had sent her on a mission that took her far, many weeks and months away from home. *Aywa*, I told you she was missing only for to divert you from her mission. *Wallah*, this daughter of mine is more courageous, more cunning, more generous and strong than a man. That is why I raised her, not only in her mother's tent, but also in my *maq'ad* ... *Aywa*, do you think only you Yahod raise daughters to be soldiers?' ... Like this, her father talked, until he had convinced Hilal that he had no cause to harm his daughter, for she only followed his orders. Her father also convinced the whole tribe, and he slaughtered twenty or maybe two hundred goats to honor her return. For seven days and seven nights people feasted, sang, and told stories in his *maq'ad* ...

"But then, one day, a week or two before her wedding day, her cousin who was bound to her in marriage when he and she were twelve-fifteen years old, suddenly came to her father's *maq'ad* and said, 'I cannot marry your daughter for she is blemished.'

"Her father looked at his daughter's cousin. *Wallah*, he looked at him long and hard, and then he said, '*Aywa*, I see why you cannot marry my daughter. *Aywa*, I see, and I agree that you should not marry my daughter. For her horizon is wide and your horizon is narrow.' *Wallah*, her father did not talk empty for he refused all the men who came to marry his daughter.

"For a year or two, or maybe three, he refused every man, until Abu Salim came to him and said, 'My son is blemished, for he went to see the world against my wishes. But his horizon always stretched wide, and now, after he went to see the world, his horizon is much too wide to marry any maiden but your daughter.'

"That is all I know to tell. Now, will you give me your camera Polaroid?"

"*Wallah*, you are a good storyteller," I say, handing her the camera.

A'ida presented me with her silver anklet—to repay me for the Polaroid, I assume. "No need, *yaa*-A'ida. Your story was more than enough payment."

"Stories are for *keif*—sheer pleasure, not for camera Polaroids," A'ida replied.

28

"Bukra—tomorrow—*Inshallah*, Salim will come home," his mother, Azzizah, kept saying day after day. If she expected him to show up this day instead of the next she gave no sign of it. Today, she and A'ida, with her little ones, went to comb the mountains and wadis for firewood. The older children went to tend the goat herd. As soon as all the others had left, Tammam went to the lookout point.

For an hour or so she waited at the point. Then, like a superstitious, love-sick girl who believes her prince comes only when she doesn't wait for him, she whipped herself into a frenzy of work. Time and again she lugged jerricans of water up to the compound. Then, she did the laundry, washing every piece of clothing she and her infant daughter owned. Next she washed her welcome-carpets, and every pot and pan and tray, and spoon, and tea glass and coffee demi-tasse. And another jerrican went to bathe little Salimeh. In the high heat of noon, she dressed her infant daughter in the new woolen dress and jacket I had brought her from Canada. Then Tamman asked me to bathe her. Afterwards, she groomed herself, braided her hair, kohled her eyes, applied red polish to her nails and her infant's, dabbed on them both so much essence of rose that the compound smelled like a florist's. By then none of us—Tammam, little Salimeh, or I— could keep our eyes open.

It saps you, the desert heat, and the climb from the waterhole to the compound is a hell of a workout. It's quite the fat farm, this compound. The longer I stay, the looser my jeans get. Also, the more easily I doze off, and the longer and longer my stretches of lethargy become—Bedouinism, it's called in The Land.

By the time she heard a man approaching, Tammam's housekeeping efforts were invisible—everything was once again coated in dust and sand.

"*Rajol*—man—approaching," Tammam muttered, half-asleep. Then she jumped up and got the fire going in her honor fire-circle. Quick-fast she rinsed the teapot and filled it with the water she had muled here, spit-and-polished her infant girl, and primped, adjusting her veils and shawls, her jewels *jingle-jangling*.

A minute or two later, a Badu shows up, looking like an extra from *Lawrence of Arabia*—long flowing robes in muted desert colors, embroidered in gold thread; silver and turquoise on the handle of his *shibriyya*—dagger—and its holster and belt; spanking-white *kaffiyye* belted with a white silk *agal*; and biblical sandals, like mine, made in Israel by Nimrod.

Salim. I sensed in him what I knew only too well in myself—the anxiety, the expectations, the memories, the fatigue that accompanies you home after a year or two. The rush of adrenalin and city energy... He was restless, impatient, awkward, choked by restraint as he exchanged salutations-greetings-blessings with Tammam.

She poured tea, silent-proper, dropping her eyes when he looked at her.

"How beautiful the child." He broke the silence.

"Her name is Salimeh," said Tammam. The strain in her voice frightened little Salimeh, who started to cry. Tammam pulled out a breast to pacify her. "The infant loves you, *yaa*-Salim. She was crying only because..."

"How are you, Tammam? How are you?—*Keif enti, keif enti, yaa-Tammam?*" Salim kept asking her.

Tammam replied with silence, her head bent low. She was crying, it seemed. But her eyes were dry when she looked at him and whispered, "How are you, *yaa*-Salim?—*Keif enta, yaa-Salim... keif enta... keif enta?...*"

Now the silence was his and he dropped his head. I was intruding, I felt.

"*Shvi shvi*—sit, sit," he muttered in Hebrew when I rose to my feet.

Without saying a word, like a Badawia, I walked away. They didn't call me back.

Not long after I reached my "private" nook at the huge outcrop of granite boulders, it sounded like a *maq'ad* full of men were heading to the compound. Tammam seemed tense when I rejoined her and Salim. And the closer the sound of the men's voices and footsteps got to the compound, the angrier Salim looked and the more he resembled his father, Abu Salim.

So many black veils, shawls, and capes had Tammam thrown over her head, and little Salimeh, she looked like a ghost's shadow carrying off a hapless infant, rising to her feet to greet more men than I had ever seen up here in the compound. All except Abu Salim, Akram, and Abu Hasan muttered a greeting-blessing while shaking her hand, or rather the black shawl that covers it—like an ultra-orthodox Jew would the hand of a woman he thinks is unclean—or incendiary, such a flame to his twig, one touch will start a forest fire … Tammam remained standing until all the men were seated on her welcome-carpets, and only then did she fold her legs and start to brew another pot of tea. God only knows how she could see-breathe through all the layers of black covering her eyes, face, head, and little Salimeh …

Silence—only the mountain echo of a shepherd child yelling-singing in the wadi below.

Imsallam Suleman Abu Salim looks like he has aged ten years in less than a day. His face is drawn, pained, old; slumping with tiredness, he stares past his son, Salim, as if he has no strength to endure the sight of him. Because Salim ran off to see the world? Because Salim fathered Tammam's child? Because Abu Salim took for himself this girl-wife his son had been engaged to marry since they were children? Salim is the very most best tracker in the whole world, according to Mutt and Jeff. Surely he could have covered his tracks for another year or two—maybe ten. Why didn't he? Was he homesick, missing his home ground, his mother, father, sisters, *hamula*—clan—Tammam? Did he return to spare them years of shame and worry, or was he simply tired of wandering from waterhole to waterhole, furtively, driven to become a fugitive by the storytelling of his father's enemies?

The *jingle-jangle* of jewels, coins, and beads announced the Badawias' return to the compound. A'ida and her infants joined our fire-circle, but Azzizah clearly wanted to greet her son in the privacy of her tent.

"Your mother is back in her tent," muttered Abu Salim, as if Salim was a child and had to be told to go to his mother to pay his respects. For a moment Salim seemed to resent it; next moment it looked like he was thinking: *Wallah*, I am home—and like a good boy he does what his mother wants when his father wants him to.

As soon as Tammam had served tea to the men around her fire-circle, Abu Salim told her to build a cooking fire.

"But the water will boil out before the herd returns," she muttered—thinking that Abu Salim would slaughter a goat to honor his son, I guess, just as the father of the blemished bride did to honor and celebrate his daughter's homecoming...

His son's homecoming, Abu Salim had no intention of honoring with anything more than coffee.

Azzizah comes to help Tammam prepare the usual for supper. Something terrible must have happened during her reunion with Salim in her tent. Her eyes are like open wounds. And Salim looks almost as if, like Tammam's brother, Akram, he thought his mother had conspired to get rid of her junior co-wife. Perhaps he regrets that he hadn't made love with Tammam as rumored, that he would rather be tested for proof than be married to anyone just to put the rumor to rest. Perhaps he has come home to exact justice—to make sure his mother's wish comes true and his father divorces Tammam, so that he, Salim, can marry her; otherwise he'll tell the whole desert that the rumor his mother had fabricated is true. It's as if he would rather die than let her reap satisfaction from the seeds of her poison. Can this be the basis of the reunion between mother and son?

Ah, the fury of a woman scorned is nothing compared with that of sons and daughters who have a mother to blame for all the wrong in the world.

"*Yaa*-Salim! Salim!" The joy of the shepherd-children returning with the goat herd filled the compound.

"You see? I told you. I knew Salim would bring a lot of candies."
Mutt and Jeff both offer me a fistful of toffees. Then they point to
the Badu that everyone round the fire-circle was calling "El-Hajj,"
meaning he had made the pilgrimage to Mecca. "That is my father,"
says Jeff. "My father also," mutters Mutt.

Three dozen people, give or take, including children, were in
the compound now. Some of the children chose to eat with the
men around the coffee-honor fire. Others joined the women
around the cooking fire.

"Tell us of your journey, *yaa*-Salim," said Azzizah's uncle, with
the seashell hearing-aid.

"*Ghul*—tell on . . . *Tell on.*" The mountains answer the Badu's
command.

"First, I went to the holy city, *Al-Quds*—Jerusalem," Salim went
on to tell in the lilting voice of Badu legend-telling. "And there, in
the holy mosques with the huge domes all covered in silver and
gold, I prayed shoulder to shoulder with a thousand worshippers."

"*Yaa-Allah! Yaa-Allah!*" the mountains exclaimed.

Only Abu Salim and Azzizah appeared unmoved, as though
Salim's recounting of his defiance heaped insult on injury.

And then, almost as if to impart to them how God had punished him for defying them, Salim went on to tell how he had
wandered in the land of Israel without food and shelter for days
and nights until he had earned money to survive. No one had
invited him to visit-stay, not even the men who had worked with
him in the dockyards in Eilat, Ashdod, and Haifa.

"*Aywa . . . aywa . . . ,*" muttered Abu Salim, knowingly, like a man
who should have been obeyed.

"*Aywa*—yes," agreed Salim, lighting a Yahodi cigarette and con-
tinuing to tell how he couldn't stomach the Yahodi food, "for the
Yahod cook, not on fire like us Badu, but on fuel called electricity
that robs the food of taste. But often, late at night, I would walk
and walk until I reached a stretch of open space, and there I would
build a fire, brew tea, prepare pita—just like here at home. And
sometimes I would fall asleep by the fire under the sheltering sky,

just like here, and I would sleep sound. *Wallah* ... sleepless, restless, were most of the nights I stayed inside a dwelling-place made of concrete or stone, like most Yahodi dwelling-places in Israel. Such places are good for winter-cold, but in summer-heat are so stifling, you cannot breathe. Out in the open, it would often be dangerous to sleep. For Yahod called 'policemen' would fall upon you and say you could be charged with an offense called trespassing, meaning crossing over to a place belonging to someone, just as our passageways belong to us."

"They imprisoned you, *yaa-Rabb* ... May a drought strike their towns ... May the Angel of Death snatch their breath," Azzizah's uncle cursed and the mountains boomed after him.

"*Aywa*—yes," said Salim. "They detained me until the Yahodi who was paying me for my working came and swore that I was not of the Arabs they call terrorists. *Wallah*, what destruction these terrorists wreak on the Yahod ..."

"For the Yahod did not kill the children of the Arabs who had killed their children in Ma'alot," says Abu Salim, flinging his cigarette butt into the fire.

"*Ghul*—tell on," Tammam's brother urges Salim. "Did you see the moving pictures?"

"*Yaa*-Allah ... *Yaa*-Allah," Mutt and Jeff exclaimed after they heard Salim tell about moving pictures, where people pay money to see story-acting, and places called restaurants, where people pay money to eat, and places called cafés, where people pay money to drink coffee.

"*Yaa-Rabb* ... *Yaa-Rabb*," the mountains mimic. "People pay money for honor? For *keif*—sheer pleasure?"

"*Aywa*," says Salim. "Nothing is free except a bathing beach or two, and beautiful green places called 'woods' or 'forests', and oases full of shrubs, bushes, flowers, and trees, called 'parks'. But people have no time to enjoy the beautiful free 'parks' and free 'woods'. Time escapes in their cities and towns. For they work all the time, like *fellahin*, else they battle like Badu warriors of old ... *Aywa*, they are not lovers of joy, but I wish you could see how they made the

Negev green, and rain did not fall there for six-seven years, just like here. *Aywa*, that is why I purchased there in the Negev-desert-city called Bir Sab'a—Beer Sheba—a generator and a drill, and also a pump, so that our well also will yield water in years of drought."

The mountains echo Abu Salim as he coughs and coughs…

Mutt and Jeff followed their grandfather, Abu Salim; their father, El-Hajj; and their uncle, Salim, to Azzizah's tent. They will all sleep there tonight, I assume. A'ida, her husband, and children had retired to their tent. The other Badu guests went to sleep in their compounds or *maq'ad*s. Only Tammam's brother, Akram, stays here with Tammam, her infant, the goats, and me.

"I was told you were gone to greet Salim, to escort him home. Did you happen to see my father when you went to escort Salim?" Tammam asks her brother.

"Yes," replies Akram, wrapping himself with one of her welcome-carpet-blankets.

"Did he, my father, send anything for me?" Tammam whispers to her brother.

"Go to sleep, *yaa*-Tammam," her brother whispers back.

"Did my father send nothing for me, not even a greeting-blessing?" whispers Tammam.

Akram replies with silence. And the mountains respond.

29

"Salim refused to fetch his bride, therefore Abu Salim had dispatched five men, my husband among them, to fetch her instead," A'ida tells me, whispering, though her infant and I are her only audience here in the cool shade beside her tent. All day she has been embroidering a cape she plans to wear at the wedding, which, according to her, "is all too fast approaching now."

You wouldn't know it from Azzizah and Tammam. Neither one is preparing anything for the wedding. Ever since Salim arrived, Azzizah has been sticking close to Tammam, almost like a guard, a protector, a warden.

The wedding is the last thing on Salim's mind as well, it seems. From first light till dusk, he has been working at the waterhole, trying to assemble the generator, the drill and pump, from rusty, second-hand parts. His clansmen helped for a couple of days, then they lost heart, saying, "Someone sold a story to Salim. A waterhole dried-up by drought is a waterhole dried up by drought—no machine will ever change that."

Only Tammam's brother, Akram, worked side by side with Salim. Like Salim, he had changed out of his finery and wore now a faded *jalabeeya* and a tattered white *kaffiyye* wrapped around his head. He and Salim are obviously close friends: both slept down at the *maq'ad* after Salim's first night home and both ate by the waterhole.

And whenever Tammam came to draw water or to deliver a bundle of pitas to them, or to build a cooking fire for them and brew tea and cook rice, both Akram and Salim would frown with worry, seeing Tammam wilting by the day ... And even when Salim and Tammam caressed each other with their eyes, they exchanged sorrow for sorrow, or so it seemed.

"Why did Salim refuse to fetch his bride?" I ask A'ida, a fountain of information now that I have presented her with my camera

Polaroid. "Does he want to finish his waterhole project before he gets married?"

"*Laa*—no. Salim didn't want to fetch her so soon after their betrothal ceremony," A'ida replies.

"Their betrothal ceremony? When and where was it held?"

"Two-three days, or maybe it was four-five days before Salim came home, that he had been summoned to appear before the father of the bride," A'ida whispers. "But Salim, like most bridegrooms, was shy to go there alone. That is why his father, Abu Salim, dispatched Tammam's brother, Akram, to flank Salim on his right, and on the left rode Salim's brother-in-law, El-Hajj...

"It was from him, from El-Hajj, that my husband had learned how the father of the bride had handed Salim the *gasala*, meaning 'the green sprig that he had cut off, for to reap,' just as in the marriage covenant he was cutting off his daughter from himself, for Salim to reap...

"O, how sorrowful was the father of the bride, sorrowful and solemn as he handed Salim the *gasala*, and loud for all to hear he said, 'This is the *gasala* of my daughter. All wrong-doing, offenses, or sins committed against her, and all responsibility to fulfill her needs, feed and water and clothe her, cross over from now on from my neck to your neck...'

"Salim was shy like every groom, but his hand did not tremble when he accepted the *gasala*, placed it under his headband—his *agal*, then, loud and clear for all to hear, he pledged: 'I, Salim, receive your daughter in the tradition of Allah and his prophet Mohammad...'

"The bride was present also—tall and graceful as a palm. Salim was wise to glance not at her, only at her kinsmen. For a woman's sons possess the character of her kinsmen. *Aywa*, I often heard my father say, 'Link your son... oh, link him with well-founded kin... for nobility stems from woman's thighs, as fire stems from tinder...'

"Salim has reason to rejoice, *Wallah*. For her kinsmen's reputation exceeds even the powerful and the noble reputation of his own father, Abu Salim. But Salim had admonished all in his party not to rejoice, for that was sure to offend the bride's kin, all of whom were sorrowful, for they were losing a beautiful, noble daughter, giving her away to another family ... giving away the best of her, the promise of her womb, the nobility bred in her bones ...

"Yet, for as long as time will be remembered, it is they and their blood-kin, not her husband and his blood-kin, who forever will be held responsible for her conduct ... *daimann*—forever and ever, long after she dies, for generations and generations, till the end of time, it is they who are bound to uphold her honor and avenge her blood ...

"*Aywa*, so aggrieved are a daughter's parents when they marry her off, neither one can suffer her wedding, nor can any of her kinsfolk ... O, all too alone a bride follows her groom. Her sons will forever belong to her husband, not to her, not even if he were to divorce her. Forever—*daimann*, her sons will serve to strengthen her husband's kin, not her own ...

"*Aywa*—stay here for the wedding and with your own eyes you will see. Not even one of the bride's kinsfolk will come to celebrate her wedding." A'ida helps herself to one of my few remaining cigarettes, lights it under her veil, and takes a break from her embroidering. It seems to be done in the same tribal pattern and tribal colors used on Azzizah's cape and Tammam's, and on the dusty cape A'ida is wearing now. A closer look reveals that, by choice or by chance, for variety or because she ran out of red thread, A'ida has embroidered a section in purple, and has changed the pattern, or the pattern changed while her mind wandered. Regardless, you can't fail to notice that her embroidery is as different as she is from Azzizah and Tammam, even from herself a day or two ago ...

⚜

From dawn to dusk, the mountains replay the clamor of hammer on steel and iron at the waterhole. Day in, day out, the banging and clanging go on and on, even in my sleep. Then, suddenly, it stopped, and the mountains echoed children's joyful voices: "She is here! The bride is here!"

"The bride is on her way," A'ida cried out, gliding off to the lookout point.

It was the most beautiful time of day at the compound, the time when the low slanting rays reveal the hues of the ancient wealth embedded in the granite surround—the best time of day to see from the lookout point in all directions.

From the direction of the waterhole, Azzizah rushed to the compound. Her son, Salim, ran into her tent, then out, lugging black and white bundles. He dumped them into his camel's saddlebags, then rode off, raising a lot of dust—and chuckles from A'ida.

"Look at how eager Salim is to take possession of his bride— the very bride he had refused to fetch," she muttered under her veil. "Look at how fast he gallops now to possess her ..."

"To possess her with a *gasala*—a green sprig, or with his *zubi*?" I ask her, and she cracks up.

"... Really, like a ram in heat—a ram whose *zubi* is as erect as his horn, Salim is galloping to posses his bride ...," A'ida goes on, between laughs. Abruptly, as soon as the shifting wind brings us the *jingle-jangle* of Azzizah's jewels, A'ida falls silent.

"I asked my son, Salim, to take possession of his bride at this bend of the wadi, below our lookout point, so that we women could see," Azzizah says, then darts to the edge of the escarpment to catch a closer look.

"Azzizah is not proper. She should be honoring her son's bride— running down to accompany her, not standing here, watching like a guest," A'ida whispers. Next breath she goes on to ululate ear-piercing trills that bounce from mountain to mountain.

Azzizah rushed over to A'ida and demanded she stop ululating—"rejoicing, when the bride is agonizing." But A'ida trills on. A healthy pair of lungs she's got. And now Azzizah utters her own long, high-pitched trill—a signal to Tammam to stay away? Confusing as hell to Tammam, these mixed messages, I imagine, but a fitting overture to what is to come.

The girl-wife is only sixteen-seventeen years old—eighteen at most. And even if there is not a grain of truth in the rumor, all eyes will be watching her at Salim's wedding. If, as custom dictates, the bride will move here, day in, day out, Tammam will have to face her. And in the night, the sound from the tent of Salim and his bride will wash over her, like tears.

"Look . . . look how eager is Salim, arriving before his bride." A'ida points to the bend of the wadi below, as two camel-riders come into view. It is impossible to see their faces from the look-out point, but one is holding black and white bundles, so I assume he must be Salim. The other, wearing blue, must be Tammam's brother, Akram, dressed in his new Prince of Saudia outfit.

"Salim was wise to ask Tammam's brother, Akram, to help him take possession of the bride," A'ida whispers to me.

"Help him take possession? How?" I ask her, but she just lets out a trill that shakes the mountains, as, down in the bend of the wadi, six camels decorated with red carpets and white flags appear.

"That is the bridal procession," A'ida then explains. "The one wearing black is the bride. All the others are Abu Salim's men." She and Azzizah ululate my ears off while Salim and Akram ride toward the bridal procession; like a raiding bandit, Salim throws the black bundle over the bride's head, then the white one. And then Salim rides on her right, and Akram on her left, until, a minute or two later, they all disappear around the wadi's bend.

"I guess Salim did not wish us to see him taking possession of his bride," I say to A'ida.

"But he did," she tells me. "Salim took possession of his bride by throwing his black *abaiah*—cloak—over her head. And Akram helped him by being his tongue, telling his bride, 'This is Salim's *abaiah*—cloak—a cover for you, for your honor, from this day onward'. And after Salim threw the white cloth over his bride, Akram, speaking for him, told her, 'Rejoice in Salim and do not reject him'. And she did not reject him—not yet."

"You mean the bride can still reject Salim?"

"*Wallah*, she can," replies A'ida. "And if Salim will not be wise, the bride might yet reject him. For he has rewarded Tammam all to much, by asking her brother, Akram, to be his tongue. *Aywa*, by doing that Salim has elevated Tammam's brother to great success, for only successful men are ever asked to do favors. Now others will ask Tammam's brother for favors and help, and the more favors Akram will do, the more people he will help, the more successful he will become. Salim was wise to give Tammam such a present for his wedding. For Tammam loves her brother, and his success and happiness are bound to gladden her..."

On our way to the tents, A'ida offered to help Azzizah pitch the bridal tent, before the procession reaches the compound. "A tent should always stand out for the bride," says A'ida.

"The bride will stay in my tent," Azzizah tells her. "Come to welcome the bride in my tent," Azzizah invites A'ida and me, ignoring A'ida's "not proper," like a true aristocrat.

In honor of the bride, Azzizah has spread on the gravel ground of her tent her most beautiful and colorful hand-woven welcome-carpets. Now that all was dusted and cleaned, the grinding stones Azzizah keeps at one side of her tent and the battered old trunk that stands in the opposite corner looked like precious antiques. And outside, near the entrance, next to the scorched fire-circle, her scorched coffee *bakraj* was gleaming in spots, like ancient brass polished and repolished. So did the round bronze tray upon which sparkled the newly clean porcelain demi-tasse coffee-honor cups. And next to it another bronze tray, this one holding the tea glasses, and a blue enamel tea kettle, chipped as ever. And that's it—Azzizah's possessions.

"Where is the blemished bride? Where is she? I wish to see her blemish!" The retarded child-boy yells, storming into Azzizah's tent, his dusty feet messing up the carpets.

"Allah, o Allah, the *djinn*-demon is controlling the child's tongue," his mother mutters to Azzizah.

"The child is late in growing from child to boy," Azzizah tells A'ida, "but he is not far wrong. Clearly the bride is blemished, just as you and I are blemished.

"We are all blemished," Azzizah says to the child.

"We are?" the child says. "You too?"

"*Aywa*—yes," Azzizah chuckles.

"Show me your blemish," he says, laughing when she shows him her creased face. "You are Azzizah," he says, embracing her, nearly tears her nose off, pulling her nose ring, "I want also a ring in my nose," he screams, and his mother starts berating her daughter, hiding behind the tent flaps.

"I told you to keep him away, to take him to the waterhole, occupy him there," she tells her scrawny daughter.

"I tried . . . tried, but . . ." The little girl starts to cry. Her bony hands look like twigs about to snap as she carries her screeching infant brother. He weighs more than her, or so it appears.

"Hand him to me," A'ida, taking pity on her, says, sighing and pulling out a breast. The infant's lips grab the nipple and the screeching stops. But her retarded son continues to scream and kick and punch his scrawny sister. Her arms flail to restrain him from tearing out her hair, nose, eyes . . . The girl-child is sobbing now and yelling that she cannot drag him outside, that he's stronger than her, and that she wants to welcome the bride, like the women here in the tent . . . A'ida spews a volley of curses, but doesn't send her daughter away. Instead she fires a look at Azzizah as if it's Azzizah's fault that her son cannot grow from child to boy; she nearly tears his arm off dragging him out of the tent, her infant still at her breast.

"Not proper for a guest to do work," Azzizah tells the girl-child, who is cleaning up after her brother by force of habit. "Not proper for a guest to do work," Azzizah tells her again. And the over-worked girl-child—her face a mess of tears, dust, and flies—grins happily. It's probably the first moment of peace she has had in days. "Where are all the other children?" Azzizah asks her, busy now building a tea fire.

"They ran out to escort the bride," replies the girl, as the ground shakes with hooves of goats returning to the compound.

Tammam glides over to Azzizah's tent. She has obviously tried to put on her best face, and must have stopped at the waterhole to do her hair and makeup; her eyes are kohled too heavily, betraying the tension in her. Even her voice is muted with emotions restrained as she recounts how she heard the ululating and drove the herd back home.

Azzizah pours Tammam a glass of sweet tea, unloads Salimeh from her arms, and tells her, "I thought you meant to stay away with the herd three days and three nights." Why? What brought her back? A'ida's trill? Not proper to ask questions...

The Badawias are draped—in veils, shawls, full-length *thowbs*, and capes. All you can see are eyes—eyes showing nothing but deference now that Imsallam Suleman Abu Salim has showed up.

He is majestic in the regalia for his son's wedding. The silver and gold embroidery that borders the brown *abaiah*—cloak—Abu Salim has draped over his sand-colored *jalabeeya*, cut from heavy wool and custom made by the best of tailors, is museum-worthy. His scowling face is clean-shaven, the scar above his jaw glistening red. He wears the usual scruffy, dusty shoes, missing their laces.

Storming into the tent again, the retarded child-boy stops in his tracks when he sees Abu Salim. "*Wallah*, you are beautiful," he tells Abu Salim. "My mother also dressed up beautiful for the wedding," the child-boy adds. And really A'ida has returned to the tent, looking beautiful in the new embroidered cape.

Abu Salim rests his hand on the child's shoulder and tells him, "The bridal tent is no place for a man. Are you a man or a woman? Do you want to sit with Salim and us men, or with the bride and the women?"

"I want to sit with you," mutters the child. "I will be quiet, quiet-good with you..."

Abu Salim orders Azzizah to open her battered old trunk. And, like Santa Claus, he starts dispensing gifts—first, to his senior wife; then, to his girl-wife—festive *thowbs*, shawls, and capes!

So, that's why the two Badawia co-wives didn't bother to bead and to embroider wedding clothes. Despite the joyful squealing, something in their response says the surprise is *pro forma*, that Azzizah's trunk has been filled with presents from Abu Salim before—presents to be used as carrot and/or a stick, reward and/or punishment...

"I give you no wedding trinkets because you are a man," Abu Salim says to the retarded child-boy, as he hands Tammam a set of festive clothes for her daughter, and to A'ida a turquoise stone set in a silver filigree ring. Last, he presents to me—a stunning hand-worked, full-length, wide-flowing *thowb*!

"Why do you look surprised?" he says to me. "Did you think we Badu have no manners? We do not honor our wedding guests with gifts?"

"You better not wear this new *thowb* Abu Salim has presented to you, for you might trip, just as you did when you had tried on Tammam's clothes," Azzizah says to me. She, Tammam, and I laugh, remembering that day with nostalgia already.

"It is not because you might trip that you would be wise not to wear your new *thowb* to the wedding, but because we Badawias would rather a stranger-woman sit on our welcome-carpet as you do—with your boots on, not proper—than like a Badawia, wearing our clothes and our jewels to lure our men," says A'ida.

I ask her if guests present no gifts to the bride and groom at Badu weddings. And she looks at me as if I accused her of being stingy, then says, "The gifts we will present Abu Salim will be over and above the gifts he had presented us when we had celebrated the circumcision of our son."

"What would be the proper wedding gift for me to present?" I ask her.

"The proper gift is something led—meaning, a goat or a sheep, or a camel," A'ida replies. "A camel I doubt any man would be willing to sell you. But a goat you could buy from Azzizah or Tammam, or from one of the neighboring Badawias."

"How much would a goat cost?"

"Ask Abu Salim or my husband," she says. "Only men know the current price."

I also changed clothes for the wedding. But the blouse, jeans, and scarf are not exactly fresh—they're as stained and full of sand and spark holes as Badu clothes. How many days, weeks, have I been here? And why? For whose benefit do I write-to-remember?

Can I help Tammam? Does she need help? Does Azzizah? Abu Salim? And even if I can help, should I? At what point does interference become welcome? Just like on my first day here, I feel like a stranger, an intruder, an ignoramus. I don't think I'll ever know these true Arabs...

It's time to leave, I feel. I'm homesick, lonely. People are getting married, starting a new life, a long journey... till death do us part...

"Look! *Wallah*, look! The bridal procession!" cries A'ida's girl-child.

The Badawias cover up, shawl over veil, as if any man could see them sitting cooped up here in Azzizah's tent—the bridal tent.

Standing at the entrance, the girl-child acts like a radio commentator at a royal wedding, broadcasting to the sequestered Badawias: "The camels are kneeling... And now Abu Salim himself is helping the bride to dismount... *Wallah*, how beautiful the bride, how tall—taller than Salim... *Wallah*, how beautiful her veil and dresses, how beautiful her procession: the white flags, the red carpets... But Salim is still dressed in his ugly old work clothes... I wish he will dress beautiful. I love his homecoming clothes..."

"Salim is dressed proper-wise," A'ida tells her child-daughter. "Only a man overly pleased to enter his bride would dress up for his wedding."

"Hush, hush..." her little daughter whispers, "Salim is now escorting his bride here, to this tent."

He leaves her at the entrance of the bridal tent—the women's tent—and joins the men.

"*Mabrouka al-arus*—blessed be the bride," A'ida cries, punctuating it with a long, high-pitched trill. She wasn't exaggerating when she told me the blemished bride is as graceful and as tall as a palm. Her demeanor is regal. Greeting the Badawias, she has to bend to touch her forehead to the forehead of each Badawia in turn. She murmurs blessings—sort of like Moses meeting his father-in-law: "... Did obeisance, kissed, asked about each other of their welfare and then they came into the tent..."

The bride exchanged salutations with the child-girl, and me last. Her voice is richly timbred and deeply resonant like a cello's. There is no trace of shyness in her voice, or in her eyes. She does not avert or hide her glance, like Badawias do, but confronts with them, in pride and arrogance, like a Badu man. And maybe because of the story that precedes her, I see in her eyes the embers of the fire that drove her to cross borders and to be bewitched by a lover. In that glow you can imagine a Badawia maiden, tethered to her own rock of isolation, leaving her parents, her tribe, her goats, and running off to Jordan with some guy she just met. How many of us Western, "liberated," women would have the fire, the faith, the madness to do that ... And even if her father did send her on a mission, it takes *muruah*—courage, balls—to cross a couple of deserts all alone at night—and it would have been at night; she's too remarkable, too memorable, to get away with crossing borders by day. *Wallah*, what a wife Abu Salim has chosen for his son.

And what a punishment he has chosen for Tammam—a woman who would make his adulterous wife grateful to be allowed her subservience.

Azzizah may have initiated this match to save her son's life, and if she did it to punish Tammam, she gives no indication of it. It worries her, no doubt, the look in Tammam's eyes, which seems to say that love is too high a price to pay for life.

"Sit, stay," Azzizah urges her neighboring Badawias. But the Badawias mutter, "*La*—no ... We should leave you alone with the bride." "Sit-stay," Azzizah insists, time and again, and finally the neighboring Badawias relent.

"It is not proper to crowd the bridal tent," A'ida whispers close to my ear. "The women guests should be sitting in the women-guest-tent, and the men in the wedding-celebration-tent."

"*Wallah, Wallah,* they are approaching to present the sacrifice," cries the girl-child from her watch at the entrance.

"Already? So soon? *Wallah,* Salim must be overeager to marry ..." The neighboring Badawias whisper and giggle under their veils.

"We Badu celebrate two-three days, even a week, before sacrificing to sanctify the marriage. Not one hour or less, like here," A'ida whispers in my ear.

At the entrance of the tent, Salim and Akram present a goat; it is trembling, as if sensing it is about to be sacrificed.

The women fall silent. All have modestly covered up, shawl over face veil, except the bride and Azzizah.

Taking advantage of my androgynous status here, I step out of the women's tent to watch the men crowding around Salim, restraining the sacrificial goat while Akram pulls out his *shibriyya*—dagger—and, loud, for all the women in the tent to hear, he says: "This is Salim's sacrifice for his bride, in keeping with tradition of Allah and the prophet."

"*Allahu akbar*—Allah is great!" the mountains thunder after the men.

"I slaughter you . . . Allah deems you pure-proper for slaughter." Akram bends over the trembling goat.

"*Allahu akbar*—Allah is great," the mountains thunder again as Akram slits the goat's throat.

The mountains spin.

Death throbs.

Silence.

Salim dips his hand into the blood spurting from the neck of the dying goat, then he enters the women's tent and sprinkles the blood over his bride. Leaving the women's tent, he rejoins the men.

"Why did he sprinkle blood on his bride?" I whisper to A'ida.

"That is the custom," she whispers back. "A marriage of two families must be sealed with blood."

"You mean the marriage is sealed already?"

"*Aywa*, half-sealed, all too soon," replies A'ida. "Now the wedding feast will begin. But it is only when and if Salim will enter his bride, plant a child in her womb, only then will the marriage be fully sealed."

"Women are not allowed to slaughter, butcher, and cook meat," explains A'ida's husband, as he begins to build a cooking-fire next to Tammam's tent.

The compound looks divided. There seem to be two separate camps—one of women, one of men—and only the children and the stranger-guest could cross over from one to the other.

Salim's brother-in-law, El-Hajj, Mutt and Jeff's father, helps Tammam's brother to butcher the goat and dump the meat into a pot of boiling water.

Abu Salim leads his thoroughbred camel over to Salim. He unbuckles his *shibriyya*—dagger—and hands it to Salim. Now, for all to hear, he tells his son, "I have married you off, armed you, and provided you with a mount."

"*Wallah*, Abu Salim wants all to hear that he had fulfilled his obligation to his son," whispers A'ida. Her husband and Akram carry a tray laden with boiled goat meat over to the women's tent.

The children choose to eat with the men—"Because the choice cuts are always on the men's tray," Mutt and Jeff explain, carrying trays piled with rice and pita over to the men's fire-circle.

I choose to eat with the women. They were crowded close to the tray—hungry and rarely given a chance to eat meat—not one of them noticed that I had no space. Only the bride: in her cello-rich voice she asked the women to make room for me. But, after all that, I couldn't bring myself to touch a morsel. I saw on that tray the terrified goat, quivering now with globs of yellow fat. And the Badawias are licking fingers shiny with grease and digging those same fingers back into the food.

The bride must have seen a stranger or two at her father's *maq'ad*. She selected a lean morsel of meat and handed it to me, saying, "*Koli... koli*—eat ... eat." She didn't see the hair stuck to the meat, I guess. In order not to offend her, I force the morsel down, then before she hands me more, I mutter, "I've had my fill, feasted with the children and the men." Her eyes said she saw through my story. But polite-proper, she said nothing. She was dressed in traditional tribal black, embroidered, not in red thread, like the married Badawias, but in blue, the color signifying maidenhood. Some of the neighboring women wore long striped coats; others, colorful embroidered jackets. All had tied hand-woven tassels to their braids.

After the trays of meat and rice were polished off and the greasy fingers wiped clean with pita, bitter coffee with no sugar, then sweet tea, with triple sugar, was consumed. And then they sang, "Abu Salim's kinsfolk are people of tradition. Praise Allah for their good reputation..." Again and again, the same refrain.

Azzizah and Tammam kept rinsing glasses and serving.

The bride kept checking her wristwatch, as if afraid she'd miss her honeymoon flight to Niagara Falls.

"Why is she looking at her wristwatch?" I whisper to A'ida.

"*Allah aref*—God knows," she whispers back. Her little daughter nearly knocks us over when she runs in and whispers, "Salim left for the mountains, riding on his new thoroughbred camel."

"Already?" mutters A'ida. "I see Salim cannot wait to find out if his bride will submit to him, or if she will reject him—flee from him in the mountains and seek protection with an elder who can convince her father to release her from obligations he made without consulting her... Salim should not be entering her tonight, for it is shameful to enter a bride when wedding guests are still celebrating. A proper man will wait a week, a month, even two, after his wedding guests have departed. But if Salim suspects his bride will flee from him, he might force-enter her tonight and then, even were she to desert him, her womb will be swollen with his child and his honor will be upheld..."

The bride is gliding out to the ditch—to relieve herself, I guess. But the little girl comes running back and whispers, "Tammam's brother and Salim's brother-in-law, El-Hajj, waited not far from the entrance, and as soon as the bride emerged, they whisked her off on a camel decorated with carpets and flags."

"Did they appear to be guarding the entrance? Abducting the bride?" A'ida asks her daughter.

"No," replies the little girl. "They were just waiting to escort her to meet Salim in the mountains."

"How did the bride know they were waiting so soon after the feast?" A'ida wonders.

"She must have heard the camel approaching the tent," whispers the little girl. I don't say anything about Salim and his bride synchronizing their watches . . .

Mutt and Jeff pulled my cassette recorder out of my brown knapsack and then asked my permission to cassette-record stories and songs. Right away, all the children formed a third circle in the compound, a children's circle, around the cassette recorder. And on cassette after cassette, they record the same story, the same song, the same refrain, the same melody. It's my last set of batteries. Won't last long. I'm spent, like them. If the Jeep was here, I'd be going home this minute.

I gave the kids all the cassettes they had recorded, except one—I don't know why I wanted to keep it since I didn't know if the Badu would ever let me declassify any cassettes or writing-to-remember. I also saved a notebook full of what the children call writing— mostly doodling, but a few drawings of themselves, dwarfed by their goats, and by adults looming larger than tents, camels, airplanes, Jeeps—almost as large as the mountains. Why do Badu children draw themselves so tiny and adults so big, when Badu adults rarely, if ever, say or do anything to make a child feel small. Badu adults don't spank children and only rarely raise their voices to reprimand them. The men are softer with the children than the women, and yet the children seem to take fewer liberties when the men are around.

✢

The wedding guests scattered soon after the bride departed. Azzizah's brother took off early this morning, and Tammam's brother is leaving now. The flies are sticking around for their own feast—the sun-baked sacrificial blood and the wedding trays, pots, pans, glasses, cups. No one has bothered to clean or clear anything away . . . There is no wind to usher out the flies today, no air-borne whispers of good or ill. The air sags, limp and vacant.

The Badu sleep in their wedding clothes and wear them to draw water, tend the goats, gather wood, build cooking-fires, ride to the *maq'ad*, and to do their tasks that are more important than work.

"Why do you wear your festive clothes? Is it not better to save them for the upcoming holiday?" I ask Tammam.

"Who will see tomorrow...," she replies as if life still hung in the balance. But I have yet to see a mountain Badu or Badawia seize today to spite tomorrow. These people live today for tomorrow's stories, "... for everything dies, only the stories live on."

Remembering the ruthless ambition of King David for immortality, what we lost when the first temple was destroyed; remembering the glory, the lust, the vengeance, you can begin to understand the Badu, the true Arabs.

Is that really what brought me here, in the dusty tatters of my wedding clothes?

As is the desert, the Badu are formed of contrasts—their dress, speech, noble manner as against their squalid living conditions, oppressive heat and frost, murky water, monotonous diet. The mind cannot process it and retreats to what came before: How I remember and long for an ice cube or two; a crisp, green salad; a juicy orange; a long, hot shower; a clean white towel; a bed; sheets, pillow, blanket; a chair and table; a fork and knife. Imma, Abba, Levi—I am homesick...

A'ida is packing up her tent—her love-room, her kitchen—loading all her belongings onto a kneeling camel, while her husband rests from the exertion of doing nothing. "Tying and untying is woman's work," she explains. "The tent and everything therein belongs to the woman—to me, not to my husband." Her children belong to her husband, and he is a good caring father, but feeding and caring for them is woman's work. In this the Badu are every man—our own men are no more helpful. Our own ghetto women busted their butts to raise children and earn money to support the family, while their husbands did nothing but study and pray. This anger speaks across time; I feel my mother's exhaustion in my bones...

"On your way to your home compound, would it be possible for you to stop at Hillel's-Hilal's post and tell him to dispatch my Jeep to Abu Salim's *maq'ad*? It is time I went home," I say to A'ida, during her cigarette break at the lookout point.

"*Aywa*, a guest should never visit-stay for more than three days," she says, sounding like my husband, Dave, who likes to say, "Guests, like fish, stink after three days."

"But you, yourself, stayed here many days more than three," I say.

"I came here, not to visit, but to remedy my son," she responds. Next breath she advises me to ask Abu Salim to dispatch a fast camel-rider to Hilal—"for we, encumbered by children, travel slow. Might take us a week, or maybe a month, to reach Hilal's post." She turns her back to the wind and lights a cigarette under her veil.

"Did you hear the latest?" she says when I am about to walk away, like a Badawia, without a parting word.

"Salim is escorting his bride back to her father's dwelling-place, meaning he was eager to show his bride, and her kin and his, that he is a man strong of will and character," A'ida tells me, revising her explanation yet again, as I do in these pages, reason shifting like the desert view—eternal and diurnal, timeless but responsive to the hourly changes wrought by sun, shade, and wind. "*Aywa*, the whole desert is bound to know that Salim, as befitting a true real man, is ruled not by his *zubi*, but by his noble blood, character, manners. For whoever sees or hears that he is escorting his bride back to her father's tents is bound to know that Salim will not be entering his bride there, for this will shame-offend her kinsfolk. *Aywa*, Salim may leave her a maiden there for a month, even two, but not longer, for this would humiliate her."

A'ida gives me a list of presents to purchase and bring in my Jeep when I come to visit-stay with her. "The Badu knowledge you will gain will be well worth the gold chains and the gold watches I ask you to purchase-bring," she says, urging me to leave this compound and visit hers.

"*Yarit*—I wish you could visit-stay with me, *yaa*-A'ida."

"*Yarit, Wallah*, it is unfortunate that you are a stranger ... You strangers all think you are not fortunate. My husband heard it from Salim," A'ida tells me. "In the *maq'ad*, to the men, Salim told how you strangers could be blessed with such good fortune: strong and healthy sons, unassailable reputation, trusted allies, and great wealth. But if you lack only one thing—for example, if you had a son who, like mine, cannot grow from child to boy—you would think yourself unfortunate, for you strangers expect to be blessed with everything, everything . . .

"We Badu are the opposite, *Wallah*. We Badu expect nothing, and if we are blessed with only one thing—like not having to share a husband with another wife, for example—we think ourselves fortunate."

"Is that why Azzizah and Tammam are content to share their husband, even if, as you say, it is not good?"

"*Wallah*, it is not good. But we Badu are content, if not with one thing, then with another."

A'ida chuckled under her veil. "And the heart has space to love many wives at the same time, *Wallah*, just as your heart has space to love your children, your husband, parents, sisters, brothers, friends, all at the same time . . .

"It is not good," she adds, "not good to be fiercely faithful to anything, not even to your kinsfolk, or even to your husband, or even to your son. For a reed not bending with the wind is bound to break, and a woman is like reed, and like glass; *Wallah*, once she breaks, she can never be repaired whole, complete again."

"Why did you wait until now to give me this knowledge?"

"My heart is large today." She laughs, pressing into my hand the silver ring that Abu Salim presented to her—showing him what she thinks of his gift, I guess.

"Why do you think Abu Salim invited me to visit-stay in the tents he forbids all other strangers to enter?" I ask, escorting her back to her camel moving-van.

"*Allah aref*—God knows," she replies. "Perhaps he favors you, as I do." Is that what happens when you toss a camera Polaroid into the equation? Or are prejudice, cynicism, paranoia, and fatigue getting the better of me?

"I miss you already," she says, and showers blessings upon me. I mutter blessings in return, then say, "The compound will be quiet, sad, empty, after you leave." And I mean it.

Azzizah and Tammam part from her Badu-proper—brief, formal. They simply mutter, "*Ma'assalame*—peace be with you."

"*Allah ysalmkin*—Allah shall reward you," she replies. Her husband and children leading the camel; she, holding her infant, walks behind, as is proper for a woman.

She must have told Tammam that I wished to leave, go home.

"No ... Stay, just a while longer," Tammam said to me as she, little Salimeh, and I sit by her fire-circle after nightfall. After that, for days, she dragged me along to tend the goats with her, as if I am the only friend she has in the world.

❧

"Salim went with his bride to stay-live at her father's dwelling-place, for he is needed there," Mutt and Jeff told me this afternoon. Not proper, A'ida would say, no doubt; a woman follows her husband, and a man should pitch his tent near his own father for his father's food is sweet ...

It wouldn't surprise me if Abu Salim had arranged it with the father of the blemished bride. Evoking some ancient legend or story, or maybe *dougri*—straight, man to man—he might have said: "Listen, between us, no one will marry your daughter, for she is blemished. Now, I will purchase her for the price of water rights, but on one condition—that you keep my son away from me, forever—*daimann* ... We Badu never forget and rarely forgive."

There are only absolutes in the Badu's world. There is no room for mitigation. Perhaps that is why alcohol is forbidden in Badu compounds the desert over, and prayer is unusual. Their reality—their way of life—their desert—is as much unreality as they can comprehend. Even when, with eyes etched red by sun, sand, and wind, they slumber their days away, lethargic, they wander the wasteland of time. Past, present, future—fused by desert days, by desert nights—is always within them. They do not wait, as we do, for some tomorrow when the Messiah will come, filling todays with yesterday, craning to glimpse redemption that lingers, eternally, around the next bend.

Passage

30

What a day. It started out to be no different from the day
before last: I was homesick; the compound was shrinking
by the day, and the days were stretching endless and monotonous,
as the extraordinary became ordinary. The Badu were growing
tired of their stranger-guest, I felt, maybe because I was growing
tired of being her. Or maybe we were just low-spirited now that
the wedding guests had gone and the rumor was squelched—
except in stories, perhaps—and the adrenalin rush had fizzled out
like the tail-end of pyrotechnics. Fighting off lethargy was becoming more difficult by the hour, and there were moments when
one might sanely wonder if the brewing of crisis after crisis in this
region was an attempt to boost adrenalin. Some days the Badu
slept on and off all day.

I turned in earlier and earlier each evening. Lean now, like the
Badu, my stomach had stopped rumbling. Azzizah worried over
how little I ate, how loose my clothes were on me; what worried
me was how my mind wandered, my thoughts diffused, unfocused.

At dawn, like the desert revived by dew, I would feel energetic
and go with Azzizah or Tammam to comb the dry riverbeds for
driftwood, or with Mutt and Jeff or Tammam to shepherd the goat
herd. But, soon after sunrise, we'd scramble off to the first spot of
shade we could find, and doze off.

It was at this hour, early dawn, only twenty-four hours ago, give
or take, that Tammam and I left the compound to water the goat
herd. Then we headed to the wadi of the acacias. The heat was raging
by the time we reached the "forest" of five spindly thorn trees. There,
we collected a few dead twigs and thorns and started a fire. It took
only one match, they were so dry, and the fire flamed out almost
before our tea was brewed. In the shrinking shadows, Tammam and
I, and the goats, were catching a nap. Then, from far away, a dream-
like call tore through the mountains—a call to come home.

"*Quuuuiiiick!!!! Faaaassst!!! Huuuurrrrrry baaaack hoooommmme!!!*" It sounded like Mutt and Jeff shouting. "Quick!!! Fast!!! Hurry back home!!!!"

"Salimeh! Salimeh!" Tammam, screaming hysterically, bolted for the compound. Her world had narrowed even more, it seemed. She showed no sign of concern for anyone else back home—not for Azzizah, who was looking after little Salimeh; not for Abu Salim; not for Mutt and Jeff. Any of them could have been bitten by a scorpion or snake, suffered a heart attack or stroke, or coughed himself to death. The Badawias' loyalty had thinned with blood, it seemed.

She did not turn around to check if I was catching up to her, which I almost did—for a while. My feet had learned to conquer wadis and mountains by now, but not as fast as the girl-Badawia.

"*Tammmaaaaamm!!!*" I called out to her soon after I cleared the bend of the dry riverbed, and the next bend, and the next. But I saw no sign of her, not even from the ridge overlooking the next weaving kilometer or so of this wadi and the one next to it. Nothing out here signposted east and west, north and south, and no landmark identified one mountain chain from another, one dry riverbed from another. Goat dung trailed off in each and every direction. The desert was a scalding and bleached furnace, and I had no water with me. Still, the image of Badu nobility clouded my mind and I expected at any moment that the mountains would echo Tammam's calls to me: "Nura, *yaa-okhti*—my sister—*ta'lli ahni*—come here. I'm here! Here!" I stood parched in the silence, waiting for the echo of these words that had carried us beyond The Divide, tribal hatred, bad blood . . . I waited and waited, then called out to her: "*Yaa-okhti*—my sister—*Tammmaaaaamm!!!*"

The picture I had long carried in my mind of the noble Badu—the one in which a traveler is stranded in the desert and a Badu or Badawia comes to the rescue, offering water and hospitality; the consideration Tammam had shown me day in, day out, for weeks—vanished. Now, she didn't seem to give a damn about her

393

guest, or her goats—the goats that sustain her Badu way of life. Relevance peaks and ebbs under the desert winds.

Her ear, which could pick up the soft tread of a camel fifteen to twenty minutes away, was deafened now by her fear for her girl-child. Or so it seemed.

I should have stayed in the shade of the "forest" of acacias, I berated myself. As I turned my anger from Tammam to myself, my picture of the Badu reappeared. I clung to it now, like for dear life. I was dehydrating now, and soon the sun and wind would sere my brain: I'll start drinking sand, savoring it like dream water.

I'm a goner if I stay here, I thought. The waterhole couldn't be more than an hour away, two hours at most. With the wind at my back, I could make it in an hour, I thought. Then it hit me: the wind was blowing toward the waterhole and the compound, and that is why I wasn't hearing a sound from Tammam, or from Mutt and Jeff.

I don't know how long I walked with the wind at my back, and with Arik, my guardian angel, encouraging me, before I saw Azzizah running toward me and shouting, "I found her!... I found her!..." Tammam and little Salimeh, and Mutt and Jeff joined us, looking as relieved as I felt.

When I heard we were only minutes away from the waterhole, I took a child's pride in the fact that I had navigated so well in that wilderness, at that hour, with no shade to point north. "*Wallah*, I was walking in the right direction."

"*Aywa*, you are like a Badawia now," said Azzizah. And already, at the waterhole, Azzizah, Tammam, and Mutt and Jeff embellished this whole episode into a legend-story of a rite-of-passage from dependence to independence; turned it into an allegory of the Badu's dream-of-dreams: roaming the desert free as the wind, unfettered by dependence on, and responsibility for, sister, brother, son, daughter, mother, father, clan, tribe. It was a rite-of-passage to personal freedom, guided only by the forces of destiny. According to the Badawias, it was destiny's decree that I go through that initiation, that rite-of-passage, just as I was about to take leave of them, their compound, their mountains—I had no idea then how many passages and transformations I would go through before the day was over.

"*Min zaman*—long before today—the alum crystal had revealed that no harm would befall our guest, Nura, in our home grounds, but today, *Wallah*, I feared fate held it in store for her to get lost to the desert, *yaa-Rabb*," Azzizah said, hauling yet another bucket of water. We must have consumed ten buckets there, we were so parched.

"... *Aywa*, I am sure it was decreed by fate that I would lose sight of her in the blinding heat of the high sun. Her blood on my head, I was thinking, her blood on my head, her blood on my head ... Yet faster than ever before in my life I ran. *Wallah*, how fate pushed my feet to run away from my sister Nura, so that, like a Badawia brave, she by herself could traverse *el sahrah*—the desert." Tammam spoke in the lilting cadences of Badu legend-telling, revising as she went along, like storytellers everywhere. Now I wonder if the second part of her story wasn't as true as the first— if, as she believed, she couldn't help but turn tail on me, for she was but an instrument of fate.

"It is a good omen," said Azzizah, "a good omen that it happened in the last few hours of the last day. Means good fortune coming late, but not too late, for us all, *Inshallah* ..." Her eyes blurred gladness with sadness at the thought of my leaving.

In a week or two, or at best a day or two, I hoped, Gingie would pick me up from the *maq'ad* alone, or with Riva and Mottke! No way could they be here today, I thought, even when little Jeff urged me, "Quick-fast, for Abu Salim had told me you must pack-tie your belongings, take them with you to the *maq'ad*." He was putting me on, I thought, seeing mischief in his eyes—and in the pail in his hands.

"*LLaaaaa*!—No!!!" his little brother screamed, ducking behind me, just as Jeff was aiming the pail, sending an arc of water over us both. Felt ice cold to the sun-baked skin. I laughed longer and harder than the prank warranted—overloaded emotions, needing the release.

"Pack your belongings quick-fast. *Nemshi*—let's go," Jeff urged me; swore on the life of the rain that a stranger-man awaits me in the *maq'ad*.

Up at the compound, the Badawias insisted I stay-sit with them for one glass of tea at least.

"But no one is tending the herd," I said, hating to prolong good-byes, to add yet another parting to the chain of them that formed my life.

"*Ma'alesh*—never mind the goat herd," Tammam said, building the fire.

"Abu Salim will be angry with us if we do not fetch Nura quick-fast," Mutt and Jeff said, pressing to cut our parting short.

Azzizah dispatched them to inform Abu Salim that I would be leaving the tents "in but a short while."

"*Stana*—wait a second," I said as they were about to take off. I bundled together my cassette recorder and blank tapes and handed them over. They were delighted and surprised to hear that it was my going-away present to them.

"Can we take it to the *maq'ad*? Is it really ours to keep? We won't break it, we know how to work it ... *Yaa-Allah*! *Yaa-Allah*!" they exclaimed. "May Allah reward you, *yaa*-Nura ..."

"*Mabrouk ... Mabrouk*—may you always be blessed," I told each in response.

Tammam blessed them and me, but Azzizah frowned. "Not good, not proper," she muttered under her veil, as if nothing had changed since that first morning in her compound, when she dismissed every gift I presented as "not good ... Presented not proper, for all to see ..."

"Have a heart, *yaa*-Azzizah. Let me have the pleasure of seeing how my presents please you," I told her, handing her my red duffel bag, containing my first aid kit, complete with vitamin and mineral supplements, iodine, antihistamines and antibiotics, and water-purifying tablets—all of which she recognized by now.

To Tammam I presented my warm Eddie Bauer parka, and the huge blue and white Maple Leaf hockey goalie's duffel bag she liked.

It would be useful in the tying and untying of her possessions when and if drought or any other instrument of fate forced them to move.

"Would little Salimeh like me to present to her my wristwatch, for to remember me by?"

"*Wallah*, she would," Tammam replied. Then she suggested I leave for Abu Salim my great old green sweater—"for in size as in color it bespeaks your generosity of heart..."

"*Aywa*, it would please Abu Salim. If you present it proper, not to his face," said Azzizah.

In return, Tammam gave me one of her *gun'ah*—long back veils: "So that your back be protected against evil eyes of envy and twisted tongues that weave false rumors behind a woman's back..."

Next, Azzizah gave me her spare old face veil, exquisitely worked "to cover a woman's cheek and chin—bespeaking of her pride, strength, endurance—and her nose—breath, inner life, heat, fire, soul—and her mouth—her hunger, craving, desire, sexual charm. So that your face be covered-protected against anyone out to shame you, defame your kin, your clan... And so that even a person blind in both eyes could hear the coins of your virtue—your self-restraint, modesty, deference..." Silent now, we sat around Tammam's fire-circle, as if words would have rendered our feelings trivial, would have tarnished the moment.

"Oh, eyes be strong, you cherish people and then they are gone..." Tammam broke the silence before the tea was brewed.

"*Ma'assalame*—Peace be with you wherever you go," Azzizah whispered in my ear, the proper-formal send-off.

"*Allah ysalmkin*—May Allah reward you two for the hospitality you extended to me," I responded, proper-formal.

"*Aywa*, you two! Strong-willed in send-off, shed not a tear—till after you part," Tammam muttered. Shy but delighted, she giggled under her veils when I embraced her—not proper-formal, but a good warm hug.

Azzizah, escaping my parting embrace, ran like a bashful maiden to the lookout point to catch a last glimpse of her stranger-no-stranger guest.

Tammam accompanied me as far as the last bend.

The knapsack I carried was heavy with the gifts presented to me and with all my writing-to-remember and cassette recordings. All made heavier still by the Badu's trust that I would never breathe a word of what I had seen or heard or sensed in their compound, without their permission, and the trust that my conduct, reflecting their hospitality, would do them proud, enhance their reputation and mine.

The air was alive with dream lakes, elongated and stretched wide like rippling mirrors—tauntingly unattainable. As I walked toward them, they danced away—faster, slower, always in step with my stride. The Jeep bobbed like a green dinghy, not far from the *maq'ad*. Shade and *kaffiyyes*—black and white, and in the foreground the aroma of honor-coffee brewing on a fragrant fire—to honor-welcome.

Tal.

I didn't think I'd ever see him again, except in my imagination and dreams—those realms in which I see Arik. I imagined I'd bump into him on the street, or in some lobby during intermission at some concert or movie. He probably would have asked me how my stay in the forbidden tents had gone. Then we would have parted and gone on with our separate lives—not because there were ill feelings between us, but because there weren't. It is our lives that are in conflict, not our hearts ... I had tucked him away in my heart like a treasured memory; a dream angel like the one in my childhood dream, the one who would escort me to the wilderness. The angel that you, Arik, sent to show me that love transcends time, preserving the past as a path to the future.

The wind rushed past my ears, molding my clothes to my body, making them almost invisible. Tal could see me approaching. I could feel his eyes on my face, my breasts, my thighs, as my Badu jewels *jingle-jangled* like wind chimes and the mountain chains all around seemed to swell and dip to the beat of the drum in my temples. Sweating and shivering, I struggled across the remaining distance, as the sun and shade I carried within me—Nura and Leora, observer and partici-pant, stranger-guest and woman—warred for dominance.

And Tal also held back, I felt—to protect his reputation and mine, my husband's, my tribe's, and my Badu hosts'. He sat with the Badu round the fire-circle as if nothing but the duty to escort me had compelled him to cross the distance alone. His face told of fatigue, exhaustion, the strain of staring through desert dust and sun for hundreds of kilometers. For days he hadn't shaved, and his hair, clothes, boots were gray with dust and grease. Out of his gray-ness, his eyes lit up when they met mine. I averted my glance—modest-proper.

"*Brukha ha'ba'ah*—Blessed be she arriving," he greeted me in Hebrew when I reached the fire-circle.

"*Barukh ha'nimtza*—Blessed be he found here," I returned his greeting. I had spoken in reflex, it was such a common Hebrew greeting. But it was only now for the first time that I noticed it was a blessing—that we Yahod, like the Badu, valued our greetings. I felt like I had new eyes—my vision sharpened by the wary vigi-lance of weeks with the Badu, and by love, perhaps...

Abu Salim invited me to sit in the place of honor, close to the fire and away from the smoke that was blowing into Tal's face. He was coughing like the Badu elders sitting next to him, until the wind shifted and decreed a new place of honor and a new place of coughing. The wind and the warmth radiating from the fra-grant fire had no effect on me as I shivered on my separate plane.

Tal went to the Jeep and returned with his army parka, drop-ping it over my shoulder. The Badu probably took it for some Yahodi-Israeli ritual wherein the parka of a woman's escort-guardian, like the *abaiah* Salim had dropped over his blemished bride, symbolized protection. His parka smelled of The Land, the sea, the meadows steaming after the *Yoreh*—the first of the rains.

Pouring honor all around, Abu Salim broke the silence to tell me, "I had asked your escort-guardian how fared your kinsmen, but he neither understands, nor speaks, Badu Arabic. Therefore, I give you permission to exchange words in your language."

"*Allah yasalmak*—May Allah repay you," I responded Badu-proper. And to show his clansmen how well Abu Salim had taught me *adabb*, I waited, taking a long, proper pause, before I translated his words to Tal: "Abu Salim gave me permission to ask you in Hebrew what brought you all the way here. Not bad news, I hope..."

Tal had no idea what an expression of trust it was for the Badu to give permission for me to speak in a language foreign to him. In my peripheral view, I could see him frowning as if I had turned docile, submissive. He frowned like a hawk, like one who sees nothing wrong in behaving like the Romans when in Rome, only in behaving like the Arabs when in Arab territory.

"I meant to pull you out before we lost you to the desert... Are you all right?"

"Yes... You didn't come here bearing bad news, did you?"

"I didn't."

"I'm happy to see you..."

"Ditto... Let's get out of here."

"Soon... The first of the rains have come to The Land, haven't they?"

"Yes. The first to break the drought, let's hope... How did you know it rained?" His frown deepened when he saw my head dropping, modest-proper like a Badawia's.

"The Jabbar came bearing good news. It rained in Israel!" I informed Abu Salim.

"*Allahu akbar*—Allah is great." The mountains echoed the elders sitting round the fire-circle.

"*Inshallah*, we will see the last of the drought this coming winter," said Abu Salim, by rote. Ever since his son's wedding, he has behaved as if he has saved a son but lost his story; as if nothing he could do would change the version that would remain after all else dies; as if all has been written now and was nothing like he had dreamed it would be.

For a moment, I feel he will confiscate all my cassette recordings and writing-to-remember and burn them, as if to cleanse by fire the remembering of Badu from generation to generation, forever—

daimann. But, just then, Mutt and Jeff, barely able to restrain their excitement, say, "Ask the Jabbar to give us a spin in the Jeep…"

"Too risky. It wouldn't take much for the Jeep to tip over and wipe out these kids," Tal tells me, after I translate. I can't believe my ears. Tal and I covered this whole peninsula in this Jeep, and this is the first time he has mentioned the risk.

Jabbar, the Badu named Tal. *Jabbar*—a man of great valor. And that's exactly what he wanted the Badu to think of him. That's why he decided we would traverse the treacherous wadi leading up to Abu Salim's *maq'ad* on a moonless night beset by a plague of darkness. The more courageous, daring, fearless they consider him to be, Tal believed, the more they'll think him unforgiving of anyone who holds Yahodi blood and honor cheap, and the better care they'll take to make sure that no harm befalls me in their tribal ground. He nearly killed us to impress the need for my safety on the Badu.

"Come on, Tal. A spin in this Jeep with a *Jabbar* would mean a lot to these two kids… Hillel gave them a ride in his Jeep."

"I'm not Hillel," said Tal. He is adamant. He'll explain later, he says, but now he suggests we leave, and the sooner the better.

So I tell Mutt and Jeff and the others round the fire-circle that the Jeep is not equipped with a safety bar, and that, were it to tip over, it might crush the youngsters; that is why the *Jabbar* has decided it's too great a risk to take them for a spin.

"Prudent… *Aywa*, prudent," mutters Abu Salim. "Tell him the children's blood is not on his head, nor on his son's, nor his son's sons' head."

Word for word I translate, but still Tal hesitates, as if there is trickery in the Badu's words. In this, he hasn't changed in all these weeks.

"I know these Badu kids. They are okay," I reassure him. Then, as if against his better judgment, he motions to the children to get into the Jeep, snapping at me, "Five minutes, and we're out of here." He couldn't wait to get away from that Badu fire-circle that smelled of war to him.

"... When Arabs fight Arabs," he once told me, "they cover their faces with *kaffiyyes*, so that no one can tell who has killed whom and no one can avenge blood. But when Arabs fight us, they're not afraid to show their faces. They know us ... They know we don't believe in blood revenge. It took us a bit of time to realize that the Arabs thought we were weak, that we had no *muruah*—balls—because of that. Now they know that reprisal will follow every terrorist action, but often too quick and too hard. If we are not careful we will soon be like them ..."

"Us, them"—entrenched in the language. Theirs, ours—The Divide ... If I had learned anything in the forbidden tents, it was that The Divide can be bridged, one on one, if not by "us and them."

I remained in the *maq'ad* while Tal took Mutt and Jeff for a spin. Soon after the wind dispersed the Jeep's dusty contrail, Abu Salim told me to follow. Badu-proper, I asked no questions, but simply followed Abu Salim in a daze of confusion and excitement sparked by the friction of quick transition to and from different lifetimes, centuries, cultures, genders. Abu Salim stopped by his she-camel, and there—away from prying eyes—he pulled out of the pocket of his *jalabeeya* the wallet I had asked him to safe-keep for me on that moonless night when Tal and I had arrived at his *maq'ad*. The wallet bulged with my passports and "just in case" money.

"You better count the money, make sure not a dollar is missing," Abu Salim said, in jest or in earnest, I couldn't tell.

I stuffed the bulging wallet into my knapsack and asked him not to offend me, not to add to the sorrow I felt on leaving.

"*Laa!*—No! Every parting leads to a greeting, and every end to a start," he said, sounding like some TV guru.

"Are you ready? Now I shall give you knowledge of preparing to start," Abu Salim told me as I was about to climb into the Jeep. I pulled my pen out, told Abu Salim I was ready, and on the canvas door of the Jeep I scribbled his preparation for starting: "*Bismillah el rahman el rehim*—In the name of Allah the merciful and the compassionate: That is what you must say at the start of a journey, or a greeting message, or at the start of everything ..."Say it!" Abu

Salim insisted, and after I did, he said, "Now you are prepared to embark . . . Peace be with you . . ."

Before I could return his blessing, the mountains thundered and trembled. The engine clanked a crescendo, then uttered a deafening silence. Grease and gasoline billowed, choking the lungs. I tried to unhook the clamps that fasten the plastic windows to the canvas doors, but my fingers were sabotaged by the bouncing, tilting, and sliding of the Jeep, as though the gravel were ice, pocked by potholes, and no guardrail around the slopes, dropping to canyons too deep to see bottom.

Tal was in his element now, one-on-one with the roller-coaster wadi. Nose down, at top speed the Jeep threatened to roll over; Tal touched the brakes and, ass-backwards, the Jeep dove; and just when it looked like we were plunging into the purple abyss of the next world, it spun and slid, carrying us headlong toward the granite mountain ribs . . . The gear in the back was jiggling loose, and the wind whistled through every crack in the canvas top and rusty frame. With an explosive whoosh, the canvas door on my side burst open, and Tal spun us in the opposite direction so that I wouldn't fly out. I braced myself as the Jeep slid sideways, burning rubber, kicking up more dust than a whole herd of goats, and a barrage of gravel and granite.

"Are you all right?" He shouted over the noise of the engine.

"Yes. You?"

"What?! What?!" He is exhilarated, flushed with the lifeblood of challenge, adventure, danger, the extraordinary . . .

"*Shushhhhh*, the whole desert can hear you. Badu ten-fifteen minutes from here can hear you. These mountains are dotted with Badu compounds and lookout points, and now, in the slanting rays, is the best time to see . . ." I scan the mountain crests, the cliffs, the slopes, at every bend on the wadi but can't tell from the riverbed which is our lookout point. I see no sign of Azzizah, Tammam, little Salimeh, no lone acacia, no sign of life.

"Don't lean on the door! The damn latch is loose!" Tal yelled out at each turn of the dry riverbed. At every one, I waved my *kaffiyye*, just in case it was the bend below the lookout. And at every green spot I saw spinning of top of a granite cliff, I yelled out to him, "Stop! Stop!" But I saw no black shawl waving back. And after a few stops he said, "If you tell me what you're looking for, I might be able to help you find it."

I had no doubt he'd find the lookout point in no time. He knew the terrain by heart.

"Did we pass the bend of the wadi directly below a lone acacia tree, or is it still ahead of us?"

"Why do you ask?" He answered a question with a question, like a true Yahodi.

How I wanted to reply, to share with him everything I had learned and experienced—most of all, the feeling that the bridge over The Divide was within reach. And I was aching to ask him: Did your friend Hillel tell you about the hornet's nest you dropped me into? About the rumor that demanded vengeance? Why didn't you drive over to the *maq'ad* and get me? Were you bedridden from more surgery on your knees? But the Badu's warning silenced me: "Woe to you and your children's children— for five generations your blood will be exposed if you betray to anyone what you saw, heard, sensed in our tents." I couldn't even tell him that, without betraying trust, exposing his and my blood—not without permission from Abu Salim or from his son or from his son's sons. A Badu gag order, after all the years I had been voiceless in The Land . . . every word I groped for came in Badu Arabic, English, or Hebrew.

"I wish . . . but I can't . . . can't say a word about the tents. Don't ask me why."

"Yes. It must be hard to articulate," he said. "That often happens. After a grueling mission, the mind blanks out the minute you reach home base and you can take a breath without fear that a bullet will make it your last."

"It wasn't like that at all . . ." What brings you here, instead of Gingie, this time? How have you been? I wanted to ask him. But I sensed he was about to reach out to me. As I was about to receive

404

him, I saw he had changed his mind—withdrew, as if he feared God would strike us dead ... As if it suddenly hit him that he must have been out of his mind to traverse this desert himself for— what? ... As if he saw the dust on my *abaiah* and smelled Badu, Arab—enemy. As if I had stepped out of a Purim play, bejeweled and bangled with Badu finery. And like that on a cheap Purim mask, my hair was braided straw; and like a borrowed Purim cos- tume, my layers of clothes were layered with dust, dotted with spark holes, stained by ashes, and caked by mud. My desert boots and the bottoms of my jeans were ringed with mud from the waterhole down by the dry riverbed that twists and turns at the foot of the mountains—but on the other side, in another century, where water is wasted as if there is no tomorrow and silence and stories roll on and on into the forever of tomorrows.

How Tamman would love to ride in this Jeep. All that is new and untried draws her. It would have amazed the Badawias to see the glance he shot at me when I finished my cigarette and, instead of putting it out in the wobbly empty pop-can wired to the hole that was once an ashtray in the dashboard, I flung the cigarette out the window.

"You shouldn't litter," he advised me, and I stifled a laugh. He saw the desert like a stranger, didn't use it like a Badu—like you use a person you really love. He saw it as some ancient relic too precious to use, even to touch, or a holy ground you take your shoes off before entering ... like the welcome-carpet the Badu fold their legs upon only fifty meters from the ditch they use as a garbage dump and open sewer. A thing and its opposite, like sun and shade, the Badu, their desert, their way of life, *Wallah*.

Badu law is as blunt as Badu manners are subtle. We Yahod are the opposite—our manners blunt, our law subtle ... Different worlds, and I couldn't switch off one and switch on the other. Instead they merged, and I shivered and sweated by turns.

Azzizah and Tamman would have left the lookout point by now to round up their parched goats, I was thinking, as round and round the Jeep went, round one mountain chain after another, all looking the same, all leading nowhere, it seemed. The engine, like a jackhammer, throbs in my temples and the exhaust fumes spin me dizzy—

"You better stop, Tal." The mountains sent back the memory of clanking and shouting and the wind returns the nauseating fumes. As he switched off the ignition key, I ran behind the Jeep and puked; when I caught my breath, out I spewed a volley of curses in Badu Arabic, English, and Hebrew. Tal laughed as he handed me a water canteen he had filled in Eilat. The water was still cold and fresh—clear, not murky, not tasting of mud, and there was not one goat hair in the whole canteen.

"Take it slow," he kept saying, as my hands shook. "It's probably the bends—and fatigue, and one cigarette too many on a stomach that didn't appreciate the Badu's diet, by the looks of it." I had disappeared down to the bone, he said, all cheekbones and legs like the tall, slender women Giacometti sculpts. Blood rushed to his face as he spoke, so unaccustomed was he to traveling alone with a woman, to commenting on her looks.

"You must be exhausted, too. When did you leave the city, or did you set off from your kibbutz?" I asked him as I sponge-bathed my face and neck with my dampened *kaffiyye*. It felt great, but the dust trails my *kaffiyye* painted on my face cracked him up. I laughed with him. "First drop of fresh water I've had in … What day is today?"

"Day forty of your stay here in Sinai, give or take a day or two."

"Feels like forty years, and four days, at once. But, really, what's the date today?" I couldn't imagine him counting the days. He pulled the number forty out of Exodus, I thought. He liked to believe that the magnet that had drawn me to Sinai was the urge to return to The Land—through the door our ancestors, the Children of Israel, had used to repossess the Promised Land, "Sinai, not a bad door," he had told me a few days after we had crossed that threshold. "A bit rusty, but it might strip you of pride …" Pride is the difference between a newcomer and a dropout, he believes. "Both are just as homesick, but a dropout comes to The Land arrogant and proud, like a husband who takes his wife for granted," he had told me, "whereas a newcomer comes to The Land humble, like a lover courting. That's why most newcomers succeed where most dropouts fail."

"Well, you can't say I'm returning to The Land proud and arrogant this time," I said. He remembered and laughed.

"If we give it a bit of a push now, barring the unforeseen we'll make it to Hillel's post before nightfall. You'll be able to take a long hot shower," he said. "And if the phone is working, you'll be able to call anyone you wish in The Land—even in Canada."

You could become jet-lagged, just from the thought of crossing a thousand or so years, let alone oceans and continents, in less than a minute. You dial a few numbers and, presto, Nura, the stranger-guest, is Leora: Levi's mother, Dave's wife, Arik's war-widow, his parents' daughter-in-law, my parents' daughter, Riva's dropout friend...

Oh, Arik, don't tell anyone but, *Wallah*, what a vacation I had in the tents—a vacation from trying to overcompensate for your loss with your parents and mine, your brother and my sister, your son and mine; from overcompensating for my dropping out and for my marrying Dave; from overcompensating Dave for my requiem years...

For a flash, as I was about to climb back into the Jeep I saw how minuscule the granite mountains are—like tiny ant hills, and Tal and I like a couple of ants much smaller than the piece of straw we're dragging, and vulnerable to the sun and shade—both wearing dark *djinn*-demon protective eyes. I laughed and laughed; never before had I felt such a release, from much more than the shackles of remembering, duty, propriety, the conventional, the mundane, the trivial. Never before had I felt so happy to be alive. Never before will I be the same Leora, I felt, delighted with this new sensation of freedom.

Tal watched me, with the wise amusement of an old man who had been through it all.

The Jeep looked like it hadn't been touched since we parted.

Just like then, the sleeping bags filled the gap between our seats; the green toolbox was stashed under my seat and, under his, the army holdall containing the classified maps and cartons of ammunition. And behind the rolled-up sleeping bags, within easy reach from my seat, the carton containing our "snack bar," or "combat rations." And on the two-by-four, supporting the canvas roof, the list we had scribbled of the names we gave to the chunks of desert we had crossed, and the "restaurants" we stopped at, and the "hotels" we checked into. And next to that list, on the canvas roof, that portrait I drew, like a child—exaggerating his furrowed brow and square jaw and the dent in his nose. And next to the jerricans in the back, the white and red first-aid box, my brown knapsack, his khaki paratrooper's kitbag, and loads of provisions to spare. He had changed nothing in the Jeep, knowing all too well the bliss of finding something constant and familiar in the pervasive otherness of a journey. That was his gift to me, one of many . . .

As the shadows stretched long, the Jeep circled and circled, the cliffs spinning all around us sunset gold. Then, Tal shouted over the clank of the engine: "The Gates of the Wadi . . ."

I hardly recognized the place. Here you could see how fast the drought was drying up waterholes, forcing Badu by the thousands to move, to change their way of life and cluster together for survival. The shanty town of sorts that only forty days ago had sprawled no farther than the banks of this wide dry riverbed, now covered the slopes of the mountains that encircled the Gates. Defeat was carried on the wind in the stench of sewage mixed with the smoke from cooking-fires fueled by goat and camel dung, and the sweat born out of misery and resignation. In the flat of the wadi, not one water tank, like forty days ago, but three huge ones trucked over by Israel, looking like three white islands in a sea of black goats. Countless shepherd-children and -women stood there, waving at the Jeep. If A'ida, her husband, and children were among them, I didn't see them. It took the Jeep a minute to pass that sprawling shanty metropolis—a minute, and then there was no sign of a goat or a Badu. Another minute, and the night swallowed the straggling rays of the sun. In that instant, the temperature dropped thirty degrees or so, and with it the noise of the engine, it seemed. The high beams revealed the dry riverbed sloping gentle, wide, and full of tracks: wheels, camels, goats, men's shoes, children's bare feet, and Badawias' sandals. Azzizah and Tammam wouldn't believe that the Jeep had rolled in to the Gates of the Wadi by sundown. It takes two days at least to cover the distance by camel. They are probably eating supper now—rice and tea. We should have left a carton of provisions back at the *maq'ad*, I was thinking, and must have said it out loud.

"What?! Couldn't hear. Speak louder." Tal shouted over the engine clamor, his eyes locked on to the high beams, pushing back the night as if to make room for the Jeep. The soft green light that spilled from the dashboard dials colored his t-shirt, green now, like the hair and the goose-bumps that swelled on his arms. Wrapped in his parka and in myself, I had forgotten how cold the night wind had become.

I could live in his enormous parka, and I had to fold my legs under me like a pillow to sit tall enough for my arm to encircle his shoulders with warmth. His hair was a tangled mass of dusty curls. His neck tasted of salt, and I could feel every shiver of mine echo in him ...

31

"The desert is wasted on tourists," Hillel told us. "They can't wait to get out of the crowded city, but the minute they see the wilderness, deserted, they start looking for a crowd of Israelis...as if we Israelis couldn't have pulled through the decades of war without some secret thing going for us, something besides courage. But no one clings to Israelis for safety like us Israelis. Comes night and every Israeli who travels the desert likes to camp in my backyard."

It has nothing to do with him being an Israeli-Yahodi, Azzizah would have told him; it is because he sits too close to plentiful drinking water. The closer you squat to a water source, the more certain you are to be burdened with guests. That is why Abu Salim's tents were not pitched close to the well. Hospitality is sacred, but, *Wallah*, even an oil-rich sheikh couldn't afford to shelter, feed, entertain every thirsty mouth in the desert. If Azzizah were to see how plentiful the water is at Hillel's Nature Conservancy post, she would have been glad of the gold she wears to ward off the evil eye of envy. Water was so freely expended at Hillel's post, even to quench the thirst of flowerbeds. To protect the flowers, they had put up tall bamboo fences and had transplanted acacia and salvadora trees, at least half of them dying of transplant shock. And to make the post smell like home—why else?—they also planted jasmine climbers.

Hillel lived in bachelor quarters that looked like they'd seen more than a tourist-girl or two. These girls must have hated to tear themselves away, waiting until the last minute before their tourist truck, Jeep, or Rover was ready to push off, then packing in a hurry, their expensive French perfumes and lotions forgotten and left behind in the medicine cabinet over the sink. Those loaded shelves imparted a warning to any girl who assumed she had set up camp at Hillel's place permanently. Hillel liked his encounters brief, it seemed. He needed the freedom of movement of a one-night stand, a short jaunt through foreign territory where you have neither the vocabulary nor the time, need, ability to bullshit.

"Only a man cursed by fate or possessed by demons," Abu Salim had once told me, "would, like Hilal, roam in the desert year after year with no wife, no sons, no parents, and no friends—other than stranger-tourists and Badu who tie-and-untie... Only a man possessed by demons, would, like Hilal, waste the passion of his youth on the protection of trees, the very trees that Allah had planted in Sinaa for to fuel Badu fires..." Hillel's endangered-species list was endangering them, Abu Salim had told him; instead of trees and birds, Hillel and the likes of him should put the Badu on his endangered-species list.

They were first and foremost on his list, Hillel had told the Badu in response. But the Badu don't trust Hillel.

If Azzizah were to see the scratches on his hands... "Those scratches on your hands look angry enough to fester. The sooner they are treated with antibiotic ointment, the better," I told Hillel.

"Her head is still in the tents," Hillel said to Tal, just like a Badu man, talking about a woman as if she were not there. A tetanus shot he'd had to take for the scratches on his hands, Hillel added.

It was an eagle that had scratched his hands, Hillel went on to say. His face lit up when he told how, while he was driving in Wadi R. just before noon today, he had noticed the eagle was injured and had trapped the great bird with his bare hands... "A vet is treating it now. That's why the post looks deserted. Everyone ran to the infirmary to watch. It's not every day you can look an eagle in the eye."

Hillel brewed coffee like a Badu, to honor his guests; in preparing his ritual, he used a gas burner and, like a Yahodi, spiked honor with sugar and cardamon. On a round tray, like a Badu, he served up honor, but, like a Yahodi, on a coffee table.

It was the first table I had seen in weeks. The first chairs, walls, ceiling, floor, bed, cupboard, doors, windows, books, paintings, records, stereo, electric lights, running water...

Gushing from the showerhead, hot or cold at a twist of a tap, clockwise, counter-clockwise. Ten jerricans' worth must have run down the drain before I could step into the shower stall. Tammam would have to sweat ten hours to haul that much water uphill to the tents. And here, jerrican after jerrican splashed away, down the drain, while I stood outside the stall like a child, reluctant, as if water were fire.

Stepping in was like crossing a border to a world in which time ran so fast it stood still. The rushing spray felt like an infusion of life, of energy. (*Wallah*, how industrious the Badu would be if their tents had running water like the homes of the tourists who fly to the desert and say that the Badu are lazy and filthy ...) Brown water spiraled down the drain; weeks' worth of dust resisted my lathering and scrubbing. It seemed to come out of my pores, from some hidden source.

"The towels are clean," Hillel said when he offered me the use of his shower—in keeping with the tradition of desert hospitality dating back to the days of our forefather Abraham. His tourist-girls must have left their towels behind too. Huge foreign towels, smelling like they had just been pulled out of a washer-drier in Canada, were hanging on a row of hooks on the bathroom door. They were jammed together and as soon as I touched one, the rest slipped down to the wet floor. As I was about to hang them back up, a naked woman appeared at the door—out of nowhere, like a ghost, it seemed, the maiden of Shulem, the dancer of two camps, come to life. Fair of hair, dark of skin, her body sensuous, her eyes ethereal. At first glance, she looked as stunned as I felt, then she laughed with me as I recognized that she was my image, reflected in the full-length mirror on the bathroom door, unveiled by the tumbling towels.

"Your reflection is mirrored in people's eyes, not in glass," I could almost hear Azzizah saying, or was it my mother who liked to say it? Azzizah would suffer from claustrophobia in that bathroom, it was so small. You couldn't get dressed without bumping into the sink, the toilet bowl, the shower stall, the door handle.

The door was hollow—a door/no door that admitted the words Tal and Hillel were exchanging in the living room, but deadened the sound. There was no mountain echo here—no breathing space and no resonance. It took a bit of time for the ear to adjust—it sounded like Hillel was asking Tal if I had mentioned the letter he had smuggled to me in the tents. Tal, in response, said, "What letter?" or "Smuggled, why?" or—I couldn't really make out what he said.

The letter. As if the courage, or the madness, that had kept me going in the tents had been washed away in the shower, I was sweating now as I struggled into a clean change of clothes, the same layers upon layers I had worn in the tents and the only clean clothes in my knapsack. I was like a walking hourglass, the sand trickling through with my every move onto the polished ballata-marble floor with each step I took from Hillel's bathroom to his living room.

"I'm sorry," I apologized.

"It's all right. It happens whenever I come in from the desert, too," Hillel said.

Whatever Tal heard Hillel say while I was taking a shower had angered him. His jaw was clenched when I rejoined them.

"The Badu see today with one eye, and eternity with the other," Hillel was saying as I sat down.

Tal's eyes met mine, inquiring, "How are you, Leora?" How are you? How are you? like Salim had asked Tammam at their reunion.

"A person could get killed for spreading such stories," Hillel went on. "But a story classified, highly secret, is the hardest thing for a Badu to keep... Left, right, and center, the Badu betray each other's confidence, even at the risk of getting killed. Still, the Badu trust only their own, not one of us. How can you blame them when we lock a Badawia up in an insane asylum, not because she is ill, hysterical or violent, but because we caught her crossing the border. Shame on us..."

"*Yaa-Allah ... yaa-Allah*!!" I exclaimed inside. Hillel was at the tail end of the story A'ida had told me of the blemished bride.

Tal lit a cigarette, puffed and puffed, then said, "It wouldn't surprise me if that border-crossing Badawia, Salim's bride, had appeared to be a basket case by the time she'd crossed the minefields at that border, and the fields of barbed wire. That border fence alone could drive you nuts for a few hours, if not days."

"I didn't see her crossing the border," said Hillel. "But, at the mental hospital, I saw her sitting in a large room full of lunatics, looking like an island of sanity and dignity... Her father is what the Badu call *Sheikh ma'roof*, meaning: the sheikh recognized by the Badu to be their leader, the sheikh who doesn't cooperate with the authorities; like the official one who we call sheikh—the one we had appointed to lead their tribe and represent them—the one who complies with us..."

"You mean the Badu have two sheikhs at once?" I asked Hillel. He and Tal looked at me like my sister and Arik's brother do whenever they think me too naïve for words.

"So, in the tents also, I see, the Badu classify this bit of information, just as we do in The Land," Hillel muttered to Tal as if I were invisible.

Did you know how ill I was in the tents? Did you inform Tal? Why didn't one of you pull me out then? How did you know I had entered the tents "knowing nothing..." as the Badawias said... nothing about the rumor?... The fevered questions circled in my mind in an angry ululation. I was in no shape to deal with them. It was a relief to be invisible in this room.

"The Badu dislike their official sheikh much more than we do; he sells them out, they think. Yet they treat him like a sheikh because they know that if he doesn't accommodate us, they will not get their free water tank week after week." Hillel said, as he refilled his wine glass and Tal's, then poured me some of the red cabernet that Tal had presented to him on our arrival. "That's the language of the region, the desert, Arabia, the Levant; the language of the *souk*—the market. Their official sheikh speaks this language all too fucking well. He probably bleeds the Badu, just as he bleeds us. His sons roam the desert in Peugeot pickup trucks, he in a chauffeur-driven air-conditioned limousine. Their unofficial sheikh rides a thoroughbred camel, which probably costs more than the limo."

The wine was starting to get to him, Hillel said. He had never seen a Badu drunk, he said. He himself drank beer from time to time, but rarely wine, and never anything stronger. "The desert is intoxicating enough..." A glass or two of wine seemed to be enough to loosen Hillel's tongue, or maybe the wine was just an excuse to talk and talk, and keep us there with him. He rambled on, a lonely man, homesick, missing old friends like Tal, who had gone through fire with him, understood in blood missions behind Their lines, the Yom-Kippur War...

"You haven't seen nobility till you see that unofficial sheikh," Hillel went on. "No one could buy him. I wasn't surprised when he told me he had dispatched his daughter to Jordan, even though it was probably a made-up story to redeem her reputation and spare her life... just as Abu Salim had probably invented the story about his son running off to see the world, to spare the lives of his son and girl-wife. That's how the Badu survive, circumvent their strict laws: They invent stories, like Scheherazade, and by accepting two sheikhs. One sheikh collaborates; the other does not compromise. And if the ruling authorities don't like it, they go and lock up his daughter in an insane asylum, knowing full well that if the Badu hate anything, it is to be locked up, confined..."

Mutt and Jeff's father was caught smuggling a quarter of a million dollars' worth of drugs—hashish or heroin, or both—Hillel told Tal. He's out on bail. Abu Salim paid a fortune to bail him out. That's why Abu Salim is flat broke these days. His clan, too. They all chipped in.

"*Yaa-Allah*," I thought. "I know nothing about the Badu."

"Jail, bail—both are a sort of professional hazard to the Badu, almost a given part of their smuggling. But a crazy house... If we locked up every girl who lost her head to a prick, we wouldn't have space for the real lunatics." Hillel laughed at the thought, lit a cigarette, took a long sip of wine. "Can you imagine how fucking surprised I was when a psychiatrist friend called me up and said he had a Badawia in his ward? I told him he's probably got some nut thinking she's a Badawia. But I knew he could tell a true Badawia when he saw one, so I drove up north and saw the sheikh's daughter sitting in that ward ... She probably thinks now that all of us Yahod are deranged ..."

Heaping virtually everything in his fridge onto the table, Hillel said, "I heard Gingie was slapped with a criminal record. Overnight, our lawmakers declared it illegal to build new settlements in the West Bank in order to woo Egypt back to the peace table. Next, Egypt won't even consider coming to the table until we pull out of the West Bank altogether ... We might as well hand the Arabs the key to The Land. No way in hell can we defend her, if we give up the West Bank."

"We'll have nothing to defend if we keep the West Bank," Tal said. "Nothing, but a cancer, wasting our moral fiber, to defend our rule over nearly a million Arabs in the West Bank."

"Tell me, why do you peaceniks make noise about the West Bank Arabs but never about the Sinai Badu? No peacenik ever mentions the legitimate rights of the Sinai Badu to Sinai. Why?" Hillel was waxing rhetorical while he and Tal prepared supper, chain-smoking and sipping cabernet ... Like the Badu, Hillel wouldn't allow me to do any work; he regarded me as a guest; a woman-guest he ignored, like a Badu does a woman in public. Addressing Tal, Hillel continued to say, "I can understand why Egypt would hold it against the Badu for being the only Arabs in this region to live in peace with us, but you peaceniks ... It's beyond me why you don't make noise for the whole world to hear that, if Egypt wants to have peace with us, she'll have to guarantee water, food, medicine, and schools for the Badu. Or better yet, include the Badu in the peace talks. That's what the Badu want. That's what they tell me, as if I could get through to the top people, as if there is someone with a bit of sense there up at the top."

"I'd settle for a bit of sense down here," Tal muttered. "Egypt can't support her fifty million inhabitants in the style we've led the Sinai

Badu to be accustomed... We win a few battles and we think we can dictate terms, not only for peace, but for a way of life... Would you like Egypt to dictate to you how to treat the Badu or any person who lives in your land? This desert belongs to Egypt. Or are you with Gingie in the belief that it's part of 'Greater Israel'?"

"Here's to this beautiful gem of a post we built in Egypt, like in our slavery days." Hillel raised a full glass to that. His post, living quarters, infirmary, and office were built to look like Abu Salim's *maq'ad*, Hillel said, then laughed cynically. "We built nothing but the very best here in Sinai. Time and again our government gives Sinai to Egypt, only for us to reconquer Sinai. Time and again we forget...," he added. Then he lit another cigarette.

Hillel was puffing away, so were Tal and I, and the smoke couldn't escape on the breeze here, like in the compound. Here, like in tents, the night wind was cold, but here all the windows were closed against it. Through the smoke, Tal gave me a strange apologetic look, then he said, "The forgetting that got us into trouble is forgetting that the Sinai War was a mistake. We wasted too many lives to protect this buffer zone. We lost fewer men in the '67 war when we didn't have Sinai as a buffer zone. We occupy a desert much bigger than our Land, and we grew accustomed to power, just as your Badu grew accustomed to our hospitals, water, and schools... We were better off without all that power, and maybe the Sinai Badu would also be better off without our schools, helicopter ambulances, water..."

"Oh, I wish I was a dreamer like you, *yaa*-Francawi," Hillel replied. "Francawi," Hillel called Tal, because Tal's parents came from the French-speaking part of Belgium, I assumed.

"If you know the Badu, you know the Arabs, *yaa*-Francawi; I've been here five years and learned that the Arabs see us as strangers who pose a threat, not only to their way of life, but to their future, their story... The minute they see us as vulnerable or weak, they'll pounce with all they've got. But who can hang tough forever? Who wants to hang tough forever? I wish I believed in miracles, *yaa*-Francawi... Who was it who said that you must believe in miracles in order to be a realist in The Land?"

417

"My father," said Tal. "He was quoting Ben-Gurion; I didn't know it till long after my father got killed ... Can you imagine what miracles we could work in The Land if we invested in peace merely half the effort we invest in war? I didn't check the Badu as you did, but I know the Negev Badu are true Arabs as much as the Sinai Badu. Yet they serve in our army, sit in our Knesset, on our labor unions and town councils, they live in peace with us. That's more than good enough for me ..."

The two of them were engaged in men-talk while doing woman's work—Abu Salim would have collapsed from laughing to see the Jabbar and Hillel prepare supper, like Tammam and Azzizah. Well, not exactly like them—each ingredient and dish lent the fragrance of home to Hillel's place. That supper tasted like suppers used to taste when I was a child, when food tasted like food—tomatoes like tomatoes, eggs like eggs, bread like bread ... And, like in a dream— the dream that taunted me in the tents—the table was heaped with fresh vegetables, cheese, lebben, bread and butter, plates, forks, spoons, knives ... They had diced tomatoes, cucumbers, and onions; grated in carrots and radishes; added pitted olives, green and black, a dash of salt, olive oil, and fresh lemon juice—just like my mother does. The omelet was as fluffy as hers, and Hillel's generosity and hospitality as boundless as the emptiness beyond Abu Salim's *maq'ad*.

And, like in the Badu compound, I couldn't phone anyone anywhere. The phone at the post, a field phone, was reserved for incoming calls—except for emergencies.

"The Canadian wants you to phone him as soon as you can," Hillel said, addressing me this time. "The Canadian," Hillel calls Professor Russell, like the Badu call him "El Bofessa." "The Canadian inquired about you on the phone, regularly," Hillel shook his head. "The Canadian abused your trust ... inexcusable, not to mention the rumor to you, and to so blatantly admit it to me, without shame or compunction ..."

A Mountain Badu would kill anyone who defamed him as Hillel did Russell—even before he went on to tell about the day he returned to the post from a home visit up north, in Haifa, and first heard that Abu Salim had finally tracked down his son, Salim. Next he heard that Tal had dropped by the post the night before and had left him a note, requesting he watch over a woman friend who had been invited to stay in Abu Salim's forbidden tents. A day later he got a phone call from the Canadian, asking, "Did you hear, by any chance, if a war widow who had dropped out to Canada made it again to Abu Salim's forbidden tents?"

"'Yes, she did,' I told the Canadian," Hillel said. "'Son of a gun,' the Canadian mutters, 'that woman has more *muruah* than ten men...' 'Did you tell her what she was walking into? A rumor that might end up in a double execution?' I ask him. 'No,' the Canadian replies. Inexcusable!" Hillel looked at me as if he expected me to echo him in denouncing Russell.

It seemed ridiculous for Hillel to be ranting to me—who was kept in the dark about the mission that would claim Arik's life—about the sin of omission.

Tal expected the same reaction from me as Hillel did, or so I read in his eyes—bloodshot, like the Badu's. The desert, knowing no discrimination, favors all eyes equally, puts all hearts to the same test. Isn't that why the Badu hold in high value such qualities of heart as generosity and nobility, courage and endurance?

"A woman's place is inferior to man, but not her heart," Abu Salim had told me, as did his wives—even his grandsons, little Mutt and Jeff, quoting him perhaps. For sure, Tammam and Azzizah suffered from no inferiority complex, and neither did A'ida or any Badawia I had met in the forbidden mountains—a place I would never have revisited had Russell not encouraged me, for whatever reason, it didn't matter now.

True, Russell should have told me of the rumor, even if, as many of those rumors that swarm in the desert, this one, too, was as harmless as a fly. And, yes, Hillel exposed his blood for generations when he attempted to make up for Russell's error in judgment; but it was likely not the first time an error in judgment had backfired on Hillel. This one cost nothing compared with others. Why, any day any one of us could put a foot wrong...

Both Hillel and Russell have rolled in the desert for years to study-understand the Badu—the true Arabs—but have been admitted only to *maq'ads*—guest-receiving-places—where Badu men say, especially to important guests, whatever they think their guests want to hear. So each stranger-guest who visits the same Badu *maq'ad* leaves with a different story. Russell's story has been told and published the world over. Hillel's—only his friends, relatives, and tourists know of Hillel's Badu knowledge. People tend to take the written over the spoken word, even though it came from Bible that the Lord sayeth, not scribbleth ... Russell probably treats Hillel not as a worthy rival and colleague, but as he had treated me—with that aloof disdain of an Anglo-Saxon newcomer trying to out-native the natives. And from what I've seen so far, Hillel wouldn't suffer it gladly. I'd bet Hillel wouldn't suffer gladly anyone who treats him like a Badu treats a woman, like he and Tal treated me.

All evening, the two of them ignored me like the Badu in the *maq'ad*, so I kept my mouth shut like in the *maq'ad*, and just listened, observed, spoke when spoken to, and formed assumptions to fill in the blanks. The minute you shut a person out of any circle— family, friends, or the hub of power—that person will start to second-guess those who have closed ranks. The heart, afraid of chaos, darkness, loose ends, craves closure, light, order. Isn't that why the least predictable rulers are the most terrifying?

No one can keep a woman guessing like a Badu, and no one can second-guess a man like a Badawia. Azzizah once told me she had learned to second-guess Abu Salim so well, she had stripped him of all his power; and, seeing that, she stopped. "Even when the heart fears the dark, it is better to gather patience and wait. Better still is to trust completely, submit," she had told me. "For fate rules over men and women alike." It was fate, Azzizah believes, that had compelled A'ida's son to drag me over the line into the tents. She would laugh to hear Hillel say that El Bofessa expected me to be his eyes and ears in her compound. He couldn't have picked a stranger-woman more blinded and deafened by ignorance, Azzizah would tell Hillel. So would I—but I said nothing.

I couldn't really speak for Russell. I hadn't known him for more than a few weeks—he's a distant relative I'd rarely seen until I first ventured to Sinai this last spring. And I had known Hillel for only a few hours—and Tal for all of seven days. The Badu, I have known just long enough to realize that I don't know them. And, really, who do I know? Even Riva, Mottke, and Gingie I can't say I know intimately; how could I, when, for more than twenty years now, we have lived on different continents. We meet once or twice a year, and I call them long distance at least once a month, when I discover that I don't speak the language—the day-to-day language, the language of intimacy. And how could I begin to know the Canadian Yahodi I married when I can't forgive myself for marrying him. And Levi, when I can't forgive myself for dragging him to exile when he was an infant . . . Who would have thought that exile meant being shut out from everyone, even yourself?

And The Land, like a proud lover—jealous and monogamous—won't take you back once you are unfaithful with another land. It is as if she is afraid, like a vain lover, that you will see how the years have ravaged her. She might let you in for a visit, but as soon as she grows tired she kicks you out, giving preference to those who stayed with her in sickness and in health and to the newcomers who have no memory of her beauty twenty or thirty years ago. The vain bitch dooms her dropouts to remember her forever young and innocent, vital and full of hope, dreams, and promise.

As if silence were a sin, Tal and Hillel stared at me. "Doesn't it bother you at all, Professor Russell's abuse of your trust in him, if nothing else?" said Tal.

"I got over it weeks ago," I replied.

"She's caught a dose of Bedouinism," Hillel said. "Apathy is the symptom of Bedouinism. A professional hazard—it hits most of us when we sit in Badu tents a bit too long . . .

"You've got to fight it," Hillel told me. "Give in to apathy now and, before you know it, someone will kick your face in, and you won't feel it. You won't care."

Only a minute ago, he and Tal shut me out, as if I was invisible; now they expect me to assert myself, not only like a woman, and not like any man, but like a man who had seen his father allow himself to be kicked from ghetto to ghetto and then to the camps. The meek could not inherit this land. Chances are they'll get killed crossing the street on a green light.

"I don't understand half of what has happened to me in the past few months," I heard my voice, sounding like that of the androgynous stranger the Badu thought I was—a woman but not a woman; not a man but like a man; a Yahodiya but, not like a Yahodiya; not a Badawia and not a Canadian but like a Canadian and like a Badawia—my voice slid from one gender, tribe, and place to another. "Maybe I'm on a roll in terms of grace—if there is such a thing. I don't know why the Badu invited me to enter tents they forbid all other strangers to enter. Or why would Yahodi men I hardly know have favored me with their desert experience, not to mention their time and hospitality. No matter what Russell's motives were, I will not spit into a well that has watered me ..."

Just then a commotion erupted outside—screeching brakes, running steps, and frantic whispers.

"Sounds like tourists scared of the night," Hillel said. "Like moths they're drawn to our electric lights." He rushed out to silence them before they woke up the whole post.

"Would you have entered the tents if Professor Russell had told you that you stood a fifty-fifty chance of witnessing a double murder?" Tal asked me. "Did you have the stomach for that? The *muruah*? That's what Russell should have told you instead of prodding you to enter these Badu tents. 'There's no shame in deciding to cancel or postpone.' That's what Russell should have told you. Then, if your decision had been to go and give it a try, you would have been sitting here, not with self-abnegating gratitude to Russell, Hillel, and me, but with a sense of accomplishment and confidence in yourself, your ability, your endurance and judgment. That's what Russell has denied you. The opportunity to gain self-confidence may seem like nothing much in Canada, but here it factors in survival. Egypt celebrates her defeat in the Yom-Kippur War as a great victory because she managed to shake our confidence for a week or two.

"A test of pride is what Hillel's letter represented to you. How could you leave without losing face? You gain nothing from passing that test, only more pride—the empty pride that makes a person cocky, arrogant, and aloof to mask his fear." Tal seemed to forget he was talking to a woman dropout on whom the fate of the nation did not depend. Only a man who believed that our number-one resource was ourselves could give me such a lecture.

He reminded me of Arik then—of what was, and what could have been . . . and of the arrogance of those early days when right and wrong seemed to be as clear-cut as life and death . . . What priorities we had then. How ambitious we were. How much we demanded of ourselves. That's all we Yahod have, we believed, after we saw what happened to Yahod who expected a drop of decency, humanity from others, a drop of compassion from God.

Hillel returned, beaming. "Some Yoram just learned never to take a leak on a viper. Good thing vipers are too lazy to pounce on every tourist foot they meet or we'd be busy with nothing but dispensing antidotes here. They work like magic, these antidotes, but a Badu, no matter how fast he gallops a camel, usually arrives here too late. No punishment worse than standing helpless while a Badu you know, like, and respect dies of a viper bite before your eyes . . ."

"Dies? I thought the Badu could teach us how to treat snakebites," I said. The calmness in my voice, words pouring out like dark honey from a near-empty jar, my heart pounding even slower, as in high-alert, life-and-death emergencies, was my own antidote. How could I have stayed in this snake-infested wasteland when just a mention of a viper makes me brace myself, like for an outbreak of war? "The Badu are expert snakebite healers," I had heard or read somewhere. The idea of a viper kept me up nights before I went to the desert, but once I got there I forgot they existed. And even when Mutt and Jeff had waved an empty dried-out snake skin in my face, I didn't give it another thought. Perhaps anticipating danger generates more fear than living with danger; or fear of fear itself blocks my fear of the deadly—the dead—the angel, *Wallah*.

And Riva thinks that I don't give a damn if I live or die. The desert is just an escape, like Canada, she thinks. She knows me better than I know myself, she thinks; maybe that's why Riva can't see past the Leora she thinks she knows. I'm afraid of life, Riva thinks, but death is really what I am afraid of...

Isn't that why I dropped out? Isn't that what keeps me from dropping back in—that and not pride, as Tal likes to believe. Isn't that why I married Dave, sprinting for a safety island? Isn't that why I fear to give Levi my consent to serve?

Just look at what ripples this fear has, the effect it has on Levi, Dave, my parents, Arik's, and me. It has kept me from living, that's all.

Now, if only you could overcome this fear of the angel just as you did your fear of vipers... If only you could see in its empty skin the ribbon that binds us all.

32

It was late, closer to dawn than to dusk when Tal and I reached this cove—a dream cove for lovers, carved by sea and desert, wind and wave, at the foot of the sandstone mountains that flank the shore of the Red Sea, the Gulf of Aqaba–Eilat.

And, as if it was only the previous night that we had last camped overnight—and a lifetime ago, both at once—we set camp in the same order. Parked the Jeep to shield the fire-circle from the cold night wind. Placed the cartons of provisions and cooking utensils by the back wheels. The water jerricans by the front tire, so that we could wash up next to the side mirror and away from the sleeping bags.

But this time Tal brought pillows. Yes. Even white pillow-cases and sheets, like a soldier who vowed during gruelling desert maneuvers and missions that, if he lived to travel the desert in civilian life, he'd never again rest his head on a rock or snuggle up to stones for comfort. He combed out every rock and stone from a patch of sand here at the cove, like a Japanese gardener. Next he leveled the sand, flattened the sleeping bags, zipped them open like a double bed, tucked his handgun under a pillow, and made up the bed to meet army regulations, smoothing away every crease. It's as long a journey from soldier to man, I thought, as from stranger to woman.

I half-expected him to turn his back to me, like the boys had done in the old days when we girls changed our clothes. But he stared at my naked body, as if to memorize it, as if he was leaving for battle with a feeling he'd never come back. I cursed that war souvenir—his, mine—that wouldn't let us submit to love without fear of loss . . .

Oh, take what is left of life, and enjoy it, *Wallah* . . . His eyes caressed my naked body, then his hands. And then I drew him close to me, and deep. I kissed his lips, his solid torso, then buried my face below. And he reached for me and tasted his seed on my lips. And then, without words, he knew how to tell a woman how beautiful she is, how precious to him, how strong his love for her—infinite, like the stars above, constant like the waves on our shore; enduring, like the sandstone mountains...

I couldn't fall asleep, and my tossing and turning disturbed him. But he wouldn't let me uncap the bottle of sleeping pills, or even the 777 brandy. He said he'd tell me a bedtime story instead.

I thought he was joking. But he drew me close to him and started: "Once upon a time..."

I laughed. I couldn't remember the last time, or any time, that anyone had told me a bedtime story.

"You want to laugh or to sleep?" he said, laughing himself. "Are you ready?" Like Abu Salim, in the sing-song voice of storytelling, he went on to tell: "Once upon a time, there was a land far away and so cold that all the birds had to fly south every winter, otherwise they would freeze to death. But one winter, when all the birds were well on their way to the warm lands down south, one bird remained behind, limping and helpless. One of her wings was injured. Days passed, and nights. Snow covered the grass, and our poor little bird limped frozen. She could find no shelter from the snow. Then, just as the snow reached her poor little neck and she saw her life pass in front of her eyes, our poor little bird heard a bell, *clang-clang*...

"*Clang-clang*... Rosalinda the cow was coming round the corner, and as she passed our poor little bird, her bell clapped, sounding like thunder to our little bird. But, wonder of wonders, heat suddenly wrapped our little bird and melted the snow around her. Happy that she had been spared, our bird burst into song...

"Just then a wolf heard her joyful voice and couldn't believe his ears, thinking that his rumbling stomach, winter starved, was taunting him. Still, he followed the chirping voice and found the bird, pulled her out of her warm berth, and—*chick-chuck*, he swallowed her in one gulp.

"Which goes to show you: first, not everyone who shits on you is your enemy; second, not everyone who pulls you out of shit is your friend. And third, whenever you find yourself knee-deep in shit, you shouldn't sing."

He sleeps like a seasoned commando fighter deep behind enemy lines. I can hardly hear him breathing. He is fearless in sleep, confident, trusting me to watch over him, as if I am a platoon buddy on guard duty. And I, like I did in the tents when sleep eluded me, write-to-remember...

The sun, gliding up the mountain chain across the gulf in Saudia, slicks the Red Sea gold. The mountain chain on our side glitters like a giant hall of mirrors, reflecting a hundred rising suns. And in this forever of tomorrows, Tal sleeps.

Flies, coming to life with the sun, dance on his face. He turns and tosses, as if they are but dream flies, then grabs the top sheet and pulls it over his head—shrouded in white, a man dead to the wonder of a roaring sea in the middle of the desert.

The red sea is bluer than the Mediterranean. A forest of mongrob bushes is anchored to the sea floor, even though their roots shoot up in the air, like windpipes. The lush green of the surviving salvadoras belie the fact that it hasn't rained here in the past six or seven years. Stretching endlessly north and south, the two mountain chains flanking the gulf look like fraternal twins—the one in Saudia draped in purple haze, the one on our side changing color with the angle of the sun.

All too soon, the sun reaches its summit and bleaches out the blazing sunrise colors. The mountain chains look dun-colored, like cardboard, and the gulf becomes a silvered stillness, so narrow, it seems, a person could float across and, with a few lazy strokes, touch Saudia. People say, though, that the gulf is infested with sharks.

As the sun descends behind the mountain chain on our side, the peaks in Saudia blaze sunset colors and the blue waters of the Red Sea are purpled. The more beautiful the moment, the more it pains me that I cannot share it with anyone—except Arik...

Round the clock Tal probably slept whenever he returned from missions and raids, and his kibbutz-girl, Ephrat, must have been happy to have him home—even asleep.

"A woman knows she loves a man when she cannot help but submit to him altogether," Azzizah once told me. "When that happens, she feels complete, whole, even if her man does not love her." Azzizah believes that a woman loved is but a woman flattered, but a woman loving is a woman complete, whole.

War is an aphrodisiac, you'd think, if you saw how people fall in love in war movies. In real life, statistics say, people make more babies in wartime. And even in wartime The Land is a sensuous, steaming blue place. But God knows how anyone could feel whole in wartime, complete enough to welcome a love that smells of that smell that hangs over a land where generation after generation of young men fall; where parents, thinking their sons will die before them, indulge them; where women, thinking their men will die in the next war, don't assert themselves as equals but cater to their men, denying them nothing.

Not everything that serves her nation serves a woman well, *Wallah*.

Tal's girl, Ephrat, denied Tal nothing for days, weeks, months, years. I see her waiting, trembling, for him to come home. As soon as she'd hear he'd gotten a furlough, she'd pretty herself, would fill their room with flowers, would bake him his favorite cake. He'd eat a bite, tell her it's great, what a dream to be home. Then he'd take a shower, ask her how she's been, and before she'd reply he'd fall asleep. The whole furlough he'd be too wasted to give of himself to her. And she'd say nothing, deny him nothing. After his knees went and he was discharged from active duty to return home for good, she would expect her due, but as much as he wanted to give it to her, Tal didn't know how. All too regular are the stitches and dull the colored threads that form the tapestry of ordinary home life. Tal is a warrior, not a weaver, and he needs the chaos of the heroic, the extraordinary, the Angel, to live. Is that how it happened, the rift that brought on their separation?

If peace ever breaks out here, the whole country will get divorced, and the men will take off, questing for danger, for a dose, a fix, of that Extraordinary stuff.

In the cold rays of the sinking sun, the salvadora trees, nearly chopped out of existence by the Badu, looked like desolate survivors; and the mongrob bushes, like dropouts and drifters, hiding roots in their windpipes; this cove like an orphaned beach; Tal's sleeping face like the face of indifference; and the darkness, like a fire dying—Tal's fire, my fire, God's fire.

I was too excited to sleep. And sick of writing-to-remember—hoping-to-forget, like an exile dreaming of what was, what could have been, and closing my eyes to what never was, never could be ...

I ran to the Jeep, aching to leave him to his sleep here and find my way out of this dark, cold wasteland. I hated the idea that I had to rely on him to lead me out of this wilderness, as if he were Moses.

The longer I sat in the dead dark Jeep, the more alone I felt, the more I hated him, the more demons I saw in his face, the more humiliated I felt, the angrier I got. Finally, I climbed out of the Jeep, grabbed the water jerrican by the front tire, and arced a stream of water into his sleeping face.

Even before the jerrican was half-empty, he sprang to his feet and, like a madman, half-crouching, clutched the loaded Beretta in both hands, and aimed at me as if I were an enemy infiltrator.

For a moment I just stood, defiant in anger and too stunned to move or utter a sound. I've never seen a person spring to action so fast out of a dead sleep; he was graceful like a jungle cat and had even managed to dodge most of the splash. His white t-shirt looked dry, but his face was dripping wet, and water was streaming from his hair down his temples and in the runnels between veins engorged from the adrenalin of fight-or-flight. It wasn't funny. I don't know why I laughed.

He turned his back to me and disappeared into the darkness outside the rim of the fire-circle. I thought he had gone to calm himself down in private or to relieve himself. I waited and waited, and saw no sign of him. I walked to the rim to the darkness to see where he was. The moon was not visible yet, but the sky was over-loaded with stars; no half-measures, no subtleties in this part of the world. Nature deals only in extremes here—drought and flash flood, broiling hot days and freezing cold nights. Colder still are the waters of the Red Sea; otherwise the cove would be enveloped in fog like the lake up in Algonquin, when the air is colder than the water. There, in the freezing waters of the foaming gulf, I saw him.

"*Taaaalll!*" I shouted to him, but, like in a nightmare, I couldn't hear my voice, so loud was the rush of the waves swelling in high tide. Then I lost sight of him.

"*Taaaalll!*" I called out, a wail of regret for splashing him, for laughing in his face.

Out of the darkness he appeared, still steaming after dousing his temper in the gulf.

"Don't you ever fucking do that again!" He backed me toward the fire-circle. "You don't know how lucky your are—lucky you're still breathing, lucky I've been trained to control my instincts, lucky most Unit operations are carried out at night!" He was calming down now and loosened his grip on my forearms. "Lucky I've had months of training to resist shooting the first thing that moves There, behind enemy lines, in the dark and to wait until you see the man's face ... It's you or him, more often than not, and you have to shoot. But you never forget. You lose a piece of your soul when you kill a man ..."

"You lose a big chunk of your soul when your man gets killed. Poor you, poor me. Come on, let's dump the victim shit into the Red Sea, let the waves engulf it like they did Pharaoh's chariot. What do you say?" I heard my voice now, foaming like the whitecaps.

He stared at me across the shimmering heat of my fire-circle, as if he had lost a portion of his inheritance, a spark of the eternal fire that moved David to sing and to dance and to play the harp, even after God had told him that his hands, too stained with blood spilled to secure The Land, were not fit to build the Temple. But

David didn't live to see God fuck over his Chosen people at the Shoah. Any son of David who still had a piece of soul to lose today, could have sung and danced circles around David. If there was any sign of grace in these days of madness, it was standing in front of me. Beads of water and the sweat of self-restraint trickling down his face and neck; he stood there looking like God's tear, God's remorse.

"Do you like to sing, to dance?" I said. "You and I can dance circles around King David..."

Now he looked flabbergasted, exasperated: "Are you out of your mind? Sing and dance! You wasted a jerrican of water!"

"Only half a jerrican," I said, correcting him.

It seemed odd that a man who was so wet was also thirsty, I thought, as he picked up the jerrican. Part of me said that he wasn't too wet for revenge, splash for splash. But no, I reasoned, he hasn't had a drink of water for the past few hours, and besides, he's too earnest, serious, for such childishness, I thought. Before I had a chance to think further, he splashed the rest of the water from the jerrican into my face, and onto the only clean clothes I had left and the parka he had lent me yesterday. That got through to him: he laughed and laughed as I tried to wrap my freezing bones in a sleeping bag and discovered I had dumped more water on his sleeping bag than on his sleeping face.

"Looks like you will have to dance to keep warm," he said, still laughing.

"All right. Come on, let's dance," I said.

He doubled over when my fist connected with his gut; he was solid muscle, but he didn't bother to flex for a woman. He cursed and laughed, at the ready now, with wide-open arms. Each step I took toward him, he countered with a step back... I gave him a pretty good chase up and down the beach, round and round the fire...

At the place of honor, close to the fire but away from the smoke, we wrapped ourselves in the one dry sleeping bag and opened a bottle of local brandy, brewed coffee, lit cigarettes...

"Didn't you hear the click?" he asked me.

"What click?" I replied.

He shook his head, picked up the Beretta, showed me how you load the clip, the magazine, said something about releasing a safety catch, and then I heard the click of a gun cocked to fire. He couldn't get over the fact that I hadn't hit the dust, "the natural reaction." He seemed to know the exact measure of *muruah* and discipline it took not to run for cover—and not to pull the trigger. He had survival down to a science. "I'll never forget this jerrican business," he muttered, shaking his head.

"'Never forget' are parting words … You didn't come for me to take a look, make love, sleep and leave, did you, Tal?" I said without thinking. I was sure he'd laugh, but he said nothing.

Silence. Not at all like Badu silence. His, opened the door to the emptiness of loss. And I couldn't close it.

"Best we part, you said to me forty days ago. Why didn't you leave it at that, Tal?" My voice sounded like it was coming from far beyond the reef, beyond the Gulf, carried on the night-cold wind and seeking the warmth of our fire. "I met you, loved you, parted from you, missed you, longed for you—but the circle was closed. I didn't think I'd see you again—except in my remembering, and I'm good at that—as good as you are at soldiering, maybe better … for the better part of my life it sustained me—it's quite the life-raft, let me tell you … amazing what remembering can do; creates a life of its own; a life that has no boundaries, bends to no laws of nature or man. Everything is possible in my remembering, everything is attainable, everything and everyone is alive … In my remembering I can be married to Arik and to Dave at the same time; I can straddle continents; I can see what was, what could have been, and say to myself, What a fool …, I should have, could have …, Why didn't I …, If only …, I wish … Why didn't you leave it at that? Oh, *yaa*-Tal … 'Had I not seen the sun, I could have borne the shade, but light a newer wilderness my wilderness has made …'"

"Is that what happened in the forbidden tents?" he said.

"No, that's what happened in our forbidden Jeep forty days ago, or in my remembering of it. Or maybe only here, when you aimed your Beretta at me. And I put up no defense. Such is my trust in you, *yaa*-Tal, complete trust—or love-submission, as a Badawia friend of mine would put it. Such love makes you feel complete-whole, she believes. Have you ever felt that?"

"Yeah, man, I feel complete-whole, one with the Universe," he replied in English, imitating the foreign volunteers at his kibbutz.

He was famished now and thirsty, but wouldn't drink more than a glass of water, just in case we decided to stay here at the cove tomorrow.

"Too bad we can't stay longer; the Jeep has to report for Army duty day after tomorrow," he said, cracking me up. That was a new one.

"It's no laughing matter," said Tal. "Jeeps are military vehicles—yours, too; that's why you didn't pay tax when you bought it. The army's counting on your Jeep to show up when it's called."

And if the Jeep fails to report, will the army jail it for deserting? Jail me for absconding? Jail Gingie for waiting a month to tell Tal that the Jeep was called up?

Tal divided his dry clothes between us, then started to prepare a feast—breakfast, lunch, dinner, all lost during his sleep... The hot peppers he added to the Spam—kosher turkey—made us thirstier still, but it was delicious on top of hash-brown potatoes... and the egg salad, tuna salad, avocado salad—and beer! He had brought beer, and enough juice to quench the thirst of a platoon for a week.

Later, as we were sharing a cigarette and a beer, he told me he had received a few job offers recently, one of which he might accept.

"What kind of job?"

"It's classified," he responded.

"So, that's why 'never forget,' your parting words. You're going back to combat duty," I said.

Silence. Even the Red Sea, at low ebb now, was but a whisper, a hiss, and a crackle, almost like the fire-circle.

"Did they promote you to Colonel in the Unit or at General HQ? You're leadership material, according to Yehoshua—Arik's friend, the Cabinet minister. Remember him? But that must be the last thing you aspire to, the rank of a General ... Your place is in the kibbutz, you told me ..."

He laughed, then repeated, "It's classified."

"That's more than Arik told me before he went. For all I know, the Sinai war was classified for him, too ... If I had known he was being called up to take part in the launching of an all-out war, I would have parted from him altogether differently on that morning he went. I would have cleared up a few things—the sorts of things a girl-wife leaves for tomorrow, thinking life is full of tomorrows and today is simply full—the baby is crying, the dishes are piled up high in the sink, the car won't start. How in the hell could he fly a plane when he couldn't start a stupid Mini Austin, I thought when he finally drove off.

"I phoned the whole fucking air force that night to find out what had happened to Arik ..."

"You didn't let a person sleep even then," Tal muttered, and I had to laugh. Laughter sparked in his eyes when he added, "Do you like to sing, to dance? I'll never be able to sing or dance, or draw a gun, without seeing you facing a loaded Beretta and not flinching ..."

Barefoot, we danced to the beat of the waves, our eyes closed to the future and the past, and even to the present. A moment or two later, the sea and wind conspired to kill our fire-circle, and we turned to rescue a few embers, build a fire closer to the sandstone mountains that held this cove in a protective embrace. And now when we leaned our backs against the sandstone, it felt like being in a cave, illuminated by a fragrant fire that protected the entrance. But whenever the winds from the Gulf came calling, the fire smoke nearly choked us. So we became the protectors, taking turns to guard the fire at the entrance with our backs. I'd fold into him and warm up my back, then he'd fold into me and I'd protect him from the night wind. After a couple of turns at windbreak duty, he cursed the icy darkness and took a swig or two of brandy to warm up, lit a cigarette and went on to say that he had been pressed to take on the job of heading the security for all our embassies and government agencies in Europe.

"You mean, to supervise those guys who check purses and bags?" I said.

"Yes, something like that." He laughed, then added, "Keep it to yourself, it's classified."

"Why in hell would something like that be classified?" I said.

He looked at me as though I was way out of touch with the world where soldiers of Allah conduct a *jihad*—a holy war of letter bombs, suicide bombers, ambushes like those that mowed down travelers in airports and athletes at the Olympic games.

"Sounds to me like you've decided to take on this job."

"No, I haven't," he said. "I don't know if I could live Outside, even for only two or three years. At the end of that stint, they'll probably give me the same story they did in the Unit—'You've got two or three years' experience. It would be a shame to waste it.' Then they'll press me to stay... The irony is that if I decide to take on this job, the pay is... Well, they try to compensate you for being homesick, I assume. If I don't hand it over to the kibbutz, I could come home with enough cash to purchase a few good *dunams* of land, and materials and tools to get a farm started and build a house. This job might turn out to be the opportunity of a lifetime..."

"We are in deep shit if a man like you has to leave The Land and do security work Outside so that he'll be able to afford to live in The Land. I'd rather sell the Jeep and lend you the cash than see you take a security job Outside for the pay, like a soldier of fortune..."

He laughed. "I could have bought a fleet of Jeeps if I had pocketed my army paycheck instead of handing it over to the kibbutz month after month."

"Where will you be based?"

"Somewhere in Europe. It's classified, in part to save my neck..."

"When would you have to start?"

"In three or four weeks. I'd have to take a training course in The Land. Will you be in Canada by then, or in The Land?"

"I don't know," I said. There was no word for where I was now.

The Land

33

Frantic—the people, the pace, as if The Land were a rental property, her people credit-poor, the landlord waving eviction papers and shouting, "Pay or get out!" Even in the peninsula, as soon as the Jeep rolled onto the paved highway, horns began to honk, and the tailgating, weaving, and passing were frenzied, as if the Nation itself was late for some pressing appointment. The Jeep seemed to be caught in the slipstream, coasting to hell, although Tal barely noticed. A resort with thatched roofs, like the Club Med in Hawaii, spins by, and a couple of settlements, their lush green fields and trees drawing the eye, like water a thirsty traveler.

"Eleven years of sweat and dreams," Tal called those settlements. "They'll have to go, if and when Egypt signs a peace pact with us."

It looked like the evacuation had already begun when we reached the service station by D————. The only one for hours either way, it was like a botched renovation of some dusty, ancient *khan*—a sort of motel for camel-riders. Long lineups of cars, Jeeps, trucks, command cars, tour buses, vans sat at the diesel pumps and the military pumps; the longest was at the gasoline pumps. It must have been 150° Fahrenheit in the sun. Steam was billowing up out of overheated engines, and melting asphalt sucked at desert boots, sandals, and running shoes. Hundreds of travelers lined up at the kiosk for colas that seemed to run right through them. Some couldn't endure the lineups at the banks of outdoor toilets and relieved themselves outside. Whenever the wind changed direction, the stench and the fumes, the flies and the noise, were unbearable. The fat lady running the kiosk, an accordion of chins cascading down her neck, her brows knotted in a ferocious frown, shouted from behind the cash register, "Go to Jerusalem!... Start a revolution!... Camp in Jerusalem, not here!... Camp in front of the Knesset building!... Tell your leaders to give Jerusalem to Egypt, not Sinai!"

"That's what they are doing, giving up Jerusalem!" someone shouted from the lineup.

"It's the beginning of the end!" shouted another.

"It's the end of the beginning!" shouted a third.

The closer we got to Eilat, the heavier the traffic, the more tourist tents dotted the gulf coast, and the fewer Badu encampments. And at the road-block just past the green sign that read "Welcome to Eilat" was another long lineup of cars, trucks, and Jeeps. A sort of Badu bazaar stood right by the road-block; travelers milled round mounds of *jalabeeyas, kaffiyyes*, copper trays, coffee *bakrajs*, and demi-tasse cups, miniature hand-woven saddlebags and hand-woven tents... Badu children ran up to the Jeep to make their pitch in broken English: "You wanna buy real, *Wallah*, real Badu *kaffiyye*, cheabbp... Badu *jalabeeya*... cheabbp, *Wallah*... Comaan, comaan, you wanna bbpictuoor-bbpolaroid of she— you—riding she-camel... cheabbp, *Wallah*, only sis dollah... tree dollah fer yah..."

Polaroid! I scan the Badu "cameramen" in the bazaar, and among them I see A'ida's husband, Abu Hasan, aiming the Polaroid camera I'd traded for the story of the blemished bride, at some tourist-girl sitting on his thoroughbred she-camel. He looked to be half the man he was in the compound, almost as if there is something in his home ground, the desert, the vast expanse of open space, that adds to one's stature. Or maybe there is something about The Land—her besieged borders, her beleaguered people—that cuts one down... not to mention the ever-present spirit of the great prophets, judges, kings, shepherds, carpenters, warriors, musicians, and lovers... Or maybe the Badu was made to feel small by his doing work, which his uncle, Abu Salim, believes is befitting but for a low-down *fellah*, and a woman—not a true, real man...

The new superhighway narrowed into an old, patched-up two-lane at the entrance to Eilat, the gateway to The Land. It still felt and smelled like an old frontier town—dusty, temporary, in flux. Youngsters, bent under heavy knapsacks, trudged along the cracked road. A line of cement trucks blocked the lane by a construction site. Across the road, a cement factory emitted a column of dust as tall as a mountain. A moment later, we drive by the noisy port warehouses that hide the blue waters of the Red Sea. A desert field-school spins by, then a wind-blown blue and white flag planted at a navy base, with gray gunboats anchored at the piers. Farther north, huge rusty oil tankers block the sea. But north of the port, the Gulf of Aqaba–Eilat opens up, curving like a huge horseshoe, full of sailboats, speedboats, fishing boats, and yachts. Luxury hotels hug the northern shoreline almost like in Miami Beach. But here, a hundred meters east of these hotels is an Arab country at war with you—or more correctly, the sliver of no-man's-land between the border of Israel and Jordan, between Eilat and Aqaba, the town that Lawrence of Arabia had taken from the Turks. It's one of the most unobtrusive and quiet borders in The Land. From the Jeep on almost any road in Eilat, you can see the tall palm trees shading the streets of Aqaba, and even the flower gardens in the winter villas there. It might as well be on the moon for us Israelis— except for border-crossing soldier-of-soldiers like Tal.

"Aqaba is just as dusty, noisy, and busy as Eilat. But Petra is much more beautiful than her pictures," he said. It was the first time I had heard him boasting. He knew it was a dream for ordinary Israelies like me to hike to Petra, even to Aqaba.

Reality had a hold on him as well, as was apparent from the precautions he took to prevent the Jeep and everything in it from being stolen. A wave of robberies the likes of which had never been seen was hitting The Land, at the same time as the worst wave of terrorism, Tal explained. The superhawks among the TV commentators were saying it was no coincidence, that no one but terrorists would steal an ambulance while the medics were upstairs helping a heart-attack victim. The superdoves maintain the crime spree is the work of our own home-grown Mafia. The cynics see it as a sign that our old dream is dead, long live the new dream—of being a country like any other country, complete with petty thieves and crime bosses...

A row of hotels—a few, like in Yamit abandoned at mid-construction—hugged the Bay of Eilat. The scorching Hamsin winds—the fifty winds—started to blow when Tal dropped me off at the hotel closest to the highway. While he went to contact a kibbutz classmate about delivering to her a parcel from home, I went in to use the pay phone.

Electric stars dotted the ceiling of the hotel's lobby, and the air-conditioning was cranked up as cold as the desert night wind. My father picked up the phone, shouting as if it were a megaphone, and barely hearing a word. My mother heard that I sounded good. "Thank God ... Thank God ... Thank God, you are on home ground," she said.

"Russell was trying to reach you all day today," she added, "he didn't say why, what for.

"I'll see you day after tomorrow ... Drive carefully ..." she cut me off, hung up—rushing already to prepare my homecoming feast.

I dialed the phone number Russell had left with my mother, but the line was busy, busy ...

Like magic, I dialed the long-distance operator and as soon as I say it's a collect call to Toronto, Canada, from Leora, I hear six thousand miles hissing on the line, a couple of rings, a deafening sneeze, and another, and another, and now Levi, his voice thick with a cold, chuckles and says, "Hi, sorry about that."

"That's all right," the operator says in a human voice, switches to his professional robot voice and adds, "Will you accept a collect call from Leora in Israel?"

"Hey, *Immmmmaaa*!!! You're back! Great! How was it? What a coincidence, I just flew in from ..." The kid is so happy and excited to hear from his mother he forgets to accept the charges.

"Will you accept the charges?" the robot demands.

"Sure ... Dad should be here any minute. You can't imagine how down he is when you are away. It's impossible to get a rise out of him, even when I told him he has it better than me; he, at least, has a girl to miss ..." The boy goes straight to the intimate, as if the last time we'd talked was breakfast this morning. "... And I also was away for the past three weeks, flying transport sorties for Jean up in Yellowknife, Flin-Flon, Uranium. I just got in ..." Your son will fly to the moon yet, Arik ... How can you ground a boy who gets himself a job as bush-pilot up in the cold white wilderness of the Canadian North ...

"And I thought you were sweating your butt off on your degree ..."

"Don't worry, Imma. I'll graduate with flying colors ..." Levi laughs and laughs, which starts him coughing—almost like Abu Salim. It's such a bad cough, you hold your breath, hoping he'll catch his. What a beast the phone—it shrinks and expands distance at the same time ... He was probably sleeping when I called—ten or eleven o'clock Sunday morning in Toronto; I couldn't remember if Toronto was six or seven hours behind The Land at this time of year.

"Is this a press call or a personal," a military censor interjects.

"Hey, operator, what's with this press call ... You've got your lines crossed. The other line is press; this one is personal," Levi tells the censor.

We got cut off. It took only a minute to reconnect.

"What a crazy country, I love it," Levi says. "But, you know, The Land doesn't look good from here. It looks like we say we want peace but we don't really mean it—like we aren't willing to give an inch of Sinai even for peace."

"It's not the impression you get in Sinai, especially from the Badu. And Israelis are flocking to Sinai in droves to catch the sights as if soon as the peace pact is signed, Egypt will close the border. It's so hard to imagine after all these decades of war—Egypt, as a peaceful neighbor ... But I saw Egyptian soldiers wave to me as if the peace pact was a done deal already."

"Gingie told me that he couldn't escort you to Sinai. How was his former commander? ... How was it in the desert? ... What did you learn from your stay with the Bedouins? ..." The boy wants the whole *megilah* long distance.

Long distance is no distance to him—a mere fingertip away.

The cost is irrelevant to him; his dad is loaded. But he knows his imma—raised on austerity rations—is only too aware that long distance runs five dollars a minute. Dollar time, bottom-line time, black-and-white time—life is simple time—not "primitive" simple, like Badu time—time everlasting—time for a beginning, a middle, and an end, and then some ... Time for the echo to reverberate and shake mountains of granite ...

"I'll tell you everything when I see you, Lev ..."

"You sound sad, Imma ..."

"Yes ... I feel sort of like in Sinai, where one circle closes before you glimpse the opening of the next ... And I know you won't be glad to hear that it hasn't been revealed to me whether or not to waive your exemption. I promise I'll give you a yes or a no before this month is out."

"That's terrific news, Imma. You don't know it but you've decided to give me a yes. I can hear it in your voice ..." The boy is an optimist like you, Arik. "Dad is here, Imma. He just walked in. You can't imagine how he's missed you ..."

I've missed him too, missed a husband to love. I was burning for him with a passion fired by another love. But passion is passion. Once awakened it demands action ... Isn't that why so many marry on the rebound? Any mate will do ...

"It's Imma! Dad! Imma on the phone!"

Dave didn't run to the receiver. As he always does first thing when he gets home from the steambath at the South Y, he fixed himself a scotch on ice. It seemed to take him as long as it takes Abu Salim to brew honor.

"Hello," Dave said.

And goodbye went shimmering dreams. His tone of voice said it all.

"Hello, Dave."

"Well, you certainly took your time." He sounds so down, Job is ecstatic compared with him. Parking his butt in the shade, he pushes me out to the sun, saying, "Go to the desert, stay with the Bedouins. You studied Arabic all these years—what for if not for this? You are not afraid of the desert, are you? A tough *Sabra* like you...?" That's what he told me months ago, and he didn't mean a word of it. He is barely able to conceal how it angered him that his wife had left him for nearly two months, roaming the desert—with Gingie's former commander. Levi told him, for sure.

Yet it wouldn't surprise me if, in some corner inside him, Dave was perversely proud that his wife traveled with such a hero as Gingie's former commander. He would expect nothing less of her...

"How have you been, Dave?" I decided not to start an argument long-distance. "I hope Marissa came through with the cleaning, the shopping, the cooking..."

"Yes, Marissa is fine," he said. "She's got a heart of gold, Marissa. Spoils Levi rotten. Made him chicken soup for his cold."

"Are you all right, Dave? Is everyone, everything okay at work? Family? Friends?"

"Everything, everyone, is fine."

Fine again. That's two. He's giving me his version of the silent treatment. I pretend it's Badu silence—costing five dollars a minute...

"How are your parents?" He finally dredged up a question to ask.

"They sound great. Asked me to give you their regards. What's the matter, Dave? You sound so..." Angry? No—too strong. Dead? Forget it. Despondent, down, depressed, listless, distant, critical? No way. "So tired, Dave."

"Oh, it's Sunday, you know... The steambath knocks you out..." Silence.

He's so angry at me, he's afraid to say more than a couple of words. Not even about world affairs, the Middle East, "his specialty." Not even about the peace talks. And not a question about the Badu.

"When are you planning to fly back to Toronto?" He breaks the silence... But just the thought of returning to such dishonest anger, the sorrow, pain, helplessness...

"I haven't decided yet,"

"But you are planning to come home for Christmas, New Year's, I assume," he said, as if Christmas and New Year's were his High Holidays.

Had I not phoned him, I wouldn't have known that Hanukkah is not far off, let alone Christmas. There's no sign of Christmas here, in this Holy Land.

"Why don't you fly here for your winter vacation, Dave, let's have our reunion here..."

"Not much notice," Dave muttered.

No appointment with the Angel is listed in Dave's social calendar. Life is busy—everlasting, not like a Badu, *Wallah*... A Badu walks with the shadow of the Angel on his shoulder, lives for stories to be remembered, *daimann*—forever and ever. A Badu ties-and-unties a compound without any notice. For Dave, even a month's notice is not enough.

"I can't just drop everything and fly to Israel," he said. "We can't have everything we want in life," he adds. Does he mean I can't stay, or that he can't fly over on such short notice? He doesn't explain, as if to test my loyalty—to Arik or to him, to The Land or to our marriage...

It's them or me, his silence said.

"Levi is planning to fly over next month," Dave added, as if Lev was his surrogate—his surrogate Israeli, surrogate pilot, surrogate hero. Is he still testing my loyalty: my son or my husband?

"You'll be flying over with Levi, Dave, right? You two were planning to surprise me..."

"No."

"You've decided to stay in Toronto for Christmas and New Year's alone? Why?"

"Because I have to..." *Have to* and *should*—that's Dave, and that's what he expects from his wife. *Should* be with him at Christmas, *should* live with him in exile till death do us part..., if it hasn't already.

"Dave, I can't see myself staying in Canada, especially when Levi serves his army duty—high risk or not."

"The phone is no place to discuss such matters, Leora."

"Such matters are open to discussion, then."

"Not in my opinion."

That's it. He doesn't like waves, but we can't have everything we want in life, can we? "This may be your last chance to tell me, Dave."

"Is that an ultimatum?"

"No, Dave. I know you don't like ultimatums. But I think it's way overdue that you meet me halfway ..."

"It won't work, Leora ... Going back home is a beautiful dream, but it won't work. I'd move to Israel this minute if I thought this dream of yours wouldn't be one of those that turns to rat-shit when you try to follow up on it ... And if you fail in this, you'll be left with a sense of loss worse, much worse than losing Arik ... You suffered a terrible tragedy when you lost Arik. It's as if you had a terrible accident when you were twenty, and ever since you've been paralyzed, disconnected from your mind—like you are disconnected from Israel ... The sooner you come to grips with that, Leora, the better. You are no different from most of the immigrants who come to Canada ..."

"What?!?"

"For once in your life listen to me, Leora. Your connection is to the people, not to the Nation. If your parents and friends were living in Toronto, we wouldn't be talking about moving to Israel. The day your parents and Arik's die, so will the connection you think you have with The Land."

"I *think* I have?! Next you'll be telling me that your connection with Israel is stronger, more real, than mine."

"I told you we *shouldn't* discuss it over the phone."

"Exactly."

"We'll talk about this another time. Take good care of yourself, Leora. Give my regards to your parents and Arik's ... You better say a few words to Levi now, or he'll be disappointed." And, as always, he passes me on to Lev ...

Oh, I know he is punishing me for being what he wished he was, punishing me for having been born in The Land and not in exile, for having been born to pioneers and not to immigrants, for not knowing the petty skirmishes of Christie Pits, and for going to the desert—the real desert, not the movie desert of *Lawrence of Arabia*. And even for knowing war—real war, not movie war, armchair war ... His favorite line is in *Lawrence of Arabia* where Lawrence asks a Badu why is he doing or not doing something and the Badu replies: *Because it pleases me.* That's it—no apologies, no explanations.

"Because it pleases me" is the line Dave dreams of saying, while he scurries around pleasing everyone and no one, conspiring in the pretense of being a master in his homeland, in Canada ... An unwelcome guest in Canada, he is a paid-up guest in The Land, buying a heritage on the installment plan with his U.J.A. friends. For less than the price of the landing gear of a single Skyhawk, he thinks he has roots that are stronger, more vital, than mine.

I'm paralyzed, he says, making me a mirror of himself ... I'm paralyzed, he says, then he tells me he won't move to The Land because to do so would destroy my dream. He leaves me with no hope, and for my own good, of course. Must take that extra seventh sense of his to see any good in this punishment—of me, of himself.

34

At the beach, Hamsin winds kept blowing from fifty directions and painting the daylight yellow-gray, a dusty shade between dusk and dawn. A ferocious Red Sea mounted the shore, gray walls of water breaking with a thunderous clap, before a white gusher would spike, then foam to the shore.

The tide must have swelled much higher the previous night, leaving behind evidence of the world's abuse of the sea. One of the cleanest, most cared-for shores in the Holy Land looked now like the world's garbage dump. Oil, as far as the eye could see; the wide expanse of fine sand was blackened and littered with pooling tar. And against the black-and-white background was a riot of color: torn plastic garbage bags, fragments of plastic pails or bowls or plates or records; cracked glass, pieces of torn rope, cables, crates, tapes, sweaters, hats, shirts, pants, shoes, belts, buckles; and rusted strips of tin and iron mesh and barbed wire, rusted nails, screws, bolts, locks, even cassette recorders. And shiploads of condoms, and pink and white tampon tubes, tangled in the seaweed among the empty shells and lifeless fish.

The Hamsin drove even the seagulls to seek shelter; not a soul was to be seen there, except a couple of Americans, judging by their accents. She, dressed like a bride left at the altar decades ago, a Miss Havisham, and strumming an untuned guitar that was missing two strings; he, a pot-bellied Swami with bushy gray hair and beard, kept turning like a slow-moving dervish, and wailing in English: "O Messiah, Messiah, Messiah!!! O Messiah, come on!!! Come!! O come already, Messiah, O Messiah!!! ..." The winds scattered her strumming and his wailing among the tar pools, the plastic chips, the condoms, the dead fish ...

✿

Heading to the exit from the beach, I see Tal coming toward me, almost like Arik whenever he appears in those dreams where he seems so real, so alive. I reach out to touch him and, *Poof!* he disappears. So I make no move to even acknowledge that I see Tal, and sure enough he doesn't vanish.

We used the boot scrapers that had been installed on each side of the path to the hotel, as if to make sure that no one would track into the Land any of the shit that the world was dumping on our shore.

His kibbutz classmate, waiting for us at the entrance to the hotel's bar, looked like she had stepped out of a Welcome to Arizona or California poster—long, sun-bleached hair; legs for days; sky-blue eyes; painted-on t-shirt tucked into tight blue jeans that were buckled at her boy-slim hips with a turquoise and silver belt. She was stuck in the sixties, littering her Hebrew with American flower-child words and inflections, and she punctuated almost every sentence with nervous laughter. Shy perhaps, she was even quicker to blush than Tal and me.

Tal treated her with a deference subtle as the echo of a memory—of their child years, perhaps, when he wished he were not a newcomer but, like her, born in the kibbutz. She's a third-generation *kibbutznikit*, he had told me; her grandparents were among the founders of their kibbutz.

Ever since they were in Grade 2, and until they were drafted into the army on graduating from high school, they had shared the same classrooms, dining rooms, dormitories—boys and girls showered together until they were twelve-thirteen, in their kibbutz, he said. "We kibbutz classmates grew up like multiple twins. That's why we rarely if ever intermarry, according to the social experts..."

They communicated in a language of their own. I didn't understand half of what they said to each other, even though it sounded like Hebrew; it reminded me of the first few days in the tents.

"Are you two too stoned to know how you stink, man. I'm surprised they let you sit here," she said, then introduced herself as Dorit and laughed as if desperately fighting a demon determined to reduce her to tears. What had happened to her?

Azzizah would say, "Look at her and you will see what happens when a beautiful girl does not wear amulets to ward off the Evil Eye of Envy."

Tal didn't seem to notice her strange laughter.

A handsome Swiss student, who had probably flown here to dive in the Red Sea but had run out of money, came to wait on our table. Dorit ordered beer.

"Local or export?" the waiter asked her.

"Export," she replied.

"Heineken or Amstel, or ...?" the handsome Swiss student couldn't take his eyes off her.

"Wouldn't it be a groove, man, if that waiter could ask, 'Marijuana or hash? Local or export? Acapulco Gold or Colombian shit'?" Dorit said when the waiter had gone to get our drinks. "What was the Bedouins' dope like?" she asked me, pulling out a tin box of tobacco and rolling herself a cigarette like a Badawia—and an American hippie back in the sixties.

"I didn't see any Bedouin using dope," I replied. "Badu tobacco smells like dope. Maybe that's why people think they smoke dope."

"Oh, come on. They look stoned. I have some great stuff. Would you like a joint?" she asked me. "Tal smoked, you know, only once—hash ... Man, was he hilarious, horny as hell ..."

"Did you two make love?" my eyes ask Tal.

"With Dorit? It would be like making love with my sister," his eyes reply.

Dorit dropped her eyes and blushed, as if our silent exchange had triggered something in her, made her feel like she was Outside. Turning her poster-perfect face away, she said, "*Feh*, what a punishment the stink you two dragged from the desert ... Stinks like Eilat ... What a drag Eilat ..."

What was keeping her in this town, I asked her. I had no idea what a torrent—a flash flood—my question would trigger.

First she laughed, then she said she had escaped to Eilat "because you can save money in Eilat, man. Frontier-town perks, you know ... Like, if you work in Eilat you don't have to give the lousy government half your paycheck in taxes . . . And besides, there isn't a place in The Land farther from the kibbutz than Eilat.

"There isn't a place on Earth, man, more boring than the kibbutz. Nothing to do in the kibbutz, man—just work, eat, sleep, and fuck. The good old days are over, if they ever existed. Man, if you heard my grandmother tell it, you'd think the kibbutz was founded by wild rebels who ran away from home, hiked over continents, came to The Land on foot, man; made love all night, reclaimed The Land all day, and in their spare time they gathered the tribe from all the corners of the globe, and singlehandedly defended their newborn kibbutz against tribes of marauding Arabs . . . Give me a break, man. They stopped making those movies even in Russia. And even if there is a grain of truth in these stories, they're ancient history, man. Like, the kibbutz was an experiment. Okay, the experiment succeeded, the kibbutz was established, and you know what happens to established things, man—they become like institutions, peopled by bureaucrats. That's what kibbutzniks are, man—narrow, petty bureaucrats."

She kept knocking the kibbutz, dumping on her home, Tal's home, their extended family, as if that family—and everyone she knows, including Tal—had tuned out her grating arias years ago, and she was glad to see someone actually touched, disturbed, by her tirade, flabbergasted to hear her say that her grandfather blamed the deterioration of the kibbutz on Hitler . . . "Before his death camps, only dreamers, fiery idealists, adventurers, came to settle up in The Land, in the kibbutz," she said. "But after the death camps, the kibbutz took in any survivor who had no family, no home, and no money to settle in the city. And they, the newcomers who came to settle in the kibbutz, changed it from what my grandfather calls 'an adventurous and daring idealistic experiment' to a boring established institution, man. The newcomers became a majority. They had equal votes, and you know what happens when everyone has an equal vote—like, you know, the lowest common denominator, mistaking conformity for equality, destroys anything different, special, beautiful . . . They want you to

451

be as narrow and boring as they are, man. And if you rebel, they punish you...

"You know, I wanted to study art, man, painting. So I asked for a study grant, because, you know, in the kibbutz we receive no pay for working," she went on to tell me. "You know, a person can loaf through life or work his ass off; it doesn't matter in the kibbutz, man. Each member receives the same allowance, like just cigarette money, you know. So I asked the kibbutz treasurer for a study grant, and what do you know, at the next general meeting that bureaucrat actually introduced my request, and my art teacher told them of my painting talent, but, wouldn't you know, some ass-hole griped that my talent is immaterial; the kibbutz was strapped for funds, and short of hands, and all the young members were serving army duty, others were serving in the Knesset, the labor unions, the city youth movement... Then another shit-shoveling *shmuck*, who wants me to work in the fucking cowshed, says the kibbutz is already supporting more than enough students and artists, poets, musicians, writers...

"Why not me? Man, the shit-heads voted that I have to wait, work in the fucking cowshed until the kibbutz had hands and funds to spare, meaning till I'm too fucking senile to know a paint brush from a hair brush... And then those assholes voted to spend a fucking fortune on a new tennis court, and a new Olympic-size swimming pool, and on plane tickets abroad for kibbutz members with enough seniority to be my parents...

"You were crazy, man, stupid, to give them all your army pay-checks," she said to Tal. What liberties she took; *Wallah*, what amulets Azzizah would prescribe if she were to hear how Dorit bad-mouthed her people and envied city give-me-give-me kids. "Man, you know how city parents support their children even after they leave home. Like, city parents pay their children's university tuition, set them up in business, and, you know, buy them a flat, fur-niture, the works. But when kibbutzniks leave the kibbutz, we get fuck-all, man, and at every home visit someone sticks it to you—'How can you leave when you know how short of hands we are?'

"Tal put so much money into the kibbutz's treasury, he's entitled to a loan, you know. But he's too proud to ask for a bit of a loan to help him find his footing in the city. He can't afford to see a movie, you know," she told me, laughing her disturbed, disturbing laughter.

Tal said nothing, but that didn't appear to be strange to her. He was probably the silent one in their kibbutz class, and didn't find his tongue until the Unit. The army had almost the opposite effect on them. Maybe because there is no elite unit for women in our army, and Dorit is accustomed to belonging to the elite.

Dorit got married to get out of army service, Tal had told me. She couldn't stand the army, he said. "Her luck, Dorit was stuck with officers not half as bright as she is. It nearly drove her crazy, taking orders from them."

They probably didn't defer to her, as Tal did. She couldn't ride on her grandparents' laurels in the army, but had to earn rank. Someone should have prepared her for that.

"Tal had told me you live in Toronto. Did you drive over to California?" she asked me, as if the drive from Toronto to California, like the drive from her kibbutz to Eilat, took less than a day.

"No, I flew to California, like a fat city-tourist," I replied, cracking Tal up.

"That's what I'm saving my money for, man—a one-way ticket to California. *The* place, isn't it?" she asked me, rhetorically. She knows it all, and better than you, she thinks; like a person compelled by demons she extolled exile. "Exile, man, is our homeland. Exile, man, is where we flourish," she said. "No way could Einstein be Einstein in The Land; Chagall, Shalom Aleichem, and Bob Dylan would get assigned to shovel shit in the fucking cowshed here. No accident, man, that Agnon, Buber, and Gershon Shalom were born and raised in exile. And you know, our Talmud was composed in exile, man … And even the Bible, man, some people say was edited, if not written, in exile. Shit, in the Bible itself it says the ten commandments were carved in Sinai, not in The Land.

And where was Moses born and raised? In Egypt, man, yet according to the Bible, no greater prophet had Israel than Moses, right? Man, nothing but wars to secure The Land did we have after Moses, then brothers' wars for the fucking kingdom; Solomon's prick fucked a thousand wives and fucked away the kingdom, man. Next page the temple is destroyed, and we're expelled from The Land, and that's when we started to thrive, man—in exile . . . That's when we discovered Jerusalem serves us best as an ideal, a dream, a symbol, something to strive for, to long for—not to live in, possess. Not for nothing the prayer says: Next year in Jerusalem. *Next year*, man, not this year. This year let the Arabs have The Land; for us it is poison, man, breeds only wars and generals with small hearts and no balls to admit The Land has served its purpose, sheltered the survivors of the death camps. Okay, now it's time to get out of the shelter, man, out of this fucking fortress, and go home where we belong—to California, Paris, New York, and Toronto. Right?" She laughed.

"You wouldn't know it from where I am sitting," I said when her mouth was busy with her Heineken. "We native-born Israelis sit on our suitcases, with one leg in The Land, no matter how many years ago we've dropped out. We *Sabras* don't transplant like immigrants the world over." I felt like I was seven hundred years old, cursed to see generation after generation repeat the same mistake, thinking they know better . . .

"Bullshit," Dorit snapped, and then, in that confident, know-it-all, sheltered Mayflower-child voice of hers, she said, "Our *Sabra* roots are nothing but a brainwashing job. We *Sabras* have no roots. That's what makes us special, unique, man . . . That and being shunned. We Yehudim are like weeds. No need to transplant weeds, no need to transplant us. The Gentiles pull us out of one place, but before they know it we pop up somewhere else . . .

"Tal wanted me to meet you. He thought you'd convince me to stay put in The Land," she said, giving in to her crazy laughter.

"True," his eyes told mine. "Tell her what a mistake dropping out was for you."

Sure, *man*, I thought. I'll pour my heart out to her and she'll blow her crazy laughter in my face, then tell me, "Yeah, man, if it's such a mistake, why don't you move your ass over here for good?" Or she'll tell me, "Sit here without a return ticket to Canada in your pocket, man, and then try to dissuade me from dropping out of the siege, the war, the fortress..."

Dorit wasn't accustomed to being shut out, even for a split second, her nervous laughter said, and she blushed when Tal and I communicated in a glance. Oh, how shut out she'd feel outside The Land. And transient even in The Land. Everyone she knew and loved when she grew up, and everyone she would meet like I did Tal, Hillel, Abu Salim, Azzizah, Tammam, A'ida, Mutt and Jeff... would slip past her life like the lone thorn trees along the highway, a spot of shade far in the wilderness; now you see it, now you don't.

My mind was drifting in a hundred and one directions: to my son packing up to move here, and Dorit packing up to leave; to my parents and how it would hurt them to hear Dorit bad-mouthing The Land, after the price they—and Arik—had paid to defend her freedom to talk her head off. And Dave—I could almost hear him saying, Israelis like Dorit are turning the country into rat shit... Dave can't stand the Israelis who dropped out to Canada—to him I'm not a dropout; his wife lives in Israel even when she's in Canada, he likes to say. Neither he, nor any of his U.J.A. buddies, would hire or socialize with any Israeli dropout. The more a Canadian contributed to the support of Israel, the more he preferred Israelis to be in Israel—to sustain his contribution and support, reaffirm it, validate it, and, of course, appreciate it...

Dorit's father was their history teacher in high school, Tal was saying; her father believed that, in a moment of weakness, desperation, impotence, a tribe—a nation—not unlike a person, is more prone to make a mistake that fucks them up for life: "Staying in exile was *the mistake* in our tribal history, Dorit's father believes."

"But you know I disagree with my father," Dorit said, munching the olives, pickles, peanuts the waiter brought with our second round of drinks.

"You say it just to shock. You know better than to say that exile is where we belong," Tal told her. "You know millions were slaughtered in exile—some, if not many, as gifted as Einstein. They definitely didn't thrive in exile. That one mistake decimated our Nation, scattered us, changed our thinking, destiny, mentality. One mistake, committed two thousand years ago, is still affecting our life—yours, mine—today. If, two thousand years ago, we had regrouped, rearmed, forced our way back into The Land, right after we were expelled, would anyone claim we had no right to live in The Land today?"

"Hey, cool it, man," Dorit said in English, laughing. "You don't have to fire up the troops, you're out of the fucking Unit, remember?" she told Tal, switching back to Hebrew. "Two thousand years ago the Romans were strong, man, and we were broken, defeated, destroyed by our own great hero, Bar Kokhba. Reminds me of our great heroes today..."

"Don't tell me Bar Kokhba destroyed us more than Hitler did." Tal said.

"But, Outside, some of us survived, man. Here, in Masada, we committed suicide—like crazy dope-heads, man—rather than surrender to the Romans," she said. The two of them talked about the Romans and Bar Kokhba like Monday-morning quarterbacks in Canada talk about the football games they watched on TV all day Sunday. In one breath, Dorit was talking about the Romans and suicide at Masada and, in the next breath, she told me, "You cannot imagine how we in the kibbutz trembled for Tal when he served in the army. Like, for ten fucking years, man, we didn't know what he was doing, but we knew Tal would volunteer for any shit-job the army considered vital to our security. Tal would buy that shit, we knew, man...

"*Pheew!*" She fanned herself with the laminated menu, like a lousy movie actress. "You two stink like Arabs, like *Chukh-chukhs*. You are not a *Chukh-chukhit*, are you?" she asked me, straining my tolerance and pity for her.

"No," I replied.

"Ironic, man, isn't it, how these *Chukh-chukhs* who had lived in Arab ghettos for centuries are like the Arabs they hate."

Hate. The demon of hatred hummed in her laughter. Who would have thought a daughter of the kibbutz, raised in the cradle of equality, would be so prejudiced. It seemed as if she had to knock and besmear everyone and everything in The Land to justify her decision to drop out. She smoked her cigarette, her nose up to the ceiling so as not to blow smoke into my face, her long blonde hair swinging from side to side, like the hair of the stranger-girls who "bewitch" Badu youth.

Tammam and Azzizah would be preparing supper now. I could almost smell the cooking fire. Mutt and Jeff would be crouching near it to keep warm, and be at the ready for a well-done pita. And Abu Salim would be coughing, lungs full of TB, fire smoke, and granite-mountain dust. There they were, only a couple of days away from this hotel by Jeep. "Wouldn't it be something if Abu Salim walked into this lobby," I said to Tal.

The lobby, full of tourists and locals now, all bent on having the vacation of their lives, buzzed with false gaiety of a New Year's party—at the Tower of Babel.

"Man, how could you stay with Bedouins?" Dorit said. "I shudder at the sound of Arabic, and the smell, *pheeeww...*"

"You talk of Arabs the way a Jew-hating Gentile will talk of you out west, in California," I told her. She laughed, then said, "I say it like it is, man, not like the hypocrites on the left who say we're all alike, but don't accept *Chukh-chukhs* as members in the kibbutz, let alone Arabs..."

"You don't have *Chukh-chukh* members in your kibbutz?" I ask, and she, delighted to have the chance to murder my innocence, replies, "One—a token *Chukh-chukhit*, blonde in her soul like an Uncle Tom, if you know what I mean. We're better than most, let me tell you. Most kibbutzim don't accept even token *Chukh-chukhs.*"

"Oh, come on," Tal says to her, then to me: "The fact is, *Chukh-chukhs* don't like the kibbutz. They prefer city life, private enterprise... Dorit likes to shock people," he adds, as if I hadn't noticed.

"You hypocrite!" she cried out. "What came first, the chicken or the egg. Man, did the *Chukh-chukhs* prefer city life because the kibbutz rejected them, or did the kibbutz reject them because they are not what the kibbutz would call, 'suited for communal life," she said, angry at him for stealing her weapon, her shock tactics. Then she turned to me and added, "Eilat is full of *Chukh-chukhs*, you know. You can't be a hypocrite here in Eilat, man, or it will cost you, let me tell you … I didn't know a *Chukh-chukhs* from a hole in the ground when I lived in the kibbutz. But here, I live with them, man … I can't stand this place, man. Ever since they got voting power, The Land smells like an Arab country—corrupt, backward, filthy …" She had never stepped into an Arab country but has no doubt what one smells like. It pained Tal, I sensed, to see her—like a sister to him—compelled by demons to hate her family, her people, herself …

That's how Riva would see Dorit—as the very embodiment of *self-hatred*, our tribal disease, a ghetto disease, a victim's disease. It's a tenacious virus that locks you into a vicious cycle: hearts deprived Outside become insatiable at home, and insatiable hearts are bound to feel deprived. But feeling deprived in your own home, with your own family, your tribe? Unbearable the pain, the disappointment, the virulent anger, like Dorit's—hatred with no temperance, without a drop of love—not for others, not for herself.

It's hard to believe that she and Tal grew up in the same kibbutz, shared a room, a life.

Spreads like typhoid, this self-hating virus, Riva would say. Some people catch it and some are spared. Tal was spared, but Dorit—less fortunate, less resilient—was not. Isn't that why she laughs, frantic, desperate, every second breath. Isn't that why she finds life a drag here in The Land, where people pray for a boring moment, a rest from all the "excitement."

Her job—ground hostess of Arkia—is a burden as well. "Boring, boring job," she said. "Kills my fucking face to smile all day." She couldn't understand what attracts tourists to The Land. She couldn't see the beauty or what would interest anyone here. "Nothing special about this place, man," she said, "except the fanatics. Man, what a pain. And the survivors of the death camps are also boring, frankly. Man, how many times can a person hear the same story? And what have I to do with them anyway? I mean, I have more in common with the survivors of Hiroshima. The atom bomb can blow up any minute, but the death camps were a 'Hitler thing'—ancient history, like the Spanish Inquisition... You know, patriotism feeds on such stuff, on yesterday's fires, yesterday's nightmares, yesterday's dreams. Man, patriotism leads to Hiroshima..."

"Your father is not sitting here, Dorit," Tal muttered.

She laughed and rolled another cigarette, then, turning to me, she said, "You know my father has a thing about Hiroshima and the Shoah. He wonders if the two were not connected—if the hate directed at us did not lead directly to Hiroshima. If we Yehudim are sort of the barometer of the world conscience, you know. Look at how the world treats us Yehudim and you will see a preview of how the world will treat itself... Neat, right? My parents are all right, man; they realized their dream, but that doesn't mean I have to continue it, keep their dream going. Right? They did their thing, man, and I'm doing mine."

"What is your thing?" I ask her.

"To enjoy life," she replies. "Like the art of life, you know, the music, the go-with-the-flow, letting-go, letting-be, have an open mind, open heart to the universe, the cosmos, man..." She laughs, but the sarcasm is only a veneer.

Who is she bullshitting? Me? Tal? Herself? Or is she trying to shrug off not only the ghetto and the blue-and-white heritage that her parents had loaded on her, but history itself? To be her own woman and submit to the moment—not to Fate, God, Tribe, or Man, and not to any Liberation Movement. Is that why she knocks everything, to cut herself off from anything imposed on her ever since the days of Eve, even the pull of love, union, of her womb? Is that the demon who hides in her laughter?

Good thing I was wearing gold to ward off the evil eye of envy; I so envied her for taking her birthright for granted; I so envied her for feeling she owes nothing to the living or the dead, for taking for granted even the freedom to choose her own fucking nightmares, as Arik would say, paraphrasing his beloved Conrad...

"Best thing that happened to you, leaving the kibbutz and heading to the desert like that. I never thought you had it in you," she said to Tal, as we were about to leave. "I've never seen him like this," she said to me, giving us more of her crazy laughter. She obviously meant it as a compliment to me, to Tal, as if love was an achievement.

❧

Kilometer after kilometer, straight as a ruler, the Arrava road rolled under the Jeep. There was hardly any traffic for hours, and the high beams kept battling back the darkness. Then, the headlights picked out hands waving, begging us to pull to a stop—to offer help? A lift? It was the middle of the night, in the middle of nowhere, one or two kilometers west of the Jordanian border.

"Might be an ambush," Tal muttered, pulling up into the darkness between us and the waving hands. He loaded the Beretta and tucked it in his belt. "Stay in the Jeep," he ordered me. But I climbed out with him. The sky was alive with stars. Let me not die on a night like this. Another breath and another step, and then we find two couples—middle-aged tourists.

"Do you speak English?" one of them says in an American voice.

"Yes," I reply.

"Oh, thank God. Sorry to trouble you," says their spokesman, who then explains that the hood of their rented Fiat keeps flipping up. The lock is probably jammed. Could we lend them a pair of pliers. The car-rental people had neglected to supply tools.

Tal hands me the flashlight and whispers in Hebrew, "Fetch the toolbox... I don't want you to stay here alone with them."

"They look all right, Tal."

"That's why it's called an ambush," he tells me.

I fetch the toolbox, and it takes him about a minute to free their jammed lock. He tests it a couple of times to make sure.

The tourists say they can't thank us enough. One of them offers Tal a ten-dollar tip.

"No, it's all right. Have a safe journey," Tal says to them in English.

". . . Just a token of our appreciation," says one of the tourists, handing me a pack of Marlboros.

"Hand it back to him. It might be a booby-trap," Tal says to me in Hebrew.

But I keep the pack, thank the tourists, then I walk to the Jeep. Just before Tal catches up to me, before we climb into the Jeep, I toss the pack into the night, as far as I can, away from the road, the tourists, the Jeep, and I brace myself.

Tal gives me a look and shakes his head. The dashboard dials tint his face green, the color of bounty, generosity, vitality.

"I was afraid that pack would explode," I explained.

"So why did you accept it?" he said.

"I don't know. It didn't feel right to be so on guard, suspicious, uncertain . . ."

"It better feel right," he said, switching on the ignition, pressing ahead. "It's all right to forget the wave of terror in Sinai, but, here in The Land, you'd better remember the Arabs who aim to blow up the peace talks. Beware, Leora, whenever you purchase a loaf of bread, a carton of milk, eggs, cigarettes, and whenever you open a letter or a book, or pass by a bicycle. One exploded in Mahaneh Yehudah, a couple of weeks ago, killing a few, injuring many . . ."

The darkness parted for the high beams, and sitting passive in the passenger seat for kilometers was so bewitching, I couldn't fight my yawns, my drooping eyelids.

"Let me drive for a while, Tal. It will keep me awake. I don't want to fall asleep now; it's the best part of the night—the part where you can almost see how to stop wandering in the wilderness and go home—or up to Nebo, at least . . ."

"At least?" He laughed, as if a glimpse of the promised land before you die was the most. Raising his voice over the roar of the engine, he said, "Close your circles and part from Arik, and you will be a dropout even if you return here, to The Land. That's what sets you apart, your open circles. They spur you on to settle for nothing less than Nebo, at least..."

It was one of those nights in The Land when there is no horizon, no line dividing heaven from earth, when the old moon dies and the new is born, when the heat of the desert courts and wins the cold night wind.

⚹

At the Service station by Ein Gedi, not a far distance from the fork: Jerusalem, Beer Sheba, while the Jeep was refilled, I tried again the number Russell had left with my mother. It connected me to an army base. He had been called unexpectedly for reserve duty, Russell explained. Then quick-fast, as if he had but a minute to talk he went "straight to the point," as he put it: he couldn't leave the base and had no way of conveying "two words of utmost importance "to a Negev Badu nomad named Awaad who will be waiting for him at the Hebron–Beer Sheba road tomorrow morning, 'wouldn't take more than an hour out of your way, if that, to convey two words to this Negev Badu, Awaad: stay put."

And now, before I could utter a word in response, Russell went on to fill my ears with rumor after rumor about Awaad's clan and the authorities, theirs, ours... all of which I found hard to believe, as did Russell. And yet he maintained, "the chances that the wrong done here would be converted into a wedding celebration are slim to none." That's the only reference Russell made to the rumor he had withheld from me—in my former life... or so it felt.

"Awaad's is a fugitive clan..." Russell knew it for a fact. "And there is also no doubt that a fire engulfed their tents and their belonging stored inside... They are proud Badu, but if you can spare another hour, Leora, stop at the store just a few kilometers before the meeting point with Awaad and buy a ten- or twenty-kilo sack of flour and same of rice, and a case or two of baby formula, bottles, nipples..." Russell had to say no more to catapult Awaad's fugitive clan, from the realm of the Other to the home

462

compound—Abu Salim's, Azzizah's, Tammam's—devastated by a fire that engulfed ancient treasures, bequeathed from *jil-el-jil*— generation after generation—welcome-carpets, camel saddles, tents Azzizah has been weaving day in day out, through all the days of her life, from wool she spun and hair of goats she raised … and healing potions made of leaves Azzizah had sweated to collect in treacherous canyons and cliffs … and dresses, veils, shawls, exquisitely embroidered by Azzizah and Tammam … and Tammam's most precious possession, the only possession strict nomadic law allowed Tammam and her mother to own, bequeath, and inherit: her mother's tent—touching it felt like touching her mother who died birthing her … Didn't take much to imagine Tammam's milk running dry, and little Salimeh's cries of hunger in a compound scorched to ashes …

35

Whatever I wished I had brought to Azzizah and Tammam, I purchased now for Awaad's clan.

The load slowed the Jeep, and when we reached the Hebron–Beer Sheba Road, the morning traffic forced us to a crawl; so, where we had counted on gaining time, time gained on us.

Awaad would have left before we arrived, we thought. But, as we approached the meeting place that Russell had specified on the phone, we saw a black *abaiah* arranged like a puptent. We coasted to a stop. Still, we startled the Badu.

His bloodshot eyes, full of sleep, stared at us as if seeing a pair of *djinn*-demons from a bad dream; his hands fumbled and his *kaffiyye* slipped to the ground, revealing dusty clumps of wooly black hair laced with straw. His dark stubble, like weeds that colonize a ruin, evoked not only a sense of loss, sorrow, and neglect, but also the memory of a face that had once been full of life. For the past week or two, he had probably slept in the jacket, shirt, and slacks he was wearing. The jacket and slacks had either shrunk in the wash or been borrowed from a shorter man. His scuffed, dusty army boots were laced only halfway, and probably before dawn, when it was still too dark to see that his socks were mismatched.

A Negev Badu was bound to know a word or two of Hebrew. But this Badu didn't seem to understand a word of Tal's greeting. And sure enough, after a brief exchange in Badu Arabic, he told me he had never heard of a man called Awaad or El Bofessa.

Whoever this Badu was, he had been waiting for hours in this spot to meet Russell, Tal's gut feeling insisted, whatever this Badu claimed. But he did not wave or call us back, as Tal thought he would, when we were about to drive away.

Up and down and around this spot we drove. We saw no sign of another Badu. We must have burned half a tank driving around, searching for Awaad. And we were starting to check our watches.

By three o'clock that afternoon, at the very latest, we had to be back in Tel Aviv and the Jeep had to be available for army duty or inspection. And only when we had no time to spare did Tal agree to check the spot that Russell had mentioned on the phone, one last time. Sure enough, the Badu was still sitting there.

With silence this Badu parried my questions. "*Wallah*, he is a true Arab," Abu Salim would say. "True Arabs trust no strangers—write-to-remember, *yaa*-Nura: all questions from the mouths of strangers must be parried with silence or agile words. For to give information to a stranger is to hand him a *shibriyya*—dagger. He might admire the *shibriyya's* handsome handle. Or he could, with its sharp edge, pierce your honor, and then your whole tribe would be bathed in shame. Such dishonor must be avenged…"

"It would be a shame if we would fail to meet with Awaad, very soon," I told the Badu, "for we have to leave for Tel Aviv in an hour's time, and the Jeep is loaded with provisions for Awaad's clan, even medicaments," I had to show him the sacks and the cartons and the bundles of the winter clothes, before he agreed to climb into the front seat of the Jeep. And even then the Badu said only that he could try to find an Arab who knows most everyone who dwells in the vicinity.

Trust begets trust, I muttered to Tal in Hebrew. Doesn't work with Arabs, said Tal. Still, he blindly followed the Badu's directions: Not a word did the Badu offer to explain why he was directing the Jeep, not through the dry riverbed, but up to the high ground, as if he feared a flood would flash through the wadi any second when the sky was innocent. The high ground, heaving like a wounded beast, was scabbed with boulders, and so torn by floodwaters, the Jeep nearly rolled over more than once or twice too often. The Badu skipped out of the Jeep—"For to better find a safer path," he said. "For to destroy the Jeep," Tal muttered. "The Badu is wasting his sweat, though; the Jeep is taking the high ground like a seasoned commando beast."

Hill after hill the Jeep groaned, dove, climbed, and tilted from side to side. And the Badu, walking ahead, kept looking for the

Arab who knows everyone in the vicinity, and calling out his name. But the hills seemed to be deserted. There was no response, not even an echo.

Then, suddenly, a man appeared—from nowhere, it seemed; a Badu or an Arab, I couldn't tell, nor could Tal. As soon as the Jeep crawled over to him, the Arab disappeared as he had appeared—into nowhere.

Tal pressed the brake but left the motor running. "Today's terrorists have learned to appear and disappear like that from yesterday's smugglers and raiders," he explained when the Badu vanished as well. Five minutes later he sounded the horn, non-stop, until the Badu reappeared—alone, gesturing for the Jeep to follow him. We followed without question, even though the Badu was leading us deeper and deeper into what Tal called terrorists' breeding ground. Tal had loaded his Beretta and tucked it into his belt long before the Badu met the Arab.

The terrorists' breeding ground looked like ghost pasture land, so ravaged by drought and plundered clean that there was not even the smell of a rotten morsel to draw a bird of prey.

And the sun was already high enough to erase colors, shadows, and depth. One hill looked like another to me, and Tal—I had never seen Tal coiled so tight.

"We are turning back if we don't see Awaad's compound from the crest of the upcoming hill," Tal decided, but when the wadi below the next hill was also bare of tents, he didn't quit. And like the Badu, Tal kept saying, "This next hill is the last."

It was when the Jeep crawled to the crest of the hill after "the last . . . and this time I mean it . . ." that we finally did see a compound of six or eight tents made of sackcloth, pitched at the foot of the swelling hill on the opposite bank of the dry riverbed. Tal stopped the Jeep and, looking like he couldn't believe what he was seeing, snapped at the Badu, "What in the hell is going on!"

But the Badu was running like hell to the compound.

"What did you see, Tal?" I yelled over the noise of the engine, as the Jeep dived downhill, right after the Badu. The compound bounced with the Jeep, then it blended with the sun-bleached boulders and rocks in the shimmering distance.

I didn't know how good Tal's eyesight was until we drove into the compound and found the tents deserted. Not a soul in sight, yet cooking-fires burned. That certainly didn't look right.

It didn't seem to surprise the Badu, though. "The stupidity of women knows no bounds," he said in Badu Arabic. Then he went on to explain that often when a child-shepherd finds a few goats missing from the herd, and fears his mother will beat him for his negligence, he runs back to the tents, crying such tears of woe that all the women in the compound lose their heads. "Sometimes they even forget to take their infants with them before they run to see if the whole herd is lost or injured," said the Badu. "You can be sure that if even one man was in the compound he would not leave the fires burning."

As soon as I started to translate his words for Tal, the Badu went to look for the women and children, or so it appeared.

Reality by now seemed to slither and change skins like a snake. One minute the Badu was Awaad, next minute he was not; *abaiah*—cloaks—appeared and disappeared into shimmering terrorists' breeding grounds; fires were smoldering in tents abandoned only ten-fifteen minutes ago, by the looks of it. And the wind carries sound a great distance in these barren hills, like in the desert, yet there was no sound of women, children, or goats. The only sound we heard is the Badu shouting, "Awaad!! Awaad!"

"The tent dwellers must have heard our Jeep before they abandoned their compound," I said to Tal. "They would have left someone behind if they needed access to a Jeep, and they are bound to know that a Jeep gallops faster than a camel. Even Badawias isolated in forbidden tents know that."

"You sound like a Badu tracker," said Tal. "What do you make of this?"

"I'd say these Badu left their compound because they couldn't or didn't want to receive guests. But Badu who don't want to receive guests cover their fires with sand or gravel, leave no clues that they were here but don't want or can't afford to extend hospitality."

Most tents were almost bare and just swept clean. A sackcloth was spread like a welcome-carpet next to each fire. The water jerricans were half-full, and the cooking utensils and serving trays stacked on the bare ground had just been washed, but not the tea glasses, and the flies knew where the sugar was stored. The knots in the flour sacks were tied low, and only two or three tents had a bit of rice, a few onions and cans of tomato paste, and goatskin bags of clarified butter that weighed next to nothing.

The tent dwellers—half prepared to pack up and leave, and half prepared to stay—were drinking tea when suddenly all of them took off. Why? Where?

The tents offered no clue.

Their water source was nowhere in sight. As far as the eye could see there was no trace of a tree, a bush, or a shrub to feed a fire or a goat.

And now, just as the Badu came running back, shouting a torrent of I couldn't understand what, in a cloud of dust a camel-rider galloped into the compound. A handsome Badu in his late teens or early twenties, wearing a red *kaffiyye*, blue jeans, and yellow t-shirt. He dismounted, rushed over to our Jeep, gave it a quick once-over, ignoring or not hearing the torrent of words the Badu who had led us to this compound was spewing faster than floodwaters.

The camel-rider took a close look at one of the fire-circles, and kicked another. Whatever the Badu told him annoyed the camel-rider, or so it seemed. "I heard you … I heard you …" he muttered to the Badu, as he walked over to us.

"Let's go, unload the Jeep. I heard you are pressed for time," he said to Tal and me in Hebrew. But it was the air about him, not only his Hebrew, his manner, his attitude, that breathed of familiarity—of home and trust.

"Yes. Three hours from now at the latest, this Jeep has to show up for reserve-duty or an army checkup at a base near Tel Aviv," said Tal.

"You are cutting it close," said the camel-rider, unbolting the back door of the Jeep, as if he couldn't wait to unload the provisions, see us leave—Why?

"Is this Awaad's compound?" Tal asked him.

"Yes," replied the camel-rider.

"Are you of Awaad's clan?" I asked him next.

"No. I'm of Awaad's tribe," said the camel-rider. "My name is Jum'ah," he added, extending his hand, his handshake solid.

"Is he Awaad or of Awaad's clan?" Tal asked Jum'ah—meaning "Friday"—pointing to the Badu who kept pacing back and forth at the tent farthest from us, by the Jeep.

"Are you Awaad or of Awaad's clan?" Jum'ah shouted to the Badu.

"*Laaa*—No!!!" the Badu shouted back.

"Did you happen to see anyone from this compound on your way here?" I asked Jum'ah next.

"No," he said.

"The tent dwellers can't be very far from here if their fires are not yet dead," said Tal. "Shouldn't take long to track them down, don't you think?" he asked Jum'ah.

"I'm not as fast a tracker as I was before I served as commanding officer, first lieutenant in the Engineering Corps," said Jum'ah, pulling out of his wallet an Israeli army ID card, as if we had to see it to believe that a Badu—a true Arab—could have the rank of a commanding officer in an army known to have the highest ratio of commanders per soldier. None ranked higher than Jum'ah, you'd think, had you seen how he beamed with pride. It was such a rare and hard-earned achievement; a personal and tribal feat; a triumph over decades of tribal animosity, mistrust and prejudice; a personal leap over centuries of illiteracy. "You didn't see many ID cards like this one," said Jum'ah.

"No, I haven't. All honor to you," said Tal. Then, while we unloaded the Jeep, Jum'ah told us that he was stationed up north at our border with Lebanon, and that the situation up there was such a mess, he couldn't wait for his furlough, but when it finally came and he returned home, he remembered that he had to defer to his elders even more than to his army commanders. So he took off on one of the family camels to get away from it all.

"In these hills?" said Tal.

"No. I was on my way to the Judean Desert," said Jum'ah, and then he talked about the desert, and about the drought, and about... I don't remember what else. On and on Jum'ah babbled about everything without any prodding from us. But not a word did he volunteer about the mystery that stared us in the face—live fires in a ghost compound.

Jum'ah certainly had a clue to this mystery by now, or he would have been searching for one. I had no doubt about that. If we asked him why he wouldn't share it with us, we'd be sure to offend him, if not alienate him altogether. He might want us to treat him as our equal, but treat a Badu—a true Arab—as an equal, and he thinks you treat him as your inferior. You have to elevate him or he thinks you reduce him. So you have to lay it on thick when you jack him up, make an ass of yourself—and of him. It robs you both of dignity.

We didn't press Jum'ah to answer any question he obviously didn't want to, or couldn't, touch. We trusted he was as straight with us as his umpteen conflicting loyalties allowed him to be.

The provisions we unpacked made such a large heap on the ground, it was hard to believe they had all fit in the Jeep. Jum'ah was still huffing and puffing from the effort of unloading the Jeep while talking almost without a breather, when he volunteered to escort us to the main road.

"One of us had better stay here until Awaad or someone of Awaad's clan shows up," I said to Jum'ah. "We were dispatched to this compound by a good friend of Awaad's with information we had been instructed to impart to no one but Awaad or someone of Awaad's clan," I explained. "I wish you were of Awaad's clan..."

"So do I... I understand your bind," said Jum'ah. This bind was probably child's play to him... God knows how many loyalties tugged him in different directions—loyalties to his Badu elders, his Israeli commanders; his old world, his new world...

Now Jum'ah walked over to the Badu, who was pacing in front of the tent farthest from us. If Jum'ah doesn't persuade the Badu to tell us that he is Awaad, then this Badu is not Awaad, Tal and I decided. But no matter what we decided, we couldn't shake the feeling that this Badu is Awaad, even when Jum'ah came out of that conference to tell Tal, "seems we have no options, but to split up. That Badu will drive with you to the main road. I'll stay here with Leora, back her up until she gets on a bus or a cab in Beer Sheba, tonight or early tomorrow at the latest."

"We have another option," I said. "We can track Awaad's people. It shouldn't take all that long. The Jeep will report for reserve-duty a bit late."

"And Jum'ah also will report for duty whenever it suits him, as will everyone else," said Tal. "The only other option we have is to retreat without completing this mission. Awaad will get his information another time, from someone else." Tal wouldn't venture into these West Bank hills for this mission again. Neither would I. But neither of us would retreat now, like frightened strangers, from this or any place in The Land.

"That Badu doesn't have to escort me to the main road," Tal said to Jum'ah.

"He doesn't want you to escort him!" Jum'ah shouted to the Badu.

Swearing and cursing, the Badu rejoined us to demand Tal give him a ride back to the place we had found him on the main road.

Tal agreed, then asked Jum'ah if he had any reservations about staying to back me up.

"Don't worry. Everything will be all right," Jum'ah said to us, looking as edgy as we felt.

It didn't occur to any of us that Tal should be the one to stay and I the one to drive away. If only we had known how unfortunate this would prove to be ...

36

As soon as Tal and the Badu left, Jum'ah started to follow the tracks that led from the tents. Jum'ah kept running in one direction, then another, as if he couldn't decide which tracks to follow. Then, suddenly, he dashed out, shouting at the top of his voice. I followed him until my lungs quit. The distance between us was wide when I saw black figures—a group of Badawias or maidens—running away from him, then running toward him; back and forth, back and forth.

Even after they reached their compound, they ran and paced back and forth—ten, fifteen Badawias and maidens clutching wailing infants, and with whimpering children trailing behind them. Back and forth, back and forth, as if torn between courage and fear. Their bloodshot eyes darting from one direction to another, their *thowbs* reeking of that unmistaken smell of fear. And their veils, hanging in disarray below their faces and their braids, revealed their lips—blue, as if frozen, though the sun was relentless. Back and forth, back and forth, talking as fast as they paced, a compulsive torrent of words through chattering teeth, all at once. Then a Badawia wearing a nose ring like Azzizah's—a silver half-crescent—their leader, it seemed, started to curse. Following her they raced from tent to tent, to my Jeep, to the tire tracks, then round and around the heap of provisions we had stacked on the ground.

"She brought them," Jum'ah told them, pointing to me. Then again and again he asked their leader, "What happened? What happened?"

"Sit-stay, coffee will soon be served," muttered the Badawia, like a robot programmed to receive guests. "Fetch this, fetch that ...," she told the maidens and the children, then something about goats, I think; she was talking so fast that even Jum'ah couldn't understand what she said.

"They're not accustomed to be so overpumped with adrenalin," Jum'ah muttered in Hebrew. I don't know if he was angry because it pained him or shamed him to see women and children of his tribe so afraid, or if he meant to fight fear with fear. But he nearly threw them into a panic—berating, warning, demanding these Badawias tell him what happened to "rob you of your *adabb*— nobility, character, dignity."

They huddled shivering and sweating as if they couldn't decide if it was winter or summer, let alone if Jum'ah was their guest, or the master of their compound and destiny. Before he became more annoyed or downright mean with them, the Badawias urged a maiden they called the poetess to "*Ghule, ghule*—tell him—what happened, tell him the Jeep was green... the Jeep was green."

"Green is no longer the color of bounty," the maiden said. That's all.

"Green is no longer the color of bounty, meaning... meaning... meaning, what?" Jum'ah demanded, like a Badu after a poem recited. "I am your tribesman," he added.

The Badawias' leader tried to explain. But neither Jum'ah nor I understood what she was saying until she clamped her fists to her jaw to stop her teeth from chattering.

"We thought the Jeep was colored green," she muttered, as if that explained it all.

"Yes, the Jeep *was*—is—colored green. Many Jeeps are spray-painted green," Jum'ah snapped as if he thought their fear stemmed from their ignorance, superstitions, backwardness.

"*Wallah*, we are but women," the Badawias' leader said, shifting from leg to leg, as if the earth under her bare feet was packed with snow or with smoldering coals. "We heard the Jeep, when it was far, far in the far distance. But we knew the Jeep was green... Not only because the Jeep sounded like the *green Jeeps* of the *Green Patrol*, but also because shadows were shrinking and not a man was in the compound. For that is when the Green Patrol had visited our home compound in the Negev—twice before."

"Twice before, *Wallah*," the others tremored behind her, like a chorus in a Greek tragedy.

"Yes, twice before," the Badawias' leader said to Jum'ah, quickly as if she feared he'd stop her before they were exonerated. "The first time the Green Patrol had visited our home-compound, they went on to round up nearly all the goats of all the herds owned by our clan. And just when the herds were rounded up in our home compound, a truck arrived to cart the goats away. I swear our clan had paid the ransom money that the Green Patrol demanded for our goats, *Wallah*. The Green Patrol has surely spent our ransom money, we thought the second time we heard the green Jeeps of the Green Patrol; that is why again the Green Patrol comes to round up and cart away our herds.

"But the second time, the Green Patrol blew into our home compound like a wind, *Wallah*. Like the wind, the Green Patrol collapsed the tent poles in our compound, but in such a way that the tents fell on the fires burning in front. It took the fire but a moment to swallow a tent that takes a woman three years to weave, *yaa-Rabb* ...

"And fed by the tents, the fire tongues rose and spread to swallow our provisions also, and our clothes as well. Only two carpets the Green Patrol had allowed us to salvage from the fires. That is why we all are weaving new carpets and new tents ...

"Today, also, we were going to weave on the hill where we do our weaving, when we heard the Jeep. And because the sun was high and no man was in the compound, we thought the Jeep was green. But because each time the Green Patrol had punished us more than the time before, *ya'ni*—that is, first they carted away our herds, next they destroyed our homes—we thought this time it would be our children's turn, if not our maidens', or even us women's. Therefore, quick-fast, we did not pause even to put out the fires before we escaped and went into hiding. We did not think it safe to leave our hiding-place until we heard the Jeep leaving our compound. We fled like senseless goats, perhaps, and perhaps like senseless goats we *baa* and tremble now. But that is how the Green Patrol had reduced us, I swear, *Wallah*."

"Yes, I heard you...," Jum'ah muttered as if his eyes, his blood, told him it was not just a story to spice up life; his tribeswoman would not be that afraid if it was just a story. But his head insisted it was unbelievable, it made no sense.

The curse of Arab curses: *Yakhrab beitak*—May your house be destroyed—the punishment of punishments: Nothing less than that was the destruction of their homes, the burning of their tents.

It was hard to believe that the Green Patrol would be a party to such a curse. Men like Tal and Hillel serve in the Green Patrol. That's why Russell had wondered if Awaad had not been stretching the truth when he had accused the Green Patrol of setting fire to his tents. There was little doubt, though, Russell told me on the phone last night, that the Green Patrol had harassed Awaad and his clan, but neither Awaad nor Russell knew why.

"We would be safe here in these desolate West Bank hills, we were told, the Badawias' leader continued. But with the Green Patrol you can never tell. *Aywa*—yes—green is no longer the color of bounty. Green is the color of misfortune, *Wallah*, of exile, *yaa-Rabb*, of despair. Our men would be too proud to tell it to you. But now that you heard it, tell one and all in our tribe—not how powerless our men, but how powerful the Green Patrol. Tell them also that we are scraping the bottom of the well here, and that we have nowhere else to go, and that we long to return to our home grounds in the Negev."

Her voice kept rising as, overhead, a pair of fighter were taking a dive that looked like it would end in a crash right there in the compound. The Badawias, and even the children, reacted like city people do to traffic noise. And when the jets shot up and out of sight, the Badawias and the children laughed at Jum'ah and me like city people do at country hicks.

"There is nothing to fear," their leader said, her fearful eyes addressing mine. "Nothing to fear," she was saying when I was thinking of Arik, and of Levi, diving in one of these jets... and for what? "Nothing to fear," she was saying. "Nothing to fear... the pilots practice like that every day, but not once did they drop a shell or a bomb outside the fire zone..."

Whatever they dropped, the pilots dropped it so low that it had no time to whistle; it didn't take long for the air to be full of what smelled like burning rubber or tar.

"Napalm," Jum'ah whispered to me, as if he didn't want the children to know their compound smelled of a weapon he considered to be unclean—a weapon that smelled of jungle warfare, Vietnam, wasted lives, abuse of power, and defeat. Or perhaps he whispered because he felt that he and I were bound now by what we were witnessing—and by shared culpability.

"I can't understand why *we've* been that rough on Awaad's clan, can you?" Jum'ah asked me in Hebrew.

I don't know if he said *we* because Badu also serve in the Green Patrol; or because he—like Russell—thought that his sheikh might be in collusion with the Green Patrol; and he, Jum'ah, believed in tribal responsibility, collective guilt, blame—and maybe punishment as well, as Badu have for centuries, and Awaad's clan to this day.

Yet not one person of Awaad's compound lumped me in with the Green Patrol. Badu may wait a hundred years to avenge. But Awaad's people, I think, separated the individual from the tribe, not only because their clan was small and powerless, or because they themselves were separated from their tribe, but because a human being has a deep need to have faith in human kind—such a deep need that Awaad's people believed the Green Patrol were only an instrument of fate ... that's what Jum'ah and I were to discover later.

"Nothing to fear, the smell, the smoke, the heat will soon drift away," the Badawias' leader, her eyes bulging with fear and her voice quivering, muttered to me.

"We'd better declare this area off-limits, or move this target-practice range somewhere else, before pilot error incinerates Awaad's people," Jum'ah added between spells of coughing. A rush of heat in wake of the explosion burned the oxygen out of the air.

Jum'ah didn't snap at the Badawias now when he told them that I have traveled a long and far distance to bring provisions for them, and information for Awaad.

"Allah shall reward her," the huddle muttered, Badu-proper, still sweating in fear of my green Jeep.

"Sit-stay. Awaad will soon return..." the Badawias' leader said. The others started to help her clean her tent. "But first, brew tea and coffee," said one, and then they couldn't decide whether they should wash up first, or collect the carpets they were weaving on the hill first, or collect the goats...

They were pumping the brakes. Fear, like a stalled car pushed downhill, gains a tremendous momentum that propels us all, governing our actions and emotions, dreams and thoughts, like an immutable law. We Yahod have shared the Badawias' momentum for centuries, rushing headlong down a preordained path of old habits, customs, and beliefs that most of us had left in the ghetto, and new ones not yet clearly defined. The Badawias, too, were being carried beyond their old ways—their way of life, their rituals and ceremonies, even their submission to fate or to Allah.

They submitted, it seemed, but like Sunday drivers facing a hill too steep for them—with the same sort of desperate readiness. I could see it as they attacked their chores with a frenzy bordering on panic.

Gone was their Badu time ever-lasting, gone was their gliding Badawia composure. Gone was also their suspicion and distrust of strangers. Up until now, I believed that defenses go up when you feel threatened, that you even develop a seventh sense, like Dave. But here I was learning that the opposite holds true—that fear overrides defenses. *Le'havdil*—there's no comparison—yet here I began to understand how defenseless my clan was in the pogroms, and how the grandparents I wished I'd known, and the uncles, aunts, and cousins I knew only from stories, had smelled in the boxcars rolling toward the death camps... how even the wise and the clever ones in my father's family, and my mother's, couldn't see that they would not be spared... and how it could happen that basic survival instincts—fight or flight—didn't work for millions...

By sunset, the Badawias were all kohled and veiled, their clothes washed and dry, their children bathed and combed, their herds rounded up and fed, the provisions I had brought divided. Rice was bubbling on cooking fires, pitas were being prepared. Jum'ah and I were sitting on a welcome-carpet when "our" Badu, the one Tal and I were certain was Awaad, returning with the men, walked past the compound.

"Awaad!" the Badawias' leader called after him.

"Go fetch him," she told her children when he didn't turn even his head back, but the children, sensing his anger, pretended not to hear her.

His anger permeated the whole compound.

Only the infants dared utter a sound during supper. The serving trays were nearly empty when Awaad, looking furious with Jum'ah, joined the fire-circle—his fire-circle and the Badawias' leader, his wife's. Jum'ah rose to his feet and walked to the darkness beyond the rim of the firelight.

"You offended him ... offended our guest," Awaad's wife muttered—to Awaad, herself, her children—I couldn't tell.

Fire shadows danced on his furious face when he started to eat the leftovers, and she started to roast honor-coffee. As soon as the others heard the *daqq-daqq-daqq* of coffee beans being pounded to fine powder, they started to drift from their fire-circles to Awaad's.

"Drop the curtain," Awaad ordered his wife. A minute later, a burlap flap divided their tent into two sections; then, two separate coffee fires were built and lit, one outside the front of each section. The men and the children gathered around the fire-circle in the men's section; the Badawias, the maidens, huddled inside the women's section, where the place of honor, at the opening, close to the fire and away from the smoke, was reserved for me.

"It's been a long time since we had a woman-guest," Awaad's wife explained. But soon after I folded my legs on her welcome-carpet, Awaad ordered his wife to dispatch me to his fire-circle. She grunted and grumbled under her veil, then told me, "You'll rejoin us later. The fire-circles are not far apart. Sit facing us women and it will be like you are sitting with us."

Jum'ah didn't join the fire-circle. His cigarette glowed in the darkness, though he could not help but see Awaad serving coffee-honor to make a *sulha*—a forgiveness. The delicate porcelain cup he handed to me Awaad left half-empty, in recognition of my generosity and to preserve his dignity. I sipped two such cups, then, after the third, I shook the empty cup and rested it upside down on the ground, just as Abu Salim had taught me.

"*Ghule*—tell us—what El Bofessa had told you to tell us," Awaad said. He couldn't wait now, it seemed. Neither he nor I acknowledged in any way the hours he wasted in the runaround he'd given Tal and me all morning. His face fell when I strung a long string of regards-blessings from Russell. The longer the string, the worse the news, Awaad obviously knew, as did the others around the fire-circle. One by one, the men asked me to relay to El Bofessa, his wife, his children, their regards and blessings, and the women also, from behind the burlap curtains, one by one. But when the maidens started, Awaad snapped, "*Bas*—enough."

Silence. Jum'ah lit another cigarette. Its glow was now so far into the darkness I could hardly see it.

"*Ba'ad idhnak*—with your permission, I will cassette-record for El Bofessa to hear," I broke the silence.

"You have my permission," Awaad snapped. He waited until I pressed the record button, then he exclaimed, "Oh, El Bofessa, a hawk to his friends, in support of them will run over fire, even flames..."

"Now, say what El Bofessa had dispatched you to tell ... *ghule*—tell," Awaad urged me.

"El Bofessa is serving reserve duty," I said. "That is why he dispatched me to inform you that you are to stay here. For he fears the Green Patrol will confiscate the remainder of your herds if and when you return to your home ground in the Negev."

"*Laaa*!—No!" protested the Badawias.

"But I thought the man in charge of the Green Patrol was El Bofessa's friend," Awaad said. "Surley El Bofessa told his friend, the head man of the Green Patrol, that we are scraping the bottom of the well here, and that our tents are pitched too close to a fire zone, a target-practice range ... And that we have no other place to go ..."

"Oh, life, who has sat me down square on hot ashes, why have you dashed me this way!!" implored a Badawia from the women's section of the tent.

"I am sure El Bofessa asked his Green Patrol friend why is he so bent on confiscating our goat herds," said the Badu with the hollowed cheeks, addressing me.

"'It is against the law to own goats in the Negev,' that is what the man in charge of the Green Patrol had told El Bofessa," I said. An infant, crying, startled the other infants in the women's section. Veils and necklaces *jingle-jangled* as they do when Badawias uncover the nursing slits of their *thowbs*.

"You mean all the goats the Negev over are illegal?" asked the Badu sitting to the right of Awaad.

"But surely El Bofessa told his Green Patrol friend that we Negev Badu have been raising goats for more years than a man can count, *Wallah*," said Awaad. "Surely El Bofessa told his friend that we Badu cannot live without goats. What will we sacrifice for the holy days? For honor of guests? For the sealing of marriage? How will a man purchase a bride if he has no goats? How will a woman weave a tent if she has no goat hair? What will we use for milk? For meat? For clarified butter? Surely El Bofessa told his friend all that ..."

"Oh Allah, may this head of the Green Patrol die from your sharp-poisoned spear, or the venom of a sidewinder in flight through the sand dunes," cursed one of the elders. He spat behind his back, then added, "And if two daughters has he, may the better abscond, and the other, her guardian rape on the ground."

"Patience ... patience," Awaad muttered to himself and the others. "Patience is the key to relief. "Tell on," he urged me.

"*Aywa*, the man in charge of the Green Patrol fears your goat herds would turn the fertile fields into a desolate desert again. That is what he had told El Bofessa," I said.

"Again?" said Awaad.

"Yes" I replied. "It is your goat herds have turned a fertile Negev into a desert in the first place, the man in charge of the Green Patrol had told El Bofessa; you Badu are not the sons of the desert, but the fathers of the desert, he said. But El Bofessa consulted with grazing experts in and out of The Land, and in and out of books, only to find they all agree that goat herds, small like yours, are harmless to the Negev desert. Therefore, El Bofessa wonders if you will permit him to hire a lawyer on your behalf. For he, El Bofessa, thinks, the only place you can fight the Green Patrol, and maybe even win, is in the court of law, of justice. 'Bear in mind, though,' El Bofessa had told me to tell you, 'that you may have to wait a few months, if not a few years, for your turn to be heard in the court of law.'"

"Where will we wait?" they asked me, from the men's fire-circle and the women's; and how do you fight in a court of law? And what is a lawyer? And how much money will this lawyer cost? And where will we find such a sum of money? "And anyway, no lawyer hired by a Badu will have the power to break a law created by the Green Patrol..."

"You mean the goat law is not new?" Awaad cried out when I told him the goat law was twenty-six years old.

"Why is the Green Patrol acting on this law only now, only on our clan? I am sure El Bofessa asked the man in charge of the Green Patrol," said the Badu with the hollowed cheeks.

"The answer to that lies partly with your sheikh. That is what the man in charge of the Green Patrol told El Bofessa," I said, my face burning hot and my back freezing cold.

"Cannot be," said the Badu sitting right of Awaad. "We talked with the sheikh two times, but not once did the sheikh say-tell it was not lawful to own or to raise goats."

"*Aywa*," concurred Awaad. "It was right after the Green Patrol had demanded too much money to ransom the herds they had carted away, that we went to the sheikh. And the sheikh told us that the Green Patrol demanded the money not to ransom our goats, only to pay a fine for the water we were taking from the neighboring kibbutzim."

"So we told the sheikh that no matter how much money we had offered to pay the kibbutzim for water rights, the kibbutzim refused, saying that because of the drought, they—the kibbutzim—had no water to spare," said the elder sitting right of Awaad. "We had no water to drink, *yaa-Rabb*, when the kibbutzim were watering fields, day and night, fields stretching wider than our home ground."

"We would have as much water as the kibbutzim have if we would move to the new tribal ground, the sheikh told us," said Awaad. "And so next day, all the men of the clan went to see the new tribal ground. And just as the sheikh had told us, we saw streets being paved, and houses being built, and Badu children already learning in the new school. And maybe a hundred Badu women and children, and even men, crowded in the waiting room of the new clinic, for the Badu doctor who was working there was also teaching in the big hospital in Bir Sab'a. If we move to live in this new place, our children will grow up to become doctors or engineers, or builders, or even electricians or plumbers—that's what our tribesmen who live there said. And after that they showed us how the electricity was working, and the gas and the plumbing.

"*Wallah*, we saw that the sheikh had told us no story when he had told us the new place was good," Awaad said. "That is why I, and all the men of the clan as well, thought it would offend not only the sheikh but the tribesmen who had already moved to live in the new place, and moreover, also shame the women of our clan, if we were to tell the sheikh that we could not move to live in the new tribal place because of the women."

"Our women are accustomed to cook with fire, not with electricity or with gas," the Badu with the hollowed cheeks explained. "Our women, meaning our clan—our children, our men, our maidens—are accustomed to traverse wadis, not paved streets. Our women are accustomed to roam as free as the wind from horizon to horizon, not to be cooped up within four walls and two *dunams* of land."

"Two *dunams* of land is all a man could purchase for his wife and children in our new tribal place, we were told by the sheikh's men," Awaad explained.

"What good is all the running water in the new place if a woman can raise only five, or maybe ten, goats in two *dunams* of land, when, for as long as anyone can remember, our women are accustomed to raising twenty, or maybe even thirty, goats each," said the Badu sitting right of Awaad.

"Instead of telling the sheikh all that, Awaad had asked you, El Bofessa, if you knew of a place where the Green Patrol would not be able to reach us." The toothless Badu was shouting at the cassette recorder. "And the day after, you, El Bofessa, told us: the West Bank. All the men of the clan went to look for a water source in the West Bank."

"Oh recorder, tell El Bofessa that no one, except the Arab *fellah* who owns the waterhole here, which is much too close to a target-practice range, was willing to sell us water rights in the West Bank," the Badu sitting right of Awaad said. Then, one by one, the men around the fire-circle, each in turn, asked the cassette recorder to convey a message to El Bofessa:

"Oh, recorder, tell El Bofessa that it was when we were hesitating to move to this well that the Green Patrol had set our tents on fire…"

"Oh, recorder, tell El Bofessa that a Badu can no longer be a Badu in the Negev…"

"Oh, these are times when the fox and the hyena feel sure, but when lions and hawks can barely endure."

On and on, the men lamented, until Jum'ah muttered in the darkness: "*Ashow, yaa*-Arab—wake up, *yaa*-Arabs—wake up, *Wallah.*" Only his footsteps were heard in the silence that followed.

"Roast coffee, brew tea," Awaad muttered to a couple of men when Jum'ah had folded his legs by my side.

Jum'ah pulled out a pack of local cigarettes—Times—and offered me one, almost like a peace-pipe—a *sulha*—forgiveness. I didn't ask him why he hadn't told Tal and me that the Badu was

Awaad. And he didn't ask me why we didn't entrust him with El Bofessa's message to Awaad. Jum'ah lit his cigarette and waited for me to light mine. And then he said, "The Green Patrol told you a goat story. The sheikh told you a water story. It's really a money and land story. How much money does each man of your clan have to pay for his two *dunams* of land in the new tribal place?" Jum'ah asked Awaad.

"No money," the Badu with the hollowed cheeks replied.

"You mean the sheikh was going to give each man in your clan two *dunams* of land as a gift?" Jum'ah said.

"No, *Wallah*, the sheikh knows we of Awaad's clan would never accept such gifts, and so he offered to trade us land for land," the Badu sitting right of Awaad replied.

"Your land for his, you mean?" Jum'ah said. "How many *dunams* in your land?" he asked Awaad.

"*Allah aref*," Awaad replied, and the others didn't know either.

"The land belongs to the clan ever since memory was born," the Badu with the hollowed cheeks said. "No one had measured her *dunams* since then."

"But would you say your land has a hundred or two hundred *dunams*?" Jum'ah asked him.

"I think the land of the clan is stretching wider than all the *dunams* in the new place," Awaad said. "Twice as wide, maybe even four times wider. But a land without water is worthless..."

"Not today, not in the Negev," Jum'ah said. "I think your troubles with the Green Patrol stem not from goats or from water but from the peace talks with Egypt. That is why the Green Patrol is acting only now on a law twenty-six years old. That is why the sheikh offered to trade you land for land."

Not one of Awaad's clan saw the connection. Their circuits were probably overloaded. Awaad and the others looked exhausted, crushed.

"I think your home grounds are very valuable lands, but no one knows it yet, except the sheikh. Information is powerful, *Wallah*," Jum'ah said to Awaad.

"*Aywa*—yes," Awaad muttered, then he poured a steaming glass of tea for Jum'ah "*Oshrob, oshrob*—drink, drink tea until the coffee is done," Awaad urged Jum'ah, sounding like he felt defeated, impotent, threatened, and had to assert himself as the master of the compound—to show Jum'ah who is boss, despite the power bestowed by information. Jum'ah did as he was told.

"We cannot hear, we cannot hear," the women muttered from behind the burlap flap as soon as the *daqq-daqq-daqq* started to sound again, like a drum.

"Raise your voice," Awaad ordered Jum'ah, as if he thought the women were the only allies he and his clansmen had now.

Jum'ah looked like he wished he had kept his mouth shut. Then raising his voice for all to hear, Jum'ah explained, "The government feeds information-power to the sheikh, because the government knows that the more power the sheikh has the more the tribe will fear the sheikh and obey him. But the more the tribe fears and obeys the sheikh, the more power the sheikh has to demand from the government—more information, more power: That is how the power-circle works. And so, if the sheikh had offered to trade you land for land, someone high up in the government must have informed the sheikh that a peace pact with Egypt is imminent; therefore, the government is planning to transfer all the military installations from the Sinai to the Negev, and for this purpose the government is planning to purchase every *dunam* of unsettled land in the Negev."

"*Yaa-Allah*," exclaimed the Badu and Badawias at both fire-circles.

"Do you know what the sheikh will do to you if you do not have his permission to battle the Green Patrol in the court of law?" said Jum'ah. "Do you know what favors the sheikh can receive from the Green Patrol if he stops you from starting such a court battle? Do you know what favors the sheikh receives from the government, the army, the Green Patrol, the trade unions—and from the kibbutzim as well?" Jum'ah obviously thought the kibbutzim had complained to the sheikh about the water Awaad's people were stealing. And the sheikh, instead of dispatching a water truck, had dispatched the Green Patrol to drive them from their land, to his. But Jum'ah kept it to himself.

"A sheikh, *Wallah*, his teeth are bright with gold. You hear him belch as he comes to greet. A belt he won't wear, having too much to eat," the Badu, sitting left of Awaad, muttered, then spat.

"Talk that is against your sheikh, your tribesmen, is against yourself as well," said Awaad, to the Badu on his left.

"*Aywa*—yes," the Badu with the hollowed cheeks muttered, and then he asked Jum'ah, "What would you do, were you in our place?"

"I would hire a lawyer to negotiate for my clansmen the sale of my clan's home ground," Jum'ah replied.

"But if we sell our home ground, where will we live?" the Badu with the hollowed cheeks said.

"*Allah aref*," Jum'ah replied, and then he explained. "If and when a peace pact with Egypt will be signed, the government is bound to confiscate your lands anyway, for The Land of Israel is small and settled, and only in the Negev is there space for all the Israeli's military installations.

"But, if and when a peace pact is signed with Egypt, surely there will be no need for military installations," I thought Awaad was about to say—only to hear him say, "You mean our home ground will become a fire zone?"

"Yes, a fire zone, or an air base, or a training camp," Jum'ah replied.

"You mean the kibbutzim will live near a fire zone like we do here?" Awaad said.

"*Aywa*—yes. The kibbutzim will have no choice," Jum'ah replied. Then he asked them, "Do you have a paper with writing on it called a land deed—you know, like an identity card with writing on it, that tells that you are you, a land deed tells that your lands are your lands," he explained.

"Let me have the papers with the writing on it." Awaad spoke to the women's section of the tent. Judging by the *jingle-jangle*, the Badawias all had to get up to make room for Awaad's wife. Further *jingle-jangles* said she was opening cartons or untying sacks... she lifted the burlap curtain to pass over the papers wrapped in a piece of cloth. Awaad untied the cloth and passed the contents to Jum'ah.

Jum'ah leaned closer to the fire, took a quick glance at the papers, then he asked me in Hebrew, "Doesn't look like a deed to me, but who knows what a deed from the British or the Turkish time looks like."

The papers were mostly thank-you notes in English—one from an agronomist who had apparently stayed with Awaad's clan when he had studied desert plants, and one from an ethnologist thanking them for their hospitality and for the songs and poems they had allowed him to record. The rest of the papers were articles about them and their way of life, all written by Russell, one of them published ten years ago, two years after Russell moved from Canada to The Land.

"The deed to your lands is not here," Jum'ah said, passing the papers back to Awaad. "Maybe you gave it to the sheikh—when he offered to trade you land for land, I mean. Did the sheikh not ask you to show him proof that your lands were your lands?"

"No, *Wallah*. The sheikh knows our lands were always our lands," Awaad replied. And the others laughed at the notion that anyone would not know that their lands were their lands.

They were still laughing when Jum'ah wondered aloud, "Did the Green Patrol, or the sheikh, or anyone in the past few weeks or months request or demand that you sign or put your thumbprint on a paper with writing on it that says you waive your claim to your home ground?"

"No," Awaad replied.

And now Awaad poured another round of *sulha*, offering the first cup to Jum'ah. This time Jum'ah didn't reject Awaad's offering, but when he accepted it, he looked like he thought his hosts were too forgiving, too generous, too noble, too far behind the times.

While Jum'ah was sipping his second or third cup, toddlers started to crawl back and forth from their mothers to their fathers until the burlap flap that separated the women's section of the tent from the men's was rolled up. Then one maiden after another played flute. All, as befitting Badu maidens modest-proper, averted their eyes from Jum'ah—all except the one that Jum'ah kept looking at as if he had galloped to this compound to see for himself the girl his parents had arranged for him to marry, and to his surprise they had picked for him a dream girl. The sparks that flew when his eyes and hers met, aroused even the moon—rising now, full and bright, above the hills east of the compound.

"Visit-stay ... visit-stay, the Badawias beseeched Jum'ah and me.

"The women have had no woman visitor ever since we went into hiding in these *Ad-daffah al-Gharbiyyah*—West Bank—hills ...," Awaad told Jum'ah and me. "Visit-stay ... visit-stay ..."

As soon as the children and the maidens heard me say that I'd visit-stay with them tomorrow, *Inshallah*, if it would not burden them, they whispered, giggled and laughed, unable to contain their excitement and their joy. And the women told the men to sacrifice a goat. Jum'ah and I protested that we both had had our fill of honor. But the men obeyed the women. They had probably eaten no meat since they had been driven into hiding in these West Bank hills.

37

Early next morning, Jum'ah left to gather support for Awaad's clan in the tribe. He also volunteered to call Tal before Tal reports me missing to the police or to the army. This evening, or early tomorrow, Jum'ah plans to return with wheels to escort me back to Herzliyya.

The men of Awaad's clan left shortly after Jum'ah. "To look for another well, secure other water rights," Awaad's wife told me.

It was not till I went with her to the well that I understood what scraping rock bottom meant.

Time and again, one Badawia dropped a pail tied to a long rope over the lip of the waterhole; time and again, the pail came up empty. "For the water is trapped between the rocks at the very bottom of the well," Awaad's wife explained. Finally, in desperation, the Badawias tied a rope around a child's waist and slowly and carefully lowered the child into what seemed like a bottomless pit. Then they lowered a pail and moved away from the lip of the well to afford the child enough light to see. Whenever the child cried, "I found it, I found it," the pail would be pulled up, full of murky, stale water that smelled and tasted even worse than it looked. If they were not so addicted to tea, they'd probably all be shivering and sweating with malaria by now.

The sun was high, and there was nothing to block the Hamsin—the fifty winds—as that same Badu child-boy led me to visit-stay with the shepherds of his clan. I don't know how far we walked, up and down one hill after another, one dry riverbed after another till we reached the cave where the shepherds—the maidens and children—were taking their lunch break in the cool shade.

All too soon the goats discovered there was nothing to munch in the dry riverbed below, and lunch break was over. The shepherds were about to head out separately in search of pasture, when Awaad's children insisted that, since I was their guest, I should join them, and the others insisted that I was the guest of the whole clan.

While they were debating, two or three Palestinian child-boys, shepherding a herd of sheep twice the size, at least, of all the goat herds of Awaad's clan, entered the wadi. As soon as they saw me, they told the children and maidens of Awaad's clan that their clan, as well as their *Yahodiya* guest, would not live to see tomorrow if I was not gone by early dawn.

I don't know how they knew I was a Yahodiya.

"Get rid of the *Yahodiya* or your throats will be slit," They demanded. Only children, and already so hateful—only two hours by Jeep from Mount Herzl and Arik, and the dreams buried with him—a life sacrificed so that no one would ever say anywhere in the world, "Get rid of the *Yahodiya*..." And now Levi is pressing me to allow him to court yet another sacrifice, as if military power could do anything to eradicate such hate...

"Get rid of the *Yahodiya*," the Palestinian shepherd-boys insisted when the might of the *Yahodiya*'s air force was whirling overhead and napalm was exploding only a few hills away. Children's hatred transcended the Real here, like that of those young thugs who lay in ambush at Christie Pits for Dave when he was little and beat him up to rid Canada of "dirty Jews."

"Get rid of the *Yahodiya*," the Palestinian shepherd-boys demanded, then they cursed and told the boys of Awaad's clan what they thought of their sisters, mothers, and of their female *Yahodiya* guest...

The children and the maidens of Awaad's clan cursed them back, but in whispers. "They are but *fellahin*," they told me, standing tall and glaring with disdain at the Palestinian shepherd-boys, until they disappeared behind the bend of the dry riverbed.

"*Get rid of the Yahodiya or ...*" The hills echoed after them.

"There is nothing to fear," the children and maidens of Awaad's clan assured me. But quick-fast, almost at a run, they escorted me back to their compound. The women in Awaad's compound agreed with the children and the maidens. "There is nothing to fear," they assured me, and later they explained that it was only because these Palestinians child-sheepherders were of the Palestinian clan who owned the waterhole that they told their men of the *fellahin's* empty threat.

I don't remember if it was nine or ten at night when the men of Awaad's clan returned to the compound. I do remember it was dark, the children were sleeping, and the pitas and the rice were cold...

"It was the Arab," Awaad said. He meant the Arab who had appeared only to disappear in the hills when Tal and I were crawling in the Jeep behind Awaad. "This Arab must have threatened to slit the throats of his fellow *Felastiniyiin* who live in these hills if we would not get rid of our *Yahodiya* guest. That Arab is a terrorist," Awaad said.

Jum'ah didn't get back that night.

Awaad's clan repitched their tents in a circle, tight, defensive—like in the old black-and-white cowboy movies when the wagon train was under attack. Only the goats slept in the tents; the men slept, or lay awake, in a protective circle around the women and the children. Awaad's wife stretched out between me and her husband, only a foot or two from me.

"Should we have to flee-hide, you stay between me and Awaad," she told me. And then she urged me to sleep, sleep... so that she could have a moment alone with her husband, I sensed. So, I feigned sleep. A while later I heard Awaad whisper to her that he would have to sell one of her goats or the most beautiful of her hand-woven welcome-carpets she had managed to rescue from the fire set by the Green Patrol, because it was bound to cost more money than he had to escort me to Jerusalem, or to Tel Aviv, or to wherever my escort-guardian lived.

Oh, how I cursed those Jew-hating Palestinian shepherd-boys... Their hatred poisoned me.

And, in but a few weeks from now Levi, my son—your son, Arik—will be exposed to this venom... Only a few weeks from now, for the first time in his life, Levi will see another human being, another tribe, as the enemy; or at best he'll take sides, in a way that his mother, slowly, without realizing it, has relinquished by dropping out to Canada...

It was still dark, an hour or two before dawn, when Awaad and his wife got up. I told them there was no need to escort me farther than the main road, where I could grab a bus or a cab. But Awaad insisted that my blood was on his head until my guardian released him from responsibility for my life. His wife agreed with him. Then she rolled up the most beautiful welcome-carpet she had woven and stuffed it into a burlap sack.

"But surely to hear my guardian's assurance over the telephone in Bir Sab'a is good enough," I told them. Awaad's wife agreed; Awaad couldn't help but see how she hated to part with her welcome-carpet. Still, Awaad muttered, "*Yemkin*—perhaps, maybe," and he hoisted the burlap sack up onto his back.

The Badu with the hollowed cheeks escorted Awaad and me to the main road. It shamed them both that their clan was getting rid of their *Yahodiya* guest, it seemed. In silence they walked, Badu-proper, a few paces ahead of the women, until we reached the main road; there, they stood guard in front of me until there was no sign of a vehicle on the road, and no sound of a vehicle approaching. Only then did Awaad tell me to follow him across the road.

"*Ma'assalame*—Peace be with you," the Badu with the hollowed cheeks muttered, turning back toward the compound. Awaad told me to rest my legs by the roadside, "for it might take a long time to stop a bus, taxi, truck or car," he explained.

I don't know if the buses didn't stop because Awaad was standing kilometers away from a bus stop. Or if the Arab vehicles didn't stop because he was standing with a *Yahodiya*. Or if the Yahodi vehicles didn't stop because he was an Arab. Or because he was hitchhiking like a monarch reviewing a parade. I don't remember how long we stood by the roadside before a couple of burly Yahod driving a minibus stopped to give us a lift.

As soon as the minibus gathered speed, Awaad whispered to

me to grab hold of my seat—"for every turn and bump can throw you off balance."

The soldier manning the road-block didn't wave the minibus through. I was wearing a *kaffiyye*, and the man's shirt over my jeans was large enough to pass for the smocks or the dresses many Arab girls wear as tops. And the burly Israelis in the front seat were wearing the same Western clothes that many Arab men wear. Yet, the soldier told only Awaad to show him his identity card and to untie the burlap sack.

"Is it really necessary to rub it in like this?" the burly Yahod protested. "Since when do we have a road-block here?" they asked the soldier.

The soldier said nothing and neither did Awaad. The soldier was checking the identity and the sackcloth bag of a vacant body, it seemed; Awaad had departed to the river beneath the river that the Badu keep secret from strangers.

Transplanted palm trees were fanning shade all along the new boulevard in Beer Sheba. And sprinklers were spraying the green lawns, and mothers were pushing strollers to lush parks... Not many years ago, when Arik and I were courting, Beer Sheba was a dusty desert donkey town. Even in Arik's expansive dreams, Beer Sheba had no place, and now the town was green, and teeming with people rushing to apartment blocks, factories, schools, hospitals and army bases, market places, restaurants and city hall... All mingled here—Badu men in *abia*, Palestinian Arab women in veils, tourists in shorts—and tearing by on a big shiny motorcycle, a Hasid in a black *kapotah*, white socks, and a motorcycle helmet, his black earlocks and beard flying.

As many women as men were pushing and shoving in front of the kiosk at the bus terminal, yet Awaad told me it was no place for a woman. "Wait there," he said, pointing to the front of the flower shop, where it was less crowded—and where he could watch me. For a long time Awaad waited behind the crowd at the kiosk, until the man behind the counter shouted to him in Arabic, "What do you want?"

"Two Coca-Cola...," Awaad muttered.

"What?! What?!" the man behind the counter shouted.

"Coca-Cola, two...," the crowd in front of Awaad replied.

Then, while the money Awaad had saved by hitching to Beer Sheba was being passed hand to hand from Awaad through the crowd to the man behind the counter, the two Coca-Cola bottles were being passed in the same way from the counterman to Awaad. The Badu handed me the bottle as if it contained dust that he had personally scraped off the moon.

It was with this sense of accomplishment and triumph that Awaad led me to the banks of pay-telephones. Too proud to say he didn't know how to read the numbers on the dial, or maybe even how to dial, he told me, "You will telephone but I will speak."

The only working phone was in the souvenir shop. We were going to take our place at the end of that line when the proprietor told Awaad, in fluent Arabic, that he would have to wait outside while I used the phone.

"But I am the one who has to speak in the telephone," said Awaad.

"In that case you will have to speak in another telephone," the proprietor said.

"Why, do you think I will break the telephone?! Do you think I do not know to speak in a telephone?!" Awaad cried out, his bloodshot eyes burning. He was back from the secret river beneath a river now, and he looked like he was not going to budge; he'd crossed one too many centuries already today. His anger was restrained and showed little of the frustration, humiliation, and uncertainty that he must have been feeling. Still, Yahod were not accustomed to seeing an Arab asserting his manhood, and some of the customers hurried their children out of the shop as if they thought Awaad was dangerous, volatile.

"I did not mean to offend you," the proprietor told Awaad now to mollify him. "I asked you to wait outside only because you carry this sack. You know how many booby traps are dismantled in this terminal each and every week?"

"So, you think I am a terrorist, I see. Why? Because I am an Arab?" Awaad thundered to be heard above the rumble of the buses. He didn't say he was a Badu, nor that his tribesmen served in the Israeli army, or that the sack he carried had been checked and double-checked at the road-block. "So, you, too, think I am a terrorist," Awaad said as the others left the store.

"You see how you drove my customers away." The proprietor sighed. "I knew you will drive them away. They will call the police, you know. Suspicious-looking bundles have to be reported to the police."

"Good, good," Awaad said. "The police will see I am not a terrorist."

"Where is your brain?!" the proprietor lashed out at me in Hebrew now. "How could you let this Badu Arab carry a sack into a bus terminal." *Let him,* he said, as if Awaad was a child-boy, not a full-grown man. Then the proprietor told me that Arabs have such pride and such a temper, this Badu Arab was liable to kill him if he were to tell him now that he could use the phone, even while he carried his sackcloth bundle. "So you better wait outside with his bundle," he said in Hebrew to me. And before I could tell him that Awaad doesn't know how to read the numbers on the dial, he switched to Arabic and told Awaad that he was welcome to use the phone but only on the condition that I wait outside with the sackcloth bag.

"But the man I have to speak with in the telephone does not know Arabic," Awaad said.

The proprietor now looked like he would have paid us to get the hell out of his store, out of his life. "No, no, one of you will have to stay outside with the sack," he said when Awaad put the burlap sack containing the welcome-carpet outside the store. "People call the police when they see bundles unattended. It is the unattended bundles that contain the time bombs."

Awaad didn't bother to conceal his contempt or his surprise. "So, you were not afraid of the sack when I carried it. I see, you were afraid of me," the Badu said. "You were afraid of me..." The Badu laughed. "Why were you afraid of me?" he asked the proprietor, and then he opened his *abaiah*—cloak—to show him that he didn't even carry a *shibriyya*—dagger—and next he dragged in the burlap sack to show him the "time bomb" that his wife had stuffed inside.

"How much do you want for this carpet?" the proprietor asked Awaad as if it was business as usual now that the bomb scare was over.

And Awaad seemed to be so happy to see that his wife's weaving was appreciated in this land of Coca-Cola and telephones, he was going to present the welcome-carpet to the proprietor as a gift, I thought.

But when the proprietor saw how happy Awaad looked, he probably thought the Badu was seeing a fortune in his pocket already, so he told Awaad that the carpet was stained, even a bit frayed; it would not fetch a large sum, even in the Bedouin market.

"Yes, yes," Awaad muttered, looking deflated, and then he told the proprietor that he'd have to speak in the telephone and only then would he know if the carpet was for sale.

"You mean the person on the telephone was promised the first right to purchase your carpet?" the proprietor asked Awaad.

Silence. Information is power, *Wallah*... In no way did Awaad betray that he might have to sell his wife's welcome-carpet for his bus fare and mine to my escort-guardian place...

And now the proprietor offered to speak Hebrew for Awaad on the phone. It would be better if he, a man, not me, a woman, spoke for him on the telephone, he told the Badu.

Awaad agreed. "Tell him how to find your guardian in the tele-phone," Awaad said to me.

The proprietor planned to tell my guardian that the carpet was worthless, it seemed, when he got on the phone. But, after all that, Tal was not to be found at work, or at home. So I gave the propri-etor my parents' phone number, and after he shouted, "Listen, I'm calling from Beer Sheba...," he told Awaad that my guardian told him she knew no one in Beer Sheba and then she hung up.

Just like my mother, I thought...

"But her guardian is a man, not a woman," Awaad said to the proprietor, as if saying so betrayed us both.

The proprietor swore that he had dialed the number I gave him, and then he said that he didn't want to purchase the carpet, he didn't want to speak for anyone on the telephone.

And now Awaad looked at me as if he thought I had betrayed him and the proprietor.

So I told him, "when you were not in the compound, was your wife not my guardian?"

Awaad laughed and told the proprietor, "*Wallah*, the truth is with her."

"I better phone now," I said, meaning to call Riva or Mottke, but the proprietor wouldn't let go of the phone.

"Just give me the number," he said, dialed, then shouted, "Listen, I'm calling from Beer Sheba, don't hang up, hold on ..." And after he asked Awaad what he wished to say, he shouted to Mottke, "Listen, some Arab in my store asked me to ask you if you'll assume responsibility for Leora's life ... No, she's all right ... She's all right, I tell you!!! Hold on ... Hold on ...

"I knew it, I knew it," he said to me in Hebrew, then, switching to Arabic, he told Awaad that my guardian wanted to know if the Arab was demanding ransom money.

"Ransom money, for what?" Awaad said.

And in reply, the proprietor shouted to Mottke, "No, the carpet is not for sale. She's all right, I told you ..." And then he told Awaad that my guardian was demanding to speak with me, to hear if I'm alive ...

"What's going on?" Mottke asked me on the phone.

38

"What was the phone call from Beer Sheba all about? Sounded like you were taken hostage. What's going on? ... You look terrible ..." Mottke said as I walked in to his place and Riva's—only an hour and a half after I parted from Awaad; that's all it took to cover the distance from Beer Sheba to Tel Aviv, by cab.

As soon as he heard me out, Mottke got on the phone, and first he called his old Underground friend, one of the top lawyers in the Land, and told him he needed his assistance with an urgent matter that had just come to his attention, could he come over as soon as he found a free hour or two, and could he bring with him his unlisted phone numbers. Next Mottke called his chess partner, the editor of a leading afternoon newspaper, and told him the same thing. After he had made his calls, Mottke informed me that they would be coming over this evening with the unlisted phone numbers of the "gangsters"—as he calls the members of the newly elected government.

"What for?" I ask him.

"From whom do you think the head of the Green Patrol is taking orders?!" Mottke nearly snaps my head off.

"But Awaad's sheikh might be involved in this, not only the Green Patrol," I said. "You can't go over the sheikh's head without Awaad's permission. Awaad and his clan will be punished for that. Insubordination is not lightly tolerated in Badu tribes. You can't just——"

"Awaad's people have nothing to lose," Mottke said, cutting me off. "Neither will we if the gangsters who ordered the Green Patrol to destroy Bedouin tents, like Cossacks in the pogroms, remain in power much longer ..."

I was so sure that Riva would tell Mottke to settle his account with Gingic and "his gangsters" at his own expense and not that of Awaad's people, I decided to keep my mouth shut, like a good dropout.

But when Riva came home from work and heard what I had witnessed, and what Mottke was planning to do about it, she seemed relieved to see Mottke riled up about something other than Gingie's fanatic Kippa, Yeshiva, or the criminal record he had been slapped with for erecting an illegal settlement in the West Bank. And then, frowning as if it had suddenly dawned on her that Mottke was not well or he wouldn't have come home early, she asked him, "Are you all right?"

"Yes, just a bit tired … I'm not the young surgeon I used to be …," he said, "and you?" his eyes caressing Riva.

"Drained." She and Mottke hardly see the sun, so many hours they work—he, with people terribly burned by fire; she, with war-bereaved burned out by loss. But it's their son's—Gingie's—service in the Unit, more than anything else—the wear-and-tear of fear for him, the sleepless nights, the stressful days—that had stolen the spring from their steps, the shine from their eyes, the inspiration from the myth of their invincibility. "Will they be coming for supper?" Riva asked Mottke.

"No, they'll be here soon after the evening news," Mottke replied. As ever, life takes time out for the national obsession to be on top of news events. "In tomorrow's news reports, the gangsters' abuse of this Bedouin clan will be fully exposed," Mottke decided.

"You are moving too fast for Awaad's good," I told Mottke.

"*Now* you are thinking of Awaad's good?" Mottke finally revealed why he was angry with me. "Where were you when Awaad needed you for his good? How could you allow a couple of Arab kids to intimidate Awaad's people? Why didn't you stand up for Awaad in Beer Sheba? …" And Riva said she could understand me sleep-walking through life in Canada, but not in The Land, and definitely not in the West Bank, "and in Beer Sheba—really, Leora, why didn't you stand up for Awaad?"

Because Awaad had his own legs to stand on, I wanted to tell her, and because a woman would be cutting his legs off by standing up for him … because I was Awaad's guest, and because Awaad was my guardian … because Awaad's values and way of life were not just a romantic dash of local color, or an intellectual exercise, but what made Awaad, Awaad. Take that from him and you rob him of the only thing he has left to lose. That's what I wanted to say, but doubt silenced me. Maybe I really was too passive, or seized by the Badawias' fear; fear is contagious. And maybe I was stunned, overwhelmed by what I had witnessed in Awaad's compound—every detail of which I had imparted to Riva and Mottke...

I had incited them to move way too fast, the way front-line fighters who had belonged to the privileged elite—to the ruling establishment—for more than thirty years would move. If Riva and Mottke knew what it was like to belong to a powerless minority, to be defenseless and afraid like Awaad's people, like our people in the ghettos There, they seemed to know it like a man knows what it's like to be a woman. I understood Dave better now; his inhibitions, lack of self-esteem, and yearning for dignity... The dignity that Arik had put his life on the line for, that our son Levi can't wait to battle for, that Riva and Mottke had devoted their lives to restoring and upholding. And wasn't it to assert their own dignity that the two Palestinian kids had threatened to slit the throats of Awaad's clanspeople, and mine, the same dignity that Awaad's clan was scraping rock bottom to hang on to?

Riva urged me to get out of my "filthy" clothes and jump into the shower—"while I prepare supper," she said, handing me one of her freshly laundered and pressed caftans.

I had no mind, no stomach, for supper or for a shower now. I phoned Russell instead. He had expected me to call yesterday, he said. "How did it go with Awaad?" he asked me. So I told him. And in response he just said that he had to get off the phone. His unit was engaged in night maneuvers, he explained, saved for last that he had full confidence in me.

"But I don't know what the sheikh will do to Awaad if Mottke goes over the sheikh's head. Do you?" I said.

"I will take care of the sheikh," Russell replied. Just like that, he turned Awaad's clan into a charity case, to be rescued by the white hats, as if life is a western movie.

The doorbell rang as I phoned Tal. His city roommate answered and told me he didn't know where Tal was or when he'd be back... He sounded like a friend covering for a spouse who fucks around.

Mottke waited for Riva to serve scotch to the lawyer and beer to the editor, and cheese and crackers, olives, and nuts... And then Mottke told his friends why he had invited them.

They heard him out without a comment. Then the newspaper editor said, "I don't think we should start anything before we make sure the sheikh won't take it out on Awaad's people."

"Awaad's clan has nothing to lose." Mottke gave him the same argument he had given me.

"You'll be surprised how much a person has to lose even when he thinks he has nothing left to lose," the newspaper editor responded. Mottke didn't argue after that; neither did Riva and the lawyer. Maybe because of the number tattooed on the editor's forearm. He couldn't have been more than a child, not bar-mitzvah yet, when they had shoved him into the death camps. I don't know how they could tell he was Jewish—his eyes were almost as blue as Dorit's, his hair almost as fair—and now, with his ruddy complexion, and a pot belly hanging over his low-riding belt, he looked like a lumberjack from Algonquin.

"One word from Misha, and the sheikh lays off Awaad's people," the newspaper editor told Mottke.

"Who is Misha?" I whispered to Riva when Mottke went to their bedroom to call Misha. Riva whispered back that Misha was Mottke's second or third cousin; that Misha had served with her, Mottke, and the lawyer in the Underground; and that Misha heads our Intelligence.

"You mean the sheikh works with our Intelligence?" I said.

"It appears so," Riva replied.

One word from anyone around this table to Awaad, and the sheikh will be at the mercy of Awaad's people; there was no need to ask Misha for any favors. But they followed two separate sets of rules, it seemed—one for peace and one for war, one for service-men and one for civilians. You don't breathe a word to anyone about a person who works with our military Intelligence, but if you don't raise hell about our civilian Green Patrol, you fail in your civic duty.

Mottke couldn't have spent more than two or three minutes talking with Misha. He said that Misha had already heard the whole story from a Canadian, a Professor Russell, who had called him just a little while ago ... and told him he'll expose the sheikh in the media unless Misha makes sure the sheikh lays off Awaad's clan ..."

Well, Russell said he'd take care of the sheikh, and, *Wallah,* he did.

"How does this Canadian come to know Misha, let alone Misha's unlisted phone number," the lawyer asked me, like a Canadian WASP would ask how a Jew had gained entry to a restricted club. And Russell had moved from Canada to The Land so that no one would think him not good enough to belong to any club; that is probably why he likes to rub elbows with the Establishment in The Land, which is, no doubt, where he got hold of Misha's unlisted phone number.

"You better ask Misha," I was about to tell the lawyer, but Riva said, "She wouldn't tell you even if she knew."

"For your sake, and that of Awaad's people as well," the lawyer said, as if our destinies were linked, "I suggest you tell that Canadian professor that a person could be charged with treason just for threatening to leak classified information to the press."

The lawyer called the former commander of the Green Patrol using a phone that Mottke had dragged to the dining-room table—to save himself the trouble of telling us later what the commander of the Green Patrol said. Riva told me that this commander was a retired lieutenant-colonel, or general, I can't remember his rank now; he obviously was such a high-ranking hero of such a reputation, Riva and Mottke couldn't believe that the man the Badu and Russell knew as the man in charge of the Green Patrol, and this man, were the same person. They thought "the gangsters" had replaced him with one of their own. The lawyer obviously considered the commander to be one of his own. They talked for a brief while about their respective families and mutual friends, and about their vacations to Europe ...

"We didn't gather here to travel to Europe," Mottke said when the travelogue moved on to the canals in Amsterdam and Venice.

"I assume the gangsters replaced you," the lawyer said to the hero on the phone. ". . . No, no one told me that you were replaced or going to be replaced . . . Well, if you didn't know you were replaced, you were not replaced . . ."

Now everyone, even Mottke, seemed to be wondering if I was a reliable witness. Like the bereaved, they were not ready to part from one of their own, not just yet. The lawyer first told the man in charge of the Green Patrol that he was sitting with a few friends, and then he said, "Do you know Awaad's clan?" as if he thought a man charged with the task of conserving nature and cultivating what little green there was in a desert threatened by an atomic reactor and development towns would be too busy to even notice a Bedouin clan like Awaad's.

"Do you know Awaad's clan?" the commander of the Green Patrol must have said to the lawyer. "No, I don't know Awaad's people," the lawyer said. "No, Professor Russell is not sitting here. No, I don't know the professor, but I heard you told him Awaad's people couldn't return to the Negev with their herds," the lawyer said.

"Oh, that is not accurate? Well, I'm not surprised," the lawyer said.

And for a moment he, like everyone around the dining-room table, including me, thought Russell had made a terrible mistake: He had heard the commander of the Green Patrol say *couldn't* when he had said *could*. Awaad's people *could* return to the Negev with their goat herds without any problems, whenever they wished. That's the message I should have delivered to Awaad's clan. What unnecessary pain and worry I have caused them, I thought. And already my mind had started to compute ways and means of reaching Awaad's clan first thing tomorrow—not in a green Jeep, but in a Skyhawk . . . Instead of napalm, I would be dropped onto Awaad's welcome-carpet. I was floating that high, imagining Awaad's face when he heard his problems were over. His clan could pack up, go home, and Jum'ah's maiden would sing like Miriam at the celebration around the fire—a celebration in biblical time and Skyhawk time at once, with no discord, no guilt, no blame.

I held my breath then, waited for the longest time, as the lawyer frowned, a frown that deepened by the minute. No one was prepared to hear him say, "Look, I don't know what could possibly lead the sheikh to fear that *our* Bedouins would end up like the Native Indians in America. It's bullshit, and you know it. I can't understand what you mean when you say Awaad's people are free to live in a brand-new Negev settlement. So am I, but you have no right to tell me or Awaad where we are free to live ..." The lawyer was listening now, breaking his silence by muttering: yes, yes. Each yes registered on his face as no, no, you Absalom, you Brutus, you Judas, and not because the man he was talking with was betraying Awaad's clan, but because he was betraying the lawyer's dream— the blue-and-white dream to which he, Riva, Mottke, and their Underground friends had given life; the dream of being a light to the Nation, the dream he had entrusted to the man in charge of the Green Patrol, the next generation, who had also been raised on the dream. It was a betrayal of trust—both personal and tribal.

"Yes ... yes," the lawyer said, "but if, as you say, Awaad's people were stealing water or raising goats illegally, it's up to a judge presiding in a court of law to decide how to punish them, not up to a civil servant like you. And if, as you say, Awaad's people are the best Bedouin poets and storytellers in the Negev and the burning of their tents by your men is just another one of their tales, then let me ask you, first: What do they have to gain by spreading such a tale—other than the sympathy of bleeding hearts, like mine, of course? And, second, why are they afraid of you—afraid like our people feared the Cossacks, the Gestapo—and if you think that that is a strong word, wait till you read the papers tomorrow." The lawyer went on, using words and threats I'd never heard used with any Outsider. But then, we expect more from our own. And the higher the expectation, the harder the fall.

"Leave the papers out of this," the newspaper editor said, looking like he wished the lawyer would also leave the Gestapo out of this.

"Oh, I wouldn't hang up if I were you," the lawyer was shouting now. "My friends may be out of power these days, but the law of The Land prevails..."

The lawyer moved the receiver away from his ear, and the commander of the Green Patrol was shouting so loud, we could hear him telling the lawyer that he didn't know what he was talking about, that a lot of things have changed in the Negev since his friends were voted out of power, and that he had apparently lost touch, obviously didn't know that Bedouins from all over Arabia were sneaking into the Negev and laying false claim to the unsettled Negev lands, counting on the bleeding hearts in The Land to scream that we are stealing Arab lands, just as the bleeding hearts are screaming for peace now with Egypt—a peace/no-peace that is going to cost us not only Sinai but the Negev; going to turn the Negev, "the breadbasket of The Land," into a military base, and a gold mine for the carpet-baggers from Arabia. The bleeding hearts may get their wish, but not at the taxpayers' expense—on and on the commander of the Green Patrol was yelling, while the lawyer muttered, "*Shmuck*... gangster... fascist..."

"How can you lump a Bedouin clan that has lived in the Negev much longer than you with carpet-baggers? And don't tell me Awaad's people have false claim to their lands; there is no better land title than the sheikh's offer to trade them land for land. I don't know what you have against Awaad's people, but let me tell you, if you don't compensate them—for their tents and for the pain and suffering that you and your Green Patrol have caused them —I'm going to take you to court, even if they press no charges. And if you think I don't have a case because this is a matter of your word against that of the best Bedouin storytellers in the Negev, let me tell you that this is a case of your word against that of a war widow..."

No one around the table but me seemed to think it strange, pathetic, a betrayal of the dream, that the word of a war widow would carry such weight in a court of law. As if a war that has raged for more than thirty years in a land of two-three million inhabitants spared anyone. And what does credibility have to do with the misfortunes of war? Had war bereavement, war injuries, or gunfire purified the soul, we'd be a nation of saints and no one sitting around this table would be feeling betrayed by one of our own...

Awaad's people couldn't see themselves betrayed by one of their own; they rejected the notion just as fast as the Yahod accepted it. I don't know why. Badu betray one another no more and no less than Yahod, and if Badu have been betrayed by others, so have the Yahod. But the Badu have lived for centuries in a solitude that rarely calls their self-image of nobility into question, while the Yahod have lived for centuries among neighbors who perceived them as Judases, and the Yahod have come to see themselves as their neighbors see them.

"Victims victimize," Riva said when the lawyer, hanging up, muttered, "Can you believe it? A man like him... not ashamed, no remorse, wouldn't budge. Why? He, of all people picking on a Bedouin clan like Awaad's..."

"Leave the victims out of this," the newspaper editor told Riva. "You *Sabras* don't know the meaning of words like *victim* or *victimizing*. I hope you never will...

"And why are you so mystified?" the newspaper editor said, turning to the lawyer. "You think blowing up the dwelling-place of the terrorist is a deterrent, and then you wonder why a soldier-boy who has destroyed such Arab dwelling-places is destroying Arab dwelling-places in civilian life as well."

"I gave you more credit than that," the lawyer snapped. "You and I, and thousands of others, have been called to battle Arabs for more than thirty years, but have you seen anyone shooting Arabs in civilian life?"

"The days of that miracle are numbered, I'm afraid," the editor said. "The impunity of the Green Patrol is a warning of that..."

"The impunity? Not if I can help it," Mottke said.

But the lawyer had no doubt now, he said, that the chances of Awaad's clan winning a legal battle against the Green Patrol, in or out of court, were slim to none. The goat law might be unjust, but the law had been enacted to protect the dream of turning the

Negev into the breadbasket of The Land. And it had worked. To benefit, not only the great majority, but Awaad's clan as well. And so, no matter how many environmental scientists were to challenge the law and to testify in court that goat herds the size of Awaad's posed no threat, as many kibbutzniks at least would testify that nothing could ravage a wheat field, turning it into desolate desert, like a herd of goats. Case dismissed. The goat law is upheld. Next case...

"And to sue the Green Patrol for the Bedouin tents they had destroyed was even more hopeless," the lawyer went on to say, "Primarily because the commander of the Green Patrol maintains it's an outright lie, and the only witnesses we have are Bedouin women and children who have a credibility problem, a Bedouin lieutenant who has a loyalty problem, and a war widow who has dropped out.

"This year, she roughs it for a few weeks in the desert, which hardly qualifies her as an expert on Bedouins or on hardship, or on fear. Yet, here she stands and testifies that the women of Awaad's clan were too frightened to have invented the story of the Green Patrol—that the physical evidence proves their fear of the Green Patrol was no work of the imagination.

"Well, even had she lived here, in The Land, the woman, bless her, would likely mistake the fluttering of a butterfly for a physical reaction to fear. And were she to find herself the only Israeli among Arabs in the hostile hills of the West Bank, she would no doubt see her own fear in them... And that's all it would take to dismiss Leora's testimony..."

"But that's a travesty, even more than the actions of the Green Patrol," Mottke said.

"Oh, come on," the lawyer said, "all evening you've been speaking for Leora. Why? If you didn't think she lacked conviction, credibility, integrity..."

Mottke was mute with rage.

But I... I knew no personal slight was intended or inferred in all this; the less you cared about your personal feelings, the more noble you were in The Land...the less in touch with yourself you were in Canada...the lower than low you were in the Badu tents...

Worlds apart...even the silence; Badu silence and Yahodi. Badu silence serves as a sort of shelter to cool down. Yahodi silence is like a cave of warring demons and angels: Sometimes you are uplifted to heaven, sometimes you are plunged to hell, and more often you are hovering at the midpoint, waiting for the rope to snap.

"Unattainable, what you are striving for," Riva's eyes seemed to say to Mottke. But he didn't seem to see her; didn't want to see her gradually being made more pragmatic by the passing of time, quicker to say: That's impractical, impossible; quicker to think like a can't-do Jew. Mottke will never believe that anything is impossible, unattainable.

The lawyer broke the silence. "If you were our witness—or better still, if Gingie's commander, what's his name... Tal, was our witness—we would have a case. Now we don't."

It was all too clear now what a mistake Tal and I, Jum'ah and Awaad, had made when we decided that Tal would deliver the Jeep for its reserve duty, and I'd deliver Russell's information to Awaad's clan.

"And I thought all men and women were equal in the eyes of the secular law of The Land," Mottke said. "That was the only redeeming factor in Gingie's criminal record—that all men, women, children—Bedouins, Jews, Arabs—are equal in the eyes of our law. Give me that, at least."

"Do you want me to tell you what you want to hear? Would that get me a cup of coffee?" the lawyer said.

He had to get up so that Riva could squeeze past him into the kitchen, and the editor had to get up, push his empty chair back in, and get out of the way so that I could pull the coffee service out of the cabinet.

The lawyer lit a cigarette, took a puff, then said, "The Green Patrol may settle out of court. If the press gives this story a lot of coverage, the public would demand it..."

"Demand it where? How?" the newspaper editor said. "You practically have to wait in line these days to hold a demonstration for or against trading Yamit—Sinai—for peace with Egypt. Three hundred thousands gathered today in City Square. The public fears a civil war might break out any day, and on the verge of a civil war you want the press to bleed for a Bedouin clan wronged by our boys? To demand the highest standards of moral conduct from our boys because we won't . . . we can't, let go of the yellow patch? . . . Blameless were we *There*; blameless we must be *here* . . .

"You've noticed, of course, that no one is suggesting we report that West Bank Arab shepherd boys had threatened to slit Leora's throat, and Awaad's, his people's . . . Why, because it's normal, happens every day? Or because no one at this table wants to further fuel the hatred of Arabs? . . .

"Look," the editor continued, "headlines shouting about Arabs terrorized, victimized, or harassed by Israelis are not going to do us any good, but that's what may ultimately move our government, if not to punish the Green Patrol, then at least to settle reparation on Awaad's clan—"

"Reparations?!!" Mottke looked like the demons and angels were still tugging at his soul. "You mean to tell me that Gingie, my son, gets a criminal record for building an illegal settlement but the Green Patrol, for destroying . . . gets off with reparations paid by you, me, the taxpayers!" His coffee spilled when he pushed his cup away, like a Badu who thinks the amends made to him at a *sulha* only add insult to injury. Riva didn't move; just watched the coffee spread until it looked like a huge stain of shame, and then she looked at the lawyer.

"What do you want me to tell you?" The lawyer sighed. "The court may find the Green Patrol guilty of denying Awaad's people due process of law. But as it's a first offense, chances are they'll get off with a reprimand, or at most, a symbolic fine . . ."

"It was a first offense for my Gingie, also," Mottke snapped.

"Oh, come on. Gingie had ample warning and you know it," the lawyer said. "What are you defending Gingie for all of a sudden as if you condone——"

Mottke pushed his chair away from the table, got up, left the room without a word.

"Let him be," Riva muttered—so unlike herself, my eyes searched hers for an explanation. "I'll clear it later," her eyes told mine.

Turning to the lawyer, Riva asked if he had Yehoshua's unlisted phone number. "Yehoshua is—was—so sweet on Leora, he wanted to marry her ...," she told the lawyer and the editor.

"One word from Yehoshua and Awaad's troubles are over," Riva told me, as if she suddenly saw me as having more persuasive powers than Queen Ester. It wouldn't take more than one word from me over the phone to persuade a cabinet minister to grant me half his kingdom.

"The only time I asked Yehoshua to use his influence, he did me a hell of a favor and agreed to dust off Arik's model dream town, buried in the archives of the Technion, and bury it somewhere in his ministry," I told Riva, "If that's how far he'd go for Arik—"

"The hour is getting late, Leora; you'd better call Yehoshua now," said Riva.

"Don't tell him that you are the war widow who was at Awaad's compound," the lawyer cautioned me. "Don't threaten him with the press," the newspaper editor said.

Yehoshua's unlisted number yielded only his male secretary or bodyguard. Whoever he was, he wouldn't put me through, so I gave him my name and Riva's number, and asked him to tell Yehoshua it was urgent.

Less than five minutes later, Yehoshua returned my call. "Are you all right?" he asked me.

"Yes," I replied, then I said I was calling because I'd heard he had the power to help a Bedouin clan.

"Straight as ever," he said, sounding annoyed and disappointed that even I, like every two-bit favor-seeker, was taking advantage of his cabinet post. "Shoot," he snapped.

As soon as I mentioned Awaad's clan, he gave me the number

of the commander of the Green Patrol. "You are sending me to the very man who has caused nothing but trouble for Awaad's clan," I said, and I was just starting to tell him what troubles the Green Patrol had unleashed on Awaad's clan when Yehoshua cut me off, saying, "You better live in The Land before you talk to me about wrong done to a Bedouin clan. You drop out of The Land, after the price Arik..."

"Awaad's people are running out of drinking water. Lives are at stake—"

"Good night," Yehoshua said, hanging up.

"We know what he said," Riva muttered, handing me a glass of whiskey.

Whiskey, like the water Arik's commander offered to me the night he came to tell me that Arik fell...

So, this is my longed-for, my dream land, and for this I am expected to sacrifice my son, leave my marriage, and move up to The Land—*alli*—ascend—*ollim Allu, Allo N'a'alle*—up, up, up—to the wilderness... I don't know why I return year after year, like a ball rolling back to the feet that kicked it... Will I be moving up by making a soldier of my son?... Is it necessary to make soldiers here—or is it just running in place?... Can't we preserve one tribe while still preserving another—or is annihilation of one or the other an inevitability, *yaa-Rabb*...

"There was a man, but look he is no more... Not on a silver platter shall the state be delivered; no, each man shall have to pay with his blood, each man shall have to pave with his bones..." The same tired old eulogies they dump on Arik's grave on Memorial Day. *"There was a man,"* they recite, and then they go on with their lives in a paradise fertilized with bones.

I remember your bones, Arik. They pressed too hard, too heavy on me, you thought, raising yourself up on your elbows, but I welcomed them... Your bones were too heavy only in your coffin...

"Ytgadal ve'yitkadash sheme Rabba—recite the mourners' prayer, dust to dust, shovel—shovel—*yaa-Rabb*, you are of blessed memory

now, Arik. *Zikhrono livrakhah*—third person—venerated, removed, departed, a man no more, a dream man. Feel his breath on your face and reach to touch him, and you awake with a new name, a new ring on your finger.

Your clothes smell musty and of mothballs, my Arik... even though, year in, year out, on the first day of spring, I spread them out to the sun, smooth away the creases of winter, and caress the memories, the promise, the dream that lingers... Caress the shadows—not the real thing?

Your Leora, when was she lost, Arik? It happened so fast. It was not too long ago I used to walk—like Azzizah and Tammam—barefoot on the sun-baked sands...

39

At the hotel I find a heap of pink message slips, saying to call my mother the minute I get back. On the first ring, my mother tears the receiver off the hook and snaps, "Who is it?"

"Me, Leora. What's the matter, Imma?"

"Are you all right?"

"Yes. What's wrong, Imma?"

"I was just going to phone the police…"

"The police! Why? What happened?"

"Oh, you've lived in Canada too long. Perhaps it's all right in Canada, but here, in The Land, never tell me that you are going to stop in the West Bank for an hour or two before you head home, then disappear for two days. Your sister kept telling me that you must be all right because no news is good news. But I couldn't shake the feeling that you were in trouble, in danger…"

And what was I going to tell her, that she is psychic, that a couple of Palestinian children have learned to hate Jews with such venom, they threatened to massacre a Bedouin clan for receiving a Jewish guest. I was so mired in hatred, prejudice, and bigotry, that I forgot love exists…

"I love you, Imma."

"Won't get you far. My tits are dry." She laughed.

"Did you hang up on someone who phoned you from Beer Sheba around noon the other day?"

"Oyi, it was you, Leora. Sounded like a man. A catastrophe the telephones in this Land." A catastrophe to my mother is not "the situation" in this Land, and not the West Bank, but the telephone lines.

"Go to sleep, Leora. The sun will soon be up," she said, and hung up, as though Herzliyya was long-distance, like Canada…

⚘

It was long after midnight when I tried again to reach Tal.

"Hello!!!" A female voice answered, shouting above Bob Dylan wailing about how it feels to be away from home, like a rolling stone, and above a crowd feeling good, laughing, partying.

"Is Tal home?" I ask her.

"What?! What!? I can't hear you!" she shouts. A catastrophe, the phones here, just like my mother said.

"I'd like to speak with Tal!" I shout.

Tal must have dragged the phone to some quiet corner, in his bedroom probably. He said Ephrat and a bus full of friends from his kibbutz had come to the city to attend the demonstration over trading Sinai for peace with Egypt. "Jum'ah phoned me to say you left with Awaad. What happened?" he asked me. As soon as I started to tell him what happened, someone must have opened the door and the hoopla spilled into his room. He said, "What?... What?... I'll come over with the Jeep tomorrow. The Jeep call-up was only a drill..."

Only a drill!

He couldn't hear, couldn't talk, had to get back to his guests. Abu Salim has nothing on him when it comes to hospitality.

Ephrat is like a guest to him now, a visitor. And what am I? A relic, like the biblical Hebrew tense that makes the past the present, the future.

Dave called, saying Riva had just phoned him from Tel Aviv. She told him I could use every friend I have in this world tonight. "What happened? What's going on?" he asked me, the worry clear in his voice. I told him he was right, I had severed irreversibly my connection to The Land, to myself, and to Canada. "I'm neither here nor there..."

"But to be Outside is the ultimate freedom," he said, offering pop psychology.

I wanted to tell him about Awaad, and Yehoshua, but the words wouldn't come, only the sobs—defeat, despair, loneliness, self-pity, shame, guilt.

It frightened him to hear the "tough one" in the family crying. I could hear the trembling in his breath, the fear that the marriage was challenged, would be lost. Maybe that's what moved him to tell me that he'd heard his friend Schaeffer, "a big wheel in construction, was planning to build a row of duplexes in Jerusalem. It makes no economic sense to invest a quarter of a million dollars or more in a duplex we're going to live in only six months a year, but what does economics have to do with this? Israel is still a special place, an emotional decision, and Levi will need a place to call home. And if Schaeffer is building, at least you can be sure the standard is going to be Canadian. The building lots, I hear, are in that section of Jerusalem that is becoming a Canadian colony... Schaeffer had sold five duplexes already and is keeping one for himself. I'll ask him to hold one for us—if you want, that is...". If it's not too late for us, he meant.

Jacob sorrowed but could find no solace, no comfort, no relief; for deep inside he knew his love child, his dream child, was not dead...

⚹

At 4:30 *a.m.* Riva called to say, "Let's have a pajama party."

"I'm all right," I told her.

"But I'm not. Mottke and I were too rough on you tonight, punished you for barging in with the Awaad story. No, for being with Awaad when—we needed you with us..."

She made it here, to this hotel on the beach at Herzliyya, in less than twenty minutes. And she had stopped on the way at a bakery and brought with her fresh black bread, butter, cheese, a thermos of coffee-honor... She tore off a chunk of bread, layered a half-inch of butter on it, and stuffed it into her mouth, looking like a lunatic delighted to find that she can still surprise me—her friend, her colleague, her student, her therapist—after all these years...

"It's for my future grandkids," she says, as she pulls out of her bag the cassette recorder she brings to the seminars, the therapy sessions, and the support groups she conducts. She pressed Record, as though sensing the times are coming to an end—like horses, the coming of an earthquake... For only the story remains, *Wallah.*

She slurped her coffee like Abu Salim, with much noise, then went on to say, "Day before yesterday, when you were at Awaad's, Mottke and I were watching the evening news when the bell rings and someone sounding like Gingie says, 'Open up. We can hear you're home.' It's not like Gingie to lose a key, but we open the door, and there stands Gingie with a girl who looks not a day over sixteen and beautiful like innocence itself. 'Meet Naomi,' he tells us. 'In a month she will be my wife.'"

"Oh, Riva, *mazal tov!* What a wonderful surprise," I interrupt her. She shook her head to dam her tears... Who would have dreamt Riva would be afraid to lose her son to her daughter-in-law. My Riva, the pillar of The Land, the underground fighter—a regular Yiddish *Mamush.* Gingie getting married... I taught him to ride a bike... trembled for him... And here he lives to love, to get married... "*Sh'ehiyeh bemazal*, Riva. *Sh'ehiyeh bemazal*—may the union be blessed with good fortune."

"Now you see why Gingie loves you," Riva says, dries her tears, blows her nose. "That's how he wanted me and his father to react. He expected us to wish him *mazal tov.* I don't know why I didn't. I don't know where my head was. Mottke and I are getting too old for Gingie's surprises. We haven't really recovered yet from his turning to a religious fanatic, and now his criminal record... But he was standing by the doorway, looking so happy, and she so beautiful... I should have wished them *mazal tov.* Instead I said, 'Come on in, children. Why are you standing at the door? Sit down.' And after they did, I said, 'So...' and Gingie laughs and says they just went through the whole story with her parents but, well, here's the short version: A month ago he went to one of the elders in his *yeshiva* and asked him to find him a wife. A few days later, this elder invites him over and introduces him to Naomi. He and Naomi met three times at this elder's place: Twice the elder sat in the room with them, and once he sat in the hallway, where he could see them but not hear them. This evening they decided to get married. So, first, they went to tell Naomi's parents, and now they came to tell us.

"'Naomi's parents wished us *mazal tov*, Gingie said when Mottke and I sat silent...

It smelled of the ghetto to us, Gingie's story, smelled of bondage, of helplessness, of servitude, of everything we struggled to free ourselves from. And here our son Gingie, of all people, as if he was demented, blemished, crippled, went to a matchmaker like the ultra-orthodox fanatics that Mottke hates.

"Mottke was burning inside, I knew. If I wish them *mazal tov* now, Mottke will explode in front of the girl and humiliate Gingie. So I turn to her and I ask if she, like Gingie, chose to become observant, or if she was born into an observant home. And the girl replies that she was born into a traditional home; her mother keeps kosher, but she prays in the synagogue only on the holy days. Her father, though, prays in the synagogue every *Shabbat*, but he wears no *kippa* or hat except in the synagogue. Then she said, 'My parents would have preferred me to be traditional like them, but I went all the way—it was all or nothing for me; that's how I am.'

"'How old are you?' I asked her, thinking how could such a young girl be so generous; instead of saying she thought her parents were hypocrites, she said, 'All or nothing; that's how I am.' And Gingie is beaming to see me like a regular mother-in-law grilling the bride.

"'I'll soon be twenty,' the bride replies. She'll be reduced to tears, if Mottke opened his mouth now, I think. So I step on Mottke's toe under the table, but he couldn't contain himself any longer... What pain, what disappointment, what anger...

"'And how are you planning to support her? You have a criminal record but no skill, no trade, no profession,' Mottke said, dumping on Gingie in front of her. 'In less than a year, no doubt, you will have a child. Every year a child, like your fanatic friends. Do you expect her parents and us to support you all, like your fanatic friends, are you going to live like a *shnorer*—a freeloader? And she looks like a fine girl. Do you know what a child every year might do to her? And you, every Monday and Thursday are serving reserve or building illegal settlements or sitting in your *yeshiva* day and night. In five years she'll have five children to raise all by herself... How will you support them when you can't support yourself?' That was restrained for Mottke. And Gingie—Gingie was in heaven: Both of us were behaving like regular parents.

"'You had no means of support when you married Imma,' Gingie responded. 'You were still fighting in the Underground when you married Imma. You didn't even know if you'd live to see tomorrow...' Things like that Gingie said, as if all of a sudden now he was Mottke's equal. As if all he had to do to be his father's equal was to get himself married. He should have known better.

"You know, Mottke was never the 'my son is my best buddy' type. Maybe he should have been. But Mottke and I were not kids when we had Gingie. We waited too long, perhaps... And now, remember how it bugs Mottke to hear anyone gush about the good old days. Well, he started to gush like that—maybe because he knew this was one thing Gingie wouldn't touch. I couldn't look at him when he told Gingie, 'If you knew how your mother and I had waited for you, how your mother and I had dreamed of having a son like you. You are our dream son, Gingie. Still, we waited to have you until we were not in the Underground, until the State was born. We wanted you to be free of the burden destiny had imposed on us. We took you into consideration, even before you were born. We waited until I was sure I'd finish medical school.'

"'Who asked you to?' Gingie should have said to his father. But he had that happy look on his face—that look that true believers have—and he was also happy with his girl-bride. He said nothing. He had no idea that his father had kept anything from him. Later, Mottke meant to tell Gingie. Later, after Gingie makes it through the Unit. And then he served reserve duty so often, Mottke didn't want to add to his burden. But now Gingie is getting married, and marriage smells of continuity, permanence. Maybe that's why Mottke went on to what really bothered him.

"'And let's say you do finish your study at your *yeshivah* studies in five, even ten, years. What can you do then?' Mottke asked his son. 'Will they let you serve as a rabbi, with your criminal record? Will they let you teach children? Or will they let you be a *shohet*— a ritual slaughterer—is that what you aspire to be?'

"Gingie, being Gingie, told his father, 'I aspire to be a good human being, Abba.' Then, as if he remembered his father didn't understand his language, he came down to earth and told Mottke that he planned to study Torah while living off the land, 'like you and your friends did.'

"That's all Mottke had to hear. 'My friends—your mother and I— we settled and lived off *our land*, not Arab land,' he told his son. 'We didn't kick Arabs off their land to build settlements. We purchased land in the free market with hard-earned cash. Desert land, malaria marshes, that no one wanted, that no one dreamed could be reclaimed. No one except us. You want to follow in our footsteps, then do as we did. Settle in the Galilee, in the Negev, the Jordan valley, settle in our land, not on Arab land. Not in the West Bank.'

"'Yehuda and Shomron,' Gingie said, correcting his father.

"'The West Bank,' Mottke insisted.

"They couldn't even agree now on the fucking name. Those two who had debated as only a chess master and a Talmudic scholar can. Those two who love each other like King Saul and Jonathan were fighting now as if for the kingdom and the crown, as if driven by some wild primal demon, a man's demon.

"'Yehuda and Shomron is our land, Abraham's land, Isaac's and Jacob's land, King David's land ... the Promised Land, more than the rest of the country,' Gingie told his father.

"'The Book is a book, not a contract,' Mottke snapped. 'The Book is a good book to learn that King David was an expansionist like you and your Block of the Faithful. King David was punished for that. Here is the lesson for you, Gingie. Look at the Book and you will see God will not permit expansionists to build the temple.'

"'What expansionists?!' Gingie pounced on his father. 'Yehuda and Shomron is our land, I can show you deeds from the Turkish time, never mind from the British. Legal deeds fully registered in our names to lands, homes, in Yehuda and Shomron. Arabs live there today, and when we show them the deeds, they scream we are evicting them...'

"Oh, how Mottke is going to dump on Gingie now, I thought. But Mottke saved it for later. He only said, 'Look in the Mishna and you'll see it says that the West Bank, or what you call the Shomron, lies outside the borders of The Land. The Mishna even tells you why—because no Jews live in the West Bank you call Shomron... A million Arabs live in the West Bank. The West Bank is their home; they have no other. What are you going to do with them, Gingie? Expel them, as we were expelled? Rule over them, like the Tommies ruled over us? Do you know what ruling them is doing to us? Did you see your Block of the Faithful—yourself—driving through their West Bank, like the Tommies used to drive—at full speed—and Arab children and women running away, afraid like our children and women were when the Tommies ruled The Land.'

"Of course, Mottke didn't mention that driving fast was necessary when you are being stoned, 'You call yourself religious but I saw how you and your Block of the Faithful talk down to Arabs, as if God had created them to do your dirty work, dig your ditches, build your settlements, in their West Bank while you pray, study Torah, serve in the army. These Arabs are not freeloaders. They need the money to support their children. They have no other means of support and you... you and the mob you elected, you and your government—are exploiting this...'

"Mottke, still fighting the old brother's war, calls the other Underground group, 'the mob,' 'the gangsters,' 'the terrorists,' you heard him tonight... more than thirty years ago, but Mottke can't forget. And to his son, who wasn't born then, he said, 'The Land has a face today like the mob, the gangsters, the terrorists, the manipulating demagogues that you had voted into power. They are misleading you. You got your criminal record for nothing. You are wasting your sweat, your youth. You have no future in the West Bank. One day the gangsters you voted for will be voted out, and then we will trade the West Bank for peace, just as we will be trading Sinai for peace…'

"'Like Chamberlain, you think you'll give them Sinai, Yehuda, and Shomron, and that will appease them,' Gingie told his father, 'How do you know the Arabs don't mean to slice us up like a salami? Today they want us to give them Sinai, tomorrow Yehuda and Shomron, next day Jerusalem, Tel Aviv, Haifa… How many wars do we have to fight before you'll face that fact? The Arabs claim the whole land is their homeland. They say they aim to destroy us. Why don't you take them at their word?'

"Gingie and Mottke were fighting for position like alpha males. Who would have thought Mottke would be afraid of losing his crown, and Gingie, smelling the fear, would go in for the kill? Gingie, who knew how his criminal record broke Mottke's heart, went and told his father. 'Your old friend, our Defense Minister, issues an order to troops in uniforms to come and arrest me for building a settlement. Do you know how they felt? 'Gingie, don't resist,' they told me. 'Gingie don't resist. We're with you, don't resist…' But I resisted like you and Imma when the Tommies arrested you for building settlements.'

"'Nothing of the sort!' Mottke was white hot with rage… 'Your mother and I—and our old friends, as you call them—we didn't call ourselves religious, but we did God's work. God had allowed millions to go up in smoke. We rescued the few survivors. We gave them shelter. We didn't call ourselves religious but we dreamed of being a light to the Nations. We dreamed of the brothers Ishmael and Isaac living side by side in peace. We tried to learn from the Arabs, to become their friends, and like brothers, to split The Land with them fifty-fifty. The Arabs didn't agree. They made a mistake. So give them a chance to correct it, give them an inch…'

"'After you,' Gingie said in English. You know he speaks English like a Canadian. 'After you,' he said, then switched to Hebrew and told his father, 'I don't see you giving the Galilee to the Arabs. I don't see you giving the Jordan valley or the Negev to the Arabs, and hundreds, thousands of Arabs are living there. And how did you treat them? You had given them voting rights, but your friends in power treated Arabs as if they were second-class citizens. You have allowed the Druse and the Bedouins to serve in our army, but not the Arabs. Why? You didn't think it was right for Arabs to fight Arabs? Did you ask your Arabs?'

"'Your Arabs,' Gingie called the Arabs now. Your Arabs ... And Mottke just sat there and listened, his face pale—too pale. But Gingie wouldn't stop—'Your Arabs have a child every year just like my friends, but that doesn't bother you. In thirty-forty years, your Arabs will be the majority. You gave them an equal vote, so chances are they will vote their own people into power, then your Arabs will rule over you and me, my sons, your grandsons. Is that what you want? Do you think your Arabs will treat me better than I treat them? Did your Arabs ever treat us better than I treat them? Do you know how many friends I've lost because your Arabs live here like a fifth column—serving Arabs, not us, not you, not me. And you gave them an equal vote. And what is it going to be like fifty years from now? Did you think of that when you were dreaming of brotherhood?' ... Gingie had never talked to his father like that.

"Maybe he should have—should have challenged his father, challenged us; should have told us he thought we'd fucked up, left him a messed-up legacy. Maybe he should have asserted himself as a man, should have measured himself against his father years ago ... You know how Gingie always held his father a notch above all other men. He always said his father worked miracles, laid a miraculous foundation for him to build on, healed the sick, had a conscience like a saint. 'If a man like Abba could survive in this world, then *Hashem*—God—is still in his prime. God didn't give up because of men like you,' Gingie would tell his father, even before he chose to be observant, remember? ... And even as recently as when he saw what his criminal record did to Mottke ... And now, so soon after, he was talking to his father like that. But Mottke was looking at his son as if he was the disappointment of his life.

"And the girl-bride was trying to hold back tears when Gingie told his father, 'What did you want me to be, Abba? What did you expect me to be? Did you want me, like your friends' sons, to play tennis, strive for smart furniture, fancy cars? Do you see your friends' sons digging ditches? Your kibbutzim hire anyone but Arabs to do their dirty work. Why not Arabs? Because they harbor Arab terrorists? Or because they are Arabs? The Arabs need the work, you said so yourself. Would you rather I didn't hire Arabs?

"'Only *Hashem*—God—has the wisdom to solve the conflicts in this region, Abba. Someone should pray. Does it bother you that I chose to pray? Would you wish me *mazal tov* if I, like your friends' sons, lived like the Gentiles? Is that what bothers you, that your son is a Jew?'

"That was the last straw. Mottke looked like he'd lost hope—Mottke, who always rebounded, even when all seemed lost. But he knew Gingie was as stubborn as he was—once Gingie had made up his mind to marry his girl-bride, nothing would sway him. Looked like his heart was breaking, for the girl-bride, for Gingie, for us, for her parents.

"But who would have thought that Mottke would ever tell his son, 'How can you call yourself a Jew when a Jew is, first and foremost, for peace? How can you call yourself a Jew when your West Bank settlements are blocking the path to peace? You are not half the Jew my friends' sons are. My friends' sons may play tennis, but they are for peace. They know there is no *mitzvah* greater than making peace. Ask your rabbi, your elders. And if they cannot find where it is written, then tell them to come to me and I will show them. Look in the book and you'll see it is written that King Saul had spared his enemy. I love King Saul for that. But you love King David—King David, who robbed King Saul of his kingdom; King David, who murdered his own soldier, his next-door neighbor, because he coveted his neighbor's wife. Did he inspire you to stand above the law?

"'Did you think your mother and I didn't know what you had to do in the Unit? Oh, if you knew how I wished you'd never have to hold a gun. Yes, I wished you'd rather hold a tennis racquet... If you knew how I wished you would be spared from knowing war...

"'Perhaps I had failed you,' Mottke finally told his son. 'Perhaps I should have prayed. But we have been praying for centuries and did our praying prevent the expulsions, the persecution, the ghetto, the pogroms, the death camps? And here in The Land, Jews who prayed day and night, Jews who said they studied Torah, betrayed my Underground friends to the Tommies. We had no right to reclaim The Land, they believed, wanted us to wait for the Redeemer to redeem, to wait—when each and every day thousands of Jews like them were being exterminated in death camps. That's when they had betrayed us to the Tommies...'. Mottke was going too far, much too far.

"He didn't hear me saying, 'Mottke, enough. Enough, Mottke...'. And Gingie sat there, speechless—the light gone from his face. And his eyes kept saying, 'Abba—father—Abba, be like yourself, Abba. I don't recognize you, Abba.'"

"And his bride kept wiping her tears.

"But Mottke went on to tell him, 'If you knew how I hate to see you wearing *kippah* and *tzitzit* like the *shnorers*—the ungrateful free-loaders who live at our expense, who squeeze us dry to build more and more *yeshivot*, keep their sons safe in their *yeshivot*, while you and my friends' sons do their dirty work. My friends' sons may play tennis, but they do their duty—double duty, in fact—for the *yeshivah shnorers* too. God's messengers, they called us in the War of Independence, when Jerusalem was besieged and they were trapped inside the walls, when bullets were flying—and the Tommies didn't protect them then. Your mother and I crossed enemy lines to rescue them, and they followed us then. They didn't wait for the Messiah then. They didn't seem to mind then that your mother's shirt was sleeveless; they didn't call her a whore because of that, like they do today. Today they stone me when I drive on *Shabbat*, as if I have no rights, as if this land is theirs, not mine. But you only remember when Arabs stone...

"'Oh, if you knew what dreams I had for your sons. If you knew what dreams I had for you...'.

"Mottke left the table then. He left the room, closed the door.

And Gingie...I don't know when he left, he and his girl-bride. I don't know where I was. Perhaps with Mottke. They didn't leave a note.

"They ran to her parents as if for shelter, for comfort. Soon after, her parents came over to our place. What people her parents are—straight, no nonsense. They told us they almost died when they first saw Gingie. You know he's not much to look at, and their daughter is a beauty. It disturbed them that the marriage was arranged, that so fast they wanted to marry, they didn't know each other. But they wished them *mazal tov* because they knew their daughter would not change her mind, and they didn't want to alienate her. They also liked Gingie's answers to the questions they asked him. They thought we should hear the answer he gave them to one question. Only an hour or two before their daughter and Gingie came to our place, her father had asked Gingie, 'What moved you to ask the elder to find for you a wife?'

"And Gingie's answer was: 'The times. Because I have a criminal record, it is time to take a lawful wife. Because the Nation is dividend, it is time to unite. Because we are occupied with war, it is time to be engaged with love. Because we are losing hope, it's time to have children. And because I trust in *Hashem*—God—I marry a woman I don't know.'"

"That's Gingie," I told his mother, the best of my friends, Riva.

And Riva, her eyes red-rimmed, stroked my cheek as if I was a child. "Do you know what Mottke's reaction was?" she said. "Two words—'King David,' he snapped, like a person says, 'Bullshit.'"

"So heartless was Mottke, so alien it was to be so destructive of his family, of himself... Made him sick. First time since—I can't remember when was the last time he stayed home from work. He won't make a *sulha* with Gingie even if it kills him, it seemed, when you blew in from the wilderness and, with you, Awaad, the Green Patrol, the new realities. Tighter than ever he held onto the old, until his old lawyer friend asked him, 'What are you defending Gingie for, all of a sudden?'

"Mottke left the room then, remember? He left to call Gingie... Make a *sulha* with his son..."

40

A solitary bird—a raven or falcon—flies high above a flock that keeps circling, as if in their hearts they know this is the desert they have been migrating to autumn after autumn, but their eyes insist they have come to the wrong place, their hearts have misdirected them; the ground below is no wasteland, but farm land.

How many Badu like Awaad have been uprooted by this greening of the Negev desert that we have been boasting about?

Once again Russell stops—to puke or to relieve himself. He certainly wasn't faking to get sick-leave from reserve duty. Instead of going home, he is going to intercede with the sheikh of Awaad's tribe for Awaad's clan.

It feels strange to sit in his Land-Rover and not hear him talk of the trees, plants, flowers, birds, and wadis in the regions we passed. I ask him the name of something, I don't remember what, and he mutters, "I'm not a teacher today, not a scholar." He doesn't seem to know what or who he is today.

Never before has he interfered so aggressively in Badu affairs, Russell said. He had wasted no time in broadcasting on "The Voice of Israel" how the Nation's Green Patrol had wronged Awaad's clan. And here he didn't have to explain what punishment it was to be driven from your tribal grounds. Still, the response to his broadcast has been mostly indifference. It is that indifference, as much as the torching of Awaad's tents, that is burning his dream, his reason for moving from Canada to this country; his decision to study the Badu way of life, he said. His first field trip was to Awaad's clan; whatever professional reputation he has, he owes in great part to Awaad's clan ...

"How can you live with yourself if you don't do everything in your power to help Awaad, his clan, now; but how can you live with yourself if you do interfere so aggressively in their life? I'm ashamed," he said, leaving it hanging like a sign unfinished.

"Today I see what a fanatic I have become. But how can you stand zealously against fanaticism without becoming a fanatic yourself? How can you struggle against evil without being touched by it? How can you deal with history without becoming exposed to its toxic effects?... This challenge is altogether different from the challenge I thought I'd face when I moved from Canada to The Land.

A command car manned by Israeli soldiers detailed to guard Awaad's sheikh, his family, his household, is parked just outside the stone wall that surrounds the sheikh's stone house—a stone house with a stone floor, a flat poured-concrete roof, electricity, running water, fridge, stove, cupboards, kitchen counters. Still, the women prepare food on the floor, crouching like Badawias in the open desert... How I would love to be now with my Badu family; *Wallah*, I miss them all.

The sheikh's receiving room is crowded with Badu men reclining on welcome-carpets like in desert *maq'ads*. Every wall is painted a different color; the paint is peeling, and some of the windows are cracked. The toilet is a hole in a wet brown floor—a bit of a stench, no toilet paper. A youngster brings us a jug of water and a towel; after we have cleaned up and straightened our clothes, the youngster disappears to announce our arrival.

The sheikh—clean-shaven, his shrewd eyes drooping in pockets sagging with age and fatigue, wears a black *abaiah*—cloak—embroidered with gold thread over a well-tailored gray three-piece suit and a red tie. His smile is sparkling gold and white, like his *kaffiyye*, and a diamond sparkles on his finger. He is Abu Salim's age, I guess; his bearing and manner are regal, gracious, and commanding, like Abu Salim's, but with a pot belly and without the wild streak, the dust on his *abaiah*, the creases, the stains, the fire-spark holes, the frayed hem. The sheikh doesn't really look like any Bedouin I've met before, and yet he does. And, if life were a movie, he'd look right for the part of our secret emissary to Arab leaders at war with us—is that what he does for our head of Intelligence, Misha?

Russell isn't sure for how many centuries a member of the sheikh's family has ruled Awaad's tribe; other members, sons and daughters, were married off to the ruling and royal families of the Arabian desert. Imagine the exchange of information-intelligence at those family gatherings. Outside, even feuding members wouldn't dare leak even a hint, not without the family's approval. Or so Russell maintains.

The sheikh received Russell with outstretched arms and invited him to stay for dinner. If Misha told him of Russell's blackmail-threat, there was no sign of it. Russell whispered something to the sheikh (the purpose of our visit, Russell told me later), and the sheikh led him to the living room, then ordered one of his sons to serve us coffee-honor. He'll not be long, the sheikh said, then went back to his receiving room, where he adjudicates and settles disputes; offers advice, jobs, and influence.

Everyone in the household seemed to know Russell. A hefty Badawia—the mistress of the house, the sheikh's wife, an Egyptian aristocrat, according to Russell—offers a string of blessings, then invites me to join the women, who are preparing a turkey for supper in a very dimly lit kitchen. Crouching on the floor, they are lighting a newspaper to singe the tiny fine feathers, just like my mother used to. There is much cooking to do in the sheikh's household, the Badawias say; always visitors...

The sheikh's daughter—fourteen years old, she said—wearing jeans and no veils, gave me a tour of the house. The rooms are huge: Riva's whole apartment could fit into the living room alone. Russell fell asleep on the couch; *frangi*—stranger's—furniture: couches, arm chairs, coffee tables in the living room. That's where the sheikh receives his *frangi* guests, his daughter told me. She calls him "the sheikh" when she speaks of him, and "Father" only when she addresses him. The carpets in all the rooms except the *maq'ad* are factory-made, she told me with pride. The ceiling is very high and there is only one bulb in the brass light fixture. It's dark as there are no windows in the living room, and it's cold, even though briquettes are smoldering in three braziers. You can't smell the coal for the aroma of spices and herbs drifting from the kitchen. There is a huge color TV set in the empty family room, but no telephone anywhere. The sheikh has no telephone because guests cannot take their shoes off when they visit the sheikh on the telephone, the sheikh's daughter explained. The entrance hall is carpeted in shoes, wall to wall.

Forty wives, or forty-two, or maybe thirty-seven, the sheikh has married so far to seal alliances and cement the tribe, his daughter said. He was married to her mother for only one night, and, in keeping with Badu law, her father has custody of all his children. She, like all the sheikh's daughters, lived with her mother until she was six or seven years old, then, as Badu law dictates, she came to live with her father. With his permission, she can visit her mother whenever she wants. The sheikh, when he is not traveling the world over, stays most of the time with this, his Egyptian wife, his daughter said, "For she is good"—good to all his children, grandchildren, daughters-in-law, and visitors, some of whom have stayed for years. This wife is also a good cook, and the school near her house is a good school, said the girl. But ever since the peace talks started, soldiers in a command car have had to escort her and her brothers to and from school, because the sheikh is for peace, and the Arabs against peace with Israel keep threatening to kill his children, she told me. Soon they will be moving to a new school—not because of the threats, she said, to let me know she was not afraid, but because soon they will be moving to a new house in their new tribal town.

She is the first of the sheikh's daughters to go to school, and the only one not to wear a veil. Her stepmother—the sheikh's wife—told her to do her homework in the living room by the brazier as it is too cold everywhere else. If she only knew how cold the nights were in Awaad's compound, would her goodness extend to Awaad's clan? Would she persuade her husband to bend, if Russell and I fail?

| How you are? | מה שלומך ? | كيف حالك |
| Very well, thank you. | טוב מאוד , תודה . | الحمد لله |

The above, the sheikh's daughter's scribbles to show me she knows how to write English and Hebrew, as well as Arabic.

Her father walks in and his wife points to Russell, sleeping. He was not feeling well, I whispered to the sheikh, up on my feet like the other women in the room. The sheikh invites us with a worn-out gesture of fist to sit, tells his wife to fetch him tea, sits on the carpet next to the brazier. He plays a cassette, holding the machine close to his ear in order not to disturb his guest's sleep. The sheikh is listening to messages taped far away, his daughter whispers, her stomach rumbling with hunger.

⚶

The men and women dined in the living room, but in separate circles. The food, served on round trays on the carpet, didn't taste as good as it smelled.

"No, no. You sit-dine with us," the sheikh told me when I was about to join the women's dinner circle. "*Klow, kol, koli*—eat, eat," he urged his guests, just like Abu Salim. Unlike Abu Salim, the sheikh ate with his guests, as did his sons. After dinner, his sons, the teenagers, rolled cigarettes, and the sheikh pulled out a Marlboro.

"*Ghul, ghul*—tell, tell." The sheikh is urging Russell to state the purpose of his visit in the voice Badu reserve for a storyteller—because he thinks Awaad's grievance is but a tale?

"Many years ago I went to the great big city, Al-Arish, and there I heard a story told by an old man. He and others say the story is true," Russell begins, presenting Awaad's case as a legend or a tale.

"A true story," the sheikh echoes Russell, as Badu do to spur on the storyteller, but cracking a glittering gold grin. His sons observe to learn; one of them will be the next sheikh. The *jingle-jangle* from the women's circle falls silent. *Wallah*, how Badu can't resist a story. The children switched the TV off and formed into huddle now in the doorway to the living room. The little ones crawl over to the women's circle, at the corner of the huge living room nearest to the men's circle.

Silence.

"*Aywa*—yes, it is a true story. Or so I heard some people say," Russell says in his Badu-legend-telling voice and pauses, as if he is waiting for the mountain echo to settle down, to find a home. "In those days, before the clinics and the schools," Russell continues, "before the roads and the helicopters, before the oil wealth and the no-peace-of-mind, there lived a poor man. The only money he had, he made by packing sacks with wheat or *tabin*—hay—and loading them upon a camel or a horse under the rider. He was a poor and a complaining man . . . Even to his Creator, the poor man complained, 'You who created us and then robbed us, you are the one who owes us, and not we who owe you'—like this the poor Badu complained to his Creator, until Allah revealed himself to him in a dream, and showed him a wadi, and in the wadi many springs."

"Many springs in the wadi," mutters the sheikh, like Badu listeners the desert over, to let the storyteller know they are with him and to add punch to the storytelling rhythm.

"*Aywa*," says Russell, "some springs gushing up, and some hardly dripping a drop, and men were drinking—some near the gushing springs, drinking much with no effort; and some by the barely dripping springs, drinking little with much effort. And there was a man, *kabir*—big, big man—guarding the springs. And he, the *kabir*, told the poor man, 'This is your spring,' pointing to a spring that was dripping a drop and a half a minute. And now, when the poor man saw this spring, he knew that he would never receive more than the lira and a half he had earned for a day, but this small little sum—this lira and a half—he will receive all his life. That is why, the next day, he felt happy when he stuffed sacks with hay or with wheat and he sang: *I have seen with my own eyes; no man had told me . . .* That is what he sang. And there, not far, stood a palace of some sheikh, or some officer from the authorities. No one knows exactly———"

"Meaning, it is the same thing," one of the sheikh's sons muttered.

"Perhaps," Russell replied. "But his daughter used to steal away in the night and make love with a man not her husband, so I think the palace was of some officer from the authorities, not of a sheikh...

"Have you heard this story told before?" Russell asked the sheikh, meaning is it all right to tell this story in present company.

"*Ghul, ghul,*" the sheikh muttered. "Go on, tell your tale."

"*Aywa*—yes." Russell complied. "Now, she from the palace heard the poor man's song and thought he means nothing else but that he has seen her making love and he knows everything. That is why, before the sun was high, she prepared and sent to him an *haidiah*— a present—a partridge roasted and stuffed with rice and with a gold dinar; so that he will know, understand, and shut up. But just then, someone passed by—one, Abu Ali or Abu Daud—who was hungry, and so he asked the poor man if he would sell him the roast. And the poor man said to himself: Since I am already accustomed to my pita and a half, I will be content with my pita and a half today also. And so he sold him the roast for five liras."

"*Yaa-salaam,*" exclaimed the sheikh's children. "*Haraam*—what a shame."

"But five liras was more than he earned for three days packing and loading," says Russell, "and so, next day, the poor man was even more happy, and he sang his song even more loudly: *I have seen with my own eyes; no man had told me...*

She from the palace heard and feared even more. And so, this time, she sent him, not a partridge, but a roasted goat—and inside, not one gold dinar, but two. And he who passed by—Abu Ali or Abu Daud—did not continue on his way. Having the day before found the gold dinar, he had returned to try his luck once more. So, once more, he asked, and once more the poor man sold, not for five liras but for ten. That is why, next day——"

"The poor man was even happier," cried out the sheikh's children.

"*Aywa,*" confirmed Russell. "He sang in a louder voice than ever. And she from the palace, afraid for her head, sent him, not a goat but a sheep, and inside, not two but five gold dinars. And the passerby—Abu Ali or Abu Daud—was already thinking to settle in that place. He came and bought with twenty liras——"

"And so next day, the poor man was even happier," a child-boy bubbled from the huddle at the doorway, cracking everyone up except Russell and the sheikh.

"*La*—no," Russell said. "That night, she from the palace was so afraid, she could not sleep. And thinking there was no other way to silence the poor man but to expel him from there, she ordered him brought to the palace, where he fell to his knees. But she said: Kill him on the spot."

"*Yaa*-Allah," exclaimed the sheikh's children.

"*Aywa*," said Russell, "and he, right away, started to beg mercy for his life. So she told him: 'Get up and tell what your eyes have seen.' And the poor man opened and told of his life from beginning to end, of his family, and of his dream, *ya'ni*—that is—of the dripping spring that was promised to him never to deceive. Now her mind was at ease. But she was not altogether certain yet. That is why she asked: 'Is that all you dreamt and no more?' 'No more,' he replied. She believed him, she said. Nevertheless he had to leave his work and his place, she said; if he disobeyed he would die, and if he obeys, she will fill his vessels with gold. No sooner said than she filled his saddlebags with gold, the like of which he had never seen in his life or dreams.

"And what was he to do? If he will not take, she will kill him on the spot. He will take, and perhaps Allah will not see—or perhaps Allah will see and punish. But thinking what to do, he became confused, and he grabbed the bag and ran out. But Allah, of course, knows and sees everything, and recognizes *daimann*—forever—and when the poor man reached the exit, he was met by the Angel of Death, the one who collects in his fist the souls of all men. And there at the exit, the maid found him and told her mistress. And there was nothing else to do then, but to call the officer from the authorities—and the *darwish* also. They all came and examined the man, but failed to understand, for his body showed no sign of injury or ill health, and he was not all that old. They failed to understand, so Allah sent the angel Gabriel to talk with them, and this is what the angel Gabriel said: *We have made him modest, so that he be true. And you have bribed him, so that he be false like you.*

We, today, have killed him. And you, if you are able, revive him to be as he was—true."

Silence. Uncomfortable silence. Russell had gone too far, making it all too explicit. "False like you—" you don't say to any host, let alone a sheikh, in front of his sons, daughter, wife. But no Badu would endow a stranger with the power to stain his reputation, especially a sheikh born to a dynasty of sheikhs going back five hundred years. His eyes and demeanor show nothing but that. And yet, he makes Russell sweat.

"You mean to say her highness had, in fact, killed the poor man?" one of the sheikh's sons—a teenager wearing a sort of après-ski outfit—asked Russell.

Here is Russell's chance to make amends . . . Give, *yaa*-Russell, and Awaad's clan shall receive. Bend, come on.

Silence.

I don't understand why the sheikh received Russell like a VIP in the living room, and for dinner, when he knew the purpose of Russell's visit—even if the sheikh, like Badu the desert over, held Russell in high regard, for his effort to conserve Badu culture and way of life—for telling the story that will remain when all else dies . . .

"I also heard this old man's tale in the *souk*, but with a different ending," the sheikh said, breaking the silence—to return story for story? Is Awaad's fate going to be decided by a story contest? A thousand and one Arabian nights, *yaa-Rabb*.

"*Ghul, ghul*—tell, tell on."

"Altogether different was the ending of the story I heard in the *souk*." The sheikh waited for me to press the Record button and then he starts. "In the story I heard in the *souk*," continues the sheikh, "the poor man grabs the gold and runs out of the palace to the *souk*. There, first he buys a thoroughbred she-camel, then he buys a tassled saddlebag fit for a wedding, then in this saddlebag he packs all his new-found fortune, and away to the city he went——"

"To Al-Arish," a little one pipes up.

"*Aywa*," the sheikh says, "to El-Arish. But in those days, before the clinics and the schools, before the oil wealth and the airplanes, before the cars and the roads, danger lurked around every bend of every wadi, bandits and robbers and raiders. And the poor man, dreaming of city pleasures awaiting him, fell into an ambush."

"*Yaa-salaam*," exclaims a child-boy. "An ambush."

"*Aywa*," continues the sheikh. "Yes, the poor man fell into an ambush. He was robbed of all his fortune, all his gold, and all his clothes. The poor man was left with only his camel, and he thought he had no choice but to head back to his tent——"

"Naked?"

"*Aywa.*"

"*Yaa-salaam.*"

"And back to his tent the poor man went, his new-found fortune gone, his clothes gone, his dream of the city gone. And there, sitting by the side of his tent, looking at his thoroughbred she-camel, the poor man saw the rope that binds the camel's front legs together, so that the camel will not wander too far from the tent, and not too far for him to fetch back. 'Now, this rope,' the poor man said to himself, 'next time, *Inshallah*, when I venture off to Al-Arish, I will take this rope, and I will bind it fast around my head so that my thinking will not travel ahead of me to city pleasures, but with me, my thinking will stay, to watch my surroundings, so that I will not fall into an ambush again.' And ever since then, we Badu wear a black or white *aqaal*—rope—on our *kaffiyye*—headdress.

"That is what I tell my tourist-guests, El Bofessa, and do you know what they tell me? They tell me they travel all the way to the desert, sit in Badu tents, roll in dust and goat shit, to learn from us Badu how to bind thinking, so that their thinking will not travel ahead of them.

"*Aywa, here and now*, they call roped thinking when roped thinking kept us Badu *there and then*—backward, *Wallah*, poor, weak and sick. Like caged monkeys we are for camera-clicking tourists, and a field day we are to stranger-scholars—not you, El Bofessa; you, I consider to be a true Badu historian. She, with you, is collecting for you to write-record true Badu history, like a woman collects wood for fire.

"You know, El Bofessa, your Canadian friends came to visit me, the other day. With a translator they came, for they are not schooled in Arabic like you, and astonished they were when the translator translated true, my saying words like *history* and even *zaman*—time. *Aywa*, even an everyday Badu word like *zaman*—time. Astonished they were to see a Badu sheikh thinking not roped, to hear Badu words not limited to hot-cold, sun-shade, and the hungry howling of a coyote in the night.

"Not full-grown, but like children we Badu are, they think, like infants ... *Aywa*, it is because we Badu remember like infant-children that the tourists travel all the way to Badu tents. That is what my son who studies in California told me. And I can understand. I know how powerful is the longing to long for innocent child-days, and to recapture sand shifting, shimmering like water, dream water. As powerful as the longing to love, *Wallah*. For a moment passed is a moment passed to the domain of dreams—a shimmering blue domain without dust, disappointment, sweat and pain. A shimmering blue domain impossible to recapture—in life.

"Only in what is called Art, I have heard it said, man can capture and recapture, and even reverse, the flow of time. Perhaps, in what they call Art. But not in life, *Wallah*—for loss is inherent in life—*aywa*, no one knows it better than you Yahod. That is why you Yahod direct your longing, not backward, but forward to what you call the days of redemption.

"Like the desert, we Badu are a domain that lies beyond the boundaries of *zaman*—time—that is what your friends have told me. We Badu are like Art, they think, no doubt, for they visit-stay a day, two, three, and then they leave. And if they stay a month or two, they think they are adventurous and brave, and maybe even ennobled and *nazif*—purified. For they think Badu like Awaad's clan are noble, true and pure as desert sand. When, in fact, as you and I know, El Bofessa, Awaad's way of life is as purifying and ennobling as suffering, backwardness, and poverty—which, as you know, El Bofessa, stink, corrupt, degrade, debilitate, ropes your thinking, your remembering, even your imagining.

"*Aywa*, yes, my son who studies in England told me how poor and limited are the best Badu storytellers of the Negev compared to best storytellers like Homer and Shakespeare who lived in old, gone-by days, not in backwardness, illiteracy, poverty, and suffering. But in a palace like the teller of a thousand and one Arabian nights.

"*Aywa*, I was not surprised to hear that all too few songs and stories were composed in the death camps—but that even one was composed is a miracle, I think. A miracle born of the habit of learning rooted so deep, it runs in your *Yahodi* veins. *Aywa*, it is this value of learning that has sustained you Yahod—I thought on it for many years and I came to understand that, were it not for this value of learning, you Yahod would not survive. For the first thing you have learned from your learning is that if there is no flour, there is no learning. Loss after loss you suffered, yet you Yahod survive, for you know not only to bend, but to tell the story of your loss. Sufficient, *Wallah*, even to move you to rebuild your tribal place, not as it was in old, gone-by days, but with running water and electricity.

"New-found treasures are false to Awaad, say those who live with running water and electricity, and Badu who fear Awaad's people will break if they will bend. Badu like Awaad's people who do not know to tell the story of Badu loss, Badu history. Badu who do not know they are drinking from a spring not theirs.

"*Aywa*, powerful indeed is the longing to long, and like love it blinds, if it confused the thinking of even the best of Badu historians. But in your writing of Badu history you said true, El Bofessa, that we Badu see life, not as a relinquishing, and not as capitulation, or acceptance of a drop and a half a minute, but as a struggle, first and foremost. *Aywa*, like you wrote, we Badu, know also to submit—not to roped thinking, but to the infinite possibilities *Allah* presents to man. And so, if misfortune befalls us, we true Badu know it was decreed by *Allah*. And if we succeed we think: How good, how fortunate. And if we fail, we believe we will overcome. For everything is possible, and every possible thing is expected. Yes, expected, *Wallah*, for infinite are the possibilities inherent in life."

"Even the possibility that Awaad's clan will be permitted to return to their tribal grounds?" said Russell. "Awaad's clan have water for but three or four days," Russell explained.

"*Aywa*—yes," says the sheikh. "Awaad's people would rather die of thirst than drink from their own spring. Infinite possibilities, they fear. True submission, they fear. The inevitable, they fear. The flow of time, of life, the struggle, the complexities, *Wallah* . . . I thought of it and I came to understand that they fear to leave the domain of longing . . . Awaad's clan are longing to be who they used to be when they do not remember even the story of who they used to be, *Wallah*. Noble warriors, they think they used to be, when in fact they were engaged in smuggling, raiding, and plundering, not only strangers and travelers, but each other . . . *Aywa*, to forget that, is like forgetting that you Yahod were slaves in Egypt. I have thought on that and it came to my understanding that the progress, the far-reaching advancement he made gives hope to man. Whereas longing for days that never were leads to despair, empty repetitions, impotence.

"Awaad's clan lost, not only their story, their remembering, their imagination and their ability to bend or adapt, but their *muruah*—their virility, *Wallah*. A historian has to speak for them as if they were already history—*ya'ni*, dead."

"They do not know I speak for them. I swear they did not ask me," Russell said. "But tomorrow, *Inshallah*, I plan to visit-see them and to tell them—what? What shall I tell them?"

"Leave it to me, El Bofessa, I will tell Awaad what there is to tell," said the sheikh, dismissing Russell as if he was, to him, not a historian, as he said, but a court jester invited for dinner conversation, intellectual exercise, a workout, a jousting of wits . . . And Russell fights to conceal the humiliation he feels, and the hurt, the defeat—his and Awaad's—like a clown struggling to conceal sorrow, pain, and loss.

Mind your own business was something Russell told himself;

study, observe, keep your academic distance. Now he broke his rules only to discover the sheikh doesn't take him seriously; and maybe Awaad as well, and Abu Salim, and all the Bedouins he knew, studied, observed, maintained an academic distance from.

The sheikh knows him, I thought, Badu sense-see through mountains, I thought, but the sheikh doesn't seem to sense-see that he's destroying everything Russell believes in, has worked for, has devoted his life to.

Now he is a grandfather, the sheikh, his lap full of grandchildren who have crawled from the women's circle. The women *jingle-jangle*; one is leaving—probably going to sleep. The children's huddle is scattered now, and it sounds like the TV has been switched on. The audience is over clearly. The sheikh looks surprised that Russell and I still sit here, and I'm uncertain myself. What is Russell waiting for?

It's a good thing Tal didn't come with us. A couple of naïve Canadians, he'd call us, making fools of ourselves and a fool of the sheikh. It's simply a mistake, Tal had told me, what the sheikh and the Green Patrol have been doing to Awaad's clan. Policy makers, leaders and politicians the world over make mistakes, and most hate to admit it. Ours would not own up to the mistakes they made in the Yom-Kippur War, he said; what are the chances they'll admit to this one?

The veiled Badawia who left the women's circle didn't go to sleep, but to brew a fresh pot of tea and a *bakraj* of coffee. She probably thought Russell would not leave until his honor was restored, his face saved. She handed the tray to a child-boy, and he carried it to the men's circle and placed it at the sheikh's feet. The sheikh lets it stand-settle, and the children gather again, folding their legs on the carpet this time, like grownup men. Those already seated in a circle call out to the others scattered throughout the house, "Storytelling again."

"*Ghul, ghul*," they say to Russell.

"Let him drink his coffee first," the sheikh says, pouring himself tea.

"You still suffer from your stomach ailment, I see," Russell says to the sheikh.

"*Aywa*," the sheikh replies. "It is from drinking too much coffee, the doctors say. But you know it is a professional hazard, for how can a sheikh arrange a *sulha* without coffee? And you know how very few the visitors, even kin, who would understand that I mean no offence to them, and have no displeasure with them, if I were to drink water or tea with them, instead of coffee."

As the sheikh drank his herbal tea, Russell said, "I was thinking of what you said."

"And?"

"And I think you may be right," Russell concedes, Badu-proper now. "I mean, Awaad may not know the story, but he knows the place—the desert, I mean; it is not unlike the desert that sheltered, nurtured, and instructed the Prophet himself…"

"It is not Awaad but his sheikh who is sitting in the place—*ya'ni*—in the desert," says the sheikh, "and in the tents as well, for we are the ones who are tying and untying, moving, bending with the wind, and encompassing, *Wallah*—*aywa*, all-encompassing was the vision of the Prophet, wider than wide, *Wallah*. You know, El Bofessa, if there is one thing I fear, it is the narrower-than-narrow vision of Badu like Awaad. For it is the narrower-than-narrow vision that leads to such Arab thinking as making peace means betrayal, defeat, capitulation. *Aywa*, and it is the narrower-than-narrow vision also that leads Arabs to close borders tighter than tight—not only to Yahod, but to Arabs who think forward, and who speak the language of brotherhood, like you and I here, El Bofessa. You speak like a Badu, and I like a professor. *Aywa*, El Bofessa, I know you like the desert more, much more, than you like America. But when the Hamsin winds blow the desert to your house in Tel Aviv, you close all the windows and all the doors, and even all the shutters. And then you switch on the air conditioner you shipped in from New York, do you not?"

"*Aywa*, I do, *yaa*-Sheikh. And it is then when the Hamsin winds are blowing and I switch on the air-conditioner that I best understand the thirst you have for the great gushing spring, America. But you know the story of the parched Badu," says Russell. "I speak like a Badu, you said, and so like a Badu I will tell this story."

"Listen well, my sons, for El Bofessa is going to change the story for the lesson to the sheikh—*ghul, ghul, yaa*—El Bofessa." The sheikh is patronizing now.

"But is it still a true story?" a child whispers to Russell.

"Of course," Russell replies. "It happened only a year ago, or maybe even only half a year ago it happened that a Badu had to venture into the desert—venture, I say, for he was not a Badu of the Negev, but a Badu of the tribes of the north, so far north you could almost say he was a Badu of the Galilee, where a Badu remembers how close he lives to the desert only when the fifty—Hamsin—winds are blowing, meaning, only fifty days a year."

"Only when the sun is in heat," says a little one, and the sheikh rewards the child with a sparkling diamond caress.

"*Aywa*," continues Russell. "Only when the sun in heat makes love to the desert—*ya'ni*, only when the fifty winds from the east conquer the winds from the west, did our Badu of the north remember how close he lives to the desert in the south. And having lived in a villa four stories high for thirty years already, or maybe for only ten or twenty years, he knew desert tracking no better than a *Yahodi*. And, to his misfortune—or good fortune, some would say—just when he, the Badu of the north, had to venture into the desert to attend a circumcision, or a wedding, or maybe for just to seal an agreement—no one knows for sure—the Hamsin was blowing and blowing, blowing up a sandstorm."

"*Yaa-Allah*."

"*Aywa*," Russell says. "No greater thirst knows man than the thirst of men who venture outdoors during the Hamsin. So burning hot, like a fire the Hamsin winds blow. And like a fire they suck the moisture from the air—*ya'ani*, the life from the air. And such a blinding sandstorm the fifty winds stirred up, would blind even the best of the Negev Badu trackers. So, of course, he, the Badu of the north, trying to find shelter in a cave, a crag, or Badu tent, got lost. And he also lost the waterbag he carried. By the time the Hamsin died and the sand settled, and the Badu of the north could see that he was lost, he was too weak, too dry, to move. And he was nearly dead-dry when a Badawia happened to find him. That is why some people say he was more fortunate than unfortunate. For the Badawia carried him to her tent when he was nearly dying of thirst. And he, being a Badu, even of the north, even a villa-dwelling Badu, saw how clean-pure the water in the clean glass she was offering to him. But in the clean glass itself, floating on the ever-so-clean-pure water, he saw a piece of straw. And since it was not *adabb*—polite—*ya'ni*, he knew it would offend her were he to take the piece of straw out of the glass, he said nothing, and he only sipped the ever-so-clean-pure water, ever so slowly, paying careful attention not to swallow the piece of straw. For it would choke him to death were he to swallow it, he knew.

"True, *Wallah*,"

"*Aywa*," Russell continued, "But when he recovered his fluids—*ya'ni*, his life—his curiosity pushed him, and he asked her, the mistress of the tent, how could it have been that when everything in her tent was so nice and clean, there was a piece of straw floating in the glass of water she had offered him. It was then that she knew he was a Badu of the north. And so she explained to him: A man with a thirst as great as yours was bound to gulp much too fast, and so the water was bound to have passed through you much too fast. And worse, much worse, you would have for certain suffered such a diarrhea, it would have drained off even the few drops of fluids that have kept you alive. That is why she decided to put a piece of straw in the glass of water, she told him, for she was certain that he, being a Badu, would not offend her—*ya'ni*, he would not take the piece of straw out of the glass in front of her. And ever so slowly, slowly, he would drink the water, just as she had meant him to do, for his well-being—*ya'ni*, his good health."

Silence.

"Is Awaad the piece of straw, or is he the Badawia? Or do you mean to say that the sheikh is the Badu of the north, and the lesson is drink ever so slowly from the great gushing spring, America, or else you risk losing being Badu?" the sheikh's daughter, sitting behind me now, whispered.

"*Allah aref*—it is but a story I heard Badu tell," Russell replied, up on his feet now, as was the sheikh, each casting a shadow of a piece of straw.

41

Rain! Torrents, with a power outage and farmers dancing, then crying, "Much too much. It's all or nothing—droughts or floods." Washed-out fields, washed-out roads, car accidents, flooded wadis in the Negev and the Judean deserts, mud slides in the Galilee and the Jerusalem mountains. For once, the weather made the top of the news. The forecast was for sun and cloud. It is too early to tell if the drought has broken.

No mention of rain in Sinai, but even the smallest spillover would flash-flood the wadis, replenish the waterholes, green the pasture, bring back Tammam's breast milk, her goats', and Azzizah's, bestow a new supply of fragrant driftwood—light up the fire-circles…

※

Friday, on his way home for *Shabbat*, Tal dropped me off at my hotel in Herzliyya. I was hoping he would invite me to his kibbutz for *Shabbat*, but … I wouldn't have gone anyway. My first *Shabbat* in The Land in weeks-months I wanted to be with my parents and Arik's.

My first *Shabbat* in Canada—my first *Shabbat* Outside the Land—I expected to be like *Shabbat* here in the Land. I didn't think it was extraordinary, until then, that as soon as the sun would set on Friday evening, a mysterious spirit would rise to wrap up The Land and hand her over to us youngsters, like a gift. And soon after the lighting of *Shabbat* candles, we'd break *hallah* at our parents' table, then we'd head out onto the street and find the crown of The Land—perfect peace—was ours for the taking. No buses ran, and cabs and cars were luxuries that few could afford in those days. The peaceful streets were ours—to consecrate, like *Shabbat* candles. Our white *Shabbat* shirts and blouses would glow in the darkness, as if from a light within.

We were *the promise*, the children of the covenant.

Shabbat is a non-event in Canada. Traffic does not stop, stores are not closed; Canadians on the whole don't share the dream of perfect peace—for one day a week, at least. The borders of Canada are peaceful all the time. Being alone on *Shabbat* in Canada is like being alone any day of the week; the mood answers to the moon, and not the heart. Yet, even in Canada, *Shabbat* was the loneliest of days after Arik fell.

I tried to reach his parents now. I phoned them all: Arik's parents, mine, his brother, my sister, Riva, Mottke, Gingie. No one answers. Some are probably still at work, others busy with last-minute arrangements for *Shabbat*.

I couldn't bear the thought of staying in this hotel suite alone, decided to surprise-visit Arik's parents and mine before their afternoon nap, bring them flowers for *Shabbat*, and the goodies they love from the Garden of Eden Bakery on Dizingoff Street.

Soldiers, boys and girls, crowded the *Trampiyada*—the hitchhiking stations—at the cut-off to Jerusalem, Haifa, Tel Aviv. The whole country seemed to be rushing home. The Coastal Highway was jammed, all six lanes, bumper to bumper, and nearly every car with an empty seat picked up a soldier from the *Trampiyada* and a bouquet of flowers for *Shabbat* from the Friday flower-vendors who stationed themselves not far from the hitch-hiking stations—affording two *mitzvot* at one stop, and they were cashing in on it. *Shabbat* profiteers, the cab driver called them.

No one answered the bell at Arik's parents' place.

At my parents place, my mother takes one look at me and says, "You disappeared to nothing in the desert ... you lost so much weight, were you ill?"

"No ... the Manna that drops from heaven unto the desert these days is low-fat," I reply. She chuckles, shaking her head.

At sundown she lights two *Shabbat* candles, without any ceremony, or any prayer that I can tell. Her lips move just to blow out the matchstick. Next she covers her face with both her hands and, like this, she stands in front of the glowing *Shabbat* candles—so very still, as if she was transported from this world of the breathing, to——

"Where? where are you, Imma?" I whisper to her, like when I was little.

Her hands float from her face to caress mine. "*Shabbat Shalom*," she says; her face is luminous now and her smile—as if angels had just whispered to her——

"What? Imma, what happened to you?"

"It's a secret," she replies, like she used to when I was a child.

"She communed with her fellow Lamed-vavniks—the thirty-six Righteous Ones, believed to exist secretly and to uphold the world until the days of redemption," my father says, only half in jest.

Three of the family's most treasured possessions have been set on the table at the same place ever since I was old enough to remember. By now, much of the silver patina has been polished off the two candlesticks—a wedding present to my parents from my mother's parents, as is the *Shabbat Hallah* cover, hand-embroidered by my mother's sister. She, and my mother's parents, and all her four brothers perished There in The Shoah. Their possessions plundered. Nothing remains, but these wedding gifts, and one photo of my mother's parents, and the story. These also might have vanished There, together with my parents, had it not been for a knife...

A knife unlike the knife in the story that tells how Isaac was spared, "there was no sign of Divine intervention in this case," as my father had put it. In this case it happened at a time when it seemed that, not the meek, but the mad shall inherit the earth; a time too painful for my parents to touch—even with words. Too little to understand it, but not to sense a locked door here, I was moved by curiosity to unlock it. But the more I would probe, the tighter they would lock, the more I would probe... until my father relented to open—only a crack. Only a peek into his story, yet this one, unlike the others he told, would invade my sleep, my being— so lifelike my father would appear, wielding a knife like a madman and, furious as hell, tearing into the Jewish agency in Poland, saying they are no better than the Tommies who issue to Jews all too few entry visas to The Land. "The Tommies are Gentiles but you are Jews," my father yells at them. "Jewish agents, you call yourselves?!"

He calls them A Shame to the Nation and to the name "Jewish"—all because they are selling legal-entry visas to the highest bidders instead of to the next in the line that he and my mother have been waiting in for years and years like *fabrente*—burning—idealists.

"Hand me two legal-entry visas to The Land this minute or I'll kill you," my father tells them, knife in hand. The Jewish agency clerks are so afraid of him and his knife, they hand him two entry visas to The Land. Quick before they blow the whistle to call the police, my father escapes.

But now my father has to face his father. And his father also pulls out a knife and tells my father that he'll kill him if he disobeys him and runs to partake in Alien work. Idolatry, Alien work, my father's father calls Zionism.

"Stay in Poland," my grandfather tells my father, "where it is safe, where a Jew can work and study the Torah." He orders my father to obey him, honor him, as is commanded in the Fifth Commandment or a bitter end will come to all. And maybe it did, because my father didn't obey the commandment.

It is too dark to see his parents and all his brothers and his sisters when my father tiptoes out of their lives... Not like they show in the movies: There is no warm lasting embrace, no tearful kiss, no blessing. No, like a cursed criminal my father sneaks away...

He berates himself, ever since then, for not taking—stealing—something from his parents, his brothers and sisters: a prayerbook, or just a torn page of his father's Talmud, a piece of cloth, or even a thread or a button... Because no one, and nothing remained of them, but the story...

"This is too cruel a punishment for transgressing one single commandment," my father felt, and with his father's curse still ringing in his ears, like a condemned man, my father went to seek pardon in the lists. Every day he read the lists like a Bible. He even looked for names remotely connected to his family's name, or to the name of someone—anyone—from his little Polish town. And when he sees a name similar to the names of the ones he knew There, he follows that name as if it was the pillar of fire that leads to the Promised Land.

But the pillar and the lists lead only to a graveyard in the sky. No one had survived in his little Polish town. Not even one who could tell him how, when, where—if by fire, by smoke, by God only knows why or what. Everyone my father knew There—vanished.

Now, only my mother can attest that he didn't invent them in his stories and dreams.

"Your sister went horseback riding in the Galilee this *Shabbat*. A place called Vered Ha'gallil," my mother told me this evening, as she and I were washing the dishes. The city was so still at that hour of the eve of *Shabbat* that we could hear my father turning newspaper pages in the living room.

"Your friends are in the paper, Leora," my father bellowed from the living room. "Riva and Mottke are guest-speakers at a medical conference at Beer Sheba University this weekend."

Just then, the neighbors next door started to chant *Zemirot* to welcome *Shabbat*. My father hummed along in the living room, my mother and I in the kitchen. We knew the medley by heart. My parents have had the same neighbors for more than a quarter century. Every *Shabbat*, they string one chant to another in the same order ... There was an extra peace in the timelessness.

"Arik's parents are in the Negev, at Arik's brother," my mother continued to fill me in when my father joined us for tea and honey cake. "Arik's father is recuperating there from a gall-bladder operation he underwent three weeks ago. Levi phoned him from Canada every day ... For as long as he can remember, Levi has heard them talk about Arik as if he was a saint, now he doesn't know what to do to measure up ... phones them, phones us, as if he has nothing better to do than phoning grandparents."

"No, he's just as impatient as Arik, can't wait to be part of the life here," I said.

"Yes, Levi knows that Arik was far from perfect," my father boomed, turning to me and adding, "You made sure of that. It's just a stage he's going through. At his age, I also tried to be one hundred percent perfect—like the Gentiles in my *shtetl* ... The Gentiles are a hundred-percent people, you know, I used to work with them in Poland, to get into shape for the pioneering work in The Land. You should have seen their hands, Leora. Mine in those days were two raw wounds, your mother can tell you. She used to dress my hands every night, and every morning the Polish Gentiles were surprised to see me back. We Jews were doomed to be physically and morally inferior to them, they believed. 'A Jew could never be as strong as a Gentile,' they used to tell me. 'Why are you killing yourself?' they used to say. And only four or five years later, who would have thought that not one Jew in my Polish town would be spared?

"Why only me? What a responsibility. How can a human being live with such a responsibility? And I, only a simple man. I cannot understand, neither man nor God—not our God and not the Gentiles' Lord, the Savior of the Gentiles. He was a hundred percent, a hundred percent of the time, the Polish Gentiles believed. That is why the Gentiles I knew had to be one hundred percent. If they were short even one iota, they had to confess and atone. That is what they told me.

"I was thinking of them when I was trying to be one hundred percent, and failing ... failing ... I was thinking, maybe a hundred percent is impossible for a human being to be—maybe inhuman standards the Gentiles had set for themselves—maybe that is why they dropped to such an inhuman low...

"It must be frustrating to be a Gentile, I was thinking when I was trying and failing to be one hundred percent, maybe it's even humiliating to be a Gentile, too humiliating, to fail and fail. It drives the Gentiles crazy, perhaps, and they forget that their Savior was a Jew, a humble carpenter, but one hundred percent—not only did He preach forgiveness, love; He was forgiveness and love, according to the Polish Gentiles I knew—which you cannot say even of Moses, and you know it says that Israel has no greater prophet than Moses.

"Or did the Gentiles remember all too well that their Savior was a Jew and think my father was not up to what they expect a Jew to be? A Jew should be like their Savior or not be at all—is

549

that what the Gentiles believe? Is that why they spared not one Jew in my *shtetl*—my town—There, in Poland?

"Is that what we Jews demand of ourselves—because we were spared, I mean, because of the responsibility? Is that why some of us Jews think we must be one hundred percent or not be at all? Is that why one Jew is turning against his brother?...

"You know, Leora, for many years I couldn't sleep, thinking what would they, who were not spared, wish me to do. I don't know to this day, to tell you the truth. Your mother also, for years we would sit every evening in the kitchen, talk it over, think together.

"Then, one day we heard from people who were *There* that a few Gentiles had risked their lives to shelter and rescue Jews... And so because of these Gentiles, even if there were all too few, your mother and I decided to make a *sulha*—a forgiveness—with all the Gentiles. For it says that, if in Sodom had there lived even fewer than ten decent people, Sodom would not be destroyed...

"I don't know if what your mother and I did was right or wrong. That is why I want you to remember, Leora, that we made a *sulha*—a forgiveness—with the Gentiles. Not a forgetting. Not a forgetting, even with God..."

"I remember how angry you were with God, Abba, so angry I was afraid God will punish you, kill you," I told my father, half wishing it would stop him from opening this door that he and my mother had kept locked ever since I was old enough to remember, except from one sliver of a crack—and half wishing he'd open it wide now, no matter how painful for him, my mother and me.

"Yes, it nearly killed me, my anger with God," my father went on to open the door. "You know, there is tremendous power in anger, power to reclaim The Land, perhaps... and power to destroy... And I was angry with Him long before the Shoah. We had suffered one pogrom too many for me. It boiled me mad that my father maintained, 'It's God's will.' I wanted to have nothing to do with such a God years before all The Millions were exterminated in the Shoah. So imagine now, when I discovered that of all the Jews of my *shtetl*, There, in Poland, only I was spared, almost like an insult to my father: Would I not betray my father—myself—if I make a *sulha* with God?

"I nearly went mad, searching for the answers to such questions. It was of no consolation to me that I was not alone. Each Jew, like Jacob, was wrestling with God..." My father turned to my mother. Their eyes locked, like in my child days, when they'd decide, almost like the Badu: Till here, and no more would they reveal. But now my mother nods her consent for my father to continue. My gut insisted I brace tight when my father, in that loud voice of the hard of hearing, went on to say, "Maybe because a woman was the first to have the courage to defy God and to taste the fruit of knowledge, your mother was the one who led me to make a *sulha* with God, even if He does not deserve it—to have mercy for Him... and for myself.

"Yes, it was your mother who moved me to wonder if we are not linked to God like you Leora, are linked to us. I mean, if just like you are to us, we Jews are God's unwanted children as well as His chosen, most wanted children..."

So that's what my parents had locked secret from me all these years. I didn't comprehend it at first. It slipped by me too fast to understand, too loud to hear; then, like an echo it bounced back...

"Hold it, wait till you hear me out," my father motioned with his powerful hand. "You are surprised to hear it, Leora, I see... that your mother and I wanted to lose you. But we were living in a tent at the time—with a leaking roof. It did not bother us. We were living out our dream. And your mother, just like in the stories, was building roads all day, and at night she sang in a choir. She was also a beautiful dancer. We were just starting to live.

"We were like children in those days—before the Shoah. We did not want to be burdened with an infant. Yes, burdened. That is how we saw it. We thought of a hundred reasons not to have a child, and your mother tried a hundred ways to lose you. There was not a potion she did not drink, no heavy object she did not lift. But you defied us then, and to this day we wonder if you are different because you were unwanted...

"Oh, how you tried to be wanted, liked, pleasing to us—and at the same time to defy us, rebel against us, even to rival us. Like us, you ran away from home and like us, you risked your life in the war effort. The scars on you legs are medals of honor and bravery for rescuing three children from a burning house hit by a bomb. I didn't think you had it in you, to tell you the truth, because I knew what a fear you have of death. But is it a wonder, when your parents wanted you not to be. Is it a wonder you are for being, for living—even if that means being in exile, dropping us, your parents, and The Land…

"Are you with me, Leora?" my father said, almost like Abu Salim, "Are you ready?" Like a Badu who could sense-see through mountains, he waited until I was ready, *Wallah*, to understand him, not as his girl-child, but as a parent—ready, *yaa-Rabb*, to see what a burden a child, in the every day; and by the very fact that love, if real, is a burden, be it as wanted, rewarding and enriching a love as mine of Levi; or even sustaining in the worst of times… The need emanating from him when, after Arik went, I was all too needy myself, and the responsibility—the double responsibility for countless decisions; like: Does he fly, does he not… pressed so heavy, *Wallah*, embarrassing how many times I wanted to push Levi away… Isn't that what I did when I ventured to Sinai?

"Yes, I'm with you, I hear you, Abba," I replied.

My father nodded, pressing his lips. "What do you think of this?" he was saying inside, it seemed, when his eyes went to Arik, as ever beaming happy on the wall… then, he turned to me and said, "Is it not because we Jews are God's unwanted children that we are driven to be wanted, to be liked by everyone: Jews, Gentiles, Arabs, but most of all liked by God—like my father?

"Oh, what a thing and its opposite—children unwanted, wanted. With one hand God keeps embracing us and with the other He is pushing us away. Does God think we Jews are like Him—made in His image—a kiss and a kick? Is that why God was so unsure, He needed such a show of loyalty, of trust; a sacrifice of a son? Or did God want to see what Abraham would be willing to sacrifice for him after all He sacrificed for His children?

"How many fathers do you hear saying that, especially fathers of children unwanted-wanted? . . . Your own father also, to be honest with you . . . The best of my years I felt I had sacrificed for you, as if you asked to be born. Maybe that is why sometimes I think God must have had the time of His life in the Garden, before His children came to the world—to knowledge, light, life, I mean. Must have been paradise for Him not to have to make a decision, even the decision of what to name His creatures. He left that to Man. Then, like a father growing jealous of his growing son, He says, 'Now that man has become *like one of us*, knowing good and bad, what if he should stretch out his hand and take also from the Tree of Life to eat and live forever.' After I read that saying, I could not help but wonder if God didn't punish us, because He was afraid of rivalry. Isn't that why He scattered us, his chosen-unwanted children, drove us to exile? To wait at the ready for Him—in suspense . . . Isn't *that* what drove us—still drives us—to wait confident-unconfident, worthy-unworthy, wanted-unwanted?

"Is it not this thing and its opposite that drives us to feel that whatever we do is not good enough? Is that not why we Jews are driven to push maybe too much, give too much, take too much, maybe even to talk too much . . . like me today; is it not this wanted-unwanted thing and its opposite that drives us to crave too much?

"Is it not why this table is overloaded—as if to make up for what was sacrificed, destroyed, lost, lacking, deprived, and like children on the run, or on that brink—any day, any minute may be the last. Is that not what drives us to be—to survive, to live, to know—even God—and to forgive—even God . . .

"Is it not because we Jews are His unwanted children that God, to make up for that, favored us to be His chosen, like I favor you over your sister to this day, even though your sister proved to be just as good a daughter as you, if not better? Or do I favor you because, if not for you, Leora, I don't know if your mother and I would have made a *sulha*—a forgiveness—with God? A forgiveness, but not a forgetting . . .

42

"Come on, Leora. Get in the Jeep. We are driving up to Jerusalem to pick mushrooms," Tal called up to say, as if it was only natural to pick mushrooms in Jerusalem on a Thursday that followed a rainy Wednesday. And then he said he had to attend a meeting in Jerusalem later on this afternoon, to discuss the security job. He wanted to weigh the pros and cons of that job offer once more before he committed himself at the meeting, I sensed. And so I agreed to be his sounding board—until we reached the ascent to Jerusalem. At Bet-Shemesh I'll grab a bus or a cab back to Herzliyya, I decided. I couldn't just hop into a Jeep and drive up to Jerusalem.

A trip to Jerusalem was a special event for me, an event that demanded a tremendous emotional toll.

Long before your bones, Arik, were buried in her bosom, long before I was born, I had entered her gates ... And once inside, you're trapped for life, a prisoner obsessed with rebuilding her— yet again. Destroyed twenty-two times, and twenty-two times rebuilt, defiant she stands, eternally watchful—over the ruins, over the dead, and over the living. The story lives on in her: the promise of ascent, Cain and Abel, the Covenant, the Altar, the Shrine, the Temple, King David, King Solomon, the Song of Songs, the Psalms, the Transcending Light ... Forever she will rise, and forever will she doom you, if you do or don't forget her. So jealous is Jerusalem—she loves you and hates you in equal measure. O, if I forget thee ... We are marked by this promise, Arik, you and I ... With nine measures of beauty God endowed Jerusalem, you believed, and to the rest of the world He gave only one; the same measure of suffering He gave to the world, and to Jerusalem he gave all of nine. Too much—O, Jerusalem ...

Much too much for you, Arik. The night before you went, you were given a commission to build in Jerusalem, and I remember so clearly how you feared you'd never be able to create a design worthy of her beauty... how you shivered whenever we entered her gates, how you felt bound to her by a sort of cord that couldn't be severed, by knives, guns, the mightiest of wills, and the distance of thousands of miles and years...

That cord binds you still, Arik, as she has taken you to her bosom now, for ever.

Houses have sprouted wild, like weeds, and the traffic has doubled, but otherwise, the landscape that rolled by on the old road to Jerusalem hasn't much changed since Arik's funeral—a hodge-podge of flat, battered-looking towns, dilapidated factories, and poor, unkempt farms, with fields and groves that smelled of the blood spilled to defend them, even after yesterday's rain.

And then the Jeep left the old road and took a hairpin turn that led to a valley stretching from horizon to horizon—the very place where, according to the Book, Joshua, needing extra daylight to win this valley, cried out: "Stand still, oh sun, oh moon, in the valley of Aijalon!" It doesn't take long to cross that valley today, even in a dented, reconditioned Jeep.

Tal turned onto a dust road that hugged the foot of the mountain range leading to Jerusalem, drove for a few hundred meters, parked, and if I hadn't known he had come to these woods to pick mushrooms, I would have thought he meant to go up to Jerusalem like a pilgrim—on foot, if only for part of the way.

You wouldn't recognize these mountains today, Arik. The green woods covering them now were a joke—only yesterday... Each and every Friday of my public-school days we would laugh when the teacher dragged out the blue-and-white *Keren-Kayemet* tin box and each of us dropped in a coin or two for the reforestation of these Jerusalem mountains. So devastated they looked, an ash-gray wasteland, even the teacher seemed to believe that our coins would be wasted on a futile exercise. And it was only to instill in us the habit of donating, that she passed the box; it was also part of our welcome ceremony for *Shabbat*...

Today, those saplings have grown to have the last laugh. And, almost like a gesture of gratitude to these Jerusalem mountains for accepting their roots, the pines have covered up their hard, crusty face with a fine carpet of fragrant needles, still moist from yesterday's rain.

The cloudbank today only formed and dissolved, as if to emphasize the infinite dimensions of the sky and the potency of the wind. If Azzizah and Tammam were to find themselves gliding up and down these wooded slopes, they would probably think they had died and gone to heaven... and then they'd chop at these evergreens for fragrant firewood, their goat herds would devour this green bounty, nurtured by our laughter, sweat, and dreams, and in no time these green Jerusalem mountains would be a story that lives on in a desolate mountain landscape.

Tal didn't find the pine mushrooms he was hoping to collect here. "They need another good rainfall," he decided after an hour or so of combing the woods. "You cannot imagine what a great treat these mushrooms are, served on toast," he said, like a true *Francawi*. Then, like a true *Sabra*, he reeled off the names of so many trees, shrubs, flowers, butterflies, insects, birds indigenous to our Jerusalem hills, I can't recollect now even one. His passion for The Land was sparked, not by her ancient temples, her age-old stories, the heat of her battles, the blood of brothers-in-arms, but by the Jordan valley, his home ground, where the earth was fertile, yielding, and hot as the desert. I envied him, like the frigid envy the passionate.

I didn't get out at Bet-Shemesh. And Tal pressed full speed on the new superhighway that climbs to Jerusalem, as if he was heading to any old capital city. In some spots, this new highway cut through the heart of the mountains and exposed the guts of Jerusalem—her stones. And those stones seemed to be weeping, a tear here and there as if they meant to be brave, but couldn't contain their sorrow.

It didn't move Tal. He had a scientific explanation for these tears. Like the ancient warriors, Tal is of the belief that whoever holds Jerusalem holds The Land. Her strategic seat hasn't changed through the centuries, he told me as we were entered Bab el Wad, or Sha'ar Hagai, whatever it is called today...

Yesterday's armored buses and trucks, used by those who fell trying to carry water, food, and medical supplies to Jerusalem when she was besieged in '48 and '49, had been left at the roadside since those days to commemorate them. They should be carted away with Masada and the Western Wall, or the Wailing Wall, as it is called in America, Tal said. To him, no matter what you called them, they were but symbols of ruin, failure, and defeat. He didn't like symbols of victory any better. He didn't like symbols period, he said. All too often they are mistaken for the essence, "like religious practices, for God, and for Jerusalem," he explained.

The Jeep crawled up that new superhighway as if the engine lacked that extra something required to make the climb to Jerusalem. And at the steep downhill, it seemed the brakes wouldn't hold, the Jeep would crash through the rail at the sharp turn at Motza and plunge to the deep canyon below. When the brakes did hold for the turn, Tal patted the Jeep like a rider would a horse galloping on heart alone. There isn't a bend in The Land more dangerous than this one, he explained. But it seemed he patted the Jeep too soon; at the last hill it inched up, threatening to roll back down at any moment...

You would probably love the Jeep for that suspense, Arik— "That's how you should enter Jerusalem: with fear and trembling," I can hear you saying. The gray concrete-block austerity-houses that used to make you cringe at the entrance to Jerusalem, are spruced up with Jerusalem stone today, and that old trash-heaped knoll is covered up with flowers that spell: Welcome to Jerusalem. And rose bushes in the thousands line the major roads, as if to replace the smell of gunpowder, ruin, blood.

Up on Mount Herzl, when he dropped me off at the black iron gate, Tal handed me his parka. "Can't keep a person warm on Mount Herzl, I know, no parka could... But take it—don't refuse this least of my offering," his eyes told mine. "I have many friends in this place," he said, standing pensive for a moment before heading off to his meeting.

No tourist buses are parked by the black iron gate; no clicking cameras disturb the peace for once. The wave of terror is driving tourists—and pilgrims—away, even from Jerusalem. But there is no keeping you apart from me here, my Arik. Inside my inner self I hear you say that the Galilee grave stones blend well with the Jerusalem stones supporting the terraces that divide the cemetery, sort of like screens in a huge restaurant—to make it intimate . . . and that the landscape architects had tried too hard to create the impression that this place was a park, not a mountain covered with graves; their designer flowerbeds, bushes, trees, winding paths, terraces, and steps take up too much space; the graves seem too close together and the dead have no breathing space . . .

The overall impression is of a mountain covered with one slab, like a brother's grave. How young most of the men were when they fell—some as young as seventeen, most in their early twenties. You would call himself "the old man of the mountain."

No man outranks another, up here on Mount Herzl. The generals have the same grave stone and are buried in the same row as their men. True equality here. No special plot was allotted to the heroes; like the cowards, pilots, soldiers, and sailors, they lay buried side by side, row after row—except the ones in the brother's graves, like the sailors who went down with their ship. Their grave, fashioned like a boat, seems to be sinking again today, due to yesterday's rain. Ah, well, future archeologists won't have to break their heads to figure out how these men died . . . But if those archeologists were to dig up the paths shaded by the pines planted here, they'd probably think we had developed a species of pine that doesn't shed needles. It wouldn't enter their minds that in a land where no plant was safe in any park, the grounds of a whole mountain would be so well kept, even the pine needles were swept away.

No one has touched even a leaf in this "park"—out of respect for the dead, no doubt. If half that respect was paid to the living, The Land would be like a foreign country, you would say and laugh. Ah, Arik, how you would love the silence today—only the rustling of leaves in the breeze, and my footsteps on the hard-packed earth. The few people who came to remember stand silent and stare disapproving—because my head is not covered. I am not here for them. You loved to see, touch, caress my hair ...

The graves of those who fell in the Sinai War are farthest away from the black iron entrance gate. To reach the grave stone that bears Arik's name, I have to pass through all the sections of all the wars that raged before and after the Sinai War. But because this section is at the farthest end, you have a ravine lot, Arik, with the best view in the mountain. And you would probably like the black grave stones in your section, the only one to use Golan basalt. They add a touch of elegance and variety, you would say; and since neither sun nor wind have faded or bleached the black, they give a dark, opaque, somber feel of permanence to the loss and are not overshadowed by the wreaths—after all, wreaths rot and die, but stones live forever—unless you crush them.

Pines trees were never your favorite. They smell of death, you used to say. But here they are not standing in a row, like soldiers guarding a cemetery. Only one pine stands by your gravestone. So tall it has grown over the years, it now lends not only dignity, but also a suggestion of ascent.

Your only complaint might be the wind, vicious by this ravine, and you, like most pilots, are—were—extra sensitive to winds ...

A futile pursuit of wind—that's how you'd sum up your life. Night after night, for years, you busted your butt, working the night shift to earn the tuition fees to study architecture—and what for? Dream towns displayed somewhere in the ministry. For The Land, too, you busted your gut, gave her all you had—and what did you get in return? A great view you can't see. And if you could see it, you'd say it was scientific, lifeless—a valley ringed by mountains, not a soul in sight. But if it was humanized, given a touch of the reality of life—abandoned-looking chicken coops, or army barracks—it would still not meet the standards of your perfectionism. Did you a hell of a lot of good; everything is good and perfect for you now. You have all the time in the world now. You no longer have to feel bad now that your flying and your dream-architecture left you with no time to be with Levi and me. Oh, how you busted your butt for us too—and what did that get you? Pebbles and shells from the beach in Herzliyya...

The only thing lacking in Jerusalem is the sea, you used to say. So, four or five months ago, before I first ventured to Sinai, I brought the sea to your Jerusalem. The pebbles and shells are still resting on your black grave stone. The wind hasn't carried them away. Time really does stand still for you, Arik... You would see nothing strange about a grown woman collecting pebbles and shells, like a girl-child for her boyfriend. Not if that woman was your Leora...

Aywa—yes, you gave me the childhood I never had, Arik. You gave me a corner of innocence that no one and nothing could kill... A green corner of innocence that replenishes the soul like a river the sea... *Sulha*—forgiveness—is born in that corner—forgiveness and trust, hope and dreams, and the striving to attain the unattainable... Our son, Levi, was born of that innocence. Isn't that why he wants my consent to waive his exemption? Isn't that why he wants to wrestle with Jacob's angel, wearing the shield of God and nothing else? Isn't that why he wants to face his own fears—not mine, to live his own life, and strive to attain his own dreams?

Why deny him that? He has lived to be a full-grown man, our Levi. There isn't a corner in his soul that isn't green, bountiful, full of light and the love of life. That's your gift to him, Arik... And he was your gift to me. Can you see the Book of Life there on the other side, Arik?

Can you see what is written for Levi? I'm going to count to three, and if I hear no objection from you, I'm going to give Levi my consent to serve any duty he chooses—let him make his own life-and-death decisions...

Seven times three I count. The mountain don't shake, and the wind doesn't die or change direction. The Book of Life offers no reason to fear. It's all right to call Levi and give my consent. The boy will be so elated; he won't be able to sleep. God better make sure he lives to see the dawn, rising blood-red from horizon to horizon.

No sun, no wind, no sigh, no kiss, no word, no tear gives a sign here; no rain would wash here, not up here on Mount Herzl. A generation comes and a generation goes, not here. No mountain could ever fill in the hole of loss here.

I stay by the black grave stone until the amber torch that would soon lend Jerusalem her golden glow lights up the tip of the pine like an eternal flame.

One night, min zaman—*a long time ago*—*before the great wadis were paved, before the electricity poles defaced the horizon, before Israel returned our Sinna desert to Egypt for peace, in the summer of the year nineteen hundred and seventy eight, in the seventh year of the drought… a moonless night it was, the men were discussing their affairs in the* maq'ad *without giving thought to intruding or visiting strangers. The darker the night, the farther the mountains carry sound. And so, everyone in the* maq'ad, *and in all the tents as well, could hear a Jeep climbing up and up, far away. And it soon became clear that it was the daring driving of courage, valor, and* keif—*sheer pleasure.*

As the Jeep approached the maq'ad, *the fire was burning fragrant and bright enough to see that the Jeep belonged to a* Yahodi, *for the license plate was yellow. And even though the elders were disappointed that he was not a Badu, they could not help but admire him even more.*

Right away all the elders in the maq'ad—*all the elders except Abu Salim, my father—started to fuss over the man-stranger. And, as was but proper, they paid no attention to the woman-stranger who came out of the Jeep with him. In the place of honor, they seated him. Tea they brewed to quench his thirst, and coffee to honor him.*

But Abu Salim, my father, was observing the man-stranger in one eye and the woman-stranger in the other.

She was a woman-stranger El Bofessa had equipped with his knowledge of Badu manners. My father knew, for she did not join the men like a stranger-woman. But so cold it was outside the fire-circle, she wrapped herself with a kaffiyye *headdress like a Badu man, freezing. My father could barely see her eyes and nose. He motioned to her to move closer to the fire. And only now, when she folded her legs on the welcome-carpet, Abu Salim, my father, could see by the firelight that she was the stranger-woman his wives had invited to visit-stay with them. For he could see her eyes now. And he could also see how new to the desert she was—brand new—but not the man-stranger.*

The man-stranger was a Yahodi *border-crossing soldier-of-soldiers, my father knew as soon as he saw the man-stranger sitting on the welcome-carpet in the place of honor, wearing the special desert boots that only the* Yahodi *soldiers-of-soldiers wear. Many a border and a desert his desert boots had crossed, my father could see right away. So could all the other men. That is why they called the man-stranger now yaa-Jabbar—a man of great valor.*

The Jabbar *was not flattered by their admiration and fuss, my father saw. And so, Abu Salim, my father, thought: Surely this* Jabbar *was wearing his desert boots while sitting on my welcome-carpet because he held us Badu in low regard. For we Badu, like women, live under the protection of men—his Israeli-Yahodi tribesmen.*

Gone are the days when we Badu were great warriors, my father thought, gone are the days when we Badu were feared.

"The woman in your charge is more than welcome to visit-stay in my tents a week, a month, even a year. Her blood, her honor, are on my head," my father told the stranger-man.

... Deep inside, Abu Salim, my father, was wondering now if this woman-stranger was fated to enhance the story that would remain after he dies, or to detract from it. She was fated to tell it, my father knew. That is why he welcomed her into his tents.

And that is why I, Salim, his son, give her permission now to tell all who wish to hear or read whatever she wrote-recorded in my father's tents.

Acknowledgments

To Marv Cohen, who traveled with me when I first ventured to the Sinai and was there for me to the last: Without you, my love, this book would not have been.

This novel was researched and written on two continents. In each were many who invested much effort, time and heart to assist me and strengthen my resolve to continue with the work, in particular:

The Bedouins of various tribes, clans and dwelling places, who offered me not only shelter, food and water for days and weeks, even months, but also their songs, dances, poems and legends by firecircles burning long into the night. All wished to remain nameless. All have broadened my horizon. To all I am most grateful.

Alfonso Nussbaumer, a dream of a desert guide, introduced me to the Sinai. His love of the desert and its inhabitants ignited mine. I'll always be grateful to him for that; for his sing-song telling of Bedouin legends and desert lore and for reading the manuscript to ensure that this work of fiction is true in spirit to the desert and its people. A most special thank you to Alfonso's wife, Nurit. I lost count of the times Nurit and Alfonso welcomed me, my family and friends into their home in Eilat.

Dr. Clinton Bailey, a highly acclaimed scholar of Bedouin culture and history, who lived among the Bedouin for many years, introduced me to the nomads. I am greatly indebted to him for that, and for his invaluable guidance and research material; for allowing me to quote extensively from his definitive collection of Bedouin poetry and studies; and for correcting the English transliteration of the Bedouin words that appear in this novel. My gratitude to his wife, Maya, for the kindness and hospitality she has accorded me over the years.

Ilon shared with me, in most intimate and painful detail, her personal and professional knowledge of war widowhood. No amount of gratitude can adequately express the debt I owe her.

Destiny truly favored me when I met Avi Oblas, who afforded me a rare insight into the realm of outstanding men/soldiers/kibbutzniks. I am most grateful to him for that, and for much more—not the least of which is introducing me to his brother Danny Shahaf, a high-ranking officer, now in reserve. I'm indebted to him for his recordings of soldiers' stories, and for the laughter we shared. These men are the brothers I wish I had.

A most special thank you to Jack McClelland, who read the beginnings of *Sulha* and spurred me on; and to Dennis Lee, who read the early sections, for his invaluable encouragement, comments and advice.

Haddassa Agassi Rosenberg read every line of the early drafts—argued, agreed, encouraged, and continued to offer great stores of knowledge, patience and intelligence until her last days. She was such a friend, and such a believer in *Sulha*.

No words can honor the debt I owe Casey Fuetsch. The editorial acumen, passionate, stubborn commitment and abundant vitality and enthusiasm she brought to the task—just as my own was depleted by grief—beg the notion that she was heaven-sent.

Surely the guardian angel of writers sent Anna Porter my way. I'm embarrassed to say how grateful I am to her.

My gratitude to all at Key Porter, most especially to my editor, Barbara Berson, who brought with her unique professionalism a fresh pair of eyes, an open mind and a love for the work, which sparked a huge burst of creative excitement, energy and insight to bring this novel to completion.

I am most grateful to Beverley Beetham Endersby, for her copy editing, into which she invested her eclectic array of talents, infinite patience and great care to keep the feel of modern Hebrew and ancient Badu Arabic in her beloved English.

There is a special place in my heart for my agent, Wayne Kabak. His efforts, commitment and faith sustained and replenished mine.

My thanks to Dr. Dionisius Ajius, for the Arabic lessons; and to Dr. Alean Al-Krenawi, for the transliteration of Badu Arabic.

Nana Mouskouri—not even in song could I convey how grateful I am for her support.

In addition, for their faith and assistance, my thanks to Shai Hinitz, Leslie Harris, Miri and Yaakov Malz, Nessa Rapoport, Ronen Berka, Professor Dajani-Shakeel, Professor Yvette Benayoun Szmidt, Jennifer Glossop, Linda McKnight, Elsa Franklin, Morris and Edna Goldberger, Stephanie Rayner, Dr. Laurel Shugarman, Jean Townsend and Izhak Hinitz.

Finally, and immeasurably, my gratitude to my parents, Na'vah and Israel Shtein, for their gift of life, and privilege. To Inna Shapiro, for being like a daughter to me. And to my sons, Martin Maccabi Himel and Daniel Marom, for their understanding, assistance and devotion, and for doing me proud.

Many books, as well as collections of field trip notes, studies and recordings, assisted me in my research of the desert, war, desert wars, and the Bedouin's way of life, in particular Dr. Clinton Bailey's *Bedouin Poetry, Bedouin Weddings in the Sinai and the Negev: Studies in Marriage Customs*, and *Desert Plants in Bedouin Life*; Lila Abu-Lughod's *Veiled Sentiments*; Emanuel Marx's *Bedouin of the Negev*; Shabtai Levi's *The Health, Hygiene and Medicine of the Bedouins of Southern Sinai*; David Maimon's *The Bedouin Tracker*; Gideon Kressel's *Changes in the Bedouin Society* and Izhak Nezter's *The Swearing and Licking of Fire* [from the Collected Lectures of the field school at Sde Boker]; T.E. Lawrence's *Seven Pillars of Wisdom*; H.R.P. Dickson's *The Arab of the Desert*; Alois Musil's *The Manners and Customs of the Rwala Bedouins*; Sir Richard F. Burton's *Personal Narrative of a Pilgrimage to Al-Madinah & Meccah*; *Kippur*, an account of Israel's October '73 war, by Yeshahayu Ben-Porat, Hezi Carmel, Uri Dan, Yehonatan Gefen, Eitan Haber, Eli Landau and Eli Tabor; Hanoch Bartov's *Daddo—48 years and 20 more days: The War Diary*; Haim Herzog's *The Arab-Israeli Wars*; Ezer Weizman's *The Battle for Peace*; Max Hastings' *Yoni, Hero of Entebbe; Self Portrait of a Hero, The Letters of Johnathan Netanyahu; Israeli War Widows, Beyond the Glory of Heroism* by Lea Shamgar-Handelman; and Eva Kirschner's *Study of Bereavement and Rehabilitation of War Widows in Israel*.